END OF THE
BEGINNING

END OF THE BEGINNING

HARRY TURTLEDOVE

NAL NEW AMERICAN LIBRARY

New American Library
Published by New American Library, a division of
Penguin Group (USA) Inc., 375 Hudson Street, New York, New York 10014, USA
Penguin Group (Canada), 90 Eglinton Avenue East, Suite 700, Toronto,
Ontario M4P 2Y3, Canada (a division of Pearson Penguin Canada Inc.)
Penguin Books Ltd., 80 Strand, London WC2R 0RL, England
Penguin Ireland, 25 St. Stephen's Green, Dublin 2,
Ireland (a division of Penguin Books Ltd.)
Penguin Group (Australia), 250 Camberwell Road, Camberwell, Victoria 3124,
Australia (a division of Pearson Australia Group Pty. Ltd.)
Penguin Books India Pvt. Ltd., 11 Community Centre, Panchsheel Park,
New Delhi - 110 017, India
Penguin Group (NZ), cnr Airborne and Rosedale Roads, Albany,
Auckland 1310, New Zealand (a division of Pearson New Zealand Ltd.)
Penguin Books (South Africa) (Pty.) Ltd., 24 Sturdee Avenue,
Rosebank, Johannesburg 2196, South Africa

Penguin Books Ltd., Registered Offices: 80 Strand, London WC2R 0RL, England

First published by New American Library, a division of Penguin Group (USA) Inc.

First Printing, November 2005
10 9 8 7 6 5 4 3 2 1

LIBRARY OF CONGRESS CATALOGING-IN-PUBLICATION DATA

Turtledove, Harry.
    End of the beginning/by Harry Turtledove.
      p.   cm.
    ISBN 0-451-21668-7
    1. World War, 1939–1945—Hawaii—Fiction.   2. Japanese—Hawaii—Fiction.
3. Hawaii—Fiction.   I. Title.
PS3570.U76E53   2005
813'.54—dc22   2005013935

Set in Minion

Printed in the United States of America

PUBLISHER'S NOTE
This is a work of fiction. Names, characters, places, and incidents either are the product of the author's
imagination or are used fictitiously, and any resemblance to actual persons, living or dead, business es-
tablishments, events, or locales is entirely coincidental.
    The publisher does not have any control over and does not assume any responsibility for author or
third-party Web sites or their content.

END OF THE
BEGINNING

I

COMMANDER MINORU GENDA WALKED PAST THE FRONT ENTRANCE TO IOLANI Palace. Fairy terns, almost whiter than white, floated through the blue, blue Hawaiian sky. The flag of the newly restored Kingdom of Hawaii fluttered on five flagpoles above the late-Victorian palace. Seeing that flag made Genda smile. The Hawaiians had gone out of their way to accommodate both Britain and the United States, with the Union Jack in the canton and red, white, and blue horizontal stripes filling the rest of the field.

Much good it did them, the Japanese officer thought. White men economically dominated the Kingdom of Hawaii for years before America overthrew it and brought the islands under U.S. control.

Well, things were different now. The Stars and Stripes no longer flew over Iolani Palace. The building no longer housed the Legislature of the Territory of Hawaii, as it had for decades. King Stanley Owana Laanui—King by the grace of God and, much more to the point, by that of the Emperor of Japan— reigned here now, along with his redheaded Queen Cynthia. And, where King Stanley reigned, Major General Tomoyuki Yamashita, who'd commanded the Japanese Army forces that conquered Hawaii, ruled.

Japanese soldiers stood guard at the top of the stairs leading up into the palace. They weren't big men—few of them had more than a couple of inches on Genda's five-three—but, with their businesslike Arisaka rifles, they didn't need to be. At the base of the stairs stood a squad of the revived Royal Hawaiian Guard. Putting the tall men at the bottom and the small men at the top minimized the size difference between them. King Stanley's guardsmen wore pith helmets and blue coats with white belts: purely ceremonial uniforms for purely ceremonial soldiers. They carried bayoneted Springfields—the Japanese had captured them by the thousand from the U.S. Army—but Genda had heard the rifles' magazines held no cartridges.

The Royal Hawaiian Guards came to an even stiffer brace as Genda strode by them. He nodded back, politely acknowledging the compliment. He turned a corner and then another one, heading for the back of the palace. More guards, both Hawaiian and Japanese, stood there. Another stairway led up into the building. And a shorter, narrower set of steps led *down* into Iolani Palace. Genda chose that stairway.

In the nineteenth century, the basement had been the servants' quarters. It had also housed the storerooms where the *kahili*—the feather-topped royal staffs—and the palace silver service, the wine, and other necessities were kept. Because at the last minute the architect had added a walled dry moat around the palace, the basement rooms had full-sized windows and weren't nearly so dark and gloomy as they would have been otherwise.

In front of one of the rooms along the wide central corridor stood two Japanese sailors in landing rig: their usual blues modified by black-painted steel helmets; infantrymen's belts, ammunition pouches, and canteens; and white canvas gaiters. Like the sentries outside, they carried Arisakas.

"Yes, sir? You wish . . . ?" one of them asked when Genda stopped and faced them.

He gave his name, adding, "I have an eleven o'clock appointment with Admiral Yamamoto." He didn't need to look at his watch to know he was ten minutes early. Being late to a meeting with the commander-in-chief of the Combined Fleet was inconceivable.

Both men saluted. "*Hai!*" they said in unison. The sailor who'd spoken before opened the door for him.

Admiral Isoroku Yamamoto worked at a plain pine desk, nothing like the ornate wooden dreadnought in King David Kalakaua's Library on the second floor of the palace, the one General Yamashita used. Genda thought that most unfair; Yamamoto outranked Yamashita, and should have taken over the finer work area. But he hadn't done it. He was in Hawaii only temporarily, and hadn't wanted to displace the permanent garrison commander.

Yamamoto got to his feet as Genda walked in. They exchanged bows. Yamamoto was only slightly taller than Genda, but had a wrestler's stocky, wide-shouldered body. "Sit down, sit down," he said now. "How are you feeling? Better, I hope? You *look* stronger than you did, and you have more color, too."

"I'm much improved, sir. Thank you," Genda said as he did sit. He'd had pneumonia when the Japanese Navy squared off against the U.S. forces trying to retake Hawaii. Despite the illness, he'd come up from *Akagi*'s sick bay to the bridge to do what he could to help the Japanese carriers against their American opposite numbers. He didn't take credit for the victory, but he'd taken part in it. More than a month after the fight, he was starting to feel like his old self, though he hadn't got there yet.

"Glad to hear it. I was worried about you," Yamamoto said with gruff affection. Genda inclined his head. Most of a generation younger than the admiral, he was Yamamoto's protégé. He'd planned the biggest part of the Pearl Harbor operation and the invasion of Hawaii. He'd planned them—and Yamamoto had rammed the plans through, turning them into reality. And now . . . they were meeting in the basement of Iolani Palace.

"The Americans have been very quiet since we stopped them," Genda remarked.

"*Hai.*" Yamamoto nodded. "I think they will stay quiet a while longer, too. I am going to take this opportunity to go back to Japan. Now that Hawaii is settled for the time being, we have to talk with the Army about what to do next. Australia . . . India . . . And of course they'll want to take another bite out of China, and they'll expect our help with that."

"So they will," Genda agreed. The Americans had offered to keep selling oil and scrap metal to Japan—if she got out of China. War, even a risky war like the one against the USA, had seemed preferable to the humiliation of bowing to another country's will. Did the Yankees tell Britain to leave India and her African colonies? Not likely! Did the Yankees hesitate to send in Marines when one of their little neighbors got out of line? That was even less likely. But they thought they could order Japan around. Bitterly, Genda said, "We don't have round eyes. We don't have white skin."

"True enough." Yamamoto nodded again, following Genda's train of thought. "But we've shown the world that that doesn't matter." He set both hands on the cheap pine desk. As a young officer, he'd lost the first two fingers of his left hand at the Battle of Tsushima, in the Russo-Japanese War. He'd lost two fingers—but the Russians lost most of the fleet that sailed halfway around the world to meet the Japanese. And they lost the war.

Genda had had his first birthday in 1905. Like any of his countrymen, though, he knew what the Russo-Japanese War meant. It was the first modern war in which people of color beat whites. And now the Japanese were beating the Americans and the British and the Australians, too.

Yamamoto said, "I hope I don't have to come back too soon. American radio broadcasts make it very plain the United States is not abandoning Hawaii. I hoped the USA would—I hoped our victories would make them see they could not win, and so make peace. But that hasn't happened. Karma, *neh?* They have more people and more resources and more factories—many more—than we do. My guess is that they will try to bring all of them into play. That will take some time."

"We will be building, too," Genda said stoutly.

"Hai," Yamamoto said once more. But that was only acknowledgment, not agreement, for he went on, "They can build faster than we can. I hope what we have done here in the Eastern Pacific has bought us the time to take and use the resources we need to stay a great power in the modern world. I hope so . . . but time will tell."

"We've done everything we set out to do here," Genda said.

"So we have. Now—is it enough?" Yamamoto seemed determined to be gloomy. He looked toward the west. "Back in Tokyo, they think everything is wonderful. They think the United States is at death's door. They do not understand the enemy. They may have read Sun Tzu, but they do not think what he says applies to them. Oh, no! They are far more clever than he."

Such sarcasm flayed. What Clausewitz was in the West, Sun Tzu was in the East—and had been for more than two thousand years. A military man disregarded the ancient Chinese general's thoughts on strategy and tactics only at his peril. Genda said, "Surely things are not so bad as that."

"No—they're very likely worse," Yamamoto said. "Be thankful you're well away from Tokyo. It's a poisonous place these days. Some of the poison comes from success, which makes it sweeter, but it's no less deadly on account of that. Deadlier, probably, in the long run, because success is the kind of poison that makes you blind."

"If the Germans knock the Russians out of the war—" Genda began.

"Yes, that's what the Army is waiting for. If the northern beast dies, they'll jump on the carcass and tear off slabs of Siberia. If."

"The *Wehrmacht* has a foothold in the Caucasus. They're getting close to Stalingrad. Stalin's 'not one step back' speech after Rostov fell sounded desperate."

Yamamoto only shrugged those broad shoulders. "We'll see what happens, that's all. The Germans were at the gates of Moscow last winter, and they got thrown back. They're after oil now. We have ours. If they can get theirs . . . I hope they haven't overreached, that's all."

"They keep the Americans and the British busy, too," Genda said, "which works to our advantage."

That made Yamamoto smile. He stood up and bowed to Genda, who hastily returned the gesture. "I might have known you would think clearly. With men like you here, Hawaii will be in good hands." He bowed again, a little more deeply: dismissal.

Genda left his office as if walking on a cloud. The man he admired more than anyone else in the world—the man all Japan admired more than anyone else in the world—approved of him! Most of Japan knew—or rather, knew of—Admiral Yamamoto from gushing newspaper and magazine articles. Genda knew the man himself, and found him all the more admirable for the acquaintance.

Trying to suppress a silly grin, Genda went up the stairs from the basement. He got to the top at the same time as Cynthia Laanui, the newly crowned Queen of Hawaii, came down the back stairs from the ground floor of Iolani Palace. "Your Majesty," Genda said in English, carefully keeping the irony from his voice.

"Hello, Commander Genda. How are you today?" The Queen knew him by sight; he was one of the four officers—two from the Japanese Navy, two from the Army—who'd chosen her husband from among the possible candidates for the restored Hawaiian throne. Stanley Owana Laanui—King Stanley now—was the first candidate who'd made it plain he would cooperate with Japan.

Genda didn't think Queen Cynthia knew how simple the selection criteria were. He didn't intend to enlighten her, either. "Better now, thank you," he said. He read English well but, unlike Yamamoto, spoke less fluently.

Cynthia Laanui smiled at him. She was, without a doubt, the first red-haired Queen the Kingdom of Hawaii had ever had. The smile packed a punch. She was somewhere between twenty-five and thirty, with green eyes, freckles, and, from the neck down, an abundant profusion of everything a woman ought to have.

"I want to thank you for everything you've done for my husband," she said. King Stanley was at least twenty years older than she was; Genda didn't think she was his first wife. Why he'd married her was obvious. Why she'd married him wasn't, not to Genda. But she seemed to care about him.

"Glad to help him," Genda said. "He is good man." He wouldn't have bet more than fifty sen—say, a dime in U.S. money—on that but it was polite, and it gave him the excuse to keep talking with this striking woman. She was only a centimeter or two taller than he was, too.

She wore a distinctly unqueenly sundress of thin cotton. When she nodded, everything else moved in sympathy, and the dress showed it off. Genda hoped he didn't notice too obviously. She said, "He's a *very* good man. Hawaii needs him, especially now."

Did she believe that, or was she being politic? Genda would have guessed she believed it. If she was so naive, she was liable to get badly hurt. "Good man, yes. Do many good things," Genda said. Agreement was always safe. And, as long as King Stanley did exactly what Japan told him to do, the occupiers wouldn't object if by some chance he turned out to be good, too.

Genda's agreement won him a smile brighter than the Hawaiian sunshine from Queen Cynthia. He felt as if a bomb had gone off in front of him and he'd got flash-burned. "I'm *so* glad you think so," she breathed. He'd never found the simple act of breathing so admirable before.

They chatted a little longer. Then, after another dazzling smile, she went back into the palace. Genda knew he needed to return to his duties. He waited till she'd gone all the way up the stairs, though.

THERE WAS A ZERO, swelling in Joe Crosetti's windshield. Joe peered through the Grumman Wildcat's gunsight. *Can't lead the son of a bitch too much, but if I don't lead him enough I'll miss, too.* The thought was there and then it was gone. If you got close enough, you damn well wouldn't miss. He waited till the hated enemy filled the bulletproof glass, then jammed his thumb down on the firing button atop the stick.

His wing machine gun roared. Tracers tore into the Jap. The enemy plane went up like a torch and plunged toward the Pacific. The pilot didn't have a prayer of getting out. Maybe he was dead from the burst of fire, anyway.

"Nailed the bastard!" Joe yelled exultantly. He swung the fighter back toward the carrier. Navigating over the trackless ocean wasn't easy, but he managed. There was the welcoming flight deck, dead ahead. He brought the Wildcat down toward the carrier's stern. This was the tricky part. . . .

Down! The plane's tailhook caught an arrester wire, and the machine jerked to a stop. He was down, and he was safe!

A voice spoke in his earphones: "Well, Mr. Crosetti, that wasn't too bad."

Reality returned with a bump harder than the one with which he'd landed. His Wildcat turned into a pumpkin, like Cinderella's carriage: actually, into a humble Texan advanced trainer. The flight deck became a yellow rectangle outlined on concrete. The arrester wires stretched across it were the McCoy, though. This was only the second time he'd landed using them.

His flying instructor, a lieutenant, junior grade, named Wiley Foster, went on, "I liked your attack run on the target. You got a four-oh on that one."

"Thank you, sir," Joe said.

"Don't thank me yet—I wasn't finished," Foster answered. "Your landing was okay, but nothing to write home about. You're not supposed to set down as hard as you would on a real flight deck, not yet. You need to convince me you can make smooth landings before you do rough ones."

"Yes, sir. Sorry, sir." Joe wanted to claim he'd come down that way on purpose, but he hadn't—and the flying instructor wouldn't have cared it he had.

"As for your navigation . . ." Lieutenant Foster paused significantly.

"Sorry, sir," Joe repeated, sounding as miserable as he felt. He'd struggled with navigation right from the start. A lot of the cadets at Pensacola Naval Air Station were college grads, or had at least some college. Joe had graduated from high school, but he was working in a San Francisco garage when the Japs bombed Pearl Harbor. He understood engines from the ground up, but his geometry and trig were barely enough to let him keep his head above water when it came to figuring out how to get from A to B and back again. And if he ever had to ditch in the vast, unforgiving Pacific, odds were he wouldn't keep his head above water long.

"It could have been worse," Foster allowed. "I've seen cadets try to head for Miami or New Orleans or Atlanta. But it could have been a hell of a lot better, too. If you want carrier duty, you'd better keep hitting the books hard."

"Yes, sir. I will, sir," Joe said fervently. Carrier duty—the chance to hit back at Japan as soon as he could—was the reason he'd signed up as a Navy flying cadet in the first place.

Lieutenant Foster slid back the canopy. He and Joe climbed out of the Texan. The flying instructor was a lanky six-footer. He towered over Joe, who barely made five-seven. That might have mattered if they were bashing at each other with swords. Who cared how big a pilot was? Joe had heard Southerners say, *It's not the size of the dog in the fight—it's the size of the fight in the dog.* What the Japanese had done since December 7 proved the same thing, but Joe wasn't inclined to give a bunch of goddamn Japs credit for anything.

He eyed the Texan with a mixture of exasperation and affection. It was a big step up from the sedate Stearman biplane on which he'd done his primary flight training. No sooner had that thought crossed his mind than a Yellow Peril buzzed by overhead. The Navy painted all its Stearmans a luminous yellow to warn other pilots that trainees were in the air.

Yes, the Texan was a long step up from a Yellow Peril. It was a monoplane with a real metal skin, not the doped canvas covering a Stearman. It had a machine gun in the left wing root—the one Joe had used to blast away at the target another plane towed. It had bomb racks, too. It could do a pretty good job of impersonating a warplane.

But it was only an impersonation. The Texan's engine put out half the horsepower of a Wildcat's. Its top speed was only about two-thirds of the Navy fighter's. That that all made it much more forgiving than the genuine article was only a detail to Joe.

Groundcrew men came out to detach the plane's tailhook from the wire and get it out of the way so another cadet could land on the yellow-outlined "carrier deck." Lieutenant Foster said, "How soon do you think you'll be ready to solo in a Texan?"

Joe blinked. He hadn't expected that question from Foster, especially not after the instructor reamed out his navigation. But it had only one possible answer: "Sir, I'm ready to take a swing at it right this minute if you want me to."

Foster had blond hair, a lock of which kept falling down on his forehead, and an aw-shucks smile that probably put the girls in mind of Gary Cooper. It put skinny, swarthy Joe Crosetti in mind of the Nob Hill nobs who looked down their straight noses at dagos like him. But the officer didn't give him a hard time because of his last name or his looks. Foster said, "I approve of your spirit, Mr. Crosetti. The Navy needs more men who don't hesitate. But if the flesh doesn't quite measure up to it, you're better off waiting, and the country would be better off if you did, too." Joe must have looked stubborn, or maybe angry, because the flying instructor sighed and went on, "How many memorial services have you attended since you got here?"

"Uh, a few, sir," Joe admitted. He'd been to more than a few, and he was sure Wiley Foster knew it. As soon as cadets started getting up into the air, they started finding ways to kill themselves. One midair collision between Yellow Perils had wiped out two cadets and two instructors. Cadets had crashed on the runway. They'd gone into the swamps around Pensacola Naval Air Station. A kid took a Stearman out over the Gulf of Mexico and never came back. No one ever found a trace of him—he was missing and presumed dead. All the same, Joe said, "That wouldn't happen to *me*." He had faith in his own indestructibility.

Lieutenant Foster clicked his tongue between his teeth. "That's what they all say. Sometimes it's the last thing they say." He eyed Joe. "You don't believe me, do you?"

"I can swing it," Joe said stubbornly.

Foster looked down at the card on which he'd recorded Joe's marks for the session. "Maybe you can, by God. Next time you go up, you'll go up by yourself."

"Thank you, sir!" Joe wanted to get all excited. He *did* get all excited, but he didn't let most of it show. He was damned if he'd act Italian in front of somebody who looked the way Wiley Foster did.

He did head back to the barracks at the next thing to a dead run. When he first got to Pensacola, he and his roomie had shared a tent. Some cadets still slept under canvas—no enormous handicap in the steamy Pensacola summertime. But he and Orson Sharp had graduated to better things.

By the time he got to the two-story brick barracks building, he was drenched in sweat. San Francisco hadn't come close to getting him ready for Florida heat and humidity. His father was a fisherman; he'd gone out of Fisherman's Wharf with his old man on weekends and during summers before he landed the job at Scalzi's garage. Till he got here, though, he'd never understood what a lobster went through when you dropped it in boiling water.

Heat and humidity or not, he took the stairs two at a time. He ran down the hall and threw the door open. Orson Sharp sat in a chair by his bunk, studying navigation. The cadet from Salt Lake City was big and fair and even-tempered. He didn't swear and he didn't drink coffee, let alone beer. Sharp was the first

Mormon Joe had ever met. Joe sometimes thought he was too good to be true, though he never would have said so.

"How did it go?" Sharp asked, looking up from his book.

Joe's enormous grin probably said everything he needed to say, but he spelled it out just the same: "Lieutenant Foster's going to let me solo next time I go up! I can't wait!"

His roomie's pleasure seemed entirely unalloyed. "That's terrific! I know you were hoping, but I don't think you expected it quite so soon."

"Nope. He liked my firing run at the target. I think that's what clinched it." Slower than he should have, Joe remembered Sharp had flown this morning, too. "How about you?"

"My instructor let me take it up by myself today." Sharp shrugged in wry self-deprecation. "I lived."

Joe fought down a stab of jealousy. His roommate had soloed in a Stearman a week before he had, too. Sharp did everything well and didn't fuss about anything. He was so unassuming, you almost had to act the same way around him. Joe walked over and stuck out his hand. "Way to go! Congratulations!"

"Thanks, buddy." Orson Sharp's hand was almost half again as big as his. When the cadets played football, Sharp was a lineman. Joe played end or defensive back. He was quick, but he wasn't big. "We're getting there," Sharp added.

"Yeah!" Joe said. "We've still got instrument flying to do, on the Link trainers on the ground and then up in the air, and I suppose they'll give us some flight time on F3Fs, too." The Navy's last biplane fighter had stayed in frontline service till less than two months before Pearl Harbor. Joe tried to imagine F3Fs mixing it up with Zeros. Perhaps mercifully, the picture didn't want to form. Now the F3F was a last-step trainer. Joe added two more words: "And then . . ."

"And then we see where they assign us," Sharp said. "Did you put down VC on all three lines on your preference questionnaire way back when?"

"Carrier duty? You bet your . . . You bet I did." Around his roomie, Joe didn't swear very much, either. "You?"

"Oh, sure," Sharp answered. "If they don't give me that, I don't care what I get. Everything else is a booby prize."

"I'm with you." Joe didn't give a damn about patrol planes or flying boats (no, that wasn't true—he hated Jap flying boats, because one had dropped a bomb on the house where his uncle and aunts and cousins lived, but he didn't give a damn about piloting an *American* flying boat) or anything but carrier-based air, preferably fighters.

"I hope we do end up together," Orson Sharp said seriously. "We've made a pretty good team so far."

"Uh-huh." Joe nodded. "I better get some more of that navigation under my belt, too, or else I'm not going anywhere." He pulled his own book out of the metal footlocker by his bed and sat down in a chair. He knew his roomie would give him a hand where he had trouble. He'd helped Sharp through some of the mysteries of engine maintenance. They *did* make a pretty good team. *Look out, Hirohito,* Joe thought, and dove into the book.

LIEUTENANT SABURO SHINDO RARELY GOT EXCITED about anything. Some people said the Navy pilot was a cold fish. He didn't see it like that. To his way of thinking, most people got excited over nothing.

He stood on the *Akagi*'s flight deck and looked around Pearl Harbor. The view here wasn't what it had been before Japan and the United States went to war. Then the American ships in the harbor were tied up alongside piers or rested easily at anchor. Now they were nothing but twisted, blackened, rusting metal. Some of them still leaked oil into the water. Shindo could see several of those rainbow patches. The mineral stink of the fuel oil fouled the tropical breeze.

The third wave of Japanese planes over Oahu had sunk two American destroyers in the channel leading out from Pearl Harbor to the Pacific, trapping the rest of the U.S. Pacific Fleet inside the harbor and letting the Japanese pound it to pieces at their leisure. Shindo nodded to himself. The Americans *would* have tried to sortie against the Japanese strike force. They probably wouldn't have had much luck, not without carrier support, but just as well they hadn't got the chance.

Japanese naval engineers had got the destroyers out of the channel only a few weeks before the failed American invasion. Shindo was glad they had. Now *Akagi* had somewhere local to make repairs without worrying about American submarines: the antitorpedo net was back in place at the mouth of the channel.

Shindo laughed unpleasantly. The Yankees hadn't bothered with torpedo netting for individual ships last December. They hadn't figured anyone could rig torpedoes to run in the shallow waters of Pearl Harbor. Japan taught them otherwise. The devastation here proved that.

Devastation held sway on land, too. Ford Island, in the middle of Pearl Harbor, had been palm trees and ferns where it wasn't U.S. Navy installations. Now it was rubble with greenery poking through; hardly anything held greenery in check for long here. The Americans had fought house to house in Pearl City, north of the harbor. The town where Navy personnel and the civilians who worked for them lived was as battered as the island.

And the land to the east was worse. The Americans had stored their fuel there, and Japanese bombs sent the oil and gas up in smoke. Shindo vividly remembered the smoke: the funeral pyre of U.S. ambitions in the Pacific. The great black greasy plume had stayed in place for weeks, till the fires finally burned themselves out. Nothing grew there. Shindo wondered whether anything ever would. Ford Island and Pearl City had seen war. The tank farms had seen hell.

Near those fuel tanks had stood the U.S. Navy repair facilities. The Yankees wrecked those themselves when they realized they weren't going to be able to hold Oahu. Japanese engineers were full of professional admiration for the job their American counterparts did. It made operating Pearl Harbor as a base for the Japanese Navy much harder—much harder, but not impossible.

As if to underscore that, *Akagi*'s flight deck vibrated under Shindo's feet. Metallic clatters and bangs came from below. A dive bomber had got one home on the carrier during the fight north of the Hawaiian Islands. The bomb penetrated the flight deck near the bow and exploded in the hangar. Luckily, just about all the ship's planes were in the air, defending *Akagi* or attacking the enemy's carriers. Otherwise, things would have been even worse.

Damage-control parties had got steel plates over the hole in the flight deck so the carrier could launch aircraft. That was the essential, the indispensable, repair. Everything else had waited. The crew was attending to the rest now, as best they could here in Hawaiian waters.

Zuikaku, much more badly damaged than *Akagi,* had had to limp back to Japan for repairs. That left her sister ship, *Shokaku,* the only undamaged Japanese carrier in the Eastern Pacific. Shindo muttered to himself. *Shokaku*'s fliers and sailors had less experience than *Akagi*'s. In a crisis . . .

No less a personage than Admiral Yamamoto thought a crisis unlikely any time soon. The Americans had hurt the Japanese carrier force. Japan had crushed the Americans. Two of the three U.S. carriers that had sailed from the American mainland lay on the bottom of the Pacific now. The third, hurt worse than either *Akagi* or *Zuikaku*, had barely staggered back to the West Coast. Whatever invasion fleet followed behind the carriers and their escorts had also run for home.

We smashed them, Shindo thought complacently. *If they come back here again, we'll smash them again, that's all.*

A tall, horse-faced officer came up onto the flight deck from below. Seeing Shindo, he waved and walked toward him. Shindo waved back, then saluted as the other man drew closer. "How are you feeling, Fuchida-*san*?" he asked.

"Better day by day, thanks," Commander Mitsuo Fuchida answered. He'd come down with appendicitis during the fight with the Americans. He'd completed his attack run, brought his bomber back to *Akagi,* gone straight to sick bay, and parted with the inflamed organ.

"Glad to hear it," Shindo said. He'd led *Akagi*'s fighters during the last wave of the attack on Oahu and in the recent battle against the Yankees north of Hawaii. Fuchida had been in overall command in the first wave and also, illness or no, in the fight where he'd come down sick.

"It's over. I got through it. They patched me up," Fuchida said as more clanging and banging came from the hangar deck. Fuchida smiled. "*Akagi* can say the same thing."

"I wish it weren't taking so long," Shindo grumbled. A thoroughly businesslike man, he didn't notice Fuchida's joke till it was too late to respond. Keeping his mind on business, he looked north and east. "I wonder what the Americans are doing with that beat-up flattop of theirs."

"She's under repair up in Seattle," Fuchida answered.

"*Ah, so desu?* I hadn't heard that," Shindo said.

"I just found out a few hours ago myself," Fuchida said. "One of our H8Ks spotted her. They're amazing aircraft." Enthusiasm filled his face. And the big flying boats *were* remarkable planes. Flying out of what had been the Pearl City Pan Am Clipper base, they could reach the West Coast of the USA for reconnaissance work or even to drop bombs. Fuchida had flown on one in a three-plane raid on San Francisco. That, no doubt, accounted for a good part of his enthusiasm.

It also made Shindo jealous as could be. Fuchida was very able. Nobody would have quarreled with that; Shindo certainly didn't. Because he was so able, he sometimes got to do things he wasn't strictly entitled to do. Sitting in the copilot's seat of an H8K was one of those, sure enough.

None of what Shindo thought showed on his face. That was true most of the time, but he made a special point of it now. The two of them served together, but they weren't close friends the way Fuchida and Minoru Genda were. And Fuchida had two grades on Shindo. Letting a superior see what you thought of him was never a good idea.

All Shindo asked, then, was, "What else are the Yankees doing in Seattle?"

"Working around the clock, seems like," Fuchida answered. "It's that way whenever we get a look at one of their ports. They haven't given up."

"If they want another go at us, they can have it," Shindo said. "We'll give them the same kind of lesson we did six weeks ago." He paused, eyeing Fuchida. Now the other naval aviator's face was the sort of polite blank mask behind which anything could have hidden. Shindo decided to press a little to see what was there: "We're just about back up to strength here with aircraft and pilots."

"In numbers, yes," Fuchida said. "Do you think the replacements fly as well as the men we lost? Are the bombardiers as accurate?"

So that was it. Shindo said, "They'll get better as they get more flying time. I was thinking the same thing not long ago about *Shokaku*'s crew."

"I hope so." Fuchida still sounded worried. "We don't have the fuel to give them all the practice I wish they could get."

Saburo Shindo grunted. That, unfortunately, was true. Blowing up the tank farms had hurt Japan as well as the USA—though the Americans surely would have fired them to deny them to the invaders. As things were, the Japanese in Hawaii didn't have the fuel to do all the patrolling by air or water Shindo would have liked to see. They'd spent gasoline and fuel oil like a drunken sailor to get through the last battle. Now they had to bring in more, a ship at a time. It wasn't a good way to do business, not when the merchant ships were short of fuel, too—and not when American subs would be hunting them.

"How soon will we be able to start using the oil we've taken in the Dutch East Indies?" Shindo asked.

"I'm afraid I haven't got the slightest idea," Fuchida answered. "Maybe Commander Genda would know, but I don't."

"If it's not pretty soon, why did we go to war?" Shindo grumbled.

"Because if we hadn't gone to war, we wouldn't have any oil coming in at all," Fuchida said. "And you can't very well worry about using or rationing what you don't have."

However much Shindo would have liked to argue with him, he didn't see how he could.

JIM PETERSON STOOD IN THE CHOW line with his mess kit and spoon. The rice and vegetables the Japs doled out to American POWs in labor gangs weren't enough to keep body and soul together. That didn't mean he wasn't hungry and didn't want the meager supper. Oh, no! For a little while after he ate it, he'd feel . . . not quite so bad.

He'd seen what happened when people got too weary to give a damn about food. The Japs didn't let them rest. They worked them just as hard as anybody else, and beat them if they couldn't keep up. And if the POWs died under such treatment—well, tough luck. Japan hadn't signed the Geneva Convention. As far as her soldiers were concerned, surrender was the ultimate disgrace. Having surrendered, the American soldiers and sailors on Oahu were essentially fair game.

Plop! The man four in front of Peterson got his miserable supper. *Plop!* The man three in front. *Plop!* Two in front. *Plop!* The guy right ahead of Peterson. And then, *plop!*—he got his. For ten or fifteen seconds, the world was a glorious place. He had food! He hurried off to eat it, cradling the mess tin to his chest like a miser with a sack of gold.

A lump of gluey rice and anonymous greens about the size of a softball— that was what he was getting all excited about. He knew it. It shamed him. It made him disgusted at himself. But he couldn't help it. That was how much his body craved even the scanty nourishment the Japs gave him.

For this I went to Annapolis? he thought bitterly as he shoveled glop into his face as fast as he could. He'd been a Navy lieutenant on the *Enterprise,* coming back to Pearl Harbor after delivering fighter planes to Wake Island. He'd roared off the carrier's deck to do what he could against the Japanese—and promptly got shot down. He'd thought his Wildcat was pretty hot stuff till he ran into his first Zero. It was also the last one he'd faced in the air. One was plenty. One had sure been plenty for him.

He managed to bail out, and came down on a golf course near Ewa, the Marines' airfield west of Pearl Harbor. He'd done his damnedest to get back in the air. His damnedest turned out to be no damn good. Lots of pilots— Marines, Army and Navy men—were in line ahead of him. All they needed were planes. The Japs did a hell of a job blowing those to smithereens on the ground. Japanese mastery of the air in the invasion was absolute.

Since Peterson couldn't fight the Japs in the air, he'd fought them on the ground as a common soldier. He'd even been promoted to corporal before the collapse; he still had the stripes on the sleeve of his ragged shirt. Nobody would use him as an officer on the ground, which was only fair, because he hadn't been trained for that. He would have got people killed trying to command a company.

Nobody in his shooting squad knew he'd been an officer. No sooner had he thought of the squad than he thought of Walter London. Up came his head, like a bird dog's. Where was London? There, sitting on a boulder, eating rice like everybody else. Peterson relaxed—fractionally. London was the weak link in the squad, the guy most likely to disappear if he saw half a chance—and if the other guys didn't stop him.

That was what shooting squads were all about. The Jap who'd come up with the idea must have got a bonus from the Devil. If one man escaped, all the others got it in the neck. That violated all the rules of war, of course, but the Japs didn't care. Anybody who'd seen them in action had no doubts that they would get rid of nine because the tenth vamoosed.

The sun sank behind the Waianae Range, Oahu's western mountains. The labor gang was widening the road that led to Kolekole Pass from Schofield Barracks. Why the road needed widening, Peterson couldn't see. He'd been stationed in the Kolekole Pass for a while during the fighting. Not many people wanted to get there, and he couldn't imagine that many people ever would.

But it gave the POWs something to do. It gave the Japs an excuse to work them—to work them to death, very often. Peterson laughed, not that it was funny. Working the prisoners to death was probably no small part of what the Japanese had in mind.

He finished the last grain of rice in the mess kit. He always did. Everybody always did. He remembered when he'd left food on his plate in the *Enterprise*'s wardroom. No more. No more. He got to his feet. He topped six feet by a couple of inches, and had been a fine, rangy figure of a man. Now he was starting to look more like a collection of pipe cleaners in rags. He'd lost somewhere close to fifty pounds, and more weight came off him every day. He didn't see how, but it did.

Peterson made a point of walking right past Walter London and scowling at him. Most POWs were scrawny wretches. London was skinny, but he wasn't scrawny. He was a wheeler-dealer, a man who could come up with cigarettes or soap or aspirin—for a price, always for a price. The price was commonly food.

A stream ran down from the mountains, close by the side of the road. POWs rinsed their mess tins and spoons in it, getting them as clean as they could. Dysentery wasn't bad here, but some men suffered from it—and more, weakened by hard labor, exhaustion, and starvation, came down with it all the time. You did what you could to stay clean and to keep your stuff clean. What you could do often wasn't enough.

There were no huts. There were no beds. There weren't even any blankets. In Hawaii, that mattered much less than it would have a lot of other places. Peterson found some grass and lay down. Other men were already lying close by. If they felt cold in the middle of the night, they would roll together and use one another to keep warm.

He woke in the morning twilight with a Japanese guard's boot in his xylophone ribs. The Jap wasn't kicking him, just stirring him to get him up and moving. If he kept lying there, though, he *would* get kicked. He scrambled to his feet and bowed to the guard. Satisfied, the Jap went on to prod the next closest American awake.

Peterson took his place for morning lineup. Till the men were counted, they got no breakfast. They formed up in rows of ten, which made it easy for the guards to count them. Or that should have made it easy; some of the Japs seemed to have trouble with numbers as big as ten. Maybe Peterson was just being rude in thinking so, but it looked that way to him. A lot of the camp guards seemed to be peasants from the Japanese back of beyond. They were ignorant and mean, and reveled in their petty authority over the Americans.

About one morning in three, something went wrong with the count. This was one of those mornings. Americans muttered to themselves when no guards were looking their way. "Fuck up a wet dream," somebody behind Peterson said. He couldn't remember the last time he'd had a wet dream. When you were slowly starving to death, dreams of pussy went right out the window.

The Japanese sergeant in charge of the labor gang wasn't a bad guy. At least, he could have been worse. He plainly had orders about how much he was supposed to feed the POWs and how much work he was supposed to get out of them. Like just about every Jap Peterson had seen, he conscientiously obeyed his orders. Past what he had to do, he wasn't cruel for the sake of being cruel.

He didn't beat people or behead them just because he felt like it, and he didn't let his men do anything like that, either.

Now, though, he looked about ready to explode. "Shooting squads!" he yelled: one of the handful of English phrases he knew.

Ice ran up Peterson's back. It always did when the prisoners got that command. As usual, the first thing he did was look around to see where Walter London was. He didn't spot him right away. Telling himself that didn't mean anything, he joined his comrades in misery. Along with them, he silently counted off: one, two, three, four, five, six, seven, eight . . . nine. No ten. Wherever London was, he wasn't here.

"Oh, fuck," somebody said very softly. It seemed more a prayer than a curse.

"How did he get loose?" Peterson's voice was also soft, but very grim. They'd kept a watch on London through the night, taking turns gapped out of their exhausted sleep. The man they worried about, of course, hadn't had to watch himself. He'd slept like a baby. Till last night, he'd slept like a baby.

"I had the last watch," a guy from Oregon named Terry said. Naked fear widened his eyes until you could see white all around the iris. "I guess maybe I fell asleep again, on account of the Jap kinda poked me awake this morning. I didn't think anything about it till—"

"Yeah. Till," somebody broke in. "You just put all our necks in the noose, God damn you."

"Too late to do anything about it. The asshole's gone." Peterson sounded even wearier than he felt—no mean trick. Under the laws of war, a sentry who fell asleep at his post could go up in front of a firing squad. He didn't take his buddies to perdition with him, though.

Here came the Japs. No chance to sneak in somebody from another group that had already been counted. The Japs might have trouble getting to eleven without taking off their shoes, but they knew nine, and they knew nine wasn't ten. They started pointing and yelling and jabbering in their own language.

The gang-boss sergeant tramped up. He had no trouble getting to nine and not to ten, either. The POWs stood at ramrod-stiff attention. The sergeant might not have been a bad guy, but he lost his temper now. Peterson even felt a moment's sympathy for him; he'd probably get in Dutch because of the escape, too.

"*Zakennayo!*" he yelled—a handy-dandy all-purpose Japanese obscenity. "*Baka yaro!*" he tacked on for good measure. *Idiots!* That also didn't fit the situation too badly. But cussing wasn't enough to satisfy him. He walked up to the closest POW in the shooting squad and slapped him in the face, hard.

He might not normally have beaten people, but things weren't normal now. Japanese noncoms belted their own privates when they got mad. The privates took it without blinking and went on about their business. The prisoners had to do the same, or else they *would* get shot on the spot.

Wham! Wham! Wham! The sergeant wasn't real tall, but he had a bull's shoulders. He didn't hit like somebody's girlfriend when she got mad. He was trying to knock you ass over teakettle. Peterson had just time to brace himself before he got it. His head whipped to one side. He refused to give the Jap the satisfaction of staggering, though he tasted blood in his mouth.

The damn Jap came back along the row, smacking everybody again. He screamed at the Americans. It was all in Japanese, but he illustrated with gestures. He did excellent impressions of being hanged, being shot, and having his throat cut—the last complete with gruesomely authentic sound effects. Then he pointed at the POWs. *This is going to happen to you.*

Peterson had figured it would happen right there. It didn't. The sergeant told off three guards and had them march the nine remaining members of the shooting squad back to Opana, the northernmost point on Oahu, to the POW camp where they'd been held since not long after the fighting stopped. The men got no food and no water. Whenever one of them stopped for any reason, the Japs set on him with their rifle butts.

After a day of that, Peterson decided he would take off when they stopped for the night. If they shot him trying to escape, he didn't figure he'd lost much. And they were going to do in his buddies anyway, so he couldn't get them into any worse trouble. Disappearing—if he could—looked like his best hope.

He never got the chance. The Japs herded the shooting squad into Waimea, on the north coast, just as the sun was going down. The men spent the night in one cell of the town jail—all of them crammed into one cell. The cell, naturally, had not been made with nine men in mind. They filled it to overflowing and piled onto one another when they lay down.

Nobody fed them. But, because the cell had been built by Americans and not by Japanese, it boasted a cold-water sink and a toilet. Jim Peterson drank till he thought water would start coming out of his ears. He washed his face and hands, too. Everybody else did the same thing. And none of them had heard a toilet flush for a hell of a long time.

When morning came, the Japs herded them out. They'd already used the sink again, expecting that they wouldn't get any water the rest of the day. They turned out to be right about that. And, because they didn't seem demoralized enough to suit their captors, the Japs quickmarched them north and east along the highway towards Opana. Now even slowing down meant a goose with a bayonet or a kick or a rifle butt in the kidneys or the ribs or the head.

Of course, quickmarching the prisoners meant the guards had to quickmarch, too. But they were well fed, and they hadn't been killing themselves with hard physical labor. They might have been tired by the time they got up to Opana. Peterson felt ready for the boneyard.

And the Japs were ready to give it to him, too. Everybody from the shooting squad went into punishment cells. They weren't big enough for anybody to stand up or lie down in them. The prisoners spent ten days in them, with only a little rice and a little water on which to stay alive.

When Peterson finally did emerge from his cell, he could barely stand. Everybody else in the squad was just as bad off. An officer strode up to them with an interpreter—a local Jap—in tow. That worried Peterson all by itself. If the Japs had something to say that they wanted the POWs to understand, it wasn't going to be good news.

Hand on the hilt of his sword, the officer snarled in Japanese. "You have failed in your obligation," the interpreter said. "Because you have failed, you will be punished. No longer will you be allowed the light duty you have enjoyed up till now."

Peterson didn't laugh in the man's face. If he had, the officer might have used that sword to cut off his head. He still wanted to live, though right at that minute he couldn't have said why.

Another furious-sounding spate of Japanese. "You will be sent to road building in the Kalihi Valley," the local Jap said. "This is your unbreakable sentence." He might have been sending them off to Devil's Island.

The officer growled one more time. The interpreter left it untranslated, which might have been just as well. The officer drew himself up straight, which would have been more impressive if he'd been taller than five-six. Like the rest of the men in the shooting squad, Peterson bowed. They knew what the Jap wanted.

As the officer swaggered away with the interpreter in his wake, Peterson dared breathe a sigh of relief. As far as he could see, they'd got off easy. Road building was road building. How could what they wanted him to do be any worse than what he'd been doing already?

And where the devil was the Kalihi Valley, anyway?

CORPORAL TAKEO SHIMIZU GATHERED HIS SQUAD by eye. "You boys ready to go back to Honolulu?" he asked.

"Yes, Corporal!" chorused the men under him. Of course they called out, "*Hai!*" at the top of their lungs. He was a noncom and they were only privates. If they annoyed him, he could slap them or punch them or kick them, and no one above him would say a word. No, that wasn't quite true. Lieutenant Horino, the platoon commander, would say, *Well done! Keep your men disciplined!* Certainly, though, no one above him would complain.

Odds were he wouldn't smack them around. He had a ready smile and a readier laugh. He'd been a while making corporal; his superiors came right out and said they feared he was too easygoing for the job. But he'd fought, and fought well, in China before crossing the Pacific to land on a beach not far from where he was now. Once he had the rank, he kept his squad in line well enough even if he didn't thump his men as often as some other corporals and sergeants did with theirs.

"Let's go, then," he said. His whole regiment had moved up from Honolulu to the beaches near Haleiwa on Oahu's north shore to defend against an American reinvasion. It hadn't come—the Japanese Navy had made sure it wouldn't and couldn't. Now the regiment was returning to its previous posting.

"This is pretty country. It's a shame to leave," Shiro Wakuzawa said. He wasn't wrong—it was the sort of country where ferns sprouted from the dirt thrown up in front of foxholes, where coconut palms (the ones that hadn't been knocked over when the Japanese shelled and bombed the beaches) swayed in tropical breezes, where the ocean was several improbably beautiful shades of blue. But Wakuzawa, who'd been a new conscript when he came ashore here, was such a sunny fellow that he made even Shimizu seem like a grouch.

An older private said, "I won't be sorry to get back to Honolulu. No whorehouses up here." With his meager pay, he couldn't afford to go to a brothel even once a month. But several other soldiers who had no more money nodded. Shimizu didn't try to argue with them. He also thought getting laid every once in a while was better than not getting laid at all. Getting laid regularly would have been better still. *Wish for the moon while you're at it,* he thought.

He led the squad over to where the platoon was assembling. Everyone was clean. Everyone had all his gear. Everyone could stand inspection—everyone already had stood Shimizu's inspection. Shimizu nodded to Corporal Kiyoshi Aiso, whose squad was also part of the platoon. Aiso nodded back. He was thin and leathery and tough—all in all, a more typical noncom than Shimizu.

Colonel Fujikawa, the regimental commander, condescended to speak to the assembled soldiers before they started marching down across Oahu. "Congratulations, men. You were ready for action," he said. "I know you would have mown down the Americans if they had dared return to Oahu. We will stay ready in case they decide to try again. *Banzai!* for the Emperor."

"*Banzai!*" the soldiers shouted.

The bugler blared out the order to advance. The soldiers started to march. "Be strong!" Shimizu called to his men. "You were soft as tofu on the march up here. I expect better." Garrison duty in Honolulu had left all of them soft. Shimizu had suffered on the march up to Haleiwa, too, but hadn't shown it in front of his men. If he kept up a bold front, he had no trouble ordering them around.

Everything seemed easy when he started out. He laughed at the mynah birds croaking and squawking in the rice paddies that had replaced most of the sugar cane and pineapple plantations past and through which he'd fought. Hawaii hadn't come close to feeding itself before Japan conquered it. Now it nearly could.

Little blue-faced zebra doves and ordinary pigeons pecked at the growing rice. There were far fewer of them than there had been when Shimizu came ashore. They were good to eat, and people had got hungry enough to eat them. And zebra doves in particular were very tame and very stupid and very easy to catch.

Before long, Wakuzawa started to sing. He had a fine musical voice, and could stick to the tune even when the soldiers around him—who weren't nearly so good—made a hash of it. Singing helped the kilometers go by. Shimizu had done a lot of it on endless dusty marches through China. The marches here weren't endless, thank heaven, and they weren't even dusty, for the roads were paved. But singing felt good all the same.

He thought so, anyhow. After Wakuzawa had led the men in a couple of ballads popular in Tokyo before they sailed for Hawaii, Lieutenant Horino said, "We are soldiers. If we're going to sing, we should sing Army songs."

Army songs had only one thing wrong with them: next to popular ballads, they were dull. Singing about the infantry's branch-of-service color and about dying for the Emperor and living on inside his spirit wasn't nearly so much fun as singing about women and getting drunk and looking for a chance to get rich and women again. Even the tunes were dull; they seemed more chants than proper songs. How could you care about singing something like that?

After a while, then, the men fell silent once more. Lieutenant Horino looked pleased with himself. To his way of thinking, he'd stopped a minor nuisance. Corporal Shimizu swallowed a sigh. When he was singing, he could do that and not notice the highway and each step along it. Now—thump, thump, thump—each footfall was what it was.

The soldiers trudged through Wahiawa. Like Haleiwa farther north, it wasn't anything special: not very big, not very rich. It wasn't very rich by Hawaiian standards, anyhow. But towns here never failed to remind Shimizu that America was a much richer country than Japan. Cars sat by the curb—so many! They couldn't go now, because they had no fuel, but ordinary people had been able to buy them. In Japan, cars were for rich men.

Some of the tires on these automobiles had gone flat. Some had been removed, too. Sooner or later, Malaya would give Japan rubber, but she was desperately short of it now. All those tires weren't doing the people of Hawaii any good, not when they couldn't drive the cars on which the tires were mounted. Better they should help Japan, then.

In Wahiawa, as anywhere else, civilians had to bow when Japanese soldiers went by. Local Japanese not only took it in stride, they did it properly, showing just the right amount of deference and respect. Whites and Chinese and Filipinos weren't so good, but orders were not to make an issue out of any bow that showed the right spirit.

A pretty blond woman in her late twenties—not far from Shimizu's age—bent as the soldiers went past. He remembered seeing a pretty woman with yellow hair as his regiment marched up through Wahiawa. Was this the same one? How could he tell after several weeks?

He'd seen a handful of missionaries in China. But for them, these people on Oahu were the first whites he'd ever set eyes on. They were big. He'd seen that from the moment he landed, when they started shooting at him. But big didn't mean tough—or not tough enough, anyhow. They'd fought hard, but in the end they'd surrendered.

Shimizu's lip curled. They deserved whatever happened to them after that. He couldn't imagine anything but fighting to the finish. At least then it was over. You didn't give yourself up to the foe so he could do whatever he wanted with you—and to you.

Lieutenant Horino strode along with one hand on the hilt of his sword. "Let them see who their masters are," he declared.

No one in Wahiawa showed the Japanese even the slightest disrespect. The locals would have been crazy to do so. Whoever tried it would have paid, and so would his or her family and friends and neighbors. Civilians didn't have shooting squads the way prisoners did, but the occupying authorities would have come up with something to make people remember.

Then the regiment trudged out of the town. More rice paddies replaced cane and pineapple. Men muttered about sore feet. No one would have had the energy to sing now. Shimizu didn't have the energy or the desire to order them to sing an Army song. He picked his feet up and put them down again, over and over and over.

The regiment didn't quite make it into Pearl City, let alone Honolulu, before the sun went down. Colonel Fujikawa looked unhappy. He'd also been unhappy when they failed to march from Honolulu to Haleiwa in one day. "You've got weak," he grumbled.

He was probably right, too. Oahu didn't offer marching opportunities the way, say, China did. You could march forever in China. After a lot of campaigns there, Shimizu thought he had. This place wasn't like that. You settled down and you patrolled in town, and that was that. If you did a whole lot of marching here, you marched into the Pacific.

As the men were settling down by the side of the road, an enormous flying boat landed in Pearl Harbor and taxied up to the shore at Pearl City. "I wonder what that's all about," said Senior Private Yasuo Furusawa, who was curious about everything.

"No idea," Shimizu said. "If the brass wants us to know, they'll tell us about it. As long as it's one of our planes, I won't lose any sleep about it."

It must have been a Japanese plane—no gunfire erupted, no bombs burst. He ate rice, assigned sentries, and rolled himself in a blanket as soon as it got dark. And, weary as he was, he lost not even a moment's sleep.

* * *

By now, Jane Armitage was used to Japanese soldiers tramping through Wahiawa. She was used to bowing whenever she saw them. She was used to keeping her thoughts to herself. If she didn't, someone might blab to the Japs, and what happened after that wouldn't be pretty.

And she was used to being hungry. She hated looking into the mirror in her apartment. The face that stared back was a stranger's, all cheekbones and chin and staring eyes. Only her yellow hair reminded her that she was really herself. When she got into the shower, her ribs stood out like ladder rungs. She could watch muscles move on her arms and legs.

The only thing that kept her from complete despair was that everybody in Wahiawa was in the same boat—all the locals, anyhow, for the occupiers ate well enough to keep their weight on. One scrawny wretch in a group of normal people would have drawn notice. One scrawny wretch in a group of scrawny wretches? They said misery loved company. By God, they had a point.

"Damn you, Fletch," she would whisper once in a while, when she was sure nobody could hear. Her ex-husband had been an artillery officer at nearby Schofield Barracks. He'd sworn up and down that the U.S. Army would give the Japs a black eye if they ever came anywhere near Hawaii. These days, Jane despised him more for being wrong than she did for drinking too much and generally for forgetting she existed except when he felt like a roll in the hay.

She couldn't brood for very long. She had her vegetable patch to look after. She was growing turnips and potatoes. She hated what the work did to her hands. They were hard and callused and scarred, with short nails with permanently black rims. There too, though, she wasn't the only one—far from it. Without the produce the locals grew, they might well have starved to death. The occupying forces wouldn't have shed a tear. The Japs might have laughed instead.

She hardly ever thought, *I should be teaching third grade,* any more. The elementary school was closed, by all appearances permanently. The principal . . . Jane flinched away from that thought. She still remembered the thunk of Major Hirabayashi's sword biting into Mr. Murphy's neck when the Japs caught Murphy with a radio after they ordered all sets turned in.

But the dreadful sound and the memory came back to her even when she was weeding in the little plot of ground. She'd chop through some nasty plant's

HARRY TURTLEDOVE

26

stem . . . and Murphy's head would leap from his shoulders, blood fountaining impossibly red and his whole body convulsing—but not for long, not for long.

"Your plot looks good."

Four words returned her to reality. Bad as reality was, it beat the stuffing out of what had been going on in her head. She turned. "Thank you, Mr. Nakayama," she said. She didn't have to bow to Tsuyoshi Nakayama. He was just a local Jap, a nursery man, not one of the invaders. But she did have to treat him with respect. He was Major Hirabayashi's interpreter and factotum. Get on his wrong side and you'd be sorry. Jane didn't want to find out how sorry she could be.

"Thank you for working so hard," Yosh Nakayama told her. He was about fifty, but looked older, his face tanned to wrinkled leather from a lifetime in the sun. "If everyone worked as hard as you, we would have more to eat."

He'd lost weight, too. He hadn't used his position to take special privileges—of which food came first these days, well ahead of money or women's favors. By all appearances, he didn't much want the job he had. That didn't keep him from doing it conscientiously.

Jane saw a bug. Automatically, she lashed out with a foot and squashed it. Nakayama nodded approval. "Some people don't care enough to do things right," he said. His English was slow and deliberate—fluent, but not quite the speech of someone who'd grown up with the language. "You are not like that."

"Well, I hope not," Jane said. "If you're going to do something, do it right."

He nodded again, and actually smiled. His teeth were very white, except for a couple of glinting gold ones. "Yes," he said, and went on to the next vegetable patch without another word.

Yes? Jane wondered. *Then why didn't my marriage work?* Of course, that had taken two, and Fletch hadn't exactly held up his end of the bargain. Jane wondered if he was still alive. If he was, he was probably a prisoner. She shivered under the warm Hawaiian sun. The Japs treated POWs worse than they treated civilians, and that was saying something. Gangs of prisoners occasionally shambled through Wahiawa, on their way to God knows what. She didn't like thinking that Fletch could be one of those skeletons in rags.

She didn't wish her ex-husband anything particularly bad. If she ever saw him coming up the street in one of those labor gangs, she would . . . She didn't have the faintest idea what she would do. Break down and cry, most likely. But if she broke down and cried about everything in Hawaii that upset her these days, she'd have no time to do anything else. She assassinated a weed instead.

PLATOON SERGEANT LESTER DILLON WAS NOT A HAPPY MAN. The Marines who served under him would have said he was never a happy man, but a platoon sergeant was supposed to make his men feel as if hell wasn't half a mile off. He wanted them more afraid of him, and of letting him down, than of the enemy.

He knew how that worked. He'd been a buck private himself in 1918, and his own sergeant had scared him a damn sight more than the Germans did. He'd gone over the top time after time, till a machine-gun bullet took a bite out of his leg and put him on the shelf for the rest of what the politicians had insisted was the War to End All Wars.

But his unhappiness here was at least as much personal as it was institutional. His company commander, Captain Braxton Bradford, had ordered all his noncoms not to go drinking in San Diego. Bradford's logic was crystal clear. "Y'all go drinking off the base, you'll run into sailors," he'd said—he was as Southern as his name. "Y'all run into sailors, you'll fight 'em. Tell me I'm wrong and you can go."

None of the corporals and sergeants had even tried. Les knew he wanted to punch the first swabbie he saw. One of his buddies, another platoon sergeant named Dutch Wenzel, said, "We wouldn't if those pussies hadn't blown the fight with the Japs."

"They did their damnedest," Captain Bradford answered. "Nobody can say any different."

No one contradicted that, either. It didn't matter. What mattered was that the troopship carrying the regiment had had to hightail it back to the mainland after the Navy lost. Marines didn't like running away, even for the best of reasons. There had already been a lot of brawls between angry leathernecks and sailors. Some of the sailors hadn't even been part of the failed attack on Hawaii. The Marines weren't inclined to be fussy.

And so Dillon sat in the Camp Elliott NCOs' club, soaking up a beer and pondering the unfairness of the world—a melancholy pursuit usually reserved for privates and other lower forms of life. It wasn't so much that he minded drinking with his own kind. He didn't. But the decor left a good deal to be desired. And the chances of picking up a barmaid were pretty damn slim—there were no barmaids, only Filipino mess stewards to take away empties and sometimes help the bartender by bringing out reinforcements.

When Dutch Wenzel walked into the club, Les waved to him. Wenzel ambled over. He and Dillon were two of a kind: big, fair-haired men with bronze suntans that said they spent a lot of time in the open. Wenzel was a few years younger: too young to have got into the First World War. But he'd served in Central America and in China and on several warships, just like Les.

"Bourbon over ice," he called to the barkeep, who waved back to show he'd heard. Wenzel nodded to Dillon. "Ain't this a lovely snafu?"

"What? You mean you'd rather be drinking in Honolulu?" Les said.

"Bet your ass," Wenzel replied. "And they wouldn't try and put Hotel Street off limits, either. We'd riot if they did, and so would the Navy. Army, too," he added after a moment—to a Marine, soldiers were hardly worth noticing.

"We coulda done it," Dillon said, draining his beer and holding up the glass to show he wanted another one. "If they'd landed us, we could've kicked the Japs' scrawny little ass."

"Oh, hell, yes," Wenzel said. He paused while the bartender brought his drink and a new beer for Dillon. "No doubt about it. They beat the Army, yeah, but they wouldn't've had a chance with us. Not a chance." He sounded as sure as if he were talking about the sunrise. That the Japanese had beaten the Army might almost have been proof they couldn't beat the Marines.

"Wonder how long it'll be before we have another go at the slant-eyed sons of bitches," Les said moodily, and then answered his own question: "We're gonna have to build more carriers first. God only knows how long that'll take."

"I hope they started 'em before we got whipped out there," his friend said. "Hell, I hope they started before the bombs stopped falling on Pearl Harbor."

Dillon nodded. "I wish they would've started a long time before that. Then we wouldn't've had to worry about any of this in the first place."

"Yeah, and then you wake up." Wenzel knocked back the rest of his drink. He looked over to the man behind the bar and nodded. The barkeep started making him another one. He went on, "Half the guys who joined the Corps in the Thirties did it because they were out of work—no better reason than that."

"Most of 'em turned out to make pretty fair Marines anyway," Dillon said. *He'd* signed up in a wartime burst of patriotism. He didn't ask why Dutch had. If Wenzel wanted to say, he would, but you didn't ask. The Marines weren't the French Foreign Legion, but they came closer than any other U.S. outfit.

II

THE *OSHIMA MARU* RAN SOUTH BEFORE THE WIND THAT BLEW DOWN FROM Oahu's hills. The island rapidly receded behind the fishing sampan. Jiro Takahashi tended the sails with more pleasure than he'd ever taken in riding herd on a diesel engine. Up till Hawaii changed hands, the boat, like all the sampans that set out from Kewalo Basin, had had a motor. When fuel dried up, they'd had to make other arrangements.

"I used to do this on the Inner Sea with my father when I was a boy," Jiro said. "You had to sail then—nobody could afford an engine."

His two sons, Hiroshi and Kenzo, only nodded. Neither said anything. Jiro realized he might have mentioned his time on Japan's Inner Sea a time or two—dozen—before. But that wasn't the only thing that made his sons surly. They'd both been born here on Oahu. Their Japanese was all right—Jiro had made sure of that with after-school lessons—but they both preferred English, a language in which he'd learned only a few swear words and other common phrases. They liked hamburgers and hot dogs better than rice and raw fish. Kenzo was seeing a blond girl named Elsie Sundberg. They were, in short, Americans.

Because they were Americans, they hated the Japanese conquest of Hawaii. They hardly bothered making a secret of it. They hadn't got in trouble for it, but they'd had endless rows with their father.

Jiro Takahashi had been born near Hiroshima. He'd come to Hawaii when he was still in his teens, before the First World War, to work in the cane fields, make himself some money, and go home. He'd made himself some money: enough to get out of the fields and go back to fishing, which was what he knew best. But he'd never returned to Japan. He'd married Reiko, settled down in Honolulu, and raised his family.

A sigh escaped him. "What is it, Father?" asked Hiroshi, who was standing by the rudder.

"I was just thinking of your mother," Jiro answered.

"Ah. I'm sorry," his older son said, and looked downcast. So did Kenzo. Their mother had died in the closing days of the fighting, when the Japanese bombarded Honolulu. The two of them and Jiro had been at sea. When they came ashore, that whole district was nothing but wreckage and fire. No one ever found Reiko Takahashi's body.

Even there, Jiro and his sons differed. The boys blamed Japan for bombing and shelling a defenseless city. Jiro blamed the Americans for not giving up when their cause was plainly hopeless.

He remained proud to be Japanese. He'd waved a Rising Sun flag when the Japanese Army held its triumphal parade through Honolulu after the Americans finally did surrender. Along with everyone else along the parade route, he'd gaped at the dirty, ragged, glum American prisoners herded along by Japanese soldiers with well-pressed uniforms and gleaming bayonets. The big, hulking Americans weren't cocks o' the walk any more. He still made a point of delivering fancy fish to the Japanese consulate on Nuuanu Avenue. He was, in short, Japanese to the core, and glad about what his countrymen had done.

And, being a father whose sons had ideas of their own (and what other kind of father was there?), he wasted no chance to show the younger generation it wasn't as smart as it thought it was. "These islands are going to stay in the Great East Asia Co-Prosperity Sphere," he said. "You saw what happened when the Americans tried to take them back. They couldn't do it."

"They'll try again," Kenzo said. "You can bet your bottom dollar on it."

"I'd rather bet a yen—-that's real money," Jiro said.

Before Kenzo could answer, Hiroshi spoke rapidly in English. Kenzo's reply in the same language sounded hot. Hiroshi said something else. Jiro's sons went back and forth like that whenever they didn't want him to know what was going on. Finally, Hiroshi returned to Japanese: "Father-*san*, can we please leave politics ashore? There's not much room to get away from each other here, and we all have to work together to bring in the fish."

Perhaps a bit grudgingly, Jiro nodded. "All right. We'll let it go," he said. Hiroshi had been polite enough that he couldn't very well refuse without seeming churlish even to himself. He spoke an obvious truth: "The fish do come first."

Now both his sons nodded, plainly in relief. The truth Jiro had spoken was truer than usual these days. Cut off from supplies from the U.S. mainland, Oahu was a hungry place. Without all the sampans setting out from Kewalo Basin, it would have been hungrier yet.

Sampans weren't the only fishing contraptions on the water nowadays, either. The *Oshima Maru* glided past a surfboard with a sail mounted on it to take it farther out to sea than the blond, sun-bronzed *haole* on it could have gone by paddling alone. He waved to the sampan as it went by. Jiro's sons waved back.

"Foolishness," Jiro said. That wasn't fair, and he knew it: the sailboard wasn't foolish, but it sure was funny-looking.

"I think that *haole* is the fellow we saw coming out of Eizo Doi's shop one time," Kenzo said. "I bet Doi put the mast and sail on his surfboard, the same as he did for the *Oshima Maru*."

"Could be." Jiro was inclined to think a little better of the white man on the surfboard if he'd visited a Japanese handyman. Before the war, a lot of the *haoles* on Oahu had tried to pretend the Japanese didn't exist . . . and had done their best to hold them down, not letting them compete on even terms. Well, *that* was over and done with now.

"We've got a good wind behind us," Hiroshi said.

"*Hai.*" Jiro nodded. He liked the *Oshima Maru* better as a sailboat than he had when she was motorized. She was silent now except for the thrum of the wind in the rigging and the slap of waves against her beamy hull. No diesel roar, not now. No diesel vibration felt through the soles of the feet, either—just the undulating motion of the sampan over the chop. And no stinking diesel exhaust; Jiro didn't miss that at all.

The one drawback to traveling with the wind was the obvious one: she'd been faster with the diesel. Kenzo said, "We're liable to be out two or three days finding a decent place to fish."

Jiro only grunted, not because his younger son was wrong but because he was right. "It's not just that we're slower, either," Hiroshi said. "Fewer fish close to Oahu these days, I think." Jiro grunted again; he suspected that was also true. There was a lot more fishing now than there had been before Hawaii changed hands. With American supplies cut off and with people desperate for any kind of food, they took whatever they could get from the sea. Before the war, he and his sons had thrown trash fish back into the Pacific. There were no trash fish, not any more.

Half a dozen flying fish sprang out of the water and glided through the air for a little ways before splashing into the sea once more. They did that to escape the bigger fish that were trying to catch them. The bigger fish—*aku* and *ahi* and *mahi-mahi* and even barracuda and sharks—were what the Takahashis wanted most. Kenzo dropped a hook into the water. Jiro didn't stop the sampan. They weren't far enough out to make this a really good place. But if his son wanted to see if he could snag a fish or two—well, why not?

And Kenzo did, too. The line jerked. He pulled in the fish. "*Ahi!*" he said happily, and then, in English, "Albacore." His gutting knife flashed. He tossed the entrails into the Pacific. The knife flashed again. He cut strips of flesh from the fish's side and handed them to Jiro and Hiroshi. Then he cut one for himself. They all ate. The flesh was nearly as rich as beef.

"Not American food, raw fish," Jiro jeered gently.

"Still good," Hiroshi said.

Kenzo nodded. Jiro couldn't tease them too hard about that. Even if they'd preferred burgers and fries when they could get them, they'd always eaten sashimi, too. Kenzo said, "And it's an awful lot better than what we'd get ashore." *That* might have been the understatement of the year. Rice and greens and not enough of either . . . No, Jiro couldn't argue there. Kenzo went on, "And sashimi's always better the fresher it is, and it just doesn't get any fresher than this."

"People who aren't fishermen don't know what really fresh fish tastes like," Hiroshi said. "Cut me some more, please."

"And me," Jiro said.

Kenzo did. He cut another strip for himself, too. Before long, there wasn't much left of the *ahi*. All three of the Takahashis were smiling. Jiro nodded to his older son. Hiroshi had hit the nail on the head. People who didn't put to sea had no idea how good fish really could be.

WAIKIKI BEACH STRAIGHT AHEAD. Oscar van der Kirk decided to put on a show. He had a stringbag full of fish at his feet. He made sure it was closed and tied to a peg he'd set into his sailboard. The peg was new, something he'd thought of only a little while before. Quite a few surf-riders were taking sailboards out to sea these days. Oscar had been first, though. He didn't begrudge anyone else the use of the idea, even if he might have made a nice chunk of change from it in peacetime. War and hunger had laws of their own, laws sterner and less forgiving than the usual sort.

For that matter, Oscar seldom begrudged anybody anything. He was a big, good-natured fellow at the very end of his twenties. The sun and the ocean had bleached his already blond hair somewhere between the color of straw and snow. His hide, by contrast, had tanned such a dark brown that a lot of people wondered if he was part Hawaiian in spite of that blond hair.

He could hear the waves crashing on the shore now. Soon they would lift the board—and him. They would slam him down in the Pacific and make him look like a prize chump if he wasn't careful, too. But he commonly was careful, and skillful to boot. He'd scratched out a living as a surf-riding instructor—a surf-riding show-off, if you like—for years before the Japs came, and even for a while afterwards.

The wave he rode, as tall as a man, started to lean toward the beach ahead. He stood atop the sailboard like a Hawaiian god, one hand on the mast, the other arm outflung for balance. Speed built as he skimmed along the crest. Wind in his face, shifting water under the shifting board . . . There was no sensation in the world like this. Nothing else even came close.

He knew quite a bit about other sensations, too. He'd given surf-riding lessons to a lot of wahines over from the mainland who were trying to recover from a broken heart or just looking for a romance that would be fun but wouldn't mean anything once they sailed away. His good looks, his strength, and his aw-shucks attitude meant he'd also given a lot of them lessons in things besides surf-riding.

Here came the beach. The wave was played out, mastered. The surfboard scraped against sand. Some of the men fishing in the surf clapped their hands. One of them tossed Oscar a shiny silver coin, as if he were a trained seal getting a sardine. He dug the coin out of the soft white sand. It was a half-dollar. That was real money. "Thanks, pal," he said as he stuck it in the small pocket on his swim trunks.

He took down the sailboard's mast and boom and rolled up the small sail that propelled it. Farther from the sea than the surf fishermen, a couple of

Japanese Army officers watched him. Oscar muttered to himself. He wouldn't have come in so spectacularly had he known he was under their cold stare. He felt like a rabbit hopping around while hawks soared overhead.

Then one of them tossed him a coin. The one-yen silverpiece was about the size of a quarter, and worth about as much. When he picked it up, he had to remember to bow to the Jap. The officer returned the bow, much more elegantly than he'd given it. "*Ichi-ban,*" the Jap said. "*Wakarimasu-ka?*"

Oscar nodded to show he *did* understand. *Ichi-ban* was part of the local pidgin a *kamaaina*—an old-timer in Hawaii—picked up. It meant *A number one,* or something like that.

"Thanks," Oscar said, as politely as he could. You never knew when one of these monkeys turned out to speak English. "Thanks very much."

And sure as hell, this one answered, "You are welcome." If he hadn't gone to school in the States, Oscar would have been surprised. They might even have been at Stanford at the same time; they weren't far apart in age.

Oscar carried the surfboard, mast, and rigging under one arm and the stringbag full of fish in his other hand. He hoped these Japs wouldn't give him a hard time about that. Just about all food was supposed to go into community kitchens, share and share alike. They allowed sampan fishermen enough for what they called "personal use"; the rest of the catch they bought at a fixed price, so much per pound regardless of what kind of fish it was. So far, the Japs hadn't harried the men who fished from sailboards—they didn't catch enough to make a fuss over. But the occupiers could harass them if they wanted to. They could do almost anything they wanted to.

To his relief, this pair just nodded to him as he walked by. Maybe they admired the show he'd put on, and didn't bother him because of that. Maybe . . . Who the hell knew for sure with Japs? All he knew for sure was, they weren't going to worry about his fish. That was all he needed to know, too.

He had an apartment not far from Waikiki Beach—a perfect place for a fellow who made his living surf-riding. The man who owned the building was a local Japanese who lived on the ground floor. Oscar knocked on his door. When the man answered, Oscar presented him with a couple of fat mackerel. "Here you go, Mr. Fukumoto," he said. "Another week, eh?"

His landlord examined the fish. "Okay. Another week," he said in accented English. Oscar went upstairs to his own place. He would have bet more business got done by barter than with cash these days. Money, very often, couldn't buy food.

Once back in his apartment, Oscar put some of the fish in the little icebox in the cramped kitchenette. That would feed him and his lady friend for a bit. The rest of the catch stayed in the stringbag. Out he went, bound for Honolulu, and especially for the Oriental district there, the section west of Nuuanu Avenue.

The markets in that part of town were fluctuating things, popping up now here, now there. They were, at best, marginally legal. Oscar suspected—no, he was sure—some Japanese palms got greased to make sure some Japanese eyes looked the other way. People who caught things and people who grew things traded and sold what they had. Money could buy food there, all right—if you had enough of it.

With fish in hand, Oscar could almost name his own price for it. But he wasn't out for cash, or not primarily. He traded some of his catch for tomatoes, some for potatoes, some for string beans, and some for a small, squat jug. What he had left after that . . . well, greenbacks would do.

He could have got a ride back to Waikiki, but rickshaws and pedicabs stuck in his craw. Just because you paid a man to act like a beast of burden, that didn't mean he ought to be one. While there'd been gasoline—and diesel fuel for buses—such contraptions hadn't existed in Honolulu. They did now. His own Chevy was long since *hors de combat*.

But Oscar didn't mind shank's mare. He got back to the apartment a little before Susie Higgins came in. Susie was a cute strawberry blonde, a divorcée from Pittsburgh. Oscar had taught her to ride the surf. She'd taught him a few things, too. She had both a temper and an eye for the main chance. They'd quarreled, broken up, and come back together a few weeks before.

Her eyes, as blue as a Siamese cat's, lit up when she saw the potatoes. "Spuds! Oscar, I could kiss you!" she said, and she did. "I'm so goddamn sick of rice, you wouldn't believe it."

"Rice is a lot better than empty," Oscar observed.

"My boss says the same thing," Susie answered. Though just a tourist, she'd landed a secretary's job after she and Oscar parted the first time. She'd done it with talent, too, not with her fair tanned body. As if to prove as much, she added, "Of course, his wife's Chinese, so he's used to the stuff."

"Long as my belly doesn't growl too loud, I'm not fussy," Oscar said. "I don't mind rice. As many Japanese and Chinese places as I've been to, I'd better not."

"It's not American," Susie said. "Once in a while is okay, I guess, but all the time?" She shook her head. "I feel like my eyes are getting slanty."

"Forget it, babe," Oscar told her. "You can eat rice till everything turns blue, and you still won't look like a Jap."

"Oh, Oscar, you say the sweetest things." Was that sarcasm? With Susie, it was sometimes hard to tell.

These days, she and Oscar cooked on a hot plate. He'd got that before the fighting ended, and it was one of the smarter things he'd done. You couldn't lay your hands on one for love or money these days. Gas was as kaput as gasoline or diesel fuel, but Honolulu still had electricity. A hot plate wasn't the ideal cooking tool—far from it—but it beat the hell out of a stove that didn't work.

"Now for another exciting evening," Susie said after she washed the dishes and he dried them. "We can't go out dancing because there's a curfew. We can't listen to the radio because the Japs confiscated all the sets. So what does that leave? Cribbage?" She made a face.

There was, of course, another possibility, but Oscar didn't name it. Susie was, or could be, a holy terror between the sheets, but she always liked to think it was her idea, not that she was being pushed into it. But then Oscar snapped his fingers. "Almost forgot!" he said, and showed off the jug he'd got that afternoon.

"What's that?" Susie suddenly sounded hopeful.

"It's *okolehao*," Oscar answered.

"Holy cow?" Susie frowned in confusion.

Oscar laughed, but maybe she wasn't so far wrong. "It's Hawaii hooch, Maui moonshine. They make the genuine article from *ti* root, and it'll put hair on anybody's chest." Hair would not have improved Susie's, but he didn't feel like editing himself. Instead, he went on, "God only knows how good this batch is, but it's booze. Want a slug?"

"You bet I do," she said. He poured her a knock, and one for himself, too. They clinked mismatched glasses, then sipped. Susie's eyes got enormous. She coughed a couple of times. "Holy cow!" she wheezed, and looked respectfully at the glass. "I don't think it's very good, but it's sure as hell strong."

"Yeah." Oscar was also wheezing a little, or more than a little. A Territorial Senator from Maui had once said that proper *okolehao* burned with a clear blue flame. Oscar didn't know about that. He did know this stuff burned all the way down. He took another sip. Maybe the first one had numbed him, because it hurt a lot less this time.

Susie Higgins drank some more, too. "Wow!" she said, and then, "How do you really say it?" Oscar gave her the name again. *"Okolehao,"* she repeated, and nodded to herself. "Well, you're right—that beats the dickens out of cribbage."

He poured himself some more, then held out the jug and raised a questioning eyebrow. Susie nodded again. "Here you go," he said, and gave her a hefty dose.

"If I drink all that, I'll go, all right—I'll go out like a light," she said, which didn't keep her from attacking the stuff. She smiled at Oscar—a slightly slack-lipped smile. "Doesn't taste so bad once you get used to it, does it?"

"I don't know," he said. "I think maybe the first knock put my tongue to sleep."

Susie waggled a finger at him. "Oh, it better not have, sweetheart, or I'm gonna be *real* disappointed in you." She exploded into gales of laughter. Oscar grinned back. He gave himself a mental pat on the back. Yeah, Susie could be as raunchy as all get-out . . . as long as *she* was doing the leading. If he'd said something like that to her, it would have chilled her faster than a cold shower.

Oscar's bed was crowded for two, but not too crowded, as long as they were friendly. His tongue, he discovered in due course, still worked fine. So did Susie's. They fell asleep in each other's arms, happy and more than a little sloshed.

FLETCHER ARMITAGE WAS AN OFFICER and a gentleman. That's what they told him when he graduated from West Point. He'd gone right on believing it when he got assigned to the Twenty-fourth Division's Thirteenth Field Artillery Battalion, based at Schofield Barracks. Of course, officers in Hawaii were something like sahibs in British India, with plenty of natives to do the scutwork for them. If a gentleman was someone who seldom got his hands dirty, Fletch had qualified.

Even before the fighting started, things hadn't been perfect for him. He'd been sleeping in the base BOQ; Jane had the apartment they'd shared in Wahiawa. The divorce hadn't been final when the Japs hit. He didn't suppose it had gone forward since the occupation, but so what? He wasn't married any more, and he knew it.

So what was he, then? Another slowly starving POW, that was all. He wasn't too far from Wahiawa himself right now. Some of the men in his gun crew had tried disappearing when the order to surrender went out. Fletch didn't know what had happened to them. Maybe they'd blended in among the civilians. Maybe the Japs had caught them and shot them. Either way, they were liable to be better off than he was.

"Work!" a Japanese sergeant shouted, one of the handful of English words the man knew. The POWs under his eye moved a little faster. They were digging tank traps and antitank ditches. Putting prisoners to work on war-related projects like that violated the Geneva Convention. Putting officers to work at all without their agreement also violated the Convention.

Fletch laughed, not that it was funny. The Japs hadn't signed the Geneva Convention, and didn't give two whoops in hell about it. They figured the USA might try to invade Oahu again, and they were damn well going to be ready if the Americans did. They'd had God only knew how many thousands of POWs sitting around in Kapiolani Park at the edge of Waikiki, and they'd sent out an order—work or don't eat. Nobody'd been eating much, but nobody had any doubts the Japs would be as good, or as bad, as their word.

Up went the pickaxe. Fletch had learned to let gravity do most of the work as it fell. He still wore the shirt and trousers in which he'd surrendered. They hadn't been in good shape then, and they were rags now. He hung on to them even so. A lot of the Americans in the gang worked stripped to the waist. He didn't want to do that; with his red hair and fair skin, he burned and burned, and hardly tanned at all.

Raise the pick. Let it fall. Raise the pick. Let it fall. A scrawny PFC with a shovel cleared the dirt Fletch loosened. Neither of them moved any faster than he had to. Slaves in the South must have found a pace like this: just enough to satisfy the overseer, and not a bit more.

Every so often, of course, the slaves would have slacked off too much. Then Simon Legree would have cracked his bullwhip, and things would have picked up again—till he turned his back, anyhow. The Jap sergeant didn't have a bull-whip. He had a four-foot length of bamboo instead. He would swing it like a baseball bat whenever he felt the need. It left welts at least as bad as a bull-whip's, and could knock a man off his feet.

About twenty feet away from Fletch, an American keeled over without having been walloped. "Man down!" Three or four POWs sang out at the same time. If somebody went down and they didn't sing out, they'd catch it—the Japs would figure they were colluding in his laziness.

Two guards strolled over to the fallen man. One of them stirred him with his foot. The prisoner—one more bag of bones among so many—lay there unmoving. The other Jap kicked him in the ribs. He didn't even curl up to protect himself. The Jap kicked him once more, harder. He still didn't move. Maybe he was dead already. If he wasn't, the guards took care of it. They bayoneted him, again and again.

"Too fucking cheap to waste ammo on him," the PFC with the shovel said out of the side of his mouth.

"Hey, it's more fun to stab the poor bastard," Fletch said, also *sotto voce*. He wasn't kidding; he'd seen the gusto with which the guards wielded their bayonets. This POW was too far gone to give them much sport. When they were satisfied they'd killed him, they thrust their bayonets into the dirt to get the blood off them. *Tidy SOBs,* Fletch thought disgustedly.

"Work!" the sergeant shouted again. Fletch worked—again, as slowly as he could get away with. His eyes kept going toward the dead man, who still lay in the hole the Americans were excavating. What did hard work get you here? What the luckless prisoner had got, nothing else. Of course, what did work that wasn't so hard get you? The same damn thing, only a little slower.

FROM THE COCKPIT OF HIS NAKAJIMA B5N1, Commander Mitsuo Fuchida spotted an oil slick on the surface of the Pacific northwest of Oahu. Excitement shot through him, but only for a moment. That wasn't the sign of a Yankee submarine, however much he wished it were. It was only fuel bubbling up from the *Sumiyoshi Maru*. An American sub had sunk her.

Now that Fuchida had found where she'd gone down, he flew his carrier-based bomber in a search spiral, looking for the boat that had done the deed. The *Sumiyoshi Maru* wasn't the first Japanese freighter on the way to Oahu the Americans had sent to the bottom. She was, in fact, the second ship they'd got in the past two weeks. Japanese forces in Hawaii couldn't well afford such losses. They needed food. They needed fuel. They needed aircraft to replace the ones they'd lost in the fight at the end of June. They needed munitions of every sort.

As long as everything went smoothly, the Japanese could just about keep themselves supplied. The locals had had a lean time of it—literally. Now, though, the islands were growing enough food on their own to keep people from starving. That was a relief. The American subs operating against Japanese shipping, though, were anything but.

Things would have been worse than they were if a couple of American torpedoes that squarely struck freighters hadn't been duds. When planes from the *Lexington* attacked the Japanese task force north of Oahu just after the fighting started, a torpedo that hit *Akagi* had been a dud, too. Fuchida didn't know what was wrong with the U.S. ordnance, but something clearly was.

For now, he kept scanning the Pacific. He'd been in overall charge of air operations for both the invasion of Hawaii and the defense against the U.S. counterattack. A lot of men with such exalted responsibilities wouldn't have gone out on ordinary search missions themselves. Fuchida liked to keep his hand in any way he could.

He called to his bombardier on the intercom: "See anything?"

"No, Commander-*san*," the rating answered. "Please excuse me, but I don't. How about you?"

"I wish I did," Fuchida told him. "That sub is probably fifty meters down and waiting for nightfall to surface and get away."

"I'd do the same thing," the bombardier said. "Why stick your neck out when you don't have to?"

"We'll search a while longer," Fuchida said. "The sub skipper may not think the freighter got a radio message off before she went down. If he doesn't, he might figure he's home free and head back to the U.S. mainland on the surface."

"Maybe." The bombardier didn't sound as if he believed it—which was fair enough, because Fuchida didn't believe it, either. It was possible, but not likely. The bombardier added, "Hard work!"

That implied the work was not only hard but pointless. "Can't be helped," Fuchida said. "I'd love to bomb a U.S. submarine. If I have any kind of chance, I will. Maybe it will persuade the Yankees to keep their boats away from Hawaii."

"Fat chance!" That wasn't the bombardier. It was the radioman, First Flying Petty Officer Tokonobu Mizuki. He'd been listening in from the rear of the cockpit, where he faced the way the plane had come. He and Fuchida went back a long way together, long enough to let him speak his mind to his superior: rare in any military, and especially in the obsessively hierarchical Japanese Navy.

Fuchida saw nothing but a little light chop on the surface of the Pacific. No trace of a wake, no trace of exhaust—not that a sub's diesel engine gave off much.

He eyed the fuel gauge. He still had plenty left. He intended to search as long as he could. He'd gone into battle with appendicitis, and kept doing what he had to do till he landed aboard *Akagi*. If illness hadn't stopped him, nothing less would.

There was a wake! But that was no submarine. It was a Japanese destroyer, also searching for the enemy boat. Fuchida waggled his wings to his countrymen down on the Pacific. He couldn't tell if they saw him—they weren't going to send up a flare or anything like that.

The spiral got wider and wider. Still no sign of the submarine. Fuchida muttered to himself, there in the cockpit. He hadn't really expected anything different. Subs' elusiveness was a big part of what made them so dangerous. So no, he hadn't expected anything different. But he had hoped. . . .

"Sir?" Petty Officer Mizuki said. "I've got an idea."

"I'll listen," Fuchida said.

"When night comes, we ought to send some of those big H8K flying boats along the course from here to the American mainland," the radioman said. "The submarine will be on the surface then. If one of our pilots spots it, he can make a good bombing run."

Fuchida scratched at his closely trimmed mustache. Slowly, he nodded to himself. "That's not a bad notion," he said. "Someone else may have had it already, but it's not a bad notion at all. Radio it back to Oahu. If we send out the flying boats tonight, the sub will still be close to the islands, and we'll have a better chance of finding it."

"Commander-*san*, I'll do it, but what are the odds the brass hats will pay any attention to a lousy rating?" Mizuki spoke without bitterness, but with an acute knowledge of how things worked. How frankly he spoke told how much he trusted his superior, who was, after all, a brass hat himself.

"Do this," Fuchida said after a little more thought. "Radio it back to Oahu. Do it in my name. Tell them I want it done. If nothing happens, if the flying boats don't find a sub, we'll leave it there. Failure on something like that won't hurt my reputation. But if it works, if one of them nails the enemy, I'll see that you get the credit."

"*Domo arigato,*" Mizuki said. Some officers stole credit when the men who served under them came up with good ideas. Fuchida wasn't one of that sort, and the radioman knew it. "They acknowledge, sir," Mizuki told him a few minutes later. "They promise they'll tend to it."

"Good," Fuchida said. "How does it feel to be a brass hat yourself?"

"I like it," Mizuki answered at once. "And I like it even better because I'm doing it under an assumed name." He and Fuchida both laughed.

Inexorably, the bomber's fuel ran down. Fuchida hadn't seen any sign of the American submarine. With a regretful sigh, he turned the Nakajima B5N1 back towards Oahu.

With the *Akagi* anchored in the calm waters of Pearl Harbor, landing aboard her was almost as easy as coming in on an ordinary runway. She wasn't rolling and pitching, the way she would out on the open sea. It required precision, but flying always required precision. Fuchida obeyed the landing officer's wigwag signals as if the man on the flight deck were piloting the bomber. The first arrester wire snagged the bomber's tailhook, and the plane jerked to a stop.

Fuchida slid back the cockpit canopy and climbed out of the Nakajima. So did Mizuki. The bombardier emerged a little later; he had to scramble up from his prone bombing position in the plane's belly.

Captain Kaku came across the flight deck toward Fuchida. "A good thought about the flying boats," the *Akagi*'s skipper said. "No guarantees, of course, but it's worth a try."

"That's what I thought when Mizuki here proposed it." Fuchida set a hand on his radioman's shoulder.

Kaku's eyes narrowed. "The signal came in under your name."

"Yes, sir," Fuchida agreed. "My idea was that no one would take a suggestion from a petty officer seriously. With my name attached to it, it might have a better chance of going forward."

"Irregular," Tomeo Kaku rumbled. Then, almost in spite of himself, he smiled. "Irregular, but probably effective." He nodded to the rating. "Mizuki, eh?"

"Yes, sir." The radioman saluted.

"Well, Mizuki, I think this will go into your promotion jacket," the *Akagi*'s skipper said.

Mizuki saluted again. "Thank you very much, sir!"

"You earned it," Kaku said, and he strolled off.

The petty officer turned to Fuchida. "And thank *you* very much, sir!"

"I'm glad to help, Mizuki, but I didn't do it for you," Fuchida answered. "Anything that will twist the Americans' tails—anything at all—I'm for it."

"Good. That's good," Mizuki said. "It doesn't look like they're going away, does it?"

Fuchida turned toward the north and east. He'd made that motion a good many times before. The U.S. mainland drew him the way magnetic north drew a compass needle. He sighed and shook his head. "No. I wish they were, but they aren't."

"DILLON, LESTER A." The supply sergeant behind the counter checked Les Dillon's name off a list. "Here you are. You have now been issued an M1 helmet." He handed Dillon the new helmet, and a fiber liner that went inside it.

"What the hell was wrong with my old tin hat?" Dillon grumbled. He'd worn the British-style wide-brimmed helmet since he joined the Marine Corps during the First World War. He stared suspiciously at the replacement, which was much deeper. "Looks like a damn pot, or maybe a footbath."

"Bitch, bitch, bitch," the supply sergeant said. By his craggy, weathered features, he'd been a Marine at least as long as Dillon. "For one thing, the new model covers more of your head than the old one did. For another thing, orders are that we get rid of the old ones and wear these. You don't like it, don't cry to me. Talk to your Congressman."

"Thanks a lot, pal," Dillon said. As well as being about the same age, they held the same grade. "I'll remember you in my nightmares."

"Go on." The supply sergeant jerked a thumb toward the door. "Make like a drum and beat it."

Carrying the new helmet and the liner, Dillon did. Outside, Dutch Wenzel had put on his helmet. "What do I look like, Les?"

"You look like hell, if you want to know what I think," Dillon answered. "The new helmet doesn't have anything to do with it, though."

"You're my buddy, all right." Wenzel gave him the finger. Then he pulled out a pack of Luckies, stuck one in his mouth, and offered Dillon the pack.

"Thanks." Dillon took a Zippo out of his pocket and lit both cigarettes. He sucked in smoke and then said, "What I want to know is, how come they're giving me a new helmet when I'm a couple of thousand miles away from any-body who's gonna shoot at me?"

"Beats me. Maybe they think it makes you look cute." Wenzel shook his head. "Nah, there's gotta be a reason that makes sense."

"You oughta go on the radio," Dillon said. "You'd run Benny and Fred Allen right off the air." He looked at the new helmet—the M1, the supply sergeant had called it. "Maybe they think they're changing our luck or something. I don't know why, though, honest to God. We've used the old one for twenty-five years, and there wasn't anything wrong with it." Like a lot of Marines, he was conservative, almost reactionary, about his equipment.

But Wenzel went on cracking wise. "That's what they said about this broad on Hotel Street."

"Can't make that joke on the radio," Dillon said. They both laughed. Dillon went on, "If we can get off the base this afternoon, you want to go see a Padre game?"

Wenzel nodded. "Why not? Who's in town?"

"The Solons. They're in second place," Dillon said. The closest big-league teams, the Cardinals and (stretching a point) the Browns, played just on this side of the Mississippi, and the Mississippi was a hell of a long way from San Diego. Pacific Coast League ball was pretty good, though. A lot of the players had put in time in the majors. A good many who hadn't, the younger ones, would sooner or later. And some of the ones who wouldn't lived on the West Coast, enjoyed playing here, and didn't give a damn if they ever went back East.

Lane Field lay right across Harbor Drive from the beach. The Pacific was right behind the third-base stands. If you looked out past the left-field fence, you could see the Santa Fe railroad yard. It was a long look; it was 390 down the line in left and 500 to dead center. Outfielders who played in that park had to be able to run like the devil. Catchers, on the other hand . . .

Dillon and Wenzel armed themselves with hot dogs and popcorn and beer. Les pointed to the backstop. "That's the goddamnedest thing I've ever seen in any ballpark anywhere, and I've been in a bunch of 'em."

After a swig of beer, his pal nodded. "Whoever laid out this place musta had himself a snootful." Nothing was wrong with the backstop as a backstop. That didn't mean nothing was wrong with it: it stood only about twelve feet back of the plate. Dutch Wenzel raised the bottle to his lips again. "Not a hell of a lot of wild pitches or passed balls in this park."

"That's putting it mildly," Dillon said.

The Padres took the field. The organist played the National Anthem. Boots Poffenberger loosened up on the mound for the Padres. He'd had two or three years in the big leagues, and hadn't particularly distinguished himself. He got the Solons out in the first. Tony Freitas, another big-league retread, took the hill for Sacramento. He gave up a leadoff single, but the Padre runner was out trying to steal.

When he argued, the Padres' manager came out to yell at the ump, too. He waved his arms and shouted and carried on, even though he had to know he didn't have a chance in hell of getting the umpire to change his mind. "Who is that guy?" Wenzel asked. "He's having a fit out there."

"That's Cedric Durst," Dillon answered. "He played for the Browns and the Yankees back in the Twenties."

"Oh, yeah. I remember him—sort of," Dutch Wenzel said. "He's gonna get his ass thrown out if he doesn't shut up."

"Watch your language, buddy," a man behind them said. "I've got my daughter here."

Dillon and Wenzel looked at each other. They both shrugged. A ballpark was no place for a brawl. They let it go. The man in back of them never knew how lucky he was. The Solons' first baseman ambled over to the argument to put in his two cents' worth. Pepper Martin could do that, because the veteran of the Gas House Gang also managed Sacramento.

Durst finally retreated to the third-base dugout, and the game resumed. Poffenberger was sharp, but Freitas was sharper. He hadn't done much in the majors, but he'd won twenty or more for Sacramento five years in a row, and was well on his way to doing it a sixth straight time. The Solons beat the Padres 3 to 1.

Lane Field wasn't far from the base. As Dillon and Wenzel waited with some other Marines for the bus that would take them back, Les said, "That wasn't bad."

"Nope—not half," Wenzel agreed. "Sorta reminds you what we're fighting for, doesn't it?"

"Yeah, but the goddamn Japs like baseball, too," Les said. "When I was in Peking—this was before they took it over—their soldiers had a team, and they'd play against us. They'd beat us some of the time, too, the bastards. They had a pitcher with the nastiest curve you ever saw. It just fell off the table."

"Fuck 'em. Lousy cocksucking monkeys," Wenzel said. None of the Marines standing around waiting for the bus told him to watch his language. A couple of them, including a captain, nodded emphatic agreement. The bus wheezed up, belching black smoke. Les and the rest of the leathernecks climbed aboard. With a clash of gears, it got rolling again and took them back to Camp Elliott.

As ALWAYS, KENZO TAKAHASHI was glad to escape the tent where he and Hiroshi and their father slept when they weren't aboard the *Oshima Maru*. Living and sleeping under canvas reminded him that their apartment was only ashes and charcoal, and that his mother had died in it.

And living under canvas with his father reminded him how different they were. He laughed a sour laugh. Before the war came to Hawaii, he and Hiroshi had desperately tried to get accepted as Americans. To the *haoles* who'd run things here, they were just a couple of Japs. Dad never understood why they wanted to be as American as the blond, blue-eyed kids they went to school with. He was always Japanese first.

Well, now things had gone topsy-turvy. The Japanese were on top. They'd thrown the *haoles* out of the saddle. Dad was as proud as if he'd commanded the army that fought its way across Oahu. And Kenzo . . . still wanted to be an American.

He laughed again, even more bitterly than before. He seemed doomed to swim against the current. The black-suited white executives who ran the Big Five, the companies that controlled Hawaii, hadn't wanted or known what to do with Japanese who acted American. The Imperial Japanese Army and Navy didn't want them or know what to do with them, either. The two sides probably had more sympathy for each other than they did for people like Kenzo.

Several Japanese soldiers—a patrol—came up the street toward him. He bowed, holding the canvas sack he carried under his left arm. The soldiers didn't acknowledge him, though they might have beaten him up if he hadn't bowed. They chattered among themselves in Hiroshima dialect much like the Japanese his father spoke. His and Hiroshi's were a little purer, because they'd studied with a *sensei* from Tokyo after American school was done.

Kenzo went past a couple of informal and not quite legal markets in the Oriental part of Honolulu. When the official ration meant hunger and a slow slide toward starvation, people with extra money or things to trade supplemented it when and as they could. Japanese soldiers and sailors sometimes traded in the markets, too. They got better food than civilians, but not a whole lot better. And their higher-ups no doubt got paid under the table to look the other way.

Once Kenzo got some little distance east of Nuuanu Avenue, there were no more markets. Chinese and Koreans and Japanese ran them. *Haoles* went to them, but didn't set up any in their own part of town. Kenzo didn't understand that, but he'd seen it was true.

Haoles in Honolulu mostly did their best to pretend nothing had changed since December 7. Houses were still well tended; the white clapboard ones, and the churches built in the same style, seemed more likely to belong to a New England small town than to the tropical Pacific. Lawns were bright green and for the most part short and neat.

Here and there, vacant lots reminded a passerby that war had touched this place. Almost all the houses that had stood on those lots were gone, scavenged for wood and anything else people thought they could use. More often than not, neighbors to either side kept grass and shrubbery from running wild.

Mynah birds eyed Kenzo suspiciously as he turned up a curving street not much different from others in the neighborhood. Before December 7, zebra doves would have puttered along the sidewalk, but people were eating them even faster than they bred. Mynahs, at least, had the sense to be suspicious.

Kenzo walked up a neatly kept entryway to a clapboard house much like its neighbors—a palace compared to the cramped flat where he'd grown up. He knocked on the door. A middle-aged blond woman opened it. "Hello, Mrs. Sundberg," he said.

She smiled at him—a slightly nervous smile, but a smile even so. "Hello, Ken," she answered. "Come on in." Everyone in school had called him Ken. All *haoles* everywhere did. His older brother was Hank to them, not Hiroshi. Most Hawaii-born Japanese had an American name to go with the one they'd been given at birth. Except when he was with his father, Kenzo still thought of himself as Ken more often than not. Some local Japanese, though, had dropped those American names like live grenades after Hawaii changed hands.

When Kenzo did walk inside, the New England feel only got stronger. The overstuffed furniture, the Currier and Ives prints on the walls, and the bricabrac everywhere didn't go with the palm trees and balmy breezes outside. He handed Mrs. Sundberg the sack. "I brought you this," he said, as casually as he could.

She hefted it, then looked inside. Plainly, she didn't want to, not right there in front of him. Just as plainly, she couldn't help herself. She was smiling even before she closed the sack. "Thank you very much, Ken," she said. "That's one of the nicest dolphins I've seen in a long time."

Kenzo thought the name a lot of *haoles* used for *mahi-mahi* was dumb. It confused the fish with porpoises' cousins. Telling that to Mrs. Sundberg would have been wasting his breath. He just said, "I hope you like it when you cook it up."

"I'm sure we will." Mrs. Sundberg sounded as if she meant every word of that. No wonder—people who weren't fishermen or didn't know fishermen never got fish like that, not these days. She went on, "Let me go put it in the icebox. Elsie will be out in a minute."

"Sure," Kenzo said, and he didn't smile till Mrs. Sundberg had turned her back. Bringing a good-sized fish every time he came to call on Elsie wasn't quite a bribe, but it did go a long way toward making her folks happier to see him. *The way to their hearts is through their stomachs,* he thought. It was no joke, either, not when so many stomachs in Hawaii were growling so loud these days.

Mrs. Sundberg came out with a glass it her hand. "Would you like some lemonade?" she asked.

"Sure," Ken said again. "Thanks." He sipped. It was good. Lemonade persisted where so many things had vanished. Hawaii still grew sugar, even if a lot of the cane fields had been turned into rice paddies since the occupation. And the Sundbergs had a lemon tree in their back yard. What else could you do with lemons but fix lemonade?

"Hi, Ken." Elsie walked into the living room from the back of the house.

"Hi." He could feel his face lighting up when he smiled. He'd known Elsie since they were in elementary school together. They'd been friends and helped each other with homework in high school. She was a nice-looking blonde—not gorgeous, but nice. (She looked a lot like her mother, in fact, though Kenzo never noticed that.) Before the war, she'd been a tiny bit plump. Hardly anybody was plump any more. A double chin now marked not just a collaborator but an important collaborator.

"I'll be right back," Elsie's mom said. And she was, too, before Kenzo and Elsie could do anything more than smile at each other. "Here you are, sweetie." She gave Elsie a glass of lemonade, too.

The longer Elsie and Kenzo stood around drinking lemonade and gabbing with Mrs. Sundberg, the less time they would have by themselves. Elsie's mother didn't say that was what she had in mind, but she didn't have to. Calling her on it would have been rude. Instead, Kenzo and Elsie just drank fast. Elsie handed back her empty glass in nothing flat. "We'll be off now, Mom."

"Have a nice time," Mrs. Sundberg said gamely.

Elsie didn't giggle till they were out of the house. She reached for Kenzo's hand before he would have reached for hers, before they'd even got to the sidewalk. "My mother," she said, exasperation and affection mingling in her voice.

"She's very nice." Kenzo knew better than to criticize Mrs. Sundberg. That was Elsie's job. If he did it, he might make Elsie stick up for her, which was the last thing he wanted. He picked something safer to say: "How have you been?"

"We're . . . getting along, one day at a time." Elsie disappointed him by taking that as a question about her whole family, but he couldn't do anything except squeeze her hand a little. She went on, "We trade lemons and avocados for whatever we can get to add to the ration. Mom's always glad when you bring a fish."

"I knew that. It's not like she doesn't show it," Kenzo said. Yes, for him praise was safer than blame. If he didn't bring something good whenever he called on Elsie, how would Mrs. Sundberg look at him? As nothing but a damn Jap? That was his bet.

They walked to the park at the corner of Wilder and Keeaumoku. It hadn't been maintained the way most of the lawns had. The grass was tall and shaggy. Weeds and shrubs sprouted here and there. The seat had come off one of the swings; only slightly rusty chains hung down from the bar.

But it was peaceful and quiet, and a place where Japanese soldiers were unlikely to come. Elsie didn't like being around them, and Kenzo didn't see how he could blame her. Some of the things he'd heard . . . He didn't want to think about that, or about not being able to protect her if trouble started.

White paint was starting to peel off the benches in the park. In peacetime, somebody would have fixed that up quick as you please. These days, the Honolulu city government, or what was left of it, had more urgent things to worry about. Most of them revolved around trying to persuade the occupiers to be a little less savage, a little less ruthless, than they might have been otherwise.

A bench creaked when Kenzo and Elsie sat down on it. That wouldn't have been allowed to happen in better times, either. One of these days, if things didn't get better, somebody would sit down on it and fall right through when rotting wood gave way. It might not take that long, either. Hawaii *was* tropical. If things weren't tended, they went to pieces pretty damn quick.

"How are *you*?" Kenzo asked again, this time bearing down on the last word.

"I don't even know any more," Elsie answered. "I was so disappointed when we lost those carriers, I don't know how to tell you."

"You don't need to. So was I," Kenzo said.

"I know. But . . ." Elsie paused, figuring out how to say what she wanted to say without getting him mad. She was considerate enough to do that, which was one of the reasons he liked her. Finally, she said, "Nobody can tell by looking that you don't like the people who're in charge now. With me, it's different." She patted her short blond hair.

Kenzo's laugh was as sour as the lemonade would have been without sugar. "Anybody who looks like me would have said the same thing before December 7."

"I didn't really understand it then. Now I do." Elsie's smile only lifted one corner of her mouth. "Nothing like wearing the shoe to show how much it pinches, I guess."

"No." Now Kenzo hesitated for a moment before he decided to add, "There are *haole* collaborators, too, you know."

"Oh, sure. They're worse than the Japanese ones, if you ask me." Elsie didn't even try to hide her venom. "At least people who were born in Japan can think it's their own country in charge now." That covered people like Kenzo's father. It didn't cover the Hawaii-born Japanese who also backed the occupiers. There were some. But Elsie didn't mention them, instead returning to whites who kowtowed to the Japanese authorities: "*Haoles* who suck up like that are just a bunch of traitors. When the Americans do come back, they ought to string 'em up."

Such talk might have been easier before the war. Now Kenzo asked, "You've seen dead people, haven't you?"

"Yes." She nodded and shuddered. Few people on Oahu hadn't, these days. "Even so, though. They deserve it."

"I guess so." Kenzo wondered how he'd got to talking about killing people with a pretty girl. *That* wasn't what he'd had in mind when he called on Elsie.

A white-haired lady wearing a broad-brimmed straw hat against the sun walked slowly through the shabby park. She looked at Elsie and Kenzo, sniffed, and stuck her nose in the air as she walked on.

"Sour old biddy," Elsie said.

"You know her?" Kenzo asked.

"I've seen her. She doesn't live too far from us." Elsie's sniff was a nasty imitation of the old woman's. "The next thing she likes after the turn of the century will be the first."

"Oh. One of those. There are lots of older Japanese people like that, too," Kenzo said.

Elsie started to say something. He thought he could guess what it was: that even old Japanese in Hawaii could like the way the war had gone. He would have had a hard time disagreeing with her, too. But she didn't say it. Instead, very quietly, she started to cry. "It wasn't supposed to be like this," she said. Kenzo wondered what she meant by *it*. Everything, probably. "It *wasn't*!"

"I know," he said. "Hey, I know." He slipped an arm around her. She clung to him as if he were a life preserver and sobbed into the hollow of his shoulder. "Hey," Kenzo repeated. "Hey." It wasn't really a word, just a noise to show he was there.

After a while, Elsie gulped a couple of times and raised her head. Her eyes were red. The tears had made her mascara run and scored lines through the powder and rouge on her cheeks. She stared at Kenzo from a distance of about six inches. "Oh, hell," she said. It was, as far as he could remember, the first time he'd ever heard her swear. She went on, "I must look like a raccoon."

He'd only seen pictures of raccoons, and he didn't care about them one way or the other. "You always look good to me," he said seriously.

It was easy enough to say. To say seriously . . . That was something else. She noticed, too—he could tell. Her eyes widened. Then, careless of smeared makeup and runny mascara, she let her eyelids fall. "Ken . . ." she whispered.

He kissed her. They'd kissed before, but never like this. Her arms were still around him. Now she squeezed him, too. Her lips tasted of salt. That only made them seem sweeter to him. Somewhere up in a tree, a Chinese thrush was singing. For a moment, Kenzo thought it was his own heart.

The kiss went on and on. Elsie made a little noise, half a purr, half a growl, down deep in her throat. Kenzo opened his eyes. The old *haole* lady was gone. Nobody seemed to be in the park but the two of them. Emboldened, he squeezed her breast through the thin cotton of her sun dress. She made that noise again, louder this time. Her hand came down on his, not to pull it away but to press him to her.

He set his other hand on her knee, just below the hem of her dress. Her legs drifted apart. But when he started to slide up the warm smoothness of her inner thigh, she gasped and twisted away. "No," she said. "I mean, we shouldn't."

"Why not?" Kenzo panted. "Who's gonna know?"

"Somebody might nine months from now," Elsie said. Kenzo didn't worry about nine months from now. He didn't worry about nine minutes from now, except about his chances of getting her down on the long grass. But she shook her head. "No," she repeated. "It wouldn't be right, and you wouldn't respect me afterwards."

"Sure I would." Kenzo heard the whine in his own voice. How many men had said the same thing to women over the years? Millions—it had to be millions. How many had meant it? Maybe a few. *Do I?* he wondered. He wasn't sure.

Elsie must have seen as much on his face. Tartly, she said, "If that's all you want, you can probably get it for a fish down on Hotel Street."

Kenzo's ears heated. "It's not all I want," he mumbled, though he couldn't deny he did want it. If he'd tried, the bulge in his trousers would have given him away.

He saw her eyeing the bulge, which only made his ears hotter still. But she let him down easy, saying, "Okay, Ken. I believe you. You're a good friend, too."

Too? he wondered. What was that supposed to mean? Did she mostly care about him as a friend? Or, besides caring for him as a friend, did part of her want to lie down on the grass with him? There was a lot of difference between the two—all the difference in the world. And he couldn't ask. If you had to ask, the answer was always the one you least wanted to hear.

There were ways to find out besides asking, though. He kissed her again, and she didn't pull away. But the kiss, while sweet, didn't feel like bombs going off inside his head. "I wish—" he said, and then stopped.

"What?" Elsie asked.

"I wish none of this stuff had happened, but we were going together anyhow," Kenzo said.

"That would be pretty good," Elsie agreed.

Kenzo wondered if her folks would have let her go out with him if the Japanese hadn't occupied Hawaii. But he had to admit to himself that maybe he wasn't being fair. Elsie's mom and dad had never had any trouble about the two of them studying together. On the other hand, studying and dating were two different things.

Now he was the one who kissed her with something close to desperation. Elsie gave back what he needed. It wasn't fire, or not quite. It was fun, but it was reassuring, too.

He looked at her. "You're something, you know that?" he said, and then, "I'm glad we're friends, too."

Her face lit up. At least half by accident, he'd said the right thing. "You're all right, Ken," she told him.

"Am I?" he said. But, coming from her, he believed it. From anybody else, he wouldn't have. He knew that. He grinned—grinned like a fool, probably. "This is an awful nice park, you know that?" he blurted. Elsie nodded, much more seriously than the foolish thought deserved. Then they looked at each other and both started to laugh.

MINORU GENDA HAD HAD A COT INSTALLED in his office, not far from Iolani Palace. Before he took it over, it had belonged to a U.S. Navy officer. In Japan, it would have been large and luxurious even for a man of flag rank. Genda believed the previous occupant was a USN lieutenant. That spoke volumes about the wealth each country enjoyed.

The cot was U.S. issue, and considerably more comfortable than anything the Japanese military used. Genda smiled to himself. Quite a few Japanese recruits had never slept in a bed with legs till they joined the Army or Navy. He'd come from a good family. He hadn't had that embarrassment, anyway.

Thanks to the cot, and to food he had sent in, he didn't have to go back to his quarters nearly so often as he would have otherwise. That meant he could use the time he would have spent going back and forth for work. If he woke up in the middle of the night—and he often did—he didn't have to lie there uselessly staring up at the ceiling. He could turn on a lamp and attack the paperwork that never stopped piling up or pore over a map, wondering how the Americans would try to be difficult next.

At the moment, the Yankees were doing what they could with submarines. They seemed to have stolen an idea from the U-boats that harried shipping in the Atlantic. If they could cut Hawaii off from resupply from Japan, the islands would be much easier to take back.

They weren't as good at the job as the Germans. They didn't have enough boats to send out wolf packs, and their torpedoes left a lot to be desired. But they were doing what they could, and it was plenty to pinch if not to strangle. Sending a few of their subs to the bottom would work wonders for Japanese morale.

It would—if anyone could figure out how to do it. So far, the Navy hadn't had much luck, and the Army was starting to grumble. Petty Officer Mizuki's idea of sending H8Ks up the track of an escaping enemy sub had produced an attack, but no oil slick or wreckage on the surface the next morning. Either the enemy boat got away clean or the anxious pilot had attacked something that wasn't there. The Americans usually talked too much about their losses, but they weren't admitting they'd had any lately.

Genda had been puzzling till nearly midnight over what Japan could do to protect her ships. When he lay down, he looked forward to getting up before sunrise and getting right back to work. No one had ever accused him of not doing everything in his power, and no one ever would.

As things worked out, he woke up long before he expected to. At half past one, air-raid sirens started howling. Genda did his best to work them into a dream about an attack on the *Akagi*, but after a few seconds his eyes opened. Staring up into the darkness, he needed another moment to remember where he was, and why. Then he swore and jumped out of the cot.

The sirens kept wailing. Orders were to shelter in a cellar till the all-clear sounded. Genda was not about to obey orders like that. He threw on his trousers, rushed downstairs, and hurried out into the quiet streets to find out what was going on.

"Careful, sir," said a sentry outside the building.

"Where are the enemy airplanes?" Genda demanded.

Before the sentry could answer, antiaircraft guns around Pearl Harbor opened up. A fireworks display of traces and bursting shells lit up the western sky. Half a minute later, the *crump!* of bursting bombs added to the din.

"*Zakennayo!*" Genda exclaimed in dismay. "They're going after *Akagi*!"

American flying boats didn't have the astounding range of H8Ks. They would need refueling from a submarine to reach Hawaii from the U.S. mainland, and probably another refueling to make it home again. As long as the enemy flying boat found the submarine in the vastness of the Pacific, though, that wasn't an insurmountable problem.

The Yankees must have decided the same thing. Yes, they were doing their best to make nuisances of themselves.

Commander Fuchida had laughed when he told of suddenly appearing over San Francisco harbor in an H8K and bombing U.S. warships there. Now the shoe was on the other foot—and Genda didn't like the way it felt.

Long after the American raiders must have disappeared, antiaircraft fire kept throwing up shells over Pearl Harbor. Shrapnel clattered down on Honolulu streets and rooftops. A chunk of steel falling from a few thousand meters would kill a man as dead as any rifle bullet.

Realizing he couldn't do anything useful where he was, Genda went back into the office building and climbed the stairs as fast as he'd descended them. He flipped on the light in his office. Blackout curtains kept it from leaking out into the street. Right this minute, that probably didn't matter. Having struck once, the Americans wouldn't be back tonight.

Genda picked up the telephone. "Get me Pearl Harbor!" he snapped when an operator came on the line.

"Who is this?" The operator sounded rattled. "Are you authorized to be telephoning during an emergency?"

"This is Commander Genda," Genda said coldly. "Put me through at once, before I ask who *you* are."

"Uh, yes, sir." Now the operator sounded terrified. Genda wanted him to sound that way.

"Pearl Harbor—Ensign Yasutake here." The youngster who picked up the phone at Pearl Harbor, by contrast, almost squeaked with excitement.

After giving his name again, Genda asked, "What's going on over there? Is the carrier all right?"

"Uh, yes, sir. A couple of near misses, but no hits," Yasutake said, and Genda breathed a sigh of relief. The ensign went on, "Uh, sir, how did you know the Americans would attack *Akagi*?"

"Because she's the most valuable target there. Why come all that way if you're *not* going to attack the most valuable target?" Genda said. "And the Yankees are bound to know she's there, too." He was sure Oahu—and, indeed, all the Hawaiian Islands—crawled with American spies. A hidden wireless set in the mountains, a few quick code groups, and . . . trouble. "I don't suppose we managed to knock down the American flying boat, did we?"

"No, sir. Or at least we didn't see any sign of it," Ensign Yasutake answered.

Genda sighed. "Too bad. Still, it could be worse. They didn't hurt us badly, either." *Even if they did scare us out of a year's growth.* "You're sure *Akagi* is all right?"

"Oh, yes, sir. No new damage," Yasutake said. Genda hung up. For the next little while, people would be running around like chickens that had just met the chopper. One of the things the Army would be screaming about was that the U.S. flying boat managed to catch the Navy napping. And the Army would have more of a point than Genda wished it did.

His own phone rang. In the after-midnight quiet, the jangle made him jump. He picked up the telephone right as the second ring started. "Genda here."

"This is Fuchida."

"Good to hear your voice. I'm glad you're all right. I'm glad *Akagi*'s all right."

Commander Fuchida laughed. "I might have known you'd already know. But we were lucky, Genda-*san*—no more than lucky. If the Americans had aimed better, they could have done a lot of harm. We have to get some of those electronic range-finding sets out here from the home islands. Then we won't be blind to attacks till they're on top of us."

That marched well with Genda's thoughts. "I'll do what I can," he promised. "I'll send a message to Admiral Yamamoto. If anybody can get some of those sets out here, he's the man. I wish the Americans weren't ahead of us there— they're already running, while we've just started to walk."

"Walking is one thing," Fuchida said. "Thinking we can stand around is something else again."

To that, Genda said the only thing he could: *"Hai."*

III

JIRO TAKAHASHI CARRIED A PLUMP *AHI* UP NUUANU AVENUE TOWARD THE JAPA-
nese consulate. The Rising Sun had always flown above the consulate, reminding him of the land he'd left when he was younger than Hiroshi and Kenzo
were now. These days, the Rising Sun waved above Iolani Palace and all over
Hawaii. That made Jiro proud, even if it appalled his sons.

Even before the war started, Jiro had brought fine fish to the consulate. The
men who served Japan deserved the best, and talking with them had given the
fisherman a taste of home, so he'd been glad to do it. Since the war started,
things were different. Jiro was pleased that his fish helped keep Consul Kita
and Chancellor Morimura from going hungry.

Japanese soldiers in their dark khaki uniforms stood guard outside the consulate. Along with the palace and the leading warship in Hawaiian waters, it
was one of the places where policy for the islands got hammered out. A sentry
pointed toward Jiro. "Here comes the Fisherman!" he exclaimed.

By the way he said it, it might have been Takahashi's name. All the sentries
called Jiro the Fisherman. They bowed as he drew near. "*Konichiwa,*
Fisherman-*sama,*" one of them said.

That was laying it on thick. The Fisherman or Fisherman-*san*—Mr.
Fisherman—was fine. Fisherman-*sama* . . . As Jiro bowed back, he said, "You
boys must be hungry if you start calling me Lord Fisherman."

The sentries laughed. "We're always hungry, Fisherman-*sama,*" said the one
who'd used the name before.

They probably were, too. Japanese soldiers got better rations than local civilians, but still ate lots of rice and not much of anything else. The sentries came from the same class as Jiro, and from the Hiroshima area, too. When he could, he brought them something. Today, though, he bowed again, apologetically. "Please excuse me, friends. Next time for you, if I get the chance. Maybe the men inside will share this *ahi* with you." He held up the fish.

"Fat chance!" two soldiers said at the same time. One of them added, "Those stingy bastards don't know how lucky they are to have you for a friend."

"No, I think I'm the lucky one," Jiro said. The sentries only jeered. But he meant it. "These are important people from the home islands, and they're glad to see me. Of course I'm lucky."

"They're glad to see your fish, anyhow," a sentry said.

"We're not going to convince him," another one said. "Let's just let him through. He'll find out for himself sooner or later." They stood aside. Jiro walked past them and into the consular compound.

A clerk greeted him: "Good day, Takahashi-*san*. How are you?"

"Pretty well, thanks. I'd like to see Consul Kita, if I may." Jiro held up the *ahi* again to explain why.

"I'm so sorry, but the consul isn't here right now," the clerk said. "He's still out on the golf course. He won't be back till this evening."

"The golf course," Jiro muttered. He knew Kita was fond of the Western game, but he'd never understood why. Whacking a ball with a stick till it fell into a hole? What was the point, besides giving you an excuse to waste time whenever you felt like it?

"Chancellor Morimura is in, though," the clerk said helpfully. "I'm sure he'd be glad to help you." He was looking at the *ahi*, not at Jiro. Maybe the sentries knew what they were talking about after all.

Tadashi Morimura was studying a map of Pearl Harbor when the clerk led Jiro into his office. Morimura was tall and handsome, with a long face and an aristocrat's cheekbones and eyebrows. He couldn't have been more than thirty. "Good to see you, Takahashi-*san*," he said, rising and bowing. "That's a handsome fish you have there. Do you want me to take charge of it till the consul comes back?"

"Yes, please," Jiro said.

Morimura didn't take it in his own hands (interesting hands, for his left index finger was missing the first joint). He called a clerk, who carried it off to the refrigerator. Had he dismissed Jiro right after that, the fisherman might have decided the consular staff did value him for his fish alone. But the chancellor—who held a title that sounded impressive but could have meant anything—said, "Please sit down, Takahashi-*san*. I'm glad to see you. I was thinking about you earlier today, as a matter of fact."

"About me?" Jiro said in surprise as he sank into a chair.

"*Hai*—about you." Morimura nodded. "Do you know Osami Murata?"

Jiro shook his head. "*Gomen nasai*, but I'm afraid I don't. Could you tell me who he is?"

"He's a broadcaster, a radio man," Morimura said. "He usually works out of Tokyo, where he lives, but he's here in Hawaii now. He's doing some shows about the islands since we took them away from the Americans. You would be a good man for him to interview. You could tell him—you could tell all of Japan—what things are like."

"They would hear me back in Japan?" Jiro said.

"That's right." Morimura smiled and nodded. His smile was exceptionally charming; it made his big eyes light up. "They'd hear you all over the world, in fact. That's how short-wave radio works."

"All over the world? Me?" Jiro laughed at that. "I can't even get my boys to pay attention to me half the time."

"Didn't they pay attention when you were in the *Nippon jiji*?" Morimura asked slyly.

"Well . . . some." Takahashi didn't want to say what kind of attention he'd got from Hiroshi and Kenzo after they saw his interview in the Japanese-language newspaper. They'd warned him against being a collaborator. *How can I be a collaborator? Japan is my country,* he thought. But his sons didn't see it that way.

"We'll set up an interview," Tadashi Morimura said. "Are you free tomorrow afternoon, Takahashi-*san*?"

"I ought to be out catching fish," Jiro said uncertainly.

Morimura winked at him. Jiro blinked. Had he really seen that? The chancellor said, "Can't you send your sons out on the *Oshima Maru* by themselves for one day?"

Jiro was flattered that the consular official remembered the name of his sampan—flattered almost to the point of blushing and coughing and stammering like a schoolboy. "I suppose I could," he said, and knew that he would. Hiroshi and Kenzo would be astonished when he didn't want to put to sea with them; he'd never been a man to shirk work, and, say what they would about him, they couldn't claim he had. But they were no happier with his company than he was with theirs. Their hearts wouldn't break to make a fishing run without him. If they brought in a good catch, they wouldn't let him forget it, either.

He shrugged broad shoulders. He'd survived worse things than that. "What time would you want me here, Morimura-*san*?" he asked.

"Come at two o' clock," Morimura answered. "But not here. Go to the KGMB studio. That's where he will want to do the interview. Have you got the address?"

"I'm sorry, but no." Not speaking English and not caring for the music KGMB played, Jiro had no idea where the station was. Morimura gave him the address. It wasn't too far from the consulate. "I'll be there," he promised.

And he was. His sons both stared at him when he told them to take the *Oshima Maru* out on their own. But they didn't argue very hard or ask very many questions. That saddened Jiro without much surprising him.

Nobody could stay sad for long around Osami Murata. "What, no fish for *me*?" he exclaimed when Morimura introduced Jiro to him. "I'm so insulted, I'm going to commit *seppuku*." He mimed slitting his belly, then laughed uproariously. "Now, Takahashi-*san*, let's figure out what we're going to talk about when we get you in front of the mike."

He was a whirlwind of jokes and energy. Jiro could no more help being swept along than his sampan could have in a gale. He wasn't even nervous when Murata plopped him down in a chair in front of a mike in a room whose likes he'd never seen before. The ceiling, three of the walls, and even the inside of the door were covered by what looked like cardboard egg cartons.

Noticing his stare, Murata said, "Stuff deadens sound." He pointed to the fourth wall, which was of glass and let Jiro see into the adjoining room. "Those are the engineers in there. If they're very, very good, maybe we'll let them out again once the show is over."

Did he mean it? He might—some of them were *haoles*, and had surely been doing their jobs here before the Japanese came. Or he might be fooling again, trying to put Jiro at ease.

"Nervous?" Murata asked. When Jiro nodded, the broadcaster poked him in the ribs and made funny faces. *Haoles* were often boisterous and foolish. Jiro didn't know what to make of a Japanese who acted like that. Murata scribbled some notes, then pointed to a light bulb that wasn't shining just then. "When that comes on, we'll start. All right?"

"*Hai.*" Jiro didn't know whether it was all right or not. He didn't know which end was up just then.

The bulb lit up. It was red. "This is Osami Murata, your man on the go," Murata said glibly, leaning toward the microphone. "I've gone a long way today—here I am in Honolulu, in the Kingdom of Hawaii. I'm talking with Jiro Takahashi, who's been here a lot longer than I have. Say hello to the people back in the home islands, Takahashi-*san.*"

"Hello," Jiro said weakly. Here in Hawaii, his old-fashioned Hiroshima accent was nothing out of the ordinary. Most Japanese who'd come here started out from that part of the country. Murata's elegant tones, though, told the world he hailed from Tokyo. They made Jiro acutely self-conscious.

Murata winked at him again. It didn't help much. The broadcaster said, "Why did you move to Hawaii all those years ago?"

"To work in the fields here," Jiro answered. "The money was better than I could get back home, so I thought I'd try it."

"And how did you like it?"

"Hard work!" Jiro exclaimed, and Murata laughed in surprise. Takahashi went on, "As soon as I could, I got away from cane and pineapple. I rented a fishing boat till I could finally afford to buy one. Put everything together and I've done all right for myself."

"A man who works hard will do all right for himself wherever he is," Murata said. Jiro found himself nodding. The younger man asked him, "Did you ever think about going back to Japan?"

"I thought about it, yes, but by then I'd married and settled down and had a couple of boys," Jiro answered with a shrug. "Looks like I'm here for good. Karma, *neh*?"

"*Hai,*" Murata said. "But Japan has reached out to you, and you're under the Rising Sun again. What do you think about that?"

He'd mentioned the Kingdom of Hawaii, but now he didn't bother pretending the islands were under anything but Japanese control. "I'm glad," Jiro said simply. "Japan is my country. I want her to do well."

"That's good. That's what we like to hear," Murata said effusively. "And your family thinks the same way?"

"I lost my wife in the fighting, but I know she would have agreed with me," Jiro said. And that was true. Reiko was also from the old country, and from his generation. Of course she would have been happy to see Japan take over from the United States.

"I'm so sorry to hear of your loss, Takahashi-*san*." Osami Murata sounded as if he meant it. "And what about your sons?"

Jiro might have known he would ask that. Jiro *had* known he would ask it. Answering it wasn't easy, though. Carefully, Takahashi said, "I always tried to raise them as good Japanese. They went to Japanese school every day after American school was over. They learned to read and write, and they speak with a better accent than the sorry one I've got."

"You're just fine the way you are, Takahashi-*san*," Murata said easily. If he noticed that Jiro hadn't really said how his sons felt about the Japanese occupation of Hawaii, he didn't let on. One of the men on the other side of the glass gave him a signal. He nodded to show he'd got it, then turned back to Jiro. "Do you have anything to say to the folks back home?"

"Only *Banzai!* for the Emperor, and that I'm proud to be a Japanese subject again," Jiro answered.

"Thank you, Jiro Takahashi!" Murata said. The red light went out. The broadcaster leaned back. "There. That's done. I think it went well. *Arigato*."

"You're welcome," Jiro said automatically. "They really heard me in Japan?"

"They really did, unless the atmospherics are just horrendous—and they've been good lately," Murata said. "I'm glad Chancellor Morimura arranged for you to meet me. You're exactly what we needed."

Nobody had ever said anything like that to Jiro before. "The way I talk—" he began.

Murata waved that away. "Don't worry about it. Not everybody comes from Tokyo. This is better. It will remind people the whole country is together here."

The whole country . . . A slow smile spread over Jiro's face. "Being part of Japan again feels good."

Osami Murata smiled, too. "It ought to," he said, and set a hand on Takahashi's shoulder. "You don't want to be an American, do you?"

"I should hope not," Jiro said quickly. Hiroshi and Kenzo had other ideas, but at least he hadn't had to come out and say so on the radio.

*   *   *

WHEN JIM PETERSON LOOKED AT THE JUNGLE-COVERED Koolau Range from a distance, he'd always thought how lush the mountains seemed. Now, up at the end of the Kalihi Valley to drive a tunnel through them, he had a different view of the jungle.

Green hell.

When he thought of a jungle, he thought of trees full of tasty fruit, of animals making a racket and common enough to be easily caught. What he thought of and what he got in the Kalihi Valley were two different things. Nobody had done much with the valley till the Japs decided to drive a road up through it and to tunnel through the mountains. Almost all of the trees in the valley were Oahu natives, and they didn't have much in the way of fruit.

As for the animals, he'd seen a few mongooses—mongeese?—skulking through the ferns. Every now and then, he spotted a bird up in the trees. And that seemed to be it. He and his companions in misery had little chance to supplement the tiny rice ration the guards doled out. It was live on that or die.

Actually, it was live on that *and* die. A man couldn't possibly do hard physical labor on what the Japanese fed him, not if he was going to last very long. Of course, if a man didn't do hard physical labor on what they fed him, they'd kill him on the spot. That put the POWs in the Kalihi Valley in an interesting position.

Green hell, again.

It rained a lot of the time up in the mountains. When it didn't rain, water dripped from the trees. Peterson's clothes started to rot and fall apart even faster than they had when he was in a less muggy part of the island. Some of the men he worked with, men who'd been in the valley longer, were next to naked. Odds of getting anything from the Japs? Two chances—slim and none.

The prisoners slept in bamboo huts thatched with whatever leaves and branches they could throw on top. It was about as wet inside the huts as outside. The bunks were better than lying in the mud, but only a little. "Jesus!" Peterson said, looking down at his hands as light leached out of the sky. They'd been battered and callused before he got here. They were worse now. The Japs here pushed POWs harder than they had anywhere else. This was punishment work, what prisoners did if the occupiers decided not to shoot them. Whether that was a mercy was an open question.

Somebody got up and shambled off toward the latrine trench. Most of the men who'd been here for a while had dysentery. Some of the new fish had already come down with it. Peterson hadn't yet, but figured it was only a matter of time.

"Jesus!" he said again, and then, "God damn Walter London to hell and gone."

"Amen," said Gordy Braddon, who came from his shooting squad. "And if that son of a bitch was in hell screaming for water, I'd give him gasoline to drink. Ethyl, no less."

"Yeah," Peterson said savagely. "Wasn't for him, we'd be...." His voice trailed away. Even without London's escape, their predicament wouldn't have been anything wonderful. But it would have been better than this. Anything would have been better than this.

He'd had that thought before. He'd had it several times since the surrender, in fact. Every damn one of them, he'd been wrong. If he turned out to be wrong again ... *I'm a dead man,* he thought.

He might easily end up a dead man even if there was nothing worse than this. He knew that, too. And when he flopped back onto the bunk and closed his eyes, he sure as hell slept like a dead man.

A Jap banging a shell casing with a hammer made him pry his eyes open the next morning. Groans rose in the hut from those with the energy to give them. Not everybody sat up despite the racket of iron smashing against brass. The Japs came in and started kicking people. That got most of the POWs up and moving. One scrawny fellow just lay there. The guard who'd been shouting at him and booting him gave him a yank. He fell on the ground—plop.

The guard felt of him, then straightened up. *"Shinde iru,"* he said, and jerked a thumb toward the door, as if to add, *Get rid of the carrion.*

"Poor Jonesy," said somebody behind Peterson. "He wasn't a bad guy."

Although the dead Jonesy couldn't have weighed more than a hundred pounds, four POWs carried him out. Peterson was one of them. They were all just shadows of their former selves, and fading shadows at that. The graveyard didn't have individual graves, just big trenches. Flies buzzed around them, even though the Japs did put down quicklime after a fresh corpse went in.

Thump! In fell the dead Jones. They tried not to put him on top of anybody else, but the trenches were filling up. Despite the lime, the stench was bad. "Could be one of us next," a bearer said.

Stubbornly, Jim Peterson shook his head. "As long as we're strong enough to carry, we won't die right away. I aim to last till the US of A comes back."

"How long do you figure that'll be?" the other man asked him. He didn't say, *Ever?*—which was something.

Peterson shrugged. "Damfino. I'm gonna stick it out, that's all. The Japs are putting us in graves, but I'm gonna spit on one of theirs, by God."

Even saying that was taking a chance. If one of the other three corpse-haulers ratted on him to the Japs, they might kill him out of hand. But they probably wouldn't. He couldn't do anything to them, no matter what he said. Odds were they'd just beat him up and put him back to work till he couldn't work any more.

"We better get back," he said. "If we aren't at the lineup, they won't feed us."

That got his companions in misery moving. Losing out on food was the worst thing that could happen to you here, worse even than a beating. Food kept your motor turning over. Assuming you wanted to go on living, that was good. As Peterson and the other three walked back, men from another hut came past them with a dead body even skinnier than Jonesy's had been. Peterson heard the final thud as it went in. He didn't look back.

The count for his hut was fouled up, as it often was when somebody died. The Japs always got all hot and bothered when they saw fewer men than they expected. They knew Jonesy was dead, but that somehow didn't seem to matter. They had to fuss and fume and gabble and wave their hands till they remembered that so many live guys minus one dead guy equaled the number of guys swaying in front of the hut.

Rain started coming down when the POWs finally trudged off to get their morning rice. This wasn't "liquid sunshine." Up here in the mountains, when it rained it rained like a son of a bitch. Peterson's shoes squelched in the mud. It leaked in through growing gaps between uppers and soles. Pretty soon, those shoes were just going to fall apart. He didn't know what he'd do then. No, actually he did know: he'd damn well go barefoot.

For the first few minutes after food hit his stomach, he felt almost like a human being. He headed for the tunnel site.

Gangs who'd got there before him had built the road up to the mountains. It wasn't paved, but it was heavily graveled—usable in all weather, without a doubt. If the tunnel ever went through, the Japs would have a shortcut between Honolulu and Kaneohe on the east coast of Oahu.

Did they care? Were the POWs working on the tunnel for its sake or just to work on something till they dropped? Some of each, was Peterson's guess.

From his point of view, it hardly mattered. Whether the Japs cared about the tunnel or not, the POWs were going to work till they dropped.

Guards didn't carry picks and shovels. They carried rifles and, sometimes, axe handles. If they didn't like the way a POW was moving, they'd whack him with one or the other, or sometimes haul off and kick him. A prisoner couldn't strike back. If he did, the guards would bayonet him and let him die slowly. They knew which wounds would kill in a hurry, and avoided those.

There weren't that many guards. Peterson sometimes thought a concerted rising here might succeed. If it did, though, so what? The prisoners would still be stuck at the ass end of the Kalihi Valley, and the Japs could easily seal off the outlet . . . whereupon everybody here would starve, since living off the land was impossible. *Damned if we do, damned if we don't,* he thought.

They did—and they were damned. Peterson grabbed a pick and shouldered it like a Springfield. Torches and candles threw the only light once Peterson and his gang got into the tunnel. Shadows swooped and leaped as men trudged past the flickering flames. Roman slaves sent to the mines must have looked on scenes like this. Peterson wondered whether anyone since had.

The sound of picks biting into volcanic rock drew him onward. Shovelers loaded the chunks the pickmen loosened into wicker baskets. Haulers lugged the spoil out of the tunnel, one basketload. The POWs argued about which job was worst. Because they argued, they switched off every so often.

There was the face of the excavation. Peterson swung up his pick and brought it forward. When he pulled it loose, basalt or granite or whatever the hell this stuff was came with it. A shoveler used his spade to get the stuff away from Peterson's feet. Peterson swung up the pick again.

As it did on a road gang, work had a pace here. Prisoners growled at anybody who worked too fast. They had reason to growl: if one guy did it, the Japs would expect everybody else to. Why give the slant-eyed monkeys the satisfaction of busting your balls for their lousy tunnel? Besides, a lot of POWs *couldn't* do anything more than they were doing. If the Japs made them work harder, they'd die sooner than they would have otherwise.

Up. Forward. *Thunk!* Pull. Clatter. Pause. Up. Forward. *Thunk!* . . . After a while, the work, like a lot of work, developed its own rhythm. Peterson fell into the almost mindless state any endlessly repetitive labor can bring on. Not thinking was better. If time just went by, he didn't dwell on how tired or how hungry or how filthy he was.

And then he brought himself up short, so suddenly that he almost slammed the pick down on his own foot. Aside from the self-inflicted wound, that would have earned him a thumping from the guards. To them, anybody who hurt himself was trying to shirk, and they made would-be shirkers sorry.

But if they were serious about wanting this tunnel to Kaneohe, wouldn't they be using a lot more dynamite and maybe jackhammers and a lot less of this hand labor out of ancient days? Of course they would. Anybody with an ounce of sense would. The Japs didn't have a lot of their own bulldozers, but they sure used the ones they'd captured here to fix up airstrips and to dig out field fortifications. They were bastards, yeah, but they weren't stupid bastards.

Which meant the tunnel was—had to be—designed first and foremost to work POWs to death. That made perfect sense, and nothing else did, and if he hadn't been so weary and starved he would have seen it right away.

It also made no damn difference, not in what he had to do. The air stank of sour sweat and rock dust and burning fat. The rubble on the tunnel floor poked and gouged his feet through the soles of his shoes. What would happen when the shoes gave up the ghost? Things would get even nastier, that was all.

Up. Forward. *Thunk!* Pull. Clatter. Pause. Up. Forward . . .

LIEUTENANT SABURO SHINDO LOOKED OUT across the airstrip at Haleiwa. It was beautiful, no doubt about that: green grass, a creamy beach, and then the blue, blue Pacific. What worried him were the things the blue, blue Pacific hid.

He forgot about the view and glowered at the mechanics he'd summoned. "Don't tell me it isn't an authorized modification," he snapped. "I want a bomb rack on my Zero, and I want a bomb rack on every Zero at this airstrip. *Wakarimasu-ka?*"

"Yes, of course we understand, Lieutenant-*san,*" one of the mechanics answered. "But think of the drawbacks. What happens if you get into a dogfight with an American plane? Think how much the weight and drag of a bomb would hurt you."

"If I run into an American, I can dump the bomb," Shindo said. "But I need something to let me go after submarines—or surface ships, if the Yankees stick their noses into these waters again. You're not going to tell me the bomb rack will slow me down much by itself, are you?" His glare warned that they'd better not tell him any such thing.

And the chief mechanic shook his head. "Oh, no, sir. But what about a malfunction? How could you land on a carrier with an unreleased bomb?"

"Carefully, I suspect." Shindo's voice was dry.

Had the mechanic been an officer, he would have had plenty to say. His face made that very plain. Since he was only a rating, "Sir, that's not funny" had to suffice.

"I didn't say it was," Shindo answered. "What other way would you expect me to land after those conditions? And after I get down—because I *will* get down—the first thing I will do is come after the thumb-fingered idiots who mounted a malfunctioning piece of equipment on my plane. So it had better work, the first time and every single time after the first. Do you understand *that*?"

The mouthy mechanic bowed. So did all his friends. They had to know Shindo wasn't kidding. If something went wrong with the bomb rack, he *would* come after them, probably with his sword. And no Japanese military court was likely to convict an officer for anything he did to ratings.

"Good." Shindo nodded coldly to them. "You can't tell me there's no scrap metal to do the job, either. Hawaii has more scrap metal than a dog has fleas."

They bowed again. Their faces showed nothing, nothing at all. Shindo knew what that meant. They hated his guts, but discipline kept them from showing it. For a moment, that tickled him—but only for a moment. A mechanic who didn't like a pilot had a million ways to take his revenge. Planes broke down a million ways. If an accident wasn't quite an accident . . . who'd know? Yes, who'd know, especially if the evidence, if there was any evidence, lay at the bottom of the Pacific?

Shindo bowed back. It went against his grain, but he did it. The mechanics flicked glances at one another. *"Domo arigato,"* he said. Their eyebrows sprang up like startled stags. Superiors were not in the habit of thanking inferiors so warmly. He went on, "We all serve the Empire of Japan, and we should always do everything we can to help her."

"Hai." Several of the stolid men in coveralls spoke up. The word could have been no more than acknowledgment, but he thought it was also agreement. They did love the Empire, no matter what they thought of him. And they had to know he felt the same way about his country.

"Good," he told them. "Very good. Take care of it. We never can tell when the Americans will come sneaking around again."

They did what he told them. If they did it more for Japan than for him, he didn't mind. If anything, that made it better. If they did it for Japan, they were likelier to forget their anger at him.

A couple of days later, though, he did get a telephone call from Commander Fuchida. "What's this I hear about fitting bomb racks to your fighters up there?" Fuchida asked.

Shindo slowly nodded to himself. *I might have known,* he thought. Mechanics had more ways than sabotage to make their displeasure felt. Gossip could be just as dangerous. "It's true, sir," Shindo told the senior air officer. "I want to be in a position to kill a submarine if I spot one. I can't dive like an Aichi, but I'll get the job done."

He waited. If Fuchida said no, to whom could he appeal? Commander Genda? Not likely, not when Genda and Fuchida were two fingers of the same hand. Captain Toda? Would he overturn a ruling his air experts had made? Again, not likely. Admiral Yamamoto? Shindo was not the least bold of men, but he quailed at that. Besides, Yamamoto was back in Japan, and would surely defer to his men on the spot.

But Fuchida said, "All right, Shindo-*san,* go ahead and do it. The more versatility we can give our aircraft here, the better off we'll be."

"Thank you, sir!" Shindo said in glad surprise. "I had the same thought myself." He hadn't, not really; his own ideas centered on finding new ways to strike the enemy. Keeping a superior sweet never hurt, though, especially when he'd just given you what you wanted.

"I've been sub-hunting myself, but I haven't had any luck. Nobody's had a whole lot of luck hunting subs, and the Army isn't very happy with us on account of that," Fuchida said. "Anything that gives a plane that spots a sub a chance to sink it sounds good in my book."

"We agree completely." This time, Shindo was telling the truth. He and Fuchida talked a little while longer before the senior officer broke the connection.

A smile of satisfaction on his face, Shindo hung up, too. He started to get up and throw the news in the mechanics' faces. So they thought they could go behind his back, did they? Well, they had another think coming!

After a couple of steps, Shindo checked himself. He laughed an unpleasant laugh. Better if he kept his mouth shut. Let the mechanics find out for themselves that Fuchida had come down on his side. They would, soon enough.

Then they would spend some time worrying about whether he knew what they'd done. He laughed again. Yes, letting them stew was better.

He could tell when they learned what Fuchida had said. They'd worked on the bomb racks before that, but in slow motion. All at once, they got serious about the project. Things that shouldn't have taken very long suddenly *didn't* take very long. Only a few days later than they would have if they'd worked flat-out from the start, they had the racks on every Zero at Haleiwa.

Shindo was the first man to test one. He didn't want any of the people he led doing something he wouldn't or couldn't do himself. He had the armorers load a light practice bomb into the rack and took his Zero up. It did feel a little sluggish with the bomb attached; the mechanics were right about that. The problem wasn't bad, though.

He picked a target not far from the airstrip; a boulder poking up through the grass did duty for a surfaced submarine. He thumbed the new button the mechanics had installed on the instrument panel. The bomb fell free.

He didn't hit the boulder, but he frightened it. A sub made a much bigger target, and he would have been carrying a much bigger bomb. If he'd put that bomb so close to a submarine, he was sure he would have hurt it.

Back to the airstrip he went; there wasn't a lot of fuel for practice. Ground-crew men guided his plane back to its camouflaged revetment. In spite of the fuel shortage, he told his pilots, "I want all of you to get as much practice as you can. This is important. The better you get when it doesn't count, the better you'll do when it does."

The pilots nodded, almost in unison. Most of them were veterans of the Pearl Harbor strikes that had opened the war in the Pacific. They knew what meticulous planning and preparation were worth.

Let me find a submarine, Shindo thought. *Let me find one, and I'll give it a nasty surprise.*

WERE THOSE THE CRATERS of the moon down there? Joe Crosetti knew better, but the bombing range had sure as hell taken a beating. He held the Texan in a dive, watching height peel off the altimeter. When he got down to 2,500 feet, he released the bomb that hung beneath the trainer.

The Texan wasn't a dive bomber, any more than it was a fighter. But it could impersonate either. Joe pulled back hard on the stick to bring the plane's nose up and get it out of the dive. When you were down to half a mile off the ground, you didn't have much margin for error, even in a plane a lot more sedate than one you would take into combat.

"Not bad, Mr. Crosetti," the instructor said—about as much praise as he ever gave. "Take her back to the base and land her."

"Aye aye, sir." Joe had to look around to figure out where he was and in which direction Pensacola Naval Air Station lay. That didn't matter much here—he had plenty of landmarks to guide him back. With only ocean between his plane and a carrier, it might not be so good.

Some guys seemed to have a compass between their ears. They always knew right where they were and how to get where they were going without fuss, muss, bother, or visible calculation. Joe suspected Orson Sharp was like that. His roomie was a strange bird, but a damn capable one. He wished *he* could find home as automatically as he reached into his pocket for a half-dollar. But navigation didn't come easy for him.

That didn't mean he couldn't navigate, only that doing it was hard work. He put the Texan down in a landing he was proud of. If he'd been that neat when he soloed in it . . . But he had more experience now. The more experience he got, the more he realized how much it mattered.

"I know you want to be a fighter jockey," the instructor said as they climbed out of the Texan.

"Yes, sir," Joe agreed.

"That's fine," the older man told him. "But if you don't get what you want, you can strike at the enemy in a dive bomber, too. If anything, you can strike harder. Fighters fight other airplanes. Dive bombers fight the ships that carry airplanes."

"Yes, sir," Joe said again. It wasn't that the other officer was wrong—he wasn't. But Joe had had his heart set on flying a fighter since before he volunteered for the naval aviation program. Oh, sure, a Dauntless could make a Jap battlewagon or carrier very unhappy—but it was such a lumbering pig in the air next to a Wildcat!

"Okay." The instructor sounded wryly amused. No doubt he knew just what Joe was thinking. Fighter pilots got the glory, and glory could look mighty good to a kid getting close to finishing flight school.

Joe hustled back to his dorm room to work on trig problems he'd have to turn in that afternoon. No, navigation wasn't easy for him. That just meant he had to sweat it out the hard way.

The door flew open. In burst Orson Sharp. Joe stared at him. Joe, in fact, dropped his pencil. His roommate looked excited, and Sharp was usually cool as a cucumber. "What's up?" Joe asked.

"You haven't heard?" Sharp demanded.

"Nope." Joe shook his head. "If I had, would I be asking you?"

"No, I guess not." The kid from Utah nodded to himself. "Word is, we're going to have one of the pilots off the *Yorktown* talk to us this afternoon."

"Wow!" Joe forgot all about trigonometry. This was bigger news than any navigation problem. The *Yorktown* lay at the bottom of the Pacific, somewhere north of Hawaii. The Japs had sunk her in the failed U.S. attack against the islands. "Not many of those guys left."

Orson Sharp nodded. "I should say not. They had to ditch in the ocean and hope a destroyer would pick them up." That wasn't the only reason there weren't many *Yorktown* pilots left. Japanese fliers had taken a savage toll on them. Sharp didn't mention that, and Joe didn't dwell on it.

Cadets weren't in the habit of ditching classes anyhow, but the hall where the pilot would speak was packed tighter than a cable car with a tourist convention in town. The navigation instructor, whose class the pilot was taking, was a dour lieutenant commander named Otis Jones. He'd pulled every string he knew how to pull to get sea duty, but he was still here. That no doubt helped make him dour. All the same, Joe was convinced he'd been born with a lemon in his mouth.

Now he said, "Gentlemen, it is my privilege to present to you Lieutenant Jack Hadley, formerly of the USS *Yorktown*, soon to return to one of the carriers now building. Lieutenant Hadley!"

Hadley came out and saluted Jones. The cadets gave the fighter pilot a standing ovation. He eyed them with an aw-shucks grin. He wasn't much older than they were; some of them might have been older than he was.

"Thanks, guys," he said. Like his clean-cut blond good looks, his flat vowels said he came from somewhere in the Midwest. Being around cadets from all over the country had made Joe way better at placing accents than he'd ever needed to be back in San Francisco. Hadley went on, "Why don't all of you sit down again? And if you don't mind too much, I'm gonna do the same thing."

No matter what Lieutenant Commander Jones said, Hadley wasn't going back to sea right away. He walked with a pronounced limp and carried a cane. A nasty burn scar showed below his left shirt cuff; Joe wondered how far up his arm it went, and what other wounds his summer whites concealed. When Jones brought him a chair, he sank into it rather stiffly, and sat with his left leg, the bad one, out straight in front of him.

"Thank you, sir," he said to Jones, who nodded brusquely and sat down himself at a front-row desk he'd saved with a homemade RESERVED sign. Jack Hadley looked out at the crowded room again. "You've got to remember, gentlemen: I don't have a whole lot of experience against the Japs myself. But what I've got is more than most Americans have, so here's how it looks to me.

"First thing you need to remember is, the Japs aren't a joke. Forgetting that is the fastest way I know to get yourselves killed. All the jokes we made up till last year about them being little bucktoothed guys with funny glasses flying planes made out of tinfoil and scrap iron—all that stuff's a bunch of hooey. They're lousy back-stabbing so-and-sos, yeah, but they're awful good at what they do. They flew rings around us out there."

He paused, a look of intense recollection on his face. Joe wondered exactly what his mind's eye was seeing. Whatever it was, it didn't seem pleasant. Hadley's left arm twitched a little. Maybe that meant something, maybe it didn't. The injured pilot was the only one who knew for sure.

After a silence that lasted a few seconds too long for comfort, Hadley went on, "The Japs are no joke, and their planes are no joke, either. You've probably heard a thing or two about what the Zero can do." He paused again, this time waiting for nods. When he got them, he resumed: "Well, everything you've heard is true. That's one hell of an airplane. It's faster than a Wildcat, it climbs better, and it can turn inside you like you wouldn't believe—and a Wildcat's pretty maneuverable all by itself. If you try and dogfight a Zero, you are fitting yourself for a coffin. Don't do it. You won't do it more than once."

Again, he seemed to look at something only he could see. This time, he explained what it was: "They told me the same thing I'm telling you. I didn't want to listen. I figured no Jap in the world had my number. Shows what I know."

He gathered himself. "*Don't* dogfight them," he repeated. "If you're taking notes, write that down. If you're not taking notes, write it down anyway." He tried the aw-shucks grin again. It came out strained. "You've got two edges, and only two. A Wildcat can outdive a Zero. You can make a firing run from above and behind. Or, if you're in a lot of trouble, you can dive out of there, and most of the time you'll get away."

Joe waited to hear what the other edge was. While he waited, he underlined what he'd written about not dogfighting. But Hadley seemed to have dried up. Lieutenant Commander Jones had to prompt him: "Lieutenant . . . ?"

"Huh?" Jack Hadley came back to himself from wherever he'd gone. "Oh. Sorry, sir. I was thinking about . . . battle damage, you might say. Yeah. Battle damage." Was he talking about what had happened to himself, to his airplane, or to the whole fleet the USA sent against Hawaii?

Did it matter?

Hadley gathered himself again: "There's one other thing you can do to at least help keep those monkeys off you. A pilot named Jimmy Thach thought it up, and the Thach Weave does some good, anyway." He briefly described the system, explaining how a threatened plane's sharp turn away from the enemy would alert the other pair in a four-plane element to turn towards it and give them a good shot. "This isn't perfect, not even close," he finished. "It takes really tight teamwork and a lot of practice to work well. But it does give us some kind of chance against a superior airplane, and we hardly had any before."

He took questions then. Several people, Joe among them, asked about the Thach Weave. Hadley painfully levered himself to his feet and drew diagrams on the blackboard. They helped; Joe hadn't been able to visualize the tactic well from words alone. The circles and arrows helped him see what needed doing. Whether he could do it, and do it in coordination with other pilots—well, that might be a different question. But he was practicing formation flying, too, so he figured he'd get the hang of it.

Then Orson Sharp said, "Sir, would you tell us about your ditching?"

Before Hadley said anything, he sat down again. Again, his bad leg stuck out in front of him. He reached out and touched that stiff knee. "I'd already got this by then. Damn bullet came in from the side. The armor in the seat is good; the stuff in the cockpit's not so hot. Tell you the truth, that damn Jap filled the plane full of holes. My engine was starting to cook. Thank God those radials are air-cooled, though. A liquid-cooled engine would've lost its coolant and frozen up on me long before, and I'd've gone into the drink too far from home.

"As it was, I nursed her back toward where our ships were at. I was hoping we still had a working carrier, but no such luck. Every time the flames got going in the cockpit, I'd use the extinguisher to put 'em out—mostly." He looked down at his burned arm. Joe couldn't tell if he knew he was doing it.

"I put her in the water as slow and smooth as I could," Hadley said. "Then I pushed back the cockpit—that still worked great, in spite of all the damage I'd taken—dragged myself out, and managed to inflate my life raft. A destroyer picked me up—and here I am."

He gave them that farmboy grin one more time. He made it sound easy. How much fear and pain hid behind the smiling façade? Enough so that even somebody like Joe Crosetti, who'd never seen combat, could tell they were there. But, since Jack Hadley pretended they weren't, everybody else had to do the same thing.

Could I do that? Joe wondered. He hoped so, but he was honest enough to admit to himself that he had no idea.

JANE ARMITAGE STOOD in line to get what the community kitchen in Wahiawa dished out for supper. As usual, what plopped onto her plate would have been the butt of a Catskills comic's joke. *The food here is lousy—and such small portions.* She got a boiled potato bigger than a ping-pong ball but smaller than a tennis ball, some greens that might have been turnip tops or might have been weeds, and, unusually, a chunk of fish a little larger than a book of matches.

By the way the fish smelled, it hadn't been caught yesterday—or the day before, either. Jane didn't complain. Wahiawa was as near in the middle of Oahu as made no difference. It wasn't very far from the Pacific—nothing on the island was—but fish of any sort seldom got away from the coast. Too many hungry mouths, especially in Honolulu.

Other people were as glad to see the treat as she was. "Isn't that something?" was what she heard most often. She sat down at one of the tables scattered around the elementary-school playground and dug in.

The fish had an undertaste of ammonia that went with the way it smelled. If she'd got it in a restaurant before the occupation, she would have angrily sent it back. Now she ate every crumb, all of the nondescript and rather nasty greens, and every bit of potato. She didn't lick the plate when she was through, but some people around her did.

Haoles mostly sat together. So did local Japanese. So did Chinese. So did Filipinos. So did Wahiawa's handful of Koreans—as far away from the local

Japanese as they could. Not all the local Japs collaborated with Major Hirabayashi and the occupiers—far from it—but enough did that people from other groups were leery about having too much to do with them.

Jane sat and listened to the chatter around her—in English and otherwise. Blaming the local Japanese for all the troubles in Wahiawa wasn't fair. Some of them really did see Japan as their country, more than they saw the USA that way. How could you blame them, when a lot of *haoles* had gone out of their way to make it plain they didn't think Japs were as good as they were?

And besides, the local Japanese weren't the only collaborators. Sitting one table away from Jane was Smiling Sammy Little, who'd sold jalopies to servicemen from Schofield Barracks before the invasion. He hadn't quite been a loan shark, but his interest rates were as high as the law allowed, and a lot of his cars were lemons. He was still smiling these days. With next to no gas on the island, he didn't sell cars any more. But the Japs were glad to buy what he had for them.

Jane hated him much more than she did someone like Yosh Nakayama. Smiling Sammy didn't remember or care that he was supposed to be an American. If the Russians or the Ethiopians or the Argentines had invaded Hawaii, he would have sucked up to them, too.

". . . Egypt . . ." ". . . outside of Alexandria . . ." ". . . Montgomery . . ." Jane got tantalizing bits of conversation from the table on the other side of her. She tried to listen without paying obvious attention. Somebody over there either had an outlawed radio or knew someone else who had one. News that wasn't Japanese propaganda did circulate in spite of everything the occupiers could do to stop it.

She swore under her breath. They were talking in low voices, and she couldn't hear as much as she wanted. *What* was going on outside of Alexandria? Had the Germans broken through at last? Or had Montgomery somehow held them? She couldn't make it out.

She looked back toward the pans and kettles where the cooks had fixed the evening slop. She hoped for dessert, even though she knew what it would be. If this nightmare ever ended, she'd taken a savage oath never to touch rice pudding again for the rest of her life. Hawaii still had sugar, and it had some rice. Boil them together till they were something close to glue, and there was a treat that counted as one only because there were no others.

Jane looked down at her arms. Every time she did, she thought she was a little skinnier than before. How long could that go on before nothing was left of her, or of anyone else? Not forever, and she knew it too well. And so she didn't despise even the sweetish library paste that went by the name of rice pudding. Calories were calories, wherever they came from.

But the cooks gave no sign of having any dessert at all to dish out today. She swore again, not quite so softly. She was so tired of being hungry all the time. And she was just so tired. . . .

Had it been less than a year ago that she'd walked into a restaurant and ordered a T-bone too big to finish? She hadn't thought anything of it. She hadn't even asked for a bag to take home the leftovers. *Christ, what a fool I was!* Had she eaten beef since the Japs occupied Wahiawa? She didn't think so.

She carried her plate and silverware to the dishwashers. Everyone took turns at that. One of the women was saying something to another one when she walked over to them. They both clammed up before she could hear what it was. They started again when she walked off and got too far away to make out what they were saying.

Her stomach knotted, and for once it wasn't the wretched food. Were they gossiping about her? About somebody she knew, somebody they knew she knew? About whatever was happening outside of Alexandria?

Whatever it was, she'd never know. They didn't trust her enough to let her in on it. Before the war, she'd talked with her third-graders about the difference between freedom and dictatorship. She'd talked about it, yeah, but she hadn't understood it. The difference lay in what people said to one another, and in what they didn't say when other people might hear. It lay in trust.

And trust, in Wahiawa, was as dead as comfortable American rule over Hawaii. If the United States came back, if the Stars and Stripes once again flew over the school and the post office and Schofield Barracks, would that trust return? How could it, once it was so badly broken?

But if it didn't, would the islands ever really be free again?

FLETCH ARMITAGE WAS SICK OF DIGGING. He would have been sick of digging even if he weren't doing it on starvation rations. He looked like a skeleton with callused hands. The Japs didn't care. If he got too weak to dig, they wouldn't put him in the infirmary till his strength came back. They'd just knock him over the head, the way you would with a dog that got hit by a car. Then they'd give his shovel to somebody else, and use that poor, miserable bastard up, too.

And why not? As far as they were concerned, prisoners were fair game. They had tens of thousands of them. If they worked POWs to death, they wouldn't have to worry nearly so much about plots and escape attempts. Skeletons with callused hands didn't have the energy or the strength to try anything drastic. All the energy they had was focused on staying alive, and they had to put all their strength into the work. If they didn't, the Japanese noncoms who lorded it over them made them pay.

This was going to be a gun emplacement. It was nicely sited: on the south side of a low hill, to make it harder to spot from the north—the probable direction of any invasion—but there'd be an observer at the top of the hill to guide the firing. He'd be hard to spot, too, especially once they got done camouflaging his position; running a phone line between the one place and the other would be easy as pie. Fletch had a thoroughly professional appreciation of what the Japs were doing right here.

He didn't appreciate having to work on it. Making him do that went dead against the Geneva Convention. The Japs were proud that they hadn't signed it. Anybody who complained on that particular score caught hell—or even more hell than anybody else caught.

Odds were the phone line the Japs used to link the top of the hill and the gun emplacement would be captured American equipment. They were using as much of what they'd grabbed here as they could.

And they were fortifying Oahu to a fare-thee-well. The United States had put a lot of men, a lot of equipment, and a lot of ships in Hawaii. Having done that, the Americans smugly decided no one would have the nerve to attack them here. *And look what that got us,* Fletch thought, turning another shovelful of earth.

The Japs labored under no such illusions. They knew the USA wanted Hawaii back. If the Americans managed to land, they would have to fight their way south an inch at a time, through works their own countrymen had made. Every time Fletch stuck his shovel in the ground, he gave aid and comfort to the enemy.

He didn't like feeling like a traitor. He didn't know what he could do about it, though. If he didn't do what the Japs told him to, they would kill him. It wouldn't be as neat or quick as knocking him over the head, either. They would make him suffer so nobody else got frisky ideas.

"*Isogi!*" the closest Jap noncom shouted. Like everybody else who heard him, Fletch worked faster for a while. He didn't look back to see if the bandy-legged bugger was yelling at him in particular, he just sped up. Looking back suggested to the Japs that you had a guilty conscience. It gave them an excuse to wallop you, as if they needed much in the way of excuses.

Ten minutes later, Fletch did look back over his shoulder. The Jap was standing there spraddle-legged, his back to the POWs, taking a leak. Fletch promptly eased off. He wasn't the only one who did.

One of the fellows in his shooting squad was a tall, sandy-haired guy from Mississippi named Clyde Newcomb. "Lord almighty," he said, wiping his sweaty face with his filthy sleeve. "Now I know what bein' a nigger in the cotton fields feels like."

Fletch dug out another shovelful of dirt and flung it aside. "I do believe I'd sell my soul to be a nigger in a cotton field right now," he said, "as long as it was a cotton field on the mainland."

"Well, yeah, far as the work goes, I would, too," Newcomb said. "I wouldn't ask more'n about a dime for it, neither. But that's not what I meant. Nobody ever *treated* me like a goddamn nigger till I stacked my Springfield and surrendered. We ain't nothin' but dirt to the Japs, an' low-grade dirt at that."

"So you Southern guys treated niggers like dirt?" Fletch didn't care much one way or the other, but anything you could talk about helped make time go by, and that was all to the good.

"You're agitatin' me." Newcomb spoke without heat. "But seriously, you gotta let the niggers know who's boss. You don't, and pretty soon they'll start thinkin' they're just as good as white folks."

"You mean like the Japs here in Hawaii started thinking they were just as good as *haoles*?" Fletch asked. Whites here hadn't lynched local Japanese, the way whites lynched Negroes in Mississippi. They'd found other, not quite so brutal, ways to keep them in their place. Even so, they were paying now for what they'd done then. If the Japs here had been treated better, there would be fewer collaborators these days.

Clyde Newcomb gave him a funny look. "Yeah, kind of—only niggers really *are* down lower than we are."

Fletch took it no further. What was the point? Newcomb was so blind to some things, he didn't even know he couldn't see them. *And we're supposed to win this war? God help us!* Did the Japs have clodhoppers like Newcomb running around loose? Maybe they did. Some of these guards sure acted as if a rifle was far and away the most complicated thing they'd ever had to worry about. Fletch hoped so. If the other side's yahoos didn't cancel out ours, we were in a hell of a lot of trouble.

Another load of dirt flew from Fletch's shovel, and another, and another. Every so often, a noncom would yell at the POWs to hurry up again. And they would . . . for a little while, or till he turned his back. Even if Newcomb didn't know his ass from third base, it was the rhythm of a cotton field, but of a cotton field back in slavery days before the Civil War. Nobody here worked any harder than he absolutely had to.

The overseers knew it as well as the slaves. They made an example out of somebody who moved too slowly to suit them—or maybe somebody chosen at random—almost every day. And they were more savage than the overseers of the American South. Negro slaves had been expensive pieces of property; overseers back then could get in trouble for damaging them. None of the Japs cared what happened to POWs here. The more of them who dropped dead, the happier they seemed.

A whistle blew when the sun went down. The work gang lined up for the little lumps of rice and greens that wouldn't have been enough to keep men alive if they'd lain around doing nothing. Then they slept. Exhaustion made bare ground a perfect mattress. Fletch closed his eyes and he was gone.

When he dreamt, he dreamt of Jane. That hadn't happened in a while. But he didn't dream of her naked and lively in the bedroom, the way he had after they first broke up. He couldn't remember the last time he'd dreamt of Jane—or even of a Hotel Street hooker—that way.

This dream was even more excruciatingly sensual, and filled him with an even more desolate sense of loss. He dreamt of Jane naked and lively . . . in the kitchen. She was fixing him the breakfast to end all breakfasts. Half a dozen eggs fried over medium—just the way he liked them—in butter. A dozen thick slices of smoke-rich bacon, hot fat glistening on them. A foot-high pile of golden flapjacks slathered in more butter, yellow as tigers, and real Vermont maple syrup. Wheat toast with homemade strawberry preserves. Coffee, as much as he could drink. Cream. Sugar.

"Oh, God!" He made enough noise to wake himself up. He looked down to see if he'd come in his pants. He hadn't. He was damned if he knew why not.

CORPORAL TAKEO SHIMIZU LED HIS SQUAD on patrol down King Street. The Japanese soldiers marched in the middle of the street; there was no wheeled traffic to interfere with them except for rickshaws, pedicabs, and the occasional horse-drawn carriage or wagon. It was another perfect Honolulu day, not too hot, not too muggy, just right.

Shiro Wakuzawa's eyes swung to the right. "I still say that's the funniest-looking thing I ever saw," he remarked.

"Have you looked in a mirror lately?" Shimizu asked. The rest of the squad laughed at Wakuzawa. But it wasn't cruel laughter, as it would have been in a lot of units. Shimizu hadn't said it intending to wound. He'd just made a joke, and the soldiers he led took it that way.

And Wakuzawa wasn't far wrong. The water tower decked out with painted sheet metal to look like an enormous pineapple was one of the funniest-looking things Shimizu had ever seen, too. Senior Private Yasuo Furusawa, who had a thoughtful turn of mind, said, "What's even funnier is that it stood up through all the fighting."

He wasn't wrong, either. After bombing Pearl Harbor, Japanese planes had also pounded Honolulu's harbor district. The Aloha Tower, down right by the Pacific, was only a ruin. But the water tower, which had to be one of the ugliest things ever made, still stood.

On the patrol went. Japanese soldiers and sailors on leave scrambled to get out of their way. Since Shimizu was on patrol, he could have asked them for their papers if he felt officious. Some of them probably didn't have valid papers. If he wanted to make his superiors smile on him, catching such miscreants was a good way to do it. But Shimizu was a long way from officious, and didn't like sucking up to his superiors. He enjoyed a good time himself; why shouldn't others feel the same way?

Civilians bowed. Shimizu marched his men through one of the unofficial markets that dotted this part of Honolulu. They were technically illegal. He could have caused trouble for the locals by hauling in buyers and sellers. But, again—why? You had to go along to get along, and he didn't see how a trade in fish and rice and coconuts did anybody any harm.

Besides, this market was within sight of Iolani Palace. If the guards didn't like it, they could close it down. Shimizu snickered. The Japanese soldiers and naval landing troops at Iolani Palace were just as much a ceremonial force as the Hawaiian unit with whom they now shared their duty. They probably weren't good for much that involved actual work.

"Corporal-*san,* do those Hawaiian soldiers have live ammunition in their rifles?" Private Wakuzawa asked.

"They didn't used to, but I hear they finally do," Shimizu said. "We're pretending they're a real kingdom, so it would be an insult if they didn't, *neh?*"

"I suppose so," Wakuzawa said. "Are they reliable, though?"

Senior Private Furusawa answered that before Shimizu could: "As long as we outnumber them, they're reliable."

Everybody in the squad laughed, Shimizu included. It looked that way to him, too. "This is like Manchukuo, only more so," he said. The soldiers nodded at that; they all understood it. Manchukuo had a real army and a real air arm, not the toy force the King of Hawaii boasted. But the soldiers and fliers obeyed the Japanese officers on the spot, not the puppet Emperor of Manchukuo. And if they ever decided not to, Japan had more than enough men in Manchukuo to squash them flat.

The Hawaiians were impressive-looking men. Many of them were more than a head taller than their Japanese counterparts. But the American defenders of Oahu had been bigger than Shimizu and his comrades. *And much good it did them,* he thought.

On marched Shimizu's squad. Every so often, he looked back over his shoulder to make sure his men were parading properly. He didn't catch them doing anything they shouldn't. They always pointed their faces straight ahead, and kept them impassive. If their eyes slid to the right or the left every now and then to look at a pretty girl in a skimpy sun dress or a halter top—well, so did Shimizu's. No woman back in Japan would have let herself be seen dressed— or undressed—like that.

A Japanese captain stepped out from a side street. "Salute!" Shimizu exclaimed, and smartly brought up his own right arm.

If anyone saluted poorly or in a sloppy way, the officer could land the whole squad in trouble. If Shimizu hadn't seen him, and the men marched past without saluting . . . He didn't care to think about what would have happened then. Aside from the beating he and his men would have got, his company commander probably would have busted him back to private. How could he have lived with the disgrace?

Well, it hadn't happened. The captain saw the salutes. He must have found them acceptable, for he went on about his business without ordering Shimizu's men to halt.

"Keep your eyes open," Shimizu warned. "Later we'll be going through Hotel Street. There will be plenty of officers there, outside the bars and the fancy brothels. A lot of them won't care that they're on leave. If you don't spot them, if you don't salute, they'll make you sorry. *Wakarimasu-ka?*"

"*Hai!*" the soldiers chorused. It was a rhetorical question; by now they'd had plenty of time to learn to understand the vagaries, the vanity, and the touchy tempers of the officers under whom they served. And since those officers had essentially absolute power over them, mere understanding wasn't enough. They had to placate and propitiate those officers like any other angry gods.

They got their own back by coming down hard on the people over whom they ruled. Furusawa pointed to a *haole* man in his twenties. "He didn't bow, Corporal!"

"No, eh?" Shimizu said. "Well, he'll be sorry." He raised his voice to a shout: "You!" He also pointed at the white man.

The fellow froze. He looked as if he wanted to bolt, but he feared the Japanese would do something dreadful to him if he tried. He was absolutely right about that. He also realized what he hadn't done. He did bow now, and spoke with desperate urgency—in English, since he knew no Japanese.

That wouldn't save him. Shimizu tramped up to him and barked, "Your papers!" *He* spoke in Japanese, of course: it was the only language he knew. His tone and his outthrust hand got his meaning across. The local man pulled out his wallet and showed Shimizu his driver's license. It had his photograph on it.

Shimizu gave him a stony glare even so. The white man reached into the wallet and pulled out a ten-dollar bill. Shimizu made it disappear fast as lightning—it was more than the Army paid him in two months. Despite the bribe, he slapped the man in the face, the way he might have slapped one of his own soldiers who'd done something stupid. The white man gasped in surprise and pain, but after that he took it as well as a soldier might have. Satisfied, Shimizu nodded coldly and went back to his men.

"Come on," he told them. "Get moving." Down the street they went. He looked back over his shoulder once. The white man was staring after them, eyes enormous in a cloud-pale face.

Hotel Street was as raucous and lascivious a place as ever. Shimizu wished he were visiting it on leave and not on patrol. Music blared from the open doorways of half a dozen dives. Some of it was Japanese, the rest the syrupy-sweet tunes of the West. Shimizu had heard that Americans found Japanese music peculiar. He knew he thought Western music was strange.

Harried-looking military policemen tried to keep some kind of order. Drunk soldiers and sailors wanted no part of it. Every so often, the military policemen knocked a couple of heads together. Even that accomplished less than it would have anywhere else.

"The Americans are foolish to attack our ships," Senior Private Furusawa said. "If they dropped bombs on Hotel Street, they could wipe out all our forces." Everybody in Shimizu's squad laughed, for it was funny, but the laughter quickly stopped, for it also held too much truth.

"Here! You!" A military policeman pointed at Shimizu. "Come take charge of this man." He shook a sozzled sailor, who giggled foolishly.

"So sorry, Sergeant-*san,* but we're on patrol and we still have a lot of ground to cover. Please excuse me," Shimizu said. Because he and his men were on duty of their own, the military policeman had no choice but to nod. Shimizu didn't smile till the fellow couldn't see him any more. Saying no—being able to say no—to one of the hated military police felt wonderful. "Forward!" he called, and the patrol went on.

IV

OSCAR VAN DER KIRK AND CHARLIE KAAPU SAT IN A WAIKIKI SALOON DRINKING
what the bartender alleged to be Primo beer. Hawaii's native suds had never
been a brew to make anybody forget fancy German beer—or, for that matter,
even Schlitz. This stuff tasted more like bathwater after the University of
Hawaii football team got clean in it.

Charlie had a different opinion. "So," he asked the man behind the bar,
"how sick was the horse when he pissed in your bottles?"

"Funny," the barkeep said. "Funny like a crutch. You try getting fucking
barley these days. For beer brewed from rice, this ain't half bad."

"Beer brewed from rice is sake, isn't it?" Oscar said.

"Sort of. I have some of that, in case any Japanese officers wander in," the
bartender said. By the way he said *Japanese officers,* he meant *Japs.* But he
wouldn't say that, not around people he didn't completely trust. Oscar knew
he and Charlie weren't informers, but the barkeep didn't. Fiddling with his
black bow tie, he went on, "There are some real hops in this, though. It's doing
its best to be beer, honest."

"That's not very good," Charlie said, and then, incongruously, "Give me another one, will you?"

"Me, too," Oscar said as he emptied his glass. "Primo's closer to real beer
than what they call gin or *okolehao* is to the real McCoy these days."

"You got that right, brother." Charlie Kaapu made a horrible face.

"Yeah, well, you don't want to know some of the shit that goes into them."

The bartender set up two more beers. "Four bits," he said. Oscar slid a half-dollar across the bar. The bartender scooped it up.

Oscar raised his glass. "Mud in your eye," he said to Charlie.

"Same to you," the half-Hawaiian surf rider replied. They both drank. They both sighed. This Primo wasn't good, even if it wasn't so bad as it might have been. Charlie sighed again. "We ought to do something different," he said.

"Like what?" Oscar asked. "Just getting along is hard enough."

"That's the point," Charlie said. "That's *why* we ought to do something different."

Back when Oscar was at Stanford, his philosophy prof would have called that a *non sequitur*. Somehow, he didn't think Charlie would appreciate philosophy. "What have you got in mind?" he asked.

"We ought to go back to the north shore," Charlie said. "We haven't been up there in a hell of a long time."

Oscar stared at him. "Are you out of your goddamn mind?" he exclaimed. "The last time we did go up there, we damn near got killed." Just thinking about it brought back gut-wrenching, bladder-squeezing raw terror.

"Yeah, I know." His *hapa*-Hawaiian buddy looked vaguely embarrassed. Maybe he was remembering fear, too. But he went on, "That's another reason to go back. It's like when you fall off a horse—you get back on again, right?"

"I guess." Oscar was vague about horses. His father's construction business had been completely motorized by the time he was born. Dad went on about a competitor who'd thought trucks were only a passing fad, and stuck with horse-drawn wagons. He'd gone broke in short order.

"Sure you do." If Charlie Kaapu had any doubts, he hid them very well. "Besides, the surf down here is rotten. I want something I can get my teeth into."

"Get your face into, you mean, if you mess up," Oscar said. Charlie gave him the finger. They both laughed. Oscar took another sip of more-or-less Primo. "Besides, we're not just surf-riders, you know. We're fishermen, too."

Charlie grimaced. "Waste time," he muttered, a handy phrase that could apply to anything you didn't like. He too took a pull at his miserable excuse for a beer. "Nobody shooting at us up there nowadays."

"You hope," Oscar said. "God only knows what the Japanese are doing up there these days, though." He didn't say *Japs* in front of the barkeep, either.

"Hey, come on. Don't you want to get away from all this for a while? Or are you *married* to that gal of yours?" Charlie laced his voice with scorn.

It struck home, too; Oscar's ears heated. "You know I'm not," he said. He and Susie were getting along pretty well, which was nice, but it wasn't *married*. He jabbed a forefinger in Charlie's direction. "If we go up to the north shore, how are we gonna get there? Even if we could find gas, my Chevy's got a dead battery and four flats. Hell, it probably doesn't even have flats any more, the way the . . . Japanese"—almost slipped there—"are stripping the rubber off cars these days."

Charlie clucked reproachfully. "And here I thought you were such a big, smart *haole*."

"What do you mean?"

"You were the guy who thought up sailboards," Charlie said. "We can go on them, catch fish"—he evidently didn't mind when he was doing it for himself—"sleep on the beach, have a hell of a time. No *huhu*."

He made it sound so easy—probably a lot easier than it really would be. And he tempted Oscar, and Oscar knew damn well he was tempted. He gave back the strongest argument against the trip he could think of: "What do you want to bet the surf will stink?"

"Bet it won't," Charlie retorted. "It's October by now, man. You can get some good sets up there."

He wasn't wrong. The waves hadn't been *that* high last December, which had disappointed Oscar and Charlie but no doubt relieved the Japanese invaders. Oscar wouldn't have wanted to try to get a landing craft over thirty-foot breakers, and no doubt the Japs hadn't wanted to, either. Storms *could* start up in the Gulf of Alaska this early, and waves from those storms had a straight shot over the Pacific, all the way down to Waimea Bay.

Charlie Kaapu gave him a slightly sloshed grin. "Come on, Oscar. Don't be a grouch. We pull this off, we talk about it forever. You want to be a fisherman *all* the goddamn time? Go ride a sampan if you do."

Maybe Oscar would have said no if he hadn't had some beer himself. But he had, and he didn't like coming back to Waikiki every day any better than Charlie did. "I'll do it!" he said. "Let's leave tomorrow."

"Now you're talking! Now you're cooking with gas!" Charlie's grin got wider and more gleeful. "Can't change our minds if we go right away."

Oscar wasn't so sure. He would have to tell Susie. When he did, she was liable to change his mind for him. Charlie didn't begin to get that. Oscar didn't think Charlie had ever stayed with a girl more than a couple of weeks. Charlie no more understood settling down than a butterfly understood staying with one flower all the time. That wasn't in a butterfly's makeup, and it wasn't in Charlie Kaapu's, either.

How much of it was in Susie's nature? There was an interesting question. Oscar told her that evening, over steaks she'd cut from a tuna he'd caught and tomatoes he'd acquired for another, smaller, fish.

He stumbled and stammered more than he wanted to. She looked at him for a while, just looked at him with those eyes that always reminded him of a Siamese cat's. The mind behind the eyes was often as self-centered as a cat's, too. But all she said—all she said at first, anyway—was, "Have fun."

He let out an elated sigh of relief. "Thanks, babe," he breathed.

"Have fun," Susie repeated. "And if I'm still here when you get back, we'll pick it up again. And if I'm not—well, this was fun, too. Mostly, anyhow." And if that wasn't praising with faint damn, Oscar had never run into anything that so perfectly fit the bill.

He wondered if he ought to tell her to stay. She'd laugh at him. She was no damn good at doing what anybody told her to. He also wondered if he should can the whole thing with Charlie. The trouble with that was, he didn't want to. And if he did can it, Susie would get the idea she could run roughshod over him. Whatever else that would be, it wouldn't be fun.

"I hope you're still around," he said after that calculation, all of which took maybe a second and a half. He wondered if he ought to add anything, and decided not to. It said what needed saying.

Susie cocked her head to one side. "I kind of hope I am, too," she said. "But you never can tell."

She didn't yell, *I look out for Number One first, last, and always,* but she might as well have. It wasn't anything Oscar didn't know. Drop Susie anywhere and she'd land on her feet. That was one more way she was like a cat.

She did the dishes as well as she could with cold water and without soap. Neither she nor Oscar had come down with anything noxious, so it was good enough. He dried. He'd become domesticated enough for that. As she handed him the last plate, she asked, "You want one for the road?"

"Sure," he said eagerly, and she laughed—she'd known he would. They always got on well in bed. This time seemed special even for them. Only afterwards, while he wished for a cigarette, did Oscar figure out why. This was, or might have been, the last time.

Susie leaned over in the narrow bed and kissed him. "Trying to make me want to stick around, are you?" she said, so he didn't have to worry about *Was it good for you, too?* tonight. Not that he was going to worry about much right then anyhow. He rolled over and fell asleep.

When he got up the next morning, she was already out the door, heading for her secretarial job in Honolulu. No good-bye kiss, then, and no early morning quickie, either. But a note—*Good luck! XOXOXO*—made him hope she'd still be here when he came back from the north shore.

Breakfast was cold rice with a little sugar sprinkled on it. It wasn't corn flakes—and it sure as hell wasn't bacon and eggs—but it would have to do. He'd just finished when Charlie Kaapu banged on his door.

"Ready?" the *hapa*-Hawaiian demanded.

"Yeah!" Oscar said. They grinned at each other, then hurried down to Waikiki Beach.

As usual since the occupation, surf fishermen were already casting their bait upon the waters. They moved aside to give Charlie and Oscar room enough to get their sailboards into the Pacific. For a wonder, they also stopped casting till the two boards were out of range.

"How many times have you just missed getting hooked by the ear when you went out?" Oscar asked.

"Missed? This big *haole* reeled me in once. Bastard was all set to gut me for a marlin till he saw my beak wasn't big enough," Charlie Kaapu said.

Oscar snorted. "Waste time, fool!" They both laughed.

Once they got out past the breakers, they set their sails. Oscar was used to sailing out a lot farther than that, to get to a stretch of the Pacific that hadn't been fished to death. Instead of running with the wind today, he swung the sail at a forty-five degree angle to the wind and skimmed along parallel to the southern coast of Oahu. Charlie's sailboard glided beside his.

"You want to talk about waste time, talk about fishing," Charlie said.

"Since when don't you like to eat?" Oscar said.

"Eating is fine. Fishing is work. Would be worse if I didn't get to surf-ride there and back again." That qualifier was as far as Charlie would go. Oscar knew the native Hawaiians had fished with nets and spears. If *that* hadn't taken the patience of Job, he didn't know what would. But Charlie, like too many Hawaiians and *hapa*-Hawaiians these days, was willing to work only on what he enjoyed, and was convinced *haoles* would run rings around him everywhere else.

They sailed past Diamond Head. These days, an enormous Rising Sun floated from the dead volcano. *So much for the Kingdom of Hawaii,* Oscar thought. He didn't say anything about that. Charlie Kaapu had no use at all for King Stanley Laanui, though he thought the redheaded Queen Cynthia was a knockout. From the pictures Oscar had seen of her, he did, too.

The empty road struck Oscar like a blow. There was still traffic in Honolulu, even if it was foot traffic instead of automobiles. Here, there was just—nobody. No tourists heading up to see the Mormon temple near Laie. No Japanese dentist off to visit his mom and dad at the little general store they ran. No nothing, not hardly.

Charlie saw the same thing. "Whole island seems dead," he said, and spat into the Pacific.

"Yeah." Oscar nodded. The otherworldly pace at which things happened when you were under sail only added to the impression. The landscape changed only very slowly. The emptiness didn't seem to change at all. And then it did: Oscar and Charlie passed a long column of Japanese troops marching east. They passed them slowly, too, for the Japs marched almost as fast as they sailed. A couple of Japs pointed out to sea as the sailboards went by. Oscar said, "I'm almost even glad to see those guys, you know what I mean?"

"I know what you mean," Charlie said. "I ain't glad to see them any which way. We're lucky the bastards aren't shooting at us."

Oscar's head whipped back toward the coast. If he saw Japs dropping to one knee or even raising their rifles, he was going to jump in the water. They'd been known to kill people for the fun of it. But the soldiers in the funny-colored khaki uniforms just kept trudging along. After another moment, Oscar figured out what made the Japanese uniforms seem funny: they were of a shade different from the U.S. Army khaki he was used to. That was all.

Slowly—but not slowly enough after Charlie's comment—the soldiers fell astern of the sailboards. "We don't want to go ashore where they can catch up with us," Charlie said, and Oscar nodded once more.

When they rounded Makapu Point, Oscar saw that the lighthouse there had been bombed. That pained him. The light had been welcoming and warning ships for a long time. To see it ruined . . . was another sign of how things had changed.

Oahu itself changed on the windward coast. Oscar and Charlie got spatters of rain almost at once, and then more than spatters. It rained all the time here.

The air felt thick and hot and wet, the way it did back East on the mainland. The sea began heaving erratically, like a restless beast.

Everything he could see on the shore was lush and green. The Koolau Range rose steeply from the sea. The volcanic rocks would have been jagged, but jungle softened their outlines; they might almost have been covered in emerald velvet. Remembering a paleontology class, he pointed to the mountains and said, "They look like giant teeth from an *Iguanodon*."

Charlie Kaapu looked not at the Koolau Range but at him. "What the hell you talkin' 'bout?" he asked. Oscar decided the world could live without his similes.

He quickly rediscovered why they called this the Windward Coast: the wind kept trying to blow him and Charlie ashore. Long stretches of the coastline were rocky, not sandy. He had to keep fighting to claw his way out to sea.

Kaneohe Peninsula was the last obstacle he and Charlie got by before putting in for the evening. They barely got by it, too. If they had to put in there, they could have, at least as far as the beach went. But what had been a Marine base was manned these days by Japanese soldiers. Oscar had no desire to get to know them better.

Wrecked American flying boats still lay along the beach like so many unburied bodies. None of them had engines on their wings. Various other bits were missing from this machine or that one. As the Japs had all over Hawaii, they'd taken whatever they could use.

Light was fading when Charlie pointed to a small stretch of sand beyond Kaneohe. Oscar nodded. They both guided their sailboards up onto the beach. "Whew!" Oscar said, sprawling on the sand. "I'm whipped."

"Hard work," Charlie agreed; the phrase, translated literally from the Japanese, had become part of the local language. "Don't have much in the way of fish, either."

Before, he'd grumbled about the indignities of fishing. Oscar saw no point in reminding him of that. He just said, "We won't starve." He checked his match safe. "Matches are still dry. We can make a fire and cook what we've got."

They gathered driftwood for fuel. The rain had stopped, which made things easier. Charlie Kaapu walked along the edge of the beach. Every so often, he would bend down. He came back with some clams. "Here," he said. "We do these, too."

The clams weren't very big—only a bite or so apiece—but anything was better than nothing. After that, Oscar and Charlie lay down on the sand. That would have been comfortable enough if it hadn't rained several times. Whenever it did, it woke Oscar up. He thought about taking shelter, but there was no shelter to take. The night seemed endless.

"Some fun," Charlie Kaapu said as they put their sailboards back into the water.

Oscar couldn't help rising to that. "Whose idea was this?" he inquired sweetly. Charlie sent him a dirty look.

They spent all day beating their way northwest along the beautiful but often forbidding coast. But they didn't worry about food for long: Charlie caught a big *ahi* less than an hour after they raised their sails. "How hungry are you?" he asked Oscar.

"What do you mean?"

"Want some raw, the way the Japs eat it?"

"Sure. Why not? I've done that a few times." Carefully, because the water was still rough, Oscar guided his sailboard alongside Charlie's. The *hapa-Hawaiian* passed him a good-sized chunk of pink flesh. He haggled bite-sized pieces off with a knife. They weren't neat and elegant, the way they would have been in a fancy Japanese restaurant. He didn't care. The flesh was firm and rich and hardly fishy at all. "Might almost be beef," he remarked.

"It's okay, but it ain't that good," Charlie said. The Hawaiian side of his family would never have seen a cow till whites brought them to the islands some time in the nineteenth century. Charlie no doubt didn't worry about that one bit. He just knew what he liked. Locally born Japanese often preferred hamburgers and steaks to raw fish, too. Nowadays, a lot of them were probably pretending to a love of sushi and sashimi they didn't really have.

Because the surfers had to tack so much, they made slow progress. They needed two and a half days to round Kahuku Point near Opana, Oahu's northernmost projection. Oscar whooped when they finally did. "All downhill from here!" he said. And so it was, as far as the wind went. But getting back to the shore to sleep that night was an adventure all by itself. Big waves pounded the beaches. Oscar and Charlie took down their masts and sails before surf-riding in. Oscar would have liked to go in with the sail up, but if something went wrong it would have cost him his rigging in surf like that. He would have been stuck with no way to get back to Waikiki but lugging his surfboard down the Kamehameha Highway—a distinctly unappetizing prospect.

Charlie Kaapu did the same thing, so Oscar didn't feel too bad. Charlie was more reckless than he was.

They ate fish and clams on the beach. Charlie—reckless again—pried some sea urchins off the nearby rocks, too. He cracked them with a stone to get at the orange flesh inside. "Japs eat this stuff," he said.

Oscar never had, but he was hungry enough not to be fussy. The meat proved better than he expected. It wasn't like anything he'd tasted before; the iodine tang reminded him of the sea. "What we ought to do is see if we can get some of those plovers"—he pointed to the shorebirds walking along the beach—"and cook them."

"I wish they were doves instead," Charlie said. "Doves are too dumb for anybody to miss 'em."

The plovers weren't. They flew off before Oscar and Charlie could get close enough to throw rocks at them. "Oh, well," Oscar said. "Worth a try."

He and Charlie got to Waimea Bay the next day. Again, they took down their rigging before going ashore the first time. Oscar looked back over his shoulder as he rode toward the beach. No Jap invasion fleet this time. No Americans with machine guns in the jungle back of the beach, either.

Once up on the golden sand, they left their masts and sails there. As they went back into the Pacific, they solemnly shook hands. "Made it," Charlie said. Oscar nodded.

And then they paddled out again. The waves weren't the three-story-building monsters they were when the north shore was at its finest. They were one-and-a-half- or two-story monsters—suitable for all ordinary purposes and quite a few extraordinary ones. Skimming along at the curl of the wave, or under the curl in a roaring tube of green and white, was as much fun as you could have out of bed, and not so far removed in its growing excitement and intensity from the fun you had in bed.

"This is why we're here," Charlie said after one amazing run. Oscar didn't know whether he meant this was why they'd come to the north shore or why they'd been born. Either way, he wasn't inclined to quarrel.

Part of the excitement was knowing what happened when things went wrong. Oscar was catfooted on his surfboard—but even cats slip once in a while. Then they try to pretend they haven't done it. Oscar didn't have that chance. He went one way, the surfboard went another, and the wave rolled over him. He had time for one startled yip before he had to fight to keep from drowning.

It was like getting stuck in God's cement mixer. For a few seconds, he literally didn't know which end was up. He got slammed into the seabottom, hard enough to scrape hide off his flank. It could have been his face; he'd done that before, too. The roaring and churning dinned in his ears—dinned all through him. He struggled toward the surface. The ocean didn't want to let him up.

His lungs hadn't quite reached the bursting point when he managed to grab a breath, but they weren't far away, either. Then another mountain of water fell on him. No half-drowned pup was ever more draggled than he was when he staggered up onto blessedly dry land.

Charlie Kaapu was trotting down the beach to capture his truant surfboard. "Some wipeout, buddy," Charlie called. "You crashed and burned."

"Tell me about it," Oscar said feelingly. He looked down at himself. "Man, I'm chewed up."

"Wanna quit?" Charlie asked.

Oscar shook his head. "You nuts? This is part of what we came for, too. Thanks for snagging my board."

"Any time," Charlie said. "Not like you haven't done it for me. Not like maybe you won't very next wave." He came up and slapped Oscar on the back, being careful to pick an unabraded spot. "You're okay, ace. You're a number-one surf-rider."

"Waste time," Oscar said, trying to disguise how proud he was. "Let's go."

The Pacific stung his hide when he went out again, as if to remind him what it could do. He didn't care. He was doing what he wanted to do—Charlie was right about that. They rode the waves till they got too hungry to stand it, then went into Waimea. The little siamin place where they'd eaten on December 7 was still open. The local Jap who ran it spoke no more English than he had then. The soup had changed a bit. The noodles were rice noodles now, and the siamin was loaded with fish instead of pork. It was still hot and filling and cheap and good.

Once they'd eaten, they went back out to the ocean. They rode the surf till sundown, then went back for more siamin. Three days passed like that. Then, not without regret, Oscar said, "I better head back."

He waited for Charlie to tell him how pussy-whipped he was. But his friend just pointed west and said, "Let's sail all the way around. We can ride the surf other places, too."

"Deal," Oscar said gratefully. Not only was it a deal—it sounded like fun.

And he hadn't looked forward to beating his way back along the windward coast, anyhow.

Kaena Point, in the far west, had been the only part of Oahu where roads didn't reach, though the island's narrow-gauge railroad did round the point. As Oscar and Charlie sailboarded by, they watched POWs slowly and laboriously building a highway there. "Poor bastards," Charlie said. Oscar nodded. They were doing it all with hand tools. That had to be killing labor.

Oscar wasn't sorry to leave the prisoners behind. They reminded him how bad things really were in Hawaii these days. Being able to catch his own food, being out on the ocean so much, had shielded him from the worst of it. So had having a girlfriend at least as self-reliant as he was.

He and Charlie had made it down the coast almost as far as Waianae when they got another reminder of the war—this one, to Oscar's surprise, by sea instead of by land. A convoy of several nondescript, even ugly, *Marus* shepherded along by two destroyers chugged past them well out in the Pacific, plainly bound for Honolulu.

Those dumpy freighters might have been carrying anything: rice, ammunition, spare parts, gasoline. For all Oscar knew, they might have been crowded with soldiers. They were too far away for him to tell. He watched them for a while. So did Charlie. Neither said anything. What could you say? Those ships showed how times had changed.

And then times changed again. One of the freighters blew up—a deep, flat *crump!* that carried across the water. A great cloud of black smoke sprang up from the stricken *Maru*. Perhaps half a minute later, another ship got hit. Smoke also rose from that one, though not so much.

"Did you see that?" "Holy Jesus!" "There's a sub out there—there must be!" "*Eeeyow!*" Oscar and Charlie were both making excited noises so fast, Oscar didn't know which of them was saying what.

The Japanese destroyers went nuts. They had been sheep dogs. Now they were wolves, on the prowl for a snake in—or rather, under—the grass. They darted this way and that. One of them fired a gun—at nothing that Oscar could see.

Both torpedoed freighters settled in the water, one quickly, the other more sedately. Planes with meatballs on the wings and fuselage buzzed off Oahu and around the convoy, also searching for the American submarine. They had no better luck than the warships did.

"That freighter's still burning," Oscar said after a while.

"Oil or gas," Charlie said. "Oil, I bet—gas and it would really have gone sky-high. That's no skin off my nose. The Japs would've kept it all themselves anyway."

"Yeah," Oscar said. "Nice to see the United States hasn't given up. I mean, we know that, but it's nice to *see*."

Charlie nodded. "I want to see 'em blow King Stanley"—he laced the title with contempt—"out of one of his own guns. Serve him right."

A Zero buzzed low over the two of them. The pilot could have shot them up if he wanted to, either because he thought they had something to do with the torpedoed freighters or simply for the hell of it. But he didn't. He just kept going. Oscar breathed a sigh of relief. He and Charlie kept going, too, though much more slowly, on toward Honolulu.

PLATOON SERGEANT LESTER DILLON looked around with a distinctly jaundiced eye. "Well, here I am at this goddamn Camp Pendleton place, and I didn't make gunny to get here," he said.

Dutch Wenzel nodded gloomily. "Me, too, and I got the same beef. You know what happened, Les? We got screwed, and we didn't even get kissed."

"Damn straight we didn't," Dillon said. " 'Course, the whole Navy got screwed. Wasn't just us."

A second look around the enormous new Marine base did little to improve it in his eyes. Camp Elliott had been crowded as a sack full of cats, no doubt about it. But Camp Elliott had been right down in San Diego, not far from the ballpark, not far from the movie theaters, not far from the ginmills, not far from the whorehouses. Once you got off the base, you could have yourself a good time.

"What are we going to do for fun around here?" Les asked mournfully.

"Beats me," Dutch said. "Got a butt on you? I'm out of White Owls."

"Sure." Dillon handed him the pack, then stuck a Camel in his own mouth. Tobacco smoke soothed, but not enough. The powers that be had carved Camp Pendleton out of the northwesternmost part of San Diego County. Another name for what they'd carved it out of was the middle of nowhere. San Clemente lay a little way up the coast, Oceanside a little way down the coast. Neither could have held more than a couple of thousand people; both were towns where they rolled up the sidewalks at six o' clock. After blowing a sorrowful smoke ring, Dillon asked, "How many divisions of Marines they gonna put in here?"

"Who you think I am, FDR?" Dutch said. "They don't tell me shit like that any more'n they tell you." Having established his lack of credentials, he got down to seriously guessing: "Sure looks like it's big enough for three easy, don't it?"

Les nodded. "About what I was thinking." He tried to imagine somewhere between forty and fifty thousand horny young men with greenbacks burning a hole in their pocket descending on San Clemente and Oceanside. The picture refused to form. There was a limerick about a little green lizard that bust. That was what would happen to those quiet seaside towns. He laughed, not that the locals would think it was funny. "The Japs invaded Hawaii, and now we've invaded California."

"Heh," Wenzel said. "Well, if the guys who grow flowers and the little old ladies with the blue hair don't like us, tough beans. Let 'em go clean out those slanty-eyed bastards by themselves."

A flying boat sailed past, out over the Pacific. Les Dillon took a long look to make sure it was an *American* flying boat. The Japs had paid the West Coast a few unwelcome calls. But he recognized the silhouette. Nothing to get excited about . . . this time.

"This whole campaign is a bastard," he said, grinding out his cigarette under the heel of his boot.

"How come? Just 'cause we've gotta go a couple thousand miles before we can get hold of Hirohito's finest?" Dutch said.

"Good start," Les agreed. "But even getting there isn't enough. We've got to find some kind of way to beat down their air power. Otherwise, we're screwed again. We can't even land if we don't—or I wouldn't want to try it if they've got planes and we don't."

"Fuck, neither would I," Wenzel agreed. "That'd be a mess, wouldn't it? They'd make waddayacallit—sukiyaki—out of us."

"Yeah." Dillon watched a car roll south down Pacific Coast Highway. Idly, he wondered who had the clout to get gasoline. The highway was pretty quiet these days. He looked past it to the beach and the ocean. "How many times you figure we're gonna invade this goddamn place?"

"Till we get it right," his buddy answered, which drew a grunt and a laugh and a nod from Dillon. Wenzel added, "Thing is, when we do it for real, we only get the one chance."

That wasn't strictly true. If a U.S. landing on Oahu failed, the Americans could always lick their wounds and try again. The country could, yeah. But the Marines who got ashore in that failed effort would never try anything again afterwards. Les didn't want to think such gloomy thoughts. To keep from thinking them, he said, "Let's go over to the NCOs' club and have a beer."

"Twist my arm." Dutch Wenzel held it out. Les gave it a yank. Dutch writhed in wrestling-ring agony. "Son of a bitch—you talked me into it."

All the buildings here had the sharp-edged look of brand new construction. Most of them still had the fresh, almost foresty smell of wood newly exposed to the air, too. Not the NCOs' club, not any more. It smelled the way it was supposed to: of beer and whiskey and sweat and, mostly, of tobacco. Cigarette smoke predominated, but pipes and cigars had their places, too. The blue haze in the air was also comforting and infinitely familiar.

Noncoms sat at the bar and at tables and talked about the things that had been on noncoms' minds since the days of Julius Caesar, if not since those of Sennacherib: how their families were doing, where they were going next and how tough it was likely to be, what idiots the brass were (those last two not entirely unrelated), and how new recruits were obviously the missing link between apes and men that Darwin had sought in vain.

A gunny whose fruit salad went all the way back to the blue, yellow, and green ribbon commemorating the Mexican campaign and the occupation of Veracruz was expatiating on the latter topic. "Sweet Jesus Christ, boots nowadays don't know enough to grab their ass with both hands," he said, gesturing with a highball glass in which ice cubes clinked. "I swear to God, the *Army* wouldn't want some of these pissweeds. And we're supposed to turn 'em into *Marines*?"

He didn't bother keeping his voice low. Heads bobbed up and down all over the club, Les' among them. Nobody except another gunnery sergeant of equally exalted status could have presumed to disagree with him. Dillon, who came close both in rank and in years, wouldn't have thought of it for a moment. As far as he was concerned, the gunny was only speaking gospel truth.

But another veteran noncom said, "Gonna need to put a lot of Marines on the beach if we're gonna do the job. Up to us to make these damnfool boots into the kind of Marines they need to be."

"Some of them won't make the grade, though," said the gunny who'd been around since dirt. "Some of them *can't* make the grade."

"We'll run them off. There won't be *that* many," the other man said. "The rest'll do the job. Even as is, we're gonna have the damn Army landing right behind us, or maybe even with us."

Everyone bristled at that, though it was too likely to be true. From what Les had heard, the Japs had four or five divisions in Hawaii. Defenders needed fewer men than invaders. He'd seen that for himself when he bumped up against the krauts in the Great War. There just wouldn't be enough Marines to go around.

"So much for Germany first," he said.

"Yeah, well, I don't care what FDR says—I think the Japs screwed that one the first time they bombed San Francisco."

Les was inclined to agree with him. By the nods and the grim silence that followed, so was everybody else in the NCOs' club. No matter what the President might want, it was personal now between the USA and Japan. Hitting Hawaii was one thing, and bad enough. But killing people on the mainland— no overseas enemy had done that since the War of 1812. Everybody was hot and bothered about it. Not even a President as powerful as Franklin Delano Roosevelt could afford to ignore 130,000,000 Americans screaming their heads off.

"If those Navy pukes can just get us to Hawaii this time, we'll do the rest of the job," Les said. "Put us on the beach, and we'll take it from there."

Nobody argued with him, either.

SAILBOARD UNDER HIS ARM, Oscar van der Kirk let himself back into his own apartment. He didn't yell, "Honey, I'm home!" It was half past three in the afternoon; Susie would be at her secretarial job. The only question was whether she still lived here.

Oscar looked in the closet. Her clothes still hung there. He nodded to himself—that was good. But then he realized it wasn't the only question after all. When she came back, would she bring anybody with her? She wouldn't know he was here. That could prove . . . interesting.

"Hell with it," Oscar said. If he'd been the sort to borrow trouble, he wouldn't have spent most of his time since graduating from college as a beach bum. Whatever happened would happen, and he'd figure out what to do about it when it did, if it did.

Instead of borrowing trouble, he hopped in the shower. He had more salt on him than an order of cheap french fries. He couldn't recall the last time he'd had an order of fries, cheap or not. They were growing potatoes—he knew that. Salt was not a problem—one of the few things that weren't. But he didn't want to think about what they might use for grease these days.

The water was cold. He didn't care. He'd got used to that. It just meant he didn't dawdle, the way he would have back when things were easy. He hopped in, sluiced himself off, and got out.

Putting on clothes he hadn't worn too often lately felt good, too. He sat back on the edge of the bed to wait for Susie.

He didn't remember going from sitting to lying. He didn't hear her key in the lock. Next thing he knew, she was shaking him. "Hey," she said. "Look what the cat dragged in. So you made it back, did you?"

"Yeah." He yawned, then gave her a kiss. Her lips were red, and tasted of lipstick. Somehow, she kept getting her hands on the stuff.

"Did you and Charlie have a good time?" She sounded amused. She might have been a mother talking to an eight-year-old boy.

Oscar nodded anyway. After another yawn—he hadn't realized how tired he was—he said, "Yeah," again. This time, he added, "The best part was off the west coast, on the way back. We got to watch an American sub blow two Jap freighters to hell and gone."

Susie's eyes lit up. "That *is* good," she said. "It didn't make the papers here—why am I not surprised?" She wrinkled her nose and looked like a kid—a happy kid. "Hasn't even made the rumor mill yet," she went on, "and that's a little more surprising."

"How have you been?" Oscar asked. "It's damn good to see you again."

"I'm okay," she answered. "I missed you." She wrinkled her nose again, in a subtly different way this time, as if annoyed at herself. "I missed you more than I thought I would—and what kind of jerk am I for telling you something like that?"

"I missed you, too," Oscar admitted. "Must be love." He said the word lightly; he didn't want to leave himself open for one of the snippy comebacks she was so good at. Lightly or not, it was the first time either one of them had said that word.

Susie looked. "Yeah," she said softly. "Must be." She leaned toward him. This time, the kiss went on and on.

Some time a good deal later, Oscar remarked, "This is how we said good-bye, and now it's how we say hello. Good thing it doesn't get boring."

Susie poked him in the ribs. "It better not, Buster." And, not too long after that, he showed her it hadn't.

EVEN THOUGH HAWAII WAS NOMINALLY an independent kingdom once more, General Tomoyuki Yamashita hadn't given up his office in Iolani Palace. If King Stanley Laanui didn't care for that—well, too bad. That was Yamashita's attitude, anyhow.

The commanding general could not only outface the King of Hawaii, he could also summon a mere Navy commander like Minoru Genda whenever he pleased. Both the Hawaiian palace guards and their Japanese opposite numbers came to attention and saluted as Genda went up the front stairs and into the palace. He outranked them, anyhow.

General Yamashita was working in the Gold Room in the second floor. Not even he had had the crust to keep for himself either the library or the royal bedchambers once King Stanley and Queen Cynthia got settled into the palace. The Gold Room, which looked over the front entrance, had been the palace music room. Whatever instruments had been in there were long gone, replaced by utilitarian office furniture that seemed dreadfully out of place in such a splendid setting.

Yamashita's scowl seemed out of place in that sunny room, too. As soon as Genda came in, the general growled, "Those stinking Yankee submarines are starting to pinch us. This time they cost us oil *and* rice. And what is the Navy doing about them? Not a stinking thing, not that I can see."

"We are doing everything we can, sir," Genda replied. "We are doing everything we know how to do. If hunting submarines were easy, they wouldn't be such dangerous weapons."

That only made Yamashita more unhappy still. "How are we supposed to defend those islands if we can't supply them?" he exclaimed.

"Sir, the Americans aren't doing exactly what we expected them to." Genda didn't sound happy, either. "We looked for them to go after our principal warships. Instead, as you say, they're trying to hurt us economically, the way the Germans are trying to strangle England."

Yamashita had dark, heavy eyebrows that gave him a fearsome frown. "All right, that's what they're trying. How in blazes do you stop them?"

"I have some good news, sir," replied Genda, who'd saved it as a miser saved gold.

"Oh? What's that?" General Yamashita sounded deeply skeptical.

"One of our H8Ks on patrol northeast of the islands spotted a U.S. submarine cruising on the surface. The seaplane attacked with bombs and cannon and sank it. No possible doubt, the pilot reports."

Yamashita grunted. "All right, there's one," he admitted. "Even one is good news—I won't try to tell you any different. But how many submarines have the Americans got in these waters? How many more are they building? And how many have we sunk?"

Minoru Genda needed a distinct effort of will to hold his face steady. Those were all very good questions. He didn't have precise answers for any of them. He knew what the approximate answers were, though: *too many, too many,* and *not enough,* respectively. "We are doing everything we can, sir," he repeated. "Before long, we'll have some of that fancy electronic rangefinding gear in the H8Ks. That should help our searches."

"While the enemy is on the surface, maybe," Yamashita said. "What about when he's submerged? How will you find him then? That's when he does his damage, *neh*?"

"*Hai,*" Genda said. "But subs are slow while submerged, and have only limited range on their batteries. They do most of their traveling surfaced."

"If the Americans come back here, how do we beat them back with no fuel for tanks or airplanes?" Yamashita demanded. "By the Emperor, how do we beat them back with no fuel for *ships*? Answer me that."

"Sir, we are making our best effort." Genda said the only thing he could. "If we had not made our best effort here, we would be fighting the war now in the western Pacific, not between Hawaii and the American mainland."

All that got him was another grunt from the general. "I suppose the Army had nothing to do with the conquest of Hawaii," Yamashita said with heavy sarcasm.

The way Genda remembered things, the Army hadn't wanted much to do with Hawaii. The Army was worried about Russia, and about keeping as many men as it could in the endless China adventure. Admiral Yamamoto had had to threaten to resign before the stubborn generals would change their minds. The benefits of their change of mind were obvious—now. And now, of course, they found new things to complain about.

Genda knew only too well that he couldn't explain that to General Yamashita. The other man not only outranked him but belonged to the service he would be maligning. What he did say once more was, "Sir we are doing everything we can do, everything we know how to do. If you can suggest other things we should be doing, we will be grateful to you."

That made Yamashita no happier. "*Zakennayo!*" he burst out. "You're supposed to know what to do about submarines. If you ask me about tanks or artillery, I can give you a sensible answer. All I want to know is, why are you having a harder time now than you were against the American aircraft carriers?"

"Aircraft carriers are easier to find than submarines, sir," Genda answered. "And once we find them, we sink them. We're better than the Americans are."

"Aren't we better with submarines, too?" Yamashita asked pointedly.

"With them? Probably," Genda replied, though he wasn't altogether sure of that. "At detecting them? At hunting them? Please excuse me, sir, but there the answer is less clear. The Americans have had more combat experience in those areas than we have, both in the last war and in this one."

"Faugh!" Yamashita said—more a disgusted noise than a word. "We're getting the experience, all right—getting it the hard way. All I have to tell you, Commander, is that we'd better put it to good use."

"Yes, sir." Recognizing dismissal when he heard it, Genda got to his feet and saluted. Yamashita sent him out of the Gold Room with an impatient wave.

With more than a little relief, Genda left. Yamashita hadn't really called him in to confer; he'd called him in to rake him over the coals. And, from the Army commandant's point of view, he had every right to do so. The Navy was supposed to protect the supply line between Hawaii and the rest of the Empire of Japan. If it didn't, if it couldn't . . . *Then we have a problem, a serious problem, here,* Genda thought unhappily.

He was heading for the koa-wood stairs to make his escape when someone said, "Commander Genda, isn't it?"—in English.

He stopped and bowed. "Yes, your Majesty," he answered in the same language.

"Why are you here today?" Queen Cynthia Laanui asked.

"Military matters, your Majesty," Genda said, which was true but uninformative.

The redheaded Queen knew as much, too. She gave him an exasperated sniff. "Thank you so much," she said, her sarcasm more flaying than Yamashita's because it came from a prettier face in a softer voice. "Let me put it another way, Commander—what's gone wrong this time? You never come to the palace when things are going well, do you?"

"I should not discuss this," Genda said.

"Why not?" Now the Queen's eyes flashed dangerously. "Why shouldn't I know what's going on? Isn't Hawaii allied to Japan? If anybody ought to be kept informed, don't you think my husband and I should?"

"You—" Genda stopped. He couldn't just come out and say, *You're an American.* She was, of course: a fine, healthy specimen of an American, too. But if she was playing the role of Queen of Hawaii to the hilt . . .

"I *am* the Queen. I could order you sent to the dungeons." That dangerous flash again. Then, half a second later, Cynthia Laanui's eyes flashed again, in an altogether different way. It happened so fast, Genda wasn't sure the two flashes weren't really one—wasn't *sure,* in fact, that he hadn't imagined both of them. Except he hadn't. She repeated, "I could order you sent to the dungeons. . . ." Her nose wrinkled, and her laugh rang sweet as frangipani. "I could—except we haven't got any dungeons, and nobody would follow the order if I was dumb enough to give it. Details, details." She laughed again, on a slightly wrier note.

Genda laughed, too, and surprised himself when he did it. He bowed. "Your Majesty," he said, and meant it more than he ever had before with either of the Hawaiian puppet monarchs. He surprised himself again by telling her about the freighters that had gone down in the channel between Kauai and Oahu.

"Oh, *that,*" Queen Cynthia said, and he could not doubt she already knew about it. As if to confirm as much, she went on, "That story's all over Honolulu—probably all over Oahu—by now. You couldn't keep it a secret if you tried, not when people on the island could see the smoke." She leaned forward a little, not to be provocative—she was provocative enough just standing there—but as a friend would in conversation with another friend. "Or is the secret part that it bothers you more than you want to let on?"

"*Hai,*" Genda said before he realized he should have answered, *That's none of your business.* Then—realization piled on realization—he saw that wouldn't have helped, either. Only an immediate, convincing denial would have done him any good, and he couldn't give her one.

"Is it so very bad?" she asked quietly.

He shook his head. He wanted to shake himself, like a dog shaking off cold water. "No, not so very bad," he answered, and searched for words—not because his English was bad, but because he wanted to be most precise. "Things are not quite so good as we would like, your Majesty. This is *honto*—it is true. But we fight a war. Things in a war go exactly how we want almost never. Do you see?"

"Oh, yes. I'm not a child, Commander."

Genda bowed once more, not trusting himself to speak. Cynthia Laanui might be a great many things, but a child she definitely was not. The flowered sun dress she wore left no possible doubt of that.

Just as he straightened, her nose wrinkled in amusement again. Only after that did her face politely go almost expressionless. *She knows what I'm thinking.* That alarmed Genda, who did not want his Japanese colleagues—let alone a *gaijin* woman—able to read him like that.

He occasionally visited officers' brothels on and near Hotel Street. Like most of his countrymen, he was much more matter-of-fact about that than Americans were. What else was he supposed to do, here so far from home? But lying down with a whore was one thing. Lying down with a woman who might be interested in you for your own sake—that was something else again.

And what would lying down with a Queen be like?

Foolishness. Moonshine, he thought. Queen Cynthia Laanui hadn't been much more than polite. If she was a friendly person, that didn't mean she wanted to do anything but make conversation with him . . . did it?

She said, "Thanks for leveling with me." She paused for a moment to make sure he understood, then went on, "Do please let me know what's going on from here on out. Things will work out better for everybody if you do."

"Do you think so?" Genda couldn't have sounded more glum, more dubious, if he'd tried for a week.

Queen Cynthia laughed once more, which only made his question seem gloomier than it had. "I'm not Mata Hari, Commander," she said. "I'm not going to seduce your secrets out of you." She cocked her head to one side. "Or should I?"

How am I supposed to answer that? Genda wondered frantically. He bowed again. That was safe, it was polite (almost reflexively so for him), and it bought him time to think. Having bought it, he knew he had better use it wisely. "Whatever your Majesty wishes, of course," he murmured.

This time, Cynthia Laanui threw back her head and chortled. "Well, Commander, that proves one thing for sure," she said, and her voice suddenly held no mirth at all. "You've never been a queen, or a king, either."

"No, your Majesty, I never have," he said, and fled Iolani Palace faster than the American fleet had fled before the triumphant Japanese earlier in the year.

KENZO AND HIROSHI TAKAHASHI took the *Oshima Maru* out of Kewalo Basin by themselves. Their father had another radio talk scheduled. His words would go back to Japan and all over the world. Kenzo wished more than anything else in the world that he would just keep quiet.

Whatever Kenzo wished, he wasn't going to get it. "Dad *likes* being a celebrity," he said bitterly. He was at the rudder, Hiroshi trimming the sails. They would trade off later. By now, dealing with the sampan's rigging and the way she went under sail was second nature to both of them, though neither had known anything about handling a sailboat before Oahu ran out of diesel fuel even for fishermen. *Baptism by total immersion,* Kenzo thought: not an idea that would have occurred to him had his father stayed in Yamaguchi Prefecture instead of coming to Hawaii.

His brother only shrugged. "Dad's made his choices. We've made ours. Right this minute, I have to say his look better."

Another measure of the choices he and Kenzo had made was that they both used English. Some men even of their father's generation had become fluent in it, but Jiro Takahashi remained at home only in Japanese. In English, he understood *yes* and *no* and *thank you* and most obscenities. Except for throwing in an occasional *Oh, Jesus Christ!* and the like, he didn't speak any, though.

"We're getting away," Kenzo said. "Only thing is, I wish to God we didn't have to come back again."

Hiroshi chuckled. "Can't very well sail to San Francisco from here."

"I know." Kenzo sounded as mournful as he felt. "I've thought about it. We might be able to catch enough fish to keep us going—we probably could. But she wouldn't carry enough water to get us there."

Now Hiroshi stared at him. "You *have* thought about it."

"I said so, didn't I?" Kenzo looked back over his shoulder. The faster Oahu receded behind him, the better he liked it. "I even went to the library to dope out which way the winds blow between here and there. But I'll tell you what really put the kibosh on things for me."

"Yeah?" his brother said.

"Yeah." Kenzo nodded. "You know what they're doing with the Japanese on the mainland, right? They're throwing 'em into camps." How Imperial Japanese propaganda here in Hawaii thundered about that! At first, Kenzo had thought it was a lie. By now, he was only too sure it was true. "The U.S. Navy would probably sink us the minute they spotted us—we're Japs, right? The Japanese don't want Japs who think they're Americans, and neither do the Americans."

A fairy tern, white as snow with big black eyes, glided along with the *Oshima Maru*. After a while, the bird perched at the top of the mast. "Damn hitchhiker," Hiroshi said.

"Yeah." Kenzo left it there. Hiroshi hadn't tried to tell him he was crazy or to say the Navy would treat them fine if it found them sailing northeast. Kenzo wished his brother would have. In that case, he might have been wrong. The way things were, he knew damn well he was right.

Land slowly slid under the horizon. When you traveled under sail, nothing happened in a hurry. But for the slap of waves against the hull and the sound of the wind in the sails and the lines, the *Oshima Maru* was ghost-quiet. It was as if time itself had been yanked back to some earlier, more patient century—and which one mattered very little. Men had been sailing like this for three thousand years, probably longer.

The tern flew away. A frigatebird—by comparison, almost as big as a light plane—soared by overhead. Its red throat sac was small now, not full of air and big as a kid's balloon: the bird was looking for lunch instead of a mate. Frigatebirds were pirates. If they had their druthers, they let other birds do the hard work of diving into the sea, then robbed them of their catch.

Hiroshi's head followed the frigatebird across the sky. "Thought for a second it was an airplane," he said sheepishly.

"Uh-huh." Kenzo had made that same mistake himself a time or two. He almost let it go there. But he asked what he wanted to ask: "Whose?"

"If it was a plane, I figured it would be Japanese and hoped it wouldn't," his brother replied. "You?"

"Same thing. Not this time, though, 'cause I knew from the start it was just a bird."

Talk of planes brought Kenzo back into the middle of the twentieth century, but not for long. There were no planes overhead, so he forgot about them. All he saw now, but for the sea and the occasional bird, were a few masts from other sampans with rigs as new as the *Oshima Maru's*—and as old as time.

On he went, farther from Oahu than he would have needed to go before the war turned everything upside down. Back then, fish had been part of what Oahu ate. Now they were a vital part of what the island ate, and the sampans skimmed every fish they could from the Pacific. Even the ocean couldn't keep up with that kind of fishing forever.

What happens when we have to go so far out to sea that travel time really cuts into how much we can bring back? Kenzo wondered, not for the first time. As usual, only one answer occurred to him. *We get even hungrier, that's what.*

As his father had taught him—something he preferred not to remember— he looked for lots of boobies and other birds diving into the sea. That would tell him where the fish were likely to be. If that frigatebird was still anywhere in the neighborhood, no doubt it was doing the same damn thing.

Hiroshi suddenly pointed to starboard. "What's that?"

"Huh?" Kenzo's head had been in the clouds—except there were no clouds. He looked to the right himself. *Something* floated on the Pacific there. Gauging distance wasn't easy—nor was telling how big that thing was. "Just looks like a piece of junk to me," he said doubtfully.

"I don't think so." Hiroshi shaded his eyes with the palm of his hand. "Steer over that way, will you?"

"Okay." Kenzo did. The breeze, which had been remarkably strong and steady ever since they set out, didn't fail now. He'd half expected it would, just from the innate perversity of the world. Hiroshi swung the boom to catch it to best advantage.

The approach didn't happen in a hurry anyway. It was close to ten minutes later before Hiroshi said, "See?"

"Yeah," Kenzo answered.

"That's a life raft, or I'm a *haole*," his brother said.

"Yeah," Kenzo repeated. He waited till they'd sailed a little closer, then cupped his hands in front of his mouth and yelled, "Ahoy, the raft! Anybody there?" God only knew how long it had floated, or where it had started out. It might hold a sun-shrunken corpse—or no one at all.

He felt like cheering when a head popped up into sight. It was, he saw, a blond head. *An American head,* he thought, excitement tingling through him. "Who're you?" the fellow croaked.

"Fishermen out of Honolulu," Kenzo answered. "We'll do whatever we can for you." He waited to see if Hiroshi would say anything different. Hiroshi said not a thing.

The American flier—he couldn't be anything else—said, "Thank God." He had several days' growth of beard; the stubble glinted red-gold in the sunshine. As the *Oshima Maru* skimmed closer, Kenzo saw his eyes get wider and more avid. And then they widened again, in a different way. The man ducked back down into the raft. This time, he came up holding a .45. "You're Japs!" he yelled.

"You stupid fucking asshole!" Kenzo screamed back. His brother stared at him in horror. At the time, he wondered why. Later, he realized cussing out a guy with a gun wasn't exactly Phi Beta Kappa. But, furious still, he went on, "We're Americans, God damn you, or we will be if you fucking let us!"

By then, they were within easy range even of a pistol. The man in the raft lowered the gun. "I think maybe you mean it," he called across the narrowing stretch of water. "You couldn't sound that pissed off if you didn't."

"Right," Kenzo said tightly. If he'd had a pistol, he wasn't sure he could have kept himself from shooting the flier—he was *that* angry.

He and Hiroshi helped the man into the sampan. The flier was more battered than he'd seemed from a distance. His coveralls were tattered and torn and bloody. He gulped water as if he'd thought he would never see it again. Maybe he had. When he spoke again, his voice had changed timbre. "Jesus!" he said, and then, "Thanks, guys. If there's anything Burt Burleson can do for you, you got it." He paused. "Who are you, anyway?"

"I'm Ken," Kenzo answered. "This is my brother, Hank." He thought their Japanese names were best buried at the moment. "What happened to you?"

Burleson also shrugged. "About what you'd figure. Recon in a PBY. We got bounced and shot up four, five days ago. Managed to break away into some clouds, but we were on fire pretty good by then. Pilot tried to put her in the water. It wasn't pretty. I was tail gunner. I think I was the only guy who got out."

His face closed in on itself. "Till the two of you saw me, I wasn't sure I had the clean end of the stick, either."

"We'll do what we can for you," Kenzo said again. "Get you ashore some kind of way without anybody seeing."

"Have any food?" Burleson asked. "I managed to catch a mackerel with the line they gave me, but raw fish ain't my idea of fun."

Kenzo and Hiroshi both broke up then. Kenzo didn't know about his brother, but he felt on the ragged edge of hysteria. The flier stared from one of them to the other, wondering if they'd gone off their rockers. Maybe they had, at least a little. Carefully, Kenzo said, "Next to what you'll get on Oahu, raw fish is pretty good."

"We *are* Japanese," Hiroshi added. "We grew up eating the stuff. We don't mind it so much. And it's a hell of a lot better than going hungry."

Burleson contemplated that. He didn't need much contemplation before he nodded. "Yeah. No argument. Took me a while before I caught *anything*."

"We're gonna finish our run, too," Kenzo said. "We can't go back to Kewalo Basin without a catch. People will wonder why if we do."

"I was hoping you would think of that," Hiroshi said. Neither of them had used a word of Japanese since Burleson came aboard. They hadn't been speaking Japanese before, either, but now things had changed. It was a language they could share if they had to. It was also dangerous, because the flier still had the .45 on his hip.

He seemed tractable enough now. "Do what you need to do, sure," he said. "I'll help, best I can. I know how to gut fish. Everybody goes fishing in Minnesota."

"Minnesota." All Kenzo knew about the place was that it bumped up against Canada and it was cold as hell in the wintertime. "You're a long way from home."

"You better believe it," Burleson said. "I was thinking that when I was in the raft there. Well, I got another chance now. Thanks, guys."

He couldn't have put it any better than that. And, even though he was a long way from at his best, he did help with the gutting when the Takahashi brothers brought in their catch. Kenzo offered him a strip of prime *ahi* flesh. "Here— try this. It's a lot better than mackerel."

Burleson tasted warily, then ate with real enthusiasm. "Damned if you're not right, Ken. It's not so—fishy-like. But it's still fish. That's pretty funny, eh?"

"Steak and lamb chops don't taste the same," Kenzo said, and then wished he hadn't. He couldn't remember the last time he'd had either. But Burleson nodded, so he supposed he'd made his point.

After a while, the American flier said, "You're not throwing anything back, are you?"

"Not these days," Hiroshi answered. "We used to, sure, but now it gets eaten as long as it's not poisonous. Like we said before, nobody's fussy."

"If there were any fussy people, they starved a long time ago," Kenzo added.

"What are you going to do about me?" Burleson asked.

"Drop you on a beach somewhere and say good luck," Kenzo told him. "What else *can* we do? We'll take you to Kewalo Basin if you want to surrender to the Japanese. They'll have soldiers there to take charge of the catch."

Burt Burleson shuddered. "No, thanks. I've heard about how they treat prisoners. You guys know anything about that?"

"We've seen labor gangs. The POWs in 'em are pretty skinny. I don't think they get fed much," Kenzo said. "The soldiers who run 'em can act pretty mean, too." All that was true. If he told Burleson how big an understatement it was, the flier might not believe him.

What he did say seemed plenty. "Okay, I'll take my chances on the beach," Burleson said, and then, "Um—can you pick one close to a place with lots of white people so I blend in better?"

So they won't turn me in, he meant. But Kenzo and Hiroshi both nodded. It was a legitimate point. Hiroshi said, "Don't trust a *haole* too far just because he's a *haole.* There are more Japanese collaborators, yeah, but there are white ones and Chinese and Filipinos, too."

"Terrific," Burleson said bleakly. "Sounds like we're gonna need to clean up this joint—clean out this joint—once we get it back."

"Yeah, maybe," Kenzo said, and tried not to think about his father.

For somebody who'd sneered at raw fish, Burt Burleson put away a hell of a lot of it. Kenzo didn't begrudge him. Floating on the Pacific wondering whether you'd live or die and sure your buddies were already dead couldn't have been much fun.

Kenzo waited till sundown to start the *Oshima Maru* back towards Oahu. He wanted to get there in the wee small hours, when people were least likely to see Burleson splashing ashore. He steered by the stars. He and Hiroshi had both got pretty good at that.

Burleson stayed awake, which surprised Kenzo a little. When he asked about it, the flier laughed and said, "I slept as much as I could in that goddamn raft—what else did I have to do? I can stay awake for this. Besides"—another laugh—"now I can see where I'm going, not where I've been like in the PBY."

The moon crawled across the sky. Oahu came up over the northwestern horizon, pretty much where Kenzo had expected it to be. He steered for Ewa. There were Japanese everywhere on Oahu, of course. With the population a third Japanese, there wouldn't be many places without them. He wondered if Burleson realized that. But he would do what he could for the flier.

He almost ran the *Oshima Maru* aground doing it. That wouldn't have been so good, which was putting it mildly. But Burt Burleson went over the side with a muttered, "God bless you guys." He struck out for the beach, which wasn't very far. Kenzo steered away from the coast to give himself some sea room.

Dawn was staining the sky with salmon-belly pink when the sampan came into Kewalo Basin. Nobody got excited about that; sampans went in and came out all the time. As usual, Japanese soldiers took charge of the catch. They paid Kenzo and Hiroshi by weight, and winked at the fish the brothers carried off "for personal use." The noncoms in charge of the details got fish from the Takahashis and other fishermen to make sure they didn't fuss about things like that. One hand washed the other.

"Everything good out at sea? Spot anything unusual?" this sergeant asked.

"What could we spot? It's just lots of water." Kenzo sounded as casual as he could.

"*Hai.* Lots of water." The sergeant drew the kanji for *ocean* in the air. It combined the characters for *water* and *mother.* "You understand?"

"Oh, yes," Kenzo said. "A mother of a lot of water." The sergeant laughed at that. Kenzo added, "But nothing else." The Japanese soldier asked no more questions.

V

IF YOU PAID ENOUGH OR HAD CLOUT, YOU COULD STILL EAT WELL IN HONOLULU. If you had enough clout, you didn't have to pay through the nose. Commander Mitsuo Fuchida fell into that category. When he had Commander Genda along with him, the proprietor of the Mochizuki Tea House bowed himself almost double and escorted them to a private room.

"Thank you for coming here, gentlemen. You honor my humble establishment, which does not deserve the presence of such brave officers." He laid the ceremonial on with a trowel, bowing again and again. Fuchida had to work to keep a smile off his face. No matter how formal the man acted, his accent was that of an ignorant peasant from the south. The impulse to smile faded after a moment. Starting as a peasant, the fellow would have had trouble rising this high had he stayed in Japan.

Kimonoed waitresses fluttered over Fuchida and Genda as the two of them sat cross-legged at the low, Japanese-style table. "Sake?" one of the girls asked. "Yes, please," Fuchida said. She hurried away. He eyed the menu. "We can get anything we want—as long as we want fish."

Genda shrugged. "I've heard this place used to have fine sukiyaki. But beef . . ." He shrugged again. "Karma, *neh?*"

"*Shigata ga nai,*" Fuchida answered, which was self-evidently true: it *couldn't* be helped. "The sushi and the sashimi here are good—and look. They've got lobster tempura. If we're going to be honored guests, we ought to make the most of it."

"What's that saying the Americans use? 'Eat, drink, and be merry, because tomorrow—' " Genda didn't finish it, but Fuchida nodded. He knew what his friend was talking about.

Back came the girl with the sake. That was brewed from rice, and there was, finally, just about enough rice to go around in Oahu—and on the other islands of Hawaii, though they mattered much less to the Japanese. Fuchida and Genda both slurped noisily from their cups. The stuff wasn't bad, though it wasn't up to the best back in the home islands.

After the food came, the waitresses knew enough to withdraw and let the Japanese officers talk in peace. Fuchida spoke without preamble: "We're going to have to fight the Americans again."

"Yes, it seems so." Genda dipped a piece of tuna into shoyu heated with wasabi. He sounded as calm as if they were talking about the weather.

"Can we?" Fuchida was still blunt.

"I don't expect them to come after us right away—they're busy in North Africa for the time being," Genda answered. Fuchida nodded and sipped at his sake again. The USA had shipped an enormous army around the Cape of Good Hope and up to Egypt. Along with Montgomery's British force, they'd smashed Rommel at El Alamein and were driving him west across the desert.

Fuchida ate some sushi. He smiled. Barbecued eel had always been one of his favorites. But, again, the smile would not stay. "Did you notice one thing about that attack, Genda-*san*?"

"I've noticed several things about it—none of them good for us," Genda replied. "Which do you have in mind?"

"That it didn't use any American carriers," Fuchida answered. "What the Yankees have left, they're saving—for us."

"I'm not worried about what they're saving," Genda said. "I'm worried about what they're building. Admiral Yamamoto was right about that." He invoked Yamamoto's name as a bishop might invoke the Pope—and with just as much reverence.

"We've given them lumps twice now. We can do it again—if they don't cut us off from supplies," Fuchida said.

"You sound like you've been listening to General Yamashita," Genda said sourly. "I got an earful of that at Iolani Palace not long ago."

"I have no more use for the Army than you do. Those people are crazy,"

Fuchida said with a distinct shudder. "But even crazy people can be right some of the time."

"What worries me is, we can beat the Americans two or three more times, beat them as badly as we did in the last big fight, and what will it do for us? Buy us more time till the next battle, that's all," Genda said. "They'll just go back to building, and we can't do much to stop them. But if they beat us even once . . . If that happens, we're in trouble." He drained his little sake cup and poured it full again.

"They have a margin for error, and we don't—that's what you're saying," Fuchida said.

Genda nodded vigorously. "*Hai!* That's exactly what I'm saying, except you said it better than I did."

"We'd better not make any errors, then," Fuchida said. "We haven't yet."

"Not big ones, anyhow," Genda agreed. "And the Americans have made plenty. But we're already doing about as well as we can. The Americans aren't, not yet. They're still learning, and they're getting better."

Fuchida went bottoms-up with his sake cup. "We're in Hawaii, and they aren't. That's how it's supposed to work, and that's how it's going to keep on working." He hoped he sounded determined and not just drunk; he'd poured down quite a bit. He wondered if he would have a headache in the morning. He wouldn't be surprised if he did. Well, there were still plenty of aspirins.

Genda said, "There's a legend from the West, where every time the hero cuts off a dragon's head, two more heads grow back. That's what worries me in this fight."

The image fit the war against America much too well—so well, in fact, that Mitsuo Fuchida got drunk enough to have no doubts whatsoever he'd regret it in the morning.

AFTER PENSACOLA NAVAL AIR STATION, the Naval Training Station outside Buffalo jolted Joe Crosetti in lots of ways. First and foremost was the weather. The chilly wind of Lake Erie was like nothing he'd ever known. It was only autumn, too; winter would be worse.

Orson Sharp, who'd switched stations and squadrons along with him, took it in stride. "Can't be too much nastier than what I'm used to," he said.

It was already a lot nastier than San Francisco ever got. Joe had hardly ever worn a topcoat; a windbreaker was usually all you needed where he grew up. He was glad of his topcoat here. He had long johns, too, and expected to wear them.

Flying out over the lake felt strange. He was used to large expanses of water. The Pacific and then the Gulf of Mexico were both magnificent, each in its own way. But the idea of being up over water as far as the eye could see and knowing it was *fresh* water . . . for a Californian, that seemed as alien as Mars.

Then there was the USS *Wolverine.* She'd started life as a coal-burning side-wheeling excursion steamer, but she'd been decked over to give aspiring carrier pilots somewhere to do endless takeoffs and landings without impeding the war effort by tying up a ship that could actually go into combat. She wasn't pretty, but she got the job done.

The same held true for the Grumman F3Fs the cadets were flying. Zeros would have slaughtered them, but they were a lot hotter than Texans. And, to Joe's amazement, Lake Erie could grow some perfectly respectable waves. That meant the *Wolverine* pitched and rolled, just the way a real carrier would out in the Pacific. It also meant the apprentice pilots had to obey the landing officer as if he were God.

One of the instructors had said, "Following the landing officer's directions is the most important thing you can do—*the* most important. Have you got that? You'd better have it, gentlemen. If you don't, you'll kill yourselves and you'll cost the country thirty-one grand for a Wildcat—twice that and then some for one of the new Hellcats, if you happen to draw them—and that's not even adding in the five cents *you're* worth. When you fly up to the stern of your carrier, you are a machine. He is the man in charge of the machine. You are under his control. He can see your approach much better than you can. He can correct it much better than you can. If you trust your own judgment instead of his, you'll be sorry—but not for long."

Some guys knew better. Some guys always knew better. You didn't get to be a pilot training for carrier operations if you didn't think pretty well of your own judgment. So far, this squadron had had one guy crash on the *Wolverine*'s wooden flight deck, one guy slam head-on into the training carrier's stern, and one guy fly his F3F into Lake Erie because they did what they wanted to do and not what the landing officer told them to do. Two of them were dead. The fellow they'd fished out of the drink was still training with the rest of the cadets.

He wouldn't make that mistake again. Whether he'd make some different mistake . . . Well, at least he had the chance to find out.

Joe lined his biplane fighter up on the carrier's stern. They'd even built a little island on the port side, to give her smoke-belching stacks somewhere to go and to make her seem more like the warships she was impersonating. And—also portside—they'd built the little platform at the stern from which the landing officer directed traffic.

Another F3F was in front of Joe. The obsolescent fighter touched down on the flight deck, tires smoking for a moment, then taxied along to the far end and roared up into the sky again. Getting everybody as many repetitions as possible was the point of the exercise.

Seeing that spurt of smoke made Joe check his own landing gear again. Yes, he'd lowered it. The landing officer would have waved him off if he'd tried anything dumb like landing with it up. He knew that. Even so . . . "It's my neck," he muttered.

There were the wigwag flags—for him this time. The landing officer dipped the flags to the left. Joe straightened out the F3F. The landing officer straightened, too, and held out both flags level with his shoulders. Joe was going the way the other man wanted him to.

I am a machine, the naval air cadet told himself. *The landing officer runs me. I do what he says.* It wasn't easy. He wanted to fly the way he wanted to fly. He'd spent all this time learning to do that. Now he had to suppress a lot of the trained reflexes he'd acquired in the past months.

The wigwag flags moved in tiny circles in the landing officer's hands: speed up. Joe obediently gave the Grumman biplane a little more throttle. Those circles stopped. The landing officer urged him up a little. The F3F's stick went back; its nose rose.

Then, suddenly, the flags dropped. Joe dove for the *Wolverine*'s deck. Any carrier landing was a controlled crash. The trick was making *controlled* the key word, not *crash.* The F3F's tires hit the timbers of the flight deck. On a real carrier, a working carrier, the plane's tailhook would have snagged a wire and brought it to a halt.

Here, Joe bounced down the deck and then off again. He gunned the engine and rose into the sky yet once more. Officers on the training carrier would be grading his performance. He thought he'd done pretty well that time. They didn't always agree with him.

After three more landings and takeoffs, he got orders to return to the land base. Regretfully, he obeyed. He thought—he hoped—he improved every time. He wanted as much practice as he could get—this was as close as he could come to the real McCoy.

Finding his way across the gray waters of Lake Erie also proved . . . interesting. The *Wolverine* steamed well out of sight of land. He needed to use some of what he'd learned in navigation before he found New York again. He hoped it was New York, anyway. If he'd fouled up, it might be Pennsylvania or Ontario. Ending up not just in the wrong state but the wrong country would have damaged his career. It probably would have meant he didn't have one.

But no—he hadn't screwed the pooch this time. That was the shoreline south of Buffalo, where he belonged. He breathed a sigh of relief. He also tried to suppress the little stab of worry that went through him whenever he did this. Out in the Pacific, he wouldn't have a shoreline to recognize. If he was going to find the enemy and find his way back to his own carrier again, he'd have to be able to *use* the navigation they were trying to pound into his head.

Can I? he wondered. He hoped so. He thought so—as long as he had a little while to think while he was doing it. "The Japs may not give you that kind of time, Joe," he said in the cockpit. "Are you sure you want to go on with this?"

But that had only one possible answer. He nodded. He didn't need to speak. He'd been doing this for most of a year now. He'd torn his life to pieces to do this. He wasn't about to back away from it now. And if that meant he had to take a few chances once he got up there . . . He shrugged. Then it did, that was all. His commissioning wasn't very far away. He didn't give a damn about becoming an officer for the sake of becoming an officer—though that would have his immigrant parents walking on air.

What he gave a damn about was that becoming an officer, becoming a pilot, would give him the chance to fly off a real carrier and take the war to the Japs. He'd been waiting for that chance ever since Pearl Harbor. It was so close these days, he could taste it. He wanted it *bad*.

By now, coming down on dry land seemed routine. Instructors had talked to the cadets about stuff like that, warning them against overconfidence. Joe had heard about guys who flew their planes into the ground just out of carelessness. He watched what he was doing, but he had to make himself watch it. That probably wasn't so good.

No landing officer with wigwag flags here—just him and the F3F and the runway. He landed smoothly enough and taxied to a stop. As he killed the engine, he laughed at himself. Three years earlier, this plane had been on a carrier. If war had broken out then, say over the sinking of the *Panay,* it would have been in the front line against the Japs. Nowadays . . . Nowadays, it was good enough to train in.

Of course, Japan probably hadn't had Zeros three years earlier, either. Things happened in a hurry nowadays, and that was that.

Another Grumman biplane came in and taxied up right behind Joe's. Orson Sharp climbed out of it. "Way to go, roomie," he said. "You made those circuits and bumps look mighty good."

"Yeah?" Joe still sometimes had trouble believing his roommate was pulling for him as hard as he seemed to.

But Sharp nodded. "Oh, yeah. We do 'em here, we can do 'em anywhere." He didn't ask about his own performance. Part of that was because Joe had been in front of him in the queue and couldn't have seen him. And the other part was that the Mormon kid, unlike Joe, was confident about everything he did up there. He wasn't a showoff or anything, but he was good, and he knew it.

Groundcrew men took charge of the fighters. Joe and Sharp walked side by side to the administration building next to the field. By now, Joe was used to having his roommate tower over him. Once you got up in the air, size didn't matter any more anyway.

When they got inside, instructors separated them. Joe's raked him over the coals for not following the landing officer's signals fast enough. The gimlet-eyed men aboard the *Wolverine* had wasted no time radioing their complaints back to the base. They never did.

Joe took the heat and tried not to show how it stung. Actually, he thought he'd done pretty well. He'd done his damnedest—he knew that. If it wasn't good enough . . . He'd just have to try to improve. You couldn't argue. You had no excuses for anything less than perfection. A couple of cadets had complained and alibied when instructors criticized them. Joe didn't know where they were these days. He did know they weren't cadets any more.

When his own reaming was done, his instructor barked, "Any questions?"

"Yes, sir," Joe replied.

The instructor's eyebrows rose. More often than not—much more often than not—that was the wrong answer. But the instructor couldn't presume ahead of time. "Go ahead," he said, his voice chilly as the weather.

"Sir, we've lost a lot of carriers in the Pacific," Joe said. "My question is, when do we start getting replacements?"

"Ah." The instructor relaxed. Joe had found a question he could safely ask: it wasn't one about his own performance. Something approaching warmth entered the older man's voice as he replied, "Well, Mr. Crosetti, you have to understand I don't know a whole lot more than you do here—not officially, anyway."

"Yes, sir," Joe said eagerly. "I do follow that. But you're hooked into the grapevine, and I'm just a dumb cadet. I don't get the time of day, let alone the juicy stuff."

The instructor's face crinkled into a wide smile. Joe hadn't been sure it had room for that much amusement, but it did. The officer said, "We're not talking weeks, but we're not talking years, either." He caught himself. "I take it back. From what I hear, the first one is only weeks away. But we're looking at next summer before we have enough hulls in the water to go back and take another shot at the Japs."

"Next summer." Joe weighed that. Normally, seen with the impatience of youth, it would have seemed a million miles away. But when he looked ahead at everything he still had to do to win a place on one of those carriers . . . "Well, that doesn't sound too bad."

LIEUTENANT SABURO SHINDO HAD ALWAYS SLEPT LIGHTLY. Lately, he'd been dozing and catnapping more than really sleeping. He didn't like that at all. Air raids came every few nights now, and he expected them even on nights when they didn't come. Worry kept him awake when sirens didn't.

Tonight, though, the alarm was real. "*Zakennayo!*" he snarled as he ran for a shelter trench. "What good is it to have this fancy electronic warning if we can't shoot down the enemy airplane once we spot it?"

As if to mock him, a couple of antiaircraft guns near the Haleiwa airstrip started barking. *Wasting ammunition,* he thought scornfully: they had about as much chance of hitting that stinking flying boat as he did if he stood up and threw rocks at it.

Through the guns' racket, he caught the steady purr of the floatplane's engines. The Americans made *good* motors; by comparison, a lot of Japanese aircraft sounded like flying washing machines.

Crump! Crump! Bombs fell, not too far away. Yankee raiders hadn't hit Haleiwa for a few nights. This was the least of the airstrips on Oahu, as it had been when the Americans held Hawaii. *Maybe they thought they would catch us napping. Maybe they were right, too.*

A few more explosions, these more distant. Shindo wanted to hop in his Zero and go after the enemy seaplane. But night fighting was a risky business only now beginning to get specialists even in Europe, where there'd been more of it than anywhere else.

If he took off here, he'd be flying blind. He wouldn't have radar technicians who could guide him to his target, the way English and German night-fighter pilots did. He wouldn't have a swarm of targets to go after, either: just one seaplane on a nuisance raid. And he'd have a devil of a time getting down again, too, with all the fields on Oahu blacked out at night.

No, he had to stay where he was and do a slow burn. That, no doubt, was what the Americans had in mind. They knew how to get what they wanted, damn them.

More bombs fell, somewhere far off in the distance. Schofield Barracks? Wheeler Field? Even Honolulu? But for those distant explosions, the night was eerily silent, as most Oahu nights were. Sound could carry a long, long way.

The all-clear sounded. Shindo went back to his tent. He was too angry and too disgusted to sleep. He thought he might have had a chance to doze off—but before he could, he thought about what the Army officers stationed in Haleiwa would say. He could hear them laughing behind their hands as they asked why the Navy couldn't keep the Yankees away from Hawaii.

He'd heard those questions before. He knew what the answer was: the Pacific was too big to let anybody keep an eye on every square kilometer of it. The Americans had found that out in the biggest possible way almost a year earlier. Now they were impressing the same lesson on the Japanese.

Shindo shrugged. The Americans could be nuisances. They *were* nuisances. But they weren't going to catch Japan napping with a major attack on Hawaii. That wouldn't and couldn't happen. By now, the Japanese had picket boats out facing the Panama Canal as well as the U.S. mainland. If the Americans wanted another crack at these islands, they would have to take it against defenders who were alert and ready.

But even that knowledge didn't soothe Shindo enough to let him sleep. He fumed about tonight's raid and tossed and turned till morning painted the eastern horizon golden. Then he went to the mess and got rice with bits of salt fish in it and a cup of tea. Like tobacco, tea was a precious import. Even Japanese military personnel below officer's rank had trouble getting their hands on any.

Some of them had taken to coffee instead. That was locally grown, though not in large amounts. Shindo thought it was nasty. But it packed the same jolt as tea, or even more, so it had its uses.

A telephone call came in from Honolulu just after Shindo finished that early breakfast. Since he was expecting it, he sounded properly subordinate to Commander Fuchida. "Yes, sir," he said. "We will make a sweep to the north. . . . Oh, yes, sir. If we spot anything, we'll do our best to shoot it down or sink it."

"Good," Fuchida said. "It would be excellent if we could show that we *are* making the Americans pay."

"I understand, sir." What Shindo understood was that Fuchida's superiors were breathing down his neck. But Shindo, like any fighter pilot, did want to be up in the air going after the enemy.

He told the armorers to load a 250kg bomb on the rack he'd had installed under his Zero's belly. If he met a submarine, he wanted to be able to punish it. The bomb wouldn't handicap him against the lumbering American flying boats he was likely to meet in these waters. It would have against Wildcats, but he didn't expect to run into Wildcats. Wildcats meant carriers close by, and there were no American carriers close by.

Away he went, up into the sky. Certain officers—not Fuchida, to his credit—complained about how much gas searches used up. They didn't think enough about the cost of not searching.

As Shindo flew in a widening spiral over the Pacific, he breathed in oxygenated air with the taste of rubber. That taste and flying would always be linked in his mind. For some men, it was the smell of gasoline; for others, the throbbing roar of the engine. Not to Shindo. For him, that taste said it all.

He wanted to spot the enemy. He wanted to kill the enemy. If he saw a flying boat, he wanted to shoot it down. If he saw a submarine, he wanted to sink it. He'd flown too many searches where nothing turned up.

The thought had hardly crossed his mind when he spied motion in the air out of the corner of his eye. He started to swing his Zero in that direction, then stopped, laughing and swearing at the same time. That wasn't an enemy flying boat—that was another Japanese fighter plane, on a search spiral of its own.

No one except the Americans would have been happy with him had he gone after it and shot it down.

That the other pilot might have shot him down instead never crossed his mind. He respected the ability of every man he faced. Not taking your opponent lightly was the best way to live to a ripe old age. But, without false modesty, Shindo expected to win every aerial combat he entered. So did any good fighter pilot. Without that touch of arrogance, you couldn't do your job well.

He felt like a peregrine falcon on the prowl for pigeons. But there were no pigeons. He kept one eye on the fuel gauge. If he had to go home hungry—again—he wouldn't be a happy man.

There! What was that, four kilometers below, down on the surface of the Pacific? It wasn't a pigeon, but it might be a duck. It was somebody's submarine, sliding along on the surface as if it didn't have a care in the world.

Somebody's, yes—but whose? Japan had subs in these waters, too, to go after American warships if the Yankees tried to invade Hawaii again. But if the submarine was American . . . Saburo Shindo didn't want clodhoppers from the Army looking down their noses at his service. Sinking an American sub would be a good way to shut them up for a while.

He put himself between the sun and the boat and went down lower for a closer look. Anyone in the conning tower would have to look up into that glare, and would have a hard time spotting him. Attacking out of the sun worked against other airplanes. It ought to be just as good against a submarine.

If he attacked . . . Shooting down his own side's plane would be bad. Bombing his own side's sub would be disastrously worse. But he knew the lines of Japanese submarines very well. He had to. This one looked different. In these waters, anything not Japanese had to be American.

Shindo didn't dither. Dithering was in his nature even less than in most fighter pilots'. As soon as he was sure that boat belonged to the enemy, he dove on it. He'd never trained as a bomber pilot. His Zero didn't have dive brakes on the wings, the way Aichi dive bombers did; the design team that made the fighter hadn't figured it would need those big slotted flaps. He couldn't dive as steeply as an Aichi pilot could, either; his plane wasn't built to handle the stress of pulling out of a dive like that. He did the best he could with what he had.

The submarine swelled enormously. Shindo saw someone on the conning tower—and then, all at once, he didn't. The boat started to slide beneath the waves. They'd spotted him! But acceleration wasn't the only thing pulling his lips back from his teeth in a predatory grin. Too late! They were much too late!

He worked the bomb-release button. That was as much a makeshift as the rack under the Zero's belly; it wasn't an original part of the instrument panel. It did what it was supposed to do, though. The bomb dropped free. Shindo pulled back on the stick, wrestling the Zero's nose up before it went into the Pacific, too. The fighter's airframe groaned. No, it wasn't made for this kind of work.

But the nose *did* lift. Shindo swung the Zero into a tight turn so he could see what he'd done. When he did, he pounded a leather-gloved hand down on his thigh. The bomb had hit maybe ten meters aft of the conning tower. Men were swarming out of the sub, which was trailing smoke and sinking fast.

Shindo went around for another pass. By then, the American sailors had got into several inflatable life rafts. His thumb found the firing button on top of the stick. The Zero's machine guns chattered. Back when the fight for Hawaii was new, Shindo had let an American pilot he'd shot down parachute safely to earth. Thinking back on it, he had no idea why he'd been so soft. He shrugged, there inside the cockpit. He tried not to make the same mistake twice.

A couple of sailors in the rafts fired pistols at his plane. Had he been down there, he would have done the same thing. But he was up here instead, and so he shot up the rafts till they sank, till blood turned the Pacific red. This was why he'd come out here. If an American flying boat rescued those sailors, they would make more trouble for Japan. And if they managed to reach Oahu or another island, anti-Japanese locals, of whom there were too many, were likely to take them in. Nobody would have to worry about either of those unfortunate developments now.

Quietly pleased with himself, Shindo flew back towards Oahu.

A LONG COLUMN OF BOOTS marched through the mud in a driving rainstorm of the sort southern California Chambers of Commerce pretended this part of the country didn't get. Lester Dillon had spent enough time at Camp Elliott to know better. The youngsters who wanted to be Marines looked thoroughly miserable.

Dillon was miserable, too, but he didn't show it. As far as they were concerned, he was immune to vagaries like weather. If rain hit him and ran down the back of his neck, if his boots squelched in the mud—well, so what? He was a platoon sergeant. At the moment, he was a platoon sergeant who craved coffee with brandy in it, but these puppies didn't need to know that.

"I can't hear you!" he shouted, pitching his voice to carry even through the downpour.

The boots had been singing a marching song. Understandably, the downpour dampened their zeal. Dillon understood that, all right, but he wasn't about to put up with it. They weren't supposed to let anything dampen their zeal. That was part of what being a Marine was all about. If rain could do it, coming under fire would be infinitely worse. Coming under fire *was* infinitely worse, but they had to act as if it weren't. They roared out the song through the rain:

> Little bird with a yellow bill
> Sat outside my window sill.
> Coaxed him down with a crust of bread,
> And then I smashed his fuckin' head!

"I still can't hear you!" Dillon shouted, but not so angrily: they were loud enough to wake the dead now.

And they were getting tougher. When they started training, this tramp through the rain and muck would have prostrated them. Now they took it in stride. Few physical challenges fazed them any more. That too was part of what made them what they ought to be. But it was the easy part. A lot of them—farm boys and factory workers—had been in good shape before they started training. But being in good shape, while necessary to make a Marine, wasn't enough.

Would they stick together? Would they think of their buddies, their unit, as more important than themselves? Would they throw away their lives to save their buddies if they had to, knowing those buddies would do the same for them? Would they go forward where staying safe required hanging back?

If they managed that—if they managed it without fussing about it, without even thinking much about it—they'd be proper leathernecks.

Dillon couldn't remember how he'd absorbed the lessons he needed to have. He knew damn well they'd been in place before he ever went Over There. What he saw in France, what he did there, only confirmed what he'd already had.

"Sergeant?" one of the boots said.

"Yeah?" Dillon growled—he wanted them to think he was God, and an angry God at that.

"This is fun!" the youngster said.

That flummoxed Dillon. In all his years in the Corps, he didn't think he'd ever heard the like. "It's not supposed to be fun, goddammit," he said after that momentary amazement. "This isn't a picnic. It isn't a lark. Those Nip assholes are gonna fuckin' kill you if they get half a chance. They're good at it. That means we gotta be even better. You hear me, maggot?"

"Yes, Sergeant!" the boot bellowed. *You hear me?* had to be answered at top volume, lest worse befall.

Worse would bloody well befall here any which way. "Drop down and give me fifty pushups," Dillon growled. "Fun, my ass!"

"Yes, Sergeant!" the boot shouted again. He was a big, blond, wide-faced kid named Kowalski. Fifty pushups in the rain, in the mud, with a heavy pack on his back, were no joke. He was filthy and damn near dead by the time he finished them. Dillon wasn't sure he could have done them himself. Kowalski, though, plainly would sooner have died for real than failed. That was a Marine's way of thinking, too. He bounced to his feet after the last one, panting and scarlet but ready to go on with the march.

"Still having fun?" Dillon asked him.

By his expression, the kid wanted to say yes. But he wasn't—quite—that dumb. "No, Sergeant!" he said loudly.

"Okay," Dillon said. "Get it in gear."

After a hot shower and a clean uniform, he told the story that evening over a beer in the NCOs' club. Dutch Wenzel shook his head as if he couldn't believe his ears. "Fun?" he said. "What the fuck is the world coming to?"

"Beats me," Dillon answered. "How much fun will he think it is when his pal gets shot in the guts? How much fun will he think it is when *he* does? It's a *job,* for Chrissake. We gotta do it, and we gotta do it right, but *fun*? For crying out loud, Dutch!"

"Easy, man—easy." Wenzel raised a placating hand. "You're preaching to the choir here."

"Okay, okay. It rocked me, though, I tell you." Les shook his head, too. He still couldn't get over it. "Fun!"

"Don't blame you," Dutch said. "Even for a boot, that's pushing it. Hey—I heard something pretty good, though."

"Tell me," Dillon urged. "Maybe it'll help me get the taste of this out of my mouth."

"I hear we launched a new carrier," Dutch told him. "Gotta start making up for what the Japs nailed last summer."

Les nodded. "That's a fact—and you're right; that is good news. What are they calling this one?"

"*Essex,*" Wenzel answered. "There are supposed to be more in the pipeline, too."

"There'd better be," Dillon said. "You gotta figure we're going to lose some on the way in. We need to smash whatever they've got and have enough left over to handle their land-based air. If we don't, we shouldn't even start."

"Yeah, well, you know that, and I know that, but do they know it back in Washington?" Wenzel said.

"Beats me," Dillon said. "I'll tell you one thing, though—we're gonna find out."

JANE ARMITAGE FOUND IT HARD to believe 1943 was more than a month old. Christmas and New Year's had passed quietly. What was there to celebrate? And one day, one month, here was a lot like another. Oh, it was a little warmer in the summer, a little rainier in the winter, but, both times, only a little. She remembered Ohio. You didn't have any trouble telling summer from winter in Columbus. In Wahiawa, you could lose track without a calendar.

Flowers bloomed. Butterflies danced and bees buzzed. Snow? When the school was open, she'd had to teach special lessons about snow. The third-graders couldn't have understood half the Christmas carols if she hadn't.

Downtown Wahiawa, such as it was, had suffered since the Japanese took over. All the stores that sold new clothes, new dishes, new furniture—new anything, when you got right down to it—had gone belly-up. New stuff had come from the mainland, and nothing came to Hawaii from the mainland any more except the occasional airplane full of bombs. Much as Jane approved of those, she didn't want to buy one and take it back to the apartment.

Secondhand places, now . . . Those flourished. If you wanted a toaster or a dress or something to read, you got it secondhand. Used goods, if not abundant, were at least available. Jane sometimes felt like a ghoul when she sorted through them, for a lot of them came from the households of people who'd died in the fighting. But what could you do? Those luckless souls had no further use for their goods, and the people who were still alive desperately needed them.

When Jane saw a copy of *Murder Must Advertise* in the secondhand-book shop, she had all she could do not to jump for joy. She liked mysteries in general and Dorothy Sayers in particular, and she'd never read that one. Showing eagerness, though, would have run up the price. Nothing was fixed these days; everything depended on how much the seller thought he—or, in this case, she—thought the buyer would part with.

Jane picked up a cookbook she didn't particularly want. Cookbooks made good cover; everyone was obsessed with food these days. She poked around through the store before casually adding the mystery to the cookbook. "How much for these two, Louise?" she asked.

Louise's jaw worked. She might have been chewing gum, except there was no gum to chew. "Fifteen dollars," she said after making whatever arcane calculations she made. Those calculations worked. She wasn't as skinny as most people in Wahiawa.

"Fifteen?" Jane squeaked. "That's outrageous!" And it was. She hadn't expected Louise to say more than ten.

The bookstore owner shrugged. She chewed on the gum that wasn't there. "Twelve, then," she said reluctantly, "and you won't jew me down another dime."

"I'm not made out of money," Jane protested. Louise shrugged again. Jane asked, "How much for each of them?" That boiled down to, how well had she hidden her reaction when she saw *Murder Must Advertise*? If Louise thought she was mostly after the cookbook, she won. If the other woman knew she wanted the mystery, she didn't.

Still more jaw-working followed. Louise was calculating what the traffic would bear. "Eight for this one, four for the other," she said at last.

She wanted more for the cookbook. Jane didn't cheer, even if she felt like it. Instead, she looked disappointed. "That's too much," she said, sending a longing glance toward the book full of recipes for Chinese chicken wings and Polynesian pork chops and bananas on the half shell and fish with pineapple sauce and suffering bastards.

"Take it or leave it." Louise had the business manners of a snapping turtle.

Sighing, Jane put the cookbook back on the table where she'd found it. "I guess I can afford this one," she said, tapping the mystery. "I sure wish you'd done it the other way, though."

Louise looked smug. Jane gave her a five-dollar bill and got back two halves in change. She left the store in a hurry, before Louise figured out she was really ready to jump for joy.

The Japs had confiscated radios. A bomb had fallen on the local movie house. Making time go by was one of the hardest things you could do these days. A good book would kill several hours. If it was good enough, you could read it more than once, too. Jane could hardly wait to get back to her place, open up the novel, and be transported from Oahu to a larger, cooler, foggier isle.

But she hadn't slipped the surly bonds of reality yet. Up the street came a work gang of American POWs herded along by Japanese guards with bayoneted rifles. She eyed them with horrified fascination. As always, they reminded her how things could have been worse.

She was thin. They were emaciated. Her clothes were worn. They still had on the tattered remnants of whatever they'd been wearing when they surrendered. She made do with cold-water showers without soap. By the way they looked—and smelled—they hadn't bathed for more than a year. Some of them stood defiantly erect, and marched as if on parade at Schofield Barracks. Others, plainly, were on their last legs, and could barely stagger along.

One of them fell down in the middle of the street. Two Japanese guards stood over him, screaming what had to be curses. When he didn't get up, they started kicking him. They paused after a minute or so to see if he would rise. He tried, but couldn't get past his knees. They kicked him some more and paused again. When he still didn't get up, two of them bayoneted him. He groaned and thrashed and bled.

Jane's nails were short these days—whose weren't?—but they bit into her palms anyhow. The Japs didn't put the POW out of his misery. They left him there to die slowly. Then, laughing, they got the rest of the prisoners moving again.

It wasn't Fletch, Jane thought as she willed her hands to uncurl. Whenever prisoners of war went through Wahiawa, she couldn't help scanning their faces to see if she spotted her ex-husband. As decrepit and shaggy as the POWs were these days, he might have stumbled past her without her even recognizing him. She wondered why she bothered. She had no idea whether he was alive. She didn't love him any more. Even if she did, what could she do for him? Nothing. Less than nothing. And if the Japs here found out she was an officer's wife—even if she and Fletch had been getting a divorce—they might make things unpleasant for her. *More unpleasant,* she thought with a shiver.

But she couldn't help looking. Getting a divorce wasn't as final as lawyers made it out to be. She wished it were.

By the time the guards were out of sight, the prisoner they'd butchered had stopped moving. Sooner or later, someone would drag the body out of the street. Jane looked away from it as she scurried back to her apartment. What worried her was how little the atrocity upset her. She'd already seen too many others.

MARCHING UP THE KAMEHAMEHA HIGHWAY was more fun than paving it or building gun emplacements for the Japs. That was how Fletcher Armitage measured his life these days. He wasn't quite so exhausted when he marched as when he worked. He didn't starve quite so quickly, either. These were things to treasure, though he wouldn't have thought so before December 7, 1941.

He understood Einstein better than he'd ever dreamt of doing. There was bad, and then there was worse. What would have looked like the worst thing in the world to him before the Japs overran Oahu now didn't seem bad at all. If that wasn't relativity, what the hell was it?

When the POWs worked, the guards pushed them hard. Why not? The Japs didn't do any road work or digging themselves. But when they marched, the pace stayed bearable. If the Japs made the prisoners doubletime, they would have to doubletime themselves, and they wouldn't have cared for that one bit. A few of them were actually plump.

Fletch's standards about what constituted a proper human form had changed radically since the surrender—so radically, he didn't altogether realize it himself. The Americans with whom he labored seemed normal to him. They were, after all, the people he saw every minute of every day. He forgot how scrawny they were because they surrounded him.

But they made the Japs, some of whom were prewar average and a handful even heavier than that, seem grotesquely obese by comparison. Why didn't they fall over dead from carting that extra weight around all the time?

Intellectually, Fletch knew he'd had that much flesh himself once upon a time. Emotionally, he didn't, wouldn't, couldn't believe it. If everyone who mattered to him seemed made of sticks and twigs, then anyone who didn't had to have something wrong with him.

"Wahiawa ahead," somebody said.

"Hot damn." That wasn't Fletch; it was a Texan named Virgil Street. He added, "Who gives a damn, anyways? We went through this lousy place fallin' back when we still had guns in our hands. Goin' through it forwards doesn't mean anything, on account of the Japs got the guns now."

Fletch kept his mouth shut. Wahiawa meant something to him. He wondered if he'd see Jane. He also wondered if she'd care if she saw him. Not likely, he feared. He never had figured out why she dumped him. He hadn't seen it coming. (That he hadn't seen it coming said a good deal about him, but one of the things it said was that he wouldn't understand what it said.) He still loved her, as much as he had before. If only . . .

He laughed. He had a picture of the Jap sergeant who bossed the work gang letting him fall out for a heart-to-heart with his ex. It was right next to his pictures of Santa Claus, the Easter Bunny, and the Tooth Fairy.

And even if the sergeant did, would Jane listen to him? That was another fat chance. She hadn't wanted to hear a word he said, not after she threw him out of the apartment. Suddenly and powerfully, he wanted a drink. Thinking of Jane made him think of bourbon. He'd done a hell of a lot of drinking after she dumped him. What with forcibly separating him from hooch, the Japanese invasion might have saved him from turning into a lush.

"Shit," he muttered. Without even thinking, he could have named a dozen pretty damn good officers, all the way up to bird colonel, who drank like fish. If that wasn't a great Army tradition, he didn't know what was. He would sooner have sacrificed his liver for his country than what he was going through now.

As the POWs came into Wahiawa, the guards strung themselves out along either side of the slow-moving column. When they were out in the country, the guards mostly relaxed. Prisoners couldn't very well run, and couldn't disappear for long. Here, though, there were side streets to duck down, houses and apartments to break into, all sorts of places to hide. The Japs weren't dummies. They could figure that out as well as white men could.

They could do all kinds of things as well as white men could, and maybe better. Back before the shooting started, Fletch wouldn't have believed it, any

more than any other U.S. Army officer would have. To him, Japs had been little bucktoothed monkeys who could turn out cheap copies of just about anything, but who flew planes made from tin cans and didn't have the balls to
fight a real war.

He knew better now. He laughed again, bitterly. One whole hell of a lot
knowing did him!

"One run, nine die!" shouted a corporal who spoke English of a sort. Everybody in each shooting squad automatically looked around to see where the
other men whose fate was tied to his were and what they were doing. Each
squad had one or two guys reckoned less reliable than the others. You wanted
to be sure they couldn't light out for the tall timber.

Fletch caught Street's eye. They nodded to each other. Everything seemed
under control. If anybody held their shooting squad together, they were the
ones. Fletch had an idea about how to lead, having been an officer. Street was a
man who commanded respect regardless of rank. There were soldiers like that.
Fletch was glad the two of them got along.

Into Wahiawa they came. Civilians on the street bowed to the approaching
Japanese. That was ingrained into everybody by now: local Japs, Filipinos, Ko-
reans, Chinamen, *haoles*. You had to show respect. The world hadn't shown
Japan respect before, and everybody was paying for it now.

Wahiawa looked poor. It looked like a mainland town where the factory
had closed down and everybody'd been out of work for a long time. Everybody
wore shabby clothes—not so bad as the rags the prisoners had on, but shabby.
People looked fearful, too, as if expecting something worse would happen if
they weren't careful. They were bound to be right, too.

"You move!" the corporal yelled, hustling them along.

Move Fletch did. If he didn't move, they would bayonet *him* on the street
and laugh while they did it. His legs and especially his feet hurt. He kept
telling himself it was only because he'd done too much work for too long on
too little food. He kept telling himself that, yes, but he had more and more
trouble making himself believe it. He was starting to get beriberi. Not only
weren't they feeding him enough, they were feeding him the wrong kind of
not enough.

A blond woman on the sidewalk bowed to the Jap soldiers. Was that Jane?
Excitement, then dejection—it wasn't. This gal was older and tougher-looking.

He'd seen worse, though. He laughed at himself. His interest in women right now had to be purely theoretical. He didn't think he could get it up if he had a crane to help.

He laughed again. "What's funny?" Virgil Street asked. Anything that made a day go by a trifle better was to be cherished. Fletch explained. The other POW snorted. "Hell, buddy, way we are now, a clapped-out fifty-cent whore'd turn up her nose at us even if we could get it up."

"Ain't that the sad and sorry truth?" Fletch looked down at himself. He doubted he weighed a hundred twenty pounds, and at least ten pounds of that were dirt. Along with everybody else in this sorry outfit, he smelled like the monkey house in the zoo. He would have killed for a sirloin, a baked potato, and pie à la mode. Hedy Lamarr dancing the dance of love in the altogether? Forget about it.

And then he *did* see Jane, and he stumbled and almost fell on his face. He recognized the sun dress she had on; she'd bought it on a shopping trip down to Honolulu, and crowed about the price for days. She was very tan. Her hands looked like hell; they were almost as battered as his own.

She saw him, too. Her jaw dropped. Her mouth shaped an O. Her eyes widened. She didn't say a thing, though. He started to scream her name—he started to, but caught himself before anything more than a gurgle escaped his lips. If he showed he knew who she was, what would happen to her? She'd catch it from the Japs, odds were.

She's alive, anyway, and she doesn't look too bad. Maybe she'd started to call him, too. If she had, she also had too much sense to finish. *I love you,* he mouthed, and wondered if she could read lips.

He must have slowed down. A guard whacked him across the shoulder blades with a length of bamboo. He staggered, but kept his feet. The bastard would have kicked him if he'd gone down. Could he have got up after a couple of good licks? He hoped so, anyhow. If he couldn't . . . Well, that would have given Jane something to watch, wouldn't it?

"You move!" the Jap corporal yelled again.

On he went; he had no choice. *Ships passing in the night,* he thought. Jane stared after him; he looked back over his shoulder once to see. But *their* ship had taken a torpedo and sunk back before the war started. Whatever he saw now, wasn't it just debris floating on the surface?

Two tears ran down his face. He wiped them away with his skinny, filthy, sunburned forearm. When he looked back over his shoulder, Jane was gone. Had she ever really been there? He knew damn well she had. Whatever the Japs had done to him, they'd never been able to make him cry.

ALL ALONE IN THE APARTMENT she'd shared with Fletch once upon a time, Jane Armitage lay on the bed they'd also shared once upon a time. Her shoulders shook. She sobbed into the pillow. He was alive. She supposed she should have been glad. She *was* glad—and then again, she wasn't. Wouldn't he have been better off dead?

She'd seen plenty of POWs. She'd imagined seeing Fletch that way. That only went to show the difference between imagination and reality. A bright-eyed skeleton with a ginger beard . . .

And he'd seen her, too. For that little stretch of time, it had been as if he'd never got drunk, as if she'd never talked to a lawyer. If he could have broken out of that sorry pack, she would have . . . She didn't know what she would have done. Whatever he wanted, probably.

He was either still lurching along or at hard labor somewhere only a couple of miles away right now. In the movies, she would have figured out a way to go to him and comfort him and feed him and get him away from the people who were making his life a hell on earth. It would have been easy as pie, and the Japs wouldn't have caught on, at least not till too late. Then they would have been left gnashing their teeth and shaking their fists as she and Fletch rode off into the sunset together.

Real life, unfortunately, didn't usually come with a Hollywood ending. The Japs were a lot tougher and smarter than the villains in the movies. She didn't have the faintest idea how she could spirit Fletch away from the work gang he was in, or even how she could get him any food. If she *did* get Fletch away, what could she do with him? Stash him here in the apartment? Then he could never go out, and she could never have anybody in. Anyone who spotted him could blackmail her forever. And a ration that wasn't adequate for one wouldn't come close to feeding two. They'd both starve. And he'd probably—no, certainly—want to sleep with her again, and, that moment of surprise on the sidewalk aside, she didn't want to sleep with him. Oh, maybe once out of pity, but no more than that, for God's sake. *And* trying to get him out and failing would lead not to one horrible death but two.

"Shit!" she said, all at once understanding why Hollywood endings were so popular. They were a hell of a lot better than the way things went when the cameras weren't rolling.

BEFORE THE JAPANESE OCCUPIED HAWAII, Jiro Takahashi had never been a man of any great consequence here. Oh, he did his work and he paid his bills and he had some friends who thought he was a pretty good fellow, but that was about it. He could go anywhere without having anyone pay special attention to him.

It wasn't like that any more. He'd been on the radio several times. He'd had his words and opinions featured in Hawaii's Japanese-language press. And he'd even had his picture and his translated words show up in Honolulu's English-language papers.

Now his fellow Japanese said, "Hello, Takahashi-*san!*" and bowed when he went by. Or they called him "the Fisherman," like the sentries at the consulate. They asked his advice for their problems. They did favors for him, and tried to have him get favors for them from the consul and his henchmen. They treated him like an important person, like a doctor or lawyer—not like a real fisherman.

He loved every minute of it.

He'd had *haoles* bow to him as if he were a senior Japanese officer. They probably wanted him to do them favors, too, the only trouble being that he had no English and hardly any *haoles* spoke Japanese. But getting respect from people who'd looked down their noses not just at him but at all Japanese before things changed was as heady as strong sake.

The only people who seemed unimpressed—to put it mildly—with his rise in the world were his sons. Hiroshi and Kenzo did their best to act as if nothing had changed, or to wish things hadn't. Once, when they were out in the *Oshima Maru* and no one else could hear, Kenzo asked, "Why couldn't you just keep your head down like most people, Father?"

"What's that supposed to mean?" Jiro answered his own question before Kenzo could: "It means you're still full of sour grapes, that's what."

"You think the Americans are gone for good," Kenzo said. "You think you can call them all the names you want. But they haven't gone away. They're sinking more and more ships these days. Their planes come over more and more often. What will you do when they take Oahu back? You'll be in more trouble than you can shake a stick at, that's what."

"They're back on the mainland." To Jiro, the U.S. mainland was as far away as the moon. "How can they come back here? Do you think I'm afraid of the bogeyman? You'd better think twice."

"They aren't the bogeyman, Father." Hiroshi backed Kenzo. "They're real." He spoke with a somber conviction Jiro couldn't dismiss, however much he wanted to.

"Oh, yes!" He still tried to laugh it off. "And I suppose you've talked to them, and they told you just what they're going to do."

Neither of his sons said anything. They only looked at each other. The breeze shifted. With automatic attention, Jiro turned to the rigging. Every bit as automatically, Hiroshi swung the rudder a few degrees to port. He and Kenzo had become good sailors, even if they liked the United States too well.

They proved right about one thing: the Americans weren't going away. Jiro had thought they would. After the beatings Japan gave them, wouldn't they see they didn't have a chance and give up? Evidently not. U.S. seaplanes buzzed over Honolulu or Pearl Harbor, dropped bombs, and flew away under cover of darkness. Or a submarine surfaced, fired a few rounds with its deck gun, and disappeared under the sea again. Or a sub *didn't* surface, but put a torpedo into a Japanese freighter—and, again, disappeared.

A couple of times, the Japanese had sunk a marauding U.S. submarine. The papers and the radio trumpeted those triumphs to the skies. Hiroshi's sardonic comment was that they wouldn't get so excited about it if it happened more often. That hadn't occurred to Jiro, and he wished it hadn't occurred to his son, either; it made an uncomfortable amount of sense.

Was there a *kami* in charge of bad timing? If there was, the spirit had its eye on the *Oshima Maru* right that minute. No sooner had Jiro worried about how Japan was really doing than Kenzo said, "It sounds like the Russians are still giving Hitler a hard time."

The Japanese-language papers that were the only ones Jiro could read had done their best to talk around that, but they couldn't get around the brute fact that Germany had got into Stalingrad, had fought a terrible battle there, and had lost it. Jiro did his best to shrug it off, and even to counterpunch: "Hitler has his war, and we have ours. Did you see how our bombers hit Australia again? More *haoles* getting what they deserve."

"*Our* bombers?" Kenzo shook his head. "They weren't mine, Father, please excuse me."

"You're Japanese, too," Jiro said angrily.

"I look like you. I speak Japanese, yes," his younger son answered. "But I speak English, too. I was born in America. I'm *glad* I was born in America."

"That silly girl you're going with has you all confused," Jiro said.

Kenzo glowered at him. "Elsie's not silly. She's about the least silly girl I ever met."

"I'm not seeing any *haole* girl, and I feel the same way Kenzo does," Hiroshi said.

Jiro went back to tending the sails. His sons just wouldn't listen to reason. One thing growing up in America had done to them: it had taught them not to respect their parents the way they would have in Japan. He and his wife had done everything they knew how to do, but America corroded good moral order—that was all there was to it.

"You don't know how lucky we are that we've come under the Emperor's rule," Jiro said.

That got squawks from both his sons. The squawks took some little will to turn into words. Kenzo got there before Hiroshi: "Some luck! If we didn't catch most of our own food, we'd be as skinny as the rest of the poor so-and-sos in Honolulu."

The ration ordinary people got *was* less than extravagant. "The Americans are sinking the ships that bring in rice," Jiro said. "Chancellor Morimura told me so himself. And besides, we don't have white men telling us what to do any more. Doesn't that count for something?"

"We have Japanese soldiers and Japanese sailors telling us what to do instead," Hiroshi said. "If we don't do it, they shoot us. The Americans never did anything like that."

"You haven't got the right attitude," Jiro scolded. His boys—now men with minds of their own—both nodded. He didn't know what to do about them. He feared he couldn't do anything.

* * *

COMMANDER MITSUO FUCHIDA BOWED TO HIS OPPOSITE NUMBER from the Army. "Good to see you again," he said.

Lieutenant Colonel Murakami bowed back in precisely the same way; their ranks were equivalent. "And you," he said, slyly adding, "Kingmaker." Fuchida laughed; along with Commander Genda and one of Murakami's colleagues, they'd chosen Stanley Laanui to head the restored—on paper, anyhow—Kingdom of Hawaii.

That, though, probably wasn't why Murakami had come to the *Akagi*—had actually set foot on a Navy ship—now. Fuchida waved him to a chair in his cramped cabin. There was no other kind on the carrier; even Captain Kaku was pinched for room. "What can I do for you?" Fuchida asked.

Before answering, Murakami looked to the closed watertight door that gave them privacy. "How long have we got before the Americans attack Hawaii again?" he asked.

"Why ask me?" Fuchida replied. "The Americans are the ones who know. You can ring up President Roosevelt and get the answer straight from him."

Instead of laughing, Murakami grimaced. "That's not as funny as it sounds, Fuchida-*san*. There was a telephone operator who passed on information to the Americans by calling California in the middle of the night when no one was paying attention to what she did. She will not call California any more—or anywhere else, either." He spoke with a grim certainty.

"I never heard anything about that," Fuchida exclaimed.

"You wouldn't. It's not something we're proud of. But I'm telling you—in confidence, I hope." Murakami waited.

Fuchida's *"Hai"* was, *Yes, I understand,* not, *Yes, I agree.* He recognized Murakami's ploy. The Army officer was telling him something he didn't know. Now Murakami hoped to hear something *he* didn't know. Bargains often went along routes like that.

When Fuchida said no more than *Hai,* Murakami sighed. "We do need this information," he said reasonably. "We have to defend this island, too—with our airplanes, and with our soldiers if the Americans manage to land."

That was polite. What he meant was, *If the Americans smash our carriers.* Since he was aboard one of them, he couldn't very well come out and say so. Commander Fuchida also sighed. "When they build enough so they think they can beat us—then they will come."

"*Domo arigato.*" Murakami's thanks were a small masterpiece of sarcasm. "And when will that be?"

"They have commissioned—we think they have commissioned—two new fleet carriers, as well as some light carriers," Fuchida answered. That was payback for Murakami's bit of news; up till now, the Navy had held the information close to its chest.

By the way the Army officer's eyes widened, it was certainly news to him. "Two?" he said. "I knew of one, but. . . ." He in turn surprised Fuchida, but not so much. The Yankees hadn't kept quiet about *Essex.* Maybe they wanted their own people to know they were building ships so they could retaliate. They'd been much more secretive about the other big carrier, and the smaller ones.

"I think our intelligence is reliable here," Fuchida said.

"*Zakennayo!*" Murakami muttered. "Two! And light carriers! How soon will they have more?" That wasn't quite fearful anticipation in his voice, but it came close.

"There I cannot tell you, not for certain." Fuchida did his best not to remember Admiral Yamamoto's worries over how fast the Americans could build things once they got fully geared up. Most experts in Japan thought Yamamoto an alarmist, but he knew the USA well—*and* he was Yamamoto. One disagreed with him at one's peril.

"What is your best estimate? What is the Navy's best estimate?" Murakami was nothing if not persistent.

"Summer." Fuchida spread his hands. "Don't ask me for anything closer than that, Murakami-*san,* because I can't give it."

The Army officer looked discontented. "General Yamashita is already assuming summer. I was hoping you could tell me more." He didn't say, *I was hoping to win points for myself if you did tell me more,* but it hovered behind his words.

"Please excuse me, but I am not a *bonz,* to lay out the future for you," Fuchida said, hoping he hid his irritation.

"Will the Navy be ready?" Murakami asked.

That did it. Fuchida was a patient man, but even patience had its limits. "No, of course not," he snapped. "We're going to go out against the Americans in a couple of rusty old tubs, and they'll sink us just like *that.*" He snapped his fingers.

Lieutenant Colonel Murakami turned red. He had brains enough to know when he'd been given the glove. His colleague, Lieutenant Colonel Minami, was all too likely to have taken Fuchida literally. "All right. All right. I know you'll do your best," Murakami said. "But will your best be good enough?"

"It always has been so far." Pride rang in Fuchida's voice; he was still affronted. "Anyone who doesn't think it will should transfer out of this kingdom—which wouldn't *be* a kingdom if the Navy didn't know what it was doing."

Murakami blushed again. "I'm not going anywhere," he said, though Fuchida had been careful not to challenge his personal courage. When the Navy officer didn't push it any further, Murakami went on, "Speaking of being stationed in a kingdom, here's something that may amuse you: King Stanley has asked for some airplanes, so Hawaii can have an air force as well as an army."

"You're joking," Fuchida said. Lieutenant Colonel Murakami shook his head. And, thinking about it, Fuchida wasn't all that surprised. King Stanley was vain. He would be the sort to want a toy air force to go with his toy Army. Fuchida asked, "What did General Yamashita say to that?" Yamashita, from everything he'd seen, had a short fuse.

But Murakami surprised him, answering, "Yamashita-*san* consulted with the Foreign Ministry, and they said to keep the Hawaiian happy if he could do it without causing us trouble. So King Stanley is getting half a dozen of our most decrepit *Hayabusas*."

"The Hawaiian Air Force." Fuchida had to smile at that. He would have screamed bloody murder, though, if King Stanley had demanded Zeros. As far as he was concerned, the Hawaiians were welcome to *Hayabusas*. The Peregrine Falcon was the Army's chief fighter plane. It was even lighter and more maneuverable than the Zero, but armed with nothing more than a pair of rifle-caliber machine guns. A Sopwith Camel rising to fight the Red Baron in 1917 had had just as much firepower. Handled well, a *Hayabusa* gave good service. Even so . . . He didn't want to criticize the plane to Murakami, who was not an aviator, but he would almost rather have gone up in a Sopwith Camel.

Murakami was smiling, too, for reasons of his own. "Do you know what the King's biggest challenge is?"

"Tell me," Fuchida urged. "I'm all ears."

"Finding pilots small enough to be comfortable in the cockpit."

Fuchida did laugh then. Hawaiians were bigger than Japanese, as the two sets of guards at Iolani Palace proved. The naval officer said, "A good thing he's sticking to Hawaiians and not using whites—although local Japanese would solve his problem for him."

"General Yamashita suggested that," Murakami said. "The King was polite about turning it down, but he did. He wants Hawaiian pilots flying for him. He has his pride, too, no matter how foolish it is."

"I suppose he does," Fuchida agreed. Much good pride would do the puppet king of Hawaii. With or without a few fighter planes to call his own, he would go on doing what Japan told him to. If he didn't . . . If he didn't, the Kingdom of Hawaii would suddenly need a new sovereign.

VI

ANYONE WHO WANTED TO HOLD AN OUTDOOR CEREMONY IN BUFFALO IN March—even at the end of March—was rolling the dice. There was a backup plan, then. Had the weather gone south (or rather, in Buffalo, gone arctic), Joe Crosetti and his fellow cadets would have received their commissions in the Castle, an impressive-looking crenellated building in the eastern part of the Front, the park that nestled up against Lake Erie.

The Castle, as far as Joe was concerned, had only one thing wrong with it: it was the headquarters of the Buffalo Girl Scouts. He could hardly imagine a less martial place to become an officer in the U.S. Naval Reserve.

But the weatherman cooperated. The day dawned bright and sunny. The mercury was in the upper forties. In San Francisco, that would have been frigid at noon. Everybody from less temperate parts of the country kept assuring him it wasn't bad at all. Since he wore a warm wool uniform, he couldn't argue with them too much.

Memorials to Buffalo units that had fought in the Civil War and the Spanish-American War were scattered over the park. They were probably easier to spot at this season of the year than in high summer, when leaves would have hidden many of them from view. Seeing them reminded Joe of what he was at last becoming fully a part of.

So did the tall bronze statue of Oliver Hazard Perry. The folding chairs for the ceremony were set up in front of it. "This is a good place for doing what we're doing," Joe said to Orson Sharp.

Sharp nodded. "I'll say. 'We have met the enemy and they are ours!' " he quoted.

Joe had forgotten that. He suddenly laughed. "And the enemy he was fighting was England, and she's the best friend we've got."

"Yeah." The young man from Utah laughed, too. "And do you remember who his younger brother was?"

"Afraid not," Joe admitted. He'd done okay in history, but he hadn't set the world on fire.

"Matthew Perry—the guy who opened up Japan," Sharp said.

"Holy Jesus!" Joe said. "Boy, he never knew how much he has to answer for, did he? He should have left it closed. That would have saved everybody a lot of trouble."

"Places, gentlemen, places," someone called in an official-sounding voice.

Places were in alphabetical order. Joe sat up near the front, his roomie toward the back. The mayor of Buffalo made a speech praising all the bright young patriots who passed through his city on their way to knocking the stuffing out of the Axis. It sounded like every other political speech Joe had ever heard until his Honor pointed to the bridge spanning the Niagara River at the north end of the Front. "That's the Peace Bridge," he said. "This end is in the United States; the other end is in Canada. We want peace all through the world, but we will have to win this war before we can get it."

Along with the other cadets, Joe applauded. Most of the clapping sounded dutiful. Joe's was a little more than that. The mayor's words echoed what he'd been thinking himself. What would Oliver Perry have made of a Peace Bridge between the USA and what was still a dominion of the British Empire? And what would Matthew Perry have made of a war between the United States and what had been a backward, hermit kingdom—especially of a war the Japanese looked to be winning at the moment? Which of the old sea dogs would have been more surprised?

After the mayor sat down, another speaker limped up to the microphone. The cadets greeted him with a hand much more heartfelt than the one they'd given his Honor. Lieutenant Zachary Gunston was a Buffalo native. Like Jack Hadley, he'd also been a Wildcat pilot in the battle in the North Pacific the summer before. Also like Hadley, he'd had to ditch his fighter, and a destroyer had plucked him from the drink.

He pointed out to the cadets. "It's up to you to carry the ball," he said. "My buddies and I, we took it as far as we could go. We didn't quite have the ma-chines we needed, and we didn't quite have the techniques we needed, either. You've learned in your training a lot of what we had to find out the hard way. Your ships will be better. Your planes will be better—I hear the fighters aboard the new carriers are a long step up from Wildcats. But in the end"—he pointed again—"it's going to be up to you, and what you've got inside you.

"We made a mistake," Gunston went on. "We figured the Japs were patsies, pushovers. We've been paying for that mistake ever since we made it. They're tougher and smarter than we ever dreamt they could be. Now it's going to be up to you to teach 'em a lesson: no matter how tough they are, no matter how smart they are, nobody sucker-punches the United States of America and gets away with it. Nobody! Am I right or am I wrong?"

"Right!" The word came out as a fierce growl from the throat of every grad-uating cadet. Joe felt like a dog snarling at another dog on the street—and God help that other sorry mutt, too!

"Okay, then, gentlemen. I think you are about ready to be commissioned now," Lieutenant Gunston said. "Please rise, raise your right hands, and repeat the oath after me." Along with his classmates, his squadmates, Joe Crosetti did. Pride tingled through him. If he had to blink rapidly several times to keep tears from forming and running down his face, he wasn't the only one. Beside him, another kid's eyelids were marching doubletime, too. When the oath was complete, Gunston looked out at the brand-new officers. "Welcome to the Navy, Ensigns! You've got a big job ahead of you."

Joe looked down at the gold stripe on his sleeve. He was as junior an officer as possible—an ensign with no seniority—but he was, by God, an officer! Crosetti the fisherman's son, an officer in the U.S. Navy! If this wasn't one hell of a country, he didn't know what would be.

"Congratulations, Ensign Crosetti," said that youngster beside Joe who'd also been blinking. He was blond and handsome and looked as if he came from a Main Line family. Maybe he did. But he wasn't any more an ensign than Joe was.

"Thanks, Ensign Cooper. Same to you," Joe said. Nobody was ragging on anybody today, and who your father was, what he did for a living, or how big a bankroll he had didn't matter. The way it looked to Joe, that they didn't, or shouldn't, matter was a big part of what the war was about.

Twisting, he looked back towards Orson Sharp. He couldn't see his roomie.

Too many other newly minted officers stood between them. Guys were starting to move around and find their special friends. Even when Joe did, he had trouble seeing past the taller people in his class. But he knew about where Sharp would be, and headed back there. Sharp was coming up toward him. They clasped hands.

"We've been waiting a long time," Joe said—it seemed like forever since he'd volunteered. "Now—"

"We get to wait some more," the ensign from Utah finished for him. "We have to get a ship. We have to get trained up on whatever we fly, whether it's a Wildcat or one of these new jobs Lieutenant Gunston was talking about. And we have to wait till enough carriers are ready to give us the best shot at licking the Japanese."

Every word of that was eminently sensible. Joe liked it no more because of that. If anything, he liked it less. "You're no fun," he said.

"I know," said Sharp, who laughed at the wet-blanket reputation he'd had all the way through the training program. "Before too long, though, the Japs will say the same thing."

"Yeah!" Joe said.

WATCHING SOME OF THE PILOTS who'd come to Hawaii as replacements, Lieutenant Saburo Shindo wondered how they'd ever made it out of flight school. They had trouble finding Haleiwa, let alone landing at the airstrip there. A few of them might never have made the acquaintance of their airplanes before these flights, or so it seemed to Shindo.

When he finally couldn't stand watching any more, he got on the telephone to Commander Fuchida. "*Moshi-moshi,*" the head of the Japanese naval air effort said. "Fuchida here."

"This is Shindo, Fuchida-*san*. What the devil's happened to flight school since we went through it?"

Mitsuo Fuchida laughed, not all together comfortably. "By all I've heard from Japan, nothing much has happened to it."

"Then what's wrong with the chowderheads it's turning out?" Shindo demanded. "Plenty of the Americans we faced were good pilots. We had better planes, and that helped a lot, but we had better fliers, too. These people . . . Yes, a Zero is better than a Wildcat, but it's not *that* much better—not enough to let these people go up against Wildcats with good pilots and hope to beat them."

"They're about the same as we were when we got out of flight school," Fuchida said.

"No!" Shindo denied the mere possibility.

But Fuchida said, *"Hai.* The difference, Shindo-*san,* is that we had plenty of combat experience against the Chinese and the Russians who flew for them before we took on the Americans. We were veterans. We were ready."

Shindo thought about it. Had he been *that* green when he left the flight school at Kasumigaura? He didn't want to believe it. He'd certainly thought he knew what he was doing. Of course, so did these gas-wasting idiots. "Maybe," he said, most grudgingly.

"With some experience, they'll do fine." Fuchida's voice was soothing. "And remember, the Yankees have taken worse combat losses than we have. If they come at us, they'll have more inexperienced pilots in the air than we do."

"I suppose so." Shindo still wasn't happy. "Have you seen these new ones, though? They haven't had much time up there, and they sure fly like it. Fuel still must be tighter than a mouse's asshole back in the home islands."

"Er—yes." Fuchida, a straitlaced sort, made heavy going of the comparison. He continued, "It shouldn't be. With the Dutch East Indies in our hands . . . That's why we fought the war in the first place."

"If the problem isn't fuel, the program's gone to the dogs," Shindo said. "It's as simple as that. I tell you, some of these people aren't ready to fly combat missions against pilots who know what they're doing."

"Get them as ready as you can, Shindo-*san,* and do it as fast as you can, too," Fuchida said. "Things are stirring in the United States. The Yankees keep launching new carriers, and they're supposed to be getting new fighters, too."

"You're full of good news today," Shindo said. "Where are *our* new fighters?"

Fuchida didn't answer that. Shindo knew why, too. The replacement for the Zero had been on the drawing boards for a couple of years. It seemed unlikely to come off the drawing boards any time soon. The Army was starting to get a new fighter. The *Hien,* with an engine based on the one that powered the German Me-109, was a much tougher plane than the *Hayabusa.* But it was also much less reliable, needed skilled mechanics—always in short supply—to keep it running, and was available in much smaller numbers than the older machine.

"One thing that will give the new pilots flight time is antisubmarine patrolling," Fuchida said. "The more enemy boats we can sink, the better off we
are. You know that."

"I know something about it," Shindo said. Despite the sub he'd sunk, the
Yankees hadn't left Hawaiian waters. They kept on with their part of the war as
if nothing had happened. Americans owned more stubbornness and more
courage than Shindo or most Japanese had expected.

"All we can do about this is the best we can," Fuchida said. "I constantly
work with the destroyer skippers so they can do a better job of attacking the
American boats. The problem is not easy. Ask the Americans themselves, or
the British, if you don't believe me. They have it in the Atlantic."

"I have more urgent things to worry about—like why my so-called replacement pilots aren't as good as they ought to be," Shindo said. "And another one
occurs to me, too: when the Americans try again, they're going to throw more
ships and planes at us than they did last time, *neh*?"

Commander Fuchida was silent for a moment. "I don't know that for a
fact," he answered cautiously when he did speak.

Shindo gave him a scornful snort. "I don't know it for a fact, either, but it's
the way to bet, eh?"

"Yes, probably," Fuchida admitted.

"All right—we're thinking the same way, then," Shindo said. "When we
came to Hawaii, we hit with everything we had. The Americans didn't the last
time, and it cost them. It was three carriers against three last time. We only
have two in these waters now. If they bring more than three, two may not be
enough. When do the reinforcements come, and how many will there be?"

Mitsuo Fuchida was silent quite a bit longer this time. "Well, that's not such
an easy question to answer, Shindo-*san*."

With another snort, Shindo said, "I'm afraid you just did."

"Things are . . . difficult." Fuchida sounded defensive, not a good sign. "The
Americans in Australia are bombing the southern coast of New Guinea as
heavily as they can. And the British are kicking up their heels in the Indian
Ocean. Admiral Nagumo's raid a year ago didn't clear them out of there. They
bombed Rangoon and even Singapore not long ago."

"I hadn't heard that," Shindo said.

"We don't go out of our way to advertise it," Fuchida said. Shindo grunted.

The other officer went on, "But what it boils down to is, our carrier forces are stretched thinner than we wish they were."

"Wonderful," Shindo said sardonically. "The Americans are building new carriers as fast as they can, aren't they?" He didn't wait for an answer, not that Fuchida tried to deny it. Instead, not trying to hide his anger, he plowed ahead: "Where the devil are *our* new carriers, Fuchida-*san*?"

"We've launched *Taiho*," Fuchida told him. "She's supposed to be a step up from *Shokaku* and *Zuikaku*."

A step up from Japan's newest, strongest fleet carriers would make *Taiho* a formidable ship indeed. But launching a carrier and putting her into action were two different things, as Shindo knew only too well. "When will we be able to get some use out of her?" he asked.

Unhappily, Fuchida answered, "Early next year, I hear."

"Wonderful," Shindo said again, with even more sarcasm than before. "All right, then. Let me ask a different question, sir. When do we get *Zuikaku* back? It's been a long time since she limped off to the home islands to get fixed up."

"Now there I really do have good news," Fuchida said. "She is ready to return to duty now."

"Well, fine—that *is* good news. Took them long enough, but it is," Shindo agreed. "So we still have the same six fleet carriers that started the war, plus a few light carriers for small change. What can the Yankees throw at us?" He refused to count *Taiho*. She would be worth something—with luck, worth a lot—later on, but not yet.

"They have *Hornet*, if she's been repaired by now. They have *Ranger*. They have *Wasp*. They also have some light carriers. And they have whatever new fleet carriers they've built. We are just about certain of two."

Shindo brightened. "That's better than I thought. They have two oceans to cover, too."

"But the British help them in the Atlantic and cause us trouble in the Indian Ocean," Fuchida said. "This is a *world* war, Shindo-*san*. And their advantage is that they can join hands. There's too much space between us and Germany to make that easy on our side."

"*Hai,*" Shindo said. The Germans had managed to get their fancy aircraft engine and the drawings that went with it to Japan by submarine. Such ventures were all too rare, though, while America and England might have been in bed with each other. Shindo sighed. "If only the Russians had gone down. . . ."

"Yes. If," Fuchida said heavily.

That seemed unlikely to happen now. For a while there, after the disaster at Stalingrad, it had looked as if Germany would go down instead. But the Germans were nothing if not resilient. They'd stabilized the front and even regained a lot of ground. That fight had a long way to go; it remained up in the air. Even so, the quick German victory on which Japan had pinned so many hopes was nothing but a pipe dream.

And, while Germany and Russia remained locked in a death embrace, Russia and Japan were neutral. That created all kinds of ironies. Russian freighters from Vladivostok freely crossed the Pacific to the West Coast of the USA even though Japan and America battled to see who would dominate the ocean. Japan did nothing to interfere with those ships. When they got to Seattle or San Francisco or Los Angeles, they took on American planes and tanks and trucks and munitions the Russians would use against Germany, Japan's ally. Then they sailed back across the Pacific, and Japan still did nothing to interfere. It was a strange business.

It was also one for which Shindo had no taste. He went back to the things over which he did have some control: "Fuchida-*san*, can you get me some extra fuel up here?"

"I don't know," Fuchida answered cautiously. "Why do you need it?"

"I want to take these puppies up and let them get some practice dogfighting me," Shindo answered. "Once they see I can shoot them down whenever I please, or near enough, they'll start to realize they don't know everything there is to know."

"That would be good," Fuchida said. "I can't promise you anything—you know how tight the gasoline situation is. But I'll try."

"We can't fight the Americans if we don't have the gas to train our pilots," Shindo said.

"Yes, I understand that," Fuchida replied. "But we can't fight them if we don't have the gas to get our planes off the ground, either. The more we use beforehand, the less we're liable to have when we need it most."

"This is no way to fight a war," Shindo said. Commander Fuchida didn't contradict him. Fuchida said nothing to reassure him, either.

* * *

IN JIM PETERSON'S MILITARY EDUCATION, he'd never learned the difference between dry beriberi and wet. Somehow, the instructors at Annapolis hadn't thought either kind important enough to put on the curriculum. That only went to show they hadn't realized slowly starving to death might form part of a naval officer's career.

Only goes to show what a bunch of ignorant bastards they were, Peterson thought as he lay in the miserable bamboo hut in the Kalihi Valley. It was raining. Of course it was raining. As far as Peterson could see, it always rained in the valley. The roof leaked. Since the Japs didn't let the POWs use anything but leaves to cover it and didn't give them much time even to put on more leaves, that wasn't the world's hottest headline, either.

Looking around, he had no trouble telling the wet beriberi cases from the dry. Men who had wet beriberi retained fluid. They swelled up in a grotesque and horrible parody of good health. Swollen or not, though, they were starving, too.

Prisoners with dry beriberi, by contrast, had a lean and hungry look. *Like mine,* Peterson thought through his usual haze of exhaustion. The pins and needles in his hands and feet were red-hot fishhooks and spikes.

The really alarming thing was, he could have been worse off. When cholera went through the camp a few weeks earlier, he hadn't caught it. He'd buried some of the dark, shrunken corpses of men who had—after he put in his usual shift at the tunnel, of course. Cholera killed with horrifying speed. You could be normal in the morning—well, as normal as POWs got, which wasn't very—and shriveled and dead by the afternoon.

One nice thing: cholera scared the Japs, too. Several guards had died just as fast as any prisoners. Beriberi, by contrast, didn't bother them at all. Why should it? They had plenty to eat, and the right kind of food, not just a starvation diet of boiled white rice and not much else.

Peterson looked around, hoping to spot a gecko. POWs ate the little lizards whenever they could catch them. Sometimes they roasted them over little fires. More often, they didn't bother. When you were in the kind of shape they were in, raw meat was as precious as any other kind.

"You know what?" Gordy Braddon asked from beside Peterson. The

Tennessean was as skinny as he was, with knees wider than his thighs. A nasty abscess ulcerated one calf. Pretty soon, the medical officer would have to cut it out to keep it from going gangrenous. A puckered red scar on Peterson's leg showed where he'd gone through that. Ether? Chloroform? The Japs had them. They laughed when the medical officers asked for some. The medical officers were lucky to get iodine, let alone anything more.

"Tell me," Peterson said after a while. Beriberi sapped the will as well as debilitating the body. Sometimes even conversation seemed more trouble than it was worth.

"We're gonna leave one man dead for every foot of tunnel we drive," Braddon said.

Peterson contemplated that. Again, he took his time. He couldn't help taking his time—his wits wouldn't work fast no matter how much he wanted them to. "One man?" he said after the slow calculations were complete. "We're liable to leave five or ten men dead for every foot of tunnel."

His companion in misery took *his* own sweet time thinking about that. "Wouldn't be surprised," he said at last. "God damn Walter London to hell and gone."

"Yeah." Even in his present decrepit state, Peterson didn't need to think that over before he agreed with it. He managed a graveyard chuckle. "Well, you know what the Japs say. 'Always prenty plisoner.'"

At the rate POWs were dying in the Kalihi Valley, he wondered how long there would be plenty of prisoners. Of course, this place was specifically designed to use them up. A lot of men who went into the ever-deepening tunnel shaft lasted only a few days. The ones who managed to get past that dreadful initiation to life here did better—if survival *was* better, which didn't always strike Peterson as obvious.

"All I want is to be alive when we take this goddamn place back," Braddon said. "Reckon I get to pay these sons of bitches back then for what they owe me."

"Yeah, that's what keeps me going, too," Peterson agreed. "Sometimes the idea of getting my own back is about the only thing that does keep me going."

He wondered whether the USA would be able to take Hawaii back. When he'd been in the POW camp up near Opana and the ordinary labor gangs, he'd had some connection with the outside world. Part of what he got was Jap propaganda, of course, but not everything was. Here and there, people had clandestine radio sets and heard the other side of the news.

Not in the Kalihi Valley. The Japs hardly bothered with propaganda here, because they didn't think the poor damned souls working on the tunnel were ever coming out. If any of the prisoners had a radio, no news from it had ever got to Jim Peterson's ear.

He started to settle down for sleep. A thrashing in the bushes made him pause. A furious grunting made him scramble to his feet. Braddon jumped up, too. So did men in worse shape than either of them. So did men in worse shape than either of them who'd been sunk deep in exhausted sleep.

That grunting meant a wild pig was out there. If they could catch it, if they could kill it, they could eat it. The mere thought of a chunk of pork drove Jim Peterson harder than any Japanese taskmaster's bamboo club.

Pigs did wander into the camp every once in a while, looking for garbage— or maybe looking to dig up bodies buried in shallow graves and do unto humans what humans were in the habit of doing unto them. The POWs had pigstickers—bamboo spears with points made from iron smuggled out of the tunnel. They hid them in the jungle; if the guards found them, they confiscated them and beat everybody in the nearest barracks. To the guards, anything that could stick a pig could also stick one of them. The guards weren't wrong, either. Peterson dreamt of spearing a couple of them. Only the certain knowledge of what would happen to him and everybody else if he tried stayed his hand.

He grabbed a spear now, and plunged into the dripping emerald jungle in the direction of the grunting. Before he got there, it rose to a furious squealing. "For Christ's sake, don't let it get away!" he shouted, and ran harder than ever.

He found where the pig was by almost falling over it. It was a boar, as nasty a razorback as ever roamed the hills in Arkansas. Two men had already driven spears into it, and hung on to them for dear life. A boar's tushes could rip the guts out of a man almost as well as a bayonet could. And a wild pig was faster and stronger than a Jap with an Arisaka.

Peterson thrust his spear into the boar's side. Much more by luck than by design, the point—which had started its career at the end of a pick—pierced the pig's heart. The beast let out a last grunt, one that seemed more startled than pained, and fell over dead.

"My God!" Peterson panted. "Meat!"

The boar was almost as scrawny as the prisoners who'd slain it. Hunger must have made it chance the camp, just as the POWs' hunger had made them attack it. More men ran up behind Peterson.

By camp custom, the prisoners who'd done the actual killing got first crack at the carcass. Also by camp custom, they took less than they might have—enough to fill their bellies once, no more—and left the rest for their comrades who hadn't been quite so fast or quite so lucky.

Peterson toasted his chunk of meat over a small fire. He wolfed it down, charred on the outside and blood-rare—close enough to raw to make no difference—inside. In happier times, people warned against pork that wasn't cooked all the way through. They talked about trichinosis. He couldn't have cared less. He would have eaten that pig knowing it had died of the black plague.

His stomach made astonished, and astonishing, noises. It wasn't used to such wealth. He had to gulp against nausea once or twice. Meat was rich fare after rice and nowhere near enough of it.

For a little while, the pins and needles in his extremities would ebb. Some of the men with wet beriberi would lose a little fluid from their limbs, and from their lungs. Their hearts wouldn't race quite so hard whenever they had to move. And then, until the next time a pig got desperate or unlucky enough to fall foul of the POWs, things would go back to the way they'd been before. You couldn't win. The most you could do was stretch the game out a little.

"By God, I've done that," he muttered. He slept better than he had in weeks. Too soon, though, his next shift came. It would have been killing work even with all the food he wanted all the time. As things were . . . As things were, by the time he finished, he wondered whether he'd stretched the game at all—and, if he had, whether he'd done himself any favors.

JANE ARMITAGE WEEDED HER TURNIPS AND POTATOES with painstaking care. Weeds grew as enthusiastically as everything else in Hawaii. She chopped and dug and chopped and dug, and didn't notice Tsuyoshi Nakayama coming up behind her till he spoke.

"Oh. Hello!" she said, hoping she didn't sound as startled as she felt. "What can I do for you?" Nakayama might have been a gardener before Hawaii changed hands. He was still a gardener, in fact, and a damn good one. But, because he was Major Hirabayashi's liaison man, he was also a major power in Wahiawa these days. You had to be careful around him.

"You don't have husband, do you?" he asked now.

Ice avalanched along Jane's spine. Had somebody else seen Fletch? Had somebody ratted on her to the Japs? Could you trust anybody at all these days? It sure didn't seem that way. "I'm not married," she said firmly, and thanked heaven she'd taken off her wedding ring as soon as she threw Fletch out of the apartment. It would have made a liar of her on the spot.

"You don't have husband, even in the Army?" Yosh Nakayama persisted.

"I'm not married," Jane said again. And the divorce would have been final by now—would have been final long since—if everything in Hawaii hadn't gone to hell the second the Japs came ashore.

"You sure?" Nakayama said.

"I'm sure." If she had to, she'd show him the papers she did have. They ought to be convincing enough, even if the final interlocutory decree hadn't been formally granted. (She wondered why they called it that. It was the decree that meant people *weren't* interlocked any more.)

The gardener who was also right-hand man to the occupiers' local commandant grunted. If that wasn't an inscrutable noise, Jane had never heard one. Nakayama said, "Maybe you should be careful for a while. You have family you can go to?"

Jane shook her head. "I just moved here a few years ago." She wished she could have the words back. They didn't quite scream that she'd come to Wahiawa as part of a military family, but that was the way to bet.

Another grunt from Yosh Nakayama. "You go somewhere else for a while? Honolulu? Waimea? Anywhere?"

She had no travel documents. She thought about what was likely to happen if she ran into a column of Jap soldiers when she didn't—or even when she did. More ice formed under her skin. "I'm staying right here."

He sighed this time instead of grunting. "If I get you papers, will you go?"

If she left, she would have to walk. The thought she'd had a moment before came back. How much good would papers do her? "No, thanks, Mr. Nakayama," she said. He'd never been *Mr. Nakayama* before the war. If she talked to him at all then, she called him *Yosh*. How could it be otherwise? She was a white woman, after all, and he was just a Jap.

Now she knew how it could be otherwise. She knew, all right, and wished she didn't.

Yosh Nakayama let out another sigh. She had the feeling he was washing his hands of her. But no, for he said, "You change your mind, you let me know right away. Right away, you hear?"

"Yes, Mr. Nakayama." Before the war, she would have added *chop-chop*, pidgin for pronto. Never mind that Nakayama didn't use pidgin, but real English—slow, sometimes clumsy, but real English. She would have said it just to keep him in his place, in her mind and in his.

He shrugged his broad shoulders now. He must have known she didn't intend to do anything of the sort. Off he went, shaking his head. She returned to weeding, but the worm of worry wouldn't leave. He'd been trying to tell her something. Whatever it was, she hadn't got the message.

The next morning, she was about to go out to the vegetable plot again when someone knocked on the door. She opened it—and found herself facing three Japanese soldiers, two privates and a noncom. "You—Jane Armitage?" In the noncom's mouth, her name was barely comprehensible.

She thought about denying it, but decided she couldn't. "Yes. What is it?"

He spoke in Japanese. The two privates lunged with their bayonets, the points stopping inches from her face. She yelped and hopped back. "You come," the sergeant said.

Jane yelped again. "I haven't done anything!" *Fletch. God help me, they must know about Fletch.*

"You come," the Jap repeated. Maybe he didn't understand what she said. Maybe—more likely—he didn't care.

Since the other choice was getting killed on the spot, Jane came. The Japanese soldiers marched her about four blocks to another apartment building, one that had stood empty since Wahiawa fell. Now it had bars on the windows and guards out in front. A sign in Japanese said something Jane couldn't read.

Three or four other parties of Japanese soldiers were also coming up to the place. Each of them had a woman with it. All the women were in their twenties or thirties. All but one were white; the other was Chinese. All of them were prettier than average. A horrid suspicion flowered in Jane. "What is this place?" she demanded.

"You come." The noncom pointed to the front door. He'd used just about all the English he had. The soldiers prodded her with the bayonets. She didn't think they drew blood, but she didn't think they would hesitate—at anything—if she balked, either. She took an involuntary step. They prodded her again, and she went inside.

Eight or ten more women already crowded the lobby, along with an equal number of soldiers to make sure they didn't go anywhere. Jane's fear grew.

Maybe this didn't have anything to do with Fletch after all, but that wasn't necessarily good news. Oh, no, not even a little bit.

*Yosh was trying to warn me. Sweet Jesus, he told me to get lost, and I didn't
listen to him.* And what was she liable to get for being stupid? In the old days,
they'd called this a fate worse than death. To her, the phrase had always been
one from bad melodrama. Now, suddenly, she understood just what it meant.
It wasn't so far wrong after all.

She looked around at her companions in misery. About half looked as terrified as she felt. They had to be the ones who'd added things up the same way
she had. The others just seemed confused. Ignorance, here, was liable to be
bliss—but not for long.

One of the Japs in the crowded lobby was a lieutenant she didn't remember
seeing before. "You will listen to me," he said in very good English. "It is not,
ah, convenient for Japanese soldiers in this part of Oahu to travel to Honolulu
for comfort and relaxation. So, we set up a comfort house here. You are chosen
to man this house."

His English might be good, but it wasn't perfect. *Manning* wasn't what the
Japs had in mind for them. What they did have in mind . . . Nobody could
keep any illusions any more. The women started screaming and cursing and
telling the lieutenant no in terms as certain as they could make them.

He let them yell for a minute or two, then spoke in Japanese to the soldiers by
him. They raised their rifles. As one man, they chambered a round. Those sharp
clicks pierced the din like a steak knife cutting tender, blood-rare prime rib. Even
at that dreadful moment, food came to the forefront of Jane's thoughts.

"Enough," the officer said. "If you do this, you will be well fed. The term of
service will be six months. You will not be liable again. If you do not . . ." He
shrugged. "If you do not, you will be . . . persuaded."

"I'd rather die!" one of the women shouted. She got the words out only a
split second before Jane would have.

With another shrug, the lieutenant barked an order in his own language.
Two soldiers handed their rifles to other men, then grabbed the woman,
threw her down on the floor, and started beating and kicking her. Her screams
and those of the other women filled the lobby. The Japanese seemed altogether indifferent.

They knew what they were doing, too. They inflicted the most pain they
could with the least real damage. When they finished, the woman lay there

crumpled and sobbing, but not too badly hurt. She was an object lesson, and a frighteningly good one.

After yet another order, the soldiers started taking women out of the lobby one by one. Some screamed and had hysterics. The Japs ignored that. Some tried to fight. The soldiers didn't put up with any nonsense. They grabbed the women's hands. If that didn't do the job, or if the women tried to kick, they beat them into submission. They didn't seem particularly malicious about it; they might have been dealing with restive horses.

When it came to be Jane's turn, she did her best to boot one of the Japs right in the balls. Her face must have given her away, because he laughed and hopped back and left her looking like a Rockette with her foot way up in the air. A second later, his buddy punched her in the jaw.

Had it been a prizefight, the referee would have stopped it and called it a TKO. She didn't fall down and she didn't pass out. But everything went blurry for a while after that. When the Japs hustled her along, her feet walked. Her will, her wits—they were somewhere far away.

She came back to herself sitting at the edge of a bed in a room with bars on the window. *I have to get out of here,* she thought, and hurried to the door. She was a little wobbly, and the side of her face hurt like hell, but she stayed on her pins. The door opened when she thumbed the latch. She hadn't been sure it would. But Japanese soldiers in the hallway leered at her when she stuck her head out. No way in hell she could get by them. She ducked back in a hurry.

Down the hall, a woman started to scream, and then another. A black, choking cloud of fear filled Jane. *I have to get away,* she thought again. What she thought she had to do and what she could do, though, were two horribly different things.

She'd just had the bright idea of using the bed for a barricade when the door opened. Too late again, just as she'd been too late figuring out what Yosh Nakayama was trying to tell her.

In strode the lieutenant who spoke English. "I decided I would start you out myself," he said, as if she ought to be honored.

"Why?" Jane whispered.

"We need comfort women," he answered. "And I liked your looks." He took a step toward her. "Let's get it over with, *neh*? Then you will know what you have to do."

"No," Jane said.

But it wasn't no. She screamed, too, adding to the chorus that had to make this building sound like one of the nastier suburbs of hell. She did her best to fight, too. Again, her best was nowhere near good enough. She took another shot to the jaw. This time, things did gray out for a little while. She came back to herself with her jeans on the floor and the Jap pumping away between her legs. That hurt, too—the pain was probably what brought her back. He didn't care if she screamed, but he slapped her when she tried to punch him.

A minute or a lifetime later, he grunted and shuddered and briskly pulled out of her. "Not bad," he said, getting to his feet and briskly doing up his trousers. "No, not bad at all."

Jane lay huddled on the bed. "Why?" she asked again. "What did I ever do to you?"

"You are the enemy," he answered. "You are the enemy, and you have lost. You do not ask why after that happens. It is part of war." He reached out and swatted her bare backside. "Maybe I will see you again." Away he went, as pleased with himself as any man is afterwards.

She lay there, trying to decide whether she wanted to kill every Jap in the world or just kill herself. When the door opened again, she gasped in horror and reached down with futile hands to try to cover herself. But the soldier who came in, although he stared and laughed, only stared and laughed. He carried a tray probably stolen from the elementary-school cafeteria. He set it down on the floor and went out.

Dully, Jane eyed it. It held more food and better food than she'd seen in months. The Jap lieutenant hadn't lied about that. For a little while, Jane didn't think she could eat. She wanted to throw up.

No matter what her mind wanted, she saw rice and vegetables in front of her. Almost without conscious thought, she found herself eating. The plate emptied in what seemed the blink of an eye. *The wages of sin are . . . lunch,* she thought, which went a long way toward telling her how punchy she was.

Food even came ahead of putting her pants back on. She was just starting to reach for the jeans when a noncom walked into the room. He laughed to find her half dressed, and gestured that she should lie down on the bed again.

"No," she said, even though he carried a bamboo stick like the ones the Jap guards used when they wanted to hurt POWs but didn't want to kill them. "I'm not going to just give it to you."

Maybe he spoke a little English. Maybe the look on her face told him she wouldn't cooperate. Either way, he did what he wanted to do. He whacked her with the stick again and again. She tried to grab it, but she couldn't. She screamed, but he ignored her. When she did her best to knee him in the crotch, he twisted to take it on the hip and slapped her in the face.

Before long, no matter how she fought, he was in her, slamming away to please himself without the faintest thought for her as anything but a piece of meat. When she thought he was distracted, she tried to bite him. Without missing a stroke, he jerked his shoulder back. Her teeth clicked on empty air. He smacked her again, and came in the same instant.

Out of the room he went, whistling one of the Japs' unmusical tunes. Jane lay on her back, his seed dribbling out of her onto the sheet. If she fought every man who came in here, she'd be dead in nothing flat. Part of her said that would be for the best, but she didn't want to die. She wanted to live till the Americans came back, and then to have her revenge.

If she just lay there and let them have her, maybe they wouldn't hit her. But could she do that without losing her mind? She had no idea of anything just then, except how many places she hurt and how disgusted with life she was.

"God damn you, Yosh," she muttered. "Why didn't you tell me what they wanted me for?" He'd probably been too embarrassed to come out and say it; middle-aged local Japanese were downright Victorian. But why, oh why, oh why, hadn't she taken the hint and lit out for the tall timber?

OSCAR VAN DER KIRK PACED HIS CROWDED little apartment like a tiger going back and forth in its cage. "For God's sake, will you cut that out?" Susie Higgins said. "You're making me nervous."

He did stop—for about thirty seconds. Then he was going back and forth again. "Something's happened to Charlie," he said.

Susie rolled her blue, blue eyes. "How can you tell?" she said in tones obviously intended for sweet reason. "He's a surf bum. He's even more of a surf bum than you are. He doesn't know today what he'll do tomorrow—and he doesn't care, either. If he disappears for a few days or a few weeks, so what? Maybe he's gone up to the north shore again or something."

"Not now." Oscar's dismissal of that was altogether automatic. "It'll be flatter than a pancake up there this time of year."

"Then he's got some other harebrained scheme going instead."

Oscar shook his head. "I don't think so. We were supposed to go out together this morning, but he didn't show. You can count on Charlie. If he says he'll be somewhere, he'll be there."

"Maybe a shark ate him."

"Maybe one did," Oscar answered. "You can joke. You don't go out there like I do. It doesn't happen very often, but it happens. Or maybe the Japs got him."

Susie snorted. "Why would the Japs want a half-breed surf-rider, for crying out loud? Get serious."

He didn't answer. He could think of some reasons. He'd had an encounter with an American sub skipper out there on the Pacific. Maybe Charlie Kaapu had, too, or with the crew of a flying boat, or. . . . Who could tell? Oscar had never said a word to anybody—Susie emphatically included—about his meeting. If Charlie had any brains, he would have kept his yap shut, too. The fewer people you told, the fewer people could blab. Living under the Japs had taught the people of Hawaii what living under the Nazis taught the people of France: keeping your head down, not drawing the occupiers' notice, was a damn good idea.

Charlie didn't even tell me anything, if there was anything to tell, Oscar thought. That hurt his feelings, even though he'd just gone through all the reasons keeping quiet was a good idea, and even though he hadn't told Charlie about the sub. Logic? None at all. At least he could laugh at himself for realizing it.

Susie was studying him. She'd never been to college—he wasn't sure she'd finished high school—but she was better at reading people than he was. "You've got that knight-in-shining-armor look on your face again," she said. "Don't do anything dumb, Oscar. You can end up dead. Easy."

"Me? Don't be silly." He laughed—uneasily. "Some knight. I'm just a surf bum myself—you said so. Besides, when did you ever see that look on me before?"

"When you took me in," Susie answered. "Oh, I knew what you wanted. Fair enough—that's the knight's reward. But a lot of people wouldn't have wanted to go on with it when things got tough. You did."

"You walked out on me," he reminded her.

"That wasn't on account of the Japs. We were driving each other squirrely," Susie said, which was true. She sent him a sidelong look. "But Charlie can't give you what I could—or he'd better not be able to, anyway."

His cheeks heated, as much in anger as in embarrassment. He was no fairy! If Susie didn't have reason to know that . . . Her eyes sparkled. She'd wanted to get under his skin, and she had. But he wasn't going to write Charlie off just because she'd annoyed him. Stubbornly, he said, "He's my buddy, darn it. I was going to go round his place, see if anybody knows anything, that's all. Safe as houses."

"And then you wake up," Susie said, which sounded a hell of a lot more caustic than *Yeah, sure.* She looked at him again. "I'm not going to be able to talk you out of it, am I?" She shook her head. "No, of course I'm not. You *do* have that look. Well, for Christ's sake be as careful as you can, you fool."

He managed a lopsided grin. "You say the sweetest things, babe. I didn't know you cared."

To his surprise—hell, to his amazement—she turned red this time. "Damn you, Oscar, sometimes you're an even bigger blockhead than usual," she muttered. He almost asked her what the devil she was talking about, but he had the feeling that would be letting her win, so he kept quiet.

When they went to bed that night, she reached for him before he could reach for her. She slid down and took him in her mouth till he was close to exploding, then straddled him and rode him like a racehorse. By the time she finished, he thought he'd just won the Kentucky Derby. She leaned forward to give him a kiss, her breasts pressing softly against his chest. "Wow!" he said sincerely.

"You've got something to remember me by, anyway," she said, "in case I never happen to see you again."

"I'll be fine," he said. Susie squeezed him and didn't answer. She'd already given him her opinion.

When morning came, she was out the door before him. Her job had regular hours, which he'd always despised. And she had to get over to Honolulu, while he only needed to wander over to the shabby part of Waikiki. Tourists, jammed hard against the beach, didn't think Waikiki had any shabby parts. The farther inland you went, though . . .

Charlie's apartment building made Oscar's seem like the Royal Hawaiian Hotel. On the mainland, stray dogs would have been sniffing at garbage on the corners in this kind of neighborhood. Here, they'd probably been caught and cooked and eaten. He didn't see any, anyhow.

A woman who looked as if she worked on Hotel Street came out of the building. "Hey!" Oscar called to her. "You seen Charlie any time lately?"

"Who wants to know?" She eyed him. "Oh, it's you. You hang around with him. Maybe you're okay." She stayed cagey, though. "How come you wanna know?"

"He owes me a bottle of *okolehao*," Oscar answered, which wasn't true but was plausible. With liquor imports from the mainland cut off, the stuff distilled from *ti* root was the best hooch around, and correspondingly important. You *would* want to find out about somebody who owed it to you.

"Yeah?" the woman said. Oscar knew what that hungry tone of voice meant: she wondered if it was still in Charlie's apartment. But her shoulders slumped as she went on, "I ain't seen him since the cops took him away night before last." Plainly, she figured that if the cops had him, they had his *okolehao*, too. Oscar would have bet the same way.

"The cops?" he said. "What do the cops want with Charlie? If you know him, you know he wouldn't hurt a fly." That wasn't a hundred percent true; when Charlie had a few too many, he'd get into bar fights. But even those were on the friendly side. He'd never ground a broken bottle into anybody's face or anything like that. Oscar didn't think he'd ever gone to jail for one.

"I don't know what's going on. I just mind my business." The woman dripped righteousness. By the way her eyes darted now here, now there, she also minded other people's business every chance she got. She said, "Maybe he couldn't pay his rent."

"Nah. They just throw your stuff out on the street then." Oscar spoke from experience. "Besides, he catches fish. Way things are now, that's a heck of a lot better than money."

"Beats me." The woman shrugged. "I gotta go, buddy. They come down on me like you wouldn't believe if I'm late." Away she went, hips working under her short dress.

"Cops?" Oscar scratched his head. Were they doing the Japs' work for them? Or had Charlie really gone and got himself in that kind of trouble? It didn't seem like him, but how could you be sure?

One way would be to go down to the police station and ask if you could bail him out. If the cops said yes, that would tell Oscar some of what he needed to find out. If, on the other hand, they said no . . . In that case, Oscar was liable to buy himself the same kind of trouble his friend had, whatever that was.

He remembered Susie's warning. He also—warmly—remembered her good-bye present. Did he want to take the chance of finding out what had happened to Charlie? It boiled down to, would Charlie take the chance for him? He knew the answer to that as soon as he formed the question.

Waikiki's police station was small and run down. The desk sergeant was a *hapa*-Hawaiian who even in these hard times seemed to overflow his chair. Oscar didn't suppose cops missed many meals, no matter what. If a local Japanese were on duty there, he didn't know what he would have done. But he did dare ask a man of Charlie Kaapu's blood what had happened to him.

The sergeant didn't answer right away. He looked at—looked through—Oscar. File cards riffled behind his impassive dark eyes. He no doubt knew who Oscar was, and that Oscar and Charlie ran around together. He might have needed to remind himself of that, but he knew. He said, "They've taken him to Honolulu." His voice, rough from years of two packs a day, revealed nothing.

"Why would they want to do that?" Oscar didn't have to fake astonishment. "What's he done? What do they think he's done? It can't be anything much—you know Charlie, don't you?"

"Sure." The cop looked through him again. "You want to spring him, right?"

"Well, of course I do," Oscar answered. "He's my pal. Can I bail him out? I'm not broke."

By the way the sergeant touched his pocket, he was going for cigarettes that weren't there. How many times had he made that gesture since Hawaii fell? From his sour expression, quite a few. "Bail him out?" he said. "I don't know about that. It, ah, isn't only the police that are interested in him."

"Who else?" Oscar knew he'd better sound naive. As if the idea were just occurring to him, he said, "The, uh, Japanese?" He'd better not say Japs around somebody who worked with them and, for all practical purposes, for them.

"That's right. He's been poking into places where he doesn't belong, sounds like," the policeman said. "So you can go there, but. . . ." His voice trailed away. He'd made the same calculation Oscar had before.

Oscar shivered. "Thanks, Sergeant," he said, and left the station in a hurry.

Into Honolulu? *Into Honolulu,* he decided, and started west. His knees weren't knocking, but he didn't know why not. He was scared green. He and Charlie had got caught in the crossfire between invading Japs and Americans right at the start of the war. He'd jumped into trenches when bombs fell not nearly far enough away. Going after his friend now, though, was consciously brave. *So this is what courage feels like,* he thought. *Not letting anybody, even me, see how frightened I am.*

Maybe it would be all right. Honolulu's police chief, still doing his job under the Japs, had come out from California not too long before the war to shape up a corrupt force, and he'd done it. The assistant chief was a full-blooded Hawaiian. Cops came from every piece in the jigsaw puzzle of nations that made up Hawaii. But if the occupiers said hop, the cops had to make like frogs.

The main station wasn't far from Honolulu Hale, the city hall. Typewriters clattered as Oscar went inside. He wondered how the police got new ribbons, or if they'd figured out a way to reink old ones.

By his looks, the desk sergeant here was at least *hapa*-Oriental. Japanese? Chinese? Korean? Oscar wasn't sure. The man's voice didn't give anything away as he asked, "What do you want, buddy?"

"You've got a friend of mine in jail," Oscar said. The sergeant raised an interrogative eyebrow. Not another muscle on his face moved. Reluctantly, Oscar named Charlie Kaapu.

That eyebrow jumped again, higher this time. Oscar wondered if the desk sergeant would yell for help, or if he'd just pull a gun and hold Oscar himself. But all he said was, "Sorry, you can't have him."

"How come? I couldn't believe he got jugged. He's the nicest guy you'd ever want to meet. What do they think he did, anyway?"

Instead of answering, the sergeant asked a question of his own: "Mac, you ever hear of the *Kempeitai?*"

Oscar shook his head. "Nope. What is it?"

"Japanese secret police. And now I'm going to do you the biggest favor anybody ever did: I'm not gonna ask you who you are. Get the hell out of here before I change my mind."

Oscar got. Once he was out of the station, he turned several corners as fast as he could, in case the sergeant did send police after him. But there was no sign of that. Oscar shivered. He hadn't learned much about winter in California or here—Susie laughed at how ignorant he was. But winter, winter unquestioned, dwelt in him now.

The *Kempeitai.* The name wasn't chilling the way, say, the *Gestapo* was—at least not to Oscar. But—secret police? It was bound to be the same kind of outfit. And it had Charlie. What *had* he done? What did they think he'd done? *What can I do to get him away?* Oscar wondered miserably. *Anything at all?*

CORPORAL TAKEO SHIMIZU HAD JUST FALLEN ASLEEP when an air-raid alarm bounced him from his cot. Wearing the thin cotton shirt and breech clout in which he'd gone to bed, he grabbed the rest of his uniform and his shoes and ran for the trenches outside the barracks hall. The Yankee marauders probably wouldn't come close, but nobody got old taking stupid chances.

Antiaircraft guns started going off. There were more of them in Honolulu these days than there had been. There needed to be more, for the Americans came over the city—and over Oahu generally—more often than they had. Machine guns started hammering, too. Tracers scribed ice-blue and yellow arcs across the sky. Through the din of gunfire, Shimizu heard the deep growl of a flying boat's engines, and then the roar of bombs going off.

Twenty minutes went by before the all-clear sounded. The guns had fired for most of that time, though the American plane was surely long gone. Shrapnel pattered down out of the sky. It might end up doing almost as much damage as the bombs.

Muttering in annoyance, Shimizu went back to bed. He hadn't been sleeping long before the air-raid sirens screeched again. *"Zakennayo!"* he said furiously. "Why doesn't the *baka yaro* in charge make up his mind?"

He found out why in short order: more U.S. aircraft were in the sky. One or two hit Honolulu, while a couple of others caused a commotion at Pearl Harbor. That meant another fireworks display off to the west.

What he wanted to see instead of more fireworks was a flying boat going down in flames. He didn't get what he wanted. After the usual delay, he did get to go back to bed.

An hour and a half later, a third wave of American planes came over Honolulu. By then, he was so tired he wanted to stay in the barracks even though the building would fall down on him if it got hit. Shouts from officers got him moving. Shouts from him helped get the men moving.

Huddling in the trench, Yasuo Furusawa said, "They want to keep us from sleeping."

"They know how to get what they want, don't they?" Shimizu growled. The

Americans weren't doing a lot of damage. They couldn't, not coming over in handfuls. But they had all the Japanese in Honolulu—maybe all the Japanese on Oahu—jumping around like fleas on a hot griddle.

He wondered if yet another set of U.S. aircraft would hit Honolulu just before dawn. None did, but a nervous gunner not far from the barracks opened up on something apparently imaginary. The gunfire didn't wake Shimizu. Shards of steel crashing down on the roof did. He went to sleep again after that, too, which proved he was made of stern—and very tired—stuff.

Getting up at dawn did nothing to improve his mood. The tea he gulped with his breakfast of rice and pickled plums didn't do nearly enough to pry his eyelids apart. He couldn't get more, either. It came from the home islands, which meant it was in short supply. That he could have any at all meant a freighter must have made it in not long before. Only officers got all they wanted.

Some officers shared the precious stuff with their men, using it as a reward for duty well performed. Unfortunately, neither Shimizu's platoon leader nor company commander seemed to have thought of that. It was going to be a sleepy, stupid day.

His squad dragged, too. Even Shiro Wakuzawa, who ordinarily was perky as you please, dragged and slumped. He said, "If the Americans do that every night, they'll drive us crazy."

"They can't do it every night." As usual, Senior Private Furusawa sounded surer of himself than his rank gave him any right to be.

"Why not?" Shimizu said, and yawned. "They've been doing it more and more lately."

Furusawa yawned, too, but politely turned his head away from his superior before he did. "But they need submarines to refuel their flying boats," he said. "They don't have planes that can make a round trip from their mainland to Hawaii. Even ours have trouble, and they're better."

"How did you hear all that?" Shimizu demanded.

"I listen a lot. I keep my head down. I keep my ears open. People who know things like to blab."

"I suppose so." Shimizu wasn't sure he would understand things even if he heard them. He was just a farmer's son. Furusawa, a city man, had the education to make sense of what came his way.

So why are you commanding him and not the other way around? Shimizu wondered. But that had an answer he understood. Experience and toughness mattered more in rank than education did.

Still, education—or maybe just raw brains—also came in handy. For three or four nights, American flying boats stayed away. But then they returned, little wave after little wave, disrupting the lives of the Japanese stationed in and around Honolulu. Shimizu really started to hate them then. He had a certain amount of trouble not hating Senior Private Furusawa, too.

COMMANDER MINORU GENDA STEPPED UP OVER THE STEEL doorsill and into the cabin that belonged to *Akagi*'s skipper. Saluting, he said, "Reporting as ordered, sir," and then, "Congratulations on your promotion."

Rear Admiral Tomeo Kaku bowed in his chair. "Thank you very much," he said, even his hard features unable to hide his pleasure. "Why don't you shut the door and then sit down? I have news you need to know."

Asking Genda to close the cabin off from the corridor meant it was secret news. Excitement and curiosity building in him, he obeyed. He wanted to sit on the edge of the seat, but deliberately sat back, making himself seem relaxed even—especially—if he wasn't. Keeping his voice as casual as he could, he asked, "What's up, sir?"

"*Zuikaku* is finally on her way back to these waters," Kaku answered, sounding pleased with himself and with the world. "The decoded message came to me not ten minutes ago. You're the first to know."

"*Domo arigato.*" Genda bowed more deeply than his superior had. "I'm very glad to hear it. About time, too, if you don't mind my saying so. They took longer repairing her than they should have."

"I agree," Admiral Kaku said. "I've growled and fussed and fumed more times than I can tell you, and it's done me no good at all. *Shigata ga nai.*" Genda nodded at that—some things *couldn't* be helped. Kaku continued, "But she's on her way at last, and she'll be here in a couple of weeks. I'd hoped they would send us *Taiho,* too, but they say she'll be shaking down for months yet." With a shrug, he repeated, "*Shigata ga nai.*"

"Too bad, sir. We could use her." Genda sighed. Everything he'd heard about *Taiho* said how much they could use her here. Among other improvements, she boasted an armored flight deck—a first for a Japanese carrier—that was supposed to protect her vitals from a 450kg bomb. Genda added, "We could use any more carriers they want to send us, big or small. The Americans are definitely getting friskier."

"I don't know what you're talking about," Kaku said, deadpan. He was so perfectly deadpan, in fact, that Genda started to believe him. Then *Akagi*'s skipper yawned a yawn that threatened to split his face in two. The Americans' nuisance raids were more than a nuisance for him. The carrier anchored at different places in Pearl Harbor every night, to give the U.S. flying boats a harder time finding and hitting her. So far, it had worked; she'd taken only incidental damage from near misses. But Admiral Kaku had to be up on the bridge whenever she was threatened. He wasn't a young man; that lack of sleep must take a toll on him.

"It's not just here, either," Genda said. "They're starting to attack our picket boats every chance they get."

"Yes, I've heard that, too." Now Kaku sounded serious, and not at all happy. "They think they can clear them out and give themselves a better chance for surprise."

"That's how it looks to me, sir." Genda also thought the Americans might be right. Japan sent out new sampans when old ones were lost, but there were always delays and foulups. The Americans might be able to build a lane through which they could get ships close to Hawaii undetected.

"I've talked with Commander Fuchida. He's talked with the people who handle our H8Ks," Admiral Kaku said. "We *will* have flying-boat patrols to cover the area no matter what. We won't get caught napping."

"That's good, sir," Genda agreed. "And the more radar sets we can get our hands on, the better. They can see farther than the naked eye can."

"I suppose so. All these gadgets," Kaku said fretfully. "It wasn't like this when my career started out, let me tell you. In those days, you really had to be able to see the enemy to hit him. None of this business of sending airplanes over the horizon to drop bombs on his head."

"Yes, sir. I've heard Admiral Yamamoto say the same thing." Genda hoped that would keep his superior happy. The difference was that Kaku sounded nostalgic for days gone by, while Isoroku Yamamoto always lived in the present—when he wasn't looking into the future. Of course, there was only one Yamamoto, which was why he commanded the Combined Fleet. Men like Kaku were absolutely necessary, but were also easier to come by.

"Admiral Yamamoto," *Akagi*'s skipper echoed musingly. "If it weren't for Admiral Yamamoto, we wouldn't be where we are now." That was true. Of course, it was also true that the Japanese wouldn't have been where they were if not for Genda himself. He was the one who'd persuaded Yamamoto to follow the air strike against Oahu with an invasion. Rear Admiral Kaku seemed unlikely to be in a position to know that. He went on, "I wonder if we would be better off if we hadn't landed. We wouldn't be stuck at the end of such a long supply line, anyhow."

"*Hai,*" Genda said, and let it go at that. As soon as he could, he excused himself and went out onto the flight deck. He found he needed fresh air. Even now, the waters of Pearl Harbor stank of fuel oil spilled in the attack a year and a half earlier. Its rainbow gleam fouled patches of what should have been blue tropical sea.

He reminded himself that Kaku was a good carrier officer. That was true regardless of whether the older man understood grand strategy. Genda remained convinced that, if Japan hadn't gone for the United States with everything she had, the Americans would have come after her the same way. With Hawaii under the Rising Sun—or even (he smiled) under its own flag once more—the USA didn't have the chance. To him, that counted for everything in the world.

Thinking of Hawaii under its own flag once more made him think of King Stanley Laanui. And thinking of King Stanley made him think of Queen Cynthia, a much more enjoyable prospect. *I need to find an excuse to get over to Iolani Palace,* he told himself. Even if it meant conferring with General Yamashita, he needed to go over there.

She hadn't so much as kissed him. He had no assurance she would. Then again, he had no assurance she wouldn't, either. One of these days soon, he intended to find out.

If she wouldn't? If she raised a fuss? The worst they could do to him was send him home. He was sure of that. And odds were they wouldn't even do so much, not with the next fight against the U.S. Navy plainly right around the corner.

VII

HARRY TURTLEDOVE

"THIS IS STUPID, OSCAR." REAL ALARM RODE SUSIE HIGGINS' VOICE. "YOU'RE going to get yourself killed, and you're going to land everybody who ever heard of you in hot water."

"Which bothers you more?" Oscar van der Kirk asked.

"You think I want the Japs breathing down my neck, you're nuts." Susie was one hard-headed gal.

Oscar couldn't even say Charlie Kaapu hadn't done anything. He didn't know that, not for sure. From what the police sergeant in Honolulu said, the Japs sure as hell thought he had. The *Kempeitai* . . . The more he repeated the name to himself, the scarier it sounded. Would they knock on his door in the middle of the night, the way the *Gestapo* was supposed to do?

"I'm just going to spread some fish around," Oscar said. "The way things are these days, food works better than cash."

"You can't even talk to the Japs," Susie said, which was largely true. "How are you going to get them to do what you want? They won't even know who you're trying to spring."

He made money-counting motions. He couldn't very well make fish-counting motions; there weren't any. "I'll manage," he said with more confidence than he felt. "Besides, they're bound to be using local clerks and such. Somebody will understand me. If you're trying to give somebody something, people always understand you."

Not even Susie tried to argue with that. She only said, "You'll get into more trouble than you know what to do with."

"You said the same thing when I went to the police station," Oscar reminded her.

She wasn't impressed. "Okay, you were lucky once. How come you think you'll be lucky twice?"

That was a better question than Oscar wished it were. Trying to make light of it, he said, "Hey, I'm lucky all the time, babe. I've got you, don't I?"

Susie turned red. She was a lot tanner than she had been when the war left her stuck in the middle of the Pacific, but the flush was still easy to see. "Damn you, Oscar, why do you have to go and say stuff like that?" she said angrily.

"Because I mean it?" he suggested.

She turned even redder. Then, very suddenly, she jumped up and dashed into the apartment's tiny bathroom. She stayed in there for quite a while, and didn't flush before she came out. Her eyes were suspiciously bright. She wagged a finger at him the way his mother had when he was four years old. "You know, it's funny."

"What is?" Oscar said. Whatever she'd been doing in there, it sure as hell wasn't laughing.

"First time I saw you, before you ever touched me or took me out on that surfboard or anything, I knew I was going to go to bed with you," she answered. "I wanted to get the taste of Rick out of my mouth as fast as I could." Rick was the ex-husband whose becoming ex- her trip to Hawaii had celebrated. She wagged that finger again. "And don't you dare say anything about getting the taste of you in my mouth."

"Me? I didn't say anything," Oscar answered as innocently as he could, though she'd done that, all right. He'd slept with a lot of women getting over their exes in a tropical paradise. That was one of the things a surf-riding instructor—a surf bum—was for.

"Oh, yes, you did." Susie sounded fierce. "You said something sweet. Going to bed with you is easy. The hard part is thinking I might . . ."

"Might what?"

"Might love you," she said in a tiny voice.

"Oh." Oscar went over to her and put an arm around her. "You know what, kiddo? I might love you, too. You know what else? I think we ought to wait and see what happens before we do anything. If it looks like the Japs'll win and keep this place, then we know where we are. If the Americans come and take it back, then we know where we are, too. Right now, it's just a mess. How can we make plans if we don't know what the heck to plan for?"

"How can we make plans if you go sticking your head in the lion's mouth?" But Susie clung to him as if he were a surfboard and the shore a long, long way away.

He kissed her. But then he said, "I've got to do it, hon. Nobody else is gonna give a darn about Charlie, but he's my friend."

She took a deep breath. Had she said, *If you loved me . . .* , they would have had a row. A few months earlier, she probably would have. Now she swallowed it instead. "I'm not going to be able to talk you out of this, am I?"

"Nope."

"Well, I'll be here if you come back, that's all." She didn't wag a finger at him this time—she poked him in the ribs. "Now I suppose you'll expect another fancy sendoff. Won't you, bub? Huh? Won't you?" She poked him again.

"Who, me?" Oscar hoped he didn't sound like somebody about to drool on the shoes he wasn't wearing. Susie laughed at him, so he probably did. Later that night, they emphatically enjoyed each other's company. Oscar slept soundly.

He went to Honolulu Hale the next morning. Life went on under the Japanese. People got married. They bought and sold property. They paid taxes on it. They got peddler's licenses. They sued one another. Most of the clerks who'd worked for the U.S. Territory of Hawaii went right on working for the Japanese Kingdom of Hawaii.

There was a new department, though. SPECIAL CASES, the sign above the door said. It wasn't quite *All hope abandon, ye who enter here,* but it might as well have been. Several people in other, safer queues looked up, startled, when Oscar walked through that door. A little old woman who seemed *hapa*-Hawaiian and maybe *hapa*-Chinese made the sign of the cross.

A clerk who might have been of the same blood glanced up from the papers on his government-issue desk. The nameplate on the desk said he was Alfred Choi. He gave a good game impression of never letting anything take him by surprise. "Yes?" he said. "You wish?"

"I have a friend who's been, uh, jailed. I don't think he's done anything, and I want to help him get out if I can," Oscar said.

"This is for the police, or for a lawyer," Alfred Choi said. Oscar unhappily shook his head. Choi looked at him, as if noting the door through which he'd come. "This man, this friend"—he made it sound like a dirty word—"has some connection to the occupying authorities?"

"Uh-huh," Oscar admitted, even less happily than he'd nodded before.

"Give me his name."

"Charlie Kaapu." Oscar wondered if Choi was going to press a secret button that sent a dozen *Kempeitai* men with pistols and samurai swords charging into the room. Nothing like that happened. The clerk got up, walked to a four-drawer filing cabinet about ten feet away, and went through the third drawer for a minute or so.

When he came back, his face was grim. "You can do nothing," he said. "I can do nothing. No one can do anything. The occupying authorities have dealt with him."

"Is he—dead?" Oscar didn't want to say the word, or even think it.

Alfred Choi shook his head. "Not yet," he said, which didn't sound good.

Maybe he was trying to put on the squeeze. Oscar hoped so; that was better than the alternative. Picking his words with care, Oscar said, "I catch a lot of fish—more than I need, sometimes."

"I have enough to eat, thank you," Choi said. "I could take fish from you. I could, ah, string you along." He used the slang self-consciously. "But since I have enough, I tell you straight out: I cannot do anything for your friend. Nobody can do anything for your friend. His case is *pau*." The Hawaiian word for *finished,* in common use in the islands, sounded dreadfully final here.

"Could I talk to anybody else?" Oscar asked.

"Do you *want* the *Kempeitai* to talk to you?" Alfred Choi sounded abstractly curious, as if he didn't give a damn one way or the other. He likely didn't. It was no skin off his rather flat nose.

"I guess maybe not," Oscar said reluctantly.

"I guess maybe not, too. This is wise." The clerk pointed to the door. "You leave through the door you came in by."

Oscar left through that door. Some of the people in the wider hall onto which SPECIAL CASES opened looked surprised anyone was allowed to leave. He decided he'd done everything he could possibly do for Charlie Kaapu. He wished he knew what Charlie had done, or what the Japs thought he'd done. And he wished he knew what they'd done to him.

* * *

THE MEMORY OF HALF-RAW, half-burnt pork was just that—a memory—for Jim Peterson these days. He was back to not so slowly starving on the usual Kalihi Valley rations, back to working himself to death too many inches at a time.

He stood in the rain for morning roll call. The Japs who did the counting had umbrellas, of course. The POWs? The mere idea was a joke. Peterson hoped the count would go smoothly. If it didn't, the Japs would probably just send the whole gang of them into the tunnel without breakfast. Prisoners starving? So what? Time lost on the tunnel? A catastrophe!

Things seemed to be moving well enough when there was a commotion to the southwest. The Japanese had the escape route well blocked off. Every once in a while, a POW grew desperate enough to try it anyway. Those who did usually got caught. Then they served as object lessons for the others. Watching them tortured to death a little at a time had given Jim Peterson more than one of his many nightmares.

This wasn't an escaped prisoner. These were new damned souls, come to take their places in hell. Along with his fellow sufferers, Peterson stared at the newcomers. "They aren't soldiers," somebody behind him said through the patter and plink of raindrops.

The man was obviously right. Instead of wearing tatters of khaki or Navy blue, they wore tatters of blue jeans and plaid or flowered shirts. Just because they were civilians didn't mean they hadn't seen their fair share of abuse and then some. They were bruised and battered and beaten. Quite a few of them limped. A lot of them had bloody mouths. They showed missing front teeth that obviously hadn't been missing long.

One of the Japs herding them forward smashed a fellow who looked half Hawaiian in the head with a rifle butt for no reason Peterson could see. The man staggered and groaned, but stayed on his feet. Peterson thought that blow would have felled an elephant. But the Japs had also put him in places where you died if you went down. This looked like one of those places for the luckless prisoner.

Somebody not far away muttered, "Look how fat they are."

They weren't fat, not really. Not even the Japanese guards, with a couple of exceptions, were fat. But they had vastly more flesh on them than the filthy, bearded skeletons already laboring in the Kalihi Valley.

Shouts in Japanese went back and forth between the soldiers bringing in the new prisoners and the guards in charge of the men already there. Those guards seemed about as delighted to see the new arrivals as a housewife would have been to find more mice marching into her kitchen.

Peterson knew why, too, or at least one of the reasons why. "If this doesn't fuck up the count . . ." he said morosely. Several men standing within earshot of him groaned. A Jap guard looked their way. They all pretended they hadn't let out a peep. After a baleful stare right out of a gangster movie, the guard looked away.

By a minor-league miracle, the new prisoners didn't foul up the count too badly. Shouting in fragmentary English, the Japs got them to line up in ranks of ten. That told the guards how many of them there were. Then the Japs went back to counting the POWs already there. They only needed to do it twice before the answer satisfied them.

Breakfast wouldn't have been more than fifteen minutes late. To the Japs, that was fifteen minutes too long. Despite groans and curses from the POWs, they headed them off toward the tunnel mouth. Curses and groans didn't count for much against fit men, fixed bayonets, and live ammunition.

The Japs drove the newcomers toward the mouth of the tunnel, too. The new fish didn't complain. They didn't know they were missing breakfast, and they didn't know what the devil they were getting into, either. "Wonder what the hell they did to get sent here," Peterson remarked.

"Must've been something juicy," Gordy Braddon said. After a meditative moment, he added, "They're the first batch of civilians ever came here. Japs must want 'em dead bad."

"Yeah—same as us," Peterson said tightly. Braddon nodded.

"What are we doing here?" asked the big half-Hawaiian guy the Jap had clouted with his rifle butt. Blood and rainwater ran down the side of his face. If he noticed, he didn't let on.

"Digging a tunnel through the mountains." Peterson found himself liking the newcomer's coolness. He added his name and stuck out a hand.

"Jim," the newcomer repeated, taking it. "I'm Charlie—Charlie Kaapu." His grip was hard and firm. Why not? He didn't have beriberi taking bites out of his strength. Not yet, anyway. If he stayed here very long, he would.

"What did you do that made 'em love you well enough to send you to this garden spot?" Peterson asked.

"Some garden," Charlie said, and laughed a loud, raucous laugh, the laugh of a man who couldn't be beaten—or at least of a man who didn't know he could. He went on, "They say I was spying for the United States."

"Yeah? Were you?" Peterson didn't ask the question. A fellow named Seymour Harper did. Peterson wasn't the only one who suspected him of snitching to the Japs, though nobody'd ever been able to nail that down for sure.

A couple of men coughed. That was about as much warning as they could give the new guy without landing in trouble themselves. It wasn't enough, not really. But Charlie Kaapu turned out not to need it. He started to shake his head, then grimaced and thought better of it. "Shit, no," he answered. "What really happened was, this Jap major's girlfriend thought I was better in bed than he was." He laughed again, complacently. "You know these Japs ain't nothin' but a bunch of needle dicks. But she got mad at him one day and told him what she thought, and the motherfucker went and grabbed me—or he had the cops do it, anyway."

Gordy Braddon said, "You had more fun getting here than we did, that's for goddamn sure." Peterson found himself nodding. He found himself smiling, too, and that wasn't something he did every day, not in the Kalihi Valley it wasn't.

Charlie was smiling, too, which only proved he'd just got here. "So how do we dig this stinking tunnel?"

They rounded the last bend in the road in front of the tunnel mouth. Jungle no longer hid the hole in the mountainside or the sorry collection of hand tools in front of it. The tools would rust in the rain, but the Japs didn't care. If a tool broke, that gave them one more excuse to take it out on a prisoner. Peterson pointed at the picks and shovels and crowbars. "Now you see it, Charlie—Devil's Island, 1943."

"Oh, boy." The half-Hawaiian started singing, "Heigh-ho, heigh-ho, it's off to work I go" in a melodious baritone. Peterson had seen *Snow White*, too—who hadn't?—but he hadn't felt like singing since he got here. He still didn't.

Inside the tunnel, torches and kerosene lamps gave just enough light to move and work by. There had been candles and lamps that burned palm oil or something like that. No more. POWs stole them to eat the tallow and drink the oil.

"You work!" If a Jap overseer was going to know any English, that was it. This one, a sergeant, brandished a length of bamboo to make sure the prisoners got the message. At one time or another, he'd already walloped everybody but the new fish at least twice.

In a low voice, Peterson said, "We don't go any faster than we have to."

Charlie Kaapu's shadow swooped and dipped along the rough black basalt of the tunnel wall as he nodded. "No *huhu,* Jim," he answered. "I get it."

But he and the rest of the newcomers still did a lot more work than any of the POWs who'd been there for a while. That wasn't because they were more diligent—Jim Peterson thought they'd all got the message about not pushing too hard. With the worst will in the world toward the Japs, though, they couldn't help themselves. They were so many Charles Atlases alongside the skeletally thin, malnourished prisoners of war. Of course a man with real muscles could outdo somebody who had nothing left between his skin and his bones.

After an eternity, the shift ended. Charlie Kaapu had got hit a couple of more times for not working fast enough to suit the guards. "You did good," Peterson told him as they stumbled back toward the camp and what would be their meager evening meal.

"Oh, yeah?" Charlie said. "How long till I look like you?"

Peterson had no real answer for that, but he knew it wouldn't be long.

ACCOMPANIED BY A PAIR of stalwart petty officers, Commander Mitsuo Fuchida bicycled through the streets of Honolulu. The petty officers weren't so much bodyguards as men who could get out in front of him and yell, "Gangway!" to clear traffic. Most places, he would have gone by car, and his driver would have leaned on the horn. That he didn't here was a telling measure of how tight fuel had got in Honolulu.

Panting a little, he stopped in front of the building where Minoru Genda had his office—stopped so abruptly that his tires drew black lines on the pale concrete of the sidewalk. "Wait for me," he told the petty officers. "I won't be very long." They nodded and saluted.

Fuchida charged up the stairs to Genda's office—and then had to charge down again when a young officer said, "So sorry, Commander-*san,* but he's not here this morning. He's gone to Iolani Palace."

"*Zakennayo!*" Fuchida snarled.

When he turned to go without another word, the junior officer said, "Sir, you're welcome to use a telephone here to call him."

"I'd better go see him," Fuchida said. If he'd wanted to telephone Genda, he

could have done it from Pearl Harbor. Some things, though, were too important to trust to wires—or to junior officers. The youngster raised an eyebrow.
When Fuchida ignored him, he sighed and went back to work.

"That *was* fast, sir," one of the petty officers remarked when Fuchida
emerged from the building.

"We're not done yet—that's why," Fuchida answered. "Genda-*san*'s not
here. We've got to head back west, over to Iolani Palace. Run interference again
for me, if you'd be so kind."

"Yes, sir," they chorused. If they sounded resigned, then they did, that was
all. What choice had they but obedience? None, and they knew it as well as
Fuchida did. They got back onto their bicycles and started bellowing, "Gangway!" some more. That, at least, seemed as if it ought to be fun. The way civilians scattered before them clearly declared who the conquerors were.

Fuchida skidded to another stop in front of the palace. The big Hawaiian
soldiers at the bottom of the front stairs came to attention and saluted as he
hurried by them. So did the Japanese troops at the top of the stairs. He paused
for a moment to ask them, "Where's Commander Genda?"

They looked at one another with expressions he found unfathomable. After
a longish pause, their sergeant said, "Is it very urgent, sir?"

"You bet your life it's urgent!" Fuchida exclaimed. "Would I be here like this
if it weren't?"

Stolidly, the noncom gave back a shrug. "You never can tell, can you, sir?
You'll likely find him in the basement."

"The basement?" Fuchida echoed in surprise. The Japanese soldiers nodded
as one. Fuchida had assumed Genda was here to talk with General Yamashita,
who had his office on the second floor. Admiral Yamamoto had used a basement office here, but the commander of the Combined Fleet was long since
back in Japan.

To make things more annoying, the front entrance didn't offer access to the
basement. Fuming, Fuchida had to go down the stairs, past the Hawaiian soldiers again, and pedal around the palace so he could go downstairs into the
lower level. What the devil was Genda doing here? And *where* in the basement
was he likely to be? That damned sergeant hadn't said.

Hawaiian bureaucrats were using some of the rooms down there. Fuchida
prowled past those. The brown men—and the white—gave him curious
looks; since Admiral Yamamoto departed, Japanese officers were seldom

seen down here. He looked into those open rooms, and did not see Commander Genda.

Fuming, he yanked open the first door to a windowless room he found—and almost got buried by an avalanche of dustpans and brooms and other cleaning gear. The Americans called a place like that *Fibber McGee's closet*; Fuchida thought the phrase came from a radio show.

He went down the hall and tried another closed door. This time, he was rewarded by a whiff of perfume, a startled female gasp, and a muttered obscenity. He shut the door in a hurry, but he didn't go away—the obscenity had been in Japanese.

Maybe I'm wrong, he thought. But he wasn't. Commander Genda came out of the small, dark room a couple of minutes later, still hastily setting his uniform to rights. He looked put upon. "What wouldn't wait till I got back to the office?" he demanded irritably.

"Nothing I can talk about till we're out of this place," Fuchida said, and then, with irritation of his own, "If you have to lay one of the maids here, couldn't you do it when you're not on duty?"

Genda didn't talk about *that* till they were out of Iolani Palace. Even then, he waved the petty officers who'd come along with Fuchida out of hearing range before saying, "I'm not laying one of the palace maids. I'm laying Queen Cynthia."

"Oh, Jesus Christ!" Fuchida had, from time to time, thought of converting to Christianity. That wasn't what brought out the oath, though. A lot of Japanese who'd been exposed to Western ways used it whether they took the religion of Jesus seriously or not.

"You're my friend. I hope you'll keep your mouth shut. Life would get more . . . more complicated if you didn't," Genda said: a commendable understatement. Occupying the islands was one thing, occupying King Stanley Laanui's wife something else again. Fuchida could imagine nothing better calculated to show what a false and useless regime the restored Kingdom of Hawaii really was. Before he could express his horror, Genda asked, "And what's the news that made you come over here and hunt me down? By the Emperor, it had better be important."

That brought Fuchida back from disasters hypothetical to disasters altogether too real. He also made sure the petty officers couldn't overhear before he answered, "The Americans put two fish into *Zuikaku* a couple of hours ago."

"What? That's impossible!" Genda exclaimed. Sadly, Fuchida shook his head. Genda went on more moderately: "That's terrible!" Fuchida could and did nod. "How did it happen? Will she sink?" Genda asked.

"How? They don't know how. They were getting close to Oahu, and *wham!*" Fuchida said. "They don't think she'll go down—she hasn't lost power, and the pumps are working. But she's not going to sail against the Americans with *Akagi* and *Shokaku,* either. She's limping in to Pearl Harbor for emergency repairs, and she may have to go back to Japan again."

"How could the Americans have got a sub in the right place to torpedo her?" Genda wasn't really asking Fuchida—he was asking an uncaring world.

Fuchida only shrugged. "Dumb luck," he said. *"Shigata ga nai."*

"Obviously it can't be helped," Genda said. "It wouldn't have happened if it could be. But I'll tell you something, Fuchida-*san*: it almost makes me wonder if the Yankees are reading our codes."

"What?" That shocked Fuchida almost as much as Genda's dalliance with the redheaded Queen of Hawaii. "Don't be silly. Everyone knows our codes are unbreakable."

"Well, yes." That Genda admitted the fact did a lot to ease Fuchida's mind. "Dreadful news, though. *Zuikaku!* We could really use her, because the Americans *are* building up for another go at us. That gets plainer every day."

"We'll be able to fly the planes off the airstrips here. . . ." Fuchida began.

Genda was a small man, and usually a mild-mannered man as well. His scowl now stopped Fuchida in his tracks. "The only way that will do us any good is if we lose the fight on the ocean. I don't want to lose the fight on the ocean," he said. "I presume we've already screamed to Tokyo that we need more carriers?"

"Oh, yes," Fuchida said. "Whether Tokyo will listen is probably a different story, though. They keep going on and on about how thin their resources are stretched."

"Our resources won't have to stretch so far if we lose Hawaii, that's for sure," Genda snapped. "Can't they see that?"

"We need more carriers. We need more trained pilots," Fuchida said. "The Americans seem to turn out as many as they want. Why can't we?"

"Admiral Yamamoto always said we couldn't hope to match them," Genda replied. "That was the main reason we gambled so much in this attack: so what they could do wouldn't matter." He sighed. "But it turns out that it *does* matter. It's just taken longer to be obvious."

Involuntarily, Fuchida looked north and east. "What do we do now?"

"The best we can," Genda told him. "What else is there?"

"You were doing the best you could with the Queen, *neh*?" If Fuchida thought about such things, he wouldn't have to think about the real troubles facing the Japanese in Hawaii—for a little while, anyway.

"It's not quite like that," Genda said with more embarrassment than Fuchida had expected from him. "She's . . . very sweet, really, and her husband doesn't understand her at all."

How many men sleeping with other men's wives had said exactly the same thing? Fuchida wondered if telling Genda as much would do any good. Since he doubted it, he reluctantly put aside his own thoughts of King Stanley's striking spouse. Duty was calling, and in a strident voice. "We've got to get you back to Pearl Harbor as fast as we can."

Commander Genda sighed once more. "Yes, I suppose so. You came out here to give me the news in person so you wouldn't have to use the telephone or the radio?"

"*Hai.*" Fuchida nodded.

"Sensible. Good security. The story will get out anyway—bad news always does—but it will take longer this way. We'll have the chance to come up with some propaganda of our own, maybe even some genuine good news."

"That's what Admiral Kaku thought." Fuchida turned to one of the petty officers. "Okano!"

"Yes, sir?" The man came to attention.

"I'm going to commandeer your bicycle for Commander Genda here. He needs to go to Pearl Harbor right away," Fuchida said. Okano nodded and saluted—again, what choice did he have? Fuchida went on, "See if you can borrow one or take one from a civilian. If that doesn't work, you'll have to walk."

"He can ride behind me, sir," the other petty officer said. "I don't mind."

The effect wouldn't be dignified, but Fuchida wasn't inclined to be fussy, not now. "All right. We'll do it that way, then," he said. "Now let's get moving."

ENSIGN JOE CROSETTI GAVE HIS FIGHTER plane a little more throttle. The F6F Hellcat responded as if angels flapped their wings harder. A slow grin stretched across Joe's face. "Wow!" he said.

He'd had some experience with Wildcats now. The F4F wasn't hopeless against the Zero—it could outdive the top Jap fighter and could take a lot more damage—but it wasn't a match for the enemy plane, either. The Hellcat . . . The Hellcat was a long step up.

It was faster than a Wildcat. It had better—much better—high-altitude performance, because its engine packed so much more power. It was even tougher than the older American plane.

Best of all, it was *his*. He didn't have a lot of time to get used to it. Before long, they'd throw him into action against the Japs. He had to be ready. He had to be, and he intended to be.

He wouldn't be alone in the sky when the clash finally came. That was the most important thing to remember. When he looked around—the cockpit gave better visibility than a Wildcat's, too—he saw a lot of other Hellcats from the *Bunker Hill* flying with him in neat formation.

Pleasure unalloyed filled his grin. Back when he volunteered to become a Navy flier, this was what he'd had in mind: roaring off a fleet carrier to take the war straight to the Japs. Plenty of guys had volunteered with the same thing in mind. Most of them hadn't made it. Some washed out of training. Some crashed. (He crossed himself, there in the cockpit, remembering the funerals he'd gone to.) And so many were flying other kinds of aircraft: flying boats or transports or blimps on antisubmarine patrol off the coasts. But here he was, by God! He'd done what he set out to do.

And there, just a few planes away, flew Orson Sharp. Actually, Joe had been surer his roomie would get a place on a carrier than he had been about himself. He was good. He knew that. Not many who'd gone through the program with him were better. The big guy from Salt Lake City was one of the few.

The formation switched from a vee to line astern as they approached the *Bunker Hill* and landed one after another. It was just like landing on the *Wolverine* on Lake Erie—except it wasn't. That was practice. Everybody knew it. You took it seriously. You had to, because you could get killed if you didn't. But it wasn't the real McCoy, all the same. This was. The *Bunker Hill* wasn't a converted excursion steamer, and she wasn't on the Great Lakes. That was the Pacific down there. Destroyers and cruisers screened the carrier, but they weren't a one hundred percent guarantee no Japanese sub could sneak in and find her. She was in the war—and so was Joe.

His mouth twisted. He'd been in the war for a while now, ever since that Jap flying boat dropped a bomb on his uncle's house after hitting San Francisco harbor. A lot of guys painted their wife's name, or their sweetheart's, on the nose of their plane. Joe's Hellcat had two names on its nose: *Tina* and *Gina*. He'd crossed the country on a train to get to his cousins' funerals.

Carrier landings were never automatic. If you thought they could be, it was your funeral—literally. When Joe's turn came, he followed the landing officer's wigwags as if he'd turned into a robot. One wing was down a little? He didn't think so, but he brought it up. He was coming in too steeply? Again, he didn't think so, but he raised the Hellcat's nose just the same.

Down came both wigwag flags. Down came Joe, in the controlled crash that was a carrier landing. One of the arrester wires caught his tailhook. His teeth clicked together, hard. He was home.

He killed the engine, pulled back the canopy, and scrambled out of the plane. Men from the flight crew hauled the Hellcat out of the way, clearing the deck for the next landing. It was all as smooth and practiced as a ballet. As far as Joe was concerned, it was just as beautiful, too.

He ran for the island, so he wouldn't be in the way if anything went wrong. When the ship wasn't launching or recovering planes, he spent as much time as he could out on the flight deck. The North Pacific felt like home to him; he'd got to know it from the deck of his father's fishing boat. Some of the guys who were first-rate pilots made lousy sailors. Not Joe. After a little boat's rolling and pitching, nothing the massive *Bunker Hill* did could faze him.

Orson Sharp had landed before him. "We're getting there," the Mormon said.

Joe nodded. "You better believe it." He'd wondered what kind of a sailor Sharp would prove—after all, his roomie had never even seen the ocean before he got to Pensacola for flight training. But Sharp seemed to be doing just fine now.

"When do you think we'll go after the Japs?" Sharp asked.

"Beats me. Why don't you get FDR on the phone?" Joe said. His buddy laughed at him. He went on, "I don't think it's gonna be real long, though. I mean, look what we're flying, and look where we're at."

It was Sharp's turn to nod. When they'd signed up to train as pilots, the Hellcat existed only on the drawing board. The *Bunker Hill* had been laid down, but only just barely. The USA hadn't been serious about the war till after the Japs hit Hawaii. If it wasn't serious now, though, it never would be.

"Look at all the other carriers we're going to have with us, too," Joe added, and his friend nodded again. Along with the *Bunker Hill* and the rest of the *Es-*

sex class—big fleet carriers that could take on anything the Japs built—there were the repaired *Hornet,* the *Ranger* brought over from the Atlantic, several light carriers built on cruiser hulls, and even more escort carriers built on freighter hulls. Both classes carried far fewer planes than a fleet carrier. The escort carriers, with a freighter's engines, couldn't make more than eighteen knots. But they could all get fighters and dive bombers and torpedo planes close to the enemy, and that was the point of the exercise.

"Soon," Orson Sharp murmured.

"Yeah." Joe heard the raw hunger in his own voice. "Soon."

BEFORE THE WAR, Kenzo Takahashi had never thought he would call on a girl carrying a sack of fish. Flowers, yes. Chocolates, sure. Mackerel? Mackerel had never once crossed his mind.

Chocolate had disappeared. He doubted any was left on Oahu. Flowers were there for the picking even now. As far as they went, Hawaii had an embarrassment of riches. Down by the harbor, Hawaiian women still made leis and sold them for a quarter or a yen, though Japanese sailors were less enthusiastic customers than American tourists had been.

But you couldn't eat flowers. (Although, these days, Kenzo wouldn't have been surprised if someone had made the experiment.) Fish made a much more practical present. Carrying them in a cloth sack let him worry less about people who might want to knock him over the head for the sake of a full belly. Even in Elsie Sundberg's neighborhood, such a thing was a long way from impossible.

None of the cars parked in front of the neat houses here had tires any more. By now, the occupying authorities had confiscated them all. None of the cars had batteries any more, either. The Japanese had taken those, too. That didn't show, though, not with a closed hood.

When Kenzo knocked on Elsie's front door, her mother opened it. She smiled. "Hello, Ken. Come in," she said.

"Thank you, ma'am." He did. As always, he had to shift gears in this neighborhood. West of Nuuanu Avenue, he was Kenzo. But this was the *haole* part of town, all right. He didn't really mind; to his way of thinking, an American needed to have an American-sounding name. He held out the sack. "I brought you folks these."

As always, a gift of food was welcome. When Elsie's mother said, "Thank you very much," she plainly meant it. She went on, "We have some ripe avocados to give you when you go."

"That'd be nice." Kenzo also meant it. Without knowing the Sundbergs, he wouldn't have had any for a long time.

"Let me get you some lemonade." Mrs. Sundberg was firm in her hospitality—and avocados and lemonade were about all she could offer. She added, "Elsie will be ready in a minute."

"Okay," Kenzo said. The lemonade would be good. One of these days, maybe Elsie would meet him at the door and just go out with him. He shrugged. He didn't plan on holding his breath. The Sundbergs clung to gentility with both hands. They didn't have much else to cling to, not with the Japanese occupation knocking what had been the ruling race and ruling class over the head.

Elsie came into the kitchen while he was drinking the sweet-tart lemonade. She had a glass, too. By now, that was part of the routine for their dates. When they finished, her mom walked them to the door, saying, "Have a good time."

"We will," Elsie told her. As soon as the door closed behind them, she asked Kenzo, "Where do you want to go?"

"I was just thinking down to the park," he answered. "We've seen all the movies on the island twice by now, and there isn't a heck of a lot else to do. We can talk and . . . and stuff."

"Yeah. And stuff," Elsie echoed in ominous tones. She knew he meant necking as well as he did. His ears got hot; he took a couple of embarrassed, shuffling steps. But then she laughed and said, "Okay, we'll do that."

A couple of kids were playing on the slide and the surviving swings when they got to the park. They sat down on a bench. The grass was even longer and more luxuriant than it had been the last time they were there. People had more urgent things than mowing it to worry about. None of the greenery had been trimmed any time lately, either.

"How have you been?" Elsie asked.

"Pretty good, except for Dad." Kenzo grimaced. "That's a big *except*, though. The more he talks to the Japanese radio, the more trouble he gets into with his big mouth. What's he gonna do when the Americans come back?"

"Do you really think they will?" Elsie asked with a bigger catch in her voice than she ever got after he kissed her.

He nodded. "I'd bet on it. All those planes coming over at night, and the subs around, and . . . all those kinds of things." He'd never said a word to any-body, not even Elsie, about the flier he and Hiroshi had rescued. What she didn't know could help keep her safe. He wondered how Burt Burleson had done once he got ashore. The Japanese hadn't bragged about capturing him, anyhow. That was something.

"God, I hope you're right," Elsie breathed. "Wouldn't it be wonderful to get things back to the way they were before all this happened?"

"Sure," Kenzo said. *Most ways,* he thought. *Would you still go out with me if things get back to the way they used to be?* He had to admit she might. They'd been good friends before. That wasn't quite the same, even if he had kissed her once.

A cloud passed in front of the sun. Rain started coming down. This was a little more than the usual "liquid sunshine." It rained hard enough to send the kids home. That didn't break Kenzo's heart. Elsie's sun dress clung to her. Kenzo admired the effect.

Elsie caught him doing it and wrinkled her nose in mock severity. Doing his best to be gallant, he said, "We can go under a tree if you want."

She shook her head. "It won't make any difference. The water'll just drip through." She was found to be right about that. She went on, "I don't mind it. It's nice and warm. And when it stops, we'll dry out pretty fast."

"Okay," Kenzo said. "In the meantime . . ." He put his arm around her. She slid toward him on the bench. He kissed her. What could be better than neck-ing in the park, even if it was raining? Actually, he knew what could be better. But Elsie didn't want to do that—or if she did want to, she pretended not to like any other well brought-up girl.

Kisses could take on a life of their own. Kenzo opened his eyes and came up for air after what seemed like forever. Elsie's eyes stayed closed, waiting for him to bend down to her again. But he didn't. Instead, softly, he spoke her name.

However softly he spoke, it wasn't the way a lover talked to his beloved. Her eyes came open, too. He pointed and said, still in a low voice, "I think you'd better get out of here."

Three Japanese soldiers were coming into the park. They weren't on patrol: they weren't carrying weapons and they weren't marching. What they were was falling-down drunk. One of them was singing something raucous.

"They won't be any trouble," Elsie said, but her voice lacked conviction.

The only way they wouldn't be any trouble was if they hadn't seen her.

Kenzo hoped that was so; they were pretty well sloshed. But, like so many things, it turned out to be too much to hope for. "Hey, sweetheart, kiss me, too!" one of them called.

"Kiss my dick!" another one added. They all thought that was funny. Kenzo didn't like the baying quality of their laughter, not even a little bit.

Elsie's face didn't change. For a foolish instant, Kenzo wondered why not. Then he realized they'd yelled in Japanese. He could go back and forth between the two languages without even realizing he was doing it. Elsie couldn't. She didn't know how lucky she was, either. "Sweetheart," he said, "you've got to get out of here *right now*."

That got through to her. She scrambled to her feet. But even then she asked, "What will they do to you if I take a powder?"

"Whatever it is, it won't be half as bad as what they'd do to you. Now get lost." He swatted her on the fanny to make sure she got the point. She yipped, but she took off. She was no dope, either. Instead of heading for any of the sidewalks, she went straight away from the Japanese soldiers, even though that was through some of the thickest bush.

"Come back!" "Where do you think you're going, you stupid bitch?" "We can catch her!" The soldiers shouted at Elsie and at one another. They pounded toward the park bench at a staggering lope. One of them fell on the wet grass. The other two hauled him upright again.

Seeing that, Kenzo waited till the very last instant before he got up and ran. He went in the same direction as Elsie had, wanting to stay between her and the soldiers. If he went any other way, they were too likely to forget about him and just keep on after her. He thought they were too drunk to catch her, but you never could tell.

He also thought they were too drunk to catch him. The Three Stooges couldn't have put on a clumsier act than that pratfall of theirs. But then he took a pratfall of his own, tripping over a root and landing *splat!* on his face. Worse yet, he knocked the wind out of himself.

He was just lurching to his feet when one of the soldiers grabbed him. "Let me go!" he yelled in Japanese. "I didn't do anything!"

They seemed momentarily startled to hear him speak their language. One of them hit him anyway. "Shut up, you bastard!" the soldier shouted. "You told the girl to get away!" He couldn't have known enough English to be sure of that, but he didn't need to be Sherlock Holmes to figure it out.

Kenzo tried to twist free. He didn't try to fight back. One against three, even three drunks, was bad odds. All he wanted to do was get away. To his dismay, he discovered he couldn't. They hit him a few more times, knocked him down, and started kicking him. That was bad. He did his best to roll into a ball and protect his head with his arms.

Then one of the soldiers said, "We're just wasting time. That stupid cunt is getting away."

They forgot about Kenzo and pounded off after Elsie. This time, Kenzo lay there for some little while before he painfully pulled himself upright again. He hoped he'd bought Elsie enough time to escape. His biggest fear had been that they would decide she *had* got away and it was his fault. In that case, they might have stomped him to death.

He spat red. He hadn't done a perfect job of covering up. And that wasn't just rainwater trickling down his jaw. Breathing hurt, too; his ribs had taken a shellacking. But he didn't feel knives in his chest when he inhaled, so he supposed nothing in there was broken. In the movies, the hero recovered from a beating as soon as it was over. Life, unfortunately, didn't imitate Hollywood. Kenzo felt like hell, or maybe a little worse.

None too steady on his feet, he lurched over to the water fountain in one corner of the park. When he turned the knob, water came out. He washed his face. It hurt. He started to dry it on his sleeve, but didn't. For one thing, his shirt was already pretty soggy. For another, he didn't want to get bloodstains on it. They hardly ever came out clean.

All he could do was hope Elsie had got home safe. He wanted to find out if she had, but he didn't do that, either. If he ran into those Japanese soldiers again, it might literally be the last thing he ever did. And he didn't want to lead them to the Sundbergs' house.

Instead, he walked back to the tent he shared with his father and brother. Nobody stared at him, so maybe he didn't look too bad. Or maybe people in Honolulu had just got used to seeing guys who'd been roughed up.

To his enormous relief, his father wasn't in the tent. His brother was. Hiroshi *did* stare at him, and exclaimed, "Jesus Christ! What happened to you?"

So much for not looking too bad, Kenzo thought. "Japanese soldiers," he answered shortly. "Could have been a hell of a lot worse. I think Elsie got away from them, and I'll be okay."

"Jesus Christ!" Hiroshi said again, and then, "You gonna tell Dad?"

"What's the use?" Kenzo said. "If I did, he'd probably say it was my own damn fault." He waited, hoping his brother would tell him he was wrong. Hiroshi didn't. Kenzo sighed, disappointed but not much surprised.

"COME ON. Let's go!" Lester Dillon shouted as the Marines in his platoon filed onto a bus. "Move it, you lazy lugs! You want to keep Hirohito waiting?"

His company commander grinned at him. "That's pretty good," Captain Bradford said.

"Thank you, sir." Dillon didn't think it was all that funny himself, but he wasn't about to say so, not if his CO liked it. He did say, "About time we got another shot at those slanty-eyed bastards."

"You better believe it," Bradford agreed. "Maybe this time the Navy'll hold up their end of the deal."

"They damn well better," Dillon exclaimed. "If they don't—"

"If they don't, I reckon they'll be too dead for us to complain about it," Braxton Bradford said. "That's how it worked out last year, anyways."

Since he was both right and an officer, Dillon let it rest there. This was a funny kind of war. If the Navy pukes didn't do their job, if they got killed, he and his buddies were pretty safe. But if the sailors and flyboys cleared the Japanese Navy out of the way in the Pacific, the Marines and the Army got to land on Oahu and tackle the Japanese Army. It only stood to reason that a lot of them wouldn't live through the campaign. But he was champing at the bit, and so was every other Marine he knew. The Army's opinion mattered to him not at all.

Does this make me patriotic, or just a damn fool? He'd got shot once, and here he was, eager to give a brand new enemy a chance to punch his ticket? He looked inside himself. He really was.

He climbed aboard the bus himself, the last man to do so. The door hissed shut. The driver put the bus in gear. Diesel engine grumbling, it started south, one of the dozens, maybe hundreds heading down from Camp Pendleton to San Diego. Pendleton had the room to train Marines by the tens of thousands. San Diego still had the port.

The convoy of buses had Pacific Coast Highway almost to itself. Gasoline rationing had made civilian traffic disappear. Les saw only a handful of cars coming north. Most of the vehicles in the other lane were trucks painted olive drab.

The Pacific was more interesting and prettier. Gulls and terns glided over-head. Waves rolled up onto the beach. In Hawaii, surf-riders would have skimmed ashore atop them. Nobody'd thought of doing that here. Every so often, a lone man or a knot of two or three friends would stand by the edge of the sea with fishing poles. Dillon saw a lot of fishermen, but he never saw anybody catch anything.

Then the buses got down into San Diego. They rolled right past the park where the Padres played. The team must have been on the road, because the ballpark was quiet and empty. Talk inside Les' bus got louder and more excited when it pulled into the harbor. He didn't see any battlewagons or carriers tied up there; they'd probably already put to sea. The harbor was full of ungainly Liberty ships and the destroyers that would escort them and—everybody hoped—keep subs away.

With a squeal of brakes that needed work, the bus shuddered to a stop. "Everybody out!" Les said. "You've got a chance to stretch your legs, so you better take it. You think we were tight in here, wait till we get on the damn troop-ship. Only difference between us and sardines there is, they won't pack us in olive oil."

Some of the Marines laughed. Most of them didn't. They'd been through last year's abortive campaign, and they knew this wasn't going to be a trip to Hawaii on a luxury liner.

They did stretch and twist when they got down on the concrete. Les low-ered his pack to the ground. Something along his spine crunched when he stretched. He was older than the men he led. He was in good hard shape for a man his age, but every now and then his body insisted on reminding him that good hard shape for a man in his forties wasn't the same as it had been when he was in his twenties. He hoped he would be able to keep up when they landed on Oahu.

If they landed on Oahu. Things had gone wrong once. He hoped they wouldn't go wrong again, but life didn't come with a money-back guarantee. *Too damn bad,* he thought.

"My company, form on me!" Captain Bradford called from a nearby bus. "We'll be boarding that ship." Since Dillon's bus stood between him and his company commander, he couldn't see which ship Bradford had in mind. It didn't matter much; Liberty ships were as like as peas in a pod, only a lot uglier.

Bradford pointed again when Les could see him. *Valdosta Liberty* was stenciled in big white letters on the black paint at the freighter's stern. But for the name, she could have been the *Alamogordo Liberty* or the *Missoula Liberty* or any of the others crowding Coronado Bay.

Up the gangplank he went. Merchant seamen in dungarees crewed the ship. He didn't much like that, but he couldn't do anything about it. The Navy had trouble finding sailors for all its new warships, let alone troopships. But if trouble came, would these civilians know what to do with the antiaircraft gun at the *Valdosta Liberty*'s bow?

Hell with it, he thought. *If they don't, some of us'll take over. Any Japs want this ship, they'll have to pay the bill for her.*

Captain Bradford, being an officer, would share a cabin with his social equals. Dillon, being a noncom, went down into the bowels of the Liberty ship with the rest of the Marines. The air down belowdecks felt still and dead. It would only get worse. They'd be sailing south, so it would get hotter. The men wouldn't have many chances to bathe. Odds were the galley would serve beans, too. *All things considered, I'd rather be in Philadelphia,* Dillon thought.

Nobody gave a damn about his opinion. He got his platoon settled in the cramped space available as best he could. The first card games started even before all the men had slung their packs up onto their bunks. The *Valdosta Liberty*'s engines came to life. He felt them through the soles of his feet as well as hearing them. The whole fabric of the ship vibrated. Then she began to move.

"Here we go again," somebody said. Les nodded. That summed it all up as well as anything.

KENZO TAKAHASHI MOVED LIKE AN OLD MAN. By late afternoon, he felt all the bruises and lumps the Japanese soldiers had given him earlier in the day. He kept walking all the same. He had to find out if Elsie was okay.

He flinched when he walked past a squad of Japanese soldiers. But he bowed, too, so they didn't bother him. He might have been bruised, but he wasn't wearing a scarlet letter (he laughed at himself for remembering American Lit at a time like this). Besides, they were on duty, not on leave and drunk. And he wasn't walking with a girl, which no doubt counted most of all.

He flinched again when he went up the Sundbergs' walk and knocked on the front door. If Elsie wasn't there . . . If she wasn't there, Mrs. Sundberg would start screaming at him, and how could he blame her?

The door opened. Elsie's mom stared out at him. Then she said, "Ken! Thank God!" and hugged him and kissed him on the cheek. She pulled him into the house and called, "Elsie! Ken's here!"

From the back of the house, Elsie squealed. She came running up to Ken, threw herself into his arms—she almost knocked him over—and gave him a kiss. It wasn't the sort of peck he'd got from her mother, either. It was the real McCoy. And Mrs. Sundberg, who stood there watching, didn't pitch a fit. She beamed at him and Elsie.

After the kiss ended, Elsie took a real look at him. "Oh, Ken!" she exclaimed. "You got hurt!"

"It's not too bad," he said, and that kiss made him less of a liar than he would have been a couple of minutes earlier. "I'm just glad you got away from those bastards, that's all." He bobbed his head toward her mother. "Excuse me."

"Don't worry about it," Mrs. Sundberg said warmly. "Elsie told me what you did. Thank you. Thank you from the bottom of my heart." She eyed him, too. "Can I get you some ice?"

"Probably too late for that," Kenzo answered. "I'll be okay in a few days. They didn't kick me in the teeth, and my ribs are just sore. Nothing's busted."

"I'm so sorry!" Elsie squeezed his hands in hers.

He shrugged. "Not your fault. Those miserable goons . . ." He couldn't call them what he wanted to, not in front of Elsie and her mother.

"They certainly are." Mrs. Sundberg's voice wasn't warm any more, not when she talked about the Japanese soldiers. She turned to Elsie. "I'm going to let the neighbors know Ken's all right, too. I'll be back in a while. I know the two of you have a lot to, uh, talk about."

He felt he'd earned his American name. Out the door Mrs. Sundberg went. Kenzo nodded to Elsie. "Hiya," he managed.

She wasn't laughing. She looked on the edge of tears. "They really could have killed you," she said.

"Yeah, well . . ." He shrugged again. It hurt. He went on, "They would have done some pretty horrible things to you, too."

Her face twisted. "You hear stories about things like that, but you don't think they can happen to you. Then they do—or they almost do." She looked down at the rug. "You hear stories about heroes, too, but you never think you know one."

"Anybody would have done the same thing," Kenzo said.

"I don't think so." Elsie sounded almost angry. "I don't think you should be so modest, either. They *could* have killed you."

It wasn't that she was wrong. On the contrary. Uncomfortably, he said, "I don't like thinking about that any better than you like thinking about, uh, the other stuff."

"Okay," Elsie said; that must have made sense to her. "What do you want to think about instead? How about this?" She kissed him again.

The kiss took on a life of its own. His arms tightened around her. She molded herself against him. He squeezed her backside, pressing her closer yet. She didn't try to pull away. She just made a wordless sound of pleasure.

They finally broke apart, but not very far. "Elsie—" he began, and stopped.

"I know, sweetheart. It's okay. It's . . . better than okay." She kissed him once more, gently this time. "You risked your life for me. That counts for a lot. Anything I can do to pay you back is pretty small stuff, anything at all."

"You don't have to do anything because of that," he said. "I didn't do it to get paid back."

"I know. It's better that way," Elsie said. "Suppose I do it because I want to, then?"

This time, he kissed her. When his hand found her breast, she didn't try to slap it away. She just made that happy noise again. He made one quite a bit like it, but deeper. After a while, his heart pounding, he asked, "What about your mom?"

Elsie laughed. "She won't be back for a while. Mom's no dummy. She didn't leave by accident. Don't worry about that."

"I'm not worried about anything," Kenzo said, which would do for an understatement till a bigger one came along.

"Come on, then." She took his hand and led him back to her bedroom.

A teddy bear almost the size of a three-year-old sat on the bed. Elsie set it on the floor with its back to the bed. Then she nodded, as much to herself as to Kenzo, and pulled the sun dress off over her head. She sat down on the edge of the bed to take off her bra and panties.

Kenzo tried not to stare as much as he wanted to. "You're beautiful," he whispered. He got out of his own clothes in a hurry.

"Oh, Ken!" Elsie said when she saw the bruises and welts on his ribs and his back and one thigh. She jumped up and kissed them one by one, so softly that her lips almost weren't there. "Is that better?" He didn't know what it did for the bruises. What it did for the rest of him was obvious. Elsie giggled.

They lay down together. It wasn't quite Kenzo's first time, but it was his first time with anybody who mattered to him, who didn't want him to go away as soon as he could so she could take on somebody else. Elsie sighed when his mouth found the pink tips of her breasts.

A little later, with him poised above her, she inhaled sharply. "Be careful," she said. "It hurts."

"I'll try," he told her, though nothing in all the world could have kept him from driving deeper then. Elsie bit her lip, but didn't say anything more. Before long, his world exploded in delight. As he came back to himself, he asked, "Are you okay?"

"I—think so," she answered. "They say it's supposed to hurt the first time, and they aren't wrong. But you're sweet." She squirmed under him. "Let me up. I don't want to leave a stain on the bedspread." When she stood up, she laughed and said, "Oops—too late. Well, cold water will get most of it out. I hope."

"Me, too." He felt foolish, and started getting dressed again. Elsie carried her clothes down the hall to the bathroom. She walked spraddle-legged, as if she'd been riding a horse for a long time. When she came back she had a wet washrag, which she used to scrub at the red stain.

"There," she said after a bit. "That's better, anyhow."

"Uh-huh." Kenzo didn't know what to do or say next. He tried, "I think maybe I better go."

"Okay," Elsie said, and then, in a different tone of voice, "I hope to God I don't catch."

"Catch? Oh!" Kenzo said. Neither of them had worried about that while it was going on. "I hope you don't, too. That would be terrible."

"It would be complicated, anyway," Elsie said.

If you knocked a girl up, you either ran away and started over somewhere else or you married her. Kenzo couldn't run far, not the way things were now. He didn't want to marry anybody yet, though he didn't suppose Elsie would be too bad. But she was dead right: no matter who ran Hawaii, a Japanese guy marrying a *haole* girl would cause complications. They'd be different complications, depending on whether the Rising Sun or the Stars and Stripes flew over the islands, but they'd always be there.

He and Elsie walked out into the front room. "We'll be careful," she said. He didn't know if she meant careful about her not getting pregnant or careful about going where Japanese soldiers could cause trouble. It struck him as a good idea either way.

"Sure," he said. "So long." He kissed her, then went out the door. He looked back when she closed it, but didn't blow her a kiss or anything. The neighbors didn't need to know. Neither did Elsie's mom—not officially, anyhow.

Corporal Takeo Shimizu led his squad through the streets of Honolulu. It was a routine patrol. Nobody gave them any trouble. By now, the locals had learned to bow and get out of the way when they saw Japanese soldiers. They hadn't needed object lessons for quite a while.

The only thing even slightly unusual that Shimizu saw was a local Japanese man, about the age of most of the privates in his squad, who walked along whistling even though a black eye and a fat lip said he'd been in a brawl and probably lost it. Shimizu almost stopped him and asked him what he was so happy about, but in the end he didn't. Being happy wasn't against the rules.

He wasn't the only one who noticed the local. "Whatever that guy's been drinking, I want some," Private Wakuzawa said.

That was funny enough to make not only Shimizu but also several other soldiers laugh. Wakuzawa was already the most cheerful man in the squad. Why did he need anything to make him happier yet? Better something like that should go to Senior Private Furusawa, who thought too much for his own good—or so it seemed to Shimizu, anyhow.

Soldiers were drilling in a park. They weren't Army men—they belonged to the special naval landing forces. They wore olive-drab uniforms, not Army khaki, and their boots were black rather than brown.

The Navy officer putting them through their paces wouldn't be satisfied with anything less than perfection, and didn't want to recognize perfection when he saw it. "You are not worthy of dying for the Emperor!" he screamed at the sweating, panting soldiers. "Not worthy, do you hear me?"

"*Hai*, Captain Iwabuchi!" the soldiers chorused.

"Then act like it, damn you!" Iwabuchi roared. "If we have to fight the

Americans, we are going to make them drown in their own blood! And how do we do that? By making them drown in *our* blood!"

"*Hai*, Captain Iwabuchi!" the troops from the naval landing force repeated.

Iwabuchi pointed toward Shimizu and his squad. "Look at those Army men! They're soft. They're ragged. Do you want to be like them? You'd better not! You have to want to die for the Emperor. You have to be *proud* to die for the Emperor! The man who does not fear death, the man who welcomes death, will surely be triumphant!"

"*Hai*, Captain Iwabuchi!" the Navy men said once more.

Shimizu was furious, though of course he did not show it in the presence of a superior. A Navy captain ranked with the commander of his regiment or any other Army colonel, too: not just a superior but an almost godlike figure. Despite that, Shimizu's own opinion of the special naval landing forces was not high. They made good enough occupation troops. But when they had to fight other soldiers, they didn't fare so well. Despite these drills, the Army did a much better job of training its men in infantry tactics than the Navy did.

Captain Iwabuchi went right on yelling at his men. They might not fight skillfully under a leader like that, but they would fight hard. They would fear him more than they feared the Americans, and they would have reason to. An officer like that would kill anybody who he thought was hanging back.

"We'll leave this place a ruin! We'll never give in!" he shrieked. "A ruin, do you hear me? Not one brick left on top of another!"

"He's not so tough," Yasuo Furusawa said, but he sidled up to Shimizu and spoke in the next thing to a whisper, taking no chances that the fanatical officer could overhear him.

"I was thinking the same thing," Shimizu answered—also in a low voice. After a moment, he went on, "Nothing wrong with dying for the Emperor, mind you. There's no better end for a Japanese soldier. It's an honor. It's a privilege." He'd had all that drilled into him in basic training, and he believed it. Even so . . . "The real point, though, is to make the enemy die for *his* country first."

"*Hai!*" Furusawa nodded. "I think that's just right, Corporal-*san*. And I don't think it ever once crossed that Captain Iwabuchi's mind."

"No, I don't, either. But all we can do about it is feel sorry for those poor Navy men."

"Maybe it won't matter," Senior Private Furusawa said. "Maybe the *real* Navy will beat the Americans on the sea, the way they did last year."

"Of course they will." Shimizu couldn't show doubt about anything like that. It would have been unpatriotic. He did think Captain Iwabuchi couldn't have been much of an officer. If he were, he would have had shipborne duty. Instead, he was stuck doing things that weren't really a Navy officer's proper job. *Serves him right,* Shimizu thought.

Even after his squad turned the corner, he could still hear Captain Iwabuchi screaming at his men and haranguing them. He might push them too far. Japanese military men were an enduring lot. They had to be. But even endurance had its limits. He wondered if Iwabuchi might suffer an unfortunate—oh, such an unfortunate!—accident. Every once in a while, things like that did happen.

The rest of the patrol stayed routine. Shimizu approved of routine. Routine meant nothing was going wrong. It also meant he didn't have to think for himself. If he didn't have to think, he couldn't make any mistakes. If he didn't make any mistakes, his own superiors couldn't start yelling at him. They wouldn't be as bad as Captain Iwabuchi, but all the same he didn't fancy an officer shouting in his face and maybe slapping him around.

He brought his men back to the barracks. He made his report to Lieutenant Horino, the platoon commander. He mentioned marching past the park where Iwabuchi was drilling his men; he couldn't very well leave it out. "Ah," Horino said. "And what did you think of that, Corporal?"

"Captain Iwabuchi is a very . . . energetic man, sir," Shimizu said carefully.

Horino laughed. "He certainly is. All right, Corporal. You may go." Shimizu saluted and left in a hurry. He'd got his message across and hadn't got in trouble for it. That would do—and then some.

VIII

LIEUTENANT SABURO SHINDO WAS LESS GLAD TO BE AT SEA AGAIN THAN HE'D EX-
pected. *Akagi* and her escorting destroyers and cruisers steamed north. So did
Shokaku, some kilometers away. They wouldn't have sortied if there hadn't
been good intelligence that the Americans were on their way again.

He wished *Zuikaku* were with them. They'd had three carriers the last time
they faced the U.S. Navy, and they'd needed all of them. The Yankees might not
be very skillful, but they didn't give up. That worried Shindo, who'd thought
conquering Hawaii would be plenty to knock the USA out of the Pacific War.

"Karma," he muttered. That submarine skipper had got lucky. He'd heard
some of his superiors wondering if the Americans had broken Japanese codes,
but he didn't believe it. How could *gaijin* ever learn Japanese well enough to do
such a thing? It had to be impossible.

Akagi and *Shokaku* steamed toward the biggest breach the Americans had
torn in the line of picket boats. It stood to reason that the Yankees would try to
send their ships through there. He would have done the same thing if he commanded the American fleet.

Commander Fuchida was pacing along the flight deck. He nodded to
Shindo. "Your planes will be ready to fight when we make contact?"

"Oh, yes, sir," Shindo answered. "Of course, sir." Shindo paused, then asked,
"Do we know how big the enemy fleet is?"

"Not exactly," Fuchida answered. "Our best guess is that it's about the same size as the one last year, maybe one carrier more. Even with only two carriers of our own, we should be able to handle that."

"Why don't we know better, sir?" Shindo asked.

"Because most of the yards where the Americans build carriers are on their East Coast," Fuchida said. "We can't do reconnaissance there, and neither can Germany."

"Their ships have to come through the Panama Canal to get at us," Shindo said. "Can't we count them once they've got to the Pacific?"

"We've tried. We haven't had much luck," Fuchida told him. "We've lost a couple of H8Ks that tried to spy on the canal. The Americans patrol aggressively in that area. We didn't get any worthwhile information, either."

"Too bad," Shindo said, which was as close as he would come to criticizing any of his superiors. He wanted to know what he was up against. Meticulous planning was a big part of what made the Hawaii operation so successful.

"*Shigata ga nai*," Fuchida said, which was true enough. He clicked his tongue between his teeth. "I do wish we had *Zuikaku* here with us, though. Well, *shigata ga nai* there, too."

"If the Yankees have the same number of carriers and the same kinds of planes as they did last year, we'll beat them again. We'll beat the pants off them."

Before Fuchida could answer, the public-address system called his name: "Commander Fuchida! Report to the bridge immediately! Commander Fuchida! Report to the—"

"Please excuse me," Fuchida said, and dashed across the flight deck towards *Akagi*'s island.

What was going on? Shindo waited for his own summons to the bridge, or perhaps for the klaxons of general quarters. Neither came, which left him stewing in his own juices. A couple of minutes later, though, *Akagi* changed course to starboard. He nodded to himself. The skipper had found out something he hadn't known before.

And then the PA system brayed to life again: "All flying crews report to the briefing room! Attention, please! All flying crews report to the briefing room at once!"

Now it was Shindo's turn to run as if possessed. He sprinted for a hatchway: the briefing room was on the hangar deck, below the flight deck. The soles of his shoes clanged on the iron treads of the stairs.

A few fliers beat him to the briefing room, but only a few. He found a seat near the front, so he could get the best look at the maps and charts and black-boards there. More and more men came in after him, all chattering excitedly. They knew they were liable to be going into action before long.

They quieted when Commander Fuchida and Commander Genda walked into the room. The man who led air operations and the man who planned them waited a few minutes to let the laggards crowd in. Then Minoru Genda spoke without preamble: "We have found the enemy."

"Ah." Shindo made the same noise as most of the men around him. The boys in Intelligence hadn't been altogether asleep at the switch, then. They really had known the Americans were coming. *Akagi* and *Shokaku* had sailed in good time to give the enemy a warm reception.

"The Americans are moving more or less along the path we anticipated," Genda went on. "A sampan just east of the ones the Yankees have been attacking spotted their ships and broke radio silence to deliver the warning. The signal cut off abruptly before the message was completed."

Saburo Shindo knew what that meant. The Yankees had spotted the sampan or traced the signal. Some good men, some brave men, were dead. Yasukuni Shrine held some new spirits.

"It appears the U.S. fleet may be somewhat larger than we expected," Commander Fuchida said. "We shall engage it even so, of course. The more damage we do to it, the harder the time the Americans will have landing on Oahu. *Banzai* for the Emperor!"

"*Banzai! Banzai!*" The cry filled the briefing room. Shindo joined it.

"Oahu has received the sampan's signal," Genda said. "Mitsubishi G4Ms are airborne, and will assist us in our attack on U.S. forces."

More *Banzai!*s rang out. Shindo joined those, too, though less whole-heartedly. The G4M was fast for a bomber, and could carry a large load a long way. There its virtues ended. It was gruesomely vulnerable to enemy fighters; with gallows humor, G4M pilots called their plane *the one-shot lighter* for the ease with which it caught fire. And a good deal of combat had proved high-level bombers had to be lucky to hit ships moving far below. Some of the G4Ms doubtless would carry torpedoes, but their pilots didn't have the practice carrier-based B5N2 fliers got.

"Range to our targets is about three hundred kilometers," Fuchida said. "We want to strike as fast as we can, before they are fully prepared."

"Suggestion, sir!" Shindo's hand shot into the air.

"Yes, Lieutenant?" Fuchida said.

"We ought to fly a dogleg to the east or west before proceeding against the enemy," Shindo said. "That way, he won't be able to follow the reciprocal of our course back to the ship, whether he picks us up visually or with his fancy electronics."

The idea seemed to take Fuchida by surprise. He talked with Genda in voices too low for Shindo to make out what they were saying. Then, with some reluctance, he shook his head. "If we had worked this out with *Shokaku* beforehand, it would be a good ploy. But we can't break radio silence to discuss it, and we can't have our planes arriving over the target after hers. A coordinated attack is vital."

"Yes, sir." Shindo wished he'd thought of it sooner, but he could see that Fuchida's reply made at least some sense.

Genda added, "Even if the Americans get through, I believe our combat air patrol should be able to handle them. Their torpedo bombers are waddling death traps, and we will be more alert for their dive bombers."

Last time, *Akagi* had been damaged, *Zuikaku* badly damaged. Shindo hoped Genda wasn't being too optimistic. But the powers that be weren't wrong when they said a quick, hard blow would serve Japan best.

"I'll be with you," Fuchida said. "Remember—carriers first. Everything else is an afterthought. Strike hard, for the Emperor's sake. *Banzai!*"

"*Banzai!*" Shindo shouted along with the rest of the fliers. "*Banzai!*"

A SCOWLING REGULAR NAVY LIEUTENANT COMMANDER PROWLED the front of the *Bunker Hill*'s briefing room. He sipped from, of all things, a glass of milk as he paced. No one laughed at him. It soothed his ulcer, which he'd got perhaps not least from contemplating the idea of a fleet carrier full of Reserve pilots.

"The Japs know we're here," he said without preamble. "One of their damn little picket boats got off a signal before we sank her. Odds are good we'll be seeing bandits before too long. They'll get their strike in on us before we can hit them. That means we probably have to take a punch and then knock them cold. Are you up for it, gentlemen?"

"Yes, sir!" Joe Crosetti's hungry howl was one among many. He'd been waiting for this day more than a year and a half, since December 7, 1941. Now the Japs seemed likely to be within arm's reach, or at least within Hellcat's reach—at last. The urge to go out and hit them all but overwhelmed him.

After another swig from that glass of milk, the briefing officer said, "Well, you'd better be. Your aircraft have cost Uncle Sam a nice piece of change. So has your training, such as it is." He had a long nose, excellent for looking down. "Add in whatever you happen to be worth and it comes to quite a sum. Try to bring it back—unless you find a good reason not to, of course."

That last sobering sentence reminded Joe this wasn't a game. They were playing for keeps, and there might be reasons not to come home. He refused to worry about it. He didn't think it would, or could, happen to him.

"Questions?" the briefing officer asked.

Nobody said anything for a little while. All Joe wanted to know was, *Where are the Japs?* The briefing office couldn't tell him that, not yet. By the looks on the other fliers' faces, they felt the same way. Then someone asked, "Sir, what do we do if we run into enemy planes on the way to their ships?"

That was a good question. Attacking the Japanese aircraft along the way might make it harder for the Japs to strike the U.S. carriers here, but it would also lessen the Americans' chances of knocking out the enemy carriers. The briefing officer frowned. "You'll have to use your best judgment on that, gentlemen. If you think you can hurt them, do it. If you think you'll have a better shot at their carriers by avoiding contact, do that."

Joe turned to Orson Sharp and whispered, "Whatever we do, we get the credit if it works out and the blame if it doesn't."

"What else is new?" Sharp whispered back, a response more cynical than he usually gave.

"For now, take your places in your aircraft," the briefing officer said. "You don't have long to wait. I'd bet my life on that." He *was* betting his life on how well some of the pilots could do against a foe who had smashed U.S. fliers whenever they met.

Not this time, Joe thought fiercely as he hurried to his Hellcat. The F6F wasn't a particularly pretty plane. The big radial engine gave it a blunt nose, like that of a prizefighter who'd stopped too many lefts with his face. A Jap Zero looked a lot more elegant. But the Hellcat had almost twice the horsepower, more firepower with its battery of heavy machine guns, sturdier construction, self-sealing fuel tanks, and good armor protecting the pilot. *The pilot.* The words weren't an abstraction to Joe, not any more. *That means me.*

He raced across the planking of the flight deck and scrambled up into his plane. He slid the canopy shut and dogged it. The cockpit smelled of leather

and avgas and lubricants: intimate odors and mechanical ones, all mixed together. Joe longed for a cigarette, but smoking around oxygen and high-octane
gas was hazardous to your life expectancy.

Sailors in yellow helmets and thin yellow smocks worn over their tunics
stood by to direct the planes' movements when they took off. Sailors in red helmets and smocks waited near the carrier's island. They were crash crews and
repairmen. The only men in blue helmets and smocks—the sailors who handled the planes while static—left on the flight deck were the pair poised to take
away the chocks that secured the lead Hellcat in its place.

"Pilots, start your engines!" It wasn't the voice of God roaring through the
loudspeakers, but that of the executive officer. On the *Bunker Hill,* as on any
ship, the skipper was God, and the exec was his prophet.

Joe knew a horrid fear that his engine wouldn't catch, that he would have to
stay behind. But it roared to life with the others. The prop blurred into near-
invisibility. Joe eyed the instruments. It wasn't a test this time; he wasn't sitting
in a simulator or a lard-butt trainer. This was for all the marbles.

The sailors in yellow formed a line across the flight deck. "Prepare to launch
planes!" came the command from the island. Joe heard it both over the loudspeakers and through his earphones. The last two men in blue took the chocks
away from the lead plane. A man in yellow walked backwards, making come-
hither motions with his hands. The Hellcat followed, also at a walking pace.

Just in front of the island stood a man with a checkered flag in his right
hand. He made grinding motions with his left. The lead plane's engine sped
up. Another roar came from the loudspeakers: "Launch planes!" The man with
the flag made more grinding motions. The lead plane's motor raced. The
checkered flag went down. The F6F raced along the flight deck, dipped as it
shot off the bow, then gained altitude again and shot up to take its place in
what would soon be the greatest assemblage of naval airpower the world had
ever known.

Plane after plane took off. After what seemed forever but was only a few
minutes, Joe's turn came. He followed the beckoning sailor in yellow to the
center of the deck, revved his engine higher and higher at the flagman's signal,
and whooped when the checkered flag dropped. Now!

Acceleration slammed him back in his seat as the Hellcat darted forward.
That sickening lurch when it went off the deck . . . He hauled back on the stick
and gave the plane all the throttle she had. Up she went. Hell, she might have

been doing the Indian Rope Trick, the way she climbed. Nothing he'd trained in even came close.

But an F6F wasn't a widowmaker, the way some hot planes were. She played tough, but she played fair. And the higher Joe got, the more of the U.S. fleet he could see spread out below him. With any luck at all, they'd give the Japs the biggest kick in the ass the world had ever known.

Along with *Bunker Hill*, *Essex* and three more brand-new fleet carriers steamed toward Hawaii. So did the repaired *Hornet*. So did *Ranger*. She wasn't an ideal combat carrier, but she could carry planes to make this big fist even bigger. And so did five light carriers, which could keep up with their bigger sisters no matter what, and close to a dozen escort carriers, which couldn't. The baby flattops would get left behind in a fast-moving action, but among them they brought almost as many planes into action as the *Essex*-class ships.

Joe spotted his element leader and took his place below and to the right of the other Hellcat. He'd wanted to lead an element—Orson Sharp led one. But wingman was what they'd given him, and he knew he had to squash that gnawing jealousy. He'd been good enough to get here, goddammit. If he did his job well, he might be leading an element pretty damn quick.

Dive bombers and torpedo planes went into formation with the fighters. The torpedo planes were new Grumman Avengers, not the lumbering Douglas Devastators that couldn't get out of their own way and had failed so miserably the year before.

"All hands! All hands! Listen up, everybody!" Excitement crackled in Joe's earphones. On the short-range, plane-to-plane circuit, the officer went on, "We've got a bearing on the Japs—a cruiser's recon plane found the bastards. I got the word just before I launched. Range about 160, maybe 170, course 200. That'll get us close enough to find 'em on our own, anyway. Let's go hunting!"

The fierce shouts that filled Joe's head made him want to snatch off the earphones. But he didn't. He added to the din. Like a swarm of bees—a big swarm of bees—the U.S. aircraft buzzed south.

Mitsuo Fuchida's B5N2 felt different with a torpedo from the way a B5N1 had with bombs slung beneath. The long, heavy torpedo made the aircraft a bit slower, a bit clumsier. He shrugged. He would do what needed doing anyway.

Patches of white, fluffy cloud sailed past every now and again. For the most part, though, the sky was clear and the sea below calm. As the Yankees had the year before, they'd picked better weather to attack Hawaii than Japan had at the end of 1941. Fuchida shrugged again. The United States *could* pick and choose. As far as he could see, Japan hadn't had a choice. Roosevelt had cut off metal shipments, frozen assets, and, most important, stopped the flow of oil, all to dislodge Japan from her rightful empire in China. If she'd bowed to U.S. extortion, she would have been America's puppet forever after. Better to fight, to seize the chance to be one of the great powers in the world.

He peered ahead, hoping to catch sight of the American ships. That was foolish, as a glance at his watch told him. He and his comrades hadn't flown nearly long enough to put the enemy in sight.

He clicked his tongue between his teeth. He didn't have so many comrades as he would have liked. Only about 120 planes were winging their way north— a third as many as had flown against Hawaii at the start of the war in the Pacific. He wished *Zuikaku* hadn't been hit. That had to be bad luck . . . didn't it? Her planes would have made this sortie half again as strong.

"Airplanes ahead!" The words in his earphones were quietly spoken, but they might as well have been screamed. Now he would see what the Americans had come up with this time.

When he found the enemy air armada, he thought for a moment he was seeing spots before his eyes. *That* many planes? He bowed in the cockpit, not to the oncoming Yankees but to Admiral Yamamoto. The commander-in-chief of the Combined Fleet had said before the war started that Japan would have six months or a year to do as she pleased in the Pacific, but things would get much harder after that. Conquering Hawaii had stretched Japan's hegemony out to a year and a half and even a little more, but Yamamoto, as usual, seemed to know what he was talking about.

As more Japanese fliers saw the Americans, questions dinned in Fuchida's earphones. He commanded the Emperor's aircraft, as he had at Pearl Harbor and in the first fight in the North Pacific. Most of the increasingly alarmed queries boiled down to, *Do we attack the enemy's planes, or do we go on to strike at his ships?*

To Fuchida, that had only one possible answer. "We go for the American carriers," he declared over the all-planes circuit. "Without carrier decks to land on, airplanes here are useless. If we sink the enemy's carriers, he cannot possibly invade Hawaii. Press on!"

The Americans should have been thinking along the same lines: so it seemed to him, anyway. But, taking advantage of their numbers, they sent some of their fighters against the Japanese strike force. Even before Fuchida called orders, some of the Zeros shot ahead to defend the precious torpedo planes and dive bombers.

They're coming very fast, Fuchida thought. The Americans had been flying higher than the Japanese. Part of that speed came from losing altitude—but only part. Alarm tingled through him. The enemy had something new. Wildcats couldn't have performed like this. Neither could Zeros.

Fuchida's B5N2 had a pair of forward-firing machine guns, plus another pair in the rear cockpit controlled by the radioman. "Be ready, Mizuki," Fuchida called through the intercom.

"What else am I going to be, sir?" the first flying petty officer replied. They'd been together a long time. Mizuki could get away with backtalk that would have sent a lot of ratings to the brig.

Fuchida didn't answer. Some of the enemy fighters ahead, he saw, *were* Wildcats, but they weren't the ones attacking the Japanese. The Americans knew Wildcats couldn't equal Zeros. They thought these new machines could.

And they might have been right. A Zero tumbled toward the Pacific, trailing smoke. Another simply exploded in midair. That pilot, at least, probably never knew what hit him. Fuchida waited to see enemy fighters going down, too. He finally spotted one, but only after several Japanese planes were lost.

The melee with the Zeros that had gone out ahead of the main force didn't last long. The Americans in the new fighters knew the planes that could hurt their ships were more important. They bored in on the Nakajimas and Aichis.

When Fuchida tried to get one of the Americans in his sights, he had trouble holding it there—it was *that* fast. He fired a quick burst, then threw the B5N2 sharply to the left. The new fighter zoomed by, close enough to give him a good look at the pilot. The plane bore a family resemblance to an oversized Wildcat, but had been refined in almost every way possible. How powerful was the engine that drove it? Strong enough to leave Zeros in the dust, plainly. That was not good news.

Mizuki fired a burst, too. His snarls came through the intercom, so he hadn't hit anything, either. Maybe he'd made the American pull away. That would be something, anyhow.

Not all the beefy new American fighters were turning away. Compared to them, the Aichis and Nakajimas the Japanese strike-force pilots flew might have been nailed in place. Dive bombers and torpedo planes fell out of the sky one after another. A few pilots cried out over the radio as they went down. More didn't have the chance.

Then, like a summer lightning storm, the Americans were gone. The rest of the Japanese no doubt as horrified and dismayed as Fuchida, they flew on. What waited for them when they found the enemy fleet?

DON'T DOGFIGHT THE JAPS. *Use your speed. Use your firepower.* People had been telling Joe Crosetti that from the minute he started training. He'd believed it, too, but only in the way he believed in the Pythagorean theorem: it was one more thing he'd learned in school.

The minute he saw Zeros maneuvering, he suddenly understood *why* everybody said the same thing about them. The Japs turned tighter than anything he'd flown probably since graduating from Yellow Perils. Get into a dogfight with them and they'd turn inside you and shoot your ass off.

Diving past them, raking them with your machine guns, standing on the Hellcat's tail to climb again for another dive—that looked like a better plan. Joe's element leader was as green as he was, but he also remembered the lessons. They zoomed past the Zeros, guns blazing, and then went after the Japanese dive bombers and torpedo planes—Vals and Kates in the reporting code they'd learned. Zeros were supposed to be Zekes, but most pilots called them Zeros anyway.

Back in school, some people couldn't remember what the big deal about the square of the hypotenuse was. Sure as hell, some of the Navy pilots here couldn't remember not to get into a turning contest with the fighters with meatballs on their wings. Some of them paid for it, too. "I'm going down!" somebody wailed. Somebody else shouted for his mother, but Mommy couldn't help him now.

As Joe made for a Kate, the plane with the torpedo under its belly opened up on him. Tracers zipped past the cockpit. He swung slightly to the left, expecting the Kate to turn to the right. But the pilot—a slightly horse-faced fellow with a mustache—pulled his plane to the left instead. That caught Joe by surprise and left him without a good shot at the Kate.

There was a flight of Vals. The dive bombers seemed to waddle through the air. Their fixed landing gear made them look like antiques. They'd done a hell of a lot of damage to Allied ships, though.

Joe's element leader bored in on them. He shot one down almost at once. They were built tougher than Zeros, but a few rounds through the engine would do the trick. Joe got one in his sights. The other thing they'd said in school was, *Get in close.* He did. The Val almost filled his sights before he thumbed the firing button on the stick.

Flames shot from the machine guns on his wings. Recoil made the Hellcat seem to stagger in the air. Joe whooped when he saw chunks of sheet metal fly off the Val. Trailing smoke, the plane spun down toward the ocean more than two miles below. "Got him!" Joe yelled. "Fucking *nailed* him!"

A moment later, a Jap in another Val almost nailed him. He'd forgotten Vals and Kates carried rear gunners. All his combat training had been fighter against fighter. The assumption was that if he could handle that, he could handle anything. And so he could—if he didn't do something idiotic. He dove to get away from the gunner.

He tried to count how many Japanese planes went down. He couldn't. Too much was happening too fast. But the Hellcats knocked down a good many. He was sure of that. He was swinging around for another go at the Kates when the squadron leader summoned the American fighters back to the Dauntlesses and Avengers they were shepherding.

"This is just act one, boys," the officer said. "We've got carriers to catch. That's the blowoff."

He was right, and Joe knew it. All the same, he hated to break away.

SABURO SHINDO WAS CALM to the point of being boring. He knew as much. He even cultivated the image. It made him all the more impressive on the rare occasions when he lost his temper—or seemed to for effect.

Now, though, he felt shaken to the core. He'd just seen his Zeros—planes that had dominated every foe they faced—hammered as if they were so many Russian biplanes. He hadn't thought it was possible, but these new American fighters could outrun, outdive, and outclimb his beloved aircraft by margins embarrassingly large. How had the Yankees done it? That there were such swarms of the new enemy planes only made things worse.

The American pilots were raw. He saw that right away. He was able to take advantage of it almost at once, getting on an enemy plane's tail and sending a burst of machine-gun fire into it. But he couldn't stay on its tail for long, because it ran away from him with effortless ease. And the machine-gun rounds didn't knock it down or set it on fire. Wildcats had been able to take a lot of damage—and needed to. By all appearances, this new and bigger fighter was tougher yet.

He used his 20mm cannon against the next American he fought. They did the trick—the enemy plane spiraled down toward the sea. But they were slow-firing and didn't have a lot of ammunition. If he ran dry with them, he was in trouble.

And he could be in trouble even if he didn't. A bullet slammed into his right wing—fortunately, out near the tip, past the fuel tank. Watching another Zero going down trailing a comet's tail of fire reminded him how inadequate the self-sealing on those tanks was. And getting hit by a burst might well make his plane break up in midair even if it didn't burn. Zeros were built light to make them faster and more maneuverable. Everything came with a price, though. If they got shot up, they often paid that price.

A horrified voice in his earphones: "What do we do, sir? They're tearing us up!"

"Protect the strike planes," Shindo answered, banking frantically to try to protect himself. "They're the ones that matter. We're just along for the ride." Even as he spoke, another Aichi dive bomber caught fire and plummeted, the pilot probably dead.

Giving the order and having it mean anything were very different. The Americans dove on the Aichis and Nakajimas, flailed them with those heavy machine guns they carried, streaked away before the protecting Zeros could do much, and climbed to deliver another punishing attack.

Then, quite suddenly, they were gone. They closed up on their own torpedo planes and dive bombers and flew on to the south, towards *Akagi* and *Shokaku*. Shindo belatedly realized that his fighters hadn't had the chance to attack the enemy's strike aircraft. The combat air patrol above the Japanese carriers would have to defend them.

And the combat air patrol above the American's carriers would have to defend *them*. Shindo's lips skinned back from his teeth in a savage smile. No one, from the Indian Ocean to the eastern Pacific here, had yet managed to keep Japanese Navy fliers from striking what they intended to strike. And, he vowed to himself, no one would now.

But how many carriers did the Yankees have, to have launched so many planes? That was also a belated question. He should have wondered sooner, but all he could do now was shrug. *However many there are, we'll deal with them, that's all. We have to.* He flew on.

ON *AKAGI'S* BRIDGE, Commander Minoru Genda got reports from the radiomen monitoring signals from the Japanese aircraft and what they could pick up from the Americans. Quietly, Rear Admiral Tomeo Kaku said, "Gentlemen, it appears likely we will soon be under attack. I rely on our airmen to hold the enemy at arm's length, and on our crew to fight the ship if for any reason the airmen are not completely successful."

"Sir, from everything I'm hearing, this attack will be larger and more severe than the one we faced last year," Genda warned. "Our intelligence estimates of what the Americans could throw at us seem too low."

Kaku shrugged. "Karma, *neh*? Things are what they are. We can't change them now. All we can do is our best, and I know we will do that."

Was he really as calm as he seemed? If he was, Genda, whose heart pounded beneath his tunic, admired him tremendously. He couldn't help saying, "I wish we had *Zuikaku* with us."

"So do I." But Kaku shrugged again. "The Yankees got lucky, and we got . . . not so lucky. That's karma, too. Here we are, and here they are, and we've got to beat them with what we have, not with what we wish we had."

The officer in charge of the recently installed radar set was a young, studious lieutenant named Tanekichi Furuta who'd studied engineering at the University of Southern California. "Sir," he said to Kaku, "we have a signal coming out of the north. Range is about a hundred kilometers and closing."

"I understand," the skipper said. He nodded to Genda. "We have about twenty minutes, Commander. Any last notions that will give us a better chance?"

"All I can think of, sir, is to tell the fighters above our carriers to hit the enemy strike planes with everything they have and to ignore the U.S. fighters as much as they can," Genda answered. "They should already know that, though."

"Very well." Kaku nodded again. "We will wait, then, and be ready to maneuver and to shoot down as many enemy planes as possible."

"Yes, sir," Genda said gravely. *Akagi* carried a dozen 120mm guns and fourteen twin 25mm mounts. She could put a lot of shells in the air. Her escorts could put up even more. How much good would all that firepower do? In the last fight, facing what was plainly a smaller strike force, two of the three Japanese carriers had been hit. Japanese fliers had given better than they got, though, so that battle proved a success. Could they do it again? Would this one?

"All ahead full," Admiral Kaku called down to the engine room. In time of need, *Akagi* could be handled almost like a destroyer. And time of need was coming. The ships ahead of the carrier started shooting. A moment later, so did the carrier herself. Puffs of black smoke appeared in the sky.

Trailing smoke, an enemy plane—one of the ferocious new fighters everyone was talking about?—cartwheeled into the sea. A great splash, and the aircraft was gone. *"Banzai!"* someone called. But how many more planes would have to fall before this battle became a success?

ONE THING JOE CROSETTI HADN'T TRAINED for was antiaircraft fire. There were obvious reasons why not. If such training got too realistic, he might have had to practice bailing out . . . if he could.

As the attack force neared the Japanese fleet, shell bursts appeared in the sky ahead of him and then all around him. When one shell burst not nearly far enough below him, it was like driving a car over a nasty pothole you hadn't seen—he bounced sharply down and then sharply up again, so that his teeth clicked together. Only after he tasted blood in his mouth did he realize he'd bitten his tongue.

A few seconds later, he got another pothole bump, and something clanged into his fuselage. "Jesus!" he yipped, anxiously scanning all the dials on the instrument panel at once. Nothing seemed wrong or out of place. He still had fuel, oil, hydraulics. . . . That clang scared him out of ten years' growth just the same.

Only one thing to do—take out his moment of panic on the Japs. The little yellow slant-eyed sons of bitches thought they owned the world. They thought they had the right to own the world, and to take whatever pieces of it they fancied. Joe was here, literally, to show them they were wrong.

Here they came. The U.S. Hellcats had ripped into the Japanese strike force.

Now it was the Japs' turn to try to knock down as many Dauntlesses and Avengers as they could before the dive bombers and torpedo planes struck at their ships.

Nobody could say the guys who flew those Zeros weren't game. Nobody could say the bastards didn't know their business, either. They understood just what they had to do, and they aimed to do it. If Wildcats and Hellcats got in their way, they fought them. Otherwise, they went for the planes that mattered more.

"Hit 'em, boys!" The squadron leader's voice rasped in Joe's earphones. "The best defense is a good offense. This is what we came for."

Joe's element leader needed no more encouragement than that. "Come on, Crosetti," he called. "Let's go hunting."

"Roger," Joe answered, and stuck with the other Hellcat when it zoomed out ahead of the American dive bombers and torpedo planes, as if to tell the Japs they'd have to go through the fighters to get where they wanted to go.

The Japanese fighters flew in what Joe thought of as a gaggle—not nearly such a rigid formation as the Americans used. It put him in mind of boxing against a southpaw: you weren't sure what was coming next. They looked as if they ought to be easy to pick off one at a time. If they were so damn easy, though, how come they'd given American pilots two successive sets of lumps around Hawaii, to say nothing of the black eye in the Philippines?

"Oh, shit!" That was the voice of Joe's element leader, and panic filled it. Joe saw why, too. A Zero had put a cannon shell into one of his wing tanks. Self-sealing was all very well, but nothing would have stopped that leak or that fire. "I'm going down!" he wailed, and he did, spinning wildly. Joe hoped to see a chute open, but there was nothing, nothing at all—just a Hellcat falling toward the sea.

An instant later, an Avenger blew up. That wasn't gasoline catching on fire; that was the torpedo slung under the aircraft blowing up. A Jap fighter must have made a lucky shot.

Joe looked around frantically for someone to latch on to. He felt naked and alone up there, the way anybody suddenly bereft of his comrade would have. For the time being, he had nobody to keep an eye out for him.

And then, suddenly, somebody was flying alongside of him. The other American pilot waved, as if to say he'd lost his leader and was looking for somebody to link up with. By the way the fellow flew, he was content to stay a wingman. That wasn't how Joe wanted to become an element leader, but one of the fastest lessons he got in combat was that nobody gave a damn about what he wanted.

Some of the Avengers had already started heading down toward the Pacific for their torpedo runs. They weren't the hopelessly slow, hopelessly clumsy Devastators that had preceded them, but they weren't any real match for Zeros, either. Several Japanese fighters dove after them.

When Joe saw that, he laughed a very nasty laugh. The Zero that could out-dive a Hellcat hadn't been born yet. He pointed, then shoved his stick forward. His fighter's nose dropped. As he dove after the Japs, his new wingman stuck like glue.

He got on a Jap's tail and thumbed the firing button. The Zero caught fire. It went straight down into the ocean. Yelling like a red Indian, he went after another one. This Jap must have spotted him at the last second, because the fellow did a flick roll and squirted away like a wet watermelon seed shot out between your fingers. One second he was there; the next, gone.

"Son of a bitch!" Joe said: frustration mixed with reluctant respect. The Zero really *was* as maneuverable as people said. Joe sure wouldn't have tried that getaway in a Hellcat, but it worked like a charm. Still, in evading him, the Jap had to break off his attack on the Avengers, so Joe figured he'd done his job.

And his altimeter was unwinding like a son of a bitch. He leveled off at under two thousand feet, then pulled the stick back and climbed. If he'd had any Japs on his tail, he would have left them behind as if they'd nailed their shoes to the floor.

As he gained altitude, he got a look at the Japanese ships not far ahead. He'd spent more than a year studying silhouettes and photos and models from every angle under the sun—and he still had a devil of a time telling destroyers from cruisers, cruisers from battleships. Even the carrier was hard to spot, and he was damned if he knew for sure which one she was.

But that wasn't his headache, not really. He needed to run out of planes before he worried about ships. He looked around for more Zeros to shoot up.

FUCHIDA HAD KNOWN IT WOULD BE BAD. The American air armada and the ferocious attack it got off against the Japanese strike force had warned him of that. But nothing in his blackest nightmares had warned him it would be as bad as *this*.

American ships stretched as far as the eye could see, as far and farther. Fuchida knew—few men knew better—the resources the Japanese Empire had available. Raw fear almost made his hand shake on the torpedo plane's stick. How were those slender resources going to stand against . . . this?

A warrior's iron steadied him. Japan had beaten the Americans before. One well-trained man who despised death was worth half a dozen of the ordinary kind. So his country's doctrine insisted, and so it had seemed up till now.

If, however, the enemy opposed you with a dozen ordinary men . . .

He shook his head. He would not think like that. The Japanese strike force had plenty, even now, to blunt the force of this attack. He believed that. He had to believe it. The alternative was feeling that rising panic again.

"Commander-*san*?" The voice on the intercom belonged to his bombardier.

"*Hai?*" Fuchida did his best to suppress what was going on inside him, but he could still hear the tension even in that one-word response.

"Sir, I was just thinking—it's a shame we can't carry two torpedoes," the rating said.

Fuchida broke up, right there in the cockpit. He didn't think he'd ever done that before. Laughter washed away the last of the fear. "*Domo arigato,* Imura-*san*," he said. "I needed that. We'll just have to do what we can with what we've got."

From the rear cockpit, Mizuki the radioman said, "That's what the man with the little dick said when he went to bed with the geisha."

Both Fuchida and Imura snorted. Fuchida's confidence, having returned, now soared. How could his country lose when it had men who cracked silly jokes in the face of death?

The Americans seemed intent on showing him exactly how Japan could lose. The destroyers and cruisers protecting the U.S. carriers—and were those battleships out ahead of them, too?—threw up a curtain of flak the likes of which he'd never seen before. That didn't worry him so much, though. The antiaircraft fire would knock down a few planes, but only a few. You went ahead and did your job and didn't worry about it. If you and an enemy shell happened to wind up in the same place at the same time, that was hard luck, and you couldn't do a thing about it.

But the Yankees, despite having dispatched such an enormous strike force against *Akagi* and *Shokaku,* also kept a formidable combat air patrol above their own fleet. Wildcats and the new fighters—whose name Fuchida did not know—tore into the attacking Japanese planes.

Mizuki's rear-facing machine guns chattered. "Scared the *baka yaro* off!" the radioman said triumphantly. And he must have, for no machine-gun bullets tore into the torpedo plane. Fuchida allowed himself the luxury of a sigh of relief. He hadn't even seen the enemy plane Mizuki fired at.

Two burning Zeros plummeted into the Pacific. Part of the problem was that the new American fighters looked a lot like bigger versions of the Wildcats with which they mingled. They were plainly descended from the planes with which Fuchida and the Japanese were familiar. But any careless Zero pilot who tried to take them on as if they were Wildcats discovered he'd made a mistake—usually his last one. Zeros could outfly the older American fighters, but not these, not these.

A piece of shrapnel clanged against Fuchida's wing. He glanced to the left. He didn't see fire. That deserved—and got—another sigh of relief from him. Then the curtain of antiaircraft fire eased. He'd brought his Nakajima past the enemy's screening ships. A carrier loomed ahead.

It threw out its own flak, of course. Tracers stabbed toward him. He ignored them. A torpedo run had to be straight. "Ready?" he called to the bombardier.

"Ready, sir," Imura answered. "A hair to the right, sir, if you please. I think she'll try to dodge to port when we launch."

Fuchida made the adjustment. The torpedo splashed into the sea. The Nakajima suddenly grew lighter, faster, and more maneuverable. Now Fuchida wished he were only a spectator, and a man who had to get out of there alive if he could. But, as the officer in overall command of the Japanese air strike, he had to linger and do what he could to direct his countrymen against the enemy. And lingering, in this neighborhood, was asking not to grow old.

"Diving against a Yankee carrier. May the Emperor live ten thousand years!" The radio call made Fuchida look around to see if he could find the attacking Aichi. But the Americans were spread out over so much ocean, he couldn't spot it. It might have been a good many kilometers away. He didn't see any sudden great plume of smoke rising from a stricken ship, either. *Too bad,* he thought.

* * *

THE PILOT IN THIS WILDCAT flew his plane as aggressively as if it were one of the new American fighters. Saburo Shindo didn't mind that at all. Aggressiveness was a great virtue in a fighter pilot—when he had the aircraft that could make the most of it. This fellow didn't, not against a Zero. Shindo got on his tail and stayed there, pumping bullets into the enemy plane till at last it caught fire and went down.

Shooting down enemy fighters was the reason he'd accompanied the Japanese dive bombers and torpedo planes against the Americans. Doing his job should have given him more satisfaction, especially since he was good at it. Today, he felt like a man snatching up whatever he could as he escaped a burning house. He might hang on to a few trinkets, a few toys, but the house would still be gone forever.

Two American fighters knocked down a Nakajima just as it started its run against an enemy ship. Shindo was too far away to help or to draw off the American planes. He could only watch helplessly.

That summed up how he felt about too much of this fight. The Japanese strike force from *Akagi* and *Shokaku* that had done such splendid work around Hawaii was getting hacked to bits before his eyes. One after another, planes tumbled into the sea. Where would more highly trained, highly experienced pilots and aircrew come from after these men were gone? He had no idea.

He also had no idea whether he would live long enough for the question to be anything but academic to him. The Americans were hitting the strike force with everything they had, and they had more than he'd ever imagined. He felt like a man who'd stuck his hand into a meat grinder.

Being an experienced fighter pilot had drilled the habit of checking six into him. That let him spot an onrushing American plane in time to pull up and roll away. The enemy zoomed by without being able to open fire on him. Had this fellow flown a Wildcat, Shindo would have gone after him in turn. But the Yankee had one of the new fighters. Chasing them in a Zero was like trying to fly up to the sun. You could try, sure, but it wouldn't do you any good.

"*Banzai!*" The victory shout made Shindo look around. He hadn't heard it nearly often enough in this fight. He felt like cheering himself when he saw a U.S. carrier on fire and listing to starboard. *Something* had gone right. About time, too.

But how many carriers formed the core of this fleet? However many there were, they far outnumbered the half dozen Japan had used to open the war against the USA. His own country had been prepared to lose a third of that force if it meant a successful attack. Would the Americans be any less ruthless in their counterattack? It seemed unlikely.

"Shindo-*san*! Are you still there? This is Fuchida."

"Yes, sir. I'm still here. What are your orders?"

"We've done everything we can here, I think—and the Americans will have done what they can do to us," Fuchida answered; Shindo wished he'd left out the second part of the observation, no matter how true it was. The strike-force commander went on, "Time to return to our ships."

"Yes, sir," Shindo repeated stolidly. Whether the Japanese carriers were still there was anybody's guess. Shindo knew as much, and no doubt Fuchida did, too. That didn't mean the senior officer was wrong. They had to try.

ALL OF *AKAGI*'S antiaircraft guns seemed to be going off at once, the heavy and the light together. The din on the bridge was indescribable. Genda and the other officers had to shout to make themselves heard. Admiral Kaku had the conn himself. Genda could do things the skipper couldn't. His strategic grasp reached from Hawaii into the Indian Ocean, while he doubted Tomeo Kaku cared a sen's worth about anything that happened beyond the ends of *Akagi*'s flight deck. But Kaku handled the carrier the way a fighter ace flew his Zero: as if the craft were an extension of his own body. Genda admired his skill and knew he would never be able to match it himself, not if he lived to be ninety.

Machine guns blazing, an American fighter raked the flight deck from no higher than the top of the island. Despite the bellowing antiaircraft guns, the enemy escaped. "That is a brave man," Genda said.

"*Zakennayo!*" somebody else replied. "How many of our brave men did he just shoot up?" Genda had no answer for that.

"Helldivers!" someone screeched. Genda involuntarily looked up, though steel armor kept him from seeing the sky. But then, he didn't need to see to imagine dive bombers racing down towards *Akagi*. He was one of the men who'd brought the technique to Japan, and he'd brought it from the USA.

Rear Admiral Kaku swung the wheel hard to port, then even harder to starboard. Muscles in his shoulders bunched as he tried to force the carrier to respond to his will at once. Bombs splashed into the sea all around *Akagi,* but the first few missed. *So far, so good,* Genda thought.

Then another shout pierced the racket on the bridge: "Torpedo! Torpedo to port!"

This isn't fair was what went through Genda's mind. *Too much happening all at once.* He and his countrymen had kept the Americans off-balance through the first two fights in Hawaiian waters. Now the shoe was on the other foot, and much less comfortable this way.

Cursing horribly, Kaku yanked the wheel to port again, intending to turn into the torpedo's path. But either that took him into the path of the dive bombers overhead or the Yankee pilots simply guessed with him and outguessed him. Three bombs hit *Akagi:* near the stern, amidships, and right at the bow.

The next thing Genda knew, he was on the floor. One of his ankles screamed at him when he tried to put weight on it. He hauled himself upright anyhow—duty shouted louder than pain. Several men were down and wouldn't get up again; the steel beneath his feet had twisted like cardboard and was awash in blood.

Kaku still wrestled with the wheel. He went on cursing for a few seconds, then said something worse than the blackest of oaths: "She doesn't answer her helm." If *Akagi* couldn't steer . . . Kaku turned to the speaking tube to shout down to the engine room. A ship could be guided, crudely, by her engines. It wasn't much, but it was what they had.

The torpedo hit then, as near amidships as made no difference.

Akagi had taken a torpedo, from a plane off the *Lexington,* during the first strike against Hawaii. That fish, like a lot of the ones the Americans used in the first months of the war, proved a dud. This one—wasn't.

Genda found himself on the floor again. Getting up a second time hurt even more than it had the first. All the same, he did it. Once he was on his feet, he wondered why he'd bothered. For a moment, he also wondered if he could stand straight. Then he realized the problem wasn't his but *Akagi*'s: the ship had a list, one that worsened every minute.

Flames were shooting up through holes in the flight deck, too. Men with hoses fought them, but they weren't having much luck.

"My apologies, Commander," Admiral Kaku said, as if he'd accidentally bumped into Genda.

"Sir, we've got to abandon ship," Genda blurted. As if to underscore his words, an explosion shook *Akagi*. Maybe that was aviation gasoline going up, or maybe it was the carrier's munitions starting to cook off.

Calmly, Tomeo Kaku nodded. "You are correct, of course. I will give the order." He spoke into the intercom, which by some miracle still functioned: "All hands, prepare to abandon ship! This is the captain speaking! All hands, prepare to abandon ship!" Bowing politely to Genda, he went on, "You should head for the flight deck now, Commander. I see you have an injured leg. Give yourself all the time you need."

"Yes, sir." Genda took one lurching stride towards a doorway twisted open. "What about you, sir?"

"What about me?" Kaku smiled a sweet, sad smile. "This is my ship, Commander."

Genda couldn't very well misunderstand that. He did protest: "Sir, you should save yourself so you can go on serving the Emperor. Japan needs all the capable senior officers she can find."

"I know you younger men feel that way," Kaku said, smiling still. "If that course seems right and proper to you, then you should follow it. As for me . . . I have made mistakes here. If I had not made mistakes, I would not be losing *Akagi*. The least I can do is atone to his Majesty for my failure. *Sayonara*, Commander."

After that, nothing would change his mind. Recognizing as much, Genda bowed and limped away. The last he saw of Rear Admiral Kaku, *Akagi*'s skipper was fastening his belt to a chair so he would be sure to go down with his ship.

When Genda got to the flight deck, he saw more flames leaping up from the bomb hit at the stern. "Come on, boys, over the side!" a petty officer shouted, sounding absurdly cheerful. "Swim away from the hull as fast as you can, mind, so the undertow doesn't drag you down when she sinks!"

That was good, sensible advice. And the ship's growing list made going over the side easier. Genda cursed when he hit the water even so. That ankle was definitely sprained, and might be broken. He rolled over onto his back and pulled away from *Akagi* with his arms.

American fighters strafed sailors in the sea. Bullets kicked up splashes only a few meters from him. He swam past a dead man leaking scarlet into the Pacific. The blood would draw sharks, but sharks, at the moment, were the least of his worries.

Their antiaircraft guns still blazing, destroyers circled the doomed *Akagi* to pick up survivors. Some men clambered up cargo nets hung from the sides. With his bad leg, Genda couldn't climb. He clung to a line till sailors aboard the *Yukikaze* could haul him up to the deck.

"*Domo arigato,*" he said. When he tried to stand on that bad leg, it wouldn't bear his weight. He had to sit and watch *Akagi* slide beneath the waves. His face crumpled. Tears ran down his cheeks. Since he was already soaking wet, only he noticed. He looked away from the carrier that had fought so long and so well, and noticed he was far from the only man off *Akagi* doing the same. She deserved mourning—and so did Admiral Kaku, who'd never left the bridge.

AN EXULTANT VOICE HOWLED in Joe Crosetti's earphones: "Scratch one flattop!" Yells and cheers and curses rang out as the enemy carrier sank.

"How do you like that, you Jap bastards?" Joe shouted. He looked around for more Zeros, and didn't see any. Some might still be airborne, but not close to him. He'd made a few runs at sailors bobbing in the sea, but decided he could hurt the enemy worse by shooting up his ships. That felt like a real duel, because the Japs shot back for all they were worth. Watching sailors scatter was a hell of a lot of fun.

After he'd made a couple of passes, an authoritative voice sounded off: "Attention, Hellcat pilots! We've got a formation of bandits coming up from the south at about 15,000 feet. Time to give them a friendly American welcome, hey?"

Joe needed a few seconds to figure out where south was. He'd got all turned around in his strafing runs. When he did, he started to climb. His new wingman still clung like a burr, which was what a wingman was supposed to do. He wondered who the guy was, and from which carrier he'd taken off.

There were the bandits, buzzing along as if they didn't have a care in the world. If they didn't, they were about to. Joe had trouble recognizing ships, but planes he knew. He clicked through a mental card file. Bombers. Twin-engined. Streamlined—they looked like flying cigars. *Bettys,* he thought. They could carry bombs or torpedoes. The point of the exercise, as far as he was concerned, was to make sure they didn't get the chance to use whatever they were carrying.

They'd seen the American fighters, and started taking evasive action. That was pretty funny. They weren't slow and they weren't completely ungraceful, but no bomber had a prayer of outdodging a fighter that wanted to come after it. The Bettys also started shooting. They carried several machine guns in blisters on the fuselage—almost impossible to aim well—and a 20mm cannon in a clumsy turret at the rear of the plane.

When Joe got on the tail of one, the Jap in that rear turret started banging away at him. The cannon didn't shoot very fast. There'd be a flash and a puff of smoke as the shell burst, then a little while later another one. Joe fired a burst as he swung the Hellcat's nose across that turret. The tail gunner stopped shooting: wounded or dead.

With that annoyance gone, Joe sawed the Hellcat's nose across the Betty's left wing root and squeezed off another burst. Sure as hell, the bomber caught fire. Intelligence said Bettys carried a lot of fuel to give them long range, and that they lacked armor and self-sealing tanks. It sure looked as if Intelligence knew what it was talking about.

He went after another bomber and shot it down just the same way. The poor bastard in the rear turret never had a chance—and once he was gone, none of the weapons the Betty carried could damage a tough bird like a Hellcat except by luck. Joe knew a moment's pity for the fliers trapped in their burning planes, but only a moment's. They would have bombed his carrier if they'd got the chance. And they would have yelled, *"Banzai!"* while they did it, too. Screw 'em.

Still . . . Three miles was a hell of a long way to fall when you were on fire.

Other U.S. pilots found different ways of attacking the Bettys. Some flew straight at the bombers and shot up their cockpits. Others climbed past them and dove like falcons stooping on doves. The unescorted Bettys were slaughtered. Watching, taking part, Joe again felt tempted to pity, but again not for long. This was the enemy. The only reason they weren't doing the same thing to him was that they couldn't. They surely wanted to.

Trails of smoke and flame told of Betty after Betty going into the Pacific. They never had a chance. They must have counted on getting close to the American fleet without being spotted. They might have done some damage if they had. The way things were, it was a massacre.

"Let's head for home, children," the squadron leader said. "We've got one enemy carrier sunk, one enemy carrier dead in the water and burning, no other carriers spotted. By the size of the enemy strike, it probably set out from two ships. We did what we came to do, in other words. We've cleared the way for things to go forward."

That sounded good to Joe. He wanted to shoot up some more Japanese ships, but a glance at the fuel gauge told him hanging around wasn't a good idea. He had to find north again, the same way he'd had to find south when he went after the Bettys.

He shook his head with amazement that approached awe. Two Bettys for sure. He thought he'd got a Zero and a Kate. One fight and he was within shouting distance of being an ace. He'd dreamt about doing stuff like that, but he'd had trouble believing it. Believe it or not, he'd done it.

He hoped Orson Sharp was okay. He'd looked around whenever he got the chance—which wasn't very often—but he hadn't spotted his longtime roomie. He kept telling himself that didn't prove anything one way or the other. Sharp was probably looking around for him, too, and not finding him.

On he went toward the north. He wondered how much damage the Jap strike force had been able to do. Less than it would have before it tangled with the American planes, that was for damn sure. And where would the Japs land now? Both of their carriers were out of business. Would they go on to Oahu? Maybe some of the Zeros could get there, but the Vals and Kates didn't have a chance. "Oh, too bad," Joe said, and laughed.

He might have been speaking of the devil, because he got a radio call on the all-planes circuit from a Hellcat a few miles ahead of him: "Heads up, boys. Here come the Japs on the way home—except they don't know home burned down. Every plane we splash now is one more we don't have to worry about later on."

Joe didn't need long to spot what was left of the enemy's air armada. He whistled softly to himself. The Japs had had a lot more planes the first time the American strike force ran into them. The U.S. fleet's antiaircraft guns and the combat air patrol must have done a hell of a job. That looked like good news.

Zeros still escorted the surviving dive bombers and torpedo planes. Hellcats roared to the attack. Joe took another look at his fuel gauge. He'd be pushing it if he gunned his bird real hard—but why was he in this cockpit, if not to push it?

He saw a Kate flying south as if it didn't have a care in the world. Was that the sneaky bastard who'd given him the slip last time by jinking left instead of right? He nodded to himself. He thought so. "Fool me once, shame on you," he said. "Fool me twice, shame on me." He goosed the Hellcat and raced toward the Jap torpedo plane.

COMMANDER MITSUO FUCHIDA'S HEART WAS HEAVY as lead inside him. He knew the strike force he led hadn't come close to defeating and driving back the U.S. fleet. In words of one syllable, the Japanese had got smashed. A glance at the battered remnants of the strike force was enough to tell him that. Far too many Japanese planes had never got to the American fleet. Of the ones that had, far too many hadn't got away.

And what would become of the ones that had done everything they were supposed to do? That was another good question, one much better than he wished it were. He'd seen the size of the American strike force when its path crossed his. What had the Yankees done to the Japanese fleet? Were any flight decks left for these few poor planes to land on?

He checked his fuel gauge. He'd been running as lean as he could, but he didn't have a chance of getting back to Oahu with what was in his tanks, and he knew it. He hadn't said anything to his radioman and bombardier, not yet. No point borrowing trouble, not when they already had so much. Maybe *Akagi* or *Shokaku*—maybe *Akagi and Shokaku*—still waited. He could hope. Hope didn't hurt, and didn't cost anything.

One of the handful of Zeros still flying with the strike force waggled its wings to get Fuchida's attention. He waved to show he'd got the signal. The pilot (yes, that was Shindo; Fuchida might have known he was too tough and too sneaky for the Americans to kill) pointed south.

Fuchida's eyes followed that leather-gloved index finger. There in the privacy of the cockpit, he groaned. Running into the U.S. strike force coming and going struck him as most unfair, though it wasn't really surprising, not when both air fleets had to fly reciprocal courses to strike their enemies and return.

"Attention!" he called over the all-planes circuit. "Attention! Enemy aircraft dead ahead!" That would wake up anybody who hadn't noticed. Then he added what was, under the circumstances, the worst thing he could say: "They appear to have seen us."

"What do we do now, Commander-*san*?" Petty Officer Mizuki asked.

"We try to get through them or past them," said Fuchida, who had no better answer. How? And what if they succeeded? Hope one of the carriers still survived? Hope some of the other ships in the Japanese fleet still survived, so he might be rescued if he ditched? That struck him as most likely, and also as a very poor best.

Reaching the Japanese fleet would be an adventure in itself. Here came the Americans. Fuchida tried to get some feel for their numbers, some feel for how many the combat air patrol over *Akagi* and *Shokaku* and the fleet's antiaircraft had shot down. It wasn't easy, not with enemy planes spread out all over the sky ahead. The shortest answer he could find was *not as many as I wish they had.*

Brave as a *daimyo*'s hunting dogs, the Zeros shot ahead to try to hold the Americans away from the Aichis and Nakajimas that might hurt enemy ships in some later fight . . . if they still had a flight deck to land on. But there weren't nearly enough Zeros to do the job. A few American fighters engaged them. That kept them busy while the other Yankees roared on toward the Japanese dive bombers and torpedo planes.

Fuchida fired a burst at an onrushing American fighter. That was more a gesture of defiance and warning than a serious attempt to shoot down the American. His B5N2 made a good torpedo plane. The Nakajima had also made a pretty good level bomber, though it was obsolete in that role now. It had never been intended to make a fighter.

After squeezing off the burst, Fuchida flung the aircraft to the left, as he had on the way north. Then he'd shaken off his attacker. This time, to his horror and dismay, the enemy went with him without an instant's hesitation. The American plane carried half a dozen heavy machine guns, not two feeble pop-guns like the B5N2.

Bullets slammed into the torpedo plane. Oil from the engine sprayed across the windshield. The bombardier screamed. So did Mizuki. Fuchida wondered why he hadn't been hit himself. It wouldn't matter for long. The plane was falling out of the sky, and he couldn't do a damn thing about it.

Still wrestling with the controls, he shouted, "Get out! Get out if you can!" The Pacific rushed up to meet him. He braced himself, knowing it would do no good.

Impact.

Blackness.

* * *

A COLUMN OF SMOKE GUIDED Saburo Shindo to *Shokaku*'s funeral pyre. The carrier burned from stem to stern. Destroyers clustered around her, taking off survivors. He supposed they would torpedo her before long. She deserved a merciful *coup de grâce,* as a samurai committing *seppuku* deserved to have a second finish him after he'd shown he had the courage to slit his own belly.

Akagi was already gone. Shindo had found no sign of the proud carrier from which he'd taken off. That made things about as bad as they could be.

Antiaircraft shells burst around him. Some of the ships down there feared he might be an American, coming back for another strike. "*Baka yaro!*" he snarled. Yes, they were idiots, but hadn't they earned the right?

He watched an Aichi go into the sea not far from a destroyer. The aircraft was lost, but the crew might live. Few strike planes had managed to come even this far. After two encounters with the U.S. strike force and after the furious defense above the American fleet, the Japanese had taken a beating the likes of which they hadn't known since . . . when? The encounter with the Korean turtle ships at the end of the sixteenth century? No other comparison occurred to Shindo, but this had to be worse.

He thought about ditching, too, thought about it and shook his head. Unlike the Nakajimas and Aichis, he had a chance to get back to Oahu. Hawaii would need as many airplanes as possible to defend her. Japan certainly wouldn't be able to bring in any more. If he could land his Zero, he should.

On he flew, then. A cruiser burned not far south of *Shokaku.* Again, lesser ships were rescuing survivors. They probably should have been fleeing back toward Hawaii, too. The Americans were bound to strike again as soon as they could. What the devil could stop them now? This whole fleet lay at their mercy.

Perhaps half a dozen other Zeros remained in the sky with him. Shindo shook his head in disbelief. Those few fighters were all that was left of two fleet carriers' worth of air power. *Zuikaku* was laid up at Pearl Harbor, a sitting duck for American air strikes. He hoped her air contingent had moved to land bases on Oahu. Even if the planes were gone, though, half of Japan's fleet-carrier strength would have to be written off. The Yankees had put more fleet carriers into this strike than Japan had left—to say nothing of their swarm of light carriers.

"What are we going to do?" he muttered. He had no idea. Whatever it was, it would be under the Army's aegis from now on. Japan's naval presence in and around Hawaii had just collapsed. A man would have to be blind to think anything different. Shindo hoped he could see trouble clearly, anyhow.

The engine on one of the surviving Zeros quit. Maybe the plane had a small fuel leak. Maybe it had just flown too hard in the battle. Either way, it wouldn't get back to Oahu. The pilot saluted as he started the long glide down to the ocean. Maybe he could ditch smoothly. Maybe a Japanese ship would find him if he did. But his chances weren't good, and he had to know it.

Shindo wondered what his own chances were. He'd flown hard, too. He throttled back even more, using just enough power to stay airborne. *Soon,* he thought. *Soon I'll see the island.*

And he did. The engine started coughing not long afterwards, but he got down on the Haleiwa airstrip. He'd flown from there during the Japanese invasion of Hawaii. Now he would have to defend it against an American return he'd never really expected.

IX

JANE ARMITAGE WAITED FOR NIGHTFALL WISHING SHE WERE DEAD, THE WAY SHE did every day. A couple of the women who'd been dragooned into the Japs' military brothel had found ways to kill themselves. Part of her envied them, but she didn't have the nerve to follow in their footsteps. She told herself she wanted to stay alive to see the USA avenge itself on Japan. That was true, but most of what held her back was simple fear.

She looked out through the barred window of her room. Another perfect late afternoon in Wahiawa. Not too hot, not too cold, not too muggy, not too dry. Blue sky. A few white clouds. Bright sunshine. This hell of a place was all the more hellish for sitting in the middle of paradise.

Japanese soldiers hurried by. Wherever they were going, they didn't have time to pause for a fast fuck. Some of them acted antsy, jabbering away in their incomprehensible language, sometimes even shouting at one another. She hoped they had plenty to be antsy about.

A knock on the door. That wasn't a horny Jap. Soon, yes, but not yet. That was supper. She opened the door. A tiny, gray-haired Chinese woman handed her a tray. She didn't speak any English. The Japs made sure of such things. How much practice had they had running brothels like this? Plenty, plainly.

Supper was better and there was more of it than if she'd still been working her little vegetable plot. She didn't care. The rice and fish and cabbage tasted like ashes in her mouth. She wasn't getting close to enough to eat for *her* sake. Oh, no. The Japs just didn't want her to be too skinny to please her . . . customers.

The Chinese woman came back in a bit to take the tray to the kitchen. She held up her hand with fingers and thumb outspread. Jane nodded dully. Next Jap soldier or sailor in five minutes.

She took off the men's pajamas that were all they let her wear and lay down on the bed naked. Some days she couldn't stand it and she fought, knowing fighting was hopeless. The Japs beat her up and then did what they wanted anyway. Today she didn't have it in her to fight. If she did her best to believe it wasn't happening, she could get through till they let her quit. Then she could go to sleep . . . and have another day just like this one to look forward to.

Another knock on the door, this one peremptory. Jane didn't say anything. She just lay there. The door opened anyhow, of course. In came a Jap. He smiled at her nakedness. She pretended he wasn't there, and kept on pretending even when he dropped his pants and got on top of her.

He did what he did. His weight was heavy on her, his breath sour in her face. He squeezed her breasts, but not quite painfully hard. It could have been worse. It had been worse, plenty of times. A slightly better than average rape. Oh, joy. He grunted and jerked and then pulled out and got off her, a stupid grin on his face. Up came his trousers. Out the door he went, without a backwards glance.

Half a minute later, another one of those here-I-come knocks. She hadn't even had time to douche, not that that would have done much against either disease or getting knocked up. In came the next one: an older man, a sergeant. She flinched inside, and hoped it didn't show. The older guys were more likely to be mean. They fed off fear, too.

This one let his trousers fall around his ankles in the middle of the little room and motioned for Jane to get down on her knees in front of him. She tried not to let him know she understood. She particularly hated that. She had to *do* it, not let it be done to her. She wanted to bite down *hard* every single time, too. Only the fear of what they'd do to her if she did held her back.

When she kept acting stupid, the sergeant yanked her out of bed and put her where he wanted her. He was shorter than she was, but strong as an ox. He motioned that he'd slap her into the middle of next week if she didn't get down to business. Hating him, hating herself more, she did. At least he wasn't very big. She gagged less that way. She wished she had enough Japanese to tell him what a little prick he was.

She hadn't got very far when he suddenly pushed her away. *That* was out of the ordinary. He waddled the three or four steps to the window, pants still at half mast, and stared out. That was when Jane realized the deep bass rumble she felt as much as heard was real, was outside herself, not the product of her own mind grinding itself to pieces.

The Jap twitched as if he'd stuck his finger into an electric socket. He said something that should have set the peeling wallpaper on fire. Then, still cussing a blue streak, he pulled up his pants and dashed out of the room.

Jane jumped to her feet and ran to the window. Anything that would make him give up on a blowjob halfway through was something she had to see.

And she did. The sky was full of planes flying in from the northwest. They were a long way up, but they didn't look like any she'd ever seen before. That and the Jap's reaction made a sudden wild hope spring to life in her. *Are they American?* she thought. *Please, God, let them be American. I stopped believing in You when You did this to me, but I'll start again if they're American. I swear I will.*

Antiaircraft guns in and around Wahiawa started banging away. The racket sounded like the end of the world, but it was the sweetest music Jane had ever heard.

Whatever this was, it wasn't just a nuisance raid like the one the year before. There were dozens and dozens, maybe hundreds, of planes up there. Nobody could have sent so many without meaning business.

Jane blinked. From what she knew about the state of the art—which, as an officer's more or less ex-wife, was a fair amount—nobody could have sent that many planes from the mainland at all. B-17s that flew into Hawaii did so un-armed, with no bomb load, and arrived almost dry just the same. Or they had . . . in 1941. This was 1943. The state of the art must have changed while she wasn't looking.

And it had, by God—by the God she began believing in again with all her heart and all her soul and all her might. The bombers started unloading on Wheeler Field and Schofield Barracks, just the other side of the Kamehameha Highway from Wahiawa.

The brothel shook. The window glass rattled. A not *very* badly aimed bomb would turn that glass into shrapnel—and might turn her into hamburger. She backed away from the window, tears streaming down her face. All at once, she wanted to live. And if that wasn't a miracle, what would be?

Screams and cheers from other rooms said she wasn't the only one, either.

Then she heard another kind of scream: one of pain, not joy. One of the women trapped there must have started celebrating even with a Jap in her room. That was foolish, which didn't mean Jane wouldn't have done the same damn thing.

More bombs burst, and still more. It sounded as if the Americans were really giving it to the airport and the barracks. "Kill 'em all!" Jane yelled. "Come on, damn you! Kill 'em all!"

KENZO AND HIROSHI TAKAHASHI HAD THE *OSHIMA MARU* to themselves. Kenzo didn't know exactly where his father was: at the Japanese consulate, the radio studio, maybe even Iolani Palace. His old man was in tight with the occupying authorities—and in hog heaven. The less Kenzo heard about it, the better he liked it.

Hiroshi was at the rudder, Kenzo minding the sampan's sails—or rather, not minding them very well. "Pay attention, goddammit!" Hiroshi barked. "Stop mooning about your girlfriend—she isn't here."

"Yeah," Kenzo said. But he couldn't stop thinking about Elsie. Going to bed with a girl would do that. He wasn't likely to forget the set of lumps those Japanese soldiers had given him, either. If that had turned out even a little different, they would have kicked him to death.

He'd hoped his old man could do something about that—find out who the soldiers were, get them in trouble, *something*. No such luck. The way his father looked at things, the beating was his own damn fault. If he hadn't got the soldiers mad at him, they would have left him alone. That they'd wanted to gang-rape his girlfriend had nothing to do with anything.

"Pay attention," Hiroshi said again. "We're not just running before the wind this time."

"I know. I know." Kenzo couldn't very well help knowing. They had the wind to starboard. They were sailing west to try their luck in the Kaieiewaho Channel, between Oahu and Kauai. They hadn't caught much sailing south lately; those waters were getting fished out. Not so many sampans headed this way: that was what Hiroshi had concluded after listening to a good deal of fishermen's gossip. Kenzo hoped his brother turned out to be right.

"What's going on there?" Hiroshi pointed north, towards Oahu.

"Huh?" Kenzo had been thinking about Elsie again. His eyes followed Hiroshi's forefinger. "Son of a bitch!" he said.

A swarm of Japanese planes was rising from what had been Hickam Field near Pearl Harbor. As the two Takahashi brothers watched, they shook themselves out into formation and flew north.

"Some kind of drill?" Kenzo hazarded.

"Maybe." Hiroshi didn't sound convinced. "They're always grousing about how they don't have a hell of a lot of gasoline, though. That's a lot of planes to send up on an exercise."

"Yeah. But what else could it be?" Kenzo answered his own question before his brother could: "Maybe the good guys are getting frisky again." *The good guys.* He'd thought of the USA that way even before the Japanese soldiers literally jumped on him with both feet, of course. Now his feelings for the country in which he was born had doubled and redoubled. So had his fear that he wouldn't get credit for those feelings no matter what. If the Americans came back to Hawaii—no, *when* they came back—what would he be? Just another Jap, and one whose father was a collaborator.

For now, he needed to remember he was a fisherman first and foremost. The winds got tricky as the *Oshima Maru* rounded Barbers Point, at the southwestern corner of Oahu, and even trickier once they passed Kaena Point, the island's westernmost extremity. By then it was late afternoon.

"Don't you think we ought to get more out into the middle of the channel before we drop our lines?" Kenzo asked.

Hiroshi shook his head. "That's what everybody else does."

As far as Kenzo could see, everybody else did it for a perfectly good reason, too: the fish were most likely to be there. But he didn't argue with his brother. He'd argued with too many people over too many things lately. "Okay, fine," he said. "Have it your way." They were sure to catch enough to keep themselves eating. If they didn't catch more than that, Hiroshi would have to go out into the middle of the channel . . . wouldn't he?

He dumped bait—minnows and offal—into the Pacific. He and Kenzo lowered the lines into the blue, blue water. "Now we wait," Hiroshi said, a sentence that could have passed from one fisherman to another anywhere in the world since the beginning of time.

A mackerel leaping out of the water not far from the sampan told Kenzo catchable fish swam nearby. It told Hiroshi the same thing; he looked as smug as their father did when Japan figured out some new way to make things tough on the USA. Kenzo damn near told him so, but that would have started an argument, too.

When they hauled up the lines, they brought in *ahi* and *aku* and *mahi-mahi*—and some sharks with them. The next little while was the frantic part of the operation. They gutted fish and got them in the storage hold as fast as they could. One of the sharks, about a three-footer, almost bit Kenzo and kept flopping and thrashing even after he'd torn out its insides.

"Damn things really don't die till after sundown," he said.

"You'd better believe it. They—" Hiroshi broke off. He cocked his head to one side. "What's that?"

"I don't hear anything." Kenzo paused—he'd just made a liar of himself. "Oh, wait a minute. Now I do. Sounds like thunder."

Hiroshi snorted, and with reason: the day was fine and clear, with hardly a cloud in the sky. "Pick something that makes sense, why don't you?"

"Okay. Maybe it's bombs." Kenzo said the first thing that popped into his mind. Once he'd said it, though, he realized how much sense it made. The low rumbles were coming from the direction of Oahu, sure as hell. Hope tingled through him. "Maybe the Americans are *really* paying a call."

"It'd be a big one if they are," Hiroshi said, which was true, for the noise went on and on. Since neither one of them could do anything about it, they both went back to gutting fish.

A few minutes later, Kenzo looked east again. When he didn't return to work right away, Hiroshi looked that way, too. They whistled softly at the same time. Thick columns of black, greasy-looking smoke were climbing up over the Waianae Range. "That is an air raid, a damn big one," Kenzo said. After gauging the position of the smoke plumes, he added, "Looks like they're pounding the crap out of Schofield and Wheeler."

"Looks like you're right," Hiroshi said once he'd made the same calculations. "They've got to be hitting other places, too, only we can't see those from where we're at."

"Yeah." Kenzo hadn't thought of that, but his brother was bound to be right. Wheeler Field was one of the most important airstrips on Oahu. If the Americans hit that one, they'd hit Hickam and Ewa and Kaneohe and the others, too. And if they were hitting airstrips like that . . . "Maybe the invasion's really on!"

"Maybe. Jesus Christ, I hope so," Hiroshi said. "About time, if it is."

The intermittent thunder of explosions ceased. But the rumble from the east didn't. If anything, it got louder. Kenzo suddenly pointed. "Will you look at that?"

"Jesus Christ!" Hiroshi said again, this time in tones approaching real reverence. The sky was full of planes, streams of them, and they were flying west, from Oahu toward Kauai. That took a lot of them right over the *Oshima Maru.*

Kenzo and Hiroshi stared up in open-mouthed awe. Kenzo had seen pictures of B-17s before the war started. Some of the big four-engined bombers matched what he remembered of those pictures. Others were a new breed, with longer, narrower wings and tails with twin rudders. The roar of the engines overhead seemed to make the sampan vibrate.

"Where are they going to land?" Hiroshi whispered.

"Beats me," Kenzo answered. He hadn't known Kauai had an airstrip long enough to land planes that big. Maybe the Japanese had built one, although he thought they'd done as little as they could on all the islands except Oahu. Still, he didn't figure that swarm of bombers would have headed for Kauai if they didn't have somewhere to put down.

"We'll tell our grandchildren about this day," Hiroshi said.

"Yeah." Kenzo nodded. "Let's just hope we live to have 'em."

WHEN CORPORAL TAKEO SHIMIZU HEARD THE AIR-RAID sirens go off, he didn't worry much. *Another American nuisance raid,* he thought. The Americans sent seaplanes over Hawaii the way Japan sent them over the U.S. West Coast. They'd drop a few bombs, and then they'd either get shot down or go away.

But orders were orders. "Come on," he called to his men. "Out of the barracks and into the trenches. Put the cards and the *go* boards away. You can pick up the games when you come back."

Grumbling, the soldiers followed him outside. Grumbling even more, they scrambled down into the trenches they'd dug in the lawn in front of the stucco building. People who stained their uniforms swore. Sure as sure, they'd get gigged for dirty clothes at roll call tomorrow morning.

When Shimizu heard aircraft engines overhead, he was relieved at first. "Hear how many there are?" he said. "Those must be our bombers coming back from the practice run they were on."

"I don't think so, sir, please excuse me," Senior Private Furusawa said. "This is a deeper noise. Our engines have a higher pitch."

Shimizu listened a little longer. The noise *did* seem different. Still . . . "Sounds like a lot of planes to me, not the ones and twos the Yankees send. They don't usually come by daylight, either. Are you saying—?"

Before he could finish, antiaircraft guns started banging. The gunners didn't think the planes overhead were Japanese. And Shimizu heard the flat, harsh *crump! crump! crump!* of bursting bombs. He heard more of those explosions than he ever had when the Japanese were conquering Hawaii.

He looked up into the sky. His jaw dropped. Those weren't American seaplanes. He'd grown familiar with their big-bellied lines. Those were bombers, monster bombers, swarms of them. Most flew to the west, in the direction of Hickam Field and Pearl Harbor. But some came right over Honolulu. And the likeliest reason they came right over Honolulu was . . .

Bombs fell from their bellies. He could see them, tumbling down through the air. And they all seemed to be falling straight toward him. *"Duck!"* he shouted, and threw himself facedown in the dirt. All of a sudden, he had more important things to worry about than getting dirt on his uniform.

The bombs' rising whistling scream made him want to scream, too. Then they hit, and he *did* scream. It didn't matter. Nobody could hear him through that thunder. The ground shook, as if in an earthquake. He'd been through some bad quakes in Japan. This was worse than any of them. When things rained down on him, he wasn't sure if he'd be buried alive.

While you were on the receiving end of a bombardment, it seemed to go on forever. At last, after what couldn't have been more than ten minutes of real time, the bombs stopped falling. At least they did close by—he could still hear explosions off to the west. *They were just paying us a social call,* Shimizu thought dazedly. *They really wanted to visit the airstrip and the harbor.*

Like a ground squirrel looking to see if the fox had really gone, he stuck his head out of his hole. The barracks had been shelled before. They'd been leveled this time. Craters were strewn over the ground around the building. So were bodies, and pieces of bodies. Other buildings nearby were smoking ruins.

Yasuo Furusawa came up beside him. The druggist's son looked around with the same horror on his face as Shimizu felt. "Oh," Furusawa said softly, and then again, "Oh." It didn't seem enough, but what else was there to say?

"Help the wounded!" officers screamed. "Get ready to move! Get ready to fight!" Shimizu didn't know how he was supposed to do all those things at once. He didn't know how he was supposed to get ready to fight at all. His rifle was in the barracks, which had started to burn. Looking down the trench, he didn't see anyone else who had a rifle with him, either.

He could do something for injured men, but not much. He bandaged wounds. He helped get people out of the trenches, and helped lift rubble so others could move them. The doctor who showed up after a few minutes quickly looked overwhelmed.

A fire engine screeched to a stop in front of the barracks. The crew—locals—started playing water on what was left of the building. That wouldn't do the rifles in there any good. It might keep the ammunition with them from cooking off, though, which would save some casualties.

Private Shiro Wakuzawa pointed west. "Look!" he said.

Shimizu did. Smoke was rising from the direction of the airfield, and from Pearl Harbor just beyond it. The American bombers had indeed hit that area harder than they'd hit Honolulu. A lieutenant started shouting at the firemen: "Don't worry about this place! Go there! There, do you hear me?" He pointed west, as Wakuzawa had.

The firemen answered him—in English. A couple of them looked Japanese, but nobody admitted to knowing the language. The officer jumped up and down, getting madder and madder. That did him no good at all. He pulled his *katana* from its sheath. The firemen backed away from him. Almost apoplectic by then, he put it back. He could kill the locals, but he couldn't get them to understand what he was talking about, and that was what he needed to do.

Other officers started screaming then. "*Zakennayo!* The rifles!" one of them howled. "How are we supposed to fight the Americans if our rifles are in there?" He pointed at the smoldering, dripping wreckage of the barracks.

Just when all the men with more gold than red on their collar tabs seemed to have lost their heads, a major said, "We have plenty of captured American rifles and ammunition at armories here in Honolulu. We can use them if there aren't any Arisakas handy. They have better stopping power than our rifles anyway."

Someone else who'd kept his wits about him added, "Whatever we do, we'd better do it fast. Night is coming, and that will make things harder. Plainly, the Yankees are going to try to invade. We'll need to be ready to march first thing in the morning."

That was how Shimizu and his squad found themselves the not too proud possessors of American Springfields. He didn't much care for his. It was larger and heavier than the Arisaka he was used to: plainly a weapon made for a bigger soldier than the average Japanese.

Yasuo Furusawa worked the bolt on his Springfield a few times. "Smooth— it's well made," he said grudgingly.

"I was thinking the same thing," Shimizu said. "It will kick like a donkey, though."

"*Shigata ga nai,* Corporal-*san,*" Furusawa said, and Shimizu had to nod.

Not getting supper couldn't be helped, either. The officers had worried about weapons first and everything else only afterwards. Shimizu was sure the regiment would start marching for its position in the northern part of Oahu as soon as it grew light, too. He wondered if he and his men would get breakfast before they set out.

As it happened, they did: rice cooked somewhere else and brought in by horse-drawn wagon. And then, some of the regiment with Arisakas and others with Springfields, all of the men in dirty, often bloodstained, uniforms, they started marching toward the positions prepared for them before the last attempted enemy invasion.

"We should have trucks," Senior Private Furusawa grumbled. "We could get there in an hour or two if we had trucks."

But they didn't—or rather, they had no fuel for them. That fire engine had been the first motorized vehicle—except for airplanes—Shimizu had seen in operation in weeks. And so . . . they marched.

To get to the Kamehameha Highway, they had to tramp past Hickam Field. A lot of airplanes remained unharmed in their revetments. The only trouble was, at the moment that did them no good at all. The American bombers had plastered the runways for all they were worth. Snorting bulldozers and swarms of men with picks and shovels—POWs, locals forced into labor gangs, and even Japanese—were doing their best to make the field usable again. Their best wasn't good enough yet.

Shimizu didn't like what he saw. How were the Japanese going to attack American ships if their planes couldn't get off the ground? For a moment, fear made his strides light. Then he remembered the aircraft carriers that had let his country conquer Hawaii in the first place. *They* would take care of the Yankees.

He marched on, feeling better.

JIM PETERSON WAS DEEP in the bowels of the Koolau Range when he heard explosions outside the tunnel mouth. He leaned on his pick for a moment, trying to catch his breath. Any excuse to pause for a little while was a good one. Every time he lifted the pick and bit into the mountainside with it, he wondered if he could do it again. The question was altogether serious. Men quietly fell over and died every day. He'd helped carry Gordy Braddon to a grave—after his usual shift was over, of course. If your knees were bigger around than your thighs, as Gordy's had been for quite a while, you weren't a prime physical specimen. By now, there were damn few prisoners in the Kalihi Valley of whom that wasn't true. It was sure as hell true of him.

The Japanese cared less about the tunnel than they did about working the POWs to death—or beating them to death or shooting them at the slightest excuse or just for the fun of it. The only way they might have got rid of the prisoners faster was by building a railroad through the jungle. Unlike the tunnel, it wouldn't have gone anywhere, but that might not have stopped them.

More explosions. "What the hell?" Charlie Kaapu said. He stood out in the mob of tunnel rats, because he was twice as strong as most of them. He hadn't been there long enough to deteriorate badly. And he'd been a civilian before, not a POW, so he'd just gone hungry; he hadn't been on a starvation diet.

"Sounds like bombs," Peterson said.

"Lots of bombs, if that's what it is," Charlie said, and Peterson had a hard time disagreeing. U.S. raids on Hawaii hadn't amounted to anything but annoyances up till now. Still more distant booms came echoing up the shaft. Whatever they were, they were too big to be just an annoyance.

The same thought occurred to somebody else. "Can't be bombs," a weary but authoritative voice said. "Wish it could, but there's too damn many of 'em. How could the USA get that many bombers over Oahu? No way, nohow. Gotta be the Japs blowing something up."

"They can blow themselves up—or just blow themselves. Don't make no difference to me," somebody else chipped in.

When the men with picks paused, the men with shovels couldn't load rubble for the men with baskets to carry out of the tunnel: there wasn't any rubble to load. And when the men with baskets didn't come staggering out of the tunnel at intervals short enough to suit the Japanese, guards came in to find out what the hell was going on. A POW near the tunnel mouth called, "Heads up!" to warn the men at the end of the shaft.

With a groan, Peterson lifted the pick. It seemed to weigh sixteen tons. He swung it back and brought it forward. It bit into the volcanic rock. Grunting, he pulled it free and swung it again.

Moments later, he heard the Japs yelling as they approached. They sounded mad as hell. They often did, but this was worse than usual. And their progress up the shaft could be noted by cries of pain from the prisoners they passed. That meant they were swinging their damn bamboo swagger sticks at whoever was unlucky enough to get within range.

They hadn't done that much for a while, not inside the tunnel. What were they so jumpy about? Peterson got a crack across the back that sent him staggering into the rough rock wall. That gave him more scrapes and lumps.

Charlie Kaapu got whacked, too. He took it with a grin, which made the guard hit him again. He kept grinning, and hefted his pick. It wasn't a threat, or didn't have to be one, for he slammed the pick into the rock a moment later. But that guard found something else to do pretty damn quick.

As soon as the Jap was out of earshot, Charlie said, "I bet the USA *is* doing something. These little cocksuckers wouldn't be so jumpy if we weren't."

Is that hope I feel? Jim Peterson wondered. He'd gone without so long, he had trouble recognizing it. He'd had grim determination to survive, but not hope. Hope was different. And yes, this *was* a dose of that fragile, precious feeling, by God.

Everybody worked harder, not because the guards were beating on people but because hope, in spite of that POW with the authoritative voice, was contagious. Men wanted to believe the Americans were on their way back, and thinking they might be made even dying prisoners stronger . . . for a little while.

When the shift ended, Peterson trudged out of the tunnel with as much spring in his step as a starving man with beriberi could have. He wolfed down his rice and nasty leaves with good appetite. But then, he was always hungry. By the time he ate, he knew the Americans *had* returned. Men too sick to labor— men who would die soon, in other words—had watched smoke rise in the southwest, from the direction of Honolulu and Pearl Harbor. Some of them had seen the bombers. Peterson couldn't see anything; it had got dark. He hardly cared. His mind's eye was in excellent working order.

The guards acted nervous at evening roll call, too. Naturally, they screwed up the count. Just as naturally, they took it out on the POWs. Peterson thought they killed a man when they knocked him down and kicked him, but he wasn't sure.

Even sleep, normally a man's most precious asset after food, went by the wayside tonight. Prisoners talked in low, excited voices, falling silent whenever a Jap stalked by. Their longings after an American victory came down to two things: steak and french fries. A few men talked about pussy, but only a few; most were too far gone to worry much about women one way or the other. Fantasies about food were much more immediately gratifying.

"Pussy's more trouble than it's worth," Charlie Kaapu opined. That surprised Peterson; Charlie, of all people here, was in good enough shape to do a woman justice—or maybe even injustice, if he saw the chance.

"It's trouble I'd like to have," somebody else said wistfully.

The big, burly—by camp standards, anyhow—*hapa*-Hawaiian shook his head. "Why you think I ended up in this goddamn place, except for pussy?"

"Tell us the story again, Charlie," Peterson said. It was better than most of the ones the prisoners told, and he hadn't heard it so often, either.

Charlie Kaapu looked disgusted with himself. "This Jap major have a blond girlfriend." He used some of the rhythms of the local pidgin without quite falling into it. Leering, he went on, "Blond girlfriend have good-looking boyfriend." He jabbed a thumb at his own chest. But then his face fell. "You go after nooky, you get stupid. I got stupid. I quarrel with the silly bitch, and she squeal on me. They grab me, they ship my ass up here. Ain't you boys lucky they do that?"

He got jeered, as he must have known he would have. As poor Gordy had said, Peterson wished *he'd* had that much fun before getting sent to the Kalihi Valley. But the news of the day left him all the more determined to outlast the Japanese.

As he and everyone else in the camp discovered much too early the next morning, the news of the day left the guards all the more determined to make sure none of the prisoners there lived through it.

JOE CROSETTI LISTENED TO THE BRIEFING OFFICER. "All right, gentlemen," the man said, and paused to swig at his milk. "We've given the Japs a left to the jaw and a right to the belly. We've sunk their carriers and we've walloped the rest of their surface ships and we've plastered their airfields on Oahu. They're on the ropes and they're wobbly, but they're still on their feet. Now we go for the KO."

Several fliers near Joe said, "Yeah!" A few others growled deep in their throats, a low animal noise he didn't think they knew they were making. He had to listen to be sure he wasn't making it himself.

"Our own losses were in the expected range," the briefing officer continued. "One light carrier sunk, an escort carrier and a fleet carrier damaged. The fleet carrier can still launch planes, and we are still in business."

More growls rose, and even a couple of whoops. This time, Joe didn't feel like joining them. The way he looked at it, the Japs had shown just how good they were. Badly outnumbered, mauled going in, they'd still managed to do real damage to the American task force. Well, those dive-bomber and torpedo-plane pilots were out of the game now, most of them for good. The ones whose planes hadn't got shot down would have had to ditch in the ocean. There couldn't have been many pickups.

"You'll know we hit their air bases on Oahu yesterday with B-17s and B-24s," the briefing officer said. "They made it all the way from the West Coast with their bombs, but they couldn't hope to get home again. That's why they headed for Kauai once the raid was done. How we got an airstrip long enough to land bombers built there under the Japs' noses is a story they'll write books about after the war. You can bet your life on that."

Of course, the bombers would still be sitting there at the end of the strip. If the Japs wanted to smash them up, they could. It must have been a one-way mission from the start. *Talk about balls-out,* Joe thought.

"Our assets on Oahu say we did a good job hitting the enemy bases, but the Japs are attempting to get them into usable shape again," the briefing officer said. "We don't want them doing that." A few grim chuckles accompanied the statement. A wry smile on his own face, the lieutenant commander went on, "Bringing carriers—to say nothing of the troopships behind us—into range of land-based air is liable to be hazardous to everybody's health." A few more chuckles, for all the world as if he were joking. "What you boys are going to do is, you're going to make damn sure that doesn't happen. Our ship's bombers are going to hit Wheeler Field again, to keep the Japs from flying off it. You fighter pilots—knock down anything that gets into the air and shoot up as much as you can on the ground. Shoot up enemy planes wherever you spot 'em, and shoot up the earth-moving machinery that lets the Japs make fast repairs. We'll hit them hard, and we'll keep hitting them till they can't hit back any more. Questions?"

"Yes, sir." A pilot raised his hand. "When do the Marines go in?"

"Day after tomorrow, if everything works the way it's supposed to," the briefing officer said. "You can make that happen. You *will* make it happen. Now go man your planes!"

As Joe hurried up to the flight deck, he fell into stride with Orson Sharp. "Day after tomorrow! We really are gonna take it back from them."

"Well, sure." Sharp looked at him. "Did you think we wouldn't?"

"Of course not!" Joe made himself sound indignant. If he'd had doubts, he didn't want to admit them even to himself, let alone to his buddy.

Hellcats buzzed overhead as he climbed into his cockpit. The combat air patrol was heavy. They were already in range of land-based air, though none had appeared yet after the naval battle. That too argued the bombers had done a good job of putting the runways on Oahu out of action for the time being.

Joe's Hellcat was gassed up and brim full of ammo. The plane had a few bullet holes that hadn't been there twenty-four hours earlier, but nothing vital had taken any damage. The engine came to life at once. Joe methodically ran through his checks—they'd drilled that into him before they let him into a Yellow Peril. Everything looked green.

Not quite so many pilots took off as had the day before. Bill Frank, who'd roomed with Joe and Orson Sharp and another guy at ground school in Chapel Hill, North Carolina, was one of the missing. Nobody'd seen his plane go down, but he hadn't landed, either. Joe tried not to think about losses. *It's a job,* he told himself. *You've got to do it. Sometimes things happen, that's all. But they won't happen to you.*

As planes began to leap into the air, Joe thought about what he would be doing. Wheeler Field. The center of the island. Between the mountain ranges. By now, after so much study, he could have drawn the map of Oahu in his sleep. Schofield Barracks and the town on the other side of the highway—Wahiawa—would guide him in if he had trouble finding the place. With the arrogance of youth, he didn't figure he would. The island wasn't very big to begin with.

And then he got the checkered flag. The Hellcat sprinted down the flight deck. There was that momentary lurch as it tried to fall into the Pacific. Joe yanked the stick back. The nose went up. The fighter zoomed away to find its fellows. Was any feeling in the world better than this? Well, maybe one.

He kept an eye peeled for ships down below. Not quite all the escorts from the Jap task force were accounted for. He figured the U.S. battlewagons and cruisers and destroyers could handle whatever was left, but why take chances? He didn't spot any major warships. They'd either gone back to the bottom or scooted back to Oahu. He did see several fishing boats. At first, he just accepted that—he was, after all, a fisherman's son. But then he remembered the Japs used those boats as pickets. They would have radios aboard. The attack from the U.S. fleet wouldn't be a surprise. If the enemy could put planes in the air, he would.

He could. And he did. Joe had just spotted Oahu, green in the distance, when a warning dinned in his earphones: "Bandits! Bandits at ten o' clock!"

Some distance back of the lead planes, Joe peered southeast till he spotted the Japanese planes. Their pilots were sly. They'd swung around toward the sun so they could come out of it and be harder to spot. Joe wished his Hellcat carried radar. Then the enemy wouldn't be able to play tricks like that. Well, they hadn't worked this time.

He glanced over at his wingman. He led an element now, instead of following in one. Survival of the fittest—or luckiest—worked in the air just the way it had in his biology textbook. The other pilot, a big blond guy from South Dakota named Dave Andersen, waved in the cockpit to show he was paying attention. Joe waved back.

Here came the Japs. Some of the fighters were Zeros. Maybe they'd made it back to Oahu after their carriers went down. Maybe they'd been based there— the Japs sure did that with their Navy planes in the South Pacific. Others were shorter, trimmer, with a smaller cockpit canopy. Silhouette recognition paid off. Those were Jap Army fighters—Oscars, in U.S. code.

Oscars were slower than Zeros. They didn't carry cannon, either, only two rifle-caliber machine guns. But they were supposed to be even more nimble and maneuverable than the Navy fighters. Having watched pilots in Zeros pull off some mind-boggling loops and turns and spins, Joe was from Missouri on that; he wouldn't believe it till he saw it for himself.

Which he did, in short order. Hellcats could outclimb and outdive Oscars with ease. But an enemy pilot who knew what he was doing could damn near fly his plane back around under itself. Hellcats flew like flycatchers. Oscars dodged like butterflies.

They couldn't hit much harder than butterflies, though. Canvas-and-wire biplanes in the last war had had just as much firepower. And Hellcats were built to take it. Oscars weren't. They were several hundred pounds lighter even than Zeros, and correspondingly flimsier. All that maneuverability came at a price. If an Oscar got in the way of a burst from a Hellcat's six .50-caliber guns, as often as not it would break up in midair.

That couldn't have been good for morale, but the Japs who flew the Army fighters had guts. They bored in on the Dauntlesses the Hellcats escorted. So did their Navy buddies in Zeros. They got a few, too, but they paid, and paid high. The Hellcats badly outnumbered them. Joe wondered how many Oscars and Zeros—and Jap bombers, too—were stuck on the ground because they couldn't take off. Lots, he hoped.

He took a shot at an Oscar. His tracers went wide. He tried to keep his nose aimed at the Jap fighter, but he couldn't. It was that much more agile in the air. In a hop and a skip, it was on his tail, those two popguns it carried blazing away. One round hit the Hellcat. Joe glanced anxiously at his gauges as he gave his plane the gun and ran away from the Oscar. No fire. No leaks. No problems. Yeah, a Hellcat could take it. And Hellcats could dish it out, too. That Jap pilot was a pro, but he'd be a dead pro in short order if he tangled with very many of the big, muscular American fighters.

There was the Koolau Range to the east, and the Waianae Range to the west. Japanese antiaircraft guns near the beach started throwing up flak. Joe swerved back and forth, just a little, to keep the gunners from being quite sure where he was going. Dave Andersen stuck with him.

Sure enough, Oahu was little. Only three or four minutes after he saw waves breaking on the beach, he was over the target. Dauntlesses screamed down out of the sky to blast the runways of Wheeler Field. Funny to think how, less than two years earlier, Japanese Vals had done the same damn thing. *What goes around comes around, you bastards,* Joe thought. *Your turn now.*

Back in December of '41, American planes had been parked on the runways wingtip to wingtip. The people in charge then worried about sabotage. They hadn't figured they'd get sucker-punched. Joe was damned if he knew why not, but they hadn't.

The Japs, unfortunately, weren't as dumb or as trusting as the Americans had been. They knew enough to build revetments, and they knew enough to camouflage them, too. But they hadn't painted a civilian bulldozer in camouflage colors—they'd left it school-bus yellow. Joe couldn't have found a juicier target in a month of Sundays. His thumb came down on the firing button. Tracers leaped ahead of the Hellcat.

A fireball spouted from the 'dozer. Joe pulled up to make sure he didn't get caught in it. He swung around for another pass at Wheeler. Shooting up what had been an American facility was fun. All the same, part of him kept imagining he'd get a bill for destroying government property.

This stuff belongs to the Japanese government now. Let them send me a bill. And let them hold their breath till I pay it!

Flak around Wheeler was heavier than it had been by the shore. The Japs knew the Americans would try to come back, and they'd done what they could to get ready. "And it's not gonna be enough, goddammit!" Joe said.

Muzzle flashes let him spot a gun's upthrust snout. *Shoot at me, will you? Shoot at my buddies? See how you like being on the other end!* The gun crew scattered as Joe opened up on them. He roared by before he could see what his bullets did to them. Maybe that was just as well. Those .50-caliber rounds were designed to pierce things like engine blocks and armor plate. What they'd do to flesh and bones hardly bore thinking about.

Several plumes of greasy black smoke fouled the blue sky. Some were from burning Jap planes caught in their revetments. Others, Joe feared, came from downed Hellcats and Dauntlesses. You couldn't do this for free, however much you wished you could.

As he climbed to make another strafing run, he got a good look at the craters pocking the runways. Even as he watched, another Hellcat shot up a bulldozer. One more cloud of smoke billowed up. Joe slammed his left fist into his thigh. One more 'dozer that wouldn't make repairs. If the Japs had to fix this mess with picks and shovels, they'd need weeks, not days.

They'd need 'em, but they wouldn't have 'em. The Marines and the Army were on the way.

"Boys, we have done what we came to do. Let's go home and gas up and do it some more." The exultant order kept Joe from heeling his fighter into another dive. He didn't complain. They had indeed done what they'd come to do.

As he flew out over the north coast, bound for the *Bunker Hill*, he spotted another well-plastered airstrip down below. *Haleiwa,* he thought. *That's what the name of that one is.* He grinned, there in the cockpit. Yeah, he knew the map, all right.

CARELESS OF—INDEED, OBLIVIOUS TO—his own safety, Lieutenant Saburo Shindo manned a machine gun near the edge of the Haleiwa airstrip. He blazed away at the American dive bombers attacking the strip—and at the fighters attacking anything around it that might make a target.

The machine gun, a Japanese weapon modeled after the French Hotchkiss, used metal strips of ammunition, not the more common belts. The loader was a Japanese groundcrew man who'd protested his unfamiliarity with the process. Shindo's pistol, aimed at his forehead, proved amazingly persuasive. Whenever the machine gun ran dry, in went another strip of cartridges. Only the ground-crew man's chattering teeth suggested he might want to be somewhere else.

One of the new American fighters—the same planes that had worked such fearful slaughter on Japan's beloved Zeros—must have spotted Shindo's tracers. On it came, straight at him, the machine guns in its wings winking balefully. He fired back, shoving down hard on the triggers till his gun unexpectedly fell silent.

"Give me another strip, you stinking son of a back-passage whore!" Lieutenant Shindo shouted.

The groundcrew man neither obeyed nor answered. Shindo glanced over to him. Bullets from the American plane's machine guns chewed up the grass and dirt all around the machine gun. One of them had caught the unwilling loader in the face. The unfortunate man no longer had a face. Not much was left of the back of his head, either. His brains and scalp spattered Shindo's coveralls.

Shoving the dead man aside, Shindo began feeding ammunition into the gun himself. That cut down his rate of fire. He did what he could, though, till the last American planes abandoned Haleiwa and headed out to sea.

Then he ran for the revetment that sheltered his Zero. Two planes nearby were burning, but his survived. He glanced back toward the runway. His mouth twisted. It was as cratered as the surface of the moon. The bulldozer that could have set things right in a hurry burned beside the runway. No one had thought to move it. *Not even me,* Shindo thought bitterly. And yet a bulldozer was, or should have been, as much a weapon of war as an airplane.

With or without the big, brutal machine, though, they had to get the airstrip ready as fast as they could. "Prisoners!" he shouted. "Have we got a gang of prisoners anywhere close by?"

TAKEO SHIMIZU HAD RAPIDLY grown to hate the American rifle he carried. It wasn't just that the Springfield was too long and too heavy for comfort. But he'd got used to all the places where his old Arisaka bumped his back when he carried it along. The Springfield hit none of them. It had its own places, and they drove him crazy—especially the one just above his kidney.

All the soldiers in his squad groused about their Springfields. He let them. If anything, he encouraged them. It gave them something to do as the northbound kilometers went by. People working in the rice paddies that had replaced sugarcane and pineapple fields paused to stare as the Japanese soldiers tramped by. The laborers—Filipinos, Koreans, Chinese, whites—had to know what the big bombing attack meant, but no one had the nerve to do anything but stare. An open jeer, here, might have touched off a massacre.

Shimizu's squad—and the rest of the regiment of which it was a part—were north of Wahiawa when he heard aircraft engines. His head came up like that of a hunting dog taking a scent. So did Senior Private Furusawa's. "Now," Shimizu said, "are those our planes or the enemy's?"

Furusawa nodded. A moment later, he said, "The enemy's! The roar is deeper than ours!"

They came out of the north. *From the sea, of course,* Shimizu thought. One second, they were tiny in the distance. The next . . . Shimizu just had time to shout, "Take cover!" before the big, blunt-nosed fighters opened up on the column of marching men.

There wasn't much cover to take. Shimizu threw himself flat by the side of the road and hoped for the best. Bullets rattled off asphalt, thudded into the ground . . . and made wet, splashy noises when they struck flesh. When a couple of them struck flesh too close to the noncom, he decided any cover was better than none. He jumped into the closest rice paddy.

Even as he crouched in the water, he unslung the Springfield and held it up to keep the muddy water from fouling the rifle. Considering how much he disliked it, that proved how thoroughly orders about maintaining a clean weapon at all times had been beaten into him.

He was far from the only soldier who went into the paddies. Not all the men were as fastidious about their rifles as he was. Some even ducked their heads under the water as planes flew by at treetop height, guns blazing. Shimizu understood that, but he wouldn't have wanted to do it himself. He assumed they fertilized the paddies here with night soil, the way they did in Japan and China.

Combat always seemed to last forever, even if in truth it was usually over in a hurry. This was hardly combat at all. Shimizu admired the handful of men who stood there and fired at the American planes. He admired them, yes, but without wanting to imitate them. The enemy here had things all his own way—and then he was gone, off to make misery somewhere else on Oahu.

Dripping and filthy, Shimizu dragged himself out of the rice paddy. Soldiers who'd flattened out and lived were getting to their feet, many of them with dazed expressions on their faces. Not all the men on the highway and by it were getting up again, though. Too many never would. The iron smell of fresh blood and the latrine stench of punctured bowels fouled the tropical air. Wounded men moaned. Bodies and pieces of bodies sprawled in ungainly postures. *What* had the Americans been firing? When one of those bullets hit a man, it tore him to pieces. The regimental physicians, those of them left alive, ran from one writhing soldier to another, doing what they could. Whatever it was, it couldn't possibly be enough.

"Forward!" called Colonel Fujikawa, the regimental commander. "We have to move forward! Are we going to defend this island against the American invaders or not?"

"*Hai!*" It was a ragged, shaken chorus, but a chorus nonetheless. Takeo Shimizu tried to ignore the wobble in his own voice when he joined it.

The American fighters strafed them again half an hour later, this time from behind. The Americans had to be flying home, back to the carriers that had brought them so close to Oahu. *Where are our carriers?* Shimizu wondered again. *What's happened to them?* The enemy planes roared off to the north, leaving many more dead and maimed behind them. Wasn't that answer enough?

Shimizu had come ashore on a north-facing beach, not two years earlier. Now he would have to keep the Yankees from doing the same. He didn't think he would have to wait for them very long, either.

*   *   *

AFTER THE *YUKIKAZE* GOT INTO PEARL HARBOR, Commander Minoru Genda demanded a car to take him to Iolani Palace. The officers there laughed in his face. American bombers had left the harbor a shambles. If there were any running motorcars, they were reserved for people more important than a mere commander off a sunken ship.

He'd had to pull strings to get his hands on a bicycle. Pedaling hurt, but the ankle wasn't broken. The *Yukikaze*'s doctor had assured him of that much, anyhow. With it tightly wrapped, he could manage. As he rolled east, he saw what the American bombers had done to Hickam Field. Many of the airplanes flying off it still survived, but the runways themselves were cratered wastelands that reminded him of the worst photos he'd seen of First World War battlefields. How soon before Japan could get those planes flying again? Soon enough to attack the enemy invasion fleet that was bound to come? He dared hope so, anyhow.

Hope, at the moment, was as much as he could do. Admiral Yamamoto had warned about this kind of U.S. response all along. The summer before, the Americans had tried to do it on the cheap, and they'd paid. And, all too plainly, they'd learned, and they'd worked. Had any of their factories and shipyards stood idle for even a moment from that day to this? Genda feared—yes, feared—not.

Honolulu itself hadn't been hit so hard. Genda pedaled past a battered barracks hall, but the bombers hadn't tried to knock the city flat. Had they wanted to, they could have done it. They'd spent their bombs more wisely, though— and then they'd flown off to Kauai! Somehow, somewhere, the Americans had managed to carve out a landing strip on the island right under Japan's nose. With Oahu secured, the Japanese hadn't worried much about the other main Hawaiian islands. That turned out to have been a mistake.

We can't afford mistakes against the Americans, Genda thought unhappily. *They're liable to beat us even if we don't make any.* He didn't think Rear Admiral Kaku had made any mistakes in the naval battle just past. That hadn't kept *Akagi* and *Shokaku* from going down. Overwhelming numbers and munitions could defeat even the finest tactics. *If we'd had twice as many carriers*—Genda broke off. He knew the answer to that. *We would have hurt the enemy more and lost all our ships anyhow.*

Maybe—probably—the fundamental mistake had been going to war against the USA in the first place. But what else could Japan have done? Let

FDR dictate what she could and couldn't do in China? For a proud and touchy empire, that would have been impossible. He sighed. Sometimes a problem had only bad solutions.

Soldiers drilled on the Iolani Palace grounds. Some were King Stanley Laanui's Hawaiians. Genda eyed them with more than a little worry. Would they really fight against the Americans? If they didn't, they might prove dangerous. Maybe giving the puppet King of Hawaii even a toy army hadn't been such a good idea.

Most of the men on the smooth green grass were Japanese, though. They weren't Army men; they belonged to the special naval landing forces, and wore greenish uniforms rather than khaki and black leather rather than brown. "What will we do to the Americans?" shouted the Navy captain leading their exercises.

"Slaughter them!" the soldiers yelled back.

"Do our lives matter?" the officer asked.

"No, Captain Iwabuchi!" the men replied. "Our lives mean nothing! Dying gloriously for the sacred Emperor means everything!"

Genda was relieved to pull up in front of the entrance and let down the bike's kickstand. It wasn't that Captain Iwabuchi and his men were wrong—far from it. But Genda had more subtlety in him than the man in charge of the special landing forces. He sighed. Much good that subtlety had done him.

The Hawaiian guards at the bottom of the stairs and the Japanese at the top saluted him as he slowly and painfully ascended. "I must see General Yamashita and the king," he told the Army lieutenant in charge of his countrymen. "At once."

"Yes, sir." The lieutenant had seen him before, and knew who he was. He sent one of his men into the palace. The soldier returned a moment later. He nodded. So did the lieutenant. "Go on up to the general's office, then."

"*Arigato gozaimasu.*" After thanking the junior officer, Genda climbed the *koa*-wood staircase to the second story. He limped into the Yellow Room, where Tomoyuki Yamashita supervised the Japanese occupation of Hawaii.

Yamashita looked up from his paperwork. "Welcome, Genda-*san*," he said. "Sit down—I can see you're hurting. Tell me how bad it is."

Genda gratefully sank into a chair. He gave the general a straight answer: "Sir, I don't see how it could be any worse. We lost both carriers we sent against the enemy, and most of the supporting ships. The Americans *will* invade. The

Army—and the special naval landing forces—will have to defeat him on the ground." The cries of the special naval landing forces floated in through the open window. The soldiers sounded ferocious. What difference, if any, that would make . . .

Yamashita grimaced. "What went wrong, Commander? We won a great victory the last time the Yankees appeared in these waters."

"Yes, sir—and we had one more carrier, and they had many fewer." The sheer size of the aerial strike force that sank *Akagi* and *Shokaku* still stunned Genda. What it said about the fleet that sent it forth was even more intimidating. And the troopships behind *that* . . .

"Very well, Commander. We will do what we can to hold this island," Yamashita said. "I am sure your Navy forces will help us. Captain Iwabuchi is nothing if not, ah, intrepid." More shouts rang out from the special landing forces.

As far as Genda could tell, Iwabuchi was a bloodthirsty fanatic. Of course, even if he was, that wasn't necessarily a drawback in a fighting man. "Between us, sir, *can* we beat back the Americans?"

"I don't know. I intend to try," Yamashita answered calmly. "Whatever we do, we buy time for our positions farther west to strengthen themselves. That was the whole point of this campaign in the first place, *neh*?"

"Yes, sir," Genda said. "I'm afraid this won't be as easy as fighting the Americans was the first time around."

"We may fail," Yamashita said. "Success or failure is karma. But no one will ever say we did not do everything we could to succeed."

Genda didn't see what he could say to that. He struggled to his feet and saluted. "Yes, sir. I had better go across the hall and brief his Majesty." He spoke without audible irony; King Stanley might have someone who understood Japanese listening. You never could tell. Genda did ask, "How is morale among the Hawaiian troops?"

"It seems all right so far," Yamashita replied. "We will use them in ways that appear most expedient." Genda understood what that meant, though a listening snoop might not have. Yamashita planned to throw the Hawaiians into the meat grinder, to use them in place of Japanese soldiers where things were hottest. That would let the Japanese last longer and stretch further. Reinforcements from the home islands were, to put it in the most optimistic terms, unlikely.

King Stanley Laanui used King David Kalakaua's library as his office. Now he sat behind the dreadnought of a desk that Genda had used with Mitsuo Fuchida and two Army officers to pick a sovereign to revive the Kingdom of Hawaii. (So far as Genda knew, none of the Japanese support ships had rescued Fuchida. He was gone, lost. He had to be. The certainty of it ate at Genda.)

The King of Hawaii looked up from whatever papers he'd been shuffling— or pretending to shuffle. Stanley Laanui was far from the most diligent administrator in the world. His eyes had always had heavy, dark pouches of flesh under them. Now they were bleary and tracked with red. When he said, "Hello, Commander Genda," his breath was sweet-sour with the reek of the fruit spirit people here insisted on calling gin.

"Good day, your Majesty." Speaking English, Genda had to be formal. He gave King Stanley a stiff, precise bow, refusing to show that the ankle troubled him.

"How bad is it?" the king asked. "It can't be good, by God. You look like a cement mixer just ran over your puppy."

"It . . . could be better, your Majesty." Genda tried to hide how shocked he was. He'd willed his face and eyes to reveal nothing. That he'd failed so badly said how much he'd been through—and probably also said the King of Hawaii was shrewder than he looked. For a man having an affair with the king's wife, that was less than welcome news.

King Stanley barked bitter laughter now. "If you say it could be better, it's even worse than I thought. When are the Americans landing?"

"In the next few days, I think. So sorry." One shock after another for Genda. If the king hadn't taken him by surprise, he wouldn't have answered so frankly.

"Christ!" Stanley Laanui burst out. "I thought I was kidding!" Those bloodshot eyes flicked back and forth like a hunted animal's. "Can you beat them? Uh—can we beat them?"

"All we can do, we will do," Genda said—a reply that sounded more promising than it was.

King Stanley, unfortunately, understood as much. "Jesus! What'll they do if they catch me?" He put a fist by his neck and jerked it upward, turning his head to the side as if hanged.

Genda did his best to look on the bright side of things: "No American soldiers are here yet. Maybe we will beat back the landing. Maybe we will beat them on the ground here. Japanese soldiers are very brave."

"Yeah, sure, Commander. I know that," King Stanley said. Under his breath, he muttered something that sounded like, *If pigs had wings* . . . If that was a proverb, it wasn't one Genda knew. The king gathered himself. "All right. We'll do what we can to give you a hand. After all, it's our necks, too, if the USA comes back."

"Thank you, your Majesty. I knew you would stand by us." Genda bowed his way out of the office. The really worrisome thing was that he was grateful for the sen's worth of support the King of Hawaii had to give. *Any port in a storm.* That was an English proverb Genda *did* know.

As he stood in the hallway, a tiny Chinese cleaning woman, easily ten centimeters shorter than he was, slipped a little piece of paper into his hand. She was smooth as a stage magician; she didn't even break stride as she walked past him. He opened it as he limped down the stairs. It had a number, nothing more. He folded it up and stuck it in a trouser pocket.

He got on the bicycle he'd managed to lay his hands on and rode around to the back of Iolani Palace. The guards at the stairs that led up and down there also saluted him. He absently returned the gesture as he went down into the basement.

The door that matched the number on the slip had a window set with wire-strengthened glass. Genda sighed to himself. Queen Cynthia wasn't going to take any chances today. He didn't suppose he could blame her, but he wished she would have. At least he would be able to speak freely behind the closed door. That too was release of a sort, though not the kind he craved.

Cynthia Laanui was more conscientious than her husband as well as more decorative. All the charities that moved food and medical supplies from hither to yon and tried to extract more ran through her. She really had done good work—and here she was, doing more. But she closed her fountain pen when Genda walked into her little office. As soon as the door clicked shut behind him, she exclaimed, "I was afraid you weren't coming back!"

So was I. But that was not a thought Genda would have shared with any woman—or with any man, unless he got drunk with a friend who'd gone through the same thing. "Here I am," he said, bowing.

"Yes—here you are . . . and you came here in a destroyer." Like any proper queen, Cynthia obviously had her spies. "Where is the *Akagi*?"

He shrugged. "Sometimes things go your way. Sometimes they go the enemy's way."

"What will you do?" she asked.

He couldn't tell whether she meant him alone or the Japanese as a whole. The answer was the same either way: "Fight."

Queen Cynthia's gingery eyebrows leaped. "Can you win?" If they couldn't win, she would face whatever the Americans chose to dish out to her husband and her. Whatever that was, Genda didn't think it would be pretty. King Stanley could at least claim he was a Hawaiian trying to regain his country's independence after half a century of U.S. occupation. It wouldn't help, but he could claim it. His wife, pure *haole*, couldn't even offer that excuse. If the Americans won, they would probably reckon her a traitor to her race.

"We will do our best. We have won before," Genda said: almost exactly what he'd told her husband.

"You'd better," she said fiercely. If she led the little Hawaiian Army, it might well fight harder than it would under King Stanley.

Genda shrugged again. "Karma, *neh*?" After that, he found only one thing left to say: "Karma too that we fell in love, *neh*?"

"Yes," Cynthia Laanui answered, and looked down at the desk. Was she remembering she was an American? She'd been willing, even eager, to forget when things were going better for Japan. Now . . . She looked up again. "What are we going to do? What *can* we do?"

He shrugged. "I do not know. Everything we can." His own chances of living through the fighting ahead were anything but good. He didn't tell her that—what was the point? No doubt she could see it for herself anyway. If he didn't live, her chances were better if no one knew she'd been sleeping with the enemy. Of course, as queen to the Japanese puppet King of Hawaii, she faced long odds, too. He got to his feet to go, and bowed once more. "Good luck."

"Same to you," she said. "I used to have it, but it seems to be gone now."

He didn't know what to say to that. He'd just got back on his bicycle when air-raid sirens began to wail. When he saw the swarms of American planes tearing up Hickam Field again, he feared Japanese luck in Hawaii was gone now, too.

FLETCHER ARMITAGE WAS DIGGING an antitank ditch north of Wahiawa when American planes roared by overhead. He wanted to laugh in the face of the worried-looking Jap guard who rode herd on him and his fellow POWs. He wanted to scream, *All right, motherfucker! You had it your way for a while. Now see how you like taking it for a change!*

He wanted to, but he didn't. He didn't get out of line at all, in fact. The Japs had been jumpy even before those planes came over. Fletch hadn't known why, but their wind was up. They started beating people up for no reason. If you gave them trouble on purpose, you'd be lucky if they just shot you. They'd probably bayonet you and leave you to die slowly under the hot sun.

And yet . . . There were a hell of a lot of prisoners and not very many guards. Before, it hadn't seemed to matter so much. The Japs were top dogs, and they knew it and so did the men they guarded. But if all of a sudden they weren't guaranteed top dogs any more, an awful lot of Americans owed them plenty—and wanted to pay it back, with interest.

More fighters and bombers flew by. The noise of explosions not too far away said something—probably Wheeler Field—was catching hell again. Unlike the big, heavy bombers the day before, these planes were coming in low. "Son of a bitch," Fletch said, staring up. "*Son* of a bitch."

"What is it?" another POW asked.

"They changed the wing emblem on our planes," Fletch answered. "They took out the red ball in the middle of the star. When did that happen?" What else had his country done while he wasn't looking—couldn't look? All at once, he felt like Robinson Crusoe, trapped on a desert island while the rest of the world went on about its business.

"No talk!" the closest Jap guard shouted. "Work!"

Like any POW, Fletch worked no harder than he had to. He doubted he weighed even 110 pounds. He had little strength and less stamina. The Japs didn't care. A lot of the work they'd had the POWs do was designed more to wear out and destroy men than for serious military reasons.

No more. Fletch could see how this ditch would slow an armored attack. The mud of the rice paddies wouldn't help tanks, either. The U.S. Army had done its best to fight when the Japanese invaded. Now the Japs were getting ready to do the same.

And they're making me help them, the sons of bitches! Fletch wanted to scream it. Under the Geneva Convention, they weren't supposed to make him do work like this. Since he was an officer, under the Geneva Convention he wasn't required to work at all. Did the Japs care? Not even slightly.

"Work!" the guard yelled again, and bashed somebody in the side of the head with the butt end of his Arisaka. The luckless POW staggered and fell to his hands and knees. The guard kicked him in the ribs, and went on kicking him till he lurched upright once more. Blood running down his cheek, the prisoner dug out another spadeful of earth. He didn't say a word. Complaining only got you deeper in Dutch. Keeping your head down as much as you could was a hell of a lot smarter.

It was most of the time, anyhow. Though Fletch obediently dug, he kept looking at that Jap guard out of the corner of his eye. He wasn't the only POW doing that, either—oh, no. Up till now, it had looked as if the Japanese would hang on to Hawaii indefinitely. That being so, you had to go along—at least some—to get along. But if this place would be under new management (or rather, the old management again) pretty soon . . .

Yeah, you slanty-eyed son of a bitch, I'll remember your face in my nightmares for the rest of my days. Do you have nightmares now, you bastard? If you don't, I bet you will pretty soon. Serves you right, too.

Along with glancing at the guard, Fletch also looked south toward Wahi-awa. Jane was still okay. He'd seen her. He knew. Maybe they could patch things up again. If Hawaii returned to the old management, why not? Anything might be possible then, anything at all.

X

PLATOON SERGEANT LES DILLON SPENT AS MUCH TIME AS HE COULD ON THE
Valdosta Liberty's deck. It was cooler and less cramped there than down below.
He went below to eat in the galley—the rule was that no food left it—and to
use the heads. He slept down there, too, and played poker. Other than that, no.
Besides, when he was below he couldn't see what was going on.

His troopship had been zigzagging west and south ever since sailing from
San Diego. Other converted freighters and liners—and the destroyers escorting them—filled the Pacific as far as his eye could see. He thought this was a
bigger fleet than the one that had sailed and then turned tail the year before.
He couldn't prove it, but it looked that way.

He was sure the course changes were quicker and more precise than they
had been the last time around. When he remarked on that, Dutch Wenzel nodded. "I guess even the swabbies can learn something if you give 'em enough
time," the other platoon sergeant said.

"Looks like you're right. Who would've believed it?" Les said. They stood
only a few feet away from a couple of the *Valdosta Liberty*'s sailors. The sailors
pretended not to hear. If they'd felt like brawling, Les was ready. What would
Captain Bradford do to him? Make him miss the invasion? Not likely! The worst
they could do to him was to send him in no matter what he did on the way.

That thought had hardly crossed his mind before the troopship's loudspeakers crackled to life. "Now hear this!" an exultant voice said. "Now hear

this! Our ships have whipped the Japanese Navy, and so we are good to proceed to our destination. Beautiful, romantic Hawaii coming up!"

The deck exploded in cheers. Sailors and Marines all yelled as if it were going out of style. Les joined in as enthusiastically as anybody else. So did his buddy. People around them were still shouting and screeching when he suddenly sobered. "What are we jumping up and down about?" he said. "We just won the chance to get our heads blown off. Aren't you glad about that?"

"Fuckin'-A I am," Dutch answered. "And so are you, you sandbagging son of a bitch. Otherwise we'd both be gunnies by now."

"Well, shit. When you're right, you're right," Les said. He and Wenzel had both turned down the chance for a third rocker under their sergeant's stripes so they could go along on the failed attack the year before instead of training boots at Camp Pendleton. Then they'd ended up at Pendleton anyhow, still at their old grade. Life was a bitch sometimes.

The racket from the *Valdosta Liberty*'s engines got louder. The ship sped up. So did all the others in the invasion fleet. Wenzel grunted. "They don't want to waste another minute, do they?"

"Would you?" Les answered. "They've wasted a year and a half already, and then some. About time we took Hawaii back. It's not *right* for Hotel Street to belong to somebody else, goddammit."

"There you go!" Dutch Wenzel laughed. "Now I know what I'm fighting for: cheap pussy and overpriced booze."

"Suits me fine," Dillon said, and Dutch didn't contradict him.

As Dillon always did when he was up on deck, he looked out into the ocean to see if he could spot a periscope. The odds were long. In this miserable tub, the odds of being able to dodge if a Jap sub did fire a torpedo were even longer. He knew all that. He looked anyhow. It was like snapping your fingers to keep the elephants away: it couldn't hurt.

"Wonder how far from Hawaii we are," Dutch said.

"Beats me," Les answered. "Ain't a hell of a lot of street signs in this part of the Pacific. We'll get there when we get there, that's all."

They got there three days later. They must have sailed past the battle between the American and Japanese carrier forces, but not a sign of it remained. The ocean kept its own secrets, kept them and buried them deep.

As the troopships approached the north coast of Oahu, the battlewagons and cruisers and destroyers that had accompanied and escorted the U.S. carriers were giving the landing beaches hell. The boom of the big guns echoed across the water. When the shells roared in, they rearranged the landscape pretty drastically.

Les watched with enthusiastic approval. "The more they knock the snot out of the Japs, the easier the time we'll have," he said.

Dive bombers took off from the carriers and pummeled what Les presumed to be Japanese positions, too. Their bombs kicked up even more dust and dirt than all that high-caliber artillery. It was, more and more, an aviator's world. *What does that make me?* Les wondered when the thought occurred to him. A minute later, he shrugged. *It makes me necessary, that's what. They can blow Hawaii to kingdom come, but I'm the poor, sorry son of a bitch who lands there with a bayonet on the end of his rifle and takes it away from the Japs. Boy, am I lucky!*

He couldn't even blame his draft board, not when he, like every other Marine, had volunteered. The Army was the place for draftees, and welcome to them.

In spite of everything U.S. aircraft had done to the island, a few Japanese planes did get off the ground and attacked the fleet. The Hellcats and Wildcats overhead went after them like dogs after marauding wolves, but they made hits, too: here a cruiser, there a troopship. When flames and smoke burst from that other ship full of Marines or dogfaces, Les swore horribly: those were his countrymen getting hurt.

Here and there along the beach, Japanese field guns fired at the fleet. Shells splashed into the water around the warships. They returned fire. The Japs might have been wiser to stay quiet. When they drew notice to themselves, bigger U.S. guns did their damnedest to smash them flat.

Somehow, Dutch looked away from the astonishing spectacle ahead. He nudged Les. "Here come the LVIs."

That made Les glance back over his shoulder, too. Sure enough, the landing craft—Landing Vehicles, Infantry, in official alphabetese—were coming alongside the *Valdosta Liberty*, as they were alongside the rest of the troopships, including the one that was on fire. Maybe that was a way to get the men off as fast as possible. Maybe it was more on the order of routine gone mad.

Whatever it was, Les didn't have time to worry about it. He nodded to the men with whom he'd be going into battle: mostly kids not old enough to vote, some of them hardly old enough to shave, leavened by a sprinkling of the old breed, veterans like himself. He'd been wondering what to tell them when the moment finally came. Now it was here. "Don't do anything stupid," he said. "Just like the book, and everything'll be jake. Right?"

Their helmeted heads bobbed up and down. Despite the most realistic training the Corps could give, most of them had no idea what being under fire was like. Their big eyes, tight lips, and somber faces said their imaginations were working overtime. Les remembered how scared he'd been when he got up to the line in France. He soon discovered everybody else was just as scared, including the Germans.

Were the Japs on the beach—and there were bound to be Japs on the beach—scared, too? They were supposed to make the Hun look like a Sunday-school teacher. *Could* they be scared? Les hoped so, but he wouldn't have bet anything above a dime on it.

"My company!" Captain Bradford shouted. "Take to the boats!"

Marines climbed over the rail and scrambled down nets stretched over the side of the *Valdosta Liberty*. Men had been moving from ships to boats like that as long as there'd been ships and boats. As far as Les was concerned, there had to be a better way. You could get smashed between ship and boat, you could fall into the water and drown, or you could fall into the boat and break your ankle. None of those helped the country one goddamn bit.

A couple of men already in the LVI steadied Dillon as he swung down from the net into the landing craft. "We got you, Sarge," one of them said.

"Thanks," Les told him—he was a long way from too proud to be glad for the help. As soon as his own feet were steady on the steel deck plates, he reached up to help other descending Marines. They got everybody into the LVI without seeing anyone hurt. Les hoped that was a good omen. He also knew damn well the record wouldn't last once they hit the beach.

Diesel engine belching and farting, the LVI pulled away from the troopship. Another one chugged up to take its place. Along with countless more, it wallowed towards Oahu. Les couldn't see out; the sides of the boat were too high. All he could see besides those steel walls were other Marines in green dungarees and jackets and camouflage helmet covers like his—and, for variety, the sailors running the LVI, who wore helmets painted battleship gray along with blue dungarees and shirts.

Even if he couldn't see out, he knew when the landing craft got close to shore. The American naval barrage fell silent, to keep short rounds from coming down on the LVIs. As soon as the warships' guns ceased fire, the Japs on shore opened up with everything they had. They'd kept a lot of their weapons quiet after all. Shells and mortar bombs started splashing down among the on-coming boats.

One burst close to Les' LVI. Fragments clattered off the boat's side, but none got through. "Thank you, Jesus," said a Marine behind the sergeant. Les found himself nodding. He'd never been a churchgoing man, but he wouldn't turn down anything he could get right now.

Every now and then, enemy rounds didn't come down among the American landing craft but on one or another of them. Then it wasn't splash-*blam!* but clang-*blam!* Les winced every time he heard that, the way he would have winced at hearing a drill in a dentist's office. And the drill might be for him next, depending on what the dentist had to say. And one of those clang-*blam!*s might be for him next, too, depending on Lord only knew what.

"Come on, goddammit. Get to the beach, goddammit," somebody was say-ing, over and over again. After a bit, Les realized the words were coming out of his own mouth. He wasn't saying anything everybody else wasn't thinking.

The LVI's bottom grated on sand. It rumbled forward anyway. It wasn't so amphibious as an amtrac, one of the tractors really designed to work on both land and water, but it could get around a bit when out of its proper element. A couple of swabbies undogged the loading gate. It kicked up a splash when it fell open; the LVI hadn't quite made it to the tide line.

"Out! Out! Out!" Captain Bradford screamed. "Spread out and get off the beach as fast as you can! Move!"

Marines poured from the landing craft. Mortar rounds were bursting on the beach, too, throwing up plumes of golden sand. Machine guns stuttered out death from the undergrowth not nearly far enough away. Japanese tracers were blue-white, not red like their American counterparts. Bullets from those machine guns and enemy rifles kicked up sand spurts, too.

Men went down. Some of them and their buddies shouted, "Doc! Hey, Doc!" for the Navy corpsmen who served the Marines. Others lay where they had fallen. No medic would help a man blown to hamburger by a mortar bomb. Neither would anything else, not till Judgment Day.

Les charged past a Japanese soldier sprawled on the ground all bloody with his long-bayoneted rifle beside him. He thought the man was dead—till a shot rang out behind him. He whirled. The round had come from an American rifle. A Marine said, "The son of a bitch was playing possum. I saw him grab for his piece, and I let him have it."

"Thanks," Les said. Had the Jap got a shot off, it would have gone into *his* back. One of those Japanese blue-white tracers snapped past his head. He threw himself down into a shell hole and fired back, muttering, "Welcome to fucking Hawaii!"

CORPORAL TAKEO SHIMIZU THOUGHT HE'D KNOWN EVERYTHING war could do. The bombardment from the U.S. Navy ships gathered off the northern beaches of Oahu showed him he was wrong. Just getting to the beaches had been a nightmare. The air attacks his regiment suffered bled it white before it ever reached its positions. And when it did . . .

If this wasn't the end of the world, you could see it from here. Shells roared in on the Japanese positions. They sounded like freight trains rumbling across the sky till they got close, when they began to scream. The guns from the destroyers and cruisers were bad enough. When the battleships opened up, you could see the huge shells coming. The earth shuddered when they hit. Fragments screamed and howled. Blast picked you up, flung you around, and slammed you down like a 250-kilo sumo wrestler on a mean drunk.

As the bombardment went on, men started screaming. Shimizu didn't blame them. He did some screaming himself, as he had when the bombers came over his barracks. Here and there, soldiers broke and ran away from the beach. Sometimes their own comrades shot them. Sometimes enemy shells took care of it before the Japanese could.

To add insult to injury, dive bombers roared down and dropped bombs on whatever the shells happened to miss. *We did this to the Americans. They fought afterwards,* Shimizu thought. *We have to do the same. But how?* He didn't dare stick his head up out of the hole where he huddled. Looking at the enemy was asking to be destroyed. Just huddling here was asking to be destroyed.

When the shelling and bombing paused, Shimizu was too shaken to respond for a moment, or maybe longer than a moment. More slowly than it should have, duty reasserted itself. "My squad!" he sang out. "Are you alive?" He supposed he should have put that better, but it was how he felt.

"Here, Corporal!" Shiro Wakuzawa called from a nearby foxhole.

"And me!" Yasuo Furusawa said. A few other men also let Shimizu know they were there. And someone not far away groaned from a wound—a bad one, if the noises he made meant anything.

That was too bad, but Shimizu had bigger worries on his mind. After things stayed quiet for a little while, he did look out toward the Pacific through the leaves and branches camouflaging his position. *"Zakennayo!"* he exclaimed.

The sea was full of ships and boats. Warships lay not far offshore. Japanese guns were still shooting, and a few vessels were on fire, but only a few. Shimizu noted the warships, yes, but they didn't hold his attention for long. Slowly wallowing toward the beaches through the waves—a much milder sea than the Japanese had faced in their winter assault—were landing craft of a variety and profusion he had never imagined. These left the trusty Daihatsu barges on which he and his comrades had come ashore far, far behind.

Some were veritable ships, big enough to hold almost anything. Shimizu didn't know what they carried, and wasn't anxious to find out. Others, smaller, pretty plainly brought soldiers to the beach. Even those were an improvement on their Japanese opposite numbers. On a Daihatsu barge, a steel shield protected the man at the wheel and the machine-gun or light-cannon crew. The soldiers the barge carried were vulnerable to enemy fire all the way in.

Not here. These landing boats had real steel sides and front, protecting the men in them. Shimizu stared in honest envy. He wished his own country could have made landing craft like them.

A few Japanese airplanes swooped low to attack the boats. They did some damage, but fearsome American fighters like the ones that had shot up Shimizu's regiment hacked several of them out of the sky. Shimizu groaned to see a beautiful Zero reduced to nothing but a slick of gasoline burning on the surface of the sea.

"Be ready!" the noncom called to whoever could hear him. "They're getting close."

Behind him, somebody with an officer's authority in his voice shouted, "The enemy must not get off the beach! We will drive him back into the Pacific! *Banzai!* for the Emperor! May he live ten thousand years!"

"Banzai!" Shimizu joined in the cry. It heartened him. If he thought about the Emperor, that enormous fleet out there and all the accompanying air power didn't seem—quite—so terrifying.

An artillery shell scored a hit on one of the landing ships. A column of smoke rose from the big vessel, but it managed to reach the beach. The doors at the bow opened. Out rumbled a tank, a snorting monster bigger and fiercer-looking than anything Japan built. On it came, sand flying up from its churning tracks.

The smaller landing boats were coming ashore, too. The men who scrambled out of them wore green uniforms, not the khaki the Americans had used before. Their helmets were also new: domed like the Japanese model rather than British-style steel derbies.

"Forward!" that officer yelled. "We must throw the invaders into the sea! I will lead you!"

Forward was the last direction Takeo Shimizu wanted to go. But *I will lead you!* was hard to ignore, and the habit of obedience to orders was as strong in him as in any other Japanese soldier. When the officer ran by, *katana* in hand, Shimizu scrambled out of his foxhole and ran after him.

Mortar bombs and artillery shells burst among the Americans on the beach. Men fell, men flew, men were torn to pieces. Machine-gun and rifle fire ripped into the Yankees, too. Not all of them went down, worse luck. A bullet cracked past Shimizu's head. He threw himself down behind a boulder. Another bullet spanged off the front of it.

He had to make himself get up and run on. Combat got no easier because he'd been away from it for a while. If anything, it felt harder. The fear came back faster. It felt worse than it had when the Japanese invaded Hawaii, much worse than it had when he fought in China.

A mortar bomb hissed down not nearly far enough away. That wasn't a Japanese round; Shimizu remembered the sound of the burst from the last time he'd fought Americans. One of his comrades started screaming. Fragments must have done their bloody work. American machine guns started stitching the air with death, too. Those big men in the unfamiliar uniforms wouldn't be easy to throw back.

Shimizu looked around him. You always wanted to see that you weren't going forward all alone. Some of his men were still with him. Good. Other Japanese farther away were advancing, too. Yes, very good.

The officer was looking around, too, when a burst from a Yankee machine gun caught him in the chest. The *katana* flew from his hand. The blade flashed in the sun as it fell to the ground. The officer twisted, staggered, and fell. He kept thrashing on the ground, but he was a dead man. At least two, maybe three, rounds had torn out through his back. As always, exit wounds were ever so much larger and bloodier than the holes bullets made going in. If one of those rounds hadn't found his heart, he would still bleed to death in short order.

Was anybody else of higher rank still up and fighting? Shimizu didn't see anyone. That wasn't a good sign, but he didn't have time to brood about it. "Come on!" he shouted. "We can do it!" Could they? They had to try.

Even though he ran forward in a crouch, a bullet caught him in the side. At first, he felt only the impact. His legs didn't want to carry him any more. He held on to his rifle as he sprawled on the ground. The pain hit then. His mouth filled with blood when he howled. He tried not to thrash like a dog hit by a truck. If he lay still, maybe he could take out one more enemy soldier.

An American in that new green uniform eyed him. Shimizu looked back, his own eyes mere slits. The American brought up his rifle to make sure of him. Shimizu tried to shoot first, but found he lacked the strength to raise the heavy Springfield. He saw the muzzle flash. Then darkness crashed down.

SABURO SHINDO SHOT DOWN HIS SECOND AMERICAN FIGHTER in the space of a few minutes. It was luck as much as anything else: he put a cannon shell through the enemy's canopy, and probably through the pilot, too. The plane, out of control, spiraled down to the Pacific.

Much good it does me, Shindo thought. Smash one ant, and the rest would still steal the picnic. The Yankees were ashore. It was the Army's fight now. The Navy had done everything it could—and failed. Shindo hated failure. He knew that none of what had happened was his fault. That didn't mean it hadn't happened, or that what sprang from it wouldn't be bad.

American landing craft littered the beaches like children's toys at the edge of a bathtub. Those ingenious boats, the great fleet of warships offshore, and the stifling enemy air umbrella overhead spoke of an industrial power and of a determination far greater than he'd imagined. He'd scorned the Americans in 1941. He didn't enjoy that luxury any more.

Tracers zipped past his Zero. He couldn't outdive or outclimb the U.S. fighter on his tail. He could outturn it, and he did, throwing his aircraft hard to the right. The American tried to stay with him, but couldn't. Only a Japanese Army Hayabusa could turn with a Zero, but a *Hayabusa* couldn't stay up with one if it did.

And Shindo and his Zero couldn't stay up with the American. He fired a burst at the enemy fighter, but it did no harm. Then the other plane sped away from his as if he were wearing heavy boots. He'd seen that before, too. It infuriated and humiliated him. None of what he felt showed on his face or in his demeanor. It seldom did.

An antiaircraft shell from one of the ships below burst too close for comfort. It didn't harm the Zero, but staggered it, as if it had rolled into a pothole in the air. He swung through some quick turns and speed changes to throw off the gunners, all the while wondering what to do next.

He couldn't harm the enemy carriers, not now. Strafing the other warships wouldn't do a thing to their big guns. He couldn't do much to the landing craft, either, and what he could do wouldn't matter; the Americans *were* on the beaches. *I have to hit them there, then,* he decided.

He came in low, machine guns hammering. His bullets sent something up in flames. Enemy soldiers scrambled for cover and flopped down when they found it. Not all of them ran. Some stood their ground and blazed away at him with small arms. They'd done the same thing during the first day of the Japanese attack on Hawaii. Anyone who thought the Americans weren't brave was a fool. They were soft, and they let themselves be captured so their enemies could make sport of them, but in action they showed plenty of courage.

Machine guns also opened up on Shindo. They put enough lead in the air to be nuisances, or worse than nuisances. A bullet clanged home, somewhere behind the cockpit. Shindo eyed his instruments. No damage showed. His controls still worked. He climbed, spun back, and made another run along the beach.

More fire answered him this time. The Americans were ready to the point of being trigger-happy. They missed him, though, missed him again and again. He watched his own bullets chew up sand, and hoped they chewed up men as well.

After one more pass along the beach, he saw he was low on gas. Time to go back and refuel. He'd got out of Haleiwa by bouncing along the grass near the damaged airstrip: if he could take off from a rolling, pitching carrier deck, he could also manage that. But he pulled up instead of trying to land where he'd got airborne. The U.S. naval bombardment had cratered the fields near the runway. He would surely flip his Zero if he tried to put it down.

If he couldn't land there, though, where could he? The next closest runway was at Wheeler Field, near the center of the island. He knew the Americans had worked Wheeler over, too, but they would have done that from the air alone. Some of the bigger naval guns might have reached it, but surely they would be concentrating on targets closer to shore. Shindo would have, were he mounting an invasion. He had to assume the Americans would do the same.

Wheeler was only a couple of minutes away. He realized at once that the runways would not serve. They'd been pounded hard, and the bulldozers that might have fixed them in a hurry had been pounded even harder. He saw several burnt-out hulks. One of them had been flipped onto its back, no mean feat with a machine so massive.

Bombs had fallen on the grass around Wheeler Field, but it wasn't—Shindo was betting his life it wasn't—an impossible landing surface. He came in as slow as he could, just above stalling speed. Down went his landing gear. He brought the fighter's nose up and the tail down, as if he were out to snag an arrester cable on a carrier deck.

He bounced to a stop. It wasn't a landing to be proud of, but he got down. For the moment, nothing else mattered. He undogged the canopy, pushed it back, and stood up in the cockpit. Groundcrew men ran toward him. "What do you need?" they shouted.

"Everything," Shindo answered. "Gas. Oil. Ammunition. A place to piss."

One of the men pointed back into the bushes. "Do it there. The Yankees won't spot you that way. And do it fast, before their planes come over again, see you, and shoot you up."

They weren't just talking about him, of course. The Americans were much more likely to spy his Zero. As Shindo went into the bushes and undid his flying suit so he could ease himself, he heard the buzz of engines overhead. But that was the familiar buzz of his own country's airplanes; the Zero and the *Hayabusa* used the same powerplant. Keeping a few planes in the air to protect what was left of Wheeler Field struck him as a good idea, though he pitied the Army pilots in their Peregrine Falcons. The fearsome new American fighters would chew them up and spit them out. Higher speed and the wing cannon gave Zeros at least some kind of chance against the enemy.

When he came out of the undergrowth, he didn't see any armorers working on those wing cannon. "What's the matter?" he demanded.

A man reloading one of his machine guns said, "So sorry, Pilot-*san,* but this has been an Army field for a while. Because *Hayabusas* don't carry cannon, I don't think we've got any 20mm ammunition."

"*Zakennayo!*" Shindo exclaimed. He thought hard. "Wait a minute. You fly *Donryus* out of here, *neh*?"

The Ki-49—its name meant Dragon Swallower—was the Army's counterpart to the Navy's G4M bomber. It was faster, but had a much shorter range. Like the G4M, it mounted a 20mm cannon for defensive armament.

"I'm an idiot!" the armorer exclaimed. He clapped a hand to his forehead, then bowed. "Please excuse me, sir. We store ammunition for bombers separately from what fighters use."

"I don't care if you stow it up your back passage," Shindo said. "Just get me some, and hurry about it."

The armorer screamed at his colleagues. One of them dashed away. He came back fast enough to satisfy even the unhappy Shindo. No enemy airplanes had shown up, which was all to the good. Shindo wondered if he'd be able to take off again without nosing down into a hole in the ground. The run was bumpy, but he got airborne.

He would take off and land on highways if he had to. All he wanted to do was hit the Americans as hard as he could for as long as he could. But how would he get refueled if he had to land on a highway? How would the armorers reload his guns? He shrugged. For now, he had fuel and ammunition—and plenty of Americans to hit. He roared back toward the landing beaches.

JIRO TAKAHASHI STARED AT THE SCRIPT in front of him in dismay. "Oh, Jesus Christ!" He looked up to Osami Murata in even greater dismay. "So sorry, Murata-*san,* but I can't say this!"

"Why not?" the radio correspondent from Tokyo asked calmly. "What's wrong with it?"

"What's wrong with it?" Jiro echoed. He hoped Murata was joking, but feared he wasn't. "It isn't true, that's what! How can you say—how can you have me say—all the Japanese in Hawaii support the Emperor against the USA?" Not all the Japanese in his own family supported the Emperor against the USA, as he knew too painfully well. He kept quiet about that. Instead, he said, "Captain Iwabuchi has put up signs all over Honolulu that anyone who causes trouble will be shot. He's put them up in English and Korean and Tagalog and Chinese *and Japanese.* He wouldn't do that if he thought all the Japanese here were loyal."

"Captain Iwabuchi has to fight." Murata was patience personified. "That's not your job. Your job is to persuade people to support the Emperor and

Japan. You've been good at it, Takahashi-*san*. Now you have to keep on doing it. We need you more than ever, in fact."

"Do you?" Jiro tried to keep the worry out of his voice. He probably ended up sounding like a machine. He knew why they needed him more than ever. The Americans were ashore on the north coast of Oahu. They hadn't come very far yet, but they plainly ruled the air here. Japan had used that edge to win after her invasion. Couldn't the United States do the same? He feared it could.

"Yes, we do." Beneath his calm, beneath his good nature, Murata showed steel. "Are you sure *you're* a loyal Japanese citizen yourself, Takahashi-*san*?"

"I should hope I am!" Jiro said.

"Well, I should hope you are, too," the radio man said. "But if you are, you're going to have to prove it." He tapped the script with an elegantly manicured fingernail. "With this!"

"Jesus Christ! Give me something I can read without wanting to go out and cut my throat afterwards!" Jiro said. "Hawaii isn't better off under the Greater East Asia Co-Prosperity Sphere than it was before. Not all Japanese here love the Emperor. I wish they did, but they don't. I don't *know* what the Koreans are doing, but I don't think they're 'flocking to volunteer along with their Japanese co-imperials.' " Koreans didn't like being part of the Japanese Empire. The Koreans in Hawaii had made no secret of being glad they weren't part of the Empire any more—except now they were again.

Murata waved Jiro's complaints aside as if they came from a little boy. "We all have to do what we can, Takahashi-*san*," he said. "We're fighting a war. It's come here again. We didn't want that to happen, but it did. We have to use every weapon we can get our hands on. Building morale, here and in the home islands, is one of the weapons we need. You're scheduled to go on the air in a few minutes. Are you going to read what you're supposed to read, or not? Reading it will help the Empire. If that doesn't matter to you . . ."

He didn't say what would happen then. By not saying, he let pictures form in Jiro's mind. Jiro didn't like any of those pictures. They started with bad things happening to him and went on to bad things happening to his sons and friends. None of those bad things would be hard to arrange, not at all. He played the last trump in his hand: "I'm going to complain to Chancellor Morimura." If he reminded Murata who his friends were, maybe the man would back off.

Instead, Murata laughed uproariously. "Go ahead, Takahashi-*san.* Go right ahead. Who do you think wrote that script, anyway?"

"Not Chancellor Morimura?" Jiro said in something not far from horror.

With more than a little malicious glee, the broadcaster from Tokyo nodded. "The very same. Now, Takahashi-*san*, enough of this nonsense. Get on with it, and no more backtalk."

Miserably, Jiro obeyed. He wondered how he could get through the program, but he'd done enough of them that he had no trouble reading the words set out before him. He thought his performance left something to be desired, but the engineer in the room next to the studio gave him a thumbs-up through the window that let the man see in.

When it was over, sweat drenched Jiro. He stumbled out of the studio. Murata waited in the hallway, all solicitude now that he'd got what he wanted. "Very good!" he said. "You see? That wasn't so hard."

"Whatever you say," Jiro answered dully.

"Yes, whatever I say." Murata had that elegant accent. He wore a fancy suit. And he had all the arrogance the Japanese conquerors had brought with them from the home islands.

Jiro had admired that arrogance when it was aimed at the local *haoles*. When it was pointed at him and fired like a gun . . . It felt different then. Amazing how different it felt. "Please excuse me, Murata-*san*. I'm going home."

"So long," Murata said, as if he and Jiro were still on friendly terms. *As if we were ever on friendly terms,* Jiro thought. Murata had used him, the way a man would use any tool that came in handy. *I was too dumb to see it. I see it now, though.* He didn't intend to say anything about it. If he did, Hiroshi and Kenzo would only laugh at him. Hearing *I told you so* from his sons was the last thing he wanted.

The thick, nasty, greasy smell of burning fuel oil filled the air. He'd got used to that after the Japanese bombed the Pearl Harbor tank farms. Then, once the tanks finally burned dry, the stink went away. Now it was back. It wasn't so strong this time, probably because Japan didn't stow nearly so much fuel here as the USA had. But the Americans had hit what there was.

Men from the special naval landing forces and civilians worked together to build barricades and machine-gun nests at street corners. The civilians hadn't volunteered for the duty, which didn't mean they could get out of it. When a *haole* man didn't move fast enough to suit one of the Navy men, he got the stock of an Arisaka rifle in the side of the head. Blood running down his cheek and jaw, the white man threw another chunk of rubble on the growing barricade, and then another.

A soldier gestured with his rifle at Takahashi. "Hey, you! *Hai*, you there! Get over here and give the Emperor a hand!"

"Please excuse me, but I just did," Jiro answered. "I just finished broadcasting for Murata-*san*."

"Now tell me one I'll believe," the Navy man said scornfully.

But one of his pals said, "Hang on—I know this guy's voice. You're the one they call the Fisherman, aren't you? I listen to you whenever I can."

"That's me," Jiro said. A few minutes before, he'd hated his connection to the Japanese radio. Now he used it, even if he did hate it. He shook his head. Life was stranger and more complicated than anyone could imagine till he'd put a good many miles under his keel.

"Let him go," the second soldier urged the first. "He's done his bit, and we've got plenty of warm bodies here."

"All right. All right. Have it your way." The first man from the special naval landing forces sounded disgusted, but he didn't argue any more. "Go on, you," he told Jiro. "You better keep your nose clean."

"*Domo arigato.* I will, thank you." Jiro got out of there in a hurry.

The Americans hadn't fought much inside Honolulu. They'd surrendered when driven back to the city's outskirts. That spared the civilian population. But surrender wasn't in the Japanese soldier's vocabulary. The special naval landing forces looked to be getting ready to battle it out house to house. Would anything be left standing by the time the battle was through? More to the point, did anybody on either side care?

JOE CROSETTI GULPED COFFEE IN THE *BUNKER HILL*'S WARDROOM. If not for java, he didn't know how the hell he would keep going. He'd heard the pharmacist's mates were giving out benzedrine tablets to pilots who asked for them. He hadn't tried to find out, not yet. He didn't think he needed *that* big a kick in the pants. It had occurred to him, though.

In the seat next to his, Orson Sharp slurped from a bottle of Coke. He was serious about staying away from the "hot drinks" that were forbidden to him, but he needed a jolt, too. A couple of empties sat by his feet.

"You're gonna be pissing like a racehorse," Joe said. "What do you do if you're up in your Hellcat and you gotta whizz?"

Sharp smiled what looked like a very secular smile. "Ever hear of a streetcar driver's friend?" he asked.

When Joe shook his head, his buddy explained the gadget. "Son of a bitch!" Joe said. "That's a great idea. But what if it comes loose when you're pulling a lot of g's? You'll have piss all over the inside of your flight suit, maybe all over the inside of the cockpit."

"Hasn't happened yet," Sharp answered, "and I've flown that plane every which way but inside out. I'm thinking of writing a testimonial for the company."

"Jeez Louise, I don't blame you," Joe said. "But what about your John Henry? How does it like the 'friend' when you weigh four times as much as you're supposed to?"

"Everything hurts then," Orson Sharp said matter-of-factly, which was true enough. "He's not bruised or anything—I'll tell you that."

"Okay. I wish I'd thought of it myself," Joe said. "Can you get 'em on the ship, or did you bring it aboard?"

"I brought mine, so I don't know if you can get them or not. You'd probably do best asking the toughest-looking CPO you can find. If he can't tell you, nobody can."

"Makes sense. CPOs know everything—or if they don't, they sure think they do," Joe said. That had been a revelation to him since boarding the carrier. When he was in flight training, almost all his instructors were officers. He'd dealt with petty officers only when navigating the maze of Navy bureaucracy. Now he saw the senior ratings were the men who held things together. They might be able to run the ship better without officers than officers could without them.

A plane roared in and landed, up above their heads. The ship shook a little, but only a little. An *Essex*-class carrier displaced upwards of 27,000 tons; a few tons of airplane weren't much next to that. Joe and Orson Sharp both said, "Dauntless," at the same time. Engine noise was a dead giveaway—if you knew what you were listening for. By now, they both did.

"How does it feel, being a veteran?" Sharp asked.

Joe considered. A yawn interrupted his consideration. "Tired," he said.

His friend nodded. "That's the truth." He took another swig from the wasp-waisted green glass bottle, then burped softly. "Excuse me." His politeness was automatic; he'd been a gentleman before he became an officer. After one more swig, he went on, "We're doing what we've got to do, though."

"Oh, hell, yes." Joe nodded vigorously. The Marines and Army men were on the ground in Oahu, and fighting their way south from the invasion beaches. It wasn't easy or cheap—*quit* didn't seem to be in the Japs' vocabulary—but they were doing it. Some Japanese submarines still prowled around, but the enemy's surface fleet in these waters had taken a KO. And enemy air power was on its last legs. Japan had proved naval air could beat the land-based variety. Now the USA was extending the lesson.

"Some of their pilots are awful good," Sharp said. "I ran into this guy in an Oscar the other day. He could make that little plane sit up and beg and darn near"—he might have been the only man on the carrier who would have said *darn near*—"wag its tail. I had two more Hellcats with me, and we couldn't touch him. He got out of stuff you couldn't get out of. We never laid a glove on him—and I landed with a hole in my prop."

"They can leave you talking to yourself, all right," Joe agreed. "With those two little machine guns, though, they have a devil of a time hurting you, and you can get away from 'em easy as pie. As long as you don't dogfight 'em, you're okay." He paused. "Did they patch you up or put a new propeller blade on?"

"New blade," Sharp told him. "I could've flown without the repair if I had to—it's only a .30-caliber hole—but why take chances? We've got the spares, and that's what they're here for."

"Better believe it," Joe said. "And pretty soon the Japs won't have any planes left, or anywhere to fly them out of if they do. I don't care how sweet a pilot you are. If you can't get off the ground, you might as well pick up a rifle and go fight with the infantry."

Before answering, Orson Sharp finished the Coke and set the bottle down by the other dead soldiers. "That's probably what happened to some of our guys after December 7." His voice was grim.

"Yeah, it probably is." Joe didn't like to think about what had happened to American servicemen of any sort since Hawaii fell, but that would have been an extra humiliation on top of all the others. Not to be able to fight the way you'd trained so hard to do . . . "Time to pay 'em back."

An hour later, he was in the cockpit again, buzzing towards Oahu. Orson Sharp was up there with him. Their orders were looser than they had been at the very start of the land campaign. They were supposed to shoot up anything that moved on the ground, knock down any planes that came up against them, and especially make sure the enemy didn't have the chance to repair his airfields.

One of those fields, the one at Haleiwa, had already fallen into U.S. hands. As Joe flew above it, he saw bulldozers and steamrollers swarming over the strip to put it back in commission. He also saw artillery coming down nearby. The field wasn't ready to use, not by a long shot. He preferred flying off a carrier deck to shellfire. Hellcats were well-protected planes, but nothing on God's green earth would save you if you stopped a 75mm round.

As if to remind him of that, puffs of black smoke from antiaircraft shells burst all around him. The Japs put up as much flak as they could. This wasn't nearly so heavy as it had been when he flew over the Japanese carriers and their escorts, though. That had been almost thick enough to walk on. It had scared him, too. Now he had its measure. You jinked a little. You sped up and slowed down. You tried not to give them a straight shot at you. Once you'd done that, you went on with your mission. Every so often, somebody got shot down. You just hoped your number wasn't up that particular day.

That thought had hardly crossed his mind when a Hellcat, trailing smoke, fell out of the sky and crashed into a rice paddy down below. No way the pilot could have got out—it happened too fast. "Oh, you poor, unlucky son of a bitch," Joe said. The flak must have murdered his engine—or murdered him, so he had no chance to pull up or bail out.

A machine gun turned its winking eye Joe's way. Those coldly frightful ice-blue Japanese tracers zipped past the Hellcat. Joe's thumb stabbed the firing button. Red American tracers jumped out ahead of the fighter. He had six machine guns, all of them firing heavier slugs than the Jap's weapon. Joe wouldn't have wanted to catch a .50-caliber round. If the wound didn't kill you, the sheer shock of getting hit was liable to.

Only a handful of Oscars and Zeros rose against the Hellcats. So did one sharp-nosed fighter of a type he hadn't seen before. That had to be a Tony, an Army machine with an engine based on the Messerschmitt-109's liquid-cooled in-line powerplant and not the radial engine that powered both other Japanese fighters. Tonys were supposed to be fast and well-armed. This one, beset by half a dozen Hellcats, didn't last long enough for Joe to tell much, though it survived more battle damage before going down than other enemy planes Joe had met.

If there were more of those, they could be a royal pain, he thought. The Tony looked a *hell* of a lot like an Me-109. Part of that, no doubt, was the engine, which dictated the shape of the plane's front end. But he still wondered whether some German engineers had stepped in and given the Japs a hand.

That wasn't his worry. He and the other Hellcat pilots took turns shooting up Hickam Field, down by Pearl Harbor. Watching Japs sprint for cover was fun. Watching some of them not make it was even more fun. It didn't feel as if he'd just shot men, any more than it had when he downed enemy airplanes. They were just . . . targets, and he was glad he'd hit them.

Someone else had set a bulldozer on fire. Joe admired the column of smoke that rose from it. As long as the Hellcats kept coming back, the Japs could only repair the runways at night. And early-morning visits by Dauntlesses made sure they'd have new damage to fix the next night.

You didn't see Japanese soldiers marching along highways by regiments any more. To Joe, that was a damn shame. They'd been awful easy to shoot up then. But they weren't fools. They'd learned better in a hurry. These days, they traveled by squads and platoons, and they stayed off the roads whenever they could. That did make it harder to strafe them. Of course, it also made it harder for them to move and to fight, which helped the gyrenes and dogfaces on the ground.

Joe looked for gun emplacements. Strafing artillery pieces was always worth doing. People said shellfire killed and wounded a lot more men than all the rounds from rifles and machine guns put together. Joe didn't know if that was true, but he'd heard it more than once.

A lot of the Japs' gun pits were in the jungle-covered mountains, and camouflaged with fastidious attention to detail. He spotted one gun only because he saw the muzzle flash. If not for that, he never would have known where it was. How they'd manhandled it up there was beyond him.

When he ran low on ammo, he flew back toward the *Bunker Hill*. One by one, his fellow pilots were breaking off, too. He laughed a little. He'd had all this training in formation flying, and here he was on his own. The Japs didn't have enough planes in the air to make neat formations necessary any more.

A destroyer was on fire, a few miles off the coast of Oahu. Some enemy pilot had managed to get through the CAP overhead. The Japs were still giving it everything they had. They didn't seem to realize they were fighting out of their weight—or else they just didn't give a damn.

Destroyers and their bigger buddies needed to stay close to shore so they could pound enemy positions with their guns. The carriers cruised farther north—with luck, farther out of harm's way. Joe didn't see any of them in trouble, and was glad not to.

He found his own ship and lined up on her stern. After that, he did exactly what the landing officer told him to do. *Not* making his own decisions never failed to rattle him. That was what he was supposed to do when he was in the air. But he had to obey here. He'd seen that ever since he first tried putting down on the placid old *Wolverine* on Lake Erie. He believed it. He just didn't like it.

The landing officer straightened him up, got his approach angle a little gentler, and then dropped the wigwag flags. Joe shove the stick forward. The Hellcat dove for the carrier's deck. The tailhook missed the first arrester wire, but caught the second one. The fighter jerked to a stop.

Joe scrambled out. The deck crew got the plane out of the way so the next Hellcat in line could land. "Anything special she needs, sir?" one of the ratings asked.

"Ammo's run dry," Joe answered. "Fuel's still okay. Engine's behaving." The petty officer waved and grinned and nodded.

Joe trotted across the planking to the island, and then down to the wardroom for debriefing. He looked around. Most of the fliers who'd gone out were back, but.... "Where's Sharp?" he asked.

"Didn't you see?" somebody said. "He took a flak hit and went down. Nobody spotted a chute, so he bought the farm for sure, poor sucker."

"Oh . . . That was him?" It felt like a blow in the belly.

"You okay, man?" the other flier asked. "You look a little green."

Numbly, Joe shook his head. He tried to put some of what he felt into words: "We were roomies at the start of training. We were buddies all the way through. He was always better in class than I was. He was always better in a plane than I was, too. And now I'm here and he's . . . gone?" He wouldn't say *dead,* dammit. He shook his head again, and stared down at the deck so the other pilot wouldn't see tears in his eyes. "I don't believe it."

"That's tough." The other man—a guy Joe hardly knew, not the way he knew Orson Sharp (had he known anybody but his kid brother the way he knew Sharp?)—spoke with rough sympathy. "We've all lost friends. Fuckin' war's a fuckin' mess. But what can you do? You gotta pick it up. You gotta suck it up. If we don't kick the Nips' yellow asses, none of this means shit."

"Yeah." Every word of that was true. None of it helped. Joe felt even more empty than he had when the Japs bombed Uncle Tony's house. He'd got that news secondhand, after it happened. This? Hell, he'd seen Sharp go down. He hadn't known who it was, though. Knowing would have been even worse, because it wasn't as if he could have done anything about it.

"Just bad luck," the other pilot said. "We'll pay 'em back, though. We'll pay 'em back, and then some."

"Sure." Joe stared down at the deck again. He imagined a house in Salt Lake City (in his imagination, it looked a lot like his house, though he knew it probably wouldn't for real). He imagined a Western Union messenger getting off a bike or out of a car—probably off a bike, with gasoline so hard to come by these days—and going to the door with a Deeply Regrets telegram from the War Department. And he imagined the lives of his buddy's parents and brothers and sisters—he had a big family—turned upside down and inside out.

Christ! They wouldn't even get to bury him. There probably wasn't enough left to bury.

If we don't kick the Nips' yellow asses, none of this means shit. There was the war, in one profane sentence. But with Orson Sharp dead, another thought filled Joe's mind. Even if they did kick the Nips' yellow asses, did any of this mean shit?

KENZO TAKAHASHI APPROACHED THE BARRICADE with more than a little trepidation. Seeing a machine gun aimed at your belly button would do that. "Who are you?" demanded one of the men behind the gun. "Why should we let you by?" Like most of the soldiers from the special naval landing force, he was both meaner and jumpier than the Army men they'd supplanted in and around Honolulu.

After giving his name, Kenzo added, "I'm Jiro Takahashi's son. Do you listen to him?"

And that did the trick, and not for the first time, either. The scowling soldier at the machine gun suddenly grinned—and all of a sudden he was a friendly kid, no older than Kenzo. "You're the Fisherman's son? You must be all right, then. Come ahead." He even gave Kenzo a hand to help him scramble up over the barricade.

It made Kenzo want to laugh and cry at the same time. He wasn't all right, not the way the soldier meant. He was rooting for the USA, not for Japan. He hated trading on his father's celebrity among the occupiers. However much he hated it, he did it, because it worked. He felt as if he were getting away with passing counterfeit money every time.

On he went. The soldiers at the next barricade, seeing that he'd passed the one before, didn't give him any trouble. That was a relief. Everybody in Honolulu, locals and occupiers alike, was nervous these days. With American planes in the air, with American troops ashore, plenty of people who'd sucked up to the Japanese were trying to figure out how to explain what they'd been up to since December 7, 1941.

The occupiers knew that perfectly well. They might be bastards, but they weren't fools. They trusted next to nobody now, and often showed mistrust by opening fire. And the way they treated locals showed no signs of getting better—if anything, it was getting worse.

Kenzo talked his way past two more barricades before he made it to Elsie Sundberg's neighborhood. No soldiers were on her street, which relieved him. Nobody else was out and about, either. That struck him as smart. This was the *haole* part of town, and the Japanese trusted whites even less than they trusted anybody else. Farther west, the occupiers had plastered up propaganda posters saying things like ASIANS TOGETHER AGAINST IMPERIALISM! in several languages. They didn't bother here. The *haoles* lay low and hoped neglect wouldn't turn to massacre.

Elsie opened the door even before Kenzo knocked. "Come in, honey," she said. "Come in quick!" He did. She shut the door behind him. The Venetian blinds were closed; nobody could see in from the street. "Are you okay?" she asked, giving him a hug.

"Me? Yeah, sure. I'm fine." Kenzo didn't say anything about running the machine-gun gauntlet on the way over here. He just clung to her.

"Hello, Ken." Mrs. Sundberg came out from the kitchen. Before he'd got Elsie away from the soldiers in the park—and before what happened afterwards—her arrival would have made him let go of her daughter as if Elsie had become red-hot. Not now. He kept on holding her, and Mrs. Sundberg didn't say boo. She just went on with the rituals of hospitality: "Would you like some lemonade?"

"Yes, ma'am. Thank you," Kenzo said. She did make good lemonade. As she went back to the kitchen to get some, he asked Elsie, "You folks have enough to eat?"

She shrugged. "We're all right. We're not great, but we're all right." She was a lot skinnier than she had been when they went to school together. He was thinner, too, but not to the same degree; there were advantages to being a fisherman in hard times.

"How are things out in the city?" Mrs. Sundberg asked, returning with lemonade for Kenzo and for Elsie. "We, ah, don't get out much these days."

"You're smart not to," Kenzo answered. "If you weren't staying close to home, I sure would tell you to." He talked about the barricades, and about how the occupation troops were getting antsier by the hour. "I think they're liable to make a big fight right here in town, and to . . . heck with civilians. It looks that way, anyhow."

"That's not good," Elsie said, which was a pretty fair understatement.

"Not even a little bit," Kenzo agreed. "It's one of the reasons I came over here—to ask if you people have any kind of hiding place you can duck into if things get really bad." He didn't go into detail about what *really bad* might mean, or how bad it might be. He had the idea he didn't know in any detail himself, and that that might be just as well for his own peace of mind.

Elsie's mother sniffed. "These houses aren't like the one in Connecticut where I grew up. They don't have a proper basement." By the way she sounded, that might have been Kenzo's fault.

By the way Elsie said, "Oh, Mom!" she must have thought the same thing.

"It's true," Mrs. Sundberg said. "And you know how much harder it made things when your father dug that hidey-hole under the walk-in closet during the . . . first round of unpleasantness." She didn't like talking—or thinking—about the Japanese invasion. Kenzo had seen that before. She would if she had to—she wasn't far enough out in left field not to believe in it or anything—but she didn't like it. It had turned her world upside down, and it meant she wasn't on top of the world any more.

When the USA finished the job here, she would be again. How would she feel about Kenzo then?

That was a worry for another day. "Hidey-hole?" Kenzo echoed.

"See for yourself." Mrs. Sundberg led him into the bedroom she shared with her husband. He'd never been in there before. The closet made him want to laugh, or to scream. All by itself, it seemed half the size of his family's apartment. Why would anybody need all that *stuff*?

The trap door in the floor, though, had to be of recent vintage. It lay under a throw rug, and was hard to spot in the gloom even with the rug off. Elsie's mom made an oddly courteous gesture of invitation. Kenzo bent and lifted up the trap door. The hinges worked without a sound. The scent of damp earth rose from below into the closet.

As Mrs. Sundberg said, the house had no basement, only a crawl space. Her husband had dug out a hole under the trap door, and had heaped the dirt he'd dug out around it to help protect it from gunfire and shell fragments. It wouldn't do much if a bomb fell on the house. For anything short of that . . .

"Wow!" Kenzo said, lowering the trap again. "That's swell!"

Mrs. Sundberg neatly replaced the rug. "Ralph was in France in 1918," she said. "He knows something about entrenching."

"He never talks about what he did in the war," Elsie said. From the times Kenzo had met him, Mr. Sundberg rarely talked about anything. He made money for the family; his wife and daughter did the talking. They all seemed content with the arrangement. Elsie went on, "This was the first time he ever did anything that showed he really had been in the fighting."

What horrors had her father seen Over There? What had he done? He probably had reasons to keep quiet. Having got a glimpse of what war looked like when the Japanese pounded Honolulu, a glimpse and a pounding that cost him his mother, Kenzo had some idea how lucky he was not to know more. No sooner had that thought crossed his mind than antiaircraft guns started hammering much too close by.

"Look, if there's any sign of trouble, you *use* that hole, you hear?" he said. "Don't wait. It's . . . pretty bad."

"We will." Elsie and her mother spoke at the same time.

"Okay. I better go, then. That's what I wanted to make sure about." What he really wanted was to take Elsie back to *her* bedroom and close the door. He couldn't say that or do anything about it, not with Mrs. Sundberg standing right there. He just dipped his head awkwardly. "Be careful."

Elsie wasn't as shy as he was. She hugged him and gave him a kiss that made him want to take her back there more than ever. And she whispered in his ear: "My time of the month came, so *that's* okay."

"Good," he whispered back. Worrying about a girlfriend was hard enough. Worrying about a girlfriend who was expecting would have been twice as bad, or maybe four times. After a moment, Kenzo kissed Elsie. Mrs. Sundberg was still standing right there, and she didn't say a word.

MAJOR GENERAL YAMASHITA HAD MOVED HIS HEADQUARTERS out of Iolani Palace and over to Pearl City. Minoru Genda wished the commanding general hadn't. For one thing, it gave him fewer excuses to visit Queen Cynthia. For another, it put the defense of Honolulu in the hands of Captain Iwabuchi and the special naval landing forces. Iwabuchi was a samurai of the old go-down-fighting school. He could not have cared less if he took all the civilians and the whole city down with him.

"We still have a lot of sailors at Pearl Harbor," Genda said. "The Americans put men like that in the line against us. If you want to do the same, sir, they are ready and willing to fight alongside your soldiers."

"They'll probably have to." Yamashita's voice was gloomy. "The American soldiers who tried fighting as infantry got slaughtered. The same will likely happen to our men." He glowered at the map spread out on a table in front of him. Blue-headed pins and pencil marks showed the American advance between the Waianae and Koolau Ranges. Despite desperate Japanese counterattacks, U.S. forces ground forward day by day. Yamashita went on, "We don't really need sailors fighting on land. We need carriers and planes."

"Yes, sir." Genda knew too well that all the carriers Japan had left, put together, couldn't launch half as many planes as the U.S. armada off the north coast of Oahu. He also knew that the planes the Japanese could launch were nowhere near a match for their American opponents. "We have requested reinforcements," he said. "So far, Tokyo has not seen fit to send them out."

Admiral Yamamoto was too smart to waste resources like that. Genda hoped he was, anyhow. There would be other battles to fight later, battles where Japan wouldn't be at such an overwhelming disadvantage. The soldiers and sailors already here could go right on delaying U.S. forces. That was what they were good for now: the land equivalent of a fleet in being. How long they could stay in being was the last important question.

General Yamashita didn't see things that way. Genda could hardly blame him. "*Zakennayo!*" Yamashita burst out. "They're playing games with my men's lives back in the home islands. I want to fight with some chance of victory. Gallant defeats make fine poetry, but the people the poems talk about don't get the chance to hear them, *neh*?"

"*Hai. Honto,*" Genda said, and it *was* true. He shrugged. "We're at the end of a very long supply line, sir."

"No." Yamashita shook his big head, as angry and frustrated as a baited bear. "We *were* on the end of a long supply line. Now the Americans have cut it off. When we took Hawaii, they couldn't bring anything in. Now we can't. This is not a good omen."

"No, sir, it's not." Genda could hardly disagree with that. "We have to hang on as long as we can."

Yamashita made a disgusted noise. "If this were some other part of the world, I'd pull back into the mountains and harass the enemy for months, maybe for years. But this is a terrible jungle to fight a war in, because you can't live in it. There's next to no game and next to no fruit."

"For a long time, we were the ones who took advantage of that, sir," Genda said. "Escaped prisoners of war can't live off the countryside, the way they can in Malaya or the Philippines."

"Prisoners." Major General Yamashita fairly spat the word. "If we lose here, there are liable to be prisoners. Japan would lose face because of that." With a scowl, he went on, "I assure you, though, Commander, I will not be one of those prisoners. If you are with me at the final moments, perhaps you would honor me by acting as my second."

"Of course, sir. It would be my privilege." Japanese officers, soldiers, and sailors were trained to commit suicide rather than letting themselves be captured. Ritual *seppuku* was a survival from samurai days. Back then, a second had used his sword to take off his companion's head after the latter began the act of slitting his belly. These days, a pistol was more common. Both weapons quickly and cleanly took the victim out of his pain. Genda felt he had to add, "I hope that day does not come."

"So do I—which doesn't mean it won't," Yamashita said.

Genda bit his lip and nodded. The time might also come when he needed a second—or, if he was rushed or in danger of falling into enemy hands, the inelegance of a pistol or a grenade might have to do. Trying to shove worry aside, he pointed at the map and said, "We may be able to hold them at the narrow-est stretch between the mountain ranges."

"Maybe." But the commanding general didn't sound as if he believed it. "Hard to hold in the face of that much air power. And the Americans' tanks are very good—even better than the Russian machines we fought in Mongolia in 1939."

Those also had to be new models, because that certainly hadn't been true of the handful of tanks the Yankees used here in 1941. Japan did not have many tanks—and the ones she did have didn't match up well against those of the other great powers. The Soviet Union had painfully proved that in the border war just before the fighting in Europe broke out.

A country needed a strong automotive industry to build good tanks in quantity. Japan didn't have one. *We would have, in a few more years,* Genda thought. His country had done so much so fast to hurl itself from feudalism headlong into the modern age. Japanese ships and warplanes and infantry weapons measured up to any in the world. But she hadn't been able to do everything at once. Now the question was, how much would that cost her?

"No more carriers, eh? No more airplanes?" Major General Yamashita said. It wasn't really a question.

"Please excuse me, sir, but I have to tell you it doesn't seem likely," Genda said.

"Too bad. They could let us make a real fight of it." Yamashita shook his head. "Now . . . Now I have a hard time holding on to hope. With the enemy in control of the air, with the enemy in control of the sea, all we can hope to do is delay the inevitable."

"I understand, sir," Genda said. "Even that can be valuable. It wins the Em-pire more time to ready itself for the battles that lie ahead."

"*Hai.* A small consolation, but a consolation." Yamashita did not sound consoled. He had to see he would die on Oahu. Genda foresaw the same fate for himself. When there was no escape, all you could do was fight. But he feared for the Empire in those coming battles. If the Americans could bring a force like this to bear wherever they chose, how could Japan hope to withstand them? And American factories and shipyards were still working at full tilt. How long before the United States could muster two such forces, or three?

How long before Japan could muster even one? That, he feared, would take much longer.

Admiral Yamamoto had foreseen all this. Even back when they were first beginning to plan the Pearl Harbor operation and the assault on Hawaii, Yamamoto had feared these blows wouldn't be enough. Their success had bought Japan almost two years to conquer and consolidate. Genda hoped his country had done enough in that time to ready itself for the blows that lay ahead.

He hoped so, yes, but he doubted he would be around to see one way or the other. "Karma, *neh*?" he said to Yamashita. "*Shigata ga nai.*" He was here because of a plan he'd offered to Admiral Yamamoto. Without it, the Japanese fleet would have struck at Oahu and then withdrawn. Genda shook his head. Bad as this was, that would have been worse. The Americans would have kept this excellent base. They would have caused Japan trouble far sooner than they were able to here in the real world.

"Things do not always happen as we wish they would," Yamashita said. "Our troubles here, the difficulties Germany is having in Russia . . ."

"Yes," Genda said. And there was another irony. Japan and the USSR were neutral. Soviet freighters could and did travel across the Pacific from Vladivostok to the U.S. West Coast and pick up arms and munitions to use against Japan's European allies. No one interfered with them in any way. War and diplomacy were curious businesses.

Antiaircraft guns started booming. Genda didn't hear American fighters roaring in at treetop height to shoot up anything that moved. Instead, the rumble of engines was deeper and quieter at the same time: the planes making the racket were flying high. To Genda's embarrassment, Yamashita realized what was going on before he did: "Their damned bombers are back!"

He moved not a muscle. When he didn't seek shelter, Genda could hardly do so, however much he wanted to. While they could still get planes off the ground, the Japanese had sent bombers of their own to Kauai to strike back at the planes that had dealt their airfields such a devastating blow. The pilots had reported wrecking a lot of them. Plainly, they hadn't wrecked enough.

Just as plainly, the American logistical push was even more impressive than Genda had thought. Those U.S. heavy bombers must have got to Kauai as near dry as made no difference. The Americans had brought along enough fuel to get a lot of them airborne again, along with bombs for them to carry.

Maybe we should have put bigger garrisons on the other islands, Genda thought. But Oahu was the one that really counted. Either Japan would have had to pull men from here or brought in more troops overall, which meant more mouths to feed. It hadn't seemed worthwhile.

The ground shook under Genda as bombs burst only a few hundred meters away. Yamashita sat, impassive, in front of the map. Maybe he'd already resigned himself to death, now or before too long. Genda supposed he ought to do the same. A warrior had to, after all. But achieving that indifference, he found, came harder than it should have.

XI

"YOU SURE YOU OUGHT TO GO TO WORK?" OSCAR VAN DER KIRK ASKED SUSIE. "These Japs in town nowadays, they've got blood in their eye."

"I'll be okay." Susie was wearing the frumpiest dress she owned, but nothing on God's green earth would make her look like Margaret Dumont. She went on, "They're not going to *shoot* me any which way," and batted those cat-blue eyes at him.

There were times when he didn't know whether to laugh or to pop her one. He ended up laughing now, because she would have hit back or thrown things if he did try to pop her. "You've got to worry about the other, too," he said stubbornly. "Some of the things I've heard about those bastards—"

Susie made an impatient gesture. "We've heard that stuff about the Japs ever since they got here."

"Some of it's true, too," Oscar said.

"Some of it, yeah, but not all of it. Most of the time, they haven't been too bad," Susie said. As far as Oscar was concerned, that was damning with faint praise, but Susie would do whatever she felt like doing. If the world didn't like it, that was the world's tough luck. As if to prove as much, she picked up her handbag, kissed him good-bye—a long, slow, delicious kiss, as if to give him something to look forward to when she got back that evening—and went out the door.

"Jesus," Oscar said hoarsely, listening to her footsteps receding down the hall. He shook his head, waiting for his heart to stop pounding. It didn't want to. Susie was a hell of a piece of work—a hell of a piece, period—no two ways about it.

Still shaking his head, he gathered up his sailboard and carried the contraption down to Waikiki Beach. To his relief, the Japs hadn't cordoned it off with barbed wire. But they did have machine-gun nests and mortar positions camouflaged with golden sand every fifty yards or so along the beach, and more of those half-soldier, half-sailor types trotting here and there.

Fortunately, one of their noncoms or ratings or whatever the hell he was had seen Oscar before. Oscar bowed to him—not easy when he had the big, clunky surfboard under one arm and the mast and rigging and sail in his other hand, but he managed. The Jap even deigned to bow back, though not so deeply. More to the point, the tough-looking little man waved him on toward the Pacific.

"Thanks," Oscar said, and then, *"Arigato."* He knew only a handful of Japanese words, but he'd learned that one long before the war started. It came in handy all kinds of places. And it sure came in handy now. The Jap's face lit up; his grin exposed several gold teeth. He bowed again, this time as equal to equal, and shouted to his men. Oscar couldn't understand any of it, but by the way they smiled and nodded it must have been good. *How to win friends and influence people,* he thought.

The Japanese had chased the fishermen off the beach, but they let Oscar paddle out to sea. They were used to him, and didn't think he was heading out to a submarine or anything like that. Only he knew about the submarine he'd met. He hadn't even told Susie, though he had asked the sub's skipper to get word to her family on the mainland that she was all right.

He ran up his mast, rigged the sail, and scooted out to sea on the breeze from off the hills in back of Honolulu. Even as the land receded, he could still hear the rumble of artillery off in the distance. It made him think about things in a way he hadn't for quite a while. If his countrymen took over again, could he patent the sailboard? If he could, there was probably money in it. He'd done without much money for a long time. Having some might be nice.

He'd got out far enough to think about dropping his hooks into the Pacific when he spotted something floating on the water. It was too small to be a boat, and it wasn't going anywhere, just bobbing on the swells. Curious, he swung the sailboard towards it.

He'd just realized it was a rubber raft when a head popped up out of it.

"Hey, mac, what the hell you call that thing you're on?" the head's possessor asked in purest Brooklynese.

"A sailboard," Oscar answered automatically. He had questions of his own: "Who are you? Are you okay? How'd you get here? Want me to help you get to land?"

"A sailboard? Ain't that somethin'? What'll they think of next?" The guy in the raft jabbed a thumb at his own chest. "Name's Nick Tversky. Yeah, I'm jake—not a fuckin' scratch on me. Sometimes you'd rather be lucky than good, ya know? Goddamn Nip flak tore hell outta my engine, but the shit all missed me. Can you get me ashore without letting everybody from Tojo on down in on where I'm at?"

"Uh . . ." Oscar paused. That would have been easy before the Americans came to Hawaiian waters. The Japs hadn't been so antsy then. They sure as hell were now. "Don't know for sure if I can sneak you in."

"Okay. Don't get your ass in an uproar about it." The downed pilot sounded a lot more cheerful than Oscar would have in his little rubber boat. He explained why: "They got PBYs doin' search and rescue. Figure I got a better chance of getting picked up than I do sneakin' past the fuckin' slanteyes. If I have to try it, I guess I can paddle that far."

"Okay," said Oscar, who was dubious. "You want me to give you a line and some hooks? You might catch something." He'd been about to start fishing himself before he spotted the life raft.

"That's white of you, buddy, but honest to God, I think I'll be fine," Nick Tversky said. He hadn't been out here long. He wasn't badly sunburned, and he hardly needed a shave. Plainly, he wasn't too thirsty, either.

Oscar didn't know what to do or what to tell him. Meeting a downed pilot was something he'd thought about now and again. Meeting a foulmouthed downed pilot who didn't want to be rescued? That was a different story. "Awful good to see the USA coming back here," he tried, adding, "About time."

"Hey, I ain't the brass. I can't do nothin' about that," Nick Tversky said. "But speakin' of brass, I figure we didn't try it for a while after we screwed the pooch the first time on account of we wanted to make sure we had the brass knucks on."

"I guess that makes sense," Oscar said. "We sure missed you, though."

"What can you do? Sometimes you just gotta stand the gaff." Tversky obviously had no idea what Oahu had been through since December 7, 1941. On the other hand, Oscar had no idea what getting shot down in a fighter plane was like. Did the two balance out? He couldn't have said, not like the scales of justice, but they probably belonged somewhere in the same ballpark.

"Good luck to you," Oscar said uncertainly, afraid he was leaving Tversky to a fate much worse than the pilot imagined.

But then Tversky let out a whoop and pointed off to the east. "There's my goddamn taxi, if I can flag it down!" Oscar looked that way. A speck in the sky swelled rapidly. It was a flying boat, all right. Was it an American flying boat? The Japs had 'em, too. Nick Tversky seemed in no doubt. He waved like a man possessed. He pulled out what looked like a pistol and fired it straight up. It turned out to be a flare gun. The flare was much less impressive than it would have been at night: a small red ball of fire. But either it or the pilot's gesticulating—he damn near capsized the raft—did the trick. The flying boat swung its blunt nose toward him. He whooped again, louder and more ferocious than an Indian in a two-reeler Western.

The PBY, if that was what it was, splashed down onto the Pacific and rumbled toward him. Somebody leaned out of a hatch—Oscar was hazy on the right name—and yelled, "What's this? Old home week?"

"He's my buddy," Tversky yelled back, and then, more quietly, "What the hell you say your name was?"

"Oscar," Oscar answered.

"Oscar here's good luck," the pilot went on. "He shows up, and then you show up."

"What the hell kind of a name for a Hawaiian is Oscar?" said the guy on the PBY.

"I'm from California," Oscar said dryly. "I've lived here eight years or so."

"Fuck me," the flier said. They took Tversky aboard the flying boat. The engines roared back to life. The big, clumsy-looking airplane lumbered over the Pacific, graceless as a goose running across the surface of a lake to take off. When it finally got airborne, it didn't seem so splendidly suited to the new medium as a goose. But it flew well enough. It kept on going in the direction it had been heading when its crew spotted the downed flier.

That left Oscar alone on the water with an empty rubber raft. "Score one for our side," he said. He'd first set eyes on Tversky less than half an hour earlier. Now the pilot was gone. In a day or so if not in mere hours, he'd be back in the war. As for Oscar . . . *I've got fish to catch,* he thought, and sailed out a little farther before dropping his lines into the sea.

He'd hoped running into Tversky would bring him good luck, but it didn't. His catch was average or slightly below. But you took what you could get. *Maybe not for too much longer. Maybe things will get back to the way they used to be.* He could hope, anyway.

He brought the sailboard back to Waikiki Beach with automatic skill he could hardly have imagined when he first thought up the gadget. As with anything else, practice made pretty darn good. Charlie Kaapu had been every bit as smooth as he was. What the devil had happened to Charlie? Oscar scowled as he took the sailboard over the breakers. Whatever it was, it wasn't anything he could fix. He'd put his own neck on the line trying. That consoled him . . . not very much.

Some of the Japs on the beach actually applauded when he came ashore. He would have liked that better if he hadn't been thinking about Charlie. He would have liked it better if he hadn't had to cough up a couple of fat mackerel to keep their goodwill, too. *Cost of doing business,* he thought. That *did* console him—some, anyway.

When he got back to the apartment, he found Susie there. By all the signs, she'd been there quite a while. She was falling-down drunk; the place reeked of the horrible fruity stuff they called gin these days. She'd never done anything like that in all the time he'd known her. "What happened?" he blurted.

She looked up from the beat-up old sofa. Her eyes didn't want to track him. "Oscar!" she said. "Thank God!" After a moist hiccup, she added, "It could've been me."

"What could have?" he asked. "What happened, babe?" He wished he had some coffee in the place, but it was harder than hell to come by these days. He'd lost the habit.

"I was going to work. To work," Susie repeated, maybe forgetting she'd just said that. "And these Japsh—*Japs*—at one of the barricades." She had to try three times before she got the word right. "These Japs, they had a girl down in the middle of the street, and they. . . . They all . . ." She didn't go on. Tears started running down her face. "It could have been me!"

"Hey," Oscar said softly. "Hey." He might have been gentling a spooked horse. *I told you so,* came to the tip of his tongue and died there, which was probably lucky for him. He'd heard that these sailor-soldiers did things like that, which was why he hadn't been thrilled when Susie headed for work in the morning. He went over and cautiously put a hand on her shoulder. She flinched, but only a little. "I'm glad you're okay," he told her. She'd earned the right to get smashed, sure as the devil.

"It could have been me," she said one more time. Then she clung to him and cried her heart out. He hadn't seen many tears from her before. "What am I gonna do?" she asked after the storm passed.

"I think you better stay in here, not let those bastards spot you," Oscar answered.

"I'll go nuts," she said. "I'll lose my tan." Snockered as she was, that seemed to matter a lot to her. But then she shuddered, remembering what she'd seen. "I'll do it."

"Okay," Oscar said. "For now, just settle down. Get some sleep if you can. You'll feel it when you wake up, I'm afraid."

"I'm not drunk!" she said irately.

"Sure, babe. Sure." Oscar lied without hesitation. *The things you do for love,* he thought with a wry smile. Then he stopped cold; as usual, the word brought him up short. But he nodded to himself. Whether the word made him nervous or not, it talked about something real. He gave Susie a kiss.

"What's that for?" she asked.

"Just because," he said. "Just because."

GUARDS HUSTLED AMERICAN POWS SOUTH, away from the American soldiers who'd landed to bring Oahu back under the Stars and Stripes. Like most— probably all—of his buddies, Fletch Armitage would sooner have run toward the Americans than away from them, shooting squads or no shooting squads. The guards might have been bastards, but they weren't stupid bastards. They could figure that out for themselves. The minute anybody got the slightest bit out of line, they opened fire. Dead prisoners marked the road back toward Honolulu.

Men slipped away anyhow, especially at night. Fletch got no sleep. Every few minutes, a rifle or a light machine gun would bark. Screams from the wounded punctuated the time between bursts of gunfire. Sometimes the Japs would let wounded men howl. Other times, they would go out and finish them off with rifle butts or bayonets. Fletch couldn't decide which noises were more horrible.

But the noises weren't what made him sit tight. A cold calculation of the odds was. Could he get away from the guards? Possible, but not likely. Once he did, could he sneak through the Japanese lines without getting murdered by ordinary enemy soldiers? Also possible, but even less likely. Put the two together, and he figured his chances were much less than drawing the king of spades to fill out a royal flush.

When the sun came up, he saw how many Americans had died trying to get away, and how many hadn't died—yet. Had he had anything in his stomach, he might have thrown it up. The Japs hadn't bothered feeding the POWs, though. It didn't look as if they were going to start now, either.

Curses and kicks got the prisoners on their feet. The guards bayoneted one man who had trouble. After that, the stronger Americans helped their weaker buddies up. "*Isogi!*" the guards shouted. How they expected the POWs to hurry was beyond Fletch, but they did.

"Bastards," somebody said. Fletch nodded. The Japs were also bastards who'd eaten; they'd brought rice along for themselves.

Before long, clouds drifted over the marching—actually, shambling—men. It started to rain. In the blink of an eye, everybody threw his head back and opened his mouth as wide as it would go. Men fell down because they couldn't see where they were going. Nobody gave a damn. Fletch got a couple of swallows before the sun came out again.

By the afternoon of the second day, they reached the outskirts of Honolulu. Fewer men had tried to run off than had the day before. They were farther from the front, and they had the horrible examples of the day before still fresh in their memories. Honolulu looked fortified to a fare-thee-well. The Americans hadn't fought in the city. They'd surrendered before drawing a couple of hundred thousand defenseless civilians into the battle. By all the signs, the Japs cared no more about civilians than they did about POWs. Fletch didn't know what would make them surrender. He couldn't think of anything that seemed likely to.

The POWs did get fed, after a fashion. They were marched past a pot of rice. Each man got a spoonful, shoved straight into his mouth by a cook who looked as if he hated them all. Everybody got the same spoon. Fletch didn't care. By then, he would have eaten rice off a cowflop. He would have thought about eating the cowflop, too.

Hardly any locals were on the street. The ones who were seemed to cling to the sides of buildings and to do their best not to make themselves conspicuous in any way. They watched the prisoners with frightened eyes.

Through Honolulu. Through Waikiki. Fletch had a pretty good notion of where they were going by then. When he turned out to be right, he started to laugh. The POW next to him must have thought he was nuts, and might not have been so far wrong. "What's so goddamn funny?" the man demanded.

"This is where I came in," Fletch answered.

Back to Kapiolani Park and the POW camp there. Back through the barbed-wire gates that had let him out when the Japs decided they'd sooner get work from their prisoners than leave them sit around idle and starving. *As long as they were going to starve us, they could use us while we wasted away. Oh, yeah. That's what you call efficiency.*

Fletch wondered why the Japanese were bringing prisoners back here now. To keep them from running off to the Americans? That was bound to be one reason. To keep the Americans from shooting them up by mistake? In spite of his misery, he laughed again. The next sign the Japs showed of worrying about what happened to POWs would be the first. To gather a lot of prisoners together in one place so they could be massacred more easily? He looked at the machine guns in the towers out beyond the barbed wire. That seemed alarmingly likely.

And what could he do about it? Not one single, solitary thing, not that he could see. The gate shut behind his gang of POWs.

He looked around. The camp wasn't so insanely crowded as it had been the last time he was here. That would have encouraged him if he hadn't feared most of the missing men were dead.

His old tent had been right about . . . here. It was gone. Somebody else had the spot now, and had run up a lean-to that looked as if it would stop leaning and start collapsing any minute now. The barracks still stood, but he didn't want anything to do with them. Any place where POWs congregated in large numbers was liable to be a place where the Japs could get rid of them in large numbers.

He didn't mind sleeping on the ground. Why should he? He'd done enough of it lately. There was bound to be canvas to scrounge, and sticks as well. Before long, he could rig some kind of shelter to keep off the rain. Till then, he wouldn't worry about it, not in this weather. Getting wet mattered much less than it would have on the mainland. He did head for the one water fountain in the park. The march down had left him dry as a bone.

Because the POW camp wasn't so crowded, the line at the fountain was shorter than it had been in days gone by. Even so, while he waited another gang of POWs came in. He finally got to the water, and drank and drank and drank.

"Been through the Sahara, buddy?" asked the guy behind him.

"Feels like it." Fletch splashed some water on his face, too. It felt wonderful. At last, reluctantly, he gave up his place.

Still more prisoners came into the camp. Fletch remembered what some crazy Roman Emperor had said, a couple of thousand years earlier. It went something like, *I wish all humanity had a single neck, so I could cut off the head at one blow.* He wished that hadn't come back to him from whatever history class he'd heard it in. It described what the Japs looked to be doing here much too well.

THE TROUBLE WITH MORTARS was, you could hardly hear the bombs coming in before they burst. Les Dillon caught a faint hiss in the air and threw himself flat just in time. The fragments from the mortar round snarled past above him. He allowed himself the luxury of a sigh of relief. The Japs had a particularly nasty little weapon the Americans called a knee mortar. It wasn't fired off anyone's knee, but one man could serve it, and every other Jap infantryman seemed to carry one. One of those bombs had almost punched his ticket.

Schofield Barracks lay not far ahead. Bombers had largely leveled the barracks halls. The Japanese didn't seem to care. They were as ready to defend rubble to the death as they would have been to save Hirohito's crown jewels.

A machine gun fired several quick bursts from the direction of the barracks—a reminder to Les to keep his head down, as if he needed one. The Japs were even tougher than he'd figured they would be. Logically, they didn't have a prayer. They had no air cover left. They had next to no armor, and what they did have wasn't good enough. If he were their CO, he would have dickered a surrender on the best terms he could get.

They didn't think that way. They didn't surrender, period. The only Japs who'd been captured were men either knocked cold or too badly hurt to get away or to kill themselves. They also took no prisoners. God help you if you tried to surrender to them. Sometimes their wild counterattacks would overrun

U.S. forward positions. Les had helped recapture one or two of those. The American corpses he'd seen made him hate the enemy instead of just being professionally interested in getting rid of him, the way he had been with the Germans in 1918. After that, he wouldn't have let any Japs give up even if they'd tried.

One of the green young Marines in his platoon, an open-faced Oklahoma kid named Randy Casteel, hunkered down near him and asked, "Sarge, how come the Japs do shit like that? Don't they know it just makes us want to fight 'em even harder?" His drawl only made him sound more horrified and more bewildered than he would have without it.

Les Dillon was bewildered, too, and he'd seen a lot more nasty things over a lot more years than Private Casteel had. "Damned if I can tell you," he answered. "Maybe they think they're scaring us when they do that kind of stuff to a body."

"They got another think comin'!" Casteel said hotly.

"Yeah, I know." Les also knew the Japs hadn't done everything to bodies. Some of those poor men—most of them, probably—were alive when the enemy got to work on them. He could only hope they'd died pretty soon. "We just have to keep pushin' and keep poundin'. They won't do anything like that once they're all dead."

"Sooner the better," Casteel said.

"Oh, hell, yes." Les felt fatherly—almost grandfatherly—as he went on, "But you got to remember not to do anything dumb, though. Killing Japs is the name of the game. Don't let them kill you. You do something stupid, they'll make you pay for it before you can even blink. Take bayonets."

Randy Casteel nodded eagerly. "Oh, yeah, Sarge. I know about that."

"Make sure you remember, dammit. The Nips have more evil tricks than you can shake a stick at," Les said. Normal bayonet drill meant keeping the cutting edge toward the ground. But the Japanese bayonet had a hooked hand guard. The Japs used it to grab on to a U.S. bayonet. A twist, and the Marine's rifle went flying. "Keep the left side of the blade toward the deck and you'll be fine."

"Yeah, Sarge," Casteel repeated. Several men had died before somebody was sharp enough to figure out a counter. To look at your average Japanese soldier, you wouldn't think he was big enough or strong enough to win a bayonet fight—but he was. Oh, brother, was he.

"Other thing to remember is, don't use the bayonet till it's your last choice,"

Les added. "Blow the little fucker's head off instead. Let's see him get sneaky trying to dodge a bullet."

In training, everybody fussed about the bayonet. In the field, it made a tolerable can opener or barbed-wire cutter. It wasn't a great combat knife; like almost all Marines, Les preferred the Kabar on his belt.

"Over here! C'mon! This way!" The call from ahead came in perfect English. Randy Casteel glanced at Les.

The platoon sergeant shook his head. "Sit tight," he said. "Another goddamn decoy." Some of the enemy soldiers knew the language, and some of the locals still worked with them and for them. The locals had grown up speaking English, so of course they had no telltale accent to give them away. If you paid attention to shouts from people you didn't know, you'd charge right into an ambush.

Les stuck his head up—just for an instant, and not in a place from which he'd looked before. Somebody in khaki was moving out there. He snapped off a shot and ducked down again. Not even the scream that followed made him take another look. The Japs should have gone in for amateur theatricals. Look at the soldier you thought you'd just killed and it was even money he'd be waiting to plant one right between your eyes.

The sun dropped down toward the Waianae Range. Les muttered under his breath. "More goddamn infiltrators after dark, sure as shit."

"Yeah, Sarge." Randy Casteel nodded. In the daytime, American firepower and airplanes dominated. At night, it was the Japs' turn. They'd sneak into the American lines by ones and twos. They'd roll grenades into foxholes or jump in with a knife. The rule now was two men in a hole, one of them awake all the time. It made war even more exhausting than it would have been otherwise, but it saved lives.

At least one American had been shot by somebody on his own side for not coming out with the password fast enough to suit a trigger-happy Marine. Les felt sorry that had happened, but not very. Anybody dumb enough to move around at night when he didn't have to and dumb enough to draw a blank on the password was probably dumb enough to get himself killed some other way if he hadn't found that one.

"You know the word for tonight?" Les asked Casteel.

"Lizard lips," the kid answered. Les nodded. Most of the passwords had l's and r's in them: those were the English sounds that gave the Japs trouble.

Darkness fell fast here. Twilight didn't linger the way it did in more northerly climes. And when it was dark, it was *dark*. The electricity was out. There was no background glow, the way there would have been if lights shone not far away. A few fires burned, but with the rice paddies wet there weren't many of those, either.

"You gonna sack out on me if I give you first watch?" Les asked. "Tell me straight. If you're beat, sleep now, and I'll get you up at midnight. I can last, and I don't want both of us screwed because you couldn't."

"If you don't mind, Sarge, I better sleep now. I'm pretty beat," Casteel said.

"Okay. Go ahead," Les told him. The kid curled up, twisted a couple of times like a dog making a nest, and was dead to the world inside of two minutes. Les knew unconsciousness would sap him just as fast and just as hard when his turn came. Bare ground? Damp ground? Rain? He'd sleep on a bed of nails like an Indian fakir.

For now, though, he had to stay awake. He stuck his head up to look out of the hole. That was all he did; anyone walking around at night was presumed to be a Jap. He peered south, his rifle close by him. Most of the fires down around Schofield Barracks seemed to be out. He muttered something foul. He might have spotted Japs sneaking forward against a background of flame. Now he'd have to do it the hard way.

He wished for the moon. It wasn't a childish wish for something he couldn't possibly get. He just wished it were in the sky. But it wasn't, and it wouldn't come up till Randy Casteel went on watch. He shrugged. Odds were the kid needed more help than he did. So he told himself, anyway.

A few strands of barbed wire looped in front of the American position. Les didn't think they would slow the Japs down. But the Marines who'd set out the wire had also hung K-ration cans partly filled with pebbles from it. With luck, a noise from those would give some warning.

Off to his left, a rifle cracked—an Arisaka. A burst from an American machine gun answered it. Les wondered if a night firefight would break out. That would be the last thing anybody needed. But the firing died away. As far as Les could tell, all it had done was scare everybody who was awake. Casteel's breathing never even changed.

Les longed for a cigarette. That would have to wait till daylight. The flash of a match and the glow of a coal just asked a sniper to draw a bead on you. He longed for a cigarette, but he wasn't dying for one.

The stars wheeled across the sky. Nothing happened, but something always could. Waiting for it, wondering when it would come and how bad it would be, wore away your stomach lining.

Out ahead, something rattled. Les' rifle was against his shoulder before he knew how it had got there. The noise might not have come from a Jap. The other night, somebody'd used up a stray cat's nine lives all at once. But you never could tell.

Was that a moving shape, there on this side of the wire? It might have been too small and low for a man, but it might not have, too. The Japs could crawl on their bellies as well as snakes. Finger tight on the trigger, Les hissed out a challenge: "Password!"

No answer. No movement. Silence. He wondered if his nerves were getting the best of him. He called the challenge again. Still nothing. But the shape of the shadows ahead looked different from the way it had before he heard that rattle. It might have been his imagination. He didn't think so. He thought it was a Jap, maybe two. The rifle bucked against his shoulder.

Japs had fine discipline—better discipline, probably, than the Marines. But holding still and not making a sound despite a wound from a high-powered .30-caliber round proved beyond this one. He groaned. Les fired again. The Jap screamed, the cry slowly subsiding into an agonized gurgle.

But sure as hell, more than one enemy soldier lurked out there in the darkness. With a bloodcurdling shriek, the Jap Les hadn't hit dashed at him. He fired once more—and missed. Night shooting was as much a matter of luck as anything else. Still shrieking, the Jap jumped down into the foxhole with him.

If Les hadn't got his M-1 up in a hurry, the Jap would have gutted him like a tuna. The knife in the enemy soldier's hand rebounded from the stock. Les had told Randy Casteel about the virtues of firing as opposed to the bayonet. He had no time to aim and shoot. He didn't even have time or room for a bayonet thrust. He used a buttstroke instead, and felt the big end of his piece slam the side of the Jap's head.

He thought—he hoped—the blow would fracture the enemy's skull. But either the Jap had a devil of a hard head or Les hadn't hit so hard as he thought he had. The Jap kept fighting, if a little dazedly. He slashed out with his knife. Les felt his tunic tear and the hot pain of a blade cutting his arm. He hissed a curse.

Then the Jap grunted, more in surprise than anything else, and went limp.

The hot-iron smell of blood filled the foxhole, as well as an earthier stink—the soldier's bowels had let go. He was dead as shoe leather before he finished crumpling.

"Hell of a way to wake somebody up," Randy Casteel said peevishly.

"Thanks, kid," Les panted. "Got a wound dressing handy? Can you stick it on my arm? He nicked me a little." He worked his hand. The fingers all opened and closed and gripped the way they were supposed to. He nodded to himself. "Doesn't seem too bad."

"Lemme see." Casteel bent to get a close look in the darkness. "Yeah, I can patch you up. You just got a star to go with your Purple Heart." He fumbled in his belt pouch for the dressing.

"All things considered, I'd rather have a blowjob," Les said, which jerked a startled laugh from the other Marine.

"What the fuck's going on?" somebody called from not far away. If he didn't like the answer, a grenade would follow the question.

"That you, Dutch?" Les said. "Two Japs, looks like. I scragged one. Other one tried to keep us company. He cut me a little, but Casteel gave him a Kabar where it did the most good."

Somebody else out there in the darkness asked a low-voiced question. Dutch Wenzel's reply was loud enough to let Les hear it: "Oh, hell, yes, sir, that's him. Ain't a Jap in the world talks English like that."

"I dusted some sulfa powder on the wound, too, Sarge," Randy Casteel said.

"Good. That's good. You did everything just right," Dillon answered. "What time is it, anyway?"

"Uh, half past ten."

"Think you can sleep another hour and a half? I'll go back on watch. I won't be able to get any shuteye for a while anyway—not till the arm quiets down a little." He said nothing about the pounding of his heart, which also needed to ease. Nothing like damn near getting killed to keep you up at night.

Casteel said, "I'll give it a try." He needed almost ten minutes to start snoring this time. Les envied him his youth and resilience. *I'm supposed to be the smart one,* he thought. *So how come I'm the one who got cut?*

THE JAPANESE OFFICER ON TOP OF JANE ARMITAGE squeezed her breasts one last time, grunted, and came. She lay there unmoving, as she had while he pumped away inside her. He didn't care, damn him. He patted her head, as if she were a dog that had done a clever trick. Then he dressed and walked out of the room.

Dully, she waited for the next violation. She knew she ought to douche, but what was the point? With so many Japs every day, douching seemed a pitiful stick in the wind against pregnancy and disease.

How long did the average comfort woman last? How long before the sheer physical endurance you needed to take on man after man after man—none of whom gave a damn about you except as one convenient hole or another—combined with mind-numbing self-loathing to make you decide you couldn't stand to go on for one more cock, let alone one more day? Jane was stubborn. The end hadn't come for her, because she still wanted to see the Japs dead more than she wanted to die herself. But new girls had replaced several from the original contingent by now, and the ones who'd left hadn't gone on rest cures. They'd died, died by their own hands.

Jane flinched when the door opened. But it wasn't another horny Jap wanting a few minutes of fun before he went back to killing American soldiers. It was one of the Chinese women who ran the soldiers' brothel for the occupiers. She fluttered her fingers, a gesture that meant Jane had taken on her last man for the day.

Wearily, she nodded. The Chinese woman closed the door and went on to the next room. *Occupiers.* The word echoed in Jane's head. In Shakespeare's day, she remembered from a lit course at Ohio State, to occupy a woman meant to screw her. Jane had never thought to see the connection so vividly illustrated in the twentieth century.

Not far away, Japanese field guns boomed, shooting at the Americans pushing down from the north. She wished the guns would blow up in the Japs' faces. She hadn't really understood the futility of wishing till she got here.

Before long, American shells screamed in. Counterbattery fire, they called it. That was what she got for being an artilleryman's wife. Ex-wife. Almost ex-wife. She shook her head in sour disbelief. She'd thought Fletch wasn't the lover she deserved. Maybe he wasn't. But a million years of Fletch would have been paradise next to what she'd gone through the past few weeks.

A white woman poked her head into the room. Beulah stayed—was stuck in—the room next door. "Come on," she said. "We might as well get something to eat."

"Okay." Jane made herself climb to her feet. More shells burst within a few hundred yards of the apartment building–turned-brothel. "I wish a couple of those would land on this place and blow it straight to hell." Even though she knew wishing was useless, she couldn't stop. What else did she have left?

Beulah only shrugged. She was broad-shouldered and stolid and, Jane suspected, not very bright. If anything, that helped her here; not thinking was an asset. "Gotta keep going," she said. "What else can we do?"

Hang ourselves. But Jane didn't say it. She'd been taught as a girl that saying something made you more likely to do it. She wasn't sure she believed that any more, not after a couple of psychology classes, but any English major would have said words had power. If they didn't, why pay attention to them in the first place?

The comfort women gathered together in what had been a storeroom and now, with the addition of chairs and tables no doubt stolen from people's homes, did duty for a dining room. Some of the women didn't want to have much to do with anybody. Jane was one of those. Others talked about what they'd done and what their Japs had done; they might have been factory workers comparing the behavior of machines. If they were going to talk, they didn't have much else to talk about.

Supper was rice and vegetables—more than Jane would have got if they hadn't kidnapped her. The Japs might not have wanted to fuck her if she looked like a starving woman. She didn't care. She wouldn't have done this for all the gold in Fort Knox. She wouldn't even have done it for a T-bone smothered in mushrooms and onions.

Somebody said, "What'll the Japs do if it looks like they're gonna get kicked out of Wahiawa?" There was something new to talk about after all.

"Please, God," somebody else said, "and soon!" A woman sitting near Jane crossed herself. That anyone could still believe in God impressed her—and horrified her, too. What did it take to get you to see nobody was on the other end of that telephone?

"Maybe they'll let us go," Beulah said.

"Not the Japs!" Jane said. "They never do anything for anybody. They do things to people instead."

"So what'll they do to us?" Beulah asked. "What can they do that they haven't already done?"

Jane winced. That question made altogether too much sense. After weeks of having to lie down for endless men she hated, what was left in the way of degradation? But someone had an answer: "They're liable to kill us all. That way, we won't be able to tell anybody what they made us do."

No one spoke for a little while. The unwilling comfort women weighed the odds. Would the Japanese murder them in cold blood? It didn't strike Jane as the least bit unlikely. Dead women told no tales. She said, "We've got to get out of here."

"How?" three women asked at the same time. The windows were barred. The doors were guarded. The Chinese women who ran the brothel for the Japs—their boss was a snake named Annabelle Chung—kept their eyes open for trouble all the time. Even talking about escaping was dangerous. Some of the miserable women in this room informed. No one knew who, but the fact seemed inarguable. What could they get that would make squealing on their fellow sufferers worthwhile? Not more food, the usual currency of betrayal in the rest of Wahiawa. Fewer horny Japs? After a while, what difference did that make? But Jane couldn't see any other reason to snitch except general meanness. Of course, that wasn't impossible, either.

No matter how many women asked the question, nobody answered it. An answer did occur to Jane: give the guards some of what she had to give the other Japanese soldiers. Before she landed here, sucking a stranger's cock to get something she wanted would no more have occurred to her than killing herself. She probably would sooner have killed herself. She remembered that, as if from very far away. Now . . . She'd had to get down on her knees so often for nothing at all, why not do it once more if she really needed to? And it wasn't as if suicide were a stranger to her thoughts nowadays.

She looked around at the other comfort women. Were they thinking along with her? How could they not be? A few weeks of this had coarsened the women it didn't kill. Some of them hadn't even bothered to put on clothes before they came to supper. There had been evenings when Jane didn't bother, either, though she'd thrown on a muumuu now. Would they all be thinking, *Well, why not? What's one more after so many?*

And if by some accident they got out of this, what would their lives be like? Jane tried to imagine wanting a man to touch her. The picture refused to form. And she tried to imagine a decent man wanting to touch her if he knew what the Japs had made her do. That picture wouldn't take shape, either. She shook her head. What was left for her? Nothing she could see.

Sometimes a woman broke down and sobbed here. Sometimes crying jags ran through them all, contagious as chicken pox. Not tonight, though. Maybe they were all trying to figure the odds.

Artillery and small-arms fire through the night didn't keep Jane from sleeping like a stone. One more thing nobody'd told her: screwing all day was hard physical labor. And it wore out the spirit much worse than the body.

No rooster announced the dawn. As far as Jane knew, all the roosters in Wahiawa except one saved for stud were long since chicken stew. Since coming here, she'd wondered once or twice if he got sick of fucking strangers all day every day. She figured the odds were against it. After all, he was a goddamn male.

Usually, the breakfast gong took the rooster's place. The women woke for that. If they didn't get breakfast, they couldn't eat till suppertime. Today, though, just as the eastern sky was beginning to go pink, four 105mm shells slammed into the brothel.

That got Jane out of bed—literally. She woke up on the floor, with one of the walls tilted sideways and with chunks of plaster falling on her head from the ceiling. Somebody was screaming, "Fire!" at the top of her lungs. Somebody else was just screaming, the agonized, unthinking cries of the badly wounded.

Jane scrambled to her feet. She cut one of them on broken glass, but she hardly cared. She let the muumuu fall over her head, then rushed out the door. It had been locked from the outside, but the blasts blew it open.

Beulah's door had come open all by itself, too. Jane looked into the room. "Let's get out of here!" she shouted. "We'll never have a better chance!"

"I guess not," Beulah said—she must have been in another line when they were handing out brains. All she had on was a pair of panties. She didn't stop for anything else. Come to think of it, that wasn't so dumb.

"Where do you think you're going?" Annabelle Chung stood in the corridor, hands on her hips. Jane wasted no time on conversation. She hauled off and belted her oppressor in the chops. The Chinese woman shrieked and staggered, but tried to fight back. Jane gave her a pretty fair one-two. Maybe she'd been listening after all when Fletch went on and on about Joe Louis and Hank Armstrong.

The Chinese woman went down on hands and knees. When she started to get up, Beulah kicked her in the ribs. That wasn't in the Marquis of Queensberry rules, but it sure as hell worked. Annabelle Chung stayed down. "Way to go!" Jane shouted.

The side of the building had a hole in it you could drive a bus through. Comfort women streamed out. Some wore muumuus like Jane; one or two were buck naked. Several of them were limping or bleeding. None of that mattered. Getting out did.

Out in the open. Two Japs had stood nearby. Only the bottom part of one of them was left. The other had had his head almost blown off. Jane looked longingly at the Arisakas by the dead men. She knew how to use a bolt-action rifle. But lots of Japs still occupied Wahiawa. Even with a rifle, she couldn't kill them all. *Oh, but I want to!* she thought. They could kill her, though, and they would if they saw her with an Arisaka in her hands. She hated to leave the rifles there, but she did.

"Let's get away!" she said. Her partners in misery didn't need the advice. They were already scattering as fast as they could. Some of them would have friends and families to go back to. Would they still be friends, would the families stay loving, when they found out what the women here had had to do? Maybe. Some of them might, anyhow. The rest? Well, they couldn't be worse than the Japs.

Jane had nothing and nobody here. Fletch was a POW if he hadn't died since she last saw him. For all practical purposes, he was an ex-husband, anyway. *Would I take him back now?* Jane laughed as she ran. That wasn't the question, was it? *Would he take me back now?* She had no idea. Everything she'd done, she'd been forced to do. Everybody had to know that. Would anyone care, or would she stay soiled in the eyes of the world for the rest of her life?

She'd worry about that later. All she wanted to do now was get away from the brothel, get away from the Japs, and let the world scorn her if it would.

More artillery shells screamed in. Jane threw herself flat before they burst. Fletch had talked about that, too, and she'd seen it worked when the Japs came down from the north. Now her own country was doing its best to kill her. She forgave it. As she lay there in the gutter with fragments of sharp steel screeching by above her head, she cried tears of pure, unadulterated joy.

LIEUTENANT SABURO SHINDO HELPED MECHANICS gut wrecked Zeros and Hayabusas, salvaging machine guns and 20mm cannon for use against the

Americans on the ground. He'd already gutted his own fighter. To his mortification, the Yankees had caught it on the ground and shot it up bad enough to keep it there for good. He'd wanted to die in the air, with luck taking a few more enemy planes with him. The *kami* in charge of such things paid no attention to what he wanted.

He couldn't remember the last time he'd seen a Japanese fighter in the air. The Americans ruled the skies now. Their fearsome planes roared over Oahu like flying tigers, shooting up anything that moved. When the Japanese landed here, Zeros dominated the air. Now Shindo was finding out how taking what he'd dished out felt. He would rather have stayed on the other end of it.

"Pass me those tinsnips," he said. The mechanic working with him did. He sliced away at the aluminum skin of a Zero's wing. The fuselage had burned. The other wing had gone up with it. This one, by a freak of war, was pretty much intact. Put that cannon in some kind of improvised ground mount and it would make a few Americans sorry they'd ever been born.

The thought had hardly crossed his mind before he heard a sound he'd come to hate: the roar of enemy engines in the air. American radials had a deeper note than their Japanese counterparts; anyone who'd heard both would never confuse the two. Shindo threw down the snips and ran for the nearest trench. The Japanese had dug lots of them when they thought they would still be able to fly out of Wheeler Field. That proved optimistic, but the trenches still gave people a place to hide when Yankee planes came over.

A few soldiers fired at the fighters and dive bombers with rifles. So Americans had fired at Zeros when the war was new: furiously, but without much hope. The Americans had knocked down a couple of Japanese planes—put enough lead in the air and you would. Much good it had done them. No doubt the Japanese here would knock down a few American planes, too, and much good that would do *them*.

In fact, the muzzle flashes told the Yankees where the trenches were. Shindo huddled in the damp-smelling dirt as heavy machine-gun slugs chewed up the ground all around him. Some of them struck home. Few men who were hit cried out, as they would have if a rifle-caliber round struck them. If a high-velocity bullet the size of a man's thumb hit you, you were usually too dead to scream.

Bursting bombs made the earth shake under him. The noise was tremendous, something beyond the normal meaning of the word. Shindo felt it through his skin as much as he heard it. Dirt rained down on him. Fragments of bomb casing howled past not nearly far enough over his head.

And then, like a cloudburst, it was over—till the next time. Shindo looked at his wristwatch. He shook his head in slow wonder. All that horror, compressed into less than ten minutes? It was as abbreviated as air-to-air combat, and seemed even slower. In the air, he could have fought back. Here, he just had to take it.

The Americans hadn't gone back to the north. They'd flown south instead, to harry Pearl Harbor and Ewa. That meant they might hit Wheeler Field again on the way home to their carriers. Shindo shrugged stoically as he climbed out of the trench. If they did, they did, that was all. He couldn't do anything about it. He could help the Army meet the U.S. invaders.

Or he thought he could. When he got a look at the fighter he'd been cannibalizing, he wasn't so sure any more. One bomb had landed right on it, another close by. One blast or the other had driven his tinsnips deep into the trunk of a palm tree, so deep he knew he'd need other tools to get them out. And the barrel of the cannon he'd been freeing had a distinct bend in it now. Nobody would use that weapon against the Yankees.

Shindo's shoulders slumped. How were you supposed to fight the enemy when he blocked things even before you did them? Again, the Americans must have been asking themselves something like that at the end of 1941. Now that it was Japan's turn, Shindo found no better answers than they had then.

JIM PETERSON STOOD AT ATTENTION WITH HIS FELLOW sufferers in the Kalihi Valley. Most of them were as skeletal as he was. Beriberi and dropsy swelled others past what was natural. A man like Charlie Kaapu, who was only gaunt, stood out as an extraordinary physical specimen.

POWs had tried to get away from this hellhole before the Americans came back to Oahu. Now, with the hope of rescue in the air, escape attempts came more often. But sick, starving men couldn't go very far very fast. They usually got caught. And when they did, they paid.

This poor fellow looked like a rack of bones. The butcher's cat would have turned up its nose at him even before the Japs beat the crap out of him. Now he was all over bruises and blood, too. They'd broken his nose. A couple of guards held him upright. He didn't seem able to stand on his own.

"What'll they do to him?" Charlie Kaapu whispered to Peterson. He'd quickly mastered the art of speaking without moving his lips.

"Don't know," Peterson whispered back. "That's why we're here, though— so they can make a show."

It wasn't much of a show. The guards let the POW fall to his knees. A lieutenant swung his sword. Peterson had heard that samurai swords would cut through anything on the first try. One more lie—or maybe the Jap hadn't taken good care of the blade. Any which way, he needed three hacks before the POW's head fell from his neck. The body convulsed, but not for long. The head just lay there. If anything, it seemed relieved the ordeal was over.

"Fuck," Charlie Kaapu whispered. Under his swarthy skin, he turned green.

He was a civilian. He hadn't seen so much. Peterson only shrugged. The Japs had done plenty worse. The lieutenant let out a torrent of Japanese. A noncom who spoke fragments of English pointed to the emaciated corpse and the pool of blood soaking into the ground under it. "You run, you—" He pointed again. That got the meaning across, but Peterson suspected some of the lieutenant's eloquence was lost in translation. *Yeah, like I give a shit,* he thought.

Off in the distance, bombs burst and .50-caliber machine guns chattered: the unmistakable sounds of American planes giving the Japs hell. The guards resolutely pretended nothing out of the ordinary was going on. The POWs had to pretend the same thing. Men who grinned or laughed caught hell. Several of them had died from it—not as spectacularly as the beheaded man, but every bit as dead. The guards were jumpy, and getting jumpier all the time, no matter what they pretended.

The sergeant with a little English pointed toward the mouth of the tunnel through the Koolau Range. "You go!" he yelled, and the POWs went.

It was madness. Peterson knew it. Everybody knew it, prisoners and guards alike. The only reason the men were digging through the mountains' bowels was so they could die from hard labor and bad food. Too many of them hadn't needed any further abuse from the Japs. The routine was deadly enough.

Besides that, even if there had been some point to all the man-killing labor, there wasn't any more. The Japanese would never get a nickel's worth of good out of the tunnel. By every sign Peterson could use to judge, they wouldn't hold Oahu. The Stars and Stripes would fly here again. Everything the POWs in the Kalihi Valley did was an exercise in futility.

They got driven to it even so. If anything, they got driven harder than ever now. The guards might have feared they would rise up if they weren't worked to death and otherwise intimidated. They might have been right, too.

Outside the tunnel mouth, Peterson grabbed a pick. Charlie Kaapu took a shovel. His face said he would sooner have bashed Japs with it than lifted chunks of rock. "Easy," Peterson murmured. A machine-gun nest covered the tools. Anybody who got out of line would die fast. So would a lot of POWs who hadn't done one damn thing.

The *hapa*-Hawaiian growled, down deep in his throat. But he carried the shovel into the tunnel instead of braining the nearest guard. Light vanished. It would have been dark in there even if Peterson had been well nourished. Night blindness had advanced with his beriberi. He couldn't see much at all.

Lamps set into the wall here and there gave just enough light to let him keep moving forward. The sound of other POWs banging away at the living rock told him he was getting close. So did a Jap's yell: "Hurry up! Faster!"

Peterson wanted to ask why. The Jap would have answered with a beating or a bayonet or a bullet. Those answers were persuasive enough, too. How could you argue with them? You couldn't, not unless you had a club or a rifle yourself. Peterson wished for a rifle. He wished for a machine gun, and the strength to fire it from the hip. You could do that in the movies. In the real world? He knew better.

A Jap hit him with a bamboo swagger stick for no reason he could see. A pick was a weapon, too. He could have broken the bastard's head. He could have, but he didn't. He didn't fear death himself, though he would surely die if he raised his hand to a guard. But the Japs would slaughter untold other POWs to avenge and punish. He didn't want to die with that on his conscience.

Instead of smashing the guard's skull, the pick bit into the rock. Pulling it free took all his strength. So did lifting it for the next stroke. How many had he made? Too many. Far too many. That was all he knew.

He grubbed rock out of the wall. Charlie Kaapu shoveled it up and dumped it into baskets. Some other poor, sorry son of a bitch carried away the spoil. Other POWs grubbed and shoveled and carried, too. The guards screamed at everybody to move faster. Dully, Peterson wondered what difference it could make. They weren't that close to punching through, or he didn't think they were. Even if they had been, what advantage could the Japs gain from moving men to the east coast? No fighting there. Could they get back over the mountains and hit the Americans in the flank? They'd done it in the west in their invasion, but they'd been up against a much weaker foe, and one who didn't control the air. Peterson didn't believe they could make it matter this time around.

Every so often, one of the laborers keeled over. The guards weren't about to put up with that—it was too much like resting on the job. They fell on the sufferers like wolves, trying to get them back on their feet with blows and kicks. Some of the POWs could be bullied upright again. Some were too far gone, and lay on the tunnel floor no matter what the Japs did. And some didn't keel over because they were tired. Some keeled over because they were dead.

The men who carried away rock also carried away corpses. That gummed up the works, because the rock accumulated. The Japs just screamed at them to move faster, too, and beat them when they didn't—SOP for Imperial Japan.

Hours blurred together into one long agony. At last, after the usual eternity, the guards let the POWs stumble out of the tunnel. They queued up for the little bit of rice the Japs grudgingly doled out. There was even less than usual today. Men grumbled—food they took seriously. The Japs only shrugged. One who spoke a little English said, "More not come. Blame Americans."

Had U.S. fighters (some of the ones Peterson had seen weren't Wildcats, but new, plainly hot machines) shot up the rice on the way to the Kalihi Valley? Or had the Japs, with more important things to worry about than a bunch of damned—literally—POWs, just not bothered sending any? Either way, it made starving to death seem almost worthwhile.

Almost.

WHEN JIRO TAKAHASHI WALKED UP NUUANU AVENUE to the Japanese consulate, he was shocked not to see the Rising Sun flying in front of the compound. Then he noticed how many bullet holes pocked the buildings. The staff must have decided not to fly the flag to keep from giving a target to the American planes now constantly overhead.

For most of the occupation, the guards in front of the consulate had been a ceremonial force. No more. They crouched in sandbagged machine-gun nests, the snouts of their weapons pointing up toward the sky. There were fewer of them than there had been. Some, Jiro supposed, would have gone up to the front. Others . . . With the buildings as battered as they were, some of those bullets would have found flesh, too.

"It's the Fisherman!" one of the guards called. The men who were left still knew Jiro. That made him feel good. The one who'd spoken went on, "You bring us some nice *ahi,* Fisherman, or even some mackerel?"

Jiro laughed nervously. He was emptyhanded, as they could see. "Not today, *gomen nasai,*" he answered. He *was* sorry, too; in better times, he would have had fish for the consul and the chancellor and often the guards as well. "Is Kita-*san* in?" he asked.

"I think so," the talky guard answered. "Go on in any which way. They'll be glad to see you. They're glad to see anybody right now." His laugh had a somber edge.

With such gallows humor ringing in his ears, Jiro did. Even some of the secretaries had put down their pens and picked up Arisakas. One of the remainder, a gray-haired fellow who would have been useless on a battlefield, said, "Oh, yes, Takahashi-*san,* the consul's here. I'm sure he'll be happy to talk to you. Please wait a moment." He hurried back to Nagao Kita's office.

Returning a moment later, he beckoned Jiro on. "Welcome, Takahashi-*san,* welcome," Kita said after they exchanged bows. "Good to see you haven't abandoned us." His words showed spirit, but his round features were thinner and less jaunty than Jiro had ever seen them.

Jiro bowed again. "I wouldn't do that, your Excellency," he said, though the thought had crossed his mind. The radio broadcasts full of lies he'd had to read still rankled.

"Plenty of people would," Kita said. "They want to forget they ever heard of Japan or the Great East Asia Co-Prosperity Sphere. Opportunists." He laced the word with scorn. "They probably have American flags in their closets, waiting to come out when the time is right."

"I'm still here," Jiro said, reflecting that both his sons thought him an idiot for clinging to the land where he was born. His still being here prompted another thought. "Please excuse me, Kita-*san,* but where is Chancellor Morimura?"

"Somewhere up at the fighting front," Kita answered. Jiro blinked; the skinny official with the doelike eyes hardly seemed a military man. But the consul went on, "I have learned he is a graduate of Eta Jima, invalided out of the Navy because of stomach trouble. He went into, ah, other work after that.

Now, though, with every man needed to hold back the Americans, he has returned to the warrior's life."

Tadashi Morimura—was that even his real name?—a graduate of the Japanese naval academy? Jiro had trouble imagining it, let alone believing it. But it was plainly true. And what "other work" had Morimura been doing? By the way Consul Kita said it, the man had been a spy. "I'm—amazed, Kita-*san*," Jiro said.

"So was I," Kita answered. "You think you know someone, and then you find you didn't know him at all." He shrugged. "*Shigata ga nai.*"

"*Hai.*" Jiro nodded. He'd thought Morimura a friend, not an operative. Things looked clearer than they had. No wonder Chancellor Morimura had introduced him to Osami Murata. He'd wanted the radio man from Tokyo to use Jiro as a propaganda tool. And he'd got what he wanted.

If I saw Morimura now, I'd punch him in the nose, Jiro thought. He laughed at himself, even here. The younger man would probably mop the floor with him. He shrugged. *Well, so what? Sometimes you have to do things like that, just to show you're no man's puppet.* He felt as if he wore strings on his wrists and ankles.

Nagao Kita might have been reading his mind. "I am sorry to have to tell you this, Takahashi-*san*," he said. "I fear it will make you less likely to stay loyal to the end."

He was right to fear that, too. But Jiro said only, "I've come this far. I can't very well jump out of the boat now." *It's too late. It wouldn't do me any good.* Because he had the consul at a momentary disadvantage, he felt he could ask, "How *does* the fighting look?"

"They push us back," Kita answered bleakly. "We fight with great courage, shouting the Emperor's name and wishing him ten thousand years. For all we do, though, they rule the skies, and they have more tanks and artillery."

"This is not good," Jiro said.

"*Honto.* This is *not* good," the consul agreed. "I don't know what we can do about it, though, except die gloriously, not retreating even a centimeter, dying rather than yielding the ground we have conquered."

That did sound glorious. It also sounded like a recipe for defeat. Modern Japan had never been defeated in a foreign war. She'd beaten China and Russia. She'd sided with the Allies in World War I, and beaten Germany in China and on the seas. The idea that she *could* lose was unimaginable—except that

Jiro had to imagine it. He asked, "What will you do, Kita-*san*, if, if—the worst happens?"

"I am a diplomat. The rules for me are different from the ones for soldiers," Kita replied. "I can be exchanged."

Jiro had an inspiration. "I am a Japanese national. Can I be exchanged, too?" If Hawaii returned to American hands, he wouldn't want to stay here. Most people would hate him for siding with Japan. They might do worse than hate him. They might decide he was a traitor and hang him or shoot him.

Consul Kita looked surprised. "Well, I don't know, Takahashi-*san*. I would have to do something like put you on my staff, I suppose."

"Could you?" Jiro asked eagerly. Going back to Japan would mean leaving his sons behind. He knew that. But Hiroshi and Kenzo had their own lives. And they were Americans, as much as he remained Japanese. They might be glad to see him go. They'd probably be relieved if he did.

"Depend on it." Kita scribbled a note to himself. "We will go on hoping that black day does not come. But if it should, we will see what we can arrange."

"*Domo arigato, Kita-san.*" Jiro bowed in his chair. There was one thing he wouldn't have to worry about. Of course, he still might get killed, but that didn't bother him the same way. It wasn't certain, and he couldn't do anything about it one way or the other. If Japan lost, though, American vengeance was as sure as tomorrow's sunrise. Now he'd done what he could to escape it.

WHEN MINORU GENDA PEDALED OVER TO IOLANI PALACE, something had changed. He needed a moment to realize what it was: the big, tough-looking Hawaiian soldiers who'd guarded the bottom of the stairway up to the front entrance were gone. He asked one of the Japanese guards at the top of the stairs what had happened to them.

"Sir, King Stanley sent them up to the front." The noncom's tone made it plain he had nothing to do with anything his superiors did. "He sent the whole Hawaiian Army to the front."

The whole Hawaiian Army had about a battalion's worth of men. "Did he?" Genda said. "Our officers approved it?"

"Sir, would those Hawaiians be there if they hadn't?" the noncom asked reasonably.

"I suppose not." Genda still had doubts, but he wasn't about to discuss them with an underofficer. The occupying authorities had let King Stanley Laanui form an army of sorts because they'd nominally restored Hawaii's independence, and independent countries always had armies—of sorts. At the time, nobody—doubtless including King Stanley—had imagined the Hawaiian Army might actually have to fight.

For that matter, nobody knew which side it would choose to fight on. Did the soldiers think of themselves as Hawaiians, loyal to the ancient kingdom, or as Americans on masquerade? Were there some who felt each way? If there were, the tiny army might have its own tiny civil war.

If it did that while it was holding some of the line . . . well, what followed wouldn't be pretty. And yet the Japanese officers who presumably knew it best had let it go forward. Genda hoped they knew what they were doing. Too late to change it now, either way.

His ankle didn't bother him too much when he went up the stairs to the library. He'd interviewed Stanley Laanui there, along with other possible candidates for the revived Hawaiian throne. Now the room again belonged to a distant relative of David Kalakaua, the King of Hawaii who'd had it built.

Seen from the front, the enormous Victorian desk behind which King Stanley sat seemed wide as *Akagi*'s flight deck. Poor *Akagi*! For a moment, pain for Genda's lost ship stabbed at him, dagger-sharp. He bowed to the king, not least to make sure his face didn't show what he was thinking. "Your Majesty," he murmured.

"Hello, Commander. Nice of you to come to see *me* for a change." Stanley Laanui slurred the words so Genda had trouble understanding them. Was he drunk this early in the morning? Whether he was or not, he alarmed the Japanese officer. Did he know about Genda's visits to Queen Cynthia? If he did, what did he aim to do about them? If he kept a pistol as well as a bottle in one of those drawers . . . But the not very kingly King of Hawaii went on, "This Captain Iwabuchi is a lot nastier than General Yamashita ever was."

Genda believed that. The commandant of the special naval landing forces struck him as hard and determined even by Japanese standards. "I am so sorry, your Majesty," Genda said. "You know he has many worries."

"Like I don't!" the king exclaimed. "They won't hang Iwabuchi if our side loses."

He was bound to have that right. Genda couldn't imagine the Japanese naval officer letting himself be captured. Iwabuchi would surely die in battle or commit *seppuku* before permitting such a disgrace. "Do not be hard on him," Genda said. "Remember, he helps defend your country."

"Oh, yeah," King Stanley said. "He'll defend it till everybody in Honolulu's dead."

Genda had no doubt Captain Iwabuchi intended to defend Honolulu just that way. "This is war, your Majesty," he said—use was making his English more and more fluent. "This is not a game. We cannot stop and ask to begin again. It goes to the end, whatever the end may be."

"If I'd figured the Americans were coming back, I don't know that I would have let you stick a crown on my noggin," Stanley Laanui said.

"Believe me, your Majesty, I do not want the Americans here any more than you do," Genda said. "Japan does all it can to beat them."

"Hawaii's doing everything it can, too," the king said. "That's why I sent my army up to join the fighting."

"Hai," Genda said, and not another word. Any other word might have been too much. But after a moment he did find a few that seemed safe: "I hope the Army will fight strongly for us."

"Why shouldn't it?" the king asked.

Genda said nothing. The question had too many answers—because the soldiers might not be loyal to the King of Hawaii, because they didn't have all the weapons they needed to fight first-rate foes like the U.S. Marines and Army, because they had no combat experience, because some of them were either cutthroats or men looking for enough to eat and not really warriors at all. They'd all been trained since they joined up, but how much did that mean?

Only one way to find out. By now they'd be up near the line. Whatever Japanese officer they reported to would use them. Why not? They would surely kill some Americans. If they died themselves, even in swarms, so what? Better them than precious, irreplaceable Japanese troops.

King Stanley was doing his best to act like a proper ally. Genda admired him for that. He also pitied him. Japan didn't want a proper ally here in Hawaii, any more than she wanted proper allies in any of the countries she'd conquered. She wanted puppets who would deliver natural resources and do as they were told.

Hawaii had no natural resources to speak of. Sugar? Pineapple? Neither would have been worth a single Japanese soldier or sailor. Hawaii's position *was* its natural resource. Under the Rising Sun, it shielded everything farther west and made it hard for the USA to help Australia and New Zealand. Under the Stars and Stripes, it was a spearhead aimed straight at the rest of the Japanese Empire.

It behooved Japan to hold on to Hawaii as long as she could, then. How long that would be . . . "We will all do the best we can, your Majesty," Genda said.

"How good is that?" King Stanley demanded. "You can hear the American guns off to the north. Sounds like they come closer every day, too. You don't see anything but American planes any more. They shoot up anything that moves. They've damn near killed me two, three times by now. How can you stop them, Commander? Answer me that, please. Answer me that."

"We will do the best we can," Genda repeated. "We have more courage than the enemy does." He believed that was true, even if the Marines were not to be despised.

The king looked at him. "What difference does courage make if they drop bombs on your head and you can't do anything about it?"

"Well . . ." The question was too much to the point. Genda found he had no answer. He feared none of his superiors did, either.

XII

LES DILLON HAD ALREADY DISCOVERED THAT SOME OF THE JAPS FIGHTING THE Marines carried Springfields, not Arisakas. That made sense; after the Army threw in the sponge here, it must have handed over a zillion rifles, plus the ammo to shoot them for a zillion years. But it made him have a harder time telling by ear who was shooting at whom.

That was doubly dangerous right now, because the enemy in front of his platoon didn't seem to be Japs at all. They spoke English as well as half the Marines, and they wore what looked like U.S. Army khaki, not the darker shade Japan preferred.

He wasn't the only one who'd noticed, either. "Who are you guys?" a Marine yelled through the racket of gunfire.

The answer came back at once: "Royal Hawaiian Army! Get the fuck off our land, *haole* asshole!" A burst from a machine gun punctuated the words.

Royal Hawaiian Army? Les blinked. He knew the Japs had given Hawaii a puppet king. He hadn't known—he hadn't dreamt—anybody besides the Japs took the King of Hawaii seriously. Not sticking his head up, he called, "Why aren't you people on our side, not the enemy's?"

That got him another burst. He'd been smart to keep low—tracers went right over his foxhole. Whoever was handling that gun knew what to do with it. "Japan never took our land away from us! Japan never took our country away from us!" another Hawaiian shouted. "The USA sure as hell did!"

Yeah, but that was a long time ago. The words died unspoken on Les' lips. It might seem a long time ago to him. To the noisy bastard on the other side of the line, it wasn't even the day before yesterday. For that matter, you couldn't talk about the Civil War with a lot of Southerners—Captain Bradford included. It wasn't the Civil War to them, either. It was the War Between the States . . . or, if they'd been drinking for a while, the War of Damnyankee Aggression. Whatever you called it, it happened long before Hawaii joined—or was joined to—the United States.

He tried another tack: "Why fight now, for Chrissake? You can't win, and you'll just get shot." He knew damn well the Japs wouldn't surrender. He'd seen them fight to the death in hopeless positions too many times to have any doubts on that score. But maybe the Hawaiians were different. If he could do things on the cheap instead of putting his one and only irreplaceable ass on the line, he would, and gladly.

No words came back this time. One more burst of machine-gun fire did. Whatever the men in front of him had in mind, surrender wasn't it. He muttered to himself. Sooner or later, he'd find out what those bastards in old-fashioned khaki were worth.

It turned out to be sooner. Not long after dark fell, a runner brought word that the Marines would go forward the next morning, half an hour after sunrise. Les almost opened fire before the man stammered out the countersign to his hissed challenge. When he got the news instead, he halfway wished he had shot the fellow.

He lay in his foxhole, trying to grab whatever uneasy sleep he could. That wasn't much. Little firefights kept breaking out all along the line. Maybe the Hawaiians knew something was up, or maybe they just wanted to prove they had balls. He would have been happy to take it on faith.

The U.S. barrage started as soon as morning twilight painted the eastern sky gray. Volley after volley of 105s crashed down on the enemy positions in front of Les and his buddies. Mortar bombs added to the weight of flying metal. He'd seen heavier bombardments in the last war, but this was plenty to cut a man into screaming hamburger if he stood up in it—and maybe if he didn't, too. The Royal Hawaiian Army wouldn't have faced artillery fire before. He wondered how the Hawaiians liked it.

Under cover of the booming guns, half a dozen Shermans clanked up toward the line. Les was glad to see the big, ugly iron monsters. They could clear out the strongpoints that survived the artillery—and some always did. And they drew enemy fire, too. Infantrymen always aimed small-arms fire at tanks. Les didn't know why—rifle and machine-gun bullets couldn't penetrate armor plate. But he'd seen it again and again. If the Hawaiians were shooting at the Shermans, they wouldn't be shooting at him so much. He approved of that. Oh, yes. He approved of that very much indeed.

His belly knotted as soon as the 105s fell silent. He knew what was coming next. And it came. Captain Bradford yelled, "Come on, men! Up out of your holes! Follow me!"

Grunting, Les scrambled out of his foxhole and ran forward. He bent over. He zigged and zagged. He knew none of that would do him a damn bit of good if the bullet with his name on it was out there flying. A Boche machine gunner had taught him that lesson once and for all time in 1918, and he still had the puckered scars to prove it.

Bullets cracked past him. The Hawaiians weren't dead, and they weren't paralyzed, either. *Too fucking bad,* he thought. When you heard a crack, a round came much too close. He ducked automatically whenever he did hear one. He'd been ashamed of that till he saw everybody else did it, too, which sure hadn't taken long.

He'd fought in trenches before, in 1918 and here. That was the worst war had to offer. The Germans had been tough. The Japs here were even worse, because they didn't give up and they kept coming at you till they were dead or you were. So he had standards of comparison. The fifteen or twenty minutes till the Marines killed the last man from the Royal Hawaiian Army were the worst minutes of his life—even worse than the time Cindy Lou Callahan's father caught them in bed together and ran for his shotgun, which went a long way towards explaining how and why Les joined the Marines.

The Hawaiians wouldn't give up, either. They wouldn't retreat. They didn't just stay in place and die. They kept making countercharges at the Marines, screaming and swearing and throwing grenades. Like anybody who'd done any fighting, Les vastly preferred bullets to his bayonet. The bayonet got blood on it in those trenches. So did his Kabar. So did the butt end of his rifle. He killed one bastard with his bare hands in an animal tangle of flying arms and legs. If he hadn't tucked his chin down tight to his chest, the enemy soldier might have broken his neck instead of the other way round.

Afterwards—but only afterwards, when the red madness of battle eased— he wondered why the Hawaiians sold their lives so dear. Did they think the

USA would hang them for traitors and they had nothing to lose? Did they really hate Americans? Or were they simply as much caught up in the madness as the men who faced them? He couldn't even ask a prisoner afterwards. There were no prisoners. Like Napoleon's guards, like the Japanese who'd given them guns, the men from the Royal Hawaiian Army died but did not surrender.

Once the last of them *had* died, Les Dillon squatted in a muddy trench and lit a cigarette. He'd just finished bandaging a Marine's leg. He hoped the man wasn't hamstrung. All he could do was hope; he was no corpsman. Another Marine who'd also come through unhurt stared at him from about ten feet away. He too had a cigarette dangling from the corner of his mouth. "Fuck," he said, and then again: "Fuck."

Les nodded. "Yeah," he said, and, "Jesus." That amounted to about the same thing. If he'd spoken first, he would have said what the younger man had.

He looked around. These torn-up trenches weren't worth a thing by themselves, any more than one German trench had been worth anything in particular during the War to End All Wars. How many men had died defending them? How many had died or been maimed taking them? He knew the answer to the last question, knew it out to the tenth decimal place: too goddamn many. He threw down the cigarette butt and lit a new one.

A runner came over from the right. "What are you guys sitting around with your thumbs up your asses for? Pick up your feet—get moving. Back where I came from, they're going forward like Billy-be-damned."

A burst of weary profanity answered him. Les said, "Cut us some slack, okay? We almost got our heads handed to us here. Those fucking Hawaiians wouldn't give up for shit."

"Goldbricks. I knew you guys were goldbricks," the runner said.

"Goldbricks, my ass," Les said. Even after a fight like the one he'd just been through, sometimes your own side was a worse enemy than the bastards who'd been trying to kill you. "What the hell you talkin' about?"

"Hawaiians," the runner sneered. "You can't bullshit me about Hawaiians— I damn well know better. We had Hawaiians in front of us, too, all decked out like the Army was when the shit hit the fan. They fired two, three shots and then threw down their pieces and threw up their hands. We musta took a company's worth o' POWs."

The man meant it. Les could see that. He and the other Marines who'd just gone through hell stared dully at the irate runner. "Fuck," he mouthed, as the youngster had a few minutes earlier. He gathered his men by eye. "Come on," he said. "We gotta get back in the goddamn war."

THINKING BACK ON THINGS, Senior Private Yasuo Furusawa couldn't account for being alive. Most of the men from his regiment had died at or near Oahu's northern beaches. They'd done everything they could to throw the Americans into the sea. They'd done everything they could—and it hadn't been enough.

Furusawa stayed alive after the first day's fighting—one of the few who did. Naval bombardment didn't kill him. Neither did U.S. air strikes. Nor did enemy artillery and small-arms fire. By the second morning, nobody survived to give him orders.

He'd retreated several times since then. For one thing, he had no one left to tell him not to. For another, he wasn't a typical soldier. Most of the men in his regiment—even most of his noncoms—had come into the Army straight off a farm. A lot of them had had to learn how to make up a bed that stood on a frame instead of just on the floor. They sucked up the indoctrination about the duty to die for their country along with the rest of their training till it became as automatic as slapping a new clip into an Arisaka.

It wasn't that Furusawa was unwilling to die for Japan. Like any soldier with a gram of sense, he knew that was always possible, often likely, sometimes necessary. But he was less inclined to die if it *wasn't* necessary than most of his comrades. Because he was a druggist's son, he'd got more education than the average conscript. And his father had taught him to think for himself in a way most Japanese didn't.

"You always have to worry. Is this the right medicine? Is this the right dosage? Will it be good for this patient? Never assume anything. Always check, always question—always." Furusawa didn't know how many times he'd heard his father say that. And the old man, being a typical Japanese father in a lot of ways, would usually follow the advice with a clout in the ear to make sure it sank in. The method was brutally simple. The Army used it, too. Like a lot of brutally simple things, it worked.

In his innocence, the younger Furusawa had gone on asking questions after he was conscripted. The Army, far more brutal than his father ever dreamt of being, soon cured him of that—at least of asking them out loud. But the habit of thought persisted. He would sometimes smile to himself when he ran into things that made no logical sense. Even smiling could be dangerous. He was convinced he got more than his share of thumps and slaps because he didn't act like a patriotic machine. Of course, he didn't know a single soldier who wasn't convinced he got more than his share of thumps and slaps, so who could say for sure?

After the Americans landed, he'd fought hard. But he'd watched other soldiers rush across open ground to try to come to close quarters with the enemy. And he'd watched rifles and machine guns and mortars and artillery shells tear them to bloody shreds before they accomplished a thing. If a sergeant or a lieutenant had shouted at him in particular—"You! Furusawa! Forward!"—he supposed he would have charged, too. No superior had. That left him to use his own judgment. And he was still alive and fighting, while flies buzzed around the bloated, stinking corpses of most of his regiment.

How long he could escape becoming a bloated, stinking corpse himself was anybody's guess. He crouched in a shell hole not far in front of the ruins of Schofield Barracks. The U.S. Army's former base had been smashed twice now, first by the Japanese when the Yankees held it and now by the Americans to keep Japan from getting any use out of it.

Several of the men nearby were stragglers and orphans like himself. Others belonged to a company whose captain wasn't shy about grabbing reinforcements wherever he could. A corporal spoke in bitter frustration: "Those stinking bastards!"

"Who?" Furusawa asked. That could have meant either the enemy or the Japanese high command.

"The Yankees," the corporal answered. "When the wind blows from them to us, you can smell their cigarettes. When was the last time *you* had one?" Naked longing filled his voice.

"Please excuse me, but I don't smoke," Furusawa said.

"*Ai!*" The noncom's disgusted grunt might have meant, *Why do they saddle me with idiots like this?* Furusawa's cheeks heated. The corporal went on, "Well, even you'll know they don't send many smokes from Japan. I haven't had one for weeks. American tobacco's good, too—better than what we use ourselves. I'm tempted to sneak over there and cut somebody's throat just so I can steal his cigarettes."

He sounded as serious as a funeral. "Are cigarettes worth risking your life for?" Furusawa asked.

"Why not? I'm going to get killed pretty damn quick anyway," the corporal said. "Cigarettes or hooch or pussy—might as well have fun while I can."

That made more sense to Furusawa than it might have to a lot of his countrymen. "You don't think we can win?" he said.

"Win, lose—who gives a shit? They'll use us up either way."

And that made sense to Furusawa, too, however much he wished it didn't. All the phrases the Japanese Army used to convince its men to fight to the end no matter what came bubbling up in his mind. He didn't bring any of them out. But even thinking them at a time like this showed he'd been more thoroughly indoctrinated than he thought. What were such words worth on a real battlefield, with the stench of death and its lesser cousin, the stench of shit, all around?

Words were worth enough to send young Japanese men into the face of enemy guns by the hundreds, by the thousands. A lot of those young Japanese men were part of that battlefield stench now. How could anything be worth more than a man's life? The words said the country was, the Emperor was. And the young men, or most of them, believed it.

He knew what questioning it here and now would get him: a bullet in front of the ear or in the back of the neck, unless some officer who heard him decided to make him into an example for other doubters. In that case, he'd die a lot slower and hurt a lot more while he was doing it.

He opened a ration can he'd taken from a dead American. A lot of the food the enemy ate was nasty, but he got lucky this time—it was chopped, salty meat. It wasn't anything he would have got back home, but it was like something he might have got. He wolfed it down. As he did, he remembered the cans of the stuff called Spam he'd found for his squad when the Japanese were conquering. He sighed nostalgically. Now that—that had been *really* good.

Not five minutes after he'd finished, the Americans started shelling the Japanese line. Furusawa huddled in his hole, right next to the can he'd dropped. Had the *kami* decided to discard him the same way? Getting discarded hadn't hurt the can. If his time was here, he hoped he would be as lucky.

Huddled next to him, the corporal who wanted a smoke said, "Stinking Hawaiians. It's their fault we're in this mess."

He didn't mean Japan. Japan's problems weren't the Hawaiians' fault. But those of this particular knot of Japanese soldiers *were*. Furusawa said the most he could for the men of the Royal Hawaiian Army: "Some of them fought well."

"And some of them damn well didn't," the noncom snarled as a nearby shell burst sent splinters screeching overhead. "Some of them ran away. *Zakennayo!* Some of them surrendered, the worthless turds." Furusawa had run away. He would have been dead if he hadn't. The corporal had probably run away, too.

Surrender . . . That was scarier than the artillery barrage. You didn't just disgrace yourself if you gave up. You disgraced your family, too. Who could say what the authorities would do to them if word that you were a prisoner got back to Japan? And it wouldn't be only the authorities. Who would go to a druggist whose son had thrown down his rifle? Who wouldn't turn away when a man like that, a man who had raised such a worthless son, walked by? Who wouldn't talk about him behind his back?—not that he wouldn't know what all his neighbors, all his former friends, were saying.

Mortar bombs hissed down along with the shells. Furusawa really dreaded mortars. You could hardly hear them coming, and they dropped straight down into foxholes. You couldn't hide from them, the way you could from ordinary artillery. If one of them decided to rip you up, there you were—sashimi—and you couldn't do a thing about it.

Then, as suddenly as a Hawaiian rain shower, the bombardment stopped. Furusawa and the corporal looked at each other, each one making sure the other was still breathing and hadn't been blown to red rags without even a chance to scream.

Shouts in harsh English came from the north. So did bursts of machine-gun fire to make the Japanese keep their heads down. And so did clanking rattles that sent fresh ice walking down Furusawa's spine. Tanks! He'd seen the new U.S. tanks before—always from some little distance, or he wouldn't be here worrying about them now. They were bigger and tougher-looking than their Japanese counterparts, not that any Japanese tanks were close by. Their cannon would wreck machine-gun nests, their machine guns would chew up infantry-men, and what could a poor damned foot soldier do about them? Not bloody much.

Furusawa popped out of his hole a couple of times to fire at the oncoming Marines. Bullets cracked past him whenever he did. He took his life in his hands even to try to shoot. But he knew the Yankees would run up and kill him if he didn't fight back. The risk of death against its certainty . . . You braced yourself, you took the risk, and you hoped for the best. If no bullet found you, you did it again.

A burst of machine-gun fire from one of the U.S. tanks almost tore his head off. He crouched in the hole, shuddering. Then the machine gun swung elsewhere, to torment other luckless Japanese soldiers.

As soon as it did, the corporal with whom Furusawa had been talking sprang up and ran toward the tank, which was horribly close. He scrambled onto the metal monster before the bow gunner could swing his weapon back to bear on him. Through the din of battle, Furusawa heard the noncom tap two grenades on his helmet, or possibly on the side of the tank, to start their fuses. He opened a hatch and chucked them in. Then he jumped down and tried to get away.

One of the American tankers cut him down with half a dozen rounds from the submachine gun he carried as a personal weapon. The grenades went off: two muffled thumps inside the big steel box. An instant later, much bigger booms followed—the grenades must have touched off the tank's ammunition. The big machine ground to a halt. A thick column of greasy black smoke rose from it.

Five men and a traveling fortress slain. The corporal's spirit would have a lot to be proud of as it took its place with so many others in Yasukuni Shrine. Furusawa admired the man's bravery, and admitted to himself he couldn't match it.

Seeing the tank go up in flames made the Yankees hesitate. It filled the Japanese with new spirit, at least for a little while. Another soldier used a bottle full of burning gasoline to disable a second tank, though Furusawa thought some of that crew got away. He hoped the new loss would make the Americans draw back. It didn't. They might have lacked the stubborn stoicism of Japanese troops, but they were brave, tough men.

"Give up!" someone shouted in Japanese. "You won't be harmed after surrender! You'll be fed and treated well."

Only a long burst of machine-gun fire answered that call. The Americans must have found a local Japanese to do their talking—to do their lying—for them. They'd done that when the American Army was advancing, too. You listened to those wills-o'-the-wisp at your peril. Furusawa had seen men do what they said and then get shot down.

Another call came from behind him: "Back here! We've got another line set up!" That was a Tokyo man talking. He didn't have the Hiroshima accent of the men from Furusawa's regiment—and of most Japanese settlers in Hawaii. That made Furusawa believe him. It also gave the senior private an excuse to retreat with his honor more or less intact.

He seized the chance, scrambling and scurrying and scuttling. Bullets whipped by him, but none bit. He flopped down into a hole deeper and much better made than the one in which he'd sheltered. This had to be a position American POWs had prepared in advance. He nodded to himself. Good. Now the Army would get some use out of all that digging.

A U.S. FIGHTER PLANE ROARED LOW OVER THE VAST POW CAMP in Kapiolani Park. Fletcher Armitage stood in line for the evening meal—whatever rice and weeds the Japs cared to give their prisoners. The plane's pilot waggled his wings as he zoomed away. When American fliers first started doing that, some of the prisoners had waved back. After the beatings the Japanese guards handed out, that stopped in a hurry.

One of the guard towers sent a stream of bullets after the fighter, but it was long gone. The machine guns in the towers bore on the camp. When the towers went up, the Japs hadn't figured those guns would need to shoot down U.S. planes. *Too bad, you bastards,* Fletch thought.

A man in front of him said, "I wonder what the hell they call that aircraft. Sure as hell didn't have anything like it when we got took."

He was right about that. It looked more businesslike than any plane Fletch had known in 1941, and its business was death.

The line snaked forward. When Fletch got up to the cooks, one of them plopped a ladleful of overcooked, gluey rice and green stuff in his bowl. The ladle was small. For all he knew, the greens were lawn trimmings. He didn't care. For one thing, he didn't get enough to matter. For another, he would have eaten all he did get. If the Japs had cooked grubs in with the gruel, he would have eaten those, too.

He savored what little he got. For a couple of hours, he wouldn't feel like a man starving to death—which he was. He would just be very hungry. To a POW in Hawaii, very hungry seemed wonderful.

Two emaciated prisoners carried an even more emaciated body to the disposal area near the perimeter. Several others lay there, some scrawnier yet. Men who should have been in the prime of life died here every day, and not a few of them. Fletch glanced warily toward the guard towers. If the Japs in them decided to open up, men inside the perimeter would die by the hundreds, by the thousands. And they were thinking about it. He could feel the tension in the air. If anything, those American fighters made it worse. The Japs were losing the fight for Oahu. The distant rumble of artillery fire and bombs going off wasn't so distant any more. If the guards wanted to take a last revenge on the POWs in their hands and under their machine guns, they could.

If they did, the Americans would avenge themselves in turn. That was obvious. It might have restrained Americans guarding Japanese prisoners. Fletch could tell the Japs didn't give a shit. They intended to fight to the death any which way. If they could get rid of men who might recover and fight them again—or just men who'd fought them in the past—they would do it, and then die with smiles on their faces.

I'll give you something to smile about, you slant-eyed mothers. Fletch's hands balled into fists. He'd had that fantasy so many times. And he couldn't do one goddamn thing to make it real. Not one. The Japs were on the right side of the wire and he was on the wrong side. He didn't have a Chinaman's chance of getting out, either. Hell, a Chinaman would have had a better chance than he did. A Chinaman might have been able to fool the guards into thinking he was another Jap. Tall, thin, freckled, and auburn-haired, Fletch made a most unconvincing Japanese.

He did what most of the POWs did most of the time: he lay down and tried to rest. The laughable rations gave them next to no energy. The less they used, the better off they were. He shook his head when that occurred to him. The less energy he used, the longer he'd last. Whether that made him better off was a long way from obvious.

But sleep had dangers of its own. When he slept, he dreamt of . . . food. He burned too low for sex to mean anything to him. But food—food was a different story. Those dreams never went away. If anything, they got worse as he got weaker. Steaks smothered in onions danced in his dreams. So did mashed potatoes and string beans. Bacon and eggs. Pancakes—mountains of pancakes smothered in melted butter and maple syrup. Cherry pie à la mode. Not slices—whole pies, with quarts of vanilla ice cream plopped on top. Coffee with cream and sugar. Beer. Brandy. Whiskey.

And when he woke up, the dreams would seem so vivid, so real. He'd be just about to dig in, just about to make up for more than a year and a half of tormenting hunger—and then he'd have his food snatched away by cruel consciousness. When a man cried in Kapiolani Park, he most likely cried after a dream of food.

Still, if you didn't dream of roast beef, sleeping was better than staying awake. General anesthesia would have been better still. The only kind the Japs offered, though, was too permanent to suit him.

When he didn't dream of food, he often did dream of combat. Sometimes he and the U.S. Army triumphed over the Japs. Waking up after those hurt almost as bad as waking up after a dream of Thanksgiving turkey with all the trimmings. Sometimes he got shot in the night or, worse, bayoneted. Returning to himself after *those* dreams came as close to relief as anything in the POW camp.

He dreamt of combat tonight. It was artillery in his head, which could be as bad as bayonets. He'd commanded a 105; he knew too well what shellfire did to human flesh. If he hadn't known before, what he'd seen in the fighting would have taught him plenty.

And when he woke, he woke from a noisy dream of combat to . . . combat. Machine guns and rifles and mortars were going off much too close by. Tracers ripped through the prisoner camp, mostly from south to north. The tracers were red. Fletch needed a moment to remember what that meant. The Japs used ice-blue tracers. Red tracers meant . . . Americans!

"Holy Jesus!" Fletch whispered. Tears filled his eyes. Maybe those were tears of weakness. He didn't care. Somebody'd remembered he and his comrades in misery existed. Somebody was trying to save them.

What might have been the voice of God but was more likely a Marine or sailor on a PA system shouted through the racket of gunfire: "Prisoners! U.S. prisoners! Move toward the beach! We'll get you out!" As if to underscore that, a mortar round hit a guard tower. It went over with a crash. There was one machine gun that wouldn't shoot back—and wouldn't shoot any POWs, either.

But the guards and soldiers around Kapiolani Park weren't about to give up without a fight. As far as Fletch could see, the Japs never gave up without a fight—never gave up, in fact. They stopped fighting only when they died. Their cold-looking tracers spat out at the attacking Americans. And, as the POWs started moving toward their rescuers, automatic-weapons fire lashed the camp.

Men died and fell wounded and screaming just as they were on the point of being rescued. The unfairness of that tore at Fletch. So did raw terror. He didn't want to be one of those casualties, not now, not at this of all moments. But the prisoners couldn't do anything to protect themselves. They had no place to hide. Bullets either nailed them or didn't. It was all luck, one way or the other.

A squad of guards rushed into the camp and turned their Arisakas on the POWs, too. They must have thought they could turn the Americans back. Instead, careless of whether they lived or died, the POWs surged toward them. Disciplined to the end, the Japs all emptied their clips at about the same time. As they were reloading, the Americans swarmed over them. The scene was straight out of Dürer or Goya: skeletons rising up to attack the living. The Japs screamed, but not for long. Fletch had always thought only artillery could tear a man to pieces. He found he was wrong. Bare hands did the job just fine.

One by one, machine guns in the guard towers fell silent, knocked out by the attackers. "Move! Move! Move!" roared the big voice on the loudspeaker. "American prisoners, move to the south!"

Tracerlight gave Fletch his first glimpse of the soldiers who'd hit the beach to liberate the POW camp. He needed a moment to recognize them for what they were. They wore dark uniforms—dark green, he thought—not the khaki that had been his color. Even their helmets were different: pot-shaped domes that covered more of the head than the British-style steel derbies Fletch and his comrades had used. For a heartbeat, he wondered if they really were Americans. But they had rifles and submachine guns in their hands, and they were shooting up the Japs. What else mattered? He would have kissed Orson Welles' Martians if they turned their fearsome heat rays on those guard towers.

These weren't Martians. They were Americans, even if they wore funny clothes. "Haul ass, youse guys!" one of them yelled in pure New York. "We got boats on the beach waitin' for yousc. Shake a leg, already!"

Fletch gave it all he could. He had the feeling a tortoise with a tailwind would have left him in the dust, but he couldn't do anything about that. The Marines had landed with bulldozers with armored driver's boxes to tear paths through the barbed wire. He stumbled out through one, stumbled across Kalakaua Avenue, and then fell down when he got to the sand.

Not all the Japs were out of action. Falling down might have saved his life— a sniper's bullet cracked past just over his head. He hauled himself to his feet and staggered on. The beach was alive with stick figures just like him.

"This way! This way!" Marines and sailors with red flashlights steered

POWs toward the boats that waited for them. "We got plenty for everybody. Don't fight! Don't trample!"

Obeying that order came hard. How could anyone stand to wait another moment to be free? As he stood there, bullets still snapping and cracking past every so often, he got a look at the boats that would take him and his partners in misery away. He knew damn well that the U.S. military had owned no such slab-sided, front-mouthed machines before the war with the Japs started. Like the airplanes, like the uniforms, these had all been designed and built from scratch while he waited on the sidelines. A career officer, he wondered if he'd have any career left even after he got his strength back.

While he was staring at the landing craft, the men who crewed them stared at the nearly rescued POWs. "You poor sorry sons of bitches," one of them said. "We ought to murder every motherfucking Jap in the world for this."

Before Fletch could say anything, one of the other Americans on the beach beat him to the punch: "Sounds good to me."

One by one, the boats filled and waddled off the beach and into the water. They were every bit as ungainly there as they were on land. Fletch's turn finally came. He climbed an iron ramp and got into a boat. A sailor was passing out cigarettes to the POWs. "Here ya go, pal," he said, and gave Fletch a light. The first drag on the Chesterfield after so long made him dizzy and light-headed and sick to his stomach, as if he'd never smoked at all. It felt wonderful.

Another sailor said, "You guys are so skinny, we can load more of you on each boat than we figured." It only went to show there were advantages to everything, even starvation. Fletch would gladly have forgone that one.

A motor started. Chains rattled. The ramp came up. Sailors dogged it shut. All of a sudden, it was the bow of the boat. Awkward as a drunken sow, the landing craft backed into the water. Beside Fletch, a man quietly started to bawl. "We're free," he blubbered. "We're really free. I didn't think we ever would be, but we are."

"Yeah," Fletch said, and then he was crying, too, joy and weakness all coming out at once. Inside a couple of minutes, half the breathing skeletons in the boat were sobbing as if their hearts would break.

Sailors dealt out more smokes. And they passed out open ration cans, too. Tears stopped as abruptly as they'd started. Everybody crowded forward, wanting his with a fierce and terrible desire. None of them would ever be the same about food again. Fletch was sure of that. Right now, they might have been hungry wolves in a cage. Not till his hands closed around a can did a low, unconscious growl die in his throat.

He ate with his fingers. The can held greasy roast-beef hash. It was the most delicious thing he'd ever tasted. He couldn't remember the last time he ate beef. Probably when his Army rations ran out. "My God," he muttered, over and over again. "My God!" That such food was out there! Even his dreams hadn't been anything like this. He cut his tongue licking the inside of the can to make sure he got every tiny scrap out of it.

The boat's motion and the rich food they weren't used to made several men seasick. After some of the stinks Fletch had known lately, that one wasn't so bad. His own stomach seemed to take the wonderful food for ballast. Nothing bothered him as the boat chugged away from Oahu. He didn't think anything would ever bother him again. He might have been wrong, but he felt that way.

After a couple of hours, his landing craft and the others came up alongside ships that took the POWs aboard. That wasn't easy. They couldn't climb nets, the way sailors and Marines did. Sailors on deck lowered slings to the boats. The sailors there fitted them around the prisoners' shoulders. The men on the ship hauled them up.

Fletch felt more like a package than the daring young man on the flying trapeze. "Careful, buddy," a sailor said as he came up over the rail. "Don't hurt yourself."

"I'm out of that goddamn camp," Fletch answered. "How could anything hurt me now?" As soon as he was safely up on deck, he asked, "Can I get some more food? Can I have a bath?"

"We got saltwater soap, and those showers are going," the sailor said. "Otherwise it's a sponge bath—too many men and not enough fresh water. Food . . . Doc's gotta say it's okay before we give you much. Sometimes you eat too much too fast, you get sick."

"I wouldn't." Fletch knew he sounded like a whiny little kid. He couldn't help it. When it came to food, he felt like a whiny little kid.

He decided to take a shower. Even he didn't believe how filthy he was. As he stripped off his rags, a sailor said, "You got anything in the pockets you need to keep? Otherwise we're gonna deep-six all of this shit."

"No, there isn't anything," Fletch answered. He wasn't used to being around well-fed Americans any more. Their fleshy bodies looked wrong, distorted. He knew the problem was in the way he looked at these strangers who'd rescued him and taken him in, not in the men themselves. Knowledge didn't change perception.

Saltwater soap was nasty stuff, but he needed something nasty to get a few layers of filth off. Lots of freed POWs scrubbed themselves in the showers. An ocean-temperature shower wasn't too bad, not when the ocean was off Hawaii. He kept flicking glances toward the naked men in there with him. He could see every bone and every tendon in their bodies. That was how Americans were supposed to look. Next to them, the sailors and Marines seemed almost . . . inflated.

After he came out of the shower and dried off, all he got in the way of clothes was a bathrobe. "Sorry, buddy," said the sailor who handed it to him. "We didn't know you guys'd be in such miserable shape."

"It's okay," Fletch said. But for modesty, going naked in this climate was no hardship. The Hawaiians had done it all the time. And he didn't need anybody else to tell him he was in miserable shape. He knew that himself.

He didn't actually see a doctor. A pharmacist's mate looked him over. "You don't seem *too* bad, all things considered," the man said after a very quick, very cursory check. "Just don't try to fatten yourself up all at once." He picked up a spray gun. "Shed the robe." He sprayed both Fletch and the garment.

Fletch's nose wrinkled. "What's that stuff?" he asked. Whatever it was, it had a harsh, chemical tang. There were other kinds of bad smells besides those that sprang from filth and death.

"Shit's called DDT—and now you know as much as you did before, right?" the pharmacist's mate said. "What you need to know is, it kills lice, mosquitoes, every kind of bug under the sun, kills 'em dead, dead, dead. You may not believe it, but you aren't lousy any more."

"What about the nits?" Fletch scratched automatically.

"Kills them, too," the sailor said. "And if a louse does somehow hatch, what's left of the DDT in your hair is plenty to make the little bastard buy the farm. I'm telling you, buddy, this shit is the straight goods."

"Yeah? What's it do to people, then?" Fletch asked.

"Diddly squat. Safe as houses. Greatest thing since sliced bread." The pharmacist's mate gave him back the robe. "Go feed your face. Not too much, though, you hear? Or you'll be sorry."

"Yes, Mother," Fletch said, which made the other man laugh. He went on to the galley. They had biscuits there, with butter and jam. Flour had vanished from Oahu even before the American surrender. It all came from the mainland—and then it stopped coming. Butter and jam were only memories, too. "Thank you, Jesus!" somebody said: as short and sincere a grace as Fletch had ever heard.

And then the cooks brought out platters of fried chicken. At the sight, at the mouth-watering smell, several POWs burst into tears. One of them said, "But what's for all the other guys?" That got a laugh and defused the tension that had built at the presence of so much food. Fletch felt the fear—somebody else might get more than he did. He had to remind himself there was plenty for everyone. His head might know that, but his belly didn't.

He snagged a drumstick. The coating of batter crunched in his mouth. Then he was eating hot chicken. He wasn't dreaming about it. It was real. Tears streamed down his cheeks. It was real. When he set the bone down, not the tiniest scrap of meat was left on it. No crumbs from the biscuits remained on his plate, either.

He leaned back in his chair. He didn't feel starved. He didn't even feel hungry. He could hardly remember what that was like. "Wow!" he said.

The man next to him grinned. "Right the first time, buddy."

A sailor came by to pick up plates. A POW stopped him, saying, "I was at the Opana camp for a while, up at the other end of the island. That place was as big as this one, maybe bigger. Have you gone after the guys there, too?"

The sailor's face clouded. "We can't," he said. "As soon as we got close to it, the Japs started shooting up the place. We weren't ready for it then—we didn't think anybody could act that bastardly. Shows what we knew." He made as if to spit on the deck, then caught himself at the last second. "Don't know for sure how many guys those fuckers murdered—gotta be thousands."

"Jesus!" The prisoner who'd asked the question crossed himself.

Fletch was horrified but not surprised. Everything the Japanese had done since taking Hawaii showed POWs were nothing but a nuisance to them. They'd starved their captives, abused them, and worked them to death. Why wouldn't they slaughter them to keep them from being rescued? It made perfect sense—if you fought the war like that.

"Thanks for getting to us before they did the same thing at Kapiolani," he said. The gob hadn't had thing one to do with it, but Fletch had enough gratitude to spread around to anybody in the U.S. military right now.

"Brass figured we'd better try," the sailor said. "I'm gladder'n hell it went as well as it did."

How many Japanese machine-gun bullets had snapped by within a couple of feet of Fletch? How many scrawny, starving men had those bullets killed? He didn't know. He wondered if anyone would ever know exactly. He knew who would, if anybody ever did: Graves Registration. And yet here he was, on an American ship, his belly full—really full!—of American food. He was gladder than hell the rescue had gone as well as it had, too.

THE GUARDS IN THE KALIHI VALLEY WERE JUMPIER than ever. That made the prisoners tunneling through the Koolau Range jumpier than ever, too—those of them who kept the strength to worry. Jim Peterson still did. So did Charlie Kaapu. Peterson admired the *hapa*-Hawaiian's strength and determination. He wished he could match them, but he'd been here much longer than Charlie, and he'd been in worse shape when he got here. His spirit was willing. His flesh? He had no flesh to speak of, not any more. He had skin, and he had bones, and only hunger between them.

"We got to get out of here," Charlie whispered to him one evening before exhaustion knocked them over the head. "We got to. Those fuckers gettin' ready to do us all in. You can see it in their eyes."

Peterson nodded. He'd had the same thought himself. Every time artillery fire got closer, every time American fighters flew by overhead, they might have been twisting a knife in the Japs' guts. The guards would lash out then, the way a kid who'd just lost a schoolyard brawl might kick a dog. They didn't have any dogs to kick, though. They had POWs instead, and kicking was the least of what they did to them.

At the same time, Peterson shook his head. Even that took effort. "Go ahead, if you think you can get away. I'd just hold you back."

"You can do it, man," Charlie said. "Gotta be tough. Get back to Honolulu, you be okay."

He might be okay if he got back to Honolulu. Flesh melted off him day by day, but he still had some. The first Jap who saw Peterson would know him for what he was—he didn't think he weighed a hundred pounds any more. And that would be all she wrote. The outskirts of Honolulu weren't more than three or four miles away. They might as well have been on the dark side of the moon, for all the good that did Peterson.

"I'm done for," he said. "Not enough left of me to be worth saving."

"Shit," Charlie said. "Don't you want to get your own back? Don't you want to watch these assholes get what's coming to 'em? How you gonna do that if you lay down and die?"

"I'm not laying down," Peterson said, remembering how fiercely he'd sworn revenge back when captivity was new. "I'm *not* laying down, dammit, but I can't go anywhere very far, either. Look at me." He held out his arm: five knobby pencils attached to a broomstick. "*Look.* How am I going to run if we get spotted?"

Charlie Kaapu looked. He swore, his words all the more terrible for being so low-voiced. "I'll go. I'll bring back help. Bet I find American soldiers in Honolulu."

Maybe he would. There'd been a hell of a lot of shooting from somewhere down that way a few nights earlier. Whatever it was all about, the guards had been even nastier since. Peterson wouldn't have imagined they needed an excuse for that, but they seemed to. He said, "If you make it, tell 'em we're up here. Far as anybody knows, I bet we've fallen off the edge of the world."

"I'll do it," Charlie said. "You really can't come, man?" Peterson shook his head again. The *hapa*-Hawaiian reached out in the darkness and set a hand on his bony shoulder. "Hang on, brother. I'm gonna get away. I'm gonna bring help."

In spite of everything, Jim Peterson smiled. "Just like in the movies."

"Fuckin'-A, man!" Charlie said. "*Just* like in the movies!"

"Well, if you're gonna do it, do it fast," Peterson said. "I don't know how much longer I'm going to last, and God only knows how long the Japs'll let anybody last."

"Cover for me at roll call in the morning," Charlie Kaapu said.

"Will do," Peterson answered, though he feared the Japs would notice Charlie was missing even if their count came out right. They had trouble telling one emaciated white man from another, yeah. *All Occidentals look alike to them,* Peterson thought, and damned if he didn't smile again. But Charlie was only half white—and only half emaciated, too, which counted for more. He stood out. He had as much *life* in him as half a dozen ordinary POWs put together. He . . .

As if to prove his own point, Peterson fell asleep then, right in the middle of a thought. He woke up some time later—he didn't know how long. Charlie Kaapu wasn't lying beside him any more. *Good luck, Charlie,* he thought, and then he fell asleep again.

Three men died during the night. The POWs who lived on carried the corpses out with them so the guards could keep the precious count straight. And those living POWs did what they could to keep the guards from noticing one of their number wasn't there and wasn't dead. They shifted around in the ranks that were supposed to be still and unmoving. The Japs clouted several of them. The guards would do that without an excuse. When they had one, they did it even more.

But they were stupider than Peterson had figured them for. He thought the Americans were going to get away with their deception, and wondered how the Japs could fail to miss what wasn't right in front of their noses. The answer wasn't all that hard to find. Their officers didn't want smart bastards here. They wanted mean bastards—and what they wanted, they got.

Still and all, the Japs would have had to be dumber than a pile of pebbles not to notice pretty damn quick that Charlie Kaapu wasn't there. They were just about to let the POWs queue up for the miserable breakfast when a corporal let out a yelp, as if somebody'd poked him with a pin: "*Kaabu!*" When the Japs tried to say *p,* it mostly came out as *b.* Peterson had got used to being called *Beterson.*

Naturally, Charlie didn't answer. The guards had the conniptions they should have had twenty minutes earlier. They started beating people in earnest, with swagger sticks, with rifle butts, and with their fists. They kicked men who fell, too. They were even more furious than Peterson had figured they would be.

And they weren't just mad at the POWs. They also screamed at one another. The men who'd been on watch during the night would surely catch holy hell. That didn't break Jim Peterson's heart. It couldn't happen to a nicer bunch of people.

The prisoners didn't get breakfast that morning. They got marched straight into the tunnel instead. The Japs cut them no slack. If anything, the guards worked them even harder than usual. Anyone who faltered got beaten or kicked without mercy. Along with taking out endless buckets of rock, the POWs dragged out several corpses.

They got no supper that night, either. Nobody dared say a word. If the Japs kept that up for another few days, they wouldn't need to worry about escapes from the Kalihi Valley any more. All the POWs here would be dead.

A few months earlier, mistreatment like this might have prompted lots of men to try to escape. No more. Next to nobody had the strength. And the guards would be shooting at their own shadows now. The prisoners went nowhere. The timing was bad.

Just before sunup the next morning, two trucks came up to the camp in the Kalihi Valley from Honolulu below. Jim Peterson and the other prisoners stared in amazement. The trucks themselves were ordinary: U.S. Army vehicles the Japs had commandeered, painting over the white star on each driver's-side door. But their being here wasn't ordinary. They were the first trucks Peterson had seen since coming to the punishment camp.

And, instead of getting the prisoners to do the work for them the way they almost always did, the Japs unloaded the trucks themselves. The contents seemed harmless enough: crates with incomprehensible Japanese squiggles on the sides. The guards lugged them over to the mouth of the tunnel. Then they set up another machine-gun position nearby, and posted several riflemen next to the crates, too.

"They treat that shit like it's the Hawaiian crown jewels," another prisoner remarked to Peterson.

"How do you know it's not?" he said. "If their side's losing, this is a hell of a place to stash 'em."

He got a lesson in the way rumors worked. By the time the POWs assembled for roll call half an hour later, everybody was convinced the Japs were going to stow the Hawaiian crown jewels in the tunnel. No one had any evidence that that was so, but nobody seemed to need any, either. In nothing flat, a chance comment swelled into one of those things everybody knew.

Another thing everybody knew was that the Japs were going to be double tough on the count this morning. Peterson and the other POWs had only been guessing about the crown jewels. What everybody knew turned out to be dead right this time. No one presumed even to twitch as the guards stalked along the prisoners' ranks. One luckless fellow who sneezed with a guard right behind him got beaten and kicked till he lay on the ground, all bloody and groaning.

Peterson shuddered to think what would happen if the Japs screwed up the count even though the prisoners were cooperating. For a wonder, the guards didn't. For what felt like an even bigger wonder, they let the POWs line up for breakfast. As always, it wasn't much and it wasn't good. After a day and a half of emptiness and brutal labor, anything at all in Peterson's belly seemed wonderful. He knew he was still a starving man. But he wasn't starving quite so fast.

After the prisoners ate, the guards pointed toward the tunnel mouth. "All go! All go!" they shouted, and, "Speedo!"—the English they used for, *Make it snappy, Mac!* Of course, a clout in the head with a rifle butt or a length of bamboo was as much a part of a universal language as a smile or a caress. Somehow, the poets had never got around to singing the praises of a good, solid wallop.

When the Japs said, "All go!" they weren't kidding. They routed out the cooks and sent them into the tunnel, too. And they made the healthier prisoners—health being very much a relative term here—carry the men who were too sick to walk but not yet dead into the shaft. "American bomber!" they said. That made Peterson wonder. For one thing, the American attackers had shown exactly no signs of caring about the Kalihi Valley. For another, up till now the Japs had shown exactly zero interest in their prisoners' safety. No, that wasn't quite true. The Japs sometimes went out of their way to decrease safety for the POWs. Improving it was another story.

More or less fortified by his more-or-less meal, Peterson attacked the rock face with a pick. Other prisoners scooped up the rock he'd torn loose, loaded it into baskets, and carried it away. Peterson heard gunshots from the direction of the tunnel mouth. He didn't think much of it—the Japs often got a wild hair up their ass—till a POW came staggering back toward the excavators. "They're killing us!" he shouted. "They're shooting us!" Then he fell over. Peterson marveled that he could have come so far so fast shot through the chest.

Work came to a ragged halt. One by one, picks and shovels fell silent. No guards lashed out with clubs or shouted, "Speedo!" and *"Isogi!"* In fact, no guards seemed to be in the tunnel at all.

When Peterson realized that, ice ran through him. "The Japs don't have the crown jewels in those boxes!" he shouted. "They've got dynamite! They're going to blow in the tunnel mouth and trap us in here!"

He threw down his pick. The steel head clanked on stone. A moment later, he picked up the tool again. It wasn't much of a weapon, but he couldn't get a better one till he knocked a Jap over the head and stole his Arisaka.

"Come on!" he yelled. "They aren't going to get away with this, God damn them!" He started back up the long, straight shaft the POWs had dug. Nor was he the only one. Everybody who still had the strength stormed up the tunnel toward the tiny circle of light at the end.

The Japs must have known something like that would happen. They'd shifted the machine guns that had protected those crates so they pointed straight down the tunnel. They fired a burst. A few rounds struck home at once. Others viciously ricocheted off ceiling, floor, and tunnel walls before finding a prisoner to wound.

That wasn't the worst of it. The worst was listening to the machine gunners laugh as they squeezed off some more rounds. In their shoes, Peterson would have laughed, too. Why not? They could fire those Nambus till the barrels glowed red, and the poor bastards they were killing couldn't even shoot back.

"We've got to keep going!" he cried. "It's our necks if we don't!"

"It's our necks if we do," somebody else said, which was just as true.

"I'd rather get shot than buried alive." Peterson wished he had some better choices, but those seemed to be the only ones on the menu.

He'd had nightmares where he was trying to run somewhere but his feet seemed stuck in quicksand. This was one of those, except it wasn't a nightmare. It was real. If he didn't get to the mouth of the tunnel before the camp guards did whatever they did, he never would.

Their machine gunners kept on shooting down the shaft. They kept on laughing between bursts, too. Then they stopped shooting. Peterson could think of only one reason why they would do that. They must have lit the fuse, and they were all running for cover.

And he was too far away. He knew he was too far away. He tried to force more speed from his poor, abused carcass, but a shuffling shamble was all it would give him. *Quicksand,* he thought desperately. *Quick—*

He was one of the leaders of the mob of POWs. He'd got within a hundred yards of the tunnel mouth when the Japanese explosives went up. The next thing he knew, it was black, and untold tons of rock were coming down on him. *Oh, good,* he thought. *At least I'm not bur*

OSCAR VAN DER KIRK JUMPED when somebody knocked on his door a little before eleven. Susie Higgins jumped higher. She'd seen horror out on the street. Oscar had just heard about it. "Who the hell's that?" she said, her voice shrill with fear.

"Don't know." Oscar heard the fear in his own voice, too. The knock came again, quick and urgent. Two years earlier, whoever it was would have just walked in. Odds were long against the door's being locked in those days.

Now . . . Now was a different story. Oscar's fear swelled with each tap. Anybody out after curfew was in trouble with the Japs. Anybody in trouble with the Japs these days was as good as dead. And so was anybody who helped someone in trouble with the Japs.

"Don't let him in," Susie whispered.

"I've got to," Oscar said. "I wouldn't let those bastards get their hands on a gooney bird, let alone a man."

Before Susie could start a fight—and before he could lose his nerve—he threw open the door. "Oscar," croaked the man in the hallway. He was about Oscar's height, but only skin and bones draped in rags. His eyes burned feverishly, deep in their sockets. A powerful stench came off him in waves, a stench that said he hadn't bathed in weeks.

"Who the—?" But Oscar broke off with the question unfinished. "Charlie? Jesus Christ, Charlie, get your ass in here!"

Charlie Kaapu gave him a ghost of the grin he knew. "Then get out of my way." Numbly, Oscar did. Charlie staggered past him and into the little apartment. If Oscar had ever wanted to see a dictionary illustration of the phrase *on your last legs,* here it was in front of him. He was so shaken, he didn't even close the door after Charlie till Susie hissed at him.

She gasped when she got a good look at the *hapa*-Hawaiian. He wasn't just four steps from starving to death. Somebody—the Japs, Oscar supposed—had been beating on him with sticks. The welts showed it: on his arms, across his face, and, visible through the holes and tears in his shirt, on his chest and back as well. He was missing some teeth he'd had when the Japs got hold of him.

He sat down on the ratty rug, as if his legs didn't want to hold him up— and they likely didn't. "You think *I* look bad, you ought to see the other poor bastards up in the Kalihi Valley," he said. "Next to them, I'm Duke goddamn Kahanamoku."

"Here." Susie ran to the icebox and pulled out a couple of ripe avocados and a mackerel.

Suddenly, Charlie's attention focused on her like a searchlight. In the presence of food, he forgot about everything else. Oscar didn't suppose he could blame him, either. "Let me have those, please," Charlie said, an unusual restraint in his voice. He sounded like a man holding himself back from leaping on what he wanted.

"I was going to do something with the fish—" Susie said uncertainly.

He shook his head. His hair and scalp were full of scabs, too. "Don't bother," he told her. "I've eaten fish Jap-style plenty of times. And I don't much want to wait, you know what I mean?"

Without a word, Susie gave him the mackerel and the alligator pears. Oscar didn't think he'd ever seen her speechless before, but she was now. Charlie made the avocados and the fish disappear in nothing flat. He ate with a single-minded concentration like nothing Oscar had ever seen. Oscar didn't try to talk with him till nothing was left but peel and seeds and bones. If he had spoken, he didn't think Charlie would have answered, or even heard him.

"Oh, Lord, that was fine." Charlie looked down at his rubbish. He'd even eaten the eyes out of the mackerel's head. "I do that for days and days at a time, I start to be a man again."

"Won't be easy, not till the Americans get here," Oscar said.

"Yeah." Charlie Kaapu nodded. "I was hoping they'd be here already—all that shooting we heard down here from up in the valley. But I see it ain't so. Some crazy Jap motherfucker almost shot me for the fun of it before I got here. 'Scuse me, Susie."

"It's okay," Susie said. "I know about the crazy Jap motherfuckers. I know more than I ever wanted to." She shuddered.

"What did they do to you, Charlie?" Oscar asked.

"Well, they taught me one thing—I ain't never gonna screw around with no Jap officer's special lady friend no more," Charlie Kaapu said. In spite of himself, Oscar laughed. So did Susie. She clapped her hands, too. Charlie went on, "But you didn't mean that. They tried to starve me to death. They tried to work me to death. When I didn't start dying fast enough to suit 'em, they tried to beat me to death, too. The other guys there were POWs who were hard cases. Imagine what I'd look like if I was there three times as long. That's them."

"My God," Susie said after trying to imagine that. "How come they aren't all dead?"

"Lot of 'em are," Charlie answered. "More dyin' every day, too. But a hard case is a hard case, and some of 'em stayed alive just to spite the Japs. This guy named Peterson shoulda been dead months ago, but he was still breathin' when I got away. One tough son of a bitch, you bet."

"What the heck did they have you doing in the Kalihi Valley?" Oscar said. "I've been up there. It's nothing but the river and trees, all the way back to the mountains."

"Don't I know it!" Charlie said. "What were we doin'? We were digging a tunnel through the mountains to the damn windward coast, that's what. Digging with picks and shovels and crowbars and baskets, mind. The Japs didn't give a shit if we ever got there. It was something to work us to death with, that's all."

"My God," Oscar muttered. People had talked about ramming a tunnel through the mountains for years. He supposed they would have got around to it sooner or later. When they did, he supposed they would have used dynamite and jackhammers and all the others tools mankind had invented to make sure jobs like that didn't take forever.

"Can I have a bath or a shower or something?" Charlie said. "I'm filthy, and I'm lousy, too. I hope you guys don't get company on account of me." Oscar hoped the same thing. He automatically started to scratch, then jerked his hand down. Out of the corner of his eye, he saw Susie doing the same thing. It would have been funny if it hadn't been so grim. And Charlie *was* filthy; the rank smell that came off him filled the apartment.

"Go ahead," Oscar told him. "I wish I had soap and hot water, that's all. You can wear some of my clothes when you come out. Toss yours out and I'll get rid of 'em."

"Will do," Charlie said. "We're about the same size—well, we used to be, anyway. I can't get over how fat people look." Oscar and Susie were both skinnier than they had been when Japan took Oahu, and they were better off than most people because Oscar caught so many fish. To a skeleton, though, a skinny man had to look fat. Charlie went into the bathroom, then stuck his head out again. "What *was* all the shooting about a couple of nights ago? That's why I thought the Army would be back here."

"They cleaned out the prison camp in Kapiolani Park," Oscar answered. *They rescued a bunch of guys who looked just like you.* He didn't say that. Except by not screwing around with women he should have left alone, Charlie couldn't help the way he looked. Oscar added, "I guess they were afraid the Japs would start killing people if they just left 'em there."

"Jeez, I believe that," Charlie said. "I was hoping I could take soldiers back to Kalihi Valley. God knows what's gonna happen to my buddies now."

He closed the door again. Water started to run. In a low voice, Oscar said, "He's gotta stay here for a while, babe. I'm sorry, but I don't know what else we can do."

Susie waved the words aside. "It's okay. You're right. We can't do anything else. My God! Did you *see* him? He looks like a photo in *Life* or *National Geographic* where they're talking about famine in India or China or somewhere like that." Now she did scratch her head. She smiled sheepishly, but said, "For heaven's sake, throw his clothes somewhere far, far away. I'm going to imagine I'm itching for the next week, whether I really am or not."

"Yeah, I know." Oscar got a flowered shirt and a pair of pants out of the closet and tossed them into the bathroom. He didn't have a belt that Charlie could use to hold up the pants; none of the ones he owned had enough holes. But a length of rope would keep his pal decent.

He glanced over at Susie. How . . . sympathetic would she feel if Charlie stayed here all the time? How would she show her sympathy? Like *that*? Oscar shrugged a mental shrug. If she did, then she did, that was all. And if she did, didn't that tell him she wasn't the girl he wanted to spend the rest of his life with?

When Charlie got out of the tub, he threw his old clothes out from behind the door. He emerged a couple of minutes later, much cleaner. Maybe because he was cleaner, maybe because of the way Oscar's shirt and pants hung on him, he looked even scrawnier than he had before.

Oscar picked up Charlie's reeking rags with thumb and forefinger, like a fussy maiden lady. He didn't care how he looked. If he'd had tongs, he would have used those. He took the clothes out to the front door of the building, poked his head outside to make sure no Japs spotted him, and threw everything into the gutter. He frantically wiped his hand against his own trouser leg as he went back to his apartment.

Charlie was telling Susie what things were like in the Kalihi Valley. She hung on his every word. Well, Charlie could tell stories with anybody this side of Will Rogers. Oscar wasn't bad, but he wasn't in Charlie's league. He shrugged to himself again. He'd see what happened, that was all. Whatever it was, he was glad Charlie had got out of the Kalihi Valley in one piece.

JANE ARMITAGE HAD MADE A LAIR OF SORTS for herself in the Wahiawa experimental planting station. A stream ran through it, so she had water. Some of the trees had fruit on them, and gave her a little something to eat. Zebra doves weren't nearly so common as they had been before the Japs invaded, but the little blue-faced birds were still around. Jane didn't dare make a fire. If you got hungry enough, you could eat them raw. Jane wouldn't have believed it, but it was true. And she was hungry enough.

She couldn't have had a simpler plan: stay out of sight and try not to die till the Americans took Wahiawa. No one seemed to have come after her or the other comfort women who'd escaped from the blasted brothel. Jane knew exactly what that meant: the Japs had more important things to worry about. They were getting screwed now instead of doing the screwing. And they had it coming to them, too.

Every so often, other people came into the station to gather fruit. Jane hid from them like an animal, cowering in the thick bushes by the stream. That was partly because she feared they might betray her to the occupiers. And it was partly because, after what the Japanese had made her do, she felt unclean. Surely anyone who knew her, anyone who knew what she'd had to do, would think she was unclean, too. From third-grade teacher to whore in one easy step . . .

The front was getting close to Wahiawa, but not fast enough to suit her. The Japs made a stand in front of the town. *They would, the bastards,* Jane thought as she got hungrier. Even though they didn't know she was here, they kept on trying to ruin her life.

They'd done it, all right. Here she was, not quite thirty, and she hoped to heaven she never saw, never touched, and most especially never tasted another cock as long as she lived. Maybe one day she'd change her mind. She laughed at that. *Yeah—when I get to be ninety. Or maybe ninety-five.*

There were times when she wouldn't have bet she could make it to her thirtieth birthday, let alone to ninety-five. Except by standing and fighting, the Japs didn't have anything to do with that. American shells had been falling on Wahiawa ever since the brothel got hit. Sometimes they fell in or near the planting station. Those fearsome crashes uprooted trees and sent shrapnel snarling through the leaves and the undergrowth. None of it hit Jane, but some came scarily close.

She'd been at the station four or five days when machine-gun bullets began snapping past overhead—because the gardens followed the course of the stream, most of the land here was lower than the surrounding countryside. Fletch had told her that when you could hear a bullet snap, it came closer than you wanted it to. She thought these bullets were wonderful. They meant the Americans were almost as close as she wanted them to be.

Then Japanese soldiers started falling back through the station. Jane hid herself as deep among the bushes as she could. She feared they would fight from the cover the exotic plants offered. The low ground, though, evidently counted for more than that. Some of the Japs paused to fill their water bottles in the stream. Then they trotted south to make a stand somewhere else.

Before long, their bullets cracked by above her head as they harassed the oncoming Americans. She lay down behind a fallen log and hoped it would protect her. Somebody set up a machine gun on the northern lip of the little valley. Its insane hammering made her fillings ache. She heard shouts that didn't sound as if they were in Japanese, and then boots padding along the trails tourists had taken to see the elephant apple and the candle tree.

Ever so cautiously, she raised her head. For a moment, fresh fear shook her. *Were* these men Americans? They were white men, and they spoke English, but she'd never seen those green uniforms before. The helmets didn't look anything like what Fletch had laughingly called his tin hat, either.

She had to nerve herself to speak. "Hello?" she said, her voice not much more than a whisper.

With frightening speed, two rifles swung to cover her. "The fuck?" one of the apparitions in green said.

"Son of a bitch! It's a broad," the other one said. "Come on out of there, lady. We goddamn near drilled you."

"*Goddamn* near," the first one agreed. "What the hell you doin' here, anyways?"

"Hiding," she answered. To her, it was the most obvious thing in the world. These—warriors—grinned as if she'd made a joke. "Who are you people, anyway?" she asked.

"Corporal Petrocelli, ma'am," one of them said, at the same time as the other answered, "Private Schumacher, ma'am." Together, they added, "United States Army."

The Army didn't wear uniforms like theirs. No—it hadn't worn uniforms like theirs. There'd been some changes made. Schumacher (who was shorter and darker than Petrocelli, which only went to show you) asked, "Any Japs around?"

Jane pointed south. "They went thataway," she said, as if she had a bit part in a B Western. "I hope you kill 'em all."

"That's what we're here for, ma'am," Corporal Petrocelli said. He looked her up and down, not like a man eyeing a woman (thank God!) but more like an engineer wondering how long a badly battered piece of machinery could keep running. Taking a couple of small cans out of a pouch on his belt, he handed them to her. "Here you go. Reckon you need these worse'n we do." Thus prodded, Private Schumacher coughed up some rations, too.

"Thank you," she whispered, on the edge of tears. Then she proved she did have a little common sense left: she asked, "How am I going to open these?"

"Here—try this." Schumacher gave her a knife—no, a bayonet, longer and slimmer than the one on his rifle. It looked much too deadly for such a mundane job, but it would probably work. He said, "Took it off a dead Jap a couple days ago. Was gonna keep it for a souvenir, but there's more. You can get some use out of it."

"Toadsticker like that'll scrag anybody who gets out of line, too," Petrocelli said.

If I'd had it back in the brothel, if I'd stuck every man that touched me . . . Jane grimaced. *If I'd done that, I'd've killed so many, the Army would probably be in Honolulu by now.*

Not far away, somebody shouted. Jane had no idea what he said. It made sense to the soldiers, though. They trotted away. Schumacher looked back over his shoulder and waved. Then they were gone.

And most of Wahiawa had to be in American hands, and Jane had a weapon and food—my God, real food! She went back into her refuge under the bushes and behind the log. Maybe she'd come out after a while, and maybe she wouldn't. In the meantime . . . She used the bayonet to open a can. It was roast-beef hash. She hadn't eaten beef in going on two years. She thought it was the most wonderful thing she'd ever tasted, which only proved how long she'd gone without.

XIII

THE AMERICANS WERE GOING TO OVERRUN WHEELER FIELD. LIEUTENANT SABURO Shindo could see as much. The Japanese on the ground were doing everything they could to hold back the enemy. They'd taken gruesome casualties, and the Yankees still moved forward. The Americans had more and better tanks than the Japanese. They had more artillery, plus Navy vessels bombarding Oahu. And they had complete control of the air.

Shindo knew how important that was. He'd enjoyed it during the Japanese conquest of Hawaii. Having American fighters and bombers overhead from dawn to dusk was much less enjoyable than being up there himself.

Now he had the chance to get up there again. The groundcrew men at Wheeler Field had cannibalized Zeros and *Hayabusas* for their weapons. They'd cannibalized half a dozen wrecked fighters to put together one that would—they hoped—fly. Shindo hadn't even had to pull strings to get to take it up against the Americans. He was, as far as he knew, the last pilot at the field alive and unwounded.

There was an American movie about a man made from parts of other men. The fighter Shindo would fly against the Americans was a lot like that. Most of it came from Zeros, with occasional pieces from *Hayabusas*. It was a deathtrap. He knew as much. Under normal conditions, he wouldn't have walked past it, let alone got into the cockpit. Now . . . The whole Japanese garrison on Oahu would die. How was the only thing that mattered. Shindo wanted to die hitting back at the enemy, hurting the round-eyed barbarians who'd dared strike against his divinely ruled kingdom.

Before he got into the Frankenstein fighter, a groundcrew man handed him a bottle of the local not-quite-gin. He wouldn't have drunk before an ordinary mission. What difference did it make now? None he could see. He'd have to be lucky to make a proper attack run. He'd need a miracle, and not such a minor one, to come back.

"Good luck. Hit them hard," the groundcrew man said as Shindo handed back the bottle. "*Banzai!* for the Emperor!"

"*Banzai!*" Shindo echoed. He climbed up into the cockpit, closed it, and dogged it shut. The engine fired up the first try. Shindo took that for a good omen. He'd been desperately short of them lately. So had all the Japanese on Oahu.

One more good omen would be taking off without blowing up. He had a hundred-kilo bomb slung under the plane. What passed for a runway was only enough grass to get him off the ground . . . he hoped. If there wasn't quite enough grass or if a wheel bumped down into a hole the grass hid—his mission would be shorter than he expected.

Despite the risks, he wished the bomb were bigger. The fighter could carry 250 kilos without any trouble, but the armorers hadn't been able to find one that size. He shrugged and adjusted the safety harness. Then he released the brakes. The plane rolled forward. He gave it more throttle. When he neared the end of the grass, he pulled back on the stick. The Zero's nose came up. He couldn't have asked for a smoother takeoff.

He got a panoramic view of the fighting as he climbed. Wahiawa was gone, lost. So were the Schofield Barracks, just north of Wheeler Field. If the mechanics had waited much longer to get busy with their wrenches and pliers and rivet guns, they wouldn't have been able to do this.

Below him, Wildcats and the new American fighters dove to shoot up a Japanese ground position. Machine-gun fire rose to meet them, but no real antiaircraft guns opened up. None of the American planes paid any attention to Shindo. If they noticed him at all, they assumed he was one of them. A Zero's size and shape were a little like a Wildcat's, but only a little. The biggest help he had was the Yankees' assumption that no more Japanese aircraft could fly. If he couldn't be Japanese, he had to be American. Logical, wasn't it? But logic was only as good as its assumptions. Since those were wrong . . .

He flew north, toward the waiting American fleet. A flight of southbound planes waggled their wings at him. Maybe they thought he was in trouble. He politely waggled back, as if to say everything was fine. They flew on. So did he. He smiled a thin smile. As he had in air battles past, he could follow their vector back to the carriers that had launched them. *"Domo arigato,"* he murmured, doubting they would be glad to have his thanks.

The rest of the U.S. task force—destroyers, cruisers, and battleships—lay close inshore, so their big guns could shell the Japanese. They went at it methodically. Why not? No one could hit back at them. Shindo didn't intend to. These ships, however impressive (and they put the biggest Japanese fleet to shame), weren't the ones that really mattered. He wanted the carriers.

They steamed farther offshore, to make sure nothing from Oahu could reach them. Lieutenant Shindo smiled again. Something from Oahu was heading their way anyhow.

There they were! They had destroyers around them to protect against submarines and to deliver antiaircraft fire. They must have long since picked him up on radar. Even if they had, though, they didn't think he was hostile.

Then he muttered, *"Zakennayo!"* The carriers still had a combat air patrol overhead. Here came a Wildcat to look him over. *Just in case,* the pilot was bound to be thinking. Shindo could survive a lot of things, but not close visual inspection. He knew the moment when the enemy flier realized what he was. The Wildcat suddenly sped up and started jinking.

The American thought he could win a dogfight. A lot of Wildcat pilots made the mistake against a Zero. They hardly ever made it more than once. This Yankee wouldn't. Shindo turned inside him, got behind him, shot him up, and sent him spinning down toward the Pacific.

But the Wildcat pilot must have radioed his buddies. They all swarmed toward Shindo. He'd just run out of leisure. Things would happen in a hurry now. He dove toward the closest carrier. The Americans still didn't space them out as widely as they should have. If the Japanese could have organized a real attack, they might have mauled this task force. As things were, Shindo could only do his best.

Antiaircraft guns opened up on him as he dove. The ships down below had finally figured out he wasn't one of theirs. The closest carrier wasn't a big one. He didn't care. If he could hit it, he would.

He pulled the bomb-release lever. The bomb fell free. It exploded on the flight deck. Shell fragments or machine-gun bullets slammed into the Zero as it zoomed away. The engine coughed. Smoke trailed from the plane.

"Karma," Shindo said. Sure enough, this was a one-way mission. He would have been angrier and more disappointed if he'd expected anything else.

He flew on toward the next nearest carrier, hoping his plane wouldn't go into the drink before he got there. A Wildcat dove on him. He did a snap roll and got away. That changed his direction. There was another carrier, not far ahead. It was landing planes, and had lots of them on the flight deck. Perfect.

He gained a little altitude, then dove as if landing himself. Inside the cockpit, he braced himself for the impact, not that that would do any good. *"Banzai!"* he shouted as the flight deck swelled below him. *"Ban—"*

JOE CROSETTI RAN FOR THE *BUNKER HILL*'S island after scrambling out of his Hellcat. He wondered why some nearby ships were firing AA like it was going out of style. He wouldn't have believed the Japs had any planes left.

What he believed didn't matter worth a damn. He got his nose rubbed in that a moment later. A sailor pointed to starboard and screamed, "Holy fucking shit, it's a Jap!"

And it was. The Zero was on fire. It skimmed low over the surface of the Pacific, straight for the *Bunker Hill*. Joe stared in helpless fascination. What the hell was that pilot thinking? He couldn't be crazy enough to try to land on an American carrier, could he? He'd get shot to pieces before he could open the cockpit. And even if that weren't so, he wasn't lined up anyway.

He rose a little, then dove for the deck. Crosetti couldn't believe he was going to crash his plane on purpose till he did it. The Zero went up in a fireball. So did half a dozen Hellcats.

"Fire!" Joe yelled. "Fire on the flight deck!"

A flightcrew man came running out of the inferno. His clothes were on fire—he might have been on fire, too. He screamed like a damned soul with devils sticking pitchforks into him.

"Down!" Joe shouted. "Down and roll!" That was what everybody got trained to do. Remembering the training when things hit the fan wasn't so easy. Joe was still in his flight suit, with the heavy leather jacket. He wasn't a big guy, but he dashed across the deck, tackled the flightcrew man, lay atop him and beat at the flames with his gloved fists. When most of the fire was out, somebody turned a hose on them for a few seconds. The man behind the hose had the sense to turn the nozzle to mist, not stream. Otherwise, the high-pressure water might have blasted them off the flight deck and into the drink.

Medics came up and hustled the burned man below. "How about you, buddy?" one of them asked Joe. "You okay?"

"Yeah, I think so," he answered dazedly. Gloves or not, he'd burned his hands. He had a burn on one cheek, too—he could feel it. But he was in one piece, nothing like the poor bastard who'd come out of that inferno.

The medic slapped ointment onto his cheek. It stung, then soothed. "You did good," the guy said, then hustled away to look for more casualties.

He wouldn't have to look far. That Jap had been a bastard, but a brave bastard. He'd done as much to the *Bunker Hill* as he could. Planes were still burning despite the ocean water the hoses poured on them. Burning gasoline and oil floated on top of the water, and had to be drowned or washed over the side.

If that Zero smashed down half a minute earlier . . . Joe shuddered. He would have been right in the middle of the fireball.

Now all he could do was help hang on to a hose that tried to defeat the flames. His burned hands screamed at him. He ignored them. The burns weren't all that bad, and he didn't think he was making them worse. He'd worry about it later any which way.

"Did you see that fucker?" asked the petty officer behind him. "You see the way he crashed that goddamn plane?"

"I sure did," Joe answered. The CPO who held the nozzle doused a burning Hellcat that might have been his. "If he'd done it a little earlier, he would have got me." There. He'd said it. The sky didn't fall. But he didn't think he would ever have the feeling that nothing could happen to him, not any more. Now he was just another—what had some wise guy called it?—another fugitive from the law of averages, that was it.

"He knew he was screwed, so he screwed us, too," the petty officer said. "How the hell do you stop a guy who already knows he's gonna buy a plot?"

"We didn't," Joe said.

"No shit!" the petty officer agreed. "Can you imagine what it would be like if a hundred o' them Jap bastards tried to crash their planes into carriers and battlewagons all at once? They could fuck up the whole goddamn U.S. Navy."

Joe thought about it. The idea was scary, but only for a moment. He shook his head. "Never happen, buddy. No way in hell. Where you gonna find a hundred guys crazy enough to kill themselves like it was close-order drill? Not even the Nips are that nuts."

"Yeah, I guess you're right," the petty officer said after some thought of his own. "You'd have to be Asiatic to do somethin' like that, and not even the Japs are Asiatic that kind of way." He pointed to an escort carrier off to starboard. A column of smoke rose from that ship, too. "Bastard must have put a bomb into her—either that or another plane got her."

"Bomb, I think," Joe said. "You can stick a bomb under just about any fighter. There was just the one plane, wasn't there?"

"Well, I *thought* so," the rating answered. "Now I ain't so sure. God, what a fucking mess this turned out to be."

He had that straight. Damage control was on the ball. They'd kept the fire from spreading, and now they just about had it out. But *Bunker Hill*'s flight deck *was* still a mess. They would have to shove six or eight planes over the side. They would have to repair the planking on the flight deck, too; some of it had caught fire. The air stank of gasoline and motor oil, of burnt paint and burnt rubber and burnt wood. And there was one more odor, too, one that made spit flood into Joe's mouth before he realized what caused it, and then made him want to be sick. The smell of burnt meat would never be the same for him again.

PLATOON SERGEANT LES DILLON CROUCHED in a shell hole just north of the Wheeler Field runways. The Japs had machine-gun nests on the other side of those battered cement strips. Before long, somebody who didn't have to do it was going to order the Marines to cross that bare ground. And they would, too, or die trying. Les didn't want to be one of the poor bastards who died trying.

He heard the sweetest sound in the world: radial engines up in the air screaming their heads off. Hellcats strafed the Jap positions. He watched those .50-caliber rounds chew up the grass over there. Then he heard different engines: Louis Armstrong instead of Benny Goodman. The Dauntlesses put bombs down right on the money and then roared away to get more ordnance and do it again.

Crossing the killing ground still wouldn't be easy. Any Jap who wasn't dead or maimed would be up and shooting the minute the Marines came out of their holes. Even the ones who were maimed would hang on to a rifle or a grenade. They weren't about to let you take them alive. That was fine with Les Dillon. He didn't want to take them alive anyhow.

A whistle sounded. Les grimaced. This was it—the moment he hadn't been waiting for. "Up, you bastards!" Captain Bradford yelled. "Are we Marines or not?"

That flicked the men's pride. The company commander had to know it would. Les sprang up and ran forward. He hunched over as low as he could and dodged from side to side. All of that did more good than snapping your fingers to keep the elephants away, but not a whole hell of a lot.

And the planes hadn't cleaned out all the Japs. He'd figured they wouldn't. Marines fell. Others flopped down to fire back. An ice-blue tracer snapped past Dillon's head. His first thought was of a firefly on benzedrine. His next was that the round had come much too close to punching his ticket. He should have thought that first, but your mind did crazy things sometimes.

Then he was in among the Japs. Some of them were real infantrymen; others, by their clothes, groundcrew for airplanes. They all fought like madmen; the next Jap with any quit in him that Les saw would be the first. But the Marines had no quit in them, either. More of them rushed up to help their buddies. The Japanese didn't get much in the way of reinforcements; Les had the feeling the ones fighting here were the last Japs standing for quite a ways.

And then they weren't standing any more. The Marines still on their feet finished off any of the enemy who still twitched. Word about the Opana POW massacre had got out. The Marines hadn't been any more inclined to take prisoners than the Japs were to be captured even before it did. Now . . . Maybe they'd follow a direct order to try to capture some enemy soldiers for interrogation. Then again, maybe not. Had the Japs won the fight, Les knew a bullet through the head was the best he could hope for. Things went downhill from there, and in a hurry, too.

Three Sherman tanks rumbled and snorted across the ruined runway. Les eyed them with a mixture of appreciation and disgust. He was glad to see them—he was always glad to see tanks, because they took so much pressure off the foot soldiers—but he would have been gladder if they'd shown up an hour earlier. They could have made taking this position a hell of a lot easier.

He wasn't the only one with that feeling, either. "Nice of you to join us, girls," a Marine lisped, giving the tankers a limp-wristed wave.

"They didn't want to get their hair mussed," another grimy, unshaven leatherneck added, even more swishily than the first one. Les started to giggle. He didn't know why, but listening to tough guys acting like a bunch of fruits always broke him up. Some fairies got into the Marines. When they were found out, they left the Corps a lot faster than they'd joined it. He'd seen that happen a few times, in China and back in the States. Some of the men who got bounced were losers for other reasons, too. Others would have made pretty fair Marines if they weren't queer.

He laughed again, on a different note. For all he knew, there was a faggot or two in the company now. As long as a man didn't advertise it—some did—how were you supposed to know?

Even while such thoughts occurred to him, he got down in a hole some Jap didn't need any more. You didn't want to be on your feet and upright when the Japs could start taking potshots at you any second. The tank crewmen, meanwhile, yelled insults back at the Marines who fought on foot. One bow gunner wanted to jump out of his tank and kick ass. The driver on that tank restrained him. He was probably lucky: ground pounders were likely to be in better shape and meaner than guys who had armor plate to hold the war at bay.

"Enough!" Les yelled. "Everybody—enough! We've got Japs to kill. You want to beat on each other, wait till we take Honolulu."

That name had enough magic to calm people down. Marines who'd been to Hawaii before thought of Hotel Street. Those who hadn't didn't, but what they had in mind was something like Hotel Street. Honolulu was the Holy Grail. There were all sorts of incentives for throwing out the Japs, booze and pussy not the smallest among them.

"Where do we go now, sir?" someone asked Captain Bradford.

"I don't have more orders yet," the company commander answered. "We did this. Now we wait and see what happens next." The men knew what to do about that. They settled themselves in the entrenchments they'd just won. Here and there, they heaved Japanese corpses out of them. They lit cigarettes. Some of them opened K-ration cans. As long as they weren't going anywhere right away, they'd make themselves as comfortable as they could. Hurry up and wait was supposed to be an Army joke, but the Marines lived by it, too.

Dutch Wenzel came up to cadge a Camel from Les. "They don't put cigars in the K-rats," Wenzel said mournfully. "You still alive? Hadn't seen you for a while, so I started to wonder."

"Well, I was the last time I looked," Dillon answered. "I wondered about you, too. Don't see somebody for a coupla hours, you figure maybe he stopped one with his chest."

"These Japs . . ." Wenzel bent close for a light, sucked in smoke, and held it as long as he could. Les wondered if he was going to finish that after he finally blew it out. Then he decided it didn't matter. Among the Marines, that was practically a complete sentence all by itself. Dutch exhaled a gray cloud and said, "You know, you can get damn near anything for cigarettes from the people here. They been without since they smoked the last of what they had. They go down on their knees to thank you if you give some away."

"Yeah?" Les leered. "You get one of these gals to go down on her knees for you? I heard of being hung like a horse, but I never heard of being hung like a Camel."

Wenzel made a horrible face, but he said, "I bet you could get sucked off for cigarettes, no shit. Tell you something—I think I'd rather get blown than lay most of these women. They're so goddamn scrawny, it'd be like laying a ladder."

Les nodded. All the civilians on Oahu were skinny. Even the Japs were skinny, and they'd had better rations than the locals. Just the same . . . "You've heard about the prisoners at that Opana place, and the ones our guys rescued down by Honolulu? Those poor mothers weren't just skinny. They were fucking starving to death for real. Goddamn Japs have a lot to answer for."

"Better believe it." Dutch smoked the cigarette down to a butt. Then he took an alligator clip out of his pocket and went on smoking it even after it got too small to hold between his fingers. That was a good idea. Les reminded himself to scrounge his own clip off a radioman or a field-telephone operator or somebody else who messed around with wires. Wenzel went on, "There was supposed to be another camp somewhere, too, one where the Japs got even with guys who got their asses in a sling at the regular places. Scuttlebutt is, that one made the others look like a rest cure."

"I heard something like that, too," Les said. "You keep hoping that crap isn't so. And then you find out it is, and that it's worse than anybody said it was, on account of nobody would've believed it if they tried to say how bad it really was."

Wenzel eyed the closest Japanese corpse. The Jap had taken one in the neck and one in the face. Either would have finished him. The one in the face had gone out through the back of his head and blown out most of his brains. Flies crawled over the blood-soaked grayish spatters. "He got it quick," Dutch observed. "After what they did at Opana, I'd like to roast 'em all over a slow fire. Not half of what they oughta get, either."

"Gonna be that kind of war, all right," Les agreed mournfully. "Back in 1918, the Germans fought hard, but they fought pretty clean. So did we, even if"—he chuckled reminiscently—"their machine gunners had a lot of trouble surrendering. Those bastards thought they could bang away till you were right on top of 'em and then put up their hands. They had more accidents. . . . But it's all gonna be like that here, and we're just starting out. Still a long way to Tokyo. Fuck, it's still a long way to Midway."

"Sir?" the radioman called to Captain Bradford.

The company commander listened and talked for a little while. Then he said, "Well, boys, we've got our orders now." He waited for the expectant mutter to die away, then went on, "We're going to do a left wheel and head for Honolulu with the rest of the guys moving south."

"What the fuck?" Les muttered. He'd figured they would keep driving straight south. He said, "Sir, what about Pearl City and Pearl Harbor?"

"They'll be taken care of, Sergeant, I promise," Bradford said. "Only difference is, we won't be the guys who do it."

"Right," Les said. Somebody somewhere way the hell up the chain of command had had himself a brainstorm. Whether it would end up being the good kind or the other kind—well, everybody would have to wait and see how that turned out. "Honolulu." Dillon tasted the word. He'd been thinking about Hotel Street not long before. He wondered what was left of it. If the damn Nips didn't shoot him first, he'd find out.

MINORU GENDA WAITED IN A HOTEL ROOM on Hotel Street. He'd brought his bicycle upstairs with him to the bare little cubicle. If he left it on the street, even chained to a lamppost, it would be gone by the time he came down. He'd paid too much for the room. He'd paid too much for the bottle of island gin he'd brought here, too. He shrugged. What did he have to do with his money now but spend it?

A knock on the door. He jumped up from the bed—the only furniture in the room but for a battered chest of drawers. Hotels on Hotel Street had only one thing in mind.

He opened the door. Queen Cynthia Laanui stood in the hallway. Probably the most recognizable woman in Hawaii, she'd taken pains not to be recognized. Her red hair was tucked up under a straw hat. Enormous sunglasses helped hide her face. She'd brought her bicycle upstairs, too. A cramped room with two bicycles in it amused Genda. Small things still could. Few big ones were amusing any more.

Queen Cynthia walked the bicycle in when Genda stood aside. He closed the door behind her and locked it. Then he took her in his arms. They kissed greedily. When they broke apart, she said, "It's not going to work, is it?" She didn't sound bitter—only very tired.

"No." Genda wished he could lie to her. Back at Pearl Harbor, Japanese officers were still busy lying to one another. They kept on believing that if this went right, and if that went right, and if they caught the Americans napping here, they might still save Oahu. American officers must have danced that dance of delusion at the end of 1941 and the start of 1942. Before long, defeat stared them in the face even so. And it would stare the Japanese in the face, too. Genda went on, "We fight hard. We are brave. But, so sorry, we cannot win. The enemy is too strong."

Saying something like that brought vast relief. His colleagues might have arrested him for telling the truth. If you didn't look at something, they were convinced, it would go away. But being convinced didn't make it true.

"What are we going to do, then?" Cynthia asked. "What *can* we do?"

What did *we* mean here? The Empire of Japan and the soon to be extinguished Kingdom of Hawaii? King Stanley and herself? Genda and herself? All of those at once? That last was Genda's guess. He said, "We all do the best we can." His answer was as ambiguous as her question.

She spotted the bottle on the chest of drawers. Two lithe strides took her to it. She yanked out the cork, swigged, and made a horrible face. "God, that's nasty," she said, coughing, and then drank again.

Genda took a pull, too. It was every bit as bad as Cynthia said it was. But the only thing worse than rotgut liquor was no liquor at all. "You have courage, not to try to get away," he said.

Her laugh was all razors and barbed wire. "Where would I go? How would I get there? Wherever it is, somebody would know my face. Your propaganda people made sure of that. I'm on postage stamps, for crying out loud. And pretty soon I'll be on post-office walls, too." Seeing that that meant nothing to Genda, she explained, "That's where we put posters of wanted criminals."

He kissed her again. "You are not a criminal to me, but you are wanted." Paying compliments in English wasn't easy for him. He hoped that one came out right.

It must have, because she turned red. But she sounded no happier as she answered, "Yeah, and that only makes me a bigger villain to the USA. Like being Queen of Hawaii wasn't bad enough, I fell for a Japanese officer. They won't know whether to shoot me or hang me."

She was probably right. No, she was bound to be right. If the Americans came back, they would have debts to pay.

He wished he could offer to take her to Japan. She deserved to escape such a fate. He didn't think the two of them would last long as a couple once she got back to the home islands. King Stanley would have to come, too. Genda's liaison with a round-eyed woman would draw much more notice, and much more censorious notice, in Japan than it did in this easygoing place. The King and Queen of Hawaii would undoubtedly go on being used for propaganda purposes: brave heads of a government in exile. Genda could see it all now.

What he couldn't see was how to get Queen Cynthia—yes, and King Stanley—away from Oahu. If he'd known how to do that, he might have had some notion of how to get away himself. But no Japanese planes had been seen in these parts since the American fleet's fighters and bombers smashed the fleet and then the land-based aircraft. An H8K flying boat *might* be able to sneak into Pearl Harbor. But the odds were long. As the Americans had shown by their landing at the Kapiolani Park POW camp, they controlled the sea and air all around Oahu, and their grip tightened by the day.

Genda didn't think Japan could scrape together enough carriers and other ships to challenge this armada, even if she abandoned the rest of the war—which she couldn't very well do. Everything Admiral Yamamoto had said about what the United States could do if roused was coming true. From Honolulu, though, Tokyo was more than 6,000 kilometers away. Even now, Hawaii shielded Japan.

Maybe a submarine could sneak in and out. None *had* come in, though. Genda didn't know if any had tried. Which would be worse, knowing some had failed or knowing his superiors far to the west hadn't dared risk any? One more question he hadn't asked himself.

"When . . . things go wrong, Japanese people often kill themselves, don't they?" By the way Queen Cynthia asked the question, she knew the answer.

"Yes, we do that." Minoru Genda nodded. He didn't go into details about *seppuku*. Women weren't expected to disembowel themselves anyway, only to slit their throats. After the nod, he shook his head, trying to shove such unpleasant, unwelcome thoughts aside. It wasn't the first time he'd had them. He said, "Too soon to worry about such things. Much too soon." He sipped from the bottle on the dresser. If he drank enough of that, he wouldn't worry about anything for a while.

Cynthia also drank. But her voice was completely sober. "Too soon to worry about it, yes. Much too soon? I don't think so."

Since Genda didn't really think it was much too soon, either, he didn't try to argue with her. He asked, "How is his Majesty?"

"He didn't think . . . this would happen when he let you put the crown on his head," she answered. Genda already knew that. She went on, "It's funny. He's at least *hapa-haole* himself, but he really is angry with *haoles* for what they've done to Hawaiians. That's genuine. A lot of him is bluff and bluster and bullshit"—maybe she felt the almost-gin after all—"but that's for real." She looked down at her ring and flushed again. "Well, he isn't angry at *all* the *haoles*."

"No one could be—can be?—could be angry at you," Genda said.

"That's sweet. You're sweet." Now Cynthia Laanui kissed him. A long time ago, someone had told him that the person who started a kiss was the one who needed it more. By the desperate way Cynthia clung to him, that held a lot of truth. When they separated, she said, "You don't know me very well. You can't know me very well, if you tell me something like that. Don't get me wrong—I like it. But I know it's silly, too."

"I don't think so." Genda was sure she was right, but he didn't care. Right now, they had nothing left but each other, and they might not have each other long, either. He gathered himself, picked her up, and carried her to the bed. He was a small man, two or three centimeters shorter than she was, but he was strong.

Their lovemaking had always had the sweetness of stolen fruit. Now, every time they touched, they knew it might be the last. The way things were these days, each joining might be the last thing they ever did. For him, and evidently for her, too, that only made the flame burn hotter.

Afterwards, a pink flush mottling the pale skin between her breasts, she said, "I wish I had a cigarette."

With the air of a successful stage magician, Genda pulled a pack of Chesterfields from a trouser pocket. "Here," he said.

Cynthia squealed and kissed him. "My God, my God, my God!" she said. "Where on earth did you get these? Where?" To hear her talk, the tobacco drought might have been worldwide, not confined to Hawaii.

Genda made a small ceremony of lighting one for her and one for himself. "A friend gave them to me," he said, and let it go at that. The friend had got them from another friend, who'd got them from a dead U.S. Marine. That might be more than Cynthia wanted to hear.

She coughed when she first inhaled. Genda had done the same thing. They'd gone without tobacco so long, it was as if they'd never smoked at all. But the second puff made her smile. "Jesus, that's good!" she said, and then, after a momentary pause, "Can I have a few to take back to Stanley? I'm sorry. I know it's greedy. But if I give him cigarettes, he won't wonder why I went out."

"Okay," Genda said. The slang made Cynthia smile. Genda didn't begrudge her five Chesterfields . . . very much. He knew she was right. If she gave the king those, he'd think she'd left Iolani Palace to get her hands on them. That she'd got them from her lover wouldn't cross his mind—or Genda hoped it wouldn't.

She smoked her cigarette down to the tiniest of butts, then stared sorrowfully at the scrap of tobacco that remained. "I feel like chewing this like a hillbilly," she said.

Although Genda knew about snuff, chewing tobacco had never caught on in Japan. The idea made him queasy—or maybe it was just the Chesterfield.

The Queen of Hawaii got out of bed and started dressing. "I'd better go back now," she said. As she had on the way from the palace to Hotel Street, she tucked her hair up under her hat and put on the sunglasses.

"We will do everything we can," Genda said. Cynthia Laanui nodded. And after they'd done that . . . Neither one wanted to dwell on what might happen then. She nodded one more time, then walked the bicycle out the door without a backward glance.

Genda waited five minutes before he dressed so they wouldn't be seen leaving together. He wrestled his own bicycle down the stairs and started back to Pearl Harbor. He hadn't gone far before he realized the great naval center was under attack. Planes roared above it: fighters strafing and dive bombers stooping on targets to drop their bombs. Japanese antiaircraft guns—and some captured from the Americans at the surrender—filled the sky with puffs of black smoke.

Naval guns were also firing on Pearl Harbor, from ranges beyond the reach of shore-based artillery. Genda wished Japan hadn't had to wreck the great coast-defense guns the USA had installed along the southern coast of Oahu. *They* would have taught those ships respect. But they could have harmed the Japanese Navy, and so Aichi dive bombers with armor-piercing bombs had blown up the casements in which they lurked.

Were those landing craft in the water? Whatever they were, they looked a lot more sophisticated than the Daihatsu barges on which Japan relied. Genda pedaled harder. He'd had permission to leave his station, but he wanted to be there to defend the harbor as long as he could. *As if one man will make any difference now,* he thought bitterly. But his legs pumped up and down all the same.

THE *BUNKER HILL* WAS A GOING CONCERN AGAIN, flight deck repaired, incinerated planes shoved into the drink, new Hellcats and Dauntlesses taken aboard. Joe Crosetti missed the fighter that had gone up in flames, but the new one would do the job just fine. He missed the men lost when that Jap crashed his Zero into the carrier far more. You couldn't replace men the way you could airplanes.

Not far away, the *Copahee* was still under repair. The escort carrier had taken a bomb from that same Jap. The guy was a son of a bitch, yeah, but he'd done a hell of a piece of work there.

Sailors on the baby flattop took off their caps and waved to Joe as he and his buddies from the *Bunker Hill* flew over them, bound for Oahu. He waggled his wings to return the compliment. By rights, the sailors could have been pissed off. How *had* that Jap got through in spite of radar and the combat air patrol overhead?

Joe feared he knew the answer. The Americans had got overconfident and fallen asleep at the switch. The blip on the radar coming in alone? So what? It was bound to be another American plane, wasn't it? Well, no. And the guys flying CAP had been slow getting a handle on it, too.

The carriers fell away behind him. So did the destroyers and cruisers screening them. He came up on the warships bombarding Oahu. Their guns thundered below him. Flame and smoke belched from the muzzles. The ships heeled in the water at the recoil. Some dug-in Japs would be catching hell.

Fewer bombardment ships remained north of Oahu. A good many had steamed around the island to pummel Pearl Harbor. Joe and his fellow fliers were on their way there, too. He'd shot up the harbor before, plenty of times. Things were different today. Marines and dogfaces were landing. They were going to take the base away from the Japs. Just about all the Japanese soldiers were at the front. What kind of fight could sailors and other odds and sods put up?

"We'll fix 'em, goddammit," Joe said. A second front here would do almost as much good as the second front in Europe Stalin kept shouting for. Catch the enemy between hammer and anvil and smash him flat. "Yeah," Joe muttered. "Yeah."

One thing the Japs had already made very plain—they had no quit in them. All the antiaircraft guns that hadn't been knocked out were banging away like nobody's business. Flying past a near miss was like driving a car over a hole in the road. You went down and then you went up again, sometimes hard enough for your teeth to click together. But you didn't pick up shrapnel from a hole in the road unless somebody'd stuck a land mine down there.

Something clanged against the new Hellcat's fuselage. Joe automatically checked the gauges. Everything looked good. These babies could take it. Hit a Zero or an Oscar with a good burst of .50-caliber bullets, and it'd break up in midair. The Army fighter the Americans called the Tony was a tougher bird, but nowhere near as tough as a Hellcat.

Orders were to shoot up anything Japanese at Pearl that might shoot back. Joe went in at not much above treetop height, machine guns blazing. He wondered if the place was worth taking away from the Nips. Two campaigns inside of two years had turned it into a pretty fair approximation of hell on earth. The water had a greasy sheen. He was so low, the odor of spilled fuel oil got into the canopy. Wrecked American and Japanese ships lay side by side, brothers in death. Before the war started, nobody except a few aviation-minded cranks had really believed airplanes could sink capital ships all by themselves.

"I believe! Oh, Lord, I believe!" Joe sounded like a Holy Roller preacher. How many hundred thousand tons of twisted steel lay below him? The last two times the U.S. and Japanese fleets clashed, neither side's ships had set eyes on the other's. Planes did all the dirty work.

Once upon a time, Ford Island, there in the middle of Pearl Harbor, had been a tropical paradise, all palm trees and bougainvillea and frangipani. Nothing green was left now, just dirt and char marks and the wreckage of buildings—and antiaircraft guns among the wreckage. Joe squeezed the firing button on top of the stick. His six .50s hammered away. The recoil made the Hellcat jerk in the air. Japs scrambled for cover. He might have been playing pinball, except those were real people down there. *Real people I hope I kill,* he thought.

Out at the edge of the harbor, landing craft were coming ashore. Some of the AA guns were firing at them instead of at the airplanes overhead. That wasn't so good. A three-inch gun could do horrible things to a boat that was meant to be equally awkward by land and sea. Joe strafed a gun from behind. He didn't think its crew heard him coming. What .50-caliber slugs did to human flesh was even worse than what antiaircraft guns did to landing craft.

Some of the ugly, boxy boats came right up the channel. Wrecks blocked bigger ships from getting in, but the landing craft scraped past them. Joe wagged his wings in salute as he shot at a Japanese machine-gun nest.

A Hellcat trailing smoke plunged into the water of the West Loch. Joe looked around. He didn't see a parachute. Maybe the poor bastard inside the plane was lucky not to get out. He would have come down in the middle of a big swarm of Japs, with a piss-poor chance of getting away. What they would have done to him before they let him die . . . Compared to that, going straight into the drink looked pretty good.

Joe made pass after pass, firing short bursts so he wouldn't overheat his guns and burn out the barrels. Finally, his ammo ran dry. He still had plenty of fuel, but so what? Unless he wanted to imitate that Jap and see how big a fire he could start, it didn't do him much good here.

It would take him home, though. He flew back over Oahu toward the *Bunker Hill.* The Japs shot at him several more times, and missed every one. Hitting a fast-moving airplane wasn't easy. Frustrated gunners on both sides could testify to that.

A few more puffs of black smoke around him, and then he was out over the Pacific. He hoped none of the American ships would fire on him. If one did, they all would, and they threw up a lot of shells and bullets. They might not get him anyway, but why take chances?

He ran the gauntlet. A CAP fighter came over to have a look at him, but it pulled away when the pilot recognized he was in a Hellcat. It waggled its wings as it went. He returned the courtesy.

As always, landing on the *Bunker Hill* meant turning off his own will and doing exactly what the landing officer told him to. Fighter pilots were a willful breed. He hated surrendering control to somebody else. But the easiest of the many ways to kill yourself on carrier duty was to think you knew better than the landing officer. However little Joe liked it, he believed it.

At the officer's signal, he shoved the stick forward and dove for the deck. "Jesus!" he said as he slammed home. His tailhook caught the second arrester wire. The Hellcat jerked to a stop.

Flightcrew men came running up as Joe opened the canopy and got out. "How'd it go, Mr. Crosetti?" one of them called.

"Piece of cake," Joe answered. "I need ammo. Then I can go back and give 'em some more. We're going to take Pearl Harbor back from those bastards— you better believe we are."

The sailors cheered. "We'll have you back in the air in nothin' flat, sir," an armorer said. "Don't you worry about a thing."

"Not me," Joe said. "That's for the guys with lots of gold braid." As an en- sign, he outranked all the ratings around him. He was an officer, of course. But he felt he was barely an officer. Just about all the others on the ship were enti- tled to give him orders.

That was a worry for another day. Now all he wanted to do was hit the Japs another lick. What would end up happening to Pearl Harbor once the Americans took it back—was also a worry for another day, and not for the likes of him.

FIGHTING WAS GETTING CLOSE to Honolulu now. The roar of battle from Pearl Harbor never went away, no matter how much Jiro Takahashi wished it would. He'd made a bet not long after the Japanese conquered Hawaii. He'd bet they were the winning side. For a while, that bet looked pretty good. It didn't any more.

He wished his sons would give him a harder time about it. He deserved a hard time for his foolishness. But they treated him sympathetically, as if he were an old rake coming back to earth after a spree with a young floozy who took him for everything but the gold in his teeth.

"*Shigata ga nai*, Father," Hiroshi said. "When the Americans come back, we just have to try to keep you out of trouble if we can."

"They can't get him for treason." Kenzo spoke as if Jiro weren't in the tent in the botanical garden. "He's not a U.S. citizen. He was just helping his own country." *No matter how dumb he was.* He didn't say that. He didn't need to say it. Everything that had happened since the Americans came back shouted it for him.

"Do you think they'll care?" Hiroshi asked. "To them, he'll be a Jap who helped the other Japs." The hateful key word was in English. His older son went on, "They'll probably deal with all the people like that, so we'd better have some good reasons why they shouldn't."

"Don't worry about me, boys," Jiro said. "Consul Kita told me he would take care of me if he could, and I'm sure he meant it."

They both stared at him. "Big deal," Kenzo said. "Kita can't even help himself now, let alone anybody else."

"That's the truth," Hiroshi agreed. "All just talk and nonsense."

"Well, I hope not," Jiro said. "The consulate is still up and running."

"Up and standing still, you mean," Kenzo said. "It hasn't got anywhere to run to. The Americans are in Pearl Harbor, Father. They'll be here in Honolulu any day now. What can Kita do?"

Jiro shrugged. He got to his feet. "I don't know. Maybe I ought to go and see, *neh?*"

"You ought to leave that place alone, Father," Kenzo said. "Haven't you got in enough trouble because you went there?"

"If America wins, you will be happy," Jiro said. "All right—be happy. I wouldn't be happy even if I never went on the radio. America is not my country. It has never been my country. I came here to make some money, not to live."

"And you made more than you ever would have in Japan," Hiroshi said.

"So what?" Jiro shrugged again. "So what, I say? I have lived for all these years in a land that does not like me, does not want me, and does not speak my language. If you want to go on being *Japs*"—he brought out the English word, too, and laced it with contempt—"in America, fine. Not for me, not if I can help it."

He pushed past Hiroshi and Kenzo and out of the tent. His sons didn't try to stop him. If they had, they would have got a surprise. They were taller and younger than he was, but he was meaner. *I raised them soft,* he thought. Most of the time, that pleased him. They didn't need to be as hard as he had. But they didn't have that toughness to fall back on, either.

The air stank of smoke, of burning. It wasn't so bad as it had been when all the fuel at Pearl Harbor burned. Then Honolulu wore a shroud for weeks, till the fires finally burned themselves out. Still, it left his lungs as raw as if he were smoking three cigarettes at the same time. He smiled wryly. He couldn't remember the last time he'd smoked one cigarette, let alone three.

Up Nuuanu Avenue he went. The guards at the Japanese consulate waved to him. "*Konichiwa*, Fisherman!" they called. "You haven't got any goodies for us today?"

"Please excuse me, no," Jiro answered. With so many American ships operating south of Oahu now, they probably would have sunk the *Oshima Maru* if he dared put to sea in her. "Is Kita-*san* in?"

"Yes—for now," a guard said. Another one sent him a reproving look, as if he might have said too much. But no one stopped Jiro from walking up the stairs and into the consulate.

When he got inside, the smell of smoke was thicker. He needed only a moment to see why: secretaries were busy tearing up papers and burning them. That sobered him. If the staff at the consulate didn't think Honolulu could hold, the game really was coming to an end.

One of the secretaries looked up from ripping reports into strips. For all Jiro knew, they were reports about him. If they were, better they should go into the fire. "Oh, hello, Takahashi-*san*," the secretary said. "The honorable consul will be glad to see you. He was just talking about you, in fact."

Maybe those reports really were about Jiro, then. "Thank you," he said, and went on into Nagao Kita's office.

"Do whatever you can to buy time. We need it," Kita was saying into the telephone when Jiro walked in. The consul waved and gestured to a chair. When he finished talking, he hung up. "Good to see you, Takahashi-*san*," he said. "Things are . . ." His little wave was more expressive than words could be.

"I see you are getting rid of your papers," Jiro said.

"Can't be helped," Kita said. "Better not to let the Americans find out some of the things we did here. Better not to let the Americans find us here, either."

"*Ah, so desu-ka?*" Jiro said. "Is there some way the Americans won't find you here?" Despite Kita's half-promise of a little while before, he did not presume to include himself among the number who might not be found here. When he talked with an important personage like the consul, he still felt very much like a horny-handed fisherman.

Nagao Kita smiled. "There is some way, yes. How would you like to stay here till tonight and come to Honolulu harbor with me? If we are lucky, a submarine will surface and take some of the people who matter to us back to Japan."

"And you really would take *me*?" Jiro hardly dared believe his ears. "*I* am a man who matters enough to go back to Japan?" He wondered what the home islands would be like. He'd been away so long. A lot had changed here in Hawaii since he came. Japan was bound to be different, too.

The consul's smile grew wider, almost filling his broad face. "I would take you. I am glad to take you, Takahashi-*san*. Your broadcasts served your country and served your Emperor well. And we have two spaces on the submarine we were not sure we would. The King and Queen of Hawaii have decided to stay here and face whatever happens."

"They are brave." Jiro thought they were also foolish. Then full understanding of what the consul had told him sank in. "I will get a place on this submarine that would have gone to the King or Queen of Hawaii? *I* will?" His voice rose to a startled squeak. It hadn't broken like that since he was nineteen years old, but it did now.

"Don't worry about it," Kita said easily. "Even if they had decided to go, we would have found a place for you one way or another."

Jiro bowed in his seat. "*Domo arigato,* Kita-san. You could put me in a torpedo tube. I wouldn't care."

"Oh, you might, if they had to shoot you at an American cruiser." Kita had a good laugh, the kind that invited everyone who heard it to laugh along. It made even a silly joke funnier than it would have been otherwise.

"I would like to go back and say good-bye to my sons," Jiro said slowly.

"Takahashi-*san*, if you were going on the submarine alone, I would tell you to go and do this," Kita answered. "We've never talked much about your sons, and one reason we haven't is that I know they think of themselves as Americans, not Japanese. I don't hold that against you. How could I, when it is true of so many of the younger generation here? I don't know that they would raise the alarm. For all I know, they probably wouldn't. But, please excuse me, I would rather not take the chance."

Jiro bowed his head. "I understand."

"Thank you," Kita said. "I do not want to make things more awkward than they have to be."

After that, Jiro had nothing to do but wait. He leafed through magazines from Japan. Everyone in them seemed happy and cheerful and prosperous. All the news was good. They talked about beating the Americans again and again. In their pages, the United States seemed a clumsy, stupid giant, not worth taking seriously. Off in the distance—but not far enough off in the distance—artillery and bombs thundered. Every so often, an American plane would roar over Honolulu. The USA made a more serious foe than the propaganda magazines cared to admit.

Darkness fell. The staff at the consulate went right on burning papers. Jiro felt useless. He didn't know enough to help. But they wouldn't want to take him back to the home islands if he were useless, would they?

He dozed in his chair. Nagao Kita shook him awake. "It's time, Takahashi-*san*," the consul—the departing consul—said.

"*Hai.*" Jiro yawned and stretched. "I'm ready." Was he? He was more ready to leave Honolulu if he could than to face the returning Americans. He supposed that made him ready enough.

The streets of Honolulu were dark and empty, but far from quiet. Off to the west, the battle for Pearl Harbor still raged. By all the signs, fighting was getting closer to the city. If that submarine didn't come in now, it would never have another chance. Jiro could plainly see that. The Japanese occupation was finished. He sighed. He wished things had turned out different. Even if he wasn't here to hear it, Hiroshi and Kenzo would be saying, *I told you so.*

Barricades and roadblocks slowed the journey down to the harbor. The special naval landing forces who manned them were alert, even jumpy. But Consul Kita talked his way past them every time.

Other little parties made their way to the harbor, too. Some of them were Japanese, others Hawaiians and even *haoles* who'd gone along with the new regime. They had a good notion of what they could expect when American rule returned. But the king and queen were staying behind. Yes, they were brave. Did they have any common sense?

He stared out past Sand Island, which helped protect the approaches to Honolulu's harbor. The Americans hadn't landed there yet; they probably hadn't thought they needed to. A Japanese garrison still held the place. If U.S.

troops had taken the island, the sub would have had a much harder time getting in—and getting out again afterwards.

Off to the west, tracers—American red and orange and Japanese blue—made a fireworks display against the night. They shed enough light to let Jiro see everyone else looked as worried as he felt. One of the Japanese, a bureaucrat in a civilian suit, said, "Where is the submarine?"

Not five minutes later, like a broaching whale but ever so much bigger, it surfaced by the pier. A hatch came open at the top of the conning tower. A moment later, several people exclaimed in disgust. Jiro didn't, but he came close. The air that wafted out of the hatch was as foul as any he'd ever smelled, and fishermen knew everything there was to know about stinks. Too many people too close together for too long, foul heads, and sour food all went into the mix. So did the stink of oil and several other things he couldn't name right away. He wondered how the sailors stood it, then decided they had to be so used to it, they didn't even notice it any more.

An officer popped out of the hatch. "Is everyone here?" he called. "We can't wait for stragglers, not if we want to get out in one piece."

"The King and Queen of Hawaii are not coming," Consul Kita said. "They have refused our invitations."

"It's their funeral," the officer said. Jiro thought that was likely true. The officer climbed out of the hatch. Sailors followed him and laid a gangplank from the pier to the sub's iron hull. The couple of dozen escapees came aboard. A sailor guided them to the ladder up to the conning tower. Another ladder led down into the dark, smelly bowels of the submarine. As people started down that ladder, the officer took their names. Nagao Kita vouched for Jiro. "Oh, yes." The officer nodded. "When we were surfaced, I would pick up his broadcasts myself. Good man."

"*Arigato,*" Jiro said shyly.

"*Do itashimashite,*" the officer answered. After the last person came aboard, he asked, "Where is Commander Genda? He's supposed to be here, too." When no one answered, the man muttered, "*Zakennayo!* The order for his recall comes from Admiral Yamamoto, no less. Well, we're not going to wait, no matter what."

Only dim orange lamps lit up the inside of the submarine. Pipes and wires ran overhead; even short men like Jiro had to duck all the time. Machinery was everywhere—above, below, and to either side. Whatever space existed for people seemed an afterthought.

The hatch clanged shut. The officer dogged it. He came down the internal ladder, his shoes clattering. He gave a series of crisp orders. The sub backed away from the pier and then went under, air bubbling out of the buoyancy tanks and water sloshing in. Slowly—Jiro gradually realized everything underwater happened slowly—it turned and started out the channel by which it had entered the harbor.

He sighed with mingled pleasure and disappointment. On the way home at last!

MINORU GENDA HAD NEVER IMAGINED he would disobey an order from Admiral Yamamoto. He looked to the commander-in-chief of the Combined Fleet as an example, a mentor, a friend. Yet the Japanese submarine had presumably come and presumably gone. Assorted dignitaries were presumably aboard the boat. He remained somewhere between Honolulu and Pearl Harbor, doing everything he could to hold back the advancing Americans.

Cynthia Laanui had nothing to do with it.

So Genda told himself, and believed he told himself the truth. The Queen of Hawaii made a wonderful diversion. He liked her more as a person than he'd thought he would, too. But none of that was reason enough to throw away his naval career.

Hawaii was.

This invasion had been Genda's idea from the beginning. He'd proposed to Yamamoto the notion of following up the air strike with ground troops. Only with Hawaii under the Rising Sun, he'd said, could it serve as Japan's shield rather than America's outstretched arm. He'd persuaded Yamamoto. Yamamoto had persuaded the Army—a harder job, since the conquest of Malaya and the Dutch East Indies and their vital resources had to move more slowly. But Yamamoto made the generals believe Japan had a better chance of keeping her conquests if she held Hawaii.

For close to two years, Hawaii had done what it was supposed to do. With a Japanese garrison here, the USA had to fight the Pacific war from its own West Coast. Its reach wasn't long enough to do Japan much harm from there.

Now, though . . . Now Hawaii was falling back into U.S. hands. Genda was no fool, but no blind optimist, either. He knew the signs of defeat when he saw them, and he saw them now. The fall of Pearl Harbor was perhaps the next to last nail in the coffin.

And if he took credit for the victory of 1941, how could he not shoulder blame for the defeat of 1943? To duck it would make him into a liar, and he refused to lie to himself. He intended to atone in his own person for his plan's failure. He thought Yamamoto would understand.

He had an Arisaka some soldier or naval landing force man would never need again. He wished he had a uniform that gave better camouflage than his Navy whites. By now, the whites had so many dirt and grass stains, they hid him better than they had a couple of days earlier. He wasn't the only man in whites to form a part of the Japanese skirmish line. That made him feel better. He wasn't the only officer determined to make the Yankees pay for everything they got.

The enemy skirmish line was a couple of hundred meters away. The Americans weren't pushing forward right this minute. Every so often, they would fire a few rifle shots or a burst from a machine gun or a Browning Automatic Rifle to discourage the Japanese from attacking. The men on Genda's side would do the same.

Genda didn't think his countrymen *could* attack. They were a motley mix of Army and Navy men. An Army captain seemed to be in local command. Genda outranked him, but didn't try to throw his weight around. The Army officer sounded capable, while he himself knew as much about infantry combat as he did about Paris fashions. He was learning fast, though.

As for the Americans . . . By all the signs, they were waiting till they built up overwhelming force. Then they would hit the Japanese line somewhere and pour through. The defenders would have the choice of dying where they stood or falling back to try to stop the enemy somewhere else. Genda had already seen the Yankees do that once. They didn't take many chances. If he'd enjoyed all their matériel, he wouldn't have taken many chances, either.

A senior private squatted in the foxhole along with Genda. He was filthy and weary, but managed a smile of sorts when he noticed Genda's eye on him. "Hard work, sir," he said wryly.

"*Hai.*" Genda nodded. In a mess like this, he worried less about rank than he would have otherwise. He said, "You look like you've done your share of hard work and then some."

"Could be, sir," the soldier answered. "I started up at the north coast—and here I am."

That was something unusual. Most Japanese soldiers who'd met the Americans on the invasion beaches were dead. Genda knew the Army preferred dying in place to retreating. Keeping his voice carefully neutral, he said, "You must have seen a lot of fighting. How did that happen, Senior Private, ah . . . ?"

"My name is Furusawa, sir." The soldier showed no reluctance to give it. He didn't seem to feel he'd done anything wrong. And he explained why: "I found all my superiors killed around me. That left me free to use my own judgment. I thought I would be more use to the Emperor killing as many Americans as I could than throwing my life away to no good purpose." By the way he eyed Genda, anyone who presumed to disagree with him would be sorry.

But Genda didn't disagree. "And have you done that?" he asked.

"Sir, I have," the soldier answered. His rifle—an American Springfield—had plainly seen a lot of use, but it was clean and in good condition. Seeing Genda's glance toward the weapon, Furusawa went on, "My unit's barracks in Honolulu were bombed, and we lost our Arisakas."

"How do you like the American piece?" Genda asked.

"It's a little heavy, sir, but not too bad," Furusawa said. "And it fires a larger-caliber round than an Arisaka, so it's got more stopping power. I do like that."

Like the rest of what Senior Private Furusawa had to say, that was more clearly reasoned than Genda would have looked for from a lowly enlisted man. And, while Furusawa's accent said he came from somewhere in the south—down by Hiroshima, perhaps—he also sounded better educated than the farmers and fishermen who made up a large part of the population there.

"Why are you only a senior private?" Genda asked, by which he meant, *Why do you talk the way you do? Why do you think the way you do?*

The younger man understood what he didn't say, which showed Furusawa *did* think that way. With a crooked smile, he replied, "Well, sir, for one thing, I was a pretty new conscript when we came here, and there weren't a lot of promotions after that. And my father is a druggist. That sort of made me a white crow to a lot of the country boys in my regiment." He echoed Genda's thought there, and continued, "Complaining wouldn't have done me much good. And keeping me down made some sense, too, because the others might not have followed me the way they would have with someone else."

Genda wondered if he himself could have spoken so dispassionately about being passed over for a promotion he obviously deserved. He doubted it. "What do you think will happen now?" he asked.

"That depends, sir. You'd know better than I do—has the Navy got enough ships and planes to beat the Americans and drive them away?"

"No." Genda spoke without hesitation.

Senior Private Furusawa shrugged. He didn't seem very surprised. "Well, in that case we'll just have to give it our best shot, won't we?" He shrugged again. "Karma, *neh*?"

He could speak indirectly at least as well as Genda. What he meant was, *We're all going to die here, and we can't do a damn thing about it.* Genda thought about that, but not for long. He didn't need long. He sighed, nodded, and said, *"Hai."*

YASUO FURUSAWA KNEW HE OUGHT TO GET AWAY from Commander Genda. The naval officer knew he'd fallen back from the north instead of senselessly charging and throwing his life away. That made Genda dangerous to him as the Japanese were driven back into Honolulu. If the officer wanted to make an example of someone, he had a nice, juicy target. And sticking around Genda endangered Furusawa in another way, too. The Navy man was a greenhorn at infantry combat. His white uniform only made things worse. He drew bullets as well as he could have without painting a target on his chest. And bullets meant for him could all too easily find someone nearby instead.

But Furusawa stayed by him. Before long, he found himself Genda's unofficial aide and orderly. Genda, he thought, was the smartest man he'd ever met. And the officer didn't seem to think he was a *baka yaro* himself. That made Furusawa proud. Right now, pride was about all any Japanese had left.

He shook his head. Japanese soldiers, or most of them, had a contempt for death the Americans couldn't begin to match. Oh, the Yankees were brave enough. He'd seen that in the first invasion, and he saw it again now. But he could not imagine an American rushing out against a tank with a flaming bottle of gasoline and smashing it down on the cooling louvers above the engine. The Japanese who did that must have known he couldn't get back to cover alive. And he didn't; the Americans shot him before he made even three steps. But their snorting mechanical monster went up in flames, and the Japanese picked off the crewmen bailing out. Without the tank, the enemy attack bogged down.

Could I do that? Furusawa wondered. His long retreat from the north left him with doubts about himself and about his courage. He didn't think he was afraid to die if his death meant something. The death of that soldier with the Molotov cocktail certainly had. He'd cost the Americans a tank and five men.

That was one side of the coin. The other side was, losing that tank and those five men wouldn't cost the USA the battle. Honolulu *would* fall. Hawaii *would* go back under the Stars and Stripes. Nobody but a blind man could believe anything else.

Well, in that case, why don't we throw down our rifles and throw up our hands and surrender? But Furusawa shook his head. No less than any other Japanese, he believed surrender the ultimate disgrace. And he didn't want to spread his own disgrace and shame to his family back in the home islands.

Besides, some of the men in charge of Honolulu might have been blind. If they didn't think they could throw the Americans back, you wouldn't know it to listen to them. The garrison commander was a Navy captain—in Army ranks, he counted as a colonel—named Iwabuchi.

"We can do it!" he shouted to anyone who would listen. "We will do it! The white men have no stomach for blood! Well, before long we will drown them in an ocean of it!"

Furusawa remembered him drilling his special naval landing forces before the Americans landed. He'd been just as fanatical then. He'd sounded like a screaming madman, as a matter of fact, and he still did. But he did more than just scream. Furusawa wouldn't have wanted to attack Honolulu. Artillery hid inside buildings here. Machine guns had elaborately interlocking fields of fire. If you took out one nest, you exposed yourself to fire from two or three others.

The only thing Captain Iwabuchi hadn't worried about in Honolulu was its civilians. If they starved, if they got shot, if they got blown to pieces—well, so what? And if a fighting man wanted a woman for a little fun before he went back to his foxhole—again, so what?

You knew what kind of screams those were when you heard them. They sounded different from the ones that came from wounded people: they held horror as well as pain. Commander Genda clucked in distress. "This is not a good way to fight a war," he said.

"Sir, this is what the Army did in Nanking, too," Furusawa said. "I hadn't been conscripted yet, but the veterans in my regiment would talk about it sometimes." Most of them had sounded pleased with themselves, too. He didn't tell Genda that.

"But American propaganda will have a field day," the Navy man said. "The Greater East Asia Co-Prosperity Sphere is supposed to protect Asia from Western imperialism. Now who will protect Asia from Japanese imperialism?"

He put his life in Furusawa's hands when he said something like that. If the senior private blabbed to someone like Iwabuchi . . . Well, one more time, so what? Genda would die a little sooner than he might otherwise, and perhaps a little more painfully. Given the perversity of war, though, neither of those was certain. None of the Japanese defenders was likely to get out of this any which way.

The Americans probed with infantry. They got a bloody nose and pulled back. Captain Iwabuchi was jubilant. "They can't stand up to us!" he shouted. "If they come again, we'll smash them again!"

Commander Genda sounded less gleeful. "They aren't done," he said to Furusawa. "They're putting a rock in their fist, that's all."

"A rock, sir?" The senior private didn't follow him for a moment.

"You'll see," Genda answered.

About fifteen minutes later, Furusawa did. American artillery started pounding the Japanese front-line positions. Furusawa had never imagined so many guns all going off at once. His own forces were not so lavishly provided with cannon. Huddling in a ball to make as small a target as he could, he felt as if the end of the world had come.

When the barrage lifted, the Americans surged forward again. Furusawa was too dazed to shoot for a little while, but Japanese machine guns opened up on the Yankees again. He was amazed he'd lived through the shelling, and even more amazed anyone else had. The automatic-weapons fire drove the Americans back again in front of his foxhole, but they broke through farther north.

"What do we do, sir?" he asked Commander Genda. "If we stay here, they'll outflank us and cut us off."

"*Hai,*" Genda answered. Any Army officer would have ordered a fight to the death where they were. Furusawa was as sure of that as he was of his own name. After a moment's thought, Genda said, "We fall back. It doesn't look like we can do much more where we are, does it?"

"Not to me, sir," Furusawa said in surprise.

To his even greater surprise, Genda smiled at him. "Well, you know more about it than I do." They fell back, passing the wreckage of a machine-gun nest that hadn't survived the barrage. Furusawa wondered if the Army would have done better with people like Genda in charge. He feared he'd never know.

XIV

WHY THIS IS HELL, NOR AM I OUT OF IT. KENZO TAKAHASHI REMEMBERED THE line from an English Lit class. It sounded like Shakespeare, but he didn't think it was. Who, then? He couldn't remember. Miss Simpson wouldn't have approved of that at all. If Miss Simpson was still alive, though, she was just as busy trying not to get blown up as Kenzo was.

He and Hiroshi didn't know where their father was. He'd headed for the Japanese consulate, and he'd never come back. Hiroshi and Kenzo both went looking for him, and neither one had any luck. Kenzo even went to the consulate himself. The guards let him in when he told them whose son he was, but nobody inside would tell him anything. Nobody of very high rank seemed to be there. He wondered where the consul and the chancellor and the other big shots were. Wherever it was, would they have taken Dad with them? Kenzo had trouble believing it.

When the big American push started, shells crashed into the refugee camp where he and his brother and their father had stayed since their apartment—and Kenzo and Hiroshi's mother—burned in the Japanese attack on Honolulu. Japanese positions were nearby, so Kenzo could see why the Americans struck. Seeing why did nothing to ease the horror.

He and Hiroshi got out unhurt. That would do for a miracle till God decide to dole out a bigger one somewhere else. He'd seen bad things when the Japanese took Honolulu. He hadn't seen the worst, because the Americans chose to surrender rather than let the worst happen to the civilians in the city.

The Japanese didn't care about civilians. They would fight as long as they had cartridges, and with bayonets after that.

And whether the Americans wanted to bring hell down on the civilians of Honolulu or not, what else were they going to do to get rid of the Japanese soldiers among them? Kenzo and Hiroshi stayed flat on their bellies all through the artillery barrage. They'd learned that much in the earlier round of fighting. It didn't always help, but it was their best hope.

Shrapnel tore through their tent and the ropes that held it up. It fell down on them, which frightened Kenzo worse than he was already—something he wouldn't have thought possible. Through the roars and crashes of exploding shells, he heard screams, some abruptly cut off.

When the shelling eased, he struggled free of the heavy canvas. The only words that came out of his mouth were, "Oh, Jesus Christ!"—something his missing father might have said. He could smell blood in the air. There lay a man gutted like an *ahi*—and there, a few feet away, lay most of his head.

Wounded men and women were worse than dead ones. They writhed and shrieked and moaned and bled and bled and bled. Kenzo bent to use a length of rope torn apart by shell fragments as a tourniquet for a woman who'd lost a big chunk of meat out of her leg below the knee. He hoped it would do her some good.

He was in the middle of that when someone shouted in Japanese: "Come on, give me a hand! Yes, you!" When he looked up, a soldier was leading Hiroshi away. The soldier had a stretcher, and needed Kenzo's brother to help him carry wounded. No doubt they would deal with soldiers first, civilians later if at all.

"Oh, Jesus Christ!" Kenzo said again. He couldn't stop them from grabbing his brother, not unless he wanted to get killed himself and probably get Hiroshi killed with him. The other trouble was, they were both too likely to get killed anyway. More American shells screamed in, some on the Japanese positions, some on the luckless refugee camp. More screams rose, many of them screams of despair. Kenzo hugged the ground next to the injured woman and hoped none of the fragments would bite him. He had no idea what else to do.

When the barrage eased, he asked the woman, "How are you?" She didn't answer. He took a look at her. A chunk of shrapnel had clipped off the top of her head. Her brains spilled out onto the dirt. Kenzo threw up. Then he spat again and again, trying to get the horrible taste out of his mouth. And then he staggered to his feet and stumbled away. Any place in the world had to be safer than where he was.

At first, his flight was blind. Before long, though, it had purpose: he headed for Elsie Sundberg's house. If anything happened to her . . . If anything happened to her, he didn't think he wanted to go on living. He'd been through a lot just then, and he was only twenty years old.

Getting to her house in eastern Honolulu was a nightmare in itself. He had to pass several checkpoints manned by special naval landing forces, and they would just as soon have shot civilians as looked at them. That was no exaggeration. Bodies lay in the street, blood pooled around them. Some of the women's skirts and dresses were hiked up. Kenzo bit his lip; the occupiers hadn't killed them right away.

Had he tried sneaking by, he was sure they would have put a bullet in him. Instead, he came up to each barricade and roadblock openly, calling, "I'm the Fisherman's son! I'm looking for my father!"

He hated using his father's collaboration in any way, but it got him by. And one of the men at a sandbagged machine-gun nest said, "Didn't he get out on the submarine the other night?"

"What submarine?" Kenzo asked—this was the first he'd heard of it.

"There was one," the landing-forces man said. Kenzo couldn't very well argue with him, because he didn't know there hadn't been one. The fellow went on, "I don't know whether your old man was on it or not, though. They don't tell guys like me stuff like that." He gestured. "Go ahead, buddy. I hope you find him. I always did like listening to him."

"Thank you," Kenzo said, wishing he hadn't heard that quite so often from Japanese military men. He could have done without the compliment. Would his father have got on a submarine—one probably bound for Japan? Muttering unhappily, Kenzo nodded to himself. His father would be able to see the jig was up here. And he must have been afraid of what the Americans would do to him when they came back. He likely had reason, too, even if he was a Japanese citizen. Collaborators would catch it.

Kenzo talked his way past another couple of Japanese strongpoints. The special naval landing forces and the soldiers they had with them seemed determined to hold on to Honolulu as long as they were still breathing and still had ammo. *God help the city,* Kenzo thought, not that God seemed to have paid much attention to Honolulu since December 7, 1941.

The fresh shell crater in the Sundbergs' front lawn made Kenzo gulp. One of the windows had only a few shards of glass in it. There was a fist-sized hole in the front door. Nobody answered when he knocked. He started to panic, but then quelled the alarm thudding through him. They'd built a hidey-hole under the house.

He tried the door. It swung open. He carefully closed it behind him, wanting things to look as normal as they could. Then he went to the closet that held the entrance to the foxhole. Sure enough, the rug over the trap door was askew.

If Elsie and her family were down there, they had to be panicking, hearing footsteps over their heads. Kenzo squatted down and rapped out *shave and a haircut—five cents* on the trap door. He didn't think any Japanese soldier would do that. When he tried to lift the trap, though, he found it was latched from below. That was smart.

He rapped again, calling, "You okay, Elsie?" Could she hear him through the floor? He called again, a little louder.

Something slid underneath him—the latch. He got off the trap door so it could go up. It did, about an inch. Elsie's voice floated out of the opening: "That you, Ken?"

"Yeah," he said, almost giddy with relief. "You okay?"

"We are now," she answered. "You gave us quite a turn there."

"Sorry," he said. "I figured I would, but it was too late by then."

"How about you?" Elsie asked.

"The Americans shelled the camp," he said bleakly. "There are machine-gun nests not far away, so they'll probably do it some more. Hank and I are okay so far. The Japanese dragooned him into being a stretcher-bearer, but he was all right last I saw him."

"What about your father?" Elsie knew where his worries lived, all right.

"I *think* he's on his way to Japan right now," Kenzo replied. "And if he is, that may be the best thing for all of us."

Elsie's mother spoke up: "If they're shelling the camp, you won't have anywhere to stay. Come down here with us."

"Are you sure?" he asked.

"Damn straight we're sure." That gruff male voice belonged to Mr. Sundberg, whom he hadn't met so often. "We owe you plenty, Ken. Maybe we can pay back a little. Come on—make it snappy."

Kenzo lifted the trap door high enough to get through it, then closed it over his own head. It was dark and gloomy under the house, and smelled of damp dirt. There'd been more digging since he last saw the shelter. Elsie squeezed his hand. "We just went down here yesterday," she said. "We've got water. We've got some food. We can last till it's over—I hope."

"And we've got a honey bucket over there in the corner, at the end of that trench." Mr. Sundberg chuckled hoarsely. "All the comforts of home."

Kenzo's nose had already noted the honey bucket. It was better than nothing. The whole setup was a lot better than staying out in the open. "Thanks," he said. That didn't go far enough. He tried again: "Thanks for looking at me and not seeing a Jap."

Elsie squeezed his hand again. Her mother said, "We'll sort that all out later. Let's see if we can live through this first." He couldn't remember the last time he'd heard such good advice.

REPLACEMENTS CAME UP TO FILL THE RANKS of Captain Braxton Bradford's company. Les Dillon looked at the new men joining his platoon with something less than delight. They were plainly just off the boat. They must have landed in the north, hopped on a truck to get down here—and now they'd go into the meat grinder. They were clean. They were clean-shaven. Their uniforms weren't filthy, and weren't out at the knees and elbows. The way the veterans looked and smelled and acted seemed to dismay them. They might have been in the company of so many wolves.

"Any of you guys ever seen combat before?" Les knew the answer would be no even before the new fish shook their heads. He sighed. Sheer ignorance was going to get a lot of them shot in the next few days. He couldn't tell them that straight out. What he said instead was, "Try and stick close to somebody who knows what the fuck he's doing. Shoot first and ask questions later. The Japs have had time to get ready for us, and they don't give up. We've got to make the damn bastards pay for what they've done to Hotel Street."

"Hotel Street, Sergeant?" a replacement asked.

Les rolled his eyes. The kid didn't even know. Wearily, Dillon said, "Best damn place in the world to get drunk and get laid. That give you the picture?" The young Marine nodded. He looked eager—*gung-ho*, people were calling it these days. Gung-ho was great if it kept you going forward. If you didn't pay enough attention to *where* you were going, though . . .

"Y'all listen up, hear me?" That was Captain Bradford. A Southern drawl often seemed to be the Marine Corps' second language. The company commander went on, "We are gonna go on through those houses and apartments in front of us, and we aren't gonna stop till we get to the rubble past 'em where the Japs bombed Honolulu a year and a half ago. We'll set up a perimeter on the edge of that zone and wait for the artillery and armor to soften up the way ahead. Questions, men?"

Nobody said anything. Les figured the new guys would keep going if they got half a chance. Marines were like that, grabbing as much as they could as fast as they could. The Army was more methodical. Dogfaces said the Marine way caused more casualties. Les thought there might be more at first, but not in the long run.

"You new men, keep your eyes open, hear?" Bradford added. "Damn Japs are better at camouflage than y'all ever reckoned anybody could be. Fuckers'll hide in a mailbox or under a doormat. Everybody watches out, everybody helps everybody else. Right?"

"Right, sir!" the Marines chorused. Les caught Dutch Wenzel's eye. The other platoon sergeant gave back a fractional nod. The replacements wouldn't know what to look for. Some of them would get educated in a hurry. Others—probably more—wouldn't stay in one piece long enough to have the chance.

Some of those houses and apartments and little shops up ahead were as innocent as they looked. Some held Jap riflemen or machine-gun positions. Japanese mortar crews would be waiting in the alleys and on the roofs. Les knew the Marines could clear them out. What the cost would be . . . That was the question.

A couple of bullets snapped past. Les was on the deck before he knew he'd thrown himself flat. It was just harassing fire, but it was from an Arisaka. He didn't believe in taking chances. Some of the new guys gave funny looks to him and the other Marines who'd flattened out. He didn't care. His mama hadn't raised him to take chances he didn't have to.

Machine guns, mortars, and some 105s opened up on the buildings ahead. Hellcats strafed them. By the time the barrage let up, they were smoking wreckage. Les wondered how anybody could tell them from the rubble farther east. He shrugged. He'd worry about that later, if at all.

"Boy, those Jap bastards must be dead meat now," a recruit said happily.

Les laughed, not that it was funny. "Yeah, and then you wake up," he said.

"They're waiting for us. You see one you think is dead, put a bullet in him. He's liable to be playing possum, waiting to shoot you in the back."

The replacement looked disbelieving. Les had neither time nor inclination to knock sense into his empty head. Captain Bradford yelled, "Forward!" and forward he went.

As usual, he ran hunched over, making himself the smallest possible target. He dodged like a halfback faking past tacklers. And the first piece of cover he saw—goddamn if it wasn't a bathtub, blown from Lord knows where—he dove behind.

Sure as hell, the shelling and strafing hadn't killed all the Japs. It hadn't even made enough of them keep their heads down. Arisakas and Springfields and Nambu machine guns opened up. Knee mortars started dropping their nasty little bombs among the Americans. So did bigger mortars farther back. Les hated mortars not only because the bombs could fall right into foxholes but also, and especially, because you couldn't hear them coming. One second, nothing. The next, your buddy was hamburger—or maybe you were.

Wounded men started screaming for medics. The Navy corpsmen who went in with Marines didn't wear Red Cross smocks and armbands or Red Crosses on their helmets. The Japs used them for target practice when they did. The medics carried carbines—sometimes rifles—too. In France in 1918, the Germans mostly played by the rules. As far as Les could see, there were no rules here. This was a very nasty war.

He snapped off a shot or two, then ran forward again. Several Marines were shooting at a ground-floor window from which machine-gun fire was coming. Les Dillon put a couple of rounds in there, too, to give the Japs inside something to think about. Two Marines crawled close enough to chuck grenades through the window. The machine gun promptly squeezed off a defiant burst. More grenades flew in. This time, the enemy gun stayed quiet.

Les ran for a doorway. Dutch Wenzel ran for one a couple of houses farther on. He stopped halfway there, yelped, and said, "Aw, shit!" His rifle fell to the pavement.

"What happened, Dutch?" Les called.

"Got one right through the hand," the other noncom answered. "Hurts like a son of a bitch. I never got shot before."

"Welcome to the club." Les wouldn't have joined if he had any choice. But an injury like Wenzel's . . . "Sounds like you got a million-dollar wound. You did your bit, it won't kill you, it'll probably heal good, and you're out of the fight for a while."

"Yeah, I already thought of that," Wenzel said. "But you know what? I'd sooner stay here with the rest of you guys. I feel like I'm getting thrown out of the game just after we went and scored six runs in the eighth."

"Stay there till we push forward some more," Les said. "Then you can get to the rear without worrying a sniper's gonna get you." *Without worrying so much,* he thought.

"Yes, Granny dear," Wenzel said. Les laughed. Like him, the other platoon sergeant was more used to giving orders than taking them.

Then the laughter died in his throat, because the door he was standing in front of opened. Had the Jap behind it been a soldier, Les would have died in the next instant. Instead, he was a skinny eight-year-old kid in ragged shorts. "Watcha doin', Mister?" he asked.

"Jesus!" Les exploded. "I almost shot you, you dumb little—" He broke off when he saw how skinny the kid was. Fumbling through the pouches on his belt, he found a K-ration can. "Here. This is chopped ham, I think. Bet you like it a hell of a lot better'n I do."

The kid's eyes got big as gumdrops. "Wow!" he breathed, as if Les had just given him the Hope Diamond. "Thanks, Mister!" He disappeared, yelling, "Mom! Mom! Guess what I got!"

You almost got a .30-caliber round in the teeth, that's what. Les' heart still thuttered. All kinds of bad things happened during a war. Even so, how could you make yourself forget you shot a little kid? Les knew he had lots of things to worry about, but that, thank God, wasn't one of them.

No MORE TAKING A SAILBOARD OUT from Waikiki Beach. The Japs had put down barbed wire and machine-gun nests and mines. Years after they were gone, some damnfool tourist would probably blow his foot off on one everybody missed till he found it the hard way.

Oscar van der Kirk wasn't especially worried about some imaginary tourist. He just didn't want to blow off his own foot crossing Waikiki Beach. He did want to live long enough to have the chance to cross it again.

Because of the fish he'd brought home, Oahu's hunger hadn't pinched him and Susie as much as it had most people. Now they had to do without, and it hurt. And they had Charlie Kaapu with them, so it hurt even more.

The only way to get food now was to go out and work. The only work was helping the Japs build more roadblocks and barricades and pillboxes to hold back the U.S. Marines and Army. Oscar thought it was a lot of work for precious little rice. Charlie started going out with him after a few days. Oscar wondered if he was strong enough to do the hauling and lifting, but he took them in stride.

"No *huhu*," he said when he and Oscar didn't happen to be close to any Japs. "Up in the goddamn tunnel, I did twice this much on a quarter the food. Everybody did."

Remembering what he'd looked like when he came out of the Kalihi Valley, Oscar believed him. He did ask, "How?"

"They'd kill you if you didn't," Charlie answered. "That whole setup was made to kill people. Either the work would do you in or the guards would. I hope our guys gutshoot every one of those bastards. They deserve it." He was normally an easygoing fellow. Not here. Not now. He meant every word of it.

But he knew how to bow and smile at the Japanese riflemen and machine gunners when he got anywhere near them. Oscar knew how to do that, too, but Charlie'd had the advanced course. Oscar could satisfy the Japs. Charlie could make them smile back and even laugh.

Sometimes he would cuss them in friendly tones while he smiled. He took his life in his hands every time he did it: some of the Japs had picked up bits and pieces of English. Oscar kept trying to warn him. And Charlie would say, "Yeah, Oscar. Sure, Oscar," and he'd go right on doing it. It was as if he had to take his revenge on them no matter what it cost him.

Off to the west, the battle for Honolulu ground on. The Americans had the artillery. They had the tanks. They had the airplanes. They even brought Navy ships off the south coast of Oahu, to blast the city with big guns. All the Japs had were the rubble and their weapons and their stubborn courage. Those were plenty to make the American reconquest a long, slow, bloody job.

"I hope they all die," Charlie said with a big grin on his face. "I hope they all die slow, and I hope they hurt all the time while they're doing it. Yes, you, too, Sergeant-*san*," he added to a Japanese noncom who walked by after fiddling with the sight on a machine gun. Hearing only the title of respect, the sergeant grinned and returned Charlie's bow.

"Ohhh, Charlie," Oscar said.

"Right, Oscar," Charlie said, and Oscar shut up.

So far, Waikiki had been only at the edges of the fight. A few overs from the U.S. bombardment of the rest of Honolulu came down there. The big raid on the POW camp in Kapiolani Park had been just east of the main part of Waikiki. Oscar began to hope his district would come through without much damage.

Artillery didn't shatter that hope. Planes from one of the carriers somewhere out in the Pacific did. In the abstract, Oscar didn't suppose he could blame the pilots. They wanted to soften up the Japs so that, when the American foot sloggers finally ground this far east, they wouldn't have to work so hard.

Oscar had got used to the roar of planes overhead. He'd even got used to the deeper tones of the new U.S. aircraft. They made Japanese aircraft sound like flying sewing machines. But the sound of dive bombers falling out of the sky straight toward him was new and altogether terrifying.

The Japs reacted before he could. Some of them dove for cover. Others either manned their machine guns and blazed away at the dive bombers or fired their rifles at them. Oscar could admire that kind of bravery without wanting to imitate it.

"Get down, you damn fool!" Charlie Kaapu yelled at him as the first bomb screamed down.

"Huh?" Oscar said brilliantly. Looking back, he had to admit it wasn't his finest hour. Charlie used the handle of his shovel to knock Oscar's legs out from under him.

Before Oscar could even squawk, the bomb hit. Blast sucked the air out of his lungs. Had the bomb burst a little closer, it would have torn them to pieces from the inside out so he drowned in his own blood. Chunks of casing screeched through the air, some of them not nearly far enough over his head.

And that bomb was only the first of eight or ten. Somebody in the Bible had wrestled with God and prevailed. Oscar felt as if he were wrestling with God and getting the crap slammed out of him. He got bounced and slapped around, and ended up all bruised and battered. He stopped complaining, even to himself, when he fetched up against the Japanese sergeant's head. The man's body was nowhere in sight. Oscar almost lost his meager breakfast.

The work he and Charlie and the rest of the Japs' forced laborers had done was smashed to hell and gone. So were a lot of Japanese soldiers and special naval landing force troops and luckless locals dragooned into working for them. And the dive bombers were only the opening act of the show. As soon as they roared away, fighters swooped low and started spraying the landscape with bullets.

Oscar watched a Jap hit by a burst literally get cut in half. The worst part was, the man's top half didn't die right away. Even though blood spilled from it—and from the rest of him—like water from a hose, he yammered something in his own language, tried to lever himself upright, and even looked around for the rifle he'd dropped. Only after most of a dreadful minute did the expression drain from his face. He slumped over again, finally seeming to realize he was dead.

"Jesus!" Oscar turned away, clapping a hand to his mouth. He'd already seen a lot of things he never wanted to see again. That one, though . . . That one topped the list.

Charlie Kaapu watched the Jap with a face that might have been carved from the basalt underlying the islands. "Serves him right," he said.

"But—" Oscar didn't have time for any more than that. Another fighter roared in, its machine guns winking fire. He folded himself into the smallest ball he could and prayed he didn't get chewed up the way the Jap had. Charlie Kaapu lay on the ground beside him, also doing his best to imitate a sowbug.

Bursts of fire from Japanese machine-gun nests answered the hail of lead from the sky. The Japs had nerve, even if Oscar thought they were short on brains. Then one of the American planes slammed into the ground and went up in a high-octane fireball. The Japs yelled like men possessed. Oscar had a hard time blaming them, too. They'd just proved they *could* hit back.

Both at the start of the Japanese invasion of Hawaii and now at the end of their tenure here, his own countrymen came closer to killing him than the Japs ever had. He waited for those fighters to come back and shoot up some more Japanese positions—positions, he hoped, a little farther away from him.

"Shit!" Joe Crosetti exclaimed when another Hellcat crashed and exploded in flames in Waikiki. He knew that could happen to him, too. He hated being reminded. Somebody wasn't going home to his mom and dad and brothers and sisters—maybe to his wife and kid. Some clerk in the War Department—some bastard thousands of miles away from the fighting and snug as a bug in a rug—would have to send out a Deeply Regrets telegram. And some family's life would turn upside down.

As Joe's thumb found the firing button and he raked the Japs below with .50-caliber slugs, he never once thought that they had moms and dads and brothers and sisters and maybe wives and kids, too. They were just . . . the enemy to him. They weren't people, the way the guys on his own side were.

And they were still doing their goddamnedest to kill him. Their pale, cold-looking tracers spat from machine guns down on the ground and probed for his fighter, trying to knock him out of the sky like that poor luckless son of a bitch who'd just bought the farm. Something clanged into the Hellcat. As always, Joe quickly scanned the instruments. Everything looked okay. The engine kept running. He reached out and patted the side of the cockpit. "Attababy!" he told the plane. They weren't just whistling *Dixie* when they said a Hellcat could take it.

Down on the ground, the Japs were sure taking it. More fires than the one from that other plane's funeral pyre were rising from Waikiki. *See how you like it, you bastards,* Joe thought. He hoped there weren't too many civilians down there. If there were, it was their tough luck. They were almost as abstract to him as the enemy. He wished the Japs would just throw in the sponge, the way some lousy pug's handlers would after Joe Louis beat the snot out of their pride and joy.

Sometimes, though, a pug stayed in there and went toe-to-toe with the champ till he got KO'ed. If the Japs wanted to do that against the USA, by God, they'd get carried out of the ring, too. Yeah, they'd landed a sucker punch at the start of the fight, but you only got one of those. And when you were up against the heavyweight champion of the world, one wasn't enough.

Joe sprayed Waikiki with bullets as big as his thumb till his guns ran dry. Then he got on the radio to his squadron leader: "Going home for more ammo."

"Roger that," the other pilot answered. "We'll keep 'em busy while you're otherwise occupied, Admiral."

"Out," Joe said with a snort. Admiral! He still aspired to a lieutenant, j.g.'s, stripe and a half on his sleeve.

A few more tracers came up at him as he flew north: Japanese holdouts still doing their damnedest to make trouble. They still held a few pockets in central Oahu where they'd been encircled and bypassed. Sooner or later, soldiers and Navy fliers would clean out those pockets. It wasn't as if the Japs could retreat to the jungle here and fight a long guerrilla war. Oahu had plenty of jungles. The only trouble, from what Joe's briefings said, was that you'd starve if you tried playing Tarzan in them.

Five minutes after he left Waikiki behind, he was out over the ocean again. Unless you flew over Oahu, you didn't realize what a small island it was. He waggled his wings as he flew past the destroyers and cruisers and battleships still firing from the north. Some of them had come around the island to hit targets near Pearl Harbor and Honolulu.

None of the ships shot at him. None of them had shot at that crazy Jap who crashed his Zero into the *Bunker Hill,* either. Bastard had extracted a high price for his worthless neck, too. He'd hurt that baby flattop along with the big fleet carrier.

Combat air patrol came by to give Joe a look-see. They hadn't done it soon enough with that Jap. Joe, of course, was harmless, at least to U.S. ships. He and the CAP planes exchanged more wing waggles and some raunchy banter over the radio. Then he flew on toward his carrier.

He still didn't like carrier landings. He didn't know a single pilot who did. He suspected there was no such animal. Like them or not, he did exactly what the nice gentleman with the wigwag flags told him to do. It worked: the landing officer didn't wave him off. When the flags dropped, so did Joe's Hellcat. His teeth clicked together as the wheels hit the flight deck. The tailhook caught. The fighter jerked to a stop.

Joe shoved back the canopy and scrambled out of the cockpit. He ran for the island as soon as his feet hit the deck planking. The faster you got away from the plane, the better off you were. The briefings had that one right. As if Joe needed the reminder, the Jap suicide pilot drove home that lesson.

"Over Waikiki, Crosetti?" the briefing officer said when Joe reported.

"Yes, sir."

The other officer—a regular and an older man—smiled. "Not the way you expected to get there, I bet."

"Sir, till the war started, I never figured I'd get there at all," Joe answered.

"Well, since you did, suppose you tell me what you saw," the briefing officer said.

"Aye aye, sir," Joe said, and he did.

AT BREAKFAST ONE MORNING on the hospital ship, Fletch Armitage realized he was making progress. Breakfast, like most breakfasts on the *Benevolence,* was scrambled powdered eggs, fried Spam, and hash browns. Nothing was wrong with the hash browns. They had crunch over greasy softness, and you could pour on the salt till they tasted just the way they were supposed to.

The powdered eggs and Spam, on the other hand . . . Up till that morning, Fletch had shoveled them into his face with reckless abandon, like a man coming back from the ragged edge of starvation. He damn well was a man coming back from the ragged edge of starvation, and he wanted to claw back from that edge just as fast as he could. He made a pig of himself at lunch and dinner and snacks in between times, too.

Some of the rescued POWs had eaten themselves right into stomach trouble. The only trouble Fletch had was gaining weight back fast enough to suit him.

This particular morning, he took a big gulp of coffee with plenty of cream (well, condensed milk) and sugar and tore into breakfast. He ate a mouthful of Spam and eggs, then paused with the oddest expression on his face. "You know what?" he said to the guy next to him in the galley.

"No," the other ex-prisoner said. "What?"

"These eggs and this meat—they're really lousy." Fletch knew he sounded astonished. He had all the food he wanted. Now he'd got to the point where he didn't just want food. He wanted *good* food. Wanting it on a hospital ship was probably optimistic, but even so. . . .

"You're right." The other man sounded as astonished as Fletch had. "I didn't even notice up till now."

"Neither did I," Fletch said. The guy to his left was just as skinny as he was. Some of the poor bastards from Kapiolani Park had actually starved to death before the U.S. Navy could throw enough food into them to keep them going. Fletch hadn't been in that boat, but he'd been in the one tied up right next to it.

"Take your plate, sir?" a Filipino mess steward asked. Fletch nodded. Good, bad, or indifferent, every scrap of food in front of him had vanished. He wondered if he would ever leave anything uneaten again. The way he felt now, he wouldn't bet on it.

As the steward also took the other former prisoner's plate, Fletch asked, "Any chance of getting fresh eggs and real ham around here?"

"Yeah," the other former POW said. Several other scrawny men nodded.

The Filipino beamed at them like a proud mother just after Junior's first steps. "Oh, my friends!" he said. "You feel better! I am so happy for you!"

"Does that mean we don't get the fancy grub?" asked the guy on Fletch's left.

"Probably," the mess steward answered, not beaming so much now. "Two thousand miles from the mainland, remember. You eat better than other people out here."

"We've earned it," Fletch said. He didn't quite feel as if he were made of pipe cleaners any more. He'd graduated to pencils—gnarled, knotty pencils, but pencils all the same. He wondered what would come next in his gradual reinflation.

What came next that day was an examination by one of the doctors on the *Benevolence*. Fletch got weighed. He had his blood pressure taken. The sawbones looked pleased. "You're getting there, Captain."

"I'm just a lieutenant," Fletch said.

"Nope." The doctor shook his head. "If you weren't a POW, you would've got the promotion by now. And so—you did."

"Thanks, Doc!" Fletch would rather have heard it from somebody besides an M.D., but he wasn't going to complain any which way. Instead of complaining, he asked, "When can I go ashore?"

"When we decide you're strong enough, and when it seems safe," the doctor answered. "I know you're feeling better—you were one of the men bitching about chow this morning, weren't you? That's a good sign. But you're not fit for active duty yet, and Oahu's no place for tourists right this minute."

"I understand that," Fletch said. "My wife's there, though—if she's still alive, anyway." He didn't say anything about the divorce that had been in progress. It wasn't final when the fighting started. Jane wouldn't have kept on with it since then . . . would she?

He'd got the doctor's attention. "Oh," the other man said. "We *are* letting men in that situation onto the island. It won't happen tomorrow, though, or the day after. You'll have some hoops to jump through as far as the paperwork goes."

"Let me at 'em!" Fletch said. "After what I went through with the Japs, I'll never worry about that kind of crap again."

"You're not the first guy I've heard that from, either," the doctor said. "One way or another, it'll get sorted out. In the meantime, try to be patient—and the breakfasts are still good for you, even if they aren't the most exciting thing in the world." All of that was undoubtedly good advice, which didn't make Fletch like it one bit better.

AFTER THE JAPS TOOK WAHIAWA, they set up a community kitchen in the elementary school to share what little there was to eat. The U.S. Army troops who retook the town kept the kitchen going. These days, it doled out K-rations and C-rations and big, tasteless chocolate bars called D-rations. The joke was that if you ate one of those, it was in you for the D-ration.

Jane Armitage was not inclined to be fussy about what kind of food she got. There was plenty of it: the only thing that mattered to her. No, one more—she didn't have to give herself to Japanese soldiers if she wanted to go on eating (to say nothing of breathing).

No one had thrown her time in the brothel in her face—yet. She didn't think any of the other women had had trouble with it, either. If the Japs dragged you in there, kept you in there with bars on the windows, and screwed you whenever they felt like it, you pretty plainly weren't collaborating. That meant you got to stand in line behind the people who damn well were.

Several women collecting their rations had hair clipped down to stubble to show what they were. They'd collaborated with the occupiers on their backs, but they'd done it for fun or for advantage, not because they had to. Most of them were local Japanese—most, but not all. One was a tall redhead who had been—maybe still was—married to somebody from Fletch's old unit. She got her food and sat as far away from everybody else as she could. Her belly bulged. The baby was due any day now. Jane would have bet anything in the world that it wouldn't have red hair.

But women who'd gone to bed with Japanese soldiers were only the small change of collaboration. Everybody stared when Yosh Nakayama came into the community kitchen. The nursery man stolidly collected his ration tins, sat down not far from Jane, and started to eat. He'd translated for Major Hirabayashi and relayed the Japanese commandant's orders to the rest of Wahiawa. But he'd also done everything he could to get crops in the ground when Oahu was hungriest, and nobody'd ever claimed he'd informed on people. Jane knew he'd done what he could to keep her out of the brothel, though she'd been too dumb to realize it till too late. Some wanted to string him up. Others thought he deserved a medal. He went on about his business, there in the eye of the storm. It wasn't as if he could hop in a plane and fly off to Tokyo.

There had been informers. Some of them had slipped out of Wahiawa before the U.S. Army came in. Jane hoped they were getting the shit bombed out of them in Honolulu. That would start to give them what they deserved. And some had tried to stay and brazen it out. Again, a lot of those were local Japanese who'd bet on the wrong horse. You could understand them even if you despised them.

But Smiling Sammy Little, who had the biggest used-car dealership in Wahiawa, was as Anglo-Saxon as George Washington. And he was in the guardhouse. He'd rolled over and wagged his tail for the Japs. They were on top, and he'd wanted to stay near the top: it seemed as simple as that. Figuring out how many people were dead because of his toadying wasn't so simple. Jane hoped he'd get it in the neck.

Somebody lit a cigarette. Jane's nostrils twitched. Along with almost all the other smokers on Oahu, she'd had to lose the habit during the Japanese occupation. The soldiers' rations included little packs of cigarettes. Jane had smoked a few. They still made her dizzy and nauseated, the way they had when she was just learning how. She intended to keep at it till it seemed natural again.

As soon as she was done eating, she went back to her apartment. As long as she stayed in there with the door locked, things had a harder time getting at her. She started to head for the bathroom, then checked herself. She'd taken endless showers. They didn't wash away the memory of all the hands that had groped her. She didn't know how many times she'd douched with salt water. That couldn't make her forget all the times she'd had to open her legs for the Japs. And, now that she had toothpaste again, she also brushed her teeth over and over. She remembered how they'd made her get down on her knees even so.

She was going to remember, going to have to deal with, all that the rest of her life. She was damned if she could see how. Maybe she was just damned, period. The Japs hadn't cared what they did to her. All they'd wanted was a few minutes of fun each. If that left her ruined for the rest of her days, so what?

She snorted. They hadn't cared about the rest of her days, not even a little bit. They'd intended to use her, use her up, and then knock her over the head. Who was she kidding? The only thing that had saved her was the U.S. reinvasion.

Slowly, she made herself straighten up and peer into the mirror over the sink. She still looked like death warmed over. But if she gave in to despair, didn't the Japs win a battle inside her head? It felt that way.

Living well is the best revenge. That held a lot of truth. She wasn't what she would have been if the Japs had left her alone, and that was a damn shame. But she wasn't a slut or a basket case just because they'd done their goddamnedest to turn her into one. And if anybody didn't like it . . . "Tough shit," she muttered. She'd never liked the way Fletch swore. Maybe now she understood it a little better than she had when they were married.

She hoped Fletch was still alive. After what she'd seen, and after the stories soldiers told about what the Japs had done at the POW camp up by Opana, she knew the odds weren't the best. She hoped anyhow. She might not have wanted to stay married to him. She didn't hate him, though, and he'd done what he could for the country.

And when he found out what the Japs had made her do, he'd probably want to spit in her eye. She sighed, wishing some of the K-rations came with a little bottle of bourbon instead of cigarettes. Somebody in Washington should have done something about that. She sure as hell needed a drink now, and she was sure plenty of servicemen needed one even worse. They had to do without, and so did she.

Life isn't fair, she thought. Her laugh was as bitter as—what was that stuff in the Bible? Wormwood, that was it. They'd used it to flavor absinthe, one more kind of booze she couldn't have. *As if I didn't find out about that the hard way.*

SANDBAGGED MACHINE-GUN NESTS AND CONCRETE pillboxes sprouted like pimples on the smooth green skin of the lawn around Iolani Palace. Trenches zigzagged from one to the next. The Japanese weren't going to give up the Kingdom of Hawaii's center of government without a fight.

Senior Private Yasuo Furusawa understood that. It was at least as much a propaganda point as a military one. As long as Iolani Palace stayed in Japanese—nominally, in Hawaiian—hands, the kingdom Japan had reestablished here remained a going concern. Strong Japanese forces also hung on in the gray, boring office buildings west of the palace. So did the remnants of the Royal Hawaiian Army. From what Furusawa had heard, some of King Stanley Laanui's Hawaiians had fought with fanatical fervor. Others, unfortunately, had hardly fought at all.

Commander Genda looked northwest, the direction from which the U.S. Marines were likeliest to come. Then he looked back over his shoulder toward the palace. Like Honolulu City Hall to the east, it hadn't been badly damaged. As if picking that thought from his informal aide's mind, Genda said, "The Americans want to keep these places in one piece if they can. They intend to use them after they finish the reconquest."

"Yes, sir." Furusawa nodded. He'd figured that out for himself. He'd also realized Captain Iwabuchi didn't intend to let the Americans have anything in Honolulu in one piece if he could help it. Here, he could. He kept insisting the Japanese would throw the Americans back. Commander Genda, Furusawa noted, claimed nothing of the sort. That also made sense to Furusawa, however little he liked it. The USA held an even more dominant position here than Japan had during the first invasion.

"How long do you think we've got, sir?" Furusawa asked.

Genda shrugged. "Your guess is as good as mine. We've already held out longer than I thought we could. The special naval landing forces are . . . dedicated men."

"*Hai*," Furusawa said. That was a diplomatic way of calling them maniacal diehards, which would have been just as true. The Army had orders against retreat. Its men knew better than to let themselves be captured. But the special naval landing forces rushed toward the enemy like lovers going to meet their beloved. They hurt the Americans, and sometimes even threw them back. The price they paid, though!

"I wish Captain Iwabuchi would not order charges," Genda said, again thinking along with him. "They are wasteful, especially when we cannot replace our losses. Better to make the Yankees come to us and pay the price."

"Would he listen if you told him something like that?" Furusawa asked.

Genda gloomily shook his head. "He would just call me soft. Maybe he would be right. I don't know anything to speak of about commanding ground troops. What's your opinion, Senior Private?"

"Mine?" Furusawa was flabbergasted. He didn't think a superior had ever asked him that before. He wished someone would have done it sooner. Now . . . "It probably doesn't matter much one way or the other, does it, sir?"

The naval officer looked at him in surprise. Furusawa wondered if he was in trouble. Then he laughed at himself. Of course he was in trouble. Before long, all the Japanese soldiers and men from the special naval landing forces would be dead. How could he land in trouble any worse than that?

After a moment, Genda started laughing, too. "Well, Furusawa-*san*, you've got the right way of looking at things—no doubt about it. All we can do here is all we can do. Once we've done it . . ." He licked his lips. "Once we've done it, they'll start defending the Empire a little closer to the home islands, that's all."

Furusawa sent him an admiring glance. Defending the Empire closer to home sounded much better than dying to the last man here. They both meant the same thing, but how you looked at it did count.

A mortar bomb crashed down not far away. Furusawa and Genda both huddled in the trench. You couldn't hear a mortar bomb coming. It announced itself by blowing up. Huddling in a trench wouldn't do you any good if the damn thing came down on top of you, either.

More mortars opened up on the Japanese positions in front of Iolani Palace. So did regular U.S. artillery pieces. You could hear those shells coming in. The louder the scream in the air, the closer to you they were. Some were very close, close enough to throw dirt on Furusawa.

"They're coming! They're coming!" someone shouted.

Furusawa popped up when he heard that. He might get killed if he did, but the American Marines would surely kill him if he waited in the hole. He squeezed off a couple of rounds from his Springfield. The U.S. barrage hadn't knocked out all the Japanese strongpoints. Machine guns spat death at the big men in green uniforms. Some fell. Some ducked into doorways or dove behind piles of wreckage. Some drew back.

"We still have teeth," Furusawa said proudly, even if he had no idea whether he'd hit any Americans.

"*Hai.*" Commander Genda jerked a thumb back over his shoulder. Smoke rose from the palace. A couple of shells had hit it. "In the end, they won't care whether they destroy it. A pity—it's a nice building. I hope . . . the people inside are all right."

He didn't talk about any one person in particular. Senior Private Furusawa had a pretty good idea which person in the palace mattered most to him, though. When Furusawa came to Hawaii from Japan, he'd never expected to meet a queen. There hadn't been any queen here then. He couldn't fault Genda's taste. Queen Cynthia was a striking woman, even if her coppery hair and green eyes made her seem more like some *kami* than a proper human being.

An American with one of their automatic rifles started squeezing off short bursts to make the defenders keep their heads down. A bullet snapped past Furusawa's ear. He ducked. So did Commander Genda. Furusawa sighed. His superior's romance probably wouldn't have ended well anyhow. It surely wouldn't now.

* * *

LES DILLON'S FIRST GLIMPSE of Iolani Palace was almost his last glimpse of anything. As he ran up Hotel Street—not the good part, worse luck—and turned right on Richards, a burst of enemy machine-gun fire cut down the Marine next to him. The man, a replacement whose name Les had never learned, probably died before he finished crumpling to the pavement. Three slugs in the chest would do that to you. Les knew he could have caught the burst as easily as the other guy. Dumb luck, one way or the other.

He dove headlong into a doorway. Letting the Japs have another good shot at him would be stupid. Not everything that happened in combat was luck, not even close. If you gave the enemy a target when you didn't have to, you almost deserved to get nailed.

The Japs kept shooting as if they thought somebody would outlaw ammunition in an hour and a half. To Les, the long bursts they fired from their machine guns showed poor training. If you fired off a whole strip of bullets, or a magazine's worth from a light machine gun, of course most of them would go high. The muzzle couldn't help pulling up. Three, four, five rounds at a crack was the right way to do it.

With all those bullets in the air, though, some had to hit something. The poor damned replacement had proved that the hard way. Calls for corpsmen rang out again and again. Les admired the Navy men who accompanied the Marines more than he could say. Combat wasn't their proper trade, but they went anywhere he and his buddies did. And they put themselves in harm's way every time they rescued a man under enemy fire. When corpsmen got liberty along with Marines, they had a hard time buying themselves drinks.

Mortars and artillery pounded the Japanese in front of Iolani Palace. Les wouldn't have wanted to be a Jap, pinned down by superior firepower and with no place to go. But he'd already seen the slant-eyed monkeys had no quit in them. Maybe that barrage knocked out some of their strongpoints, but the ones that survived kept right on shooting.

Dauntlesses roared down out of the sky to bomb the Japs. The ground shook under Les. Blast slugged him like a Sugar Ray Robinson right—and he wasn't even the target. No, he wouldn't have wanted to trade places with the Emperor's samurai.

Marines started dashing across Richards toward the palace grounds. Even after the dive bombers came in, the Japs had plenty of machine guns waiting for them. And snipers in the buildings on this side of the street took a toll, too.

A lieutenant from another company dove into the doorway with Les. "We're going to have to clear this whole block," he said.

"What? You and me?" Lieutenant or no lieutenant, Les was ready to tell him to piss up a rope if he said yes to that. Combat was one thing, and bad enough all by itself. Suicide when suicide wouldn't do you or your side any good was something else again. As far as Les was concerned, the Japs were welcome to that.

But the officer, who'd probably been born about the time when Les started going over the top in France, shook his head. "No, no, no," he said. "I've got some men following me. If they don't get chopped up too bad, they'll be along."

"Okay, sir. That's business," Les said. The junior officer wasn't asking his men to do anything he wouldn't do himself, and he'd got here ahead of them. Les asked, "How are they fixed for grenades?"

"Lots," the lieutenant said, which was the right answer. While waiting for the rest of the Marines to get there, Les kicked in the door. If Japs had lurked right behind it, he would have been dead long since. He went inside, his heart pounding. Then he had company, lots of company. It helped—some.

Clearing that block across the street from the palace grounds was as nasty a job as he'd ever been part of. The Japs, as usual, wouldn't retreat and wouldn't surrender. They had grenades, too. He would hear them banging the damn things on a helmet or against a wall to start their fuses. That would be the signal to duck into an office or back around a corner when you could, then to move forward again once the enemy grenades went off.

It might as well have been trench warfare. Along with the grenades, it came down to hand-to-hand more than once. Some Hawaiians fought alongside the Japs. Instead of being small and tough, they were big and tough, and no more inclined to surrender than Hirohito's boys.

"Just my luck," Les panted after the Marines finished a knot of them. He had blood on his bayonet and blood on his boots. The stink of it filled the air. "Some of these Hawaiian fuckers quit as soon as they got the chance—but none of the ones I ever ran into."

"Maybe they don't like you, Sarge," a Marine said.

"Wouldn't be surprised," Les said. The other leatherneck had put a bayonet into the kidneys of the Hawaiian he'd been fighting, so he couldn't complain about undue familiarity. "Got a butt on you? I'm out."

"Sure." The Marine handed him a pack.

He took one and lit it with a Zippo. "Thanks, buddy. Damn, I needed that." He gratefully sucked in smoke.

"I believe you," the other Marine said. "Some of the people here, they'd rather have cigarettes than food, and they're so goddamn skinny, they look like they oughta go into the hospital. It's a funny business."

"Yeah." Les looked down at the Camel between his index and middle fingers. A thin, curling ribbon of smoke rose from it. "Wonder how come you want 'em so goddamn bad. They don't do that much for you—not like booze or anything—but they sure get their hooks in." He shrugged. "Fuck, what difference does it make?"

"None I can see," the other Marine answered. "We're gonna have to clean out the stinking palace next, won't we? Boy, that'll be fun."

"Yeah, maybe even more fun than we just had here." Les took another drag. His eyes crossed as he tried to focus on the glowing coal. "Well, we knew pretty damn quick this was gonna be a game of last man standing. Can't be that many Japs left."

"Here's hoping," the other Marine said.

WHEN PROPAGANDA AND MILITARY NECESSITY RAN into each other, propaganda had to take a back seat. Minoru Genda understood that. Unfortunately, the Americans did, too. They were methodically knocking down Iolani Palace above his head. They might even get propaganda mileage out of that— something on the order of, *We had to destroy this historic building to liberate it.* Before long, Japan would be in no position to contradict them.

If not for the basement, which had been the preserve of servants and bureaucrats in days gone by, the palace would have been uninhabitable. As things were, Genda took refuge there with a few Japanese soldiers—his unofficial runner, Senior Private Furusawa, among them—and with King Stanley Owana Laanui and Queen Cynthia.

King Stanley was holding up better than Genda would have expected. He was holding up better than a lot of the soldiers, in fact. He gave Genda a crooked smile and said, "Well, this didn't work out the way we expected, did it?"

"Please excuse me, your Majesty, but it did not," Genda said. "Karma, *neh?* We did the best we could."

"I know. I'm not mad." Stanley Laanui laughed. "I oughta be, huh?"

"What do you mean?" Genda asked cautiously. If the King of Hawaii knew about his affair with the Queen . . . Genda almost laughed, too. What difference did it make now? No matter how you sliced it, none of them was going to live much longer. A couple of 105mm shells slammed into the palace to underscore that. Something up above Genda fell over with a crash—one of the cast-iron columns supporting the second story?

But King Stanley said, "If you'd picked somebody else to put a crown on, he'd be in the hot seat now, and I'd be off somewhere else thinking, *Better you than me, you poor, sorry bastard.*"

"You were a good king," Cynthia Laanui said. "You *are* a good king." She set a hand on his arm. Genda had to work to keep his face impassive. She might have had fun with him—she *had* had fun with him—but she did love her husband. Or if she didn't, she wouldn't show it now, not when everything was falling apart.

"No offense to you, sweetheart, but I always did want to give the USA one right in the eye," Stanley Laanui said. "I was just a little kid when that damn Dole and the rest of those pirates hijacked the kingdom, but I always figured I owed 'em one. So I tried to pay 'em back—and now they're paying me back." Up above, something else came down, hard enough to make the floor over their heads shake. Whatever it was, it had almost come through the floor.

A machine gun mounted at the edge of the dry moat began to chatter. If the U.S. Marines wanted Iolani Palace, they would have to pay the price for it. They did want it, and they were paying.

"All over now," King Stanley said. "All over." He had a U.S. Army .45 in a holster on his belt—a brute of a pistol that would knock over a horse, let alone a man. He took it out and looked at it. "Better to go this way than to let those shitheads catch me and hang me." No Japanese could have put it better.

"Yes," Cynthia said softly. She eyed the pistol with a strange fascination—half longing, half dread. "They wouldn't let us go on living for very long, and they'd have fun with us before they did hang us or shoot us. We did what we did, and it didn't quite work—you're right—and now it's time to close the door."

Stanley Laanui glanced over to Genda. "Shall I give you one between the eyes before I finish Cyndi and me?" he inquired. The way things were, he might have asked the question anyhow. But the words held a certain bitter edge. *He* does *know*, Genda thought. His gaze flicked to Cynthia. She must have realized the same thing, for she couldn't hide her surprise and alarm.

Genda decided not to show he understood everything King Stanley meant. Bowing, he said, "No, thank you, your Majesty. I will not live through defeat, either, I promise you. But we have our own way of ending."

"*Hara-kiri?*" the king asked. Genda made himself not wince as he nodded; *seppuku* was a much more elegant, much less earthy way to put it. King Stanley grimaced. "Better you than me, buddy. I want to get it over with in a hurry."

"It will be fast enough," Genda answered. He turned to Senior Private Furusawa and spoke in Japanese: "Will you please serve as my second? Things here cannot go on much longer." As if to underscore that, the machine gun at the edge of the moat started hammering away again.

"I would be honored, Commander-*san*," Furusawa said. "I will do it quickly, so you do not suffer."

"*Domo arigato,*" Genda said, and then went back to English: "It is arranged."

"Okay," Stanley Laanui said. His mouth twisted when the machine gun abruptly fell silent. "You ready, sweetheart?"

"I don't know." Queen Cynthia's voice shook. "I don't know if anybody can be ready, but you'd better not wait." She nodded to Genda. "Good-bye, Commander. We tried our best."

"*Hai. Sayonara.*" Genda looked down at the floor.

The Hawaiian royal couple went into a little room off the central hallway. A shot rang out, and then a moment later another one. Genda opened the door. If either of them needed finishing, he would take care of it. But Stanley Owana Laanui, while he might not have made much of a king, had done what he had to do here. He and his redheaded queen both lay dead, each with a neat gunshot wound to the temple—and a nasty exit wound on the other side.

"*Sayonara,*" Genda whispered again, and went back outside. He nodded to Senior Private Furusawa. "The time has come," he said, and sat cross-legged on the floor. Baring his belly, he drew his Navy-issue *katana* from its sheath. He'd never used it before. He should have had a *wakizashi*, a samurai's shortsword, but he would have to make do.

"As the blade touches you, sir?" Furusawa asked.

"Let it go in first," Genda said. "Then." He looked up to the ceiling. "With this, my death, I atone for my failure here. May the Emperor forgive me. May my spirit find its home in Yasukuni Shrine." He drove the sword home. The pain was astonishing, unbelievable. Discipline forgotten, he opened his mouth to scream. Then everything ended.

WHAT WAS LEFT OF THE TOP TWO FLOORS of Iolani Palace belonged to the USA again. Japs and Hawaiians sprawled everywhere in blood-soaked, unlovely death. So did too goddamn many Marines. Japs, and maybe Hawaiians, too, were still holed up in the basement. Every so often, they would fire up through the floor above them. That was a nasty angle when a bullet hit; two Marines, one in Les Dillon's platoon, had had their balls shot off.

The Japs had driven back three attacks on the basement from outside. Now the Americans were trying something different. Marine engineers were setting up a shaped charge on the ground floor of the palace. It would blow a big hole in the basement's roof. With luck, that would let leathernecks get down there and go toe-to-toe with the enemy.

Luck, Les thought. *Some fucking luck.* The Japs down there would die. So would a lot of Marines. He was too likely to be one of them.

Another bullet crashed up through the floor. By luck that really was good, that one missed everybody. Getting shot at from below was still goddamn scary. Several Marines fired a round or two down through the floor at the Japs they couldn't see. Then they all went somewhere else in a hurry, so the slant-eyed sons of bitches wouldn't nail them by shooting back where the bullets had gone through. Their boots clumping around overhead probably gave the enemy a hint about where they were anyway.

Through all the chaos, the engineers went on working. One of them looked up at Les and said, "Okay, we're about ready to blow this bastard."

"Hear that, people?" Les called to the other Marines. "Get your grenades ready. We'll see how many of those fuckers we can blow to hell and gone before we go down there ourselves."

Another engineer lit a fuse. The Marines drew back. After a sharp, surprisingly small *whump!,* the charge blew a hole about four feet square in the floor. Along with his buddies, Les chucked grenades through the hole as fast as he could. Some fragments came back up. They bit one man in the hand. The Marines kept on tossing grenades into the basement. They didn't want live Japs anywhere near that hole. Les didn't see how anybody could live through what the enemy was getting, but the Japs had surprised him before.

"Come on!" he said, and let himself drop through the hole. He was down there by himself for only a heartbeat. More leathernecks dropped down with him. He saw a few twisted bodies close by. Then a bullet cracked past his head. Sure as hell, some of Hirohito's warriors still had fight in them.

A Marine with a tommy gun sprayed death as if from a garden hose. After that, it was the usual chaos of a firefight, made worse because it was at such close quarters. Les was too busy to be afraid and too afraid to be anything else. He charged forward yelling like a banshee, and at least one of the fierce roars that burst from his throat started life as a terrified shriek. Even if he knew that, with luck the Japs wouldn't.

Hell, they've gotta be as scared as I am, went through his mind in one of the brief moments when he wasn't shooting or throwing a grenade into one of the rooms off the central hallway or using his bayonet. He'd already used it more here in Hawaii than he ever did in the trenches in 1918. If the Japanese soldiers he faced were afraid, they sure didn't show it. Les wasn't showing it, either, but he knew what was going on inside his own head. To him, the Japs might have been targets on the firing range, except they had the nasty habit of fighting back.

He fired and stabbed and used his rifle butt once or twice. He got a cut on one forearm, but it was hardly more than a scratch. If he wanted more oak leaves for his Purple Heart, he supposed he could get them. But he didn't much care. The Purple Heart wasn't a medal anybody in his right mind wanted to win.

More and more Marines jumped down into the basement. They went forward faster than they could get killed or wounded. Before too long, no more enemy soldiers were still standing. The Americans went through the basement, methodically finishing off wounded Japs. "Save a couple for prisoners," Les called. "The brass wants to grill 'em."

He got grumbles from the men down there with him. "After what those mothers did to our guys, they ought to grill 'em over a slow fire," one of them said.

"Save a couple," Les repeated. "Maybe what we squeeze out of 'em will save enough of our guys while we're cleaning out the last of 'em to make it worthwhile."

"Maybe." The Marine didn't sound convinced, but he didn't shoot the unconscious Jap at his feet, either. The enemy soldier showed no gunshot wounds, but he was out cold. Les wondered if he'd got the Jap with his rifle butt, or if one of the other leathernecks had done it.

He shrugged. That didn't make much difference. The fighting right here was over. He could enjoy the breather—for a little while.

"CAN YOU HEAR ME?" a voice asked in Japanese.

Yasuo Furusawa forced his eyes open. His head hurt worse than after the worst hangover he'd ever had. "*Hai,*" he whispered so he wouldn't have to hear himself. The man looking down at him was Japanese, but wore civilian clothes. They were in a tent: that was canvas behind the other man. Furusawa tried to take stock, but didn't have much luck. "What happened?" he asked at last.

"You were in Iolani Palace. Do you remember?" the other man said.

"*Hai,*" Senior Private Furusawa repeated, again as if from very far away. He remembered finishing Commander Genda. Genda had died as a samurai should. And he remembered a hole blown in the ceiling, and U.S. Marines jumping down into the palace basement roaring like tigers. He remembered trying to fight off a big one . . . and that was the last thing he *did* remember. That meant . . . "*Zakennayo!*" he exclaimed. "Am I . . . ?" He couldn't make himself say the words.

The other man nodded. "Yes, you are a prisoner of war. You were taken while unconscious. It is not your fault. You did not surrender."

That helped— about as much as bailing with a bucket helped keep a battleship afloat. "A prisoner!" Furusawa said in despair. The knowledge hurt almost as much as his head, which said a lot. Furusawa squeezed his eyes shut as shame washed over him. "My family is disgraced forever."

"Your family doesn't know," the other man said. By his old-fashioned accent—and by how thin he was—he had to be a local Japanese working with the Americans. "No one will tell them till the war is over. You can sort it out then. Meanwhile, aren't you glad you're alive?"

"No." Furusawa shook his head, which also hurt. "What . . . What will they do to me?" You could do anything to a prisoner, anything at all.

As if picking that thought from his mind, the local Japanese said, "America follows the Geneva Convention. No one will torture you for the fun of it, or anything like that. You will be questioned, but it will only be questions. Do you understand?"

"I hear you," Furusawa said wearily. He heard gunfire, too, not close enough to be alarming but not that far away, either. "We're still fighting!"

"Yes, but it's mopping up now," the other man said. "Honolulu will fall. Oahu will fall. The war will go west."

Furusawa wished he could call a local Japanese a liar. He knew he couldn't. He'd been sure Oahu would fall since his own countrymen couldn't keep the Americans off the northern beaches. Hawaii would no longer be the Empire's eastern shield. Now the USA could use the islands against Japan. *Shigata ga nai,* he thought. *He* certainly couldn't do anything about it.

"Are you hungry? Are you thirsty?" the other man asked.

"*Hai.*" Furusawa sat up on the edge of the cot where they'd put him.

"I'll get you food," the local Japanese said. "There are guards outside. Don't try to leave. It would be the last thing you did."

Furusawa hadn't thought of leaving. He barely had the strength to sit. The local Japanese went out. He spoke in English. Someone answered him in the same language. He hadn't been lying, then. Furusawa hadn't thought so. The other man came back in a few minutes with U.S. ration tins and a cup of coffee. Furusawa ate greedily. He felt a little more alive when he finished.

"You were in the palace basement, *neh*?" the local Japanese said. Furusawa nodded, and didn't wish he was dead right afterwards. The other man—who was, Furusawa slowly realized, an interrogator—went on, "Do you know what happened to the man and woman who called themselves King and Queen of Hawaii?"

"*Hai.*" Why not answer? What difference did it make now? What difference did anything make now? This felt more like a strange life after death than anything else. "He shot her. Then he shot himself. They didn't want to be captured, either."

"Well, I can believe that," the local man said. "They would have had a hard time of it." He paused to look at a notebook. Questions he wanted to ask? "Do you know who the Navy officer who committed *seppuku* was?"

"Commander Genda." With a certain mournful pride, Furusawa added, "I had the honor to act as his second."

"Lucky you." The interrogator's tone proved him more American than Japanese.

"I thought so." Furusawa paused and winced. It felt as if someone were trying to drive a blunt spike through his skull. "Please excuse me. My head hurts."

"I believe that. They say you're lucky it didn't get broken for good," the local Japanese answered. *This is luck?* Furusawa thought. The local Japanese held out two white tablets. "Here are some aspirins. They may help a little."

Poison? Furusawa wandered. But, as a druggist's son, he recognized aspirins when he saw and smelled them. He swallowed them with a last little swig of coffee. *"Arigato,"* he said. Maybe the interrogator meant it. Maybe the Americans were easier on prisoners than his own people would have been—*were.* He could hope, anyhow.

And hope was all he could do. He'd fought as long and as hard as he could, but now, for him, the war was over.

XV

KENZO TAKAHASHI WONDERED IF HE'D BEEN SMART TO MAKE SURE HIS GIRL-friend was all right. For the first few days in the shelter under the Sundbergs' house, things had been pretty quiet. He and Elsie and her folks could go up and use the bathroom. They could come out at night during lulls and get avo-cados out of the trees in the back yard. They could even sleep in beds if they wanted to, though that was risky. You could get caught when the shooting picked up again.

Now, though, the fighting had moved east. Too much of it was right in this neighborhood. The Japanese special naval landing forces didn't yield ground till they had to. By the pounding U.S. forces were giving them, they would have to before long. In the meanwhile, though . . .

In the meanwhile, what had been a quiet, prosperous residential street turned into a good approximation of hell. Shells burst all the time. Machine guns stuttered and chattered. Rifles barked. Planes flew low overhead, strafing anything Japanese that moved—and anything that moved that might be Japa-nese. Coming out would have been suicidal. Kenzo had long since lost track of how many bullets tore through the house above them.

Mrs. Sundberg cried softly. "Everything we worked so long and hard to build and get . . ." she choked out.

"Not everything," her husband said. "*We're* still here. Things are just—things." He'd always struck Kenzo as a sensible man.

"What do we do if the house catches fire?" Elsie asked.

"Get out as best we can and pray," Mr. Sundberg answered bleakly. "That's the one big worry I've got."

There were smaller ones. Mr. Sundberg had dug that narrow trench to a latrine pit. People used it when they couldn't go up above. It wasn't pleasant, or anything close to pleasant. He'd stowed bottles of water down below, but not a whole lot of food. Everybody got hungry and cranky. Kenzo also felt very much the odd man out. Elsie's folks were polite about it—he didn't think he'd ever seen them less than polite. But they and Elsie made a group he wasn't fully part of.

Her father joked about it: "If you can put up with her here, Ken, you'll never have to worry about it again."

"I think you're right," Kenzo answered. He and Elsie slept huddled together. So did her parents. They had no room for anything less intimate. Mr. and Mrs. Sundberg didn't say boo. They had to know he'd really slept with Elsie, but they didn't let on.

And then the firing got worse. Kenzo hadn't thought it could. Japanese soldiers were right outside. They shouted back and forth to one another, trying to set up a defensive line. They sounded excited and frightened, but still full of fight.

Maybe one of them smelled the stink from the latrine pit. He came over and shouted, "Who's in there?"

Elsie and her folks couldn't understand the words, but the tone made them gasp with fright. Kenzo was scared almost out of his wits, too—almost, but not quite. Trying to sound as gruff as he could, he barked, "This is a holdout position. Get lost, you *baka yaro*, or you'll give it away."

"Oh. So sorry." The soldier clumped off.

Elsie started to ask something. Kenzo held a finger to his lips. Even in the gloom under the house, she saw it and nodded. When Kenzo didn't hear any Japanese soldiers close by, he explained in a low voice. "I think you saved all of us this time, Ken," she whispered, and put her arms around him and kissed him right there in front of her parents. He was grinning like a fool when he came up for air. Maybe he wasn't such an outsider after all.

"Thanks, Ken," Ralph Sundberg said. "I don't suppose you want a kiss from me, but I'm glad you and Elsie like each other. I'll go on being glad when we get out of here, too."

"Okay, Mr. Sundberg," Kenzo answered. He couldn't have asked to hear anything better than that. If the older man really meant it . . . He hoped he got the chance to find out.

A couple of hours later, something a lot bigger and heavier than a machine-gun round smashed into the house above them. The shooting rose to a peak, then slowly ebbed. Kenzo heard fresh shouts. Some of them were the cries of the wounded, which could have come from any throat. Others, though, were unmistakably English.

"My God!" Mrs. Sundberg whispered. "We're saved!"

"Not yet," Kenzo said. And he was right. The fighting went on for the rest of the day.

As evening turned gloom into blackness, he heard a Marine outside say, "Lieutenant, I think there's Japs under this house. I'm gonna feed the fuckers a grenade."

"No! We're Americans!" Kenzo and the Sundbergs yelled the same thing at the same time. Getting killed by their own side would have been the crowning indignity.

Startled silence outside. Then: "Okay. Come out under the front steps. Come slow and easy and stick your hands in the air when you're out."

One by one, they obeyed. Scrambling out of the hole was awkward. Kenzo helped haul Elsie out. It wasn't quite so dark as he'd expected when he returned to the world outside the little shelter. Four Marines immediately pointed rifles and tommy guns at him. "You guys are Americans," one of them said to the Sundbergs. "What about this—Jap-lookin' fellow?" In the presence of two women, he left it at that.

"He's as American as we are," Mrs. Sundberg said.

"He saved all our lives when you were pushing the Japanese back through here," Mr. Sundberg added, looking back at the wreckage of his house. That must have been a tank round through it: the hole in the front wall was big enough to throw a dog through. Shaking his head, he went on, "We've known him for years. I vouch for him, one hundred percent."

Elsie squeezed Kenzo's hand. "I love him," she said simply, which made his jaw drop.

It made all the Marines' jaws drop, too. The one who'd spoken before frowned at Kenzo. "What have you got to say for yourself, buddy?"

"I'm glad to be alive. I'm twice as glad to see you guys," he answered in his most ordinary English. "I hope I can find my brother and"—he hesitated—

"my father." Sooner or later, they would find out who his father was. That might not be so good.

"Can you men spare any food?" Mr. Sundberg asked. "We got mighty hungry under there." Ration cans of hash and peaches made Kenzo forget all about what might happen later on—except when he looked at Elsie. Then he saw the bright side of the future. The other? He'd worry about it when and if it came.

By THE SOUND OF THINGS, the end of the world wasn't half a mile away from Oscar van der Kirk's apartment, and getting closer all the time. The mad, anguished fury of war seemed all the more incongruous played out in Waikiki, which would do for the earthly paradise till a better one came along.

"Japs can't last much longer," Charlie Kaapu said, looking on the bright side of things. "All over but the shouting."

"Some shouting," Oscar said.

"He pronounced it wrong," Susie Higgins said. "He meant *shooting*."

"Maybe I did," Charlie said. "Never can tell."

Plenty of shouting and shooting was going on. To any reasonable man, Charlie was right and more than right when he said things were almost over. The Japs were—had to be—on their last legs. They'd been driven out of Honolulu. Waikiki was about the last bit of Oahu they still held. Logic said that, surrounded and outgunned, they couldn't hold it long. Logic also said they should give up.

Whatever logic said, the Japs weren't listening to it. They fought from machine-gun nests and rooftops and doorways and holes in the ground. They fought with a singleminded determination that said they believed holding on to one more block for one more hour was as good as throwing the Americans into the Pacific. It seemed crazy to Oscar, but nobody on either side gave a damn about his opinion.

"I want to go out there and stab some of those little monkeys," Charlie said. "What I owe them—" He carried a little more weight than he had when he came out of the Kalihi Valley—a little, but not a lot. You couldn't put on a lot of weight in Hawaii these days no matter how you tried.

"Don't be dumb," Oscar said. "The Army and the Marines are giving you your revenge."

"And the U.S. taxpayer is footing the bill," Susie added. "How can you beat a deal like that?"

"How? It's personal, that's how," Charlie growled. As if to tell him nobody gave a damn about personal reasons, a bullet came in through the open window, cracked past the three of them, and punched a hole in the far wall. The wall already had several. All Oscar and Charlie and Susie could do was huddle here and hope they didn't get shot or blown up.

Oscar looked from Charlie to Susie and back again. As far as he knew, they hadn't fooled around on him. He was a little surprised—Susie had a mind of her own, and Charlie was a born tomcat—and more than a little glad. He'd been looking for answers. Sometimes negative ones were better than positive.

Another bullet came in through the wall. This one tore a hole in the couch. Susie yelped. So did Oscar. The U.S. taxpayer was liable to be footing the bill for wiping him off the face of the earth. "Hey!" he said.

"What?" Susie and Charlie said at the same time.

"Not you," Oscar told his buddy. He turned back to Susie. "If we get out of this in one piece, you want to marry me?"

She didn't hesitate. She rarely did. "Sure," she said. "It's not like we haven't been through a little bit together, is it?"

"Not hardly," Oscar said. Charlie whistled the Wedding March, loudly and way off tune. Oscar made as if to throw something at him. He and Charlie both laughed. Susie astonished him by starting to cry. If the war hadn't started, she would have gone back to Pittsburgh after her little fling. Oscar probably would have forgotten her by now, the way he'd forgotten a lot of girls. You never could tell how things would work out.

JOE CROSETTI SHOT UP WAIKIKI. The Japs down there stubbornly kept shooting back. It wouldn't matter much longer, though.

Enemy troops were running around the hotels by Waikiki Beach and on the beach itself, taking positions to try to defend against the landing craft coming in from the Pacific. *I've watched three invasions now,* Joe thought. *How many people can say that?*

Naval guns pounded the expensive beachfront property. A long round smashed an apartment house to smithereens a few blocks inland. Joe would have thought nothing could survive the assault from the sea and the sky.

He would have been wrong. He'd thought that before, and he'd been wrong every time. As soon as the landing craft came into range, the Japanese raked them with machine-gun fire. A field gun in the Royal Hawaiian Hotel pumped rounds at the ugly boats struggling toward the beach. Joe saw splashed from near misses, and then a boat caught fire, turned turtle, and sank, all in the wink of an eye.

"You bastards!" Joe exclaimed. He swung his Hellcat out over the ocean—and one of the landing craft opened up on him with its .50-caliber machine gun, mistaking him for a Zero. "You bastards!" he said again, this time on an entirely different note. Fortunately, the sailor with the itchy trigger finger couldn't shoot worth a damn.

And Joe spotted what he'd been looking for: the muzzle flash from the field gun. They'd put it right inside the wreckage of that big pink pile. He dove on it. His finger stabbed the firing button. Six tongues of flame flickered in front of the Hellcat's wings. As always, the fighter staggered in the air; all at once, the engine had to fight the recoil from half a dozen guns banging away like sons of bitches. Joe controlled the plane through the rough part with a touch honed by practice.

G-force shoved him down hard into his seat as he came out of the dive. The bastard of it was, he couldn't see what the hell he'd done, or even if he'd done anything. Every ten seconds took him another mile from the Royal Hawaiian.

Clang! A bullet slammed into the Hellcat. "Fuck!" Joe exclaimed. Yeah, the Japs were still doing everything they could—or maybe that was an American bullet running around loose. Either way, it was doing its best to kill him. Either way, its best didn't seem good enough. "Way to go, babe," Joe murmured affectionately, and patted the seat the way he would have patted a reliable horse's neck.

He made one more pass over Waikiki. By the time he finished that one, only two of his guns still held ammo. Time to head for home. He flew back toward the *Bunker Hill.* They'd gas him up, the armorers would reload the guns, and then he'd be off again. It was almost like commuting to work. You could get killed in a traffic smashup, too.

You could, yeah, but the jerk in the other car was just a jerk. He wasn't trying to kill you on purpose. The enemy damn well was. It made a difference. Joe was amazed at what a difference it made.

Twenty minutes later, his teeth slammed together as the Hellcat jounced home. At least he didn't bite his tongue; every once in a while you'd see a guy get out of his plane with blood dripping down his chin. Joe ran across the flight deck and down to the wardroom to debrief. Things had become routine, or pretty close, but the powers that be still wanted as many details as pilots could give.

"Did you radio the position of that field gun so a dive bomber could pay it a visit?" the debriefing officer asked.

"Uh, sorry, sir, but no." Joe thumped his forehead with the heel of his hand. "Christ, I really am an idiot!"

"Well, you did have other things on your mind," the debriefing officer said generously. "Speaking of which, you need to see Commander McCaskill in his office right away—'On the double,' he said."

"I do?" Joe yelped. Was he in trouble for not making that radio call? He didn't think he ought to be in enough trouble for the *Bunker Hill*'s commander of air operations to ream him out in person. "What for, sir?"

"He'd better be the one to tell you that," the debriefing officer answered.

Apprehensively, Joe went up to the carrier's island. He found the door to Commander McCaskill's office open. McCaskill, a craggy, gray-haired man in his early forties, looked up from his desk. "Ensign Crosetti reporting, sir," Joe said, fighting not to show the nerves he felt.

"Come in, Crosetti," the air operations commander said. "I've got something for you." Joe couldn't read anything in his voice or on his face; he would have made—probably did make—a formidable poker player.

"Sir?" Joe approached as reluctantly as a kid about to get a swat from the principal.

McCaskill reached into a desk drawer and pulled out two small boxes. He shoved them at Joe. "Here. These are yours now." Joe opened them. One held two silver bars, the other two thin strips of gold cloth. McCaskill's face had more room for a smile than Joe would have guessed. "Congratulations, Lieutenant Crosetti!" he said.

"My God, I made j.g.!" Joe blurted. It almost came out, *Holy shit!* Now *that* would have been something. He wondered if anybody ever had said something like that. He wouldn't have been surprised.

Still smiling, the older man nodded. "You earned it, son. You've done well."

"I wish Orson hadn't bought the farm," Joe said, suddenly sobered. "He would've got these way before I did."

"Oh." Commander McCaskill also sobered. After a moment's thought, he said, "I don't think you'll find anyone on this ship without absent friends." Now

Joe nodded; that was bound to be true. McCaskill went on, "If it makes you feel any better, Mr. Sharp did win his promotion—posthumously."

"Maybe a little, sir." Joe knew he had to be polite. Yelling, *Not fucking much!* would have landed him in the brig. He wondered how much consolation that promotion was for Sharp's folks back in Salt Lake. They would sooner have had their son back. Joe would sooner have had his buddy back. "Absent friends," he muttered, and then, "This is a nasty business."

"It is indeed," Commander McCaskill said. "But I will tell you the only thing worse than fighting a war: fighting a war and losing it. We're here to make sure the USA doesn't do that." Joe nodded again, not happily but with great determination.

OSCAR VAN DER KIRK CROUCHED IN THE RUBBLE of what had been his apartment building. He had one arm around Susie and the other around Charlie Kaapu. They all huddled together to take up as little space as they could. Oscar had a cut on his leg. Charlie was missing the top half-inch of his left little finger. Susie, as far as Oscar could tell, didn't have anything worse than a few bruises. She'd always been lucky.

They were all lucky. Oscar knew it. They were alive, and they weren't maimed. After everything that had hit the apartment, that was real luck. Not far away, somebody else who'd stuck it out was alternating moans and shrieks. The cries were getting weaker. Whoever it was, Oscar didn't think he'd make it.

No way to get up and see, or to help the poor bastard. You could almost walk on the bullets flying by overhead. The Marines storming up Waikiki Beach were giving it everything they had. The more lead they put in the air, the less damage the last Japanese pocket in the Honolulu neighborhood could do to them.

And the Japs were fighting back with everything they had left. That meant rifles and machine guns and knee mortars. If one of those little bombs came down on top of Oscar and Susie and Charlie . . . That would be that. Or a U.S. shell could do the job just as well, or maybe even better.

"Now we know what's worse that everything we ran into when we were surfing at Waimea!" Oscar yelled into Charlie's ear.

"Oh, boy!" Charlie yelled back.

Back in college, Oscar had read Marlowe's *Doctor Faustus*. He hadn't understood it then. Now he had understanding rammed down his throat. You really could pay too much for some kinds of knowledge. If he lived, that would be worth remembering.

The Marines were only a block or so away. Oscar could hear them shouting at one another getting a new attack ready. With luck, this one would carry them past what was left of the apartment building. With even more luck, it wouldn't kill his girl or his buddy—or him.

But he could also hear the Japs shouting a block or so to the north. It couldn't mean . . . "They sound like they're getting ready to charge, too," Susie said.

And they did. "That's crazy," Oscar said. "They'd just be killing themselves."

No sooner were the words out of his mouth than the Japanese soldiers or naval landing forces or whatever they were charged the Marines. They were screaming like banshees and shooting from the hip. It was so spectacular, and so spectacularly mad, that Oscar stuck his head up for a moment to watch. Heading the charge was a senior Japanese Navy officer in dress whites: bald and bespectacled and waving a sword. Oscar had to blink to make sure he wasn't seeing things.

Half a dozen bullets seemed to hit the officer at the same time. His body twisted horribly, as if it didn't know which way to fall. His sword went flying. And Susie grabbed Oscar and dragged him down. "Getting shot's not how you're gonna get out of proposing to me!" she yelled.

"Okay, babe. That's a deal." Oscar stayed down from then on.

By the noises, some of the Japs actually got in among the Marines. They didn't have a hope in hell of driving them back; they just died a little sooner than they would have otherwise. They probably also killed some Marines who might have lived if things went a little differently.

After that mad charge got smashed, the Marines surged forward. Only spatters of gunfire answered them. The Japs had shot their last bolt. An American in a green uniform flopped down almost on top of Oscar and Susie and Charlie. His rifle swung toward them with terrifying speed. "Don't shoot!" Oscar said. "We're on your side!"

As soon as the leatherneck got a look at Susie, the rifle stopped moving. His grin showed white teeth amidst brown stubble. "I don't care about you, pal, but I hope like hell she is," he said. "Here. Enjoy." He tossed them a pack of cigarettes and some crackers and cheese wrapped in cellophane. Then he fired a couple of rounds and ran on.

"My God!" Oscar said dizzily—and he hadn't even opened the Luckies yet. "We made it!" Susie kissed him. Charlie pounded him on the back. Nobody stuck anything up where a bullet might find it. Oscar didn't want to turn himself into a liar now, especially after Susie kissed him again.

THE JEEP THAT ROLLED SOUTH FROM HALEIWA down the twice wrecked and now restored Kamehameha Highway carried a pintle-mounted .50-caliber machine gun. The driver glanced over to Fletch Armitage. "You handle that thing if you have to, sir? Still Jap snipers around every now and then."

"I'll handle it," Fletch promised. "You think I'm skinny now, you should've seen me a month ago." He felt like a new man. If the new man tired easily and looked as if he'd blow away in a strong breeze, he still marked one hell of an improvement over the old one.

Fletch looked like a new man, too, in the olive-drab uniform that had replaced khaki while he was on the sidelines. The jeep was new, too, or new to him; none of the handy little utility vehicles had got to Oahu before the war started. The machine gun, by contrast, felt like an old friend. He could have stripped it and reassembled it blindfolded. He'd had to do that at West Point. If the instructors felt nasty, they'd remove a key part before you put it back together, and make you figure out what was wrong.

War had chewed up the landscape—chewed it up twice in less than two years. Not even Hawaii's luxuriant growth was able to cover up the latest round. Fletch looked at things with a professional eye. The Japs had fought like sons of bitches, no doubt about it. Burnt-out tanks and wrecked artillery pieces and pillboxes told how hard they had fought. So did the smell of death that fouled the warm, moist air.

The Kamehameha Highway was better than new: twice as wide, with no potholes because the paving was still so fresh. The engineers who'd put Humpty Dumpty back together again had done a hell of a job. And they'd needed to. If supplies didn't go south by the Kamehameha Highway, they didn't go south at all.

No snipers fired at the jeep. Less than an hour after Fletch got off the landing craft, he found himself in Wahiawa. "Here you go, sir," the driver said, pulling up behind the gutted corpse of a Packard that had sat by the curb since

December 7, 1941. "Good luck." He pulled a Big Little Book out of his pocket and settled down to read.

"Thanks," Fletch said tightly. He got down from the jeep. Wahiawa looked—*trampled* was the first word that came to mind. The Japs hadn't cared about civilians. To them, built-up areas made good strongpoints. The town had paid for their stand. Everybody in Hawaii had paid and paid—including, at last, the Japs themselves.

Civilians on the streets were scrawny. K-ration cans were some of the commonest trash Fletch saw. K-rations weren't delicious, but they were paradise next to what people had eaten while the Japs ruled the roost.

A brunette *haole* woman with her hair hacked off short as a Marine's shrank away from Fletch when his eye fell on her. He wondered what that was all about, but only for a moment. She must have been sleeping with the enemy. His mouth tightened, which only made the woman look more frightened as she scuttled past him. How anyone could . . . But then he sighed. Some people didn't care what they did to get by. It wasn't as if he hadn't seen that before. If your choices looked like screwing a Jap and starving to death, what would you do? He thanked God he wasn't a judge. Making Hawaii run the way it was supposed to again would take years.

His own worries were more personal. He turned west off the highway toward Schofield Barracks, which he knew were nothing but wreckage, and, more to the point, toward his old apartment building, which he hoped was still there. A lot of the places around here were okay. The Japs must not have thought they could make much of a stand in this part of town.

There it was, battered but still standing. *Just like me.* Fletch started to shake. This was harder than anything he'd done since the first time he went into combat, with Japanese fighters and dive bombers blowing up everything in sight. *And who says you're not going into combat now?* he asked himself. *Jane already blew up your heart.*

ARMITAGE was still on the mailbox in the lobby. He climbed the stairs two at a time so he wouldn't have time to think. By the time he got to the second floor, he was panting—he still wasn't in great shape. But exercise wasn't the only thing making his heart pound when he walked down the hall. He took a deep breath and knocked on what had been his own front door.

Maybe she wouldn't be home. . . . But he heard footsteps inside, so she was.

The door opened. There she was, skinny (but who wasn't skinny these days?) but still looking damn good to him. "Yes, Captain?" she said—and then she did a double take right out of the Three Stooges. "My God! Fletch! My God!" she squealed, and threw herself into his arms.

She didn't *feel* skinny. He'd forgotten how a woman in his arms did feel. Finding out again was like three shots of bourbon on an empty stomach. When he kissed her, she kissed him back—for about three seconds before she twisted away. What had been intoxication curdled. "Hello, Jane," he said sourly.

"Come in," she said, looking down at her toes and not at him. "I'm sorry, Fletch. I know what you must be thinking. But that—wasn't all about you, anyway."

"Great," he said, and she flinched as if he'd hit her. He did go in. The place didn't look too different. It smelled of wood smoke, but she sure wouldn't have been able to go on cooking with gas. "How are you?" he asked.

"I'm here," she answered. "I saw you once, with those others. . . ."

"I know. I saw you, too," Fletch said. "I must have looked like hell."

Jane nodded. "You did. I'm sorry, but you did. I didn't think anything would be left of you in a little while."

"Damn near wasn't," he said. "I was down to about a hundred pounds when the leathernecks raided the camp in Kapiolani Park and got me out." He'd put some weight back on, but he still had a long way to go. "You made it, though. Way to go."

"Way to go. Yeah. Sure." Her laugh might have been dipped in vitriol. "Fletch . . ." She stopped, then muttered, "Well, you might as well hear it from me, because you'll sure hear it."

"Hear what?" he asked, ice forming in his belly. If she'd collaborated . . . He didn't know what he'd do if she'd collaborated. Bust her in the chops and walk out, he supposed. Slam the door on this part of his life forever.

"They made me their whore," she whispered. "Comfort woman, they called it. They stuck me in a brothel, and they made me. . . . They made me fuck them and suck them, all comers welcome. There. Is that plain enough? I was doing that till the place got shelled and I could get away."

"Oh," he said, and then, "Oh, Jesus," and then, "No wonder you didn't want to kiss me."

"No wonder at all," Jane said bleakly. "Hawaii, the impregnable fortress of the Pacific." Another acid-filled laugh. "What was impregnable was me, and it's just dumb fucking luck—yeah, that's what it is, all right—I'm not carrying some Jap's bastard. I'd never know whose, either, 'cause there were too damn many to be sure."

Fletch felt like sinking through the floor. There is a peculiar, horrible helplessness unique to the man who can't protect his woman. "I'm sorry," he said in a low voice. "I'm so sorry." Part of him knew that was irrational. He'd been a POW, at least as helpless as Jane, and she'd dumped him anyhow. But he'd also been a soldier, charged with defending Hawaii against the enemy. And he'd failed. The whole Army and Navy had failed, but he didn't care about that. *He'd* failed. It was personal, which made it all the worse.

"That ought to take care of any silly foolishness about getting back together," Jane said. "You won't even want to look at me now, let alone touch me."

"Hey," Fletch said gently. Jane looked up in surprise—she must have thought he would stomp out of the place in disgust. He said, "I know all about what the Japs could make people do. They would have killed you if you didn't. You think I don't know that, too? I saw—plenty, believe me. Whatever you had to do, nobody's gonna blame you for it. I sure don't. You'll probably end up a hero, babe, and go to the mainland and make speeches about what a bunch of bastards we're fighting so people in war plants'll buy more bonds."

She stared at him. "You son of a bitch," she said, and she started to cry.

"What the—devil did I do now?" he asked, honestly bewildered.

"If you'd just walked away, it would have been over," Jane answered. "But you're—you're sweet to me." She cried harder than ever. "What am I supposed to do now? Everything that has to do with common sense says I ought to finish what I started. But then you go and you act *sweet*. What am I supposed to do about that?"

"Would you rather I slapped you silly?" Fletch inquired.

His sarcasm rolled right off her, because she nodded. "You bet I would," she answered. "If you did, I'd know where I stood—right where I always stood. It would be over. But *this*?" She stared at him again, blinking rapidly; her eyelashes were wet. "Have you grown up? Did whatever the Japs did to you finally make you grow up?"

"I don't know," he said heavily. "All I know is, I didn't die, and too many people did. No, I know one other thing—I never stopped loving you, for whatever you think that's worth. I couldn't do anything about it for weeks and months at a time, but I never stopped. Take it for what you think it's worth." He reached into his pocket. "I'd give you a drink if I had one, but all I've got are Luckies. Will a cigarette do?"

"Sweet Jesus, yes!" Jane exclaimed. "I'm getting the habit back, and I love it. There've been times when I thought about screwing a soldier for a pack. There really have. That's the other side of the coin. After so many, what's one more, especially when he's on our side? After you do . . . what I had to do, it doesn't mean what it used to."

"No, I don't suppose it would," Fletch said. "Well, I'm not asking. Leave me a couple and keep the rest of the pack. I can get more." When she took a Lucky between two fingers, he flipped a Zippo he'd got from a pharmacist's mate and lit it for her. He fired one up for himself, too. He was also getting used to them again. The nicotine buzz hit harder than he remembered from the days before the war.

Jane's cheeks hollowed as she sucked in smoke. "That's so good," she said, and then, cocking her head to one side, "What the dickens am I gonna do with you, Fletch?"

"It's your call, honey," he answered with a shrug that he hoped hid his own dreams. "I never wanted things to end. If you do . . . I guess I can't stop you. Think about it, though. Don't make up your mind right away. That's all I ask. We've both been through—too much. There's no rush. If you decide it's over, it's over. If you don't, I'll be here—till I get well enough to go back on active duty, anyhow."

"That's fair," Jane said, her voice troubled. "That's more than fair, I guess."

"Okay, let's leave it there, then." Fletch looked around for an ashtray. Jane was doing the same thing. She went back to the kitchen and came out with a saucer. They both knocked off ash and then, before long, stubbed out their cigarettes. He climbed to his feet. "I better go. I'm glad you came through . . . however it happened."

"Same to you." Looking like a soldier advancing into machine-gun fire, she stepped forward and put her arms around him. He held her, not too tight. She put her chin up.

"You sure?" he asked. Jane nodded. He kissed her, not too hard. Even with a mild kiss like that, he rose—he leaped—to the occasion. He was starting to feel well enough to know how long he'd gone without. He didn't try to do anything about it. Letting go of his not-quite-ex was hard. Holding on to her now would have been much worse. He clicked his tongue between his teeth and said, "Take care of yourself, kiddo."

"Yeah, you, too," Jane answered. "I'll see you."

"Uh-huh." Fletch left the apartment, left the apartment building, and walked back to the jeep parked on Kamehameha Highway. "Take me back to the beach," he told the driver.

Away went the Big Little Book. "Yes, sir," the soldier said, and fired up the engine.

JUSTICE OF A SORT HAD COME TO WAHIAWA. It was a rough justice, but the times it was trying to deal with had been rough, too. Jane Armitage knew that even better than most of her neighbors. Like them, she scowled at Smiling Sammy Little, who stood before his fellow townsfolk and tried to say he hadn't collaborated with the Japanese.

Smiling Sammy wasn't smiling now. The used-car dealer had on a loud checked jacket that he might have worn on his lot back in the days when Oahu had autos that ran and gas to run them. "I never hurt anybody," he insisted. "I never squealed on anybody. I never got anything special from the Japs, so help me God!"

A woman standing near Jane aimed a forefinger at him. "Look at you, you lying son of a bitch! That coat fits you!"

People muttered. It was a telling, maybe a deadly, point. Most people's clothes hung on them like tents, even after they'd been eating U.S. military rations for a while. The woman accusing Smiling Sammy had arms and legs like sticks. She was far from the only one, too. Sammy Little wasn't so chunky as he had been when he was selling cars, but he was a long way from emaciated. He'd gone through the occupation on more than rice and turnips and weeds.

"Where'd you get your chow, Sammy?" somebody called. Somebody else added, "Who'd you sell down the river for your belly?"

"I never did!" Little said. "I—I had a stash of canned goods the Japs never found. Yeah, that's it!"

The chorus of, "Liar!" that rang out had a frightening baying quality to it. Hounds might have bayed like that after treeing a raccoon, especially if they were hungry. Another chorus began: "The gauntlet! The gauntlet!"

Sammy Little licked his lips. The color drained out of his face. "No," he whispered. "I didn't do anything. I don't deserve it."

"We can hand you back to the Army," said the woman who'd pointed at him. "They'll give you a blindfold and a cigarette, or else they'll give you twenty years for sucking up to the Japs. This way, it's all over at once, and you'll probably live."

Jane didn't think anybody'd died running the gauntlet in Wahiawa, not yet. Yosh Nakayama went through almost unscathed; only a few people had wanted to take a shot at him. Most figured he'd done the best he could in an impossible situation. Other men and women, though, got badly beaten. They too probably would have faced worse from the U.S. military.

Two lines formed, from Smiling Sammy Little on one end to getting it over with on the other. The used-car salesman licked his lips one more time, then lowered his head and ran like hell between the lines. People punched him and kicked at him as he dashed by. He'd got about a third of the way before somebody tripped him. He went down with a moan. After than, a lot more of the punches and kicks landed. Jane kicked him in the ribs as he crawled past her. But he made it to the far end. He was bloodied and battered, but he was alive.

Jane kicked him only once. She despised him, but on general principles. He hadn't done anything to her personally. When two *haole* men led out a small, kind-looking Chinese woman, though . . . "Here's Annabelle Chung," one of them said. Something made a crunching noise near Jane. She realized she was grinding her teeth.

"She ran the Japs' 'comfort house' for them," the other man said. "She took their money. She brought them to the women. She made sure nobody got away, too."

"They made me do it!" Annabelle Chung said shrilly. "They said they'd kill me if I didn't!"

That might even have been true. Jane didn't know one way or the other. She didn't care, either. "So what?" she shouted. "So what, God damn you! You enjoyed seeing us in hell in there. You *enjoyed* it. How would you have liked it if the Japs did a quarter of what they did to us to you? I wish they would have."

Other women forced into prostitution screamed at Annabelle Chung, too. She started to cry. One of Jane's fellow sufferers said, "Yeah, look at those tears. What did you think we did every night after the Japs finally got through with us? I spent all that time wishing I was dead. And I spent a lot of it wishing you were dead, too."

"That's right!" Jane said. "Oh, Lord, that's just right!" Other comfort women also chimed in. The Chinese woman who'd been dragged into prostitution along with the *haoles* denounced Annabelle Chung as fiercely as any of them.

"I didn't mean anything bad," the madam said when something close to silence finally came. "I was just trying to get through it all, same as anybody else. I'm sorry."

"You're sorry you got caught," Jane yelled. "You knew what they were doing to us, and you didn't care."

"That isn't true," Annabelle Chung protested.

But a fierce, rising cry drowned her out: "The gauntlet. The gauntlet! *The gauntlet!*" People made sure Jane and the other former comfort women had good spots. They hustled Annabelle Chung to the starting point. She didn't want to go through. In her shoes, Jane wouldn't have wanted to, either. A big man finally gave her a shove. After that, it was run or die.

People were harder on the madam than they had been on Smiling Sammy Little. That probably wasn't fair; odds were he'd done more harm through the occupation than she had. But he'd been sneakier about it. He hadn't been right out there pimping for the Japanese. Saying just what he had done was hard. With Annabelle Chung, nobody had any doubts about that.

She was already staggering by the time she got to Jane. Sticking out a foot was the easiest thing in the world. Annabelle Chung went down with a wail of despair. Jane yanked at her hair—yanked some of it out. She threw it aside and kicked the Chinese woman in the side of her head. Pain shot through her foot. She didn't mind. It felt wonderful.

Annabelle Chung didn't make it to the far end of the two lines. Once she fell, the comfort women converged on her. After they finished, she lay unmoving on the ground. Jane got a good look at her then. Part of her wished she hadn't; the sight wasn't pretty. Even so . . . One of the other women said, "Not half what she had coming." Jane nodded. She'd just helped maim or kill—more likely kill—somebody, and she wasn't the least bit sorry. Maybe she should have been. Maybe she would be later. Not now, though. Oh, no. Not now.

A mynah bird hopping on the grass flew away before she got close. It was just a bird to her these days, not a potential supper. The same was true of zebra doves. The tame, foolish little birds would be everywhere again in a few years; the way they bred put rabbits to shame. She didn't mind them. Their twittering swarms would help make Hawaii feel normal once more.

Normal? Jane laughed. What was normal after close to two years of hell? Did anybody on these islands have the slightest idea? Jane knew she didn't, not any more.

From Hawaii's worries, she soon came back to her own. What was she going to do about Fletch? That she didn't disgust him still amazed her—she disgusted herself most of the time. Maybe he really did love her. How much did that matter? Enough, when she knew his flaws only too well?

Maybe. He wasn't the same person he had been before December 7, 1941, any more than she was. She wasn't the only one who'd gone through hell. He'd suffered longer than she had, if not in the same ways.

Did she want him back? Could she stand living with him? If she couldn't, could she ever stand living with anybody again? Those were all good questions. One of these days soon, she needed good answers for them.

GETTING RESCUED WITH THREE *HAOLES* who vouched for him wasn't enough to keep Kenzo Takahashi from being thrown into an internment camp behind barbed wire. He would have been angrier had he been more surprised. It was going to be open season on Japanese in Oahu for a while.

That was thanks to people like his own father. For Dad's sake, Kenzo hoped he *had* got out of Honolulu on a submarine. He wasn't in this camp. If he was still on Oahu, he'd get caught before long. God help him if he did. Better he was long gone, then. Even if he had collaborated, Kenzo didn't want him strung up.

Hiroshi was alive. He'd been in the camp longer than Kenzo had. He walked with a stick and a limp—he'd got shot in the leg after the special naval landing forces dragooned him into hauling and carrying for them. The wound was healing. He tried to make light of it, saying, "Could have been worse."

"Oh, yeah?" Kenzo said. "How?"

"They could have shot me in the head, or in the belly," his brother answered. "I saw guys that happened to." He grimaced. "Or the Marines could've finished me off when the Japanese soldiers fell back. This one bastard damn near did. I'm lying there bleeding, right, and he's got this goddamn bayonet

pᵣⁱsed to stick me"—he gestured with his cane—"and when he finds out I
s   k English he wants to know who plays short for the Dodgers."

"Pee Wee Reese," Kenzo said automatically.

"Yeah, well, I got it right, too," Hiroshi said, "but try coming up with it when
you've just been shot and some maniac wants to stir your guts with a knife. If
they gave you tests like that in school, people would study a hell of a lot harder."

"I believe it." Kenzo set a hand on his brother's shoulder. "I'm glad you're
here."

"I'm glad I'm anywhere," Hiroshi said—with feeling.

Like just about everybody on Oahu, they ate rations out of cans. Because
they'd done so much fishing, neither of them was as skinny as a lot of the Japanese in the camp. All the same, beef and pork—even beef and pork out of
cans—tasted mighty good to Kenzo.

People knew who he and Hiroshi were. They knew who their father was.
Some of them must have hoped blabbing to the authorities would win a ticket
out of camp. Kenzo never found out whether it did. He did know his name and
Hiroshi's got called at a morning lineup. When they stepped forward, they got
hustled away for interrogation.

"Your father is Jiro Takahashi, the Japanese propagandist sometimes called
'the Fisherman'?" asked a first lieutenant who couldn't have been much older
than Hiroshi.

"That's right," Kenzo said—no point denying the truth.

"Do you know his current whereabouts?" the lieutenant asked.

"No, sir," Kenzo answered.

"We heard he was on a sub headed for Japan, but we can't prove it," Hiroshi added.

"Uh-huh." The lieutenant wrote that down. "Do you have any way of
demonstrating your own loyalty to the United States of America?"

Kenzo wondered if he wanted to be loyal to a country that didn't want to
believe he was, but only for a moment. He thought about mentioning Elsie, but
figured that wouldn't do him any good—it sure hadn't yet. "That gunner we
pulled out of the Pacific," Hiroshi said. "What the heck was his name?"

Hope flowered in Kenzo. "Burleson. Burt Burleson," he said, and felt as if
he'd passed a test of his own. He and Hiroshi explained how they'd rescued the
man from the flying boat and landed him somewhere near Ewa.

The lieutenant wrote that down, too. "We will investigate," he said. "If we can't confirm your story, it will be held against you."

"Jesus Christ!" Kenzo said. "We don't know what happened to this guy once he got off the sampan. For all we know, the Japanese grabbed him ten minutes later and he's been dead for months."

"For all I know, he never existed in the first place, and you're making him up," the lieutenant said coldly. "We will investigate. In the meanwhile . . ."

In the meanwhile, they went back into the camp. Nobody wanted to have anything to do with them after that. People seemed to think collaboration was as catching as cholera. Why not? The U.S. military had the same attitude.

Eleven days later—Kenzo was keeping track—they got summoned at morning roll call again. Off they went, to be confronted by that same kid lieutenant. He looked as if he'd bitten down hard on a lemon. "Here," he said, and thrust a typed sheet of paper at each of them.

Kenzo looked down at his. It stated that he'd been certified loyal and had full privileges of citizenship in spite of his race and national origin. "Oh, boy," he said in a hollow voice. Hiroshi looked as thrilled as he sounded.

"What's the matter? You've got what you wanted, don't you?" the lieutenant said.

"What I want is for people to think I'm loyal till I do something that makes 'em think I'm not," Kenzo answered. "That's what America's supposed to be about, right? This says you thought my brother and me were disloyal till we showed you we weren't. See the difference?"

"Maybe." If the officer saw, he didn't care. "Maybe it'll work that way one of these days. I don't know. What I do know is, there were local Japs who played footsie with the occupation. Your father did. Okay, so it looks like you didn't. Terrific. You're free to go. If you want a medal for doing what any loyal American was supposed to do, forget about it."

"What do we do now?" Hiroshi asked.

"Whatever you want. Like I said, you're free to go. If you're smart, though, you'll hang on to those letters and show 'em whenever you have to." The lieutenant jerked a thumb toward the tent flap. "Go on, get out of here. Beat it."

Out they went. The guards outside started to lead them back into the internment camp. Kenzo displayed his letter. The corporal in charge of the guards read it, moving his lips. He grudgingly nodded. "I guess they're legit," he told his men.

"Fuck 'em. They're still Japs," one of the soldiers said.

"Yeah." The corporal scowled at Kenzo and Hiroshi. "I don't know how you conned your way into those papers, but you better find somewhere else to be, and I mean now."

They left as fast as they could. Hiroshi grimaced against the pain in his leg, but he didn't let it slow him down. Kenzo looked out at the wreckage of the city where he'd lived his whole life. He had to glance toward Diamond Head to get a notion of just where he was. Not enough still stood in these parts to tell him.

Later, he supposed, he would go over to the Sundbergs' and see how Elsie was doing. He wondered how often he would have to display his loyalty letter between here and there.

"Free," he said tightly. "Right."

LES DILLON'S PLATOON CAMPED on the cratered ground outside Iolani Palace. Even now, they kept sentries out. A few Japanese snipers were still running around loose. Just the other day, one of them had wounded a guy near what was left of Honolulu Hale before the Marines hunted him down and sent him to his ancestors.

The stench of death lingered in the air. A lot of bodies remained in the wreckage. Sooner or later, bulldozers would knock things down and either get them out or cover them up. It hadn't happened yet.

Somebody in a clean new uniform approached the perimeter. Seeing unfaded, untorn, unstained olive drab automatically roused Les' suspicions. Another worthless replacement for a Marine who'd known what he was doing but hadn't been lucky? But this guy walked up with an air of jaunty confidence and had a cigar clamped between his teeth.

"Dutch!" Les shouted. "You son of a bitch!"

"Yeah, well, I love you, too, buddy," Dutch Wenzel answered. His hand was still bandaged, but he showed he could open and close his fingers. "They decided not to waste cargo space shipping me back to the mainland, so here I am."

"Good to see you. Good to see anybody who knows his ass from third base," Les said. "Some of what we're getting to fill casualty slots . . ." He shook his head, then laughed. "They must've been saying the same crap about me when I went into the line in 1918."

"They were right, too, weren't they?" Wenzel said. Les affectionately cuffed him on the side of the head. Wenzel looked around. "Boy, we liberated the living shit out of this place, didn't we?"

"Bet your ass," Dillon said, not without pride. Iolani Palace would never be the same. Half of it—maybe more than half—had fallen in on itself. Somebody'd put up a flagpole on the ruins, though. The Stars and Stripes flew from it. Les figured he would start selling sweaters in hell before the old Territorial flag showed up again. Nothing like being used by a collaborator king to turn it unpopular in a hurry.

Over to the east, Honolulu Hale was in even worse shape. Being a modern building, the city hall was more strongly made than the old royal palace. That meant the Japs had used it for a fortress. After gunfire from tanks and artillery pieces leveled it, Marines and Army troops had to clear out the surviving Japs with flamethrowers and bayonets. The Stars and Stripes flew over that pile of wreckage, too. Les was proud to see the Star-Spangled Banner waving, but he wasn't sorry to have missed that fight. He'd been in enough of them, and then some.

The rest of Honolulu wasn't in much better shape. Even the buildings that still stood had pieces bitten out of them. The Japs had made a stand, or tried to, in just about every stone or brick building in town. They'd taken it out on civilians, too, which only added to the stench in the air.

Les sighed, thinking of what was left of the honky-tonks on Hotel Street: not bloody much. "This town is never gonna be the same," he said.

"This whole *island* is never gonna be the same," Dutch Wenzel said. "Pineapples? Sugar cane? All that crap's down the drain now. Nothin' but fuckin' rice paddies left. The Doles'll be *on* the dole, by God." He laughed at his own wit.

So did Les. "Who's gonna worry about any of that for a while?" he said. "Who's gonna worry about cleaning up this mess here, either? Only thing anybody's gonna give a damn about is getting this place ready to fight from. Hickam and Wheeler are up again, so the carriers don't all have to hang around, but Christ only knows how long it'll be before we can use Pearl again."

"Tell me about it," Wenzel said. "More wrecks in there—ours and the Japs'—than you can shake a stick at. All the fuel burned or blown up, the repair yards smashed to scrap . . . It'll be a while yet."

"Reckon so." Les lit a cigarette, partly to fight the stink from his friend's cigar. He looked north and west. "Even before then, we've gotta clear those bastards off of Midway and Wake—especially Midway. I won't be sorry to get rid of Washing Machine Charlie." Bettys from Midway could reach Oahu. Every few nights, a handful of them would buzz overhead, drop their bombs, and then head for home. They were only an annoyance . . . unless one of those bombs happened to come down on you.

Wenzel nodded. "Yeah, the sooner that starts, the better. And after we take care of those places—well, it's wherever we go next, that's all."

"Wherever the fuck it is, they'll need Marines," Les said positively. Dutch Wenzel nodded again. Both of them looked west, towards islands whose names and dangers they didn't know. Les blew out a cloud of smoke. "Wonder how many of us'll be left by the time it's all over. Enough, I expect." Dutch nodded one more time.

ONLY A FEW HUNDRED JAPANESE SOLDIERS AND SAILORS had been captured in the downfall of Oahu. The Americans kept them in a camp not far from Pearl City, near the northern tip of Pearl Harbor.

Yasuo Furusawa suspected one reason the Americans did that was to let their prisoners watch them at work. Getting Pearl Harbor usable again would have taken Japan years, if the Japanese had tried at all. Furusawa would have judged it an impossibly big job. The Americans threw more machines at it than he would have guessed there were in all the home islands put together. They had plenty of fuel, too, even if they were bringing every liter of it from the mainland.

And things got done. Sunken ships were raised. Some were refloated for repair. Torches attacked others, turning them into scrap metal. Buildings went up on the shore and on Ford Island. It all happened so fast, it reminded him of a movie run at the wrong speed.

"We didn't know how strong they were when we started fighting them," he said gloomily as he stood in line for rations. Even those were a sign of U.S. might. He ate more and better as an American prisoner than he had as a soldier of the Japanese Empire. He remembered what his own side had fed American POWs, and how they'd looked after a while. The comparison was daunting.

The prisoner in front of him only shrugged. "What difference does it make?" he said. "What difference does anything make? We've disgraced ourselves. Our families will hate us forever."

Even among the humiliated Japanese prisoners of war, a hierarchy had sprung up. Though only a senior private, Furusawa stood near the top of it. He'd been captured while unconscious. He couldn't have fought back. Men like him and those who'd been too badly hurt to kill themselves stood ahead of those who'd simply wanted to live, those who'd thrown away their rifles and raised their hands instead of hugging a grenade to their chest or charging the Americans and dying honestly.

Several captured prisoners had already killed themselves. The Americans did their best to stop prisoners from committing suicide. Some of the captives thought that was to pile extra disgrace on them. Furusawa had at first. He didn't any more. The Americans had rules of their own, different from Japan's. Suicide was common among his people, but not among the Yankees. He would have said they were soft had he not faced them in battle. Even the first time around, they'd fought hard. And trying to stop their reinvasion was like trying to hold back a stream of lava with your bare hands.

Every so often, prisoners got summoned for questioning. The enemy had plenty of interrogators who spoke Japanese. Furusawa wondered how many of the locals now working for the USA had served the occupation forces before. He wouldn't have been surprised if quite a few were doing their best to cover up a questionable past with a useful present.

Whatever they wanted to know, he answered. Why not? After the disaster of being captured, how could anything else matter? "Did you ever see or know Captain Iwabuchi, the commander of the defense in Honolulu?" an interrogator asked.

"I saw him several times, drilling his men. I never spoke to him, though, nor he to me. I was only an ordinary soldier, after all."

The interrogator took notes. "What did you think of Captain Iwabuchi?" he asked.

"That he asked more from his men than they could hope to give him," Furusawa said.

"Do you think there are other officers like him? Do you think there will be other defenses like this?"

"Probably," Furusawa said. By the way the local Japanese's mouth tightened, he hadn't wanted to hear that. Furusawa went on, "How else would you fight a war but as hard as you can? The Americans weren't gentle with us when they came back here, either."

"It will only cost Japan more men in the long run," the interrogator said. "You must have seen you can't hope to win when America strikes with all her power."

Furusawa had seen that. It frightened him. Even his full belly frightened him. But he said, "I am only a senior private. I just do what people tell me to do. If you had caught a general, maybe you could talk to him about such things."

"We caught a lieutenant colonel and two majors—one was knocked cold like you, the others both badly wounded," the interrogator said. "Everyone of higher rank is dead. Almost all of the men of those ranks are dead, too."

"I am not surprised," Furusawa said. "You have won a battle here. I cannot tell you anything different. But the war still has a long way to go."

They brought him back to the camp after that. He watched four-engined bombers take off from Hickam Field—one more facility repaired far faster than he would have thought possible. The huge planes roared off toward the northwest. The war still had a long way to go, and the Americans were getting on with it.

FLETCHER ARMITAGE FILLED OUT HIS UNIFORM better than he had the last time he came into Wahiawa. Looking at himself in the mirror, comparing himself to people who hadn't almost starved to death, he judged he was all the way up to very skinny. From where he'd started, that showed a hell of a lot of progress.

Wahiawa had made progress, too. They'd bulldozed rubble off the streets. Some of the long-dead automobiles parked along Kamehameha Highway were gone, too. More people were on the sidewalk. Like Fletch, they had more flesh than the last time he was here.

He tapped the driver on the shoulder. "Why don't you park?"

"Whatever you say, sir," the soldier answered cheerfully. He pulled over. Several big trucks painted olive drab rumbled by, heading south. Fletch wondered what they were carrying to Honolulu or Pearl Harbor. Both places still needed everything under the sun. He shrugged. That wasn't his worry. His worries were right here.

Walking to the apartment where he'd lived with Jane was easier this time. He didn't get tired so fast. Exercise was starting to feel good again. He wasn't doing too much without the strength to do it, the way he had while he was a

POW. No Jap sergeant was going to whack him with a length of bamboo or a rifle butt if he slowed down, either.

But he didn't have to slow down now. He went up the stairs at a good clip. He did raise his hand twice before he knocked on the door, but that was nerves, not weakness. So he told himself, anyway.

She won't be home, he thought. But the door opened. "Oh," Jane said. "It's you. Come in." She stepped aside to let him.

"You were expecting Cary Grant?" he asked with a crooked smile.

Jane laughed—sourly. "I wasn't expecting anybody. People know I had to do . . . what I did. But they know I did it, too. They don't come around much." She closed the door, then turned to look him over. "You seem better. You don't look like you'd blow away in a strong breeze any more."

"I put a roll of quarters in my pocket before I came down, just to make sure," Fletch answered. This time, Jane really laughed. His eyes traveled her. "You've always looked good to me, babe."

She stared down at the ratty rug. "Even after all that?"

"Yeah." He nodded. "I know about doing things you wouldn't do if you had a choice. Believe me, I do. The tank traps and bunkers and trenches I dug probably got our guys killed after they came back. You think I *wanted* to do that? But the Japs would've murdered me if I told 'em no, so—I dug."

Jane took that in a direction he hadn't expected, murmuring, "Killed." She eyed him. "Have you ever killed anybody? Known you killed somebody, I mean?"

Artillerymen usually fought at ranges where they couldn't see what happened when their shells came down—usually, but not always. He'd used a 105 as a direct-fire weapon when the Japs invaded Oahu. "Yeah," he said, and told her about blowing an enemy tank to hell and gone. Then he asked, "How come?"

"Because I did, too, or I think I did." She told him about Annabelle Chung. "While I was doing it, it felt like the right thing. Sometimes it still does. But sometimes I just want to be sick, you know what I mean?"

"If anybody ever had it coming, babe, she did," Fletch said. "You weren't the only one who thought so, either, if it makes you feel any better."

Jane nodded. "I tell myself that. Sometimes it helps. Sometimes it doesn't." She made a wry face. "The last couple of years, a lot of things have happened that can't be helped."

"Ain't it the truth!" Fletch said with more feeling than grammar. "But maybe some can." Awkwardly, he dropped to one knee. "Hon, since the divorce never got finished, will you please stay married to me?"

Jane stared at him. Then she started to laugh again. "You didn't do that the first time you proposed to me!"

"Well, I know you better now, and I mean it more, too," he said. "And I'll try to be a better husband, too. I won't promise the moon, but I'll try. So will you?"

"Get up, silly," she said softly. "Will I?" She seemed to be asking him as much as herself. Slowly, she nodded. "I think I will, if you're crazy enough to still want me. We'll see how it goes, I guess. And if it doesn't . . . one of us'll file papers again, that's all."

"Sure." Fletch agreed more because he didn't feel like arguing than because he wanted to think about papers and lawyers and all the other delights he'd known just before the Japs invaded. But he'd known other delights since; next to time as a Japanese prisoner, even lawyers didn't look so bad. Next to hell, purgatory probably seemed a pretty nice part of town. He grunted a little as he got to his feet. "Thank you, babe!"

"Don't thank me yet, Fletch," Jane said. "As far as I'm concerned, you're still on probation. If it works, fine. If it doesn't, I *will* go back to a lawyer." She eyed him with mock—he hoped it was mock—severity. "That's a threat, buster. You're not supposed to grin like a fool after I make a threat."

"No, huh? Not even when I'm happy?" Fletch pulled the corners of his mouth down, using one index finger for each corner. "There. Is that better?" he asked, blurrily, fingers still in place.

Jane snorted. "So help me God, you're crazy as a bedbug."

"Yes, ma'am. Thank you, ma'am." Fletch saluted her with as much precision as if he were a plebe back at West Point. "May I please kiss the bride to be, wife to be, whatever-the-heck to be, ma'am?"

Most of the time, after you'd just more or less proposed and she said yes, the answer to that was automatic. Looking at Jane's face, he knew it wasn't here. When he remembered why, some of his own joy chilled within him. But she nodded after a couple of seconds. "Carefully," she said.

"Carefully," he promised.

He held her with as much formal reserve as if they were waltzing together for the first time. She closed her eyes and raised her chin, looking about one-quarter eager and three-quarters scared to death. He kissed her. It was more than a brush of his lips across hers, but less than half of what he wanted it to be: the same sort of kiss he'd given her the last time he came back here.

When it was over, he let her go right away. "Okay?" he asked.

She nodded again. "Okay. Thank you." She looked out the window, across the room—anywhere but at him. "This won't be easy. I'm sorry. If you want to change your mind, I can see why you would."

"Not me," he said. "I figured there'd be bumps in the road. But hey—at least there's a road. The last couple of years . . ." He didn't go on, or need to. "So let's do like you said—we'll see how it goes, and we'll go from there. Deal?"

"Deal." Jane held out her hand.

Fletch shook it. "And I brought you another present, too." He pulled out two packs of Luckies.

"Wow!" She all but snatched them out of his hands. "The way things are, they're better than roses." She opened a pack and stuck a cigarette in her mouth. He lit it for her. "Wow!" she said again after the first drag.

"I better go," Fletch said. She didn't tell him to stay, however much he wished she would have. He paused with his hand on the knob. "One more thing. If they ship me out—no, when they ship me out—I'll be paying those bastards back for you."

"Yeah." Jane took another deep drag on the Lucky. "That's a deal, too, Fletch."

AUTUMN. For more than thirty years, it had been only a word to Jiro Takahashi. It was always summer in Hawaii. A little warmer, a little cooler, a little drier, a little wetter—so what? Summer, endless summer.

But now, against all odds, he was back in Japan, and he had to remember what seasons were like. Southern Honshu had always prided itself on its good weather, with the Inland Sea helping to keep things moderate. Jiro supposed it wasn't as bad here as it was up in Hokkaido, where they got real blizzards every winter. It still seemed chilly and nasty to him.

I've been spoiled, he thought.

The authorities were doing their best to keep him happy. His broadcasts from Hawaii had made him something of a celebrity in the home islands. A grumpy celebrity wasn't good.

He thought he would have been happier if they'd let him stay next door in

Yamaguchi Prefecture, where he'd been born. He'd visited his old village. He had a brother and a sister there, and a few old acquaintances. It proved more awkward than he'd expected; no one knew what to say. After so many years apart, he didn't have much in common with family or former friends.

Maybe the people who ran things were smart to keep him in a big city. He could visit again whenever he wanted to—if he wanted to. Yamaguchi Prefecture remained overwhelmingly rural. It was livelier than it had been when he left, but next to the hustle and bustle he'd known in Honolulu it seemed, if not dead, then very, very sleepy.

For instance, it had no town with first-rate broadcasting facilities. They wanted to keep him on the radio, as if his broadcasts could somehow compensate for the loss of Hawaii. Nobody ever came right out and said Hawaii *was* lost; it just stopped showing up in the news. Jiro hoped his sons had come through the fighting. He also hoped they were happy under American rule once more. He knew he wouldn't have been—and he knew the Americans wouldn't have been happy with him.

He got off the trolley at the stop closest to the studio. It was only a block or two from the domed Industrial Promotion Hall in the center of town. When he looked north, the Chugoku-sanshi Range loomed over the city skyline. The mountains didn't have snow on them yet, but they would by the time winter was over. He hadn't even seen snow since coming to Oahu. He supposed seeing it wasn't so bad. Dealing with it . . . If he had to, he had to, that was all.

"Hello, Takahashi-*san*." The local broadcaster's name was Junchiro Hozumi. He reminded Jiro of a cheap imitation of Osami Murata. He cracked crude, stupid jokes and breathed in your face to show how friendly he was. He did have a smooth baritone, though. He said, "Today shall we talk about how you came back to Japan?"

Jiro thought about that. He remembered how terribly overcrowded the submarine was, and how the stink almost knocked you off your feet. He remembered the heart-pounding fear as the boat sneaked, submerged, past the American ships that had by then surrounded Oahu. He remembered the shrill pings of the enemy's echo-tracker, and the crash and boom of bursting depth charges. He remembered how the submarine shook, as if in an undersea earthquake. And he remembered how fear turned to terror.

Did Hozumi understand what he was asking? Did he want his listeners hearing things like that? What would the government do to him—and to Jiro—

if they went out over the air? Nothing good; Jiro was sure of that. As tactfully as he could, he said, "Maybe we'd better pick something else, Hozumi-*san*."

For a wonder, Hozumi got the message. His grin was wide and friendly and showed a gold front tooth. "Whatever you say. How about being able to eat proper rice now that you're in the home islands again?"

"All right. We can do that," Jiro said. The rice here *was* better than the horrible slop he'd eaten after the occupation started. The ration was larger than the one people on Oahu had got, too—not a whole lot larger, but larger. He could talk about that and let people here think he was talking about the whole time he'd lived in Hawaii. He'd begun to understand how the game was played.

The studio reminded him of the one at KGMB from which he and Murata had broadcast. The routine seemed much the same, too. Had the Japanese borrowed from the Americans? He wouldn't have been surprised. Even the engineers' signals through the glass were the same.

"Good job," Hozumi said when the program was done. "*Good* job!"

"*Arigato,*" Jiro said. He'd got through another one, anyhow.

When he left the studio, he took the trolley down to the shore and stared out across the Inland Sea at Itaku Shima, the Island of Light. From time out of mind, the tiny island had been dedicated to the goddess Bentin. The chief temple was more than 1,300 years old. Pilgrims came to visit from all over Japan.

Hawaii didn't have anything like that. Jiro nodded to himself. Even if the weather here couldn't match what he'd left, Hiroshima wasn't such a bad place after all.